THE BRIDGE OF THE GODS

THE BRIDGE OF THE GODS

A Romance of Indian Oregon

By

FREDERIC HOMER BALCH

with an introduction by

STEPHEN L. HARRIS

WSU PRESS

Washington State University Press
Pullman, Washington

Washington State University Press
PO Box 645910
Pullman, Washington 99164-5910
Phone: 800-354-7360
Fax: 509-335-8568
Email: wsupress@wsu.edu
Website: wsupress.wsu.edu

Library of Congress Cataloging-in-Publication Data

Names: Balch, Frederic Homer, 1861-1891 author.
Title: The bridge of the Gods : a romance of Indian Oregon / by Frederic
  Homer Balch ; with an introduction by Stephen L. Harris.
Description: Pullman, Washington : Washington State University Press, [2016]
Identifiers: LCCN 2016031641 | ISBN 9780874223439 (alk. paper)
Subjects: LCSH: Indians of North America--Fiction. | Oregon--Fiction.
Classification: LCC PS1059.B42 B75 2016 | DDC 813/.4--dc23
LC record available at https://lccn.loc.gov/2016031641

INTRODUCTION.

By Stephen L. Harris

The Bridge of the Gods (1890) marks a milestone in Pacific Northwest literature: It was the first work of fiction by a Northwest writer to make Native Americans leading characters, and it was the first to celebrate the region's then little-known topography, primal forests, untamed rivers, and volcanic peaks. Even today, the book's depiction of the mighty Columbia—and the indigenous peoples who plied its sometimes treacherous waters—creates a strong impact.

The remarkably innovative author, Frederic Homer Balch (1861-1891), led a tragically short life. Struggling against the poverty and lack of education that characterized the rural Northwest frontier, Balch was determined to publicize both the area's native tribes and its landscape. While probably still in his teens, Balch had a clear vision of his authorial purpose: his "one central ambition" was "to make Oregon as famous as Scott made Scotland; to make the Cascades as widely known as the Highlands;... to make the splendid scenery of the Willamette the background for romance full of passion and grandeur."[1] By integrating the power of wilderness and human "passion," Balch succeeded in creating a fictional world in which his characters' lives are inseparable from their physical environment. Tutored through long association with native storytellers, in his fiction Balch partly adopted their worldview, in which physical matter, unseen spirit, and human minds are subtly intertwined.

---

1 Sir Walter Scott (1771-1832) was a Scottish poet and historical novelist. He wrote *Ivanhoe, Rob Roy, The Lady of the Lake,* and many other works that found international popularity.

Balch subtitled his work "a Romance of Indian Oregon." Although today's critics rarely draw the distinction, many nineteenth century writers differentiated between the novel, which emphasizes physical and psychological realism, and the romance, a form that may transcend the familiar and the probable. Like Nathaniel Hawthorne's romances, including *The Marble Faun* and *The House of Seven Gables*, *The Bridge of the Gods* portrays a fictional world that is fully naturalistic in its concrete details, but in which the supernatural—uncanny forces that impinge on human lives—plays a significant role. Setting the action in the 1690s and using both the language of myth and of plausibility, the author transforms prehistoric Oregon into a mysterious realm that encompasses both visible and invisible dimensions.

A scene early in the narrative reveals that Balch's characters inhabit a strangely fluid milieu in which matter and spirit interpenetrate. The book's hero, the idealistic minister Cecil Grey, experiences a waking vision in which he sees multitudes of Indians crossing a massive natural bridge arching over an unknown western river. The landform unveiled in this epiphany becomes the object of Grey's transcontinental quest, which eventually brings him, a missionary preaching strange doctrines of peace and love, to the Columbia region, some 3,000 miles from his New England village. Here Grey learns the bridge of his vision is *tomanowos*—a creation of the gods—and a totem of the Willamette people. The bridge's predestined fall will signify the end of both the vast Willamette tribal confederacy and its leader, the fiercely proud Multnomah.

Although Cecil Grey provides the cultural perspective of an outsider who views the Northwest's indigenous society with mixed emotions, the narrative's thematic heart is really the figure of Multnomah. A powerful chief of the Willamette alliance, Multnomah presides over a network of Pacific Coast tribes extending from Mount Shasta north to what is now British Columbia.

> He was about sixty years old, his form tall and stately, his brow high, his eyes black, overhung with shaggy gray eyebrows and piercing as an eagle's. His dark, grandly impassive face, with its imposing regularity of features, showed a penetration that read everything, a reserve that revealed nothing, a dominating power that gave strength and command to every line. The lip, the brow, the very grip of the hand on the bow told of a despotic temper and an indomitable will.

This description may echo common nineteenth-century views of the native leader, but Balch makes Mult-nomah, "the silent, the secret, the terrible," far more than a stereotypical Indian chief. A veritable force of nature, Multnomah is an egoist of cosmic stature, a tyrant who would impose his "indomitable will" not only on the living but also on the dead.

In one of the most eerily memorable scenes in western literature, Multnomah makes a night visit to Mema-loose (Chinook jargon for "dead" or "death"), one of the Columbia River islands on which the local tribes laid corpses to rest in cedar huts.[2] Defying the malevolent

---

2 Today's Memaloose Island was noted by William Clark of the Lewis and Clark Corps of Discovery on October 29, 1805, while moving downriver. The journals referred to the island as "the Sepulchar." On their return journey, Meriwether Lewis commented on the island April 15, 1806, noting "thirteen sepulchres on this rock which stands near the center of the river and has a surface of about 2 acres above high-water mark." Before Memaloose was largely submerged behind Bonneville Dam, most of the remains were removed. University of Nebraska Press / University of Nebraska-Lincoln Libraries-Electronic Text Center, *The Journals of the Lewis and Clark Expedition*, http://lewisandclarkjournals.unl.edu.

spirits of his long-deceased ancestors entombed there, which he senses are pressing invisibly upon him, Multnomah uncovers the face of his long-dead Asian wife. As the chief, by a supreme act of will, tries to wrest from her still lips a vision of the future, he hears the distant roar of avalanching rock—the collapse of the Bridge of the Gods, portending the doom of his people.

Cecil Grey arrives in Multnomah's domain just as the chief has summoned representatives of tribes under his jurisdiction to assemble on Wappatto Island (now Sauvie's Island), at the confluence of the Willamette and Columbia Rivers. A traditional meeting place of both coastal and inland tribes, among whose practices Balch is careful to differentiate, Wappatto Island is a veritable paradise, a lush setting for Multnomah's prized possession, his daughter Wallulah. A product of contrasting cultures, Wallulah is the offspring of Multnomah and an Asian wife, a princess who was sailing to marry a foreign ruler when her ship was storm-driven far off course and wrecked near the Columbia's mouth. After her mother's death, which occurs before the narrative opens, the chief keeps his daughter secluded on the island. Magnificently furnished with treasures from her mother's dowry, Wallulah's lodge contains beautifully woven carpets, tapestries, jewels, and manuscripts of poetry, which her mother had taught her to read. An oasis of peace in a warrior society, the lodge also harbors a secret that will destroy her father's people, for unopened bales of silk and other textiles stored there mask a deadly legacy from the old world.

Wallulah first appears on the flowering shores of a lake imitating the plaintive call of swans gliding by her home. On her ivory flute, the best loved of her mother's gifts, she reproduces "the very spirit" of their mournful cry. Attached to her belt by a golden chain, the flute never leaves Wallulah's side, its music accompanying her like a Wagnerian leitmotif. Only once does she let the flute fall to the ground, after Grey announces that his sense of duty will not permit him to see her again. She grips the flute defiantly when forced to marry Snoqualmie, the irascible chief of the Cayuse nation, and it remains with her to the end.

Grey's acute sense of empathy torments him with visions of Wallulah's life with Snoqualmie, who treats women as brutally as he treats his pack animals. To bear "his [sexual] touch," to sink daily deeper into the squalor of dirt and menial labor, eventually to be cast out with the "ancient withered hags, the burden bearers" who were no better than slaves, is too painful to contemplate. Intense pity and a feeling of responsibility for Wallulah's future misery poison Grey's desire for her, pitting his sensitive nature against the cold steel of his religious convictions. As Mount Hood breaks into a night eruption, Grey sees its red glare not as nature's sympathetic response to his own passion but as the imminent wrath of God on his faltering purpose. In this reaction, Balch observes, he resembles the Indians whom he had come to enlighten.

℘

Frederic Homer Balch was born in the Willamette Valley town of Lebanon on December 14, 1861, the son of James A. Balch (1825-1901) and Harriet Maria Snider Balch (1836-1891). Both natives of Indiana, they had migrated overland to Oregon, respectively, in 1851 and 1852. Exceptionally attractive in her youth, Harriet Snider was married and widowed twice before marrying James Balch.

Frederic Balch thus had two older siblings, a beloved half-sister, Allie Gallagher, who strongly encouraged his writing, and a half-brother, William Benson Helm, whose adventurous spirit he greatly admired. Although James Balch had graduated from Indiana's Wabash College and had studied law, he never applied for admission to the Oregon bar, though he briefly served as a judge in Klickitat County, Washington. Trying his hand at various occupations, from teacher, to photographer, to farmer, to cattleman, to amateur inventor, the senior Balch, despite his intelligence and talent, did not succeed at any vocation. As a result, Frederic was raised in near-poverty, with almost no formal education.

Because of Harriet's severe asthma, in 1871 the Balch family sought a drier climate east of the Cascade Range and moved to a farm near Goldendale, Washington Territory. It was on this trip that Frederic, then almost ten, first beheld the towering basalt cliffs, the silvery waterfalls, and the roaring cascades of the Columbia Gorge, an experience he never forgot. While at Goldendale, the growing boy became fascinated by the Indians living nearby and learned Chinook Jargon and some Klickitat as well.[3] Unlike many of his contemporaries, Balch showed respect for the tribal lore and customs that even then were rapidly vanishing. As his younger sister, Gertrude Balch Ingalls, later stated, no lodge or camp was too remote "if at the end of the trail he found a representative

---

3 Chinook Jargon was the trade language used in the Pacific Northwest during the late eighteenth and nineteenth century. It was comprised of a combination of several hundred native terms from the Chinook and other tribes, English, and French, and was relatively easy to learn and widely used by indigenous peoples, traders, missionaries, and pioneers. Balch included about a dozen words or phrases from Chinook Jargon in the present narrative.

of some old tribe, who remembered fragments of...legends...told by his forefathers."[4]

The Balches moved their household several more times to various sites near the Columbia, including a stay at Mount Tabor, six miles east of Portland. When the fifteen-year-old Frederic enrolled at a Mount Tabor school, his teachers were amazed at the extent of his reading: besides several of Shakespeare's plays, Scott's poetry, and Milton's *Paradise Lost*, he also had devoured Macaulay's essays on English and Roman history. Except for a brief stint at an elementary school near Goldendale years earlier, the few months at Mount Tabor (1876-1877) represented the full extent of Balch's formal instruction.[5] Taught at home by his well-educated father, young Frederic soon exhausted the family's small library and, overcoming his innate shyness, rode to distant homesteads to borrow books from other settlers. When Harriet's health again deteriorated because of the damp weather near Portland, the family returned to Goldendale, and thence to Lyle, located some forty miles distant on the Columbia River, perhaps because Harriet's brother, Jesse Snider, had settled there.

By the early 1880s, the Balch family was in extreme financial distress, partly because of a drought-induced crop failure on their Lyle farm. Then, when James Balch apparently suffered a mental crisis and was sent to live permanently with a sister in Indiana, young Frederic assumed the responsibility of supporting the family. Working on neighboring farms at harvest brought in

---

4   Gertrude Balch Ingalls, "Frederic Homer Balch," *Pacific Monthly* (Dec., 1900), 84-87. See also Alfred Powers, *History of Oregon Literature* (Portland, 1935), 326.

5   Delia M. Coon, "Frederic Homer Balch," *The Washington Historical Quarterly*, vol. 15 (January, 1924), 32-43.

little money, but railroad construction in the Columbia Gorge—the first railway on the Columbia's south bank—offered better wages. Hired by the Oregon Railway and Navigation Company, Balch broke rock for the railroad bed. Each morning he hiked downhill from his home to the river's north bank, rowed across, and put in a ten-hour day. Each evening he rowed back several miles upstream, climbed the 700-foot bluffs to the farm, and studied and wrote far into the night, shaping the novel *Wallulah*, an early version of *The Bridge of the Gods* that focused exclusively on prehistoric Indian culture. As the new track progressed farther east, Balch temporarily roomed at Columbia, a railroad camp upstream.

Much to the distress of his mother, a devout Methodist, young Balch professed agnosticism, deeply impressed by Robert G. Ingersoll, then a famous exponent of religious skepticism. About the time of his twenty-first birthday, however, he abruptly converted to Christianity. Like his later fictional creation, Cecil Grey, Balch apparently concluded that personal ambitions were incompatible with Christian practice so he renounced his literary efforts. On the December evening after announcing his conversion at a revival meeting in the Lyle schoolhouse, Balch strode to the large stone fireplace in the family home and, page by page, threw his only copy of *Wallulah* into the flames.

The sacrifice of *Wallulah* at the close of 1882 marked a decisive change in Balch's life. From the moment he burned his manuscript, Balch determined to become a Christian preacher, a lay minister who, often without pay, served small churches in settlements along the Columbia River. Traveling miles on horseback through frequently wet or freezing weather, Balch ministered to congregations from Mount Pleasant, to White Salmon, to Hood River. Initially embracing the scriptural literalism of his mother, who had often deplored the "heathen" element in his writing, Balch eventually came to champion, in his words, a "liberal Christianity"—accepting the universality of God and the brotherhood of all men, "regardless of creed, and the final redemption of the whole human race." This universalistic outlook served him well as an author, broadening his sympathies not only for Indians, but also for the wide spectrum of frontier settlers, some of whom became his parishioners. In late 1889 he took a leave of absence from the Congregational Church in Hood River to attend the Pacific Theological Seminary in Oakland, California (now the Pacific School of Religion in Berkeley), where he remained until ill health forced his return to Hood River in 1891.

While Balch was slowly attempting to reconcile his increasingly progressive Christianity with his passion to write, he also suffered intense personal grief. In rapid succession, three vibrant young women were taken from him. The first to die was his beloved half-sister, Allie Gallagher Condon, followed soon after by a favorite cousin, Mary Frances Snider, who had recently married George Lyle, son of the town's founder. The loss that most profoundly affected him, however, that taught him to "question everything but death," was the demise of Genevra Whitcomb, the daughter of a prominent Lyle family. According to members of the Whitcomb family, Genevra, outstandingly pretty and vivacious, did not reciprocate Balch's one-sided affection. She left Lyle in 1885 to attend a girls' school in The Dalles, a larger town about nine miles upriver, where she unexpectedly contracted pneumonia and died in January 1886. She was nineteen. A heavy

snowfall and sub-freezing temperatures that month iso-
lated Lyle from neighboring communities, so that after
Genevra's body was brought by a scow back to Lyle, the
Whitcomb family asked Balch to conduct her funeral.
Balch agreed, although he later remarked that it was the
worst ordeal of his life.

He managed the service well, until the coffin lid was
lifted for a last farewell. As Balch later wrote, "When I
looked upon her dead face with the little heap of salt on
the still lips, it all came back, and I knew that I was looking for the last time upon the face of the only girl I would
ever love." The sudden awareness that he felt so deeply for
Genevra came late to Balch, but it never left him. Years
later he wrote his sister Gertrude from the Oakland seminary that he had met an interesting Scottish lass who
resembled Genevra in her lively conversation, but that
the mild attraction only seemed to intensify his sense of
loss. "After all these years the girl who died at Lyle is
more to me than any girl or woman now living. If I ever
marry anyone it will have to be, I am afraid, a marriage
without love, which is not supposed to be desirable."[6]

Genevra's unexpected death left Balch utterly stricken.
After shutting himself up in his room for more than a
month, he gradually resumed his ministerial duties, not
only delivering sermons but conducting revival services
notable for their exceptionally quiet but intense spirituality. According to a friend, Jennie Jewett, who ran a popular
farm resort in White Salmon, Washington, "his one aim
seemed to be good and to do good for others." Ordained
a Congregational minister early in 1887, Balch frequently

---

6   Letter from F. H. Balch to G. B. Ingalls (1890); cited in Leonard Wiley, *The
    Granite Boulder: A Biography of Frederic Homer Balch*, published by the author
    (Portland, 1970), 119.

worked himself to exhaustion for multiple churches along the Columbia while simultaneously writing *The Bridge of the Gods*, which he completed about 1889. Juggling his authorial and pastoral duties, he sent the book out to so many different publishers—all of whom promptly mailed it back—that he was inspired to compose the jocular "Ballad of the Rejected Manuscript." By the summer of 1890, when he returned to Hood River on vacation from the Oakland seminary, Balch had apparently given up on seeing his work published.

At this low point, Nelson Brooks, a family friend and the Klickitat County Superintendent of Schools, learned of a Midwest publisher interested in Western Indian lore. In the meantime Balch's mother, living at the Lyle farm, had decided to burn the only copy of the manuscript whose repeated rejections had caused her son such disappointment. Fortunately for Northwest literature, fate intervened and an overflowing creek swept away the box in which she had placed the unpublished text. Taking off his shoes and rolling up his pants, Brooks retrieved the water-logged manuscript, which Balch recopied and sent to McClurg and Company in Chicago. Balch wrote a new preface to his story and *The Bridge of the Gods* was issued by McClurg in the fall of 1890.

Balch was convinced that the "bridge" was a historical reality and that its former existence held great meaning for the region's indigenous peoples, a confidence that contemporary scientists have confirmed. Because native languages did not have a word for "bridge," the notion that the "Bridge of the Gods" was a soaring stone arch is a later Euro-American invention. What the Indians told early trappers, missionaries, and settlers was that in ages past (the exact number of years is invariably vague) native travelers could cross the great river without wetting their feet and that the causeway on which they journeyed was *tomanowos*, a product of superhuman forces.

According to a Klickitat version of the legend, creation of the sacred landform was a divine act, but its destruction was the result of human misbehavior. In this tradition, *Tyee Sahale* (commonly translated as the "Great Spirit") had two human sons, Pahto, who controlled the area north of the Columbia, and Wyeast, who ruled the territory south of the river. The two regions were linked by the *tomanowos* causeway, over which multitudes regularly crossed the Columbia to barter and trade. As the tribes in their respective areas became increasingly greedy and aggressive, Pahto and Wyeast also competed jealously for the love of a beautiful maiden, Loowit. When the brothers' quarrel reached lethal intensity, *Tyee Sahale* angrily shook down the structure that had connected their two lands, its shattered fragments forming the Cascade Rapids. Formerly an almost impassable series of whitewater falls where the river surged over huge angular blocks, the rapids are now submerged beneath the waters impounded by Bonneville Dam. The Cascade Range, the volcanic mountains that divide Oregon and Washington, received their name from these rapids. In myth, *Tyee Sahale* punished his warring sons by transforming them into volcanic mountains: Wyeast became the lofty peak later known as Mount Hood; Pahto became broad-shouldered Mount Adams; while the alluring Loowit became the smoothly symmetrical Mount St. Helens (as she was before the eruption of 1980). Even after their metamorphosis into glaciated peaks, Wyeast, Pahto, and Loowit continued to blaze with passion, catapulting incandescent rocks down their icy slopes and devastating the countryside.

Twenty-first century geologists have validated Balch's belief in the historicity of the vanished landform, indirectly confirming the native traditions on which he based his narrative. The "bridge" legend is, in fact, a prime example of geomythology, a discipline that studies oral histories preserving memories of geologic phenomena, such as earthquakes, tsunamis, and volcanic eruptions. The geologic story of the "bridge of the gods" is as intriguing as the legends native storytellers later wove about it.

Central to the bridge's biography is the Columbia River, which empties more water into the Pacific Ocean than any other river in North or South America. Over millions of years, the Columbia's eroding power has cut the only near-sea-level passage through the still-rising Cascade Range, excavating a spectacular eighty-mile-long canyon through the mountain barrier. Ice Age floods, repeatedly released from glacial Lake Missoula in western Montana, scoured and reshaped the Columbia Gorge, widening the canyon and steepening its walls, which rise up to 4,000 feet above the river.

On the Washington (north) bank of the river the gorge walls are particularly unstable because dense, heavy volcanic rock sits on top of softer, more permeable materials. The gorge wall's upper 1,500 feet are composed of solid flows of basalt lava that erupted from vents across eastern Washington and Oregon about 15 million years ago. Underneath the lava flows is a thick layer of friable, slippery rock, old volcanic ash beds and mud flow deposits known as the Eagle Creek formation. The whole sequence of deposits is tilted gently southward so that the upper basalt flows on the north side of the Columbia slide over the lower, water-saturated Eagle Creek layer. In the words of one geologist, this section of the gorge's north wall resembles "a stack of heavily buttered pancakes on a tilted platter." Given this geologic environment, landslides are inevitable—and frequent.[7]

Geologists do not yet know what triggered the gorge's largest landslide, the Bonneville Slide, that totally dammed the Columbia River and inspired tales of the *tomanowos* landform, but they now estimate that it occurred between about AD 1416 and 1452, probably between AD 1421 and 1447. Nearly half a cubic mile of rock broke loose at or near the summits of Washington's Table Mountain and Greenleaf Peak, which stand about three miles north of the river. A complex series of rock-slide-debris avalanches moved south to block the river entirely, burying five square miles and forming a natural dam at least 200 feet high.

Trapped behind the slide barrier, the Columbia's rising waters formed a lake that extended fifty to seventy miles upstream, possibly to the site of the present John Day Dam. Donald Lawrence, the late University of Minnesota professor who researched the slide effects in the 1930s, informally dubbed the impounded waters as "Lake Balch."

Although the Bonneville Slide permanently forced the Columbia about a mile southeast of its former course, the river, probably within a few years, breached the slide's south toe, cutting a narrow channel through the rock

---

7   Jim E. O'Connor, "The Evolving Landscape of the Columbia River Gorge," *Oregon Historical Quarterly*, vol. 105 (Fall, 2004), 389-425. See also Patrick Pringle, "The Bonneville Slide," in the Columbia Gorge Interpretative Museum.

debris and initiating a major flood downstream. It is possible that part of the slide barrier remained standing after
the river incised a new passageway around its southern
margin. If so, the famed Bridge of the Gods may have
been no more than a chaotic pile of large basaltic slabs
derived from the gorge's north wall, some of which measure up to 800 feet long and 200 feet thick. This jumble
of lava blocks, too heavy to have been swept away entirely
when the slide was breached, may have remained in place
for an indefinite period, forming a conspicuous link
between tribal territories north and south of the Columbia. According to Pierre-Jean De Smet, a Jesuit missionary who visited the gorge in the 1840s, local natives
told him that the "bridge" consisted of "a long range of
towering and projecting rocks"—exactly what one would
expect of a causeway composed of angular basaltic fragments. By an interesting coincidence, Balch set the time
of the "bridge's" collapse about 1700, which is precisely
the date on which the most recent earthquake along the
Cascadia subduction zone—an estimated magnitude
9.0—convulsed the Pacific Coast from northern California to southern Vancouver Island.

However long the *tomanowos* landform endured, its
rocky remnants—creating the Cascade Rapids—permanently raised the Columbia's surface level upstream and
drowned a broad strip of forest along the former river-
banks. When Lewis and Clark traversed the Columbia
Gorge in 1805-1806, they noticed innumerable dead pine
snags standing many feet beneath the river's surface.
Although they mistakenly inferred that the river blockage
that submerged the forest had taken place only twenty
years before their expedition, the explorers correctly

recognized the nature of events that had so thoroughly transformed the river.

In his preface to *Bridge of the Gods*, Balch wrote that in his day a curious traveler plying the Columbia River "in a small boat just above the cascades" could "see submerged forest trees beneath him, still standing upright as they stood before the bridge fell in and the river was raised above them." The writer keenly felt the "weirdness" of nature's caprice, observing "fish swim among the leafless branches."

Balch's depiction of Mount Hood as a recently active volcano is also accurate. Although sheathed in glacial ice, Hood (11,239 feet) has repeatedly erupted in historic time, beginning its latest eruptive cycle about 1781-1782 and continuing intermittently until the 1860s. Thick viscous lava oozing from vents at Crater Rock, a lava dome high on Hood's south side, partly melted the volcano's ice cover, generating floods and mudflows—turbulent mixtures of water and rock fragments that flow like liquid concrete—that swept down the Sandy River and into the Columbia. In 1792, when Vancouver dispatched Lieutenant Broughton to explore the lower Columbia, Broughton found that a long sand bar extended from the Sandy's mouth across the Columbia. More than a decade later, Lewis and Clark noted that the Sandy was still choked with debris, its waters running over a wide bed of treacherous "quick Sand."

Eyewitness accounts of Mount Hood's mid-nineteenth century activity may have influenced Balch's remarkably precise description of Hood's eruptive behavior. From Tygh Ridge in September 1859, W. F. Courtney observed a night eruption: "Suddenly the heavens lit up and from the dark there shot up a column of fire. With a flash that illuminated the whole mountainside with a pinkish glare, the flame danced from the crater." For two hours the volcano continued "to blaze at irregular intervals," and the next morning Hood "presented a peculiar sight. His sides where the day before there was snow, were blackened as if cinders and ashes had been thrown out."[8] Balch's description is strikingly similar:

> From Mount Hood streamed intermittent bursts of smoke and gleams of fire that grew plainer as the twilight fell. Louder, as the hush of evening deepened, came the sullen roar from the crater of Mount Hood. Below the crater, the ice fields that had glistened in unbroken whiteness the previous day were now furrowed with wide black streaks, from which the vapor of melting snow and burning lava ascended in dense wreaths.

Courtney's report was not published until 1902, but Balch may have collected oral accounts from early settlers who had observed Hood's historic eruptions. Apparently aware that Mount Adams had been less active than Mount Hood in recent centuries, Balch was careful to differentiate between the two alpine guardians of the Columbia. While Hood radiates an incandescent glow, Adams is merely sullen, "wrapped in dusky cloud," Native testimony that Mount Adams, like Mount Hood and Mount St. Helens, had once "smoked continuously" is probably correct.

Balch had intended *The Bridge of the Gods* to be a kind of mythic prelude to more naturalistic fiction that he would write, but only *Genevieve: A Tale of Oregon* sur-

---

8   Stephen L. Harris, *Fire Mountains of the West: The Cascade and Mono Lake Volcanoes*, 3rd edition, Missoula, Montana: The Mountain Press, 2005.

vives complete. Probably begun shortly after Genevra's demise in 1886, the novel occupied Balch almost to the hour of his own death. Despite the rigors of studying for his theological degree at the Oakland seminary while suffering from tuberculosis, he devoted many evenings after class to revising this tribute to Genevra. He dedicated the work to "one, now dead, whose name gives the book its title and whose character is portrayed in its pages." The heroine, to whom he gave a more familiar form of Genevra's name, has an intelligence, grace, and simple dignity that Balch thought characterized the best type of "Oregon girl." A cornucopia of Northwest social life from Portland to Puget Sound in the late 1880s, *Genevieve* also features one of Balch's memorable Indian figures, the Princess Winemah. Although old and frail, Winemah is a formidable sorceress, sustained by her hatred of the white race who have displaced her people. Edited by Alfred Powers, then a journalism professor at the University of Oregon, *Genevieve* was published posthumously in 1932. Powers also collected several of Balch's poems and two essays, including a fictional first-person account of the Whitman Massacre, which he published in *Memaloose* (1934).

Genevieve, the most autobiographical of his fiction, testifies to the extent to which Balch identified with Indian culture. His hero (and alter ego) is Guido Colonna, the son of an Italian patriot and a Native American woman, recently returned to the Pacific Northwest after several years traveling abroad. Like his author, Colonna is determined to write about the Columbia's native inhabitants, despite the social prejudice the "half-breed" repeatedly encounters. When Balch describes Indians as "savage" or "barbarous," he is aware that is how most of his nineteenth century readers regarded them. As Ernest Ingersoll observed in 1882, "the [Oregonian] who asserts the red man's humanity and immortal worth in the eyes of his and our Creator goes flatly against" the majority opinion.[9] In *The Bridge of the Gods* when Balch writes that "[Indian culture] was a rude caricature of civilization, the picture of a society in its infancy, the rough dramatization of that phase through which every race passes in its evolution from barbarism," it is a plea to understand human unity. We all spring from ancestors who were barbarians.

Besides revising *Genevieve*, Balch devoted his final months to working on other projects, each of which was to dramatize crucial events in Pacific Northwest history. Only six chapters in a rough-draft manuscript survive of *Kenasket*, though Balch predicted that this *Tale of Oregon in 1818* would be his "shortest and...best book." Fluently mixing both historical and imaginary characters, he—with almost gritty realism—portrays the dangers and excitement of the Northwest fur trade in an era when Britain had purchased the American Fort Astoria, renaming it Fort George, and commercially dominated the entire region.

Whereas *Kenasket* describes a masculine world of intense competition and wilderness adventure, at about the same time Balch wrote his only known short story, a work that focuses exclusively on the plight of women in the contemporary Washington frontier. In "How a Camas Prairie Girl Saw the World," the author highlights the predicament of wives and daughters living in penury on remote and isolated farms, observing that their conflicts

9   Ernest Ingersoll, *Harper's New Monthly Magazine* (October, 1882), 770.

and "household tragedies [are no less] vivid and intense because the actors are clad in print or overalls." Whereas *The Bridge of the Gods* exults in the physical grandeur of a pristine landscape, the Camas girl shows the high price settlers could pay for their seclusion amid the soaring peaks and dense forest that proved formidable obstacles to an individual's artistic hopes.[10]

In March 1891 Balch became too ill to sit through a seminary class and returned to Hood River. Determined to recover from the disease that consumed him, he reassured Gertrude and his mother that he needed only a short time "to recuperate a little." He laid plans to pursue his missionary work in either Arizona or Colorado, where he hoped to find a cure—and continue rewriting *Genevieve*, finish *Kenasket*, and begin other works. In his copy of Joaquin Miller's poems, Balch sketched out the titles of other novels he had in mind: *Crossing the Plains*, perhaps incorporating his parents' memories of the Oregon Trail in the early 1850s; *A Tale of Waiilat-Pu*, depicting Marcus and Narcissa Whitman's mission of that name and of which he had already spun a narrative of the Cayuse attack; and *The Senator*, presumably a novel about then-current Pacific Northwest politics. He had many books yet to write.

Alarmed by his increasing weakness, friends almost forced Balch to enter Good Samaritan Hospital in Portland, where he died on June 3, 1891, more than six months before his thirtieth birthday. Despite the brevity of his life, Frederic Balch was a major regional writer, not only the first to cast native inhabitants in major roles in his

---

10 Stephen L. Harris, "A Northwest Tale: Frederic Homer Balch's 'Camas Prairie Girl'," *Columbia* (Spring, 1993), 37-44.

fiction, but also the first to exploit the Columbia region's physical splendor. He pioneered what no other Pacific Northwest author had done before: In *The Bridge of the Gods*, he gave the area a sense of its unique identity.

Stephen L. Harris is Professor Emeritus, Department of Humanities and Religious Studies, California State University, Sacramento, California. His dozen published books and numerous articles in periodicals focus on classical mythology, the humanist tradition in world literature, biblical interpretation, and geologic hazards in the Pacific Northwest. His interest in Frederic Homer Balch and his writings is of long standing, and he has published several articles on that topic in Oregon Historical Quarterly *and* Columbia, The Magazine of Northwest History.

"*WHAT think you now, Tohomish?*"

THE BRIDGE OF THE GODS

A Romance of Indian Oregon

By F. H. BALCH

NINTH EDITION

With eight full-page illustrations by
L. MAYNARD DIXON

CHICAGO · A. C. McCLURG & CO.
NINETEEN HUNDRED & FOUR

PUBLISHERS' NOTE

---◆---

ENCOURAGED by the steady demand for Mr. Balch's "The Bridge of the Gods," since its publication twelve years ago, the publishers have decided to issue a new edition beautified with drawings from the pencil of Mr. L. Maynard Dixon. This tale of the Indians of the far West has fairly earned its lasting popularity, not only by the intense interest of the story, but by its faithful delineations of Indian character.

In his boyhood Mr. Balch enjoyed exceptional opportunities to inform himself regarding the character and manners of the Indians: he visited them in their homes, watched their industries, heard their legends, saw their gambling games, listened to their conversation; he questioned the Indians and the white pioneers, and he read many books for information on Indian history, traditions, and legends. By personal inquiry among old natives he learned that the Bridge which suggested the title of his romance was no fabric of the imagination, but was a great natural bridge that in early days spanned the Columbia, and later, according to tradition, was destroyed by an earthquake.

Before his death the author had the satisfaction of knowing that his work was stamped with the approval of the press and the public; his satisfaction would have been more complete could he have foreseen that that approval would be so lasting.

JULY 1, 1902.

PREFACE.

————◆————

IN attempting to present with romantic setting a
truthful and realistic picture of the powerful and
picturesque Indian tribes that inhabited the Oregon
country two centuries ago, the author could not be
indifferent to the many serious difficulties inseparable
from such an enterprise. Of the literary success with
which his work has been accomplished, he must of course
leave others to judge; but he may without immodesty
speak briefly of his preparation for his task, and of the
foundation of some of the facts and legends which form
the framework of his story. Indian life and character
have long been a favorite study with him, and in these
pages he has attempted to describe them, not from an
ideal standpoint, but as he knew them in his own boyhood on the Upper Columbia. Many of the incidents
related in the story have come under his personal observation; others have been told him by aged pioneers, or
gleaned from old books of Northwestern travel. The
every-day life of the Indians, their food, their dress, their
methods of making their mats, of building their houses,
of shaping their canoes, their gambling games, their religious beliefs, their legends, their subjects of conversation, the sports and pastimes of their children, — all these
have been studied at first hand, and with the advantages
of familiar and friendly intercourse with these people in
their own homes. By constant questioning, many facts

have been gained regarding their ancestry, and the fragments of history, tradition, and legend that have come
down from them. Indian antiquities have been studied
through every available source of information. All the
antiquarian collections in Oregon and California have
been consulted, old trading-posts visited, and old pioneers
and early missionaries conversed with. Nothing has been
discarded as trivial or insignificant that could aid in the
slightest degree in affording an insight into Indian character and customs of a by-gone age.

As to the great Confederacy of the Wauna, it may
be said that Gray's "History of Oregon" tells us of an
alliance of several tribes on the Upper Columbia for mutual protection and defence; and students of Northwestern history will recall the great confederacy that the
Yakima war-chief Kamyakin formed against the whites
in the war of 1856, when the Indian tribes were in revolt
from the British Possessions to the California line.
Signal-fires announcing war against the whites leaped
from hill to hill, flashing out in the night, till the line of
fire beginning at the wild Okanogan ended a thousand
miles south, on the foot-hills of Mount Shasta. Knowing
such a confederacy as this to be an historical fact, there
seems nothing improbable in that part of the legend
which tells us that in ancient times the Indian tribes
on either side of the Cascade Range united under the
great war-chief Multnomah against their hereditary foes
the Shoshones. Even this would not be so extensive a
confederacy as that which Kamyakin formed a hundred
and fifty years later.

It may be asked if there was ever a great natural bridge
over the Columbia, — a "Bridge of the Gods," such as the
legend describes. The answer is emphatically, "Yes."
Everywhere along the mid-Columbia the Indians tell of
a great bridge that once spanned the river where the
cascades now are, but where at that time the placid

current flowed under an arch of stone ; that this bridge was *tomanowos*, built by the gods ; that the Great Spirit shook the earth, and the bridge crashed down into the river, forming the present obstruction of the cascades. All of the Columbian tribes tell this story, in different versions and in different dialects, but all agreeing upon its essential features as one of the great facts of their past history.

"*Ancutta* (long time back)," say the Tumwater Indians, "the salmon he no pass Tumwater falls. It too much big leap. Snake Indian he no catch um fish above falls. By and by great *tomanowos* bridge at cascades he fall in, dam up water, make river higher all way up to Tumwater ; then salmon he get over. Then Snake Indian all time catch um plenty."

"My father talk one time," said an old Klickitat to a pioneer at White Salmon, Washington ; "long time ago liddle boy, him in canoe, his mother paddle, paddle up Columbia, then come to *tomanowos* bridge. Squaw paddle canoe under ; all dark under bridge. He look up, all like one big roof, shut out sky, no see um sun. Indian afraid, paddle quick, get past soon, no good. Liddle boy no forget how bridge look."

Local proof also is not wanting. In the fall, when the freshets are over and the waters of the Columbia are clear, one going out in a small boat just above the cascades and looking down into the transparent depths can see submerged forest trees beneath him, still standing upright as they stood before the bridge fell in and the river was raised above them. It is a strange, weird sight, this forest beneath the river ; the waters wash over the broken tree-tops, fish swim among the leafless branches : it is desolate, spectre-like, beyond all words. Scientific men who have examined the field with a view to determining the credibility of the legend about the bridge are convinced that it is essentially true. Believed in by many tribes, attested by the appearance of the locality, and confirmed by geological investigation, it is surely entitled to be received as a historic fact.

The shipwreck of an Oriental vessel on the Oregon coast, which furnishes one of the most romantic elements in our story, is an altogether probable historic incident, as explained more fully in a foot-note on page 75.

The spelling of Indian names, in which authorities differ so widely, has been made as accurate as possible; and, as in the name "Wallulah," the oldest and most Indian-like form has been chosen. An exception has been made in the case of the modernized and corrupted "Willamette," which is used instead of the original Indian name, "Walla-met." But the meaningless "Willamette" has unfortunately passed into such general use that one is almost compelled to accept it. Another verbal irregularity should be noticed: Wauna, the name given by all the Indians in the story to the Columbia, was only the Klickitat name for it. The Indians had no general name for the Columbia, but each tribe had a special name, if any, for it. Some had no name for it at all. It was simply "the big water," "*the* river," "the big salmon water." What Wauna, the Klickitat name, or Wemath, the Wasco name, signifies, the author has been unable to learn, even from the Indians who gave him the names. They do not know; they say their fathers knew, but it is forgotten now.

A rich and splendid treasure of legend and lore has passed away with the old pioneers and the Indians of the earlier generation. All that may be found interesting in this or any other book on the Indians, compared to what has been lost, is like "a torn leaf from some old romance."

F. H. B.

OAKLAND, CALIFORNIA,
September, 1890.

CONTENTS.

Book IV.

THE LOVE TALE.

Book V.

THE SHADOW OF THE END.

ILLUSTRATIONS.

———◆———

What tall and tawny men were these,
As sombre, silent, as the trees
They moved among! and sad some way
With tempered sadness, ever they,
Yet not with sorrow born of fear.
The shadows of their destinies
They saw approaching year by year,
And murmured not.
    .   .   .   .   .   .

They turned to death as to a sleep,
And died with eager hands held out
To reaching hands beyond the deep;
And died with choicest bow at hand,
And quiver full and arrow drawn
For use, when sweet to-morrow's dawn
Should wake them in the Spirit Land.

JOAQUIN MILLER.

THE BRIDGE OF THE GODS.

BOOK I.

THE APOSTLE TO THE INDIANS.

CHAPTER I.

THE NEW ENGLAND MEETING.

Such as sit in darkness and the shadow of death. —*Bible.*

ONE Sabbath morning more than two hundred years ago, the dawn broke clear and beautiful over New England. It was one of those lovely mornings that seem like a benediction, a smile of God upon the earth, so calm are they, so full of unutterable rest and quiet. Over the sea, with its endless line of beach and promontory washed softly by the ocean swells ; over the towns of the coast, — Boston and Salem, — already large, giving splendid promise of the future ; over the farms and hamlets of the interior, and into the rude clearings where the outer limits of civilization mingled with the primeval forest, came a flood of light as the sun rose above the blue line of eastern sea. And still beyond, across the Alleghanies, into the depth of the wilderness, passed the sweet, calm radiance, as if bearing a gleam of gospel sunshine to the Indians of the forest.

Nowhere did the Sunday seem more peaceful than in a sheltered valley in Massachusetts. Beautiful indeed were the thrifty orchards, the rustic farmhouses, the meadows where the charred stumps that marked the last clearing were festooned with running vines, the fields green with Indian corn, and around all the sweep of hills dark with the ancient wood. Even the grim unpainted meeting-house on the hill, which was wont to look the very personification of the rigid Calvinistic theology preached within it, seemed a little less bare and forbidding on that sweet June Sabbath.

As the hour for morning service drew near, the drummer took his accustomed stand before the church and began to thunder forth his summons, — a summons not unfitting those stern Puritans whose idea of religion was that of a life-long warfare against the world, the flesh, and the devil.

Soon the people began to gather, — grave men and women, dressed in the sober-colored garb of the day, and little children, clad in their " Sunday best," undergoing the awful process of " going to meeting," yet some of them, at least, looking at the cool shadowed wood as they passed, and thinking how pleasant it would be to hunt berries or birds' nests in those sylvan retreats instead of listening to a two hours' sermon, under imminent danger of perdition if they went to sleep, — for in such seductive guise did the Evil One tempt the souls of these youthful Puritans. Solemn of visage and garb were the groups, although here and there the gleam of a bit of ribbon at the throat of some young maiden, or a bonnet tastefully adorned, showed that " the world, the flesh, and the devil " were not yet wholly subdued among them.

As the audience filed through the open door, the men and women divided, the former taking one side of the house, the latter the other, — the aisle forming a dividing line between them. The floor was un-carpeted, the walls bare, the pulpit undraped, and upon it the hour-glass stood beside the open Bible. Anything more stiff and barren than the interior of the meeting-house it would be difficult to find.

An unwonted stir breaks the silence and solemnity of the waiting congregation, as an official party enters. It is the Governor of the colony and his staff, who are making a tour of the province, and have stopped over Sunday in the little frontier settlement, — for although the Governor is an august man, even he may not pre-sume to travel on the Sabbath in this land of the Puritans. The new-comers are richly dressed. There is something heavy, massive, and splendid in their garb, especially in the Governor's. He is a stately military-looking man, and wears his ample vestments, his embroidered gloves, his lace and ruffles, with a magisterial air.

A rustle goes through the audience as the distin-guished visitors pass up the aisle to the front seats assigned, as the custom was, to dignitaries. Young people steal curious glances at them ; children turn around in their seats to stare, provoking divers shakes of the head from their elders, and in one instance the boxing of an ear, at which the culprit sets up a smothered howl, is ignominiously shaken, and sits swelling and choking with indignant grief during the remainder of the service.

At length the drum ceased, indicating both the arrival of the minister and the time for service to begin.

The minister took his place in the pulpit. He was a young man, of delicate mould, with a pale and intellectual face. Exquisite sensitiveness was in the large gray eyes, the white brow, the delicate lips, the long slender fingers; yet will and energy and command were in them all. His was that rare union of extreme sensibility with strong resolution that has given the world its religious leaders, — its Savonarolas and Chrysostoms; men whose nerves shrank at a discord in music, but when inspired by some grand cause, were like steel to suffer and endure.

Something of this was in the minister's aspect, as he stood before the people that morning. His eyes shone and dilated, and his slight figure gathered dignity as his gaze met that of the assembly. There was no organ, that instrument being deemed a device of the Prince of Darkness to lead the hearts of the unwary off to popery; but the opening hymn was heartily sung. Then came the Scripture reading, — usually a very monotonous performance on the part of Puritan divines; but as given in the young minister's thoughtfully modulated voice, nothing could have been more expressive. Every word had its meaning, every metaphor was a picture; the whole psalm seemed to breathe with life and power: "Lord, thou hast been our dwelling-place in all generations."

Majestic, mournful, yet thrilling with deathless hope, was the minister's voice; and the people were deeply moved. The prayer followed, — not the endless monologue of the average Puritan clergyman, but pointed, significant, full of meaning. Again his face was lifted before them as he rose to announce the text. It was paler now; the eyes were glowing and luminous; the long, expressive fingers were tremulous with excitement. It was evident to all that no common subject was to be introduced, no common effort to be made. Always composed, the audience grew more quiet still. The very children felt the hush of expectation, and gazed wonderingly at the minister. Even that great man, the Governor, lost his air of unbending grandeur, and leaned expectantly forward.

The subject was Paul's vision of the man in Macedonia crying for help. The speaker portrayed in burning words the condition of Macedonia, the heathen gloom and utter hopelessness of her people, the vision that came to Paul, and his going to preach to them. Then, passing to England under the Druids, he described the dark paganism, the blood-stained altars, the brutal priesthood of the age; and told of the cry that went forth for light, — a cry that touched the heart of the Roman Gregory into sending missionaries to show them the better way.

Like some royal poem was the discourse, as it showed how, through the storms and perils of more than a thousand years, amid the persecution of popes, the wars of barons, and the tyranny of kings, England had kept the torch burning, till in these latter times it had filled the world with light. Beautiful was the tribute he paid to the more recent defenders of the faith, and most intense the interest of the listeners; for men sat there who had come over the seas because of their loyalty to the faith, — old and grizzled men, whose youth had known Cromwell and Charles Stuart, and who had in more recent years fought for " King Monmouth " and shared the dark fortunes of Argyle.

The old Governor was roused like a veteran warhorse at the sound of the trumpet; many faces were flushed with martial ardor. The young minister paused reflectively at the enthusiasm he had kindled. A sorrowful smile flitted around his lips, though the glow of inspiration was still burning in his eyes. Would they be as enthusiastic when he made the application of his discourse?

And yet England, yea, even New England, was false, disloyal. She had but half kept the faith. When the cry of pagan England had gone forth for light, it had been heard; the light had been given. But now in her day of illumination, when the Macedonian cry came to her, she closed her ears and listened not. On her skirts was the blood of the souls of men; and at the last day the wail of the heathen as they went down into the gulf of flame would bear witness against her.

Grave and impassioned, with an undertone of warning and sorrow, rang the voice of the minister, and the hearts of the people were shaken as though a prophet were speaking.

"Out from the forests around us come the cry of heathen folk, and ye will not listen. Ye have the light, and they perish in darkness and go down to the pit. Generation after generation has grown up here in forest and mountain, and has lived and died without God and without hope. Generation has followed generation, stumbling blindly downward to the dust like the brutes that perish. And now their children, bound in iron and sitting under the shadow of death, reach out their hands from the wilderness with a blind cry to you for help. Will ye hear?"

He lifted his hands to them as he spoke; there was infinite pathos in his voice; for a moment it seemed as if all the wild people of the wilderness were pleading through him for light. Tears were in many eyes; yet in spite of the wonderful power of his oratory, there were faces that grew stern as he spoke, — for only a few years had passed since the Pequod war, and the feeling against the Indians was bitter. The Governor now sat erect and indignant.

Strong and vehement was the minister's plea for missionaries to be sent to the Indians; fearlessly was the colonial government arraigned for its deficiencies in this regard; and the sands in the hourglass were almost run out when the sermon was concluded and the minister sank flushed and exhausted into his seat.

The closing psalm was sung, and the audience was dismissed. Slow and lingering were the words of the benediction, as if the preacher were conscious of defeat and longed to plead still further with his people. Then the gathering broke up, the congregation filing out with the same solemnity that had marked the entrance. But when the open air was reached, the pent-up excitement burst forth in a general murmur of comment.

"A good man," remarked the Governor to his staff, "but young, quite young." And they smiled approvingly at the grim irony of the tone.

"Our pastor is a fine speaker," said another, "but

why will he bring such unpleasant things into the pulpit?   A good doctrinal sermon, now, would have strengthened our faith and edified us all."

"Ay, a sermon on the errors of Episcopacy, for instance."

"Such talk makes me angry," growled a third. "Missionaries for the Indians! when the bones of the good folk they have killed are yet bleaching amid the ashes of their cabins! Missionaries for those red demons! an' had it been powder and shot for them it had been a righteous sermon."

So the murmur of disapprobation went on among those slowly dispersing groups who dreaded and hated the Indian with an intensity such as we now can hardly realize.   And among them came the minister, pale and downcast, realizing that he had dashed himself in vain against the stern prejudice of his people and his age.

CHAPTER II.

THE MINISTER'S HOME.

Sore have I panted at the sun's decline,
To pass with him into the crimson West,
And see the peoples of the evening.
                                    EDWIN ARNOLD.

THE Reverend Cecil Grey, — for such was our young minister's name, — proceeded immediately after the service to his home. Before we cross its threshold with him, let us pause for a moment to look back over his past life.

Born in New England, he first received from his father, who was a fine scholar, a careful home training, and was then sent to England to complete his education. At Magdalen College, Oxford, he spent six years. Time passed very happily with him in the quiet cloisters of that most beautiful of English colleges, with its memories of Pole and Rupert, and the more courtly traditions of the state that Richard and Edward had held there. But when, in 1687, James II. attempted to trample on the privileges of the Fellows and force upon them a popish president, Cecil was one of those who made the famous protest against it ; and when protests availed nothing, he left Oxford, as also did a number of others. Returning to America, he was appointed pastor of a New England church, becoming one of the many who carried the

·flower of scholarship and eloquence into the bleak wilds of the New World.

Restless, sensitive, ardent, he was a man to whom a settled pastorate was impossible. Daring enterprises, great undertakings of a religious nature yet full of peril, were the things for which he was naturally fitted ; and amid the monotonous routine of parish duties he longed for a greater activity. Two centuries later he might have become distinguished as a revivalist or as a champion of new and startling views of theology ; earlier, he might have been a reformer, a follower of Luther or Loyola ; as it was, he was out of his sphere.

But for a time the Reverend Mr. Grey tried hard to mould himself to his new work. He went with anxious fidelity through all the labors of the country pastorate. He visited and prayed with the sick, he read the Bible to the old and dim-sighted, he tried to reconcile petty quarrels, he wrestled with his own discontent, and strove hard to grind down all the aspirations of his nature and shut out the larger horizon of life.

And for a time he was successful ; but during it he was induced to take a very fatal step. He was young, handsome, a clergyman, and unmarried. Now a young unmarried minister is pre-eminently one of sorrows and acquainted with grief. For that large body of well-meaning people who are by nature incapacitated from attending to their own business take him in hand without mercy. Innumerable are the ways in which he is informed that he ought to be married. Subtle and past finding out are the plots laid by all the old ladies and match-makers of his church to promote that desired event. He is told that he can never succeed in the ministry till he is married. The praises of Matilda Jane Tompkins or Lucinda Brown are sounded in his ears till he almost wishes that both were in a better world, — a world more worthy their virtues. At length, wearily capitulating, he marries some wooden-faced or angular saint, and is unhappy for life.

Now there was in Mr. Grey's church a good, gentle girl, narrow but not wooden-faced, famous for her neatness and her housekeeping abilities, who was supposed to be the pattern for a minister's wife. In time gone by she had set her heart on a graceless sailor lad who was drowned at sea, much to the relief of her parents. Ruth Anderson had mourned for him quietly, shutting up her sorrow in her own breast and going about her work as before ; for hers was one of those subdued, practical natures that seek relief from trouble in hard work.

She seemed in the judgment of all the old women in the church the " very one " for Mr. Grey ; and it likewise seemed that Mr. Grey was the " very one " for her. So divers hints were dropped and divers things were said, until each began to wonder if marriage were not a duty. The Reverend Cecil Grey began to take unusual pains with his toilet, and wended his way up the hill to Mr. Anderson's with very much the aspect of a man who is going to be hanged. And his attempts at conversation with the maiden were not at all what might have been expected from the young minister whose graceful presence and fluent eloquence had been the boast of Magdalen. On her part the embarrassment was equally great. At length they

were married, — a marriage based on a false idea of
duty on each side. But no idea of duty, however
strong or however false, could blind the eyes of this
married pair to the terrible fact that not only love but
mental sympathy was wanting. Day by day Cecil
felt that his wife did not love him, that her thoughts
were not for him, that it was an effort for her to act
the part of a wife toward him. Day by day she felt
that his interests lay beyond her reach, and that all
the tenderness in his manner toward her came from
a sense of duty, not from love.

But she strove in all ways to be a faithful wife, and
he tried hard to be a kind and devoted husband.
He had been especially attentive to her of late, for
her health had been failing, and the old doctor had
shaken his head very gravely over her. For a week
or more she had grown steadily worse, and was now
unable even to walk without help. Her malady was
one of those that sap away the life with a swift and
deadly power against which all human skill seems
unavailing.

Mr. Grey on returning from church entered the
living room. The invalid sat at the window, a heavy
shawl wrapped about her, her pale face turned to the
far blue line of sea, visible through a gap in the hills.
A pang wrenched his heart keenly at the sight. Why
would she always sit at that window looking so sorrowfully, so abstractedly at the sea, as if her heart
was buried there with her dead lover?

She started as she heard his footstep, and turned
her head quickly toward him, a faint flush tinging her
cheek and a forced smile quivering around her lips.
Her greeting was very gentle, and he saw that her

heart was reproaching her for being so disloyal to
him as to think of her lost lover ; and yet he felt
her fingers tremble and shrink away from his as he
took her hand.

"God forgive me ! " he thought, with infinite self-
accusation. "How repugnant I must be to her, —
an intruder, thrusting myself into the heart that is
sacred to the dead."

But he let her see nothing of this in his voice or
manner as he inquired how she had been. She replied wearily that she was no better, that she longed
to get well again and be at work.

"I missed your sermon to-day," she said, with that
strained, pathetic smile upon her lips again. "You
must tell me about it now."

He drew his chair to her side and began to give
an outline of the sermon. She listened, but it was
with forced attention, without sympathy, without in
the least entering into the spirit of what he was saying. It pained him. He knew that her nature was
so narrow, so conventional, that it was impossible
for her to comprehend his grand scheme of Indian
evangelization. But he checked his impatience, and
gave her a full synopsis of the discourse.

"It is useless, useless. They cannot understand.
A whole race is perishing around them, and they will
not put forth a hand save to mistreat a Quaker or
throw a stone at a Churchman. Our Puritanism is
like iron to resist tyranny, — but alas ! it is like iron,
too, when one tries to bend it to some generous
undertaking."

He stopped, checking back other and more bitter
words. All his soul rose up in revolt against the prej-

udice by which he was surrounded. Then Ruth spoke timidly.

"Seeing that it is so, would it not be best to let this missionary subject go, and preach on practical every-day matters? I am not wise in these things, I know; but would it not be better to preach on common subjects, showing us how we ought to live from day to day, than to discourse of those larger things that the people do not understand?"

His face darkened, though not angrily. This was the same prejudice he had just encountered in the meeting-house, though in a different form. He arose and paced back and forth with quick, impatient steps. Then he came and stood before her with folded arms and resolute face.

"Ruth, I have tried that so often, tried it with prayers and tears, but it is utterly impossible. I cannot bring myself to it. You know what the physicians say of my disease of the heart, — that my life may be very short; and I want it to be noble. I want to live for the greatest possibilities within my reach. I want to set some great work in motion that will light up thousands of darkened lives, — yea, and grow in might and power even after my lips are sealed in death."

The little figure on the chair moved uneasily under his animated though kindly gaze.

"I do not quite comprehend you. I think the best work is to do what God gives us to do, and to do it well. To me he has given to labor in caring for the house," — there was a patient weariness in her tone that did not escape Cecil, — "to you he has given the duties of a pastor, to strengthen the weak, cheer the sorrowing, comfort the old. Is it not better to do those things faithfully than to spend our time longing for some more ideal work not given us?"

"But suppose the ideal work is given? Suppose a man is called to proclaim new truths, and be the leader in a new reform? For him the quiet pastorate is impossible; nay, were it possible, it would be wrong, for would he not be keeping back the message God had given him? He would be one called to a work, yet entering not upon it; and upon him would come the curse that fell on the unfaithful prophets of old."

All the gloom of the theology of his age was on him as he spoke. Refined and poetic as was his nature, it was thoroughly imbued with the Calvinism of early New England.

She lifted her hand wearily and passed it over her aching brow.

"I do not know," she said; "I have never thought of such things, only it seems to me that God knew best when he gave us our lots in life. Surely wherever we find ourselves, there he intended us to be, and there we should patiently work, leaving our higher aspirations to his will. Is not the ideal life, after all, the one that is kindest and humblest?"

"But, Ruth," replied the minister, sadly, "while the work you describe is certainly noble, I have yet felt for a long time that it is not what God calls me to. Day after day, night after night, I think of the wild races that roam the forests to the west, of which no man knows the end. Sometimes I think that I am called to stand before the rulers of the colony and plead that missionaries be sent to the Indians.

Sometimes I feel that I am called to go and preach to them myself. Often in my dreams I plead with dark-browed sachems or with mighty gatherings of warriors to cast away their blood-stained weapons and accept Christ, till I awake all trembling with the effort. And always the deadly pain at my heart warns me that what is done must be done quickly."

The burning ardor that had given such intensity to his sermon came into his voice as he spoke. The invalid moved nervously on her chair, and he saw that his enthusiasm merely jarred on her without awakening any response.

"Forgive me," he said hurriedly, "I forgot that you were not well enough to talk of those things. Sometime when you are better we will speak of them again."

And then he talked of other and to her more interesting topics, while a keen pang rankled in his breast to find her irresponsive to that which was so dear to him.

But he was very kind to her; and when after a while the old Indian woman, Cecil's nurse in childhood and their only servant now, came to tell him that dinner was ready, he would not go until he had first brought his wife her dinner and waited on her with his own hands.

After his own repast was finished he must hasten away to preach his afternoon sermon. But he came to her first and bent over her; for though love never had been, perhaps never could be, between them, there was a deep domestic feeling in his nature.

"How good and patient you are in your sickness," he said, gazing down into the quiet, wistful face that was so honest and true, yet so thoroughly prosaic and commonplace. "What a sermon you have been preaching me, sitting here so uncomplainingly."

"Do you think so?" she said, looking up gratefully. "I am glad. I so want to do my duty by you."

He had meant to kiss her as he bent over her, though such caresses were rare between them, but there was something in her tones that chilled him, and he merely raised a tress of her hair to his lips instead. At the door he bade her a pleasant farewell, but his countenance grew sorrowful as he went down the path.

"Duty," he murmured, "always duty, never love. Well, the fault is my own that we were ever married. God help me to be true and kind to her always. She shall never know that I miss anything in her."

And he preached to his congregation that afternoon a sermon on burden-bearing, showing how each should bear his own burden patiently, — not darkening the lives of others by complaint, but always saying loving words, no matter how much of heartache lay beneath them. He told how near God is to us all, ready to heal and to strengthen ; and closed by showing how sweet and beautiful even a common life may grow through brave and self-sacrificing endurance of trouble.

It was a helpful sermon, a sermon that brought the listeners nearer God. More than one heart was touched by those earnest words that seemed to breathe divine sympathy and compassion.

He went home feeling more at peace than he had done for many days. His wife's room was still, as he entered it. She was in her easy-chair at the window, lying back among the pillows asleep. Her face was flushed and feverish, her long lashes wet with tears. The wraps had fallen away from her, and he stooped over to replace them. As he did so her lips moved in her half-delirious slumber, and she murmured some name sounding like his own. A wild throb of joy thrilled through him, and he bent closer to listen. Again she spoke the name, spoke it sorrowfully, longingly. It was the name of her lover drowned at sea.

The long, nervous fingers that held the half-drawn wraps shook convulsively as with acutest pain, then drew the coverings gently around her.

"God help her, God help her!" he murmured, as he turned softly away, his eyes filling with tears, — tears for her sorrow rather than his own.

CHAPTER III.

A DARKENED FIRESIDE.

> . . . Her way is parted from my way ;
> Out of sight, beyond light, at what goal may we meet ?
> DANTE ROSSETTI.

RUTH was much worse in the evening, but at last, after Cecil had watched at her side till a late hour, she sank into a troubled sleep. Then the old Indian servant insisted on taking his place at the sufferer's bedside, for she saw that he was much worn by the labors of the day and by anxiety for his wife. At first he refused ; but she was a skilled nurse, and he knew that the invalid would fare better in her hands than his own, so at last he consented on condition that she would call him if his wife grew worse. The woman promised, and he withdrew into the library, where a temporary bed had been made for him. At the door he turned and looked back.

His wife lay with closed eyes and flushed face amid the white pillows. The robe over her breast stirred with her difficult breathing, and her head turned now and then from side to side while she uttered broken, feverish words. By her sat the swarthy nurse, watching her every movement and ready with observant eye and gentle touch to minister to all her needs.

A yearning tenderness and pity came into his gaze. " Poor child, poor child ! " he thought. " If I could only make her well and happy ! If I could only bring her dead lover back to life, how gladly would I put her in his arms and go away forever!" And it seemed to him in some dim way that he had wronged the poor sufferer; that he was to blame for her sorrow.

He went on into the library. A lamp was burning on the table; a Hebrew Bible and a copy of Homer lay beside it. Along the walls were arranged those heavy and ponderous tomes in which the theology of the age was wont to clothe itself.

He seated himself at the table and took up his Homer; for he was too agitated to sleep. But it was in vain that he tried to interest himself in it. The rhythm had lost its music, the thought its power; it was in vain that he tried to forget himself in the reply of Achilles, or the struggle over the body of Patroclus.

Hawthorne tells us that a person of artistic temperament may at a time of mental depression wander through the Roman galleries and see nothing in the finest masterpieces of Raphael or Angelo. The grace is gone from the picture, the inspiration from the marble; the one is a meaningless collection of colors, the other a dull effigy carved in stone.

Something of this mood was on Cecil to-night. Irresponsive to the grand beauty of the poem, he felt only its undertone of heartache and woe.

" It is like human life," he thought, as he listlessly turned the pages; " it is bright on the surface, but dark and terrible with pain below. What a black mystery is life! what bitter irony of justice! Hector is dragged at Achilles' chariot-wheel, and Paris goes free. Helen returns to her home in triumph, while

Andromache is left desolate. Did Homer write in satire, and is the Iliad but a splendid mockery of justice, human and divine? Or is life so sad that every tale woven of it must needs become a tragedy?"

He pondered the gloomy puzzle of human existence long that night. At length his brain grew over-weary, and he slept sitting in his chair, his head resting on the pages of the open book.

How long he slept he knew not, but he awoke with a start to find a hand laid on his shoulder and the tall figure of the Indian woman standing beside him. He sprang up in sudden fear.

"Is she worse?" he cried. But the woman, with that light noiseless step, that mute stolidity so characteristic of her race, had already glided to the door; and there was no need for her to answer, for already his own apprehensions had replied.

He was in the room almost as soon as she. His wife was much worse; and hastening through the night to a neighboring farmhouse, he roused its inmates, despatched a messenger for the physician, and returned, accompanied by several members of the neighbor's family.

The slow moments dragged away like years as they watched around her. It seemed as if the doctor would never come. To the end of his life Cecil never forgot the long-drawn agony of that night.

At length their strained hearing caught the quick tread of horses' hoofs on the turf without.

"The doctor, the doctor!" came simultaneously from the lips of Cecil and the watchers. The doctor, — there was hope in the very name.

How eagerly they watched his face as he bent over

the patient ! It was a calm, self-contained face, but they saw a shadow flit over it, a sudden almost imperceptible change of expression that said " Death " as plainly as if he had spoken it. They could do nothing, he said, — nothing but wait for the end to come.

How the moments lingered ! Sometimes Cecil bent over the sufferer with every muscle quivering to her paroxysms ; sometimes he could endure it no longer and went out into the cool night air or into the library, where with the mere mechanical instinct of a student he picked up a book, reading a few lines in it, then throwing it aside. Yet wherever he was he felt her sufferings as acutely as when standing by her side. His whole frame was in keenest sympathy with hers, his whole being full of pain. So sharp were his sensations that they imparted an abnormal vigor to his mind. Every line his eyes met in reading stood out on the page with wonderful distinctness. The words seemed pictorial, and his mind grasped abstruse propositions or involved expressions with marvellous facility.

He noted it, and remembered afterward that he thought at the time how curious it was that his tortured sympathies should give him such startling acuteness of perception.

The slow night waned, the slow dawn crept over the eastern hills. Cecil stood with haggard eyes at the foot of the bed, watching the sleeper's face. As the daylight brightened, blending with the light of the still burning lamps, he saw a change come over her countenance ; the set face relaxed, the look lost its wildness. A great hope shone in his hollow eyes.

" She is getting better, she is coming out of her sufferings," he whispered to the doctor.

"She will be out of her sufferings very soon," he replied sadly ; and then Cecil knew that the end was at hand. Was it because the peace, the profound serenity which sometimes is the prelude of death, filling her being, penetrated his, that he grew so strangely calm? An inexpressible solemnity came to him as he looked at her, and all his agitation left him.

Her face grew very sweet and calm, and full of peace. Her eyes met Cecil's, and there was in them something that seemed to thank him for all his goodness and patience, — something that was both benediction and farewell. Her lips moved, but she was past the power of speech, and only her eyes thanked him in a tender, grateful glance.

The sun's edge flashed above the horizon, and its first rays fell through the uncurtained window full upon her face. She turned toward them, smiling faintly, and her face grew tenderly, radiantly beautiful, as if on that beam of sunshine the spirit of her dead lover had come to greet her from the sea. Then the sparkle died out of her eyes and the smile faded from her lips. It was only a white, dead face that lay there bathed in golden light.

A moment after, Cecil left the house with swift footsteps and plunged into the adjacent wood. There under a spreading oak he flung himself prone upon the earth, and buried his face in his hands. A seething turmoil of thoughts swept his mind. The past rose before him like a panorama. All his married life rushed back upon him, and every memory was regret and accusation.

"I might have been kinder to her, I might have been better," he murmured, while the hot tears gushed

from his eyes. " I might have been so much better
to her," he repeated over and over, — he, whose whole
thought had been to shut up his sorrow in his own heart
and show her only tenderness and consideration.

By and by he grew calmer and sat up, leaning
against the tree and looking out into vacancy with
dim eyes that saw nothing. His heart was desolate,
emptied of everything. What was he to do? What
was he to set before himself? He had not loved
her, but still she had been a part of his life; with
what was he to fill it now?

As he sat there depressed and troubled, a strange
thing happened.

He was looking, as has been said, blindly into vacancy. It may have been an optical illusion, it may
have been a mere vagary born of an over-wrought
brain; but a picture formed before him. In the distance, toward the west, he saw something that looked
like a great arch of stone, a natural bridge, rugged
with crags and dark with pine. Beneath it swept a
wide blue river, and on it wild horsemen were crossing and recrossing, with plumed hair and rude lances.
Their faces were Indian, yet of a type different from
any he had ever seen. The bridge was in the heart
of a mighty mountain-range. On either side rose
sharp and lofty peaks, their sides worn by the action
of water in some remote age.

These details he noted as in a dream; then the
strangeness of it all burst upon him. Even as it did
so, the vision dissolved; the bridge wavered and passed
away, the mountain-peaks sank in shadow. He leaped
to his feet and gazed eagerly. A fine mist seemed
passing before his sight; then he saw only the reach

of hill and woodland, with the morning light resting upon it.

While the vision faded, he felt springing up within him an irrepressible desire to follow it. A mysterious fascination seized him, a wild desire to seek the phantom bridge. His whole being was swayed as by a supernatural power toward the west whence the vision had passed. He started forward eagerly, then checked himself in bewilderment. What could it mean?

In the nineteenth century, one similarly affected would think it meant a fevered, a disordered brain ; but in the seventeenth, when statesmen like Cromwell believed in dreams and omens, and *roués* like Monmouth carried charms in their pockets, these things were differently regarded.

The Puritan ministry, whose minds were imbued with the gloomy supernaturalism of the Old Testament on which they fed, were especially men to whom anything resembling an apparition had a prophetic significance. And Cecil Grey, though liberal beyond most New England clergymen, was liable by the keenness of his susceptibilities and the extreme sensitiveness of his organization to be influenced by such delusions, — if delusions they be. So he stood awed and trembling, questioning within himself, like some seer to whom a dark and uncertain revelation has been made.

Suddenly the answer came.

"The Lord hath revealed his will unto me and shown me the path wherein I am to walk," he murmured in a hushed and stricken tone. "Ruth was taken from me that I might be free to go where he should send me. The vision of the Indians and the bridge which faded into the west, and the strange desire that was given me to follow it, show that the Lord has another work for me to do. And when I find the land of the bridge and of the wild people I saw upon it, then will I find the mission that God has given me to do. " Lord God of Israel, I thank Thee. Thou hast shown me the way, and I will walk in it, though all its stones be fire and its end be death."

He stood a moment with bowed head, communing with his God. Then he returned to his lonely home.

The friends whose kindly sympathies had brought them to the house of mourning wondered at the erect carriage, the rapt, exalted manner of the man. His face was pale, almost as pale as that within the darkened room ; but his eyes shone, and his lips were closely, resolutely set.

A little while, and that determined face was all sorrowful and pitying again, as he bent over the still, cold body of his dead.

CHAPTER IV.

THE COUNCIL OF ORDINATION.

Friends were assembled together; the Elder and Magistrate also
Graced the scene with their presence, and stood like the Law and
the Gospel . . . .
After the Puritan way and the laudable custom of Holland.
The Courtship of Miles Standish.

A FEW days after the funeral, letters missive from
the little society went out to all the neighboring churches, calling a council to ordain the Reverend Cecil Grey a missionary to the Indians.

It was a novel thing, in spite of the noble example
that Roger Williams had set not many years before;
and the summons met with a general response.

All the churches, far and near, sent delegates. If
one could only have taken a peep, the day before the
council, into the households of that part of New England, what a glimpse he would have gotten of Puritan
domestic life! What a brushing up there was of
black coats, what a careful starching and ironing of
bands; and above all, in Cecil's own neighborhood,
what a mighty cookery for the ordination dinner the
next day! For verily the capacity of the clerical
stomach is marvellous, and is in fact the one thing in
theology that does not change. New departures alter
doctrines, creeds are modified, but the appetite of
the clergy is not subject to such mutations.

The morrow came, and with it the expected guests. The meeting-house was crowded. There were many ministers and lay delegates in the council. In the chair sat a venerable preacher, not unknown in the records of those days, — a portly man, with a shrewd and kindly face. Sterner faces were there also. The council wore a grave aspect, more like a court of judges before whom a criminal is cited to appear than an assembly of clergymen about to ordain a missionary.

After some preliminaries, Cecil was called on to give a statement of his reasons for wishing to go as an evangelist to the Indians. He rose before them. There was a singular contrast between his slight form and expressive features and the stout frames and grim countenances of the others. But the graceful presence of the man had in it a quiet dignity that commanded the respect of all.

In obedience to the command, he told how he had thought of the unknown tribes beyond the Alleghanies, living in the gloom of paganism and perishing in darkness, till an intangible sympathy inclined him toward them, — till, as it seemed to him, their great desire for light had entered into and possessed him, drawing him toward them by a mysterious and irresistible attraction. He felt called of God to go and minister to their spiritual needs, and that it was his duty to leave everything and obey the call.

" Is this all? " he was asked.

He hesitated a moment, and then described his vision in the wood the morning of his wife's death. It made a deep impression on his hearers. There was scarcely a man in the assembly who was not tinged with the superstition of the age; and all listened, not lightly or sceptically, but in awe, as if it brought them to the threshold of the supernatural.

When the narration was ended, the chairman requested him to retire, pending the decision of the council; but first he was asked, —

"Are you willing to abide by the decision of this council, whatever it may be?"

He raised his head confidently, and his reply came frank and fearless.

"I shall respect the opinions of my brethren, no matter how they may decide; but I shall abide by the will of God and my own convictions of duty."

The grave Puritan bent his head, half in acknowledgment of the reply, half in involuntary admiration of its brave manhood; then Cecil left the room, the silent, watchful crowd that filled the aisles parting respectfully to let him pass.

"Now, brethren," said the chairman, "the matter is before you. Let us hear from each his judgment upon it."

Solemn and weighty were the opinions delivered. One brother thought that Mr. Grey had plenty of work to do at home without going off on a wild-goose chase after the heathen folk of the wilderness. His church needed him; to leave it thus would be a shameful neglect of duty.

Another thought that the Indians were descendants of the ten lost tribes of Israel, and as such should be left in the hands of God. To attempt to evangelize them was to fly in the face of Providence.

Another thought the same; but then, how about

that vision of Mr. Grey? He could n't get around that vision.

"I don't know, brethren, I don't know!" he concluded, shaking his head.

Still another declared positively for Mr. Grey. The good people of the colonies owed it to the savages to do something for their religious enlightenment. It was wrong that so little had been done. They had taken their land from them, they had pushed them back into the wilds at the point of the sword ; now let them try to save their souls. This man had been plainly called of God to be an apostle to the Indians ; the least that they could do was to bid him Godspeed and let him go.

So it went on. At length the venerable chairman, who had twice turned the hour-glass upon the table before him, rose to close the discussion. His speech was a singular mixture of shrewdness, benevolence, and superstition.

He said that, as Christians, they certainly owed a duty to the Indians, — a duty that had not been performed. Mr. Grey wished to help fulfil that neglected obligation, and would go at his own expense. It would not cost the church a shilling. His vision was certainly a revelation of the will of the Lord, and *he* dared not stand in the way.

A vote was taken, and the majority were found to be in favor of ordination. The chairman pronounced himself pleased, and Mr. Grey was recalled and informed of the result.

"I thank you," he said simply, with a glad and grateful smile.

"Now, brethren," said the worthy chairman with

much unction, " the hour of dinner is nigh at hand, and the good people of this place have prepared entertainment for us ; so we will e'en put off the ceremony of ordination till the afternoon. Let us look to the Lord for his blessing, and be dismissed."

And so with a murmur of talk and comment the council broke up, its members going to the places where they were to be entertained. Happy was the man who returned to his home accompanied by a minister, while those not so fortunate were fain to be content with a lay delegate. Indeed, the hospitality of the settlement was so bounteous that the supply exceeded the demand. There were not enough visitors to go around ; and more than one good housewife who had baked, boiled, and roasted all the day before was moved to righteous indignation at the sight of the good man of the house returning guestless from the meeting.

Early in the afternoon entertainers and entertained gathered again at the meeting-house. Almost the entire country side was there, — old and young alike. The house was packed, for never before had that part of New England seen a man ordained to carry the gospel to the Indians. It occurred, too, in that dreary interval between the persecution of the Quakers and the persecution of the witches, and was therefore doubly welcome.

When Cecil arrived, the throng made way reverently for him. Was he not going, perchance like the martyrs of old, to the fagot and the stake? To those who had long known him he seemed hardly like the same man. He was lifted to a higher plane, surrounded by an atmosphere of sanctity and heroism, and made sacred by the high mission given him of God, to which was now to be added the sanction of holy men.

So they made way for him, as the Florentines had made way for " il Frate " and as the people of God had made way for Francis Xavier when he left them to stir the heart of the East with his eloquence, and, alas ! to die on the bleak sea-coast of China, clasping the crucifix to his breast and praying for those who had cast him out.

Cecil's face, though pale, was calm and noble. All his nature responded to the moral grandeur of the occasion. It would be difficult to put into words the reverent and tender exaltation of feeling that animated him that day. Perhaps only those upon whose own heads the hands of ordination have been laid can enter into or understand it.

The charge was earnest, but it was not needed, for Cecil's ardent enthusiasm went far beyond all that the speaker urged upon him. As he listened, pausing as it were on the threshold of an unknown future, he wondered if he should ever hear a sermon again, — he, so soon to be swallowed by darkness, swept, self-yielded, into the abyss of savagery.

Heartfelt and touching was the prayer of ordination, — that God might accept and bless Cecil's consecration, that the divine presence might always abide with him, that savage hearts might be touched and softened, that savage lives might be lighted up through his instrumentality, and that seed might be sown in the wilderness which would spring up and cause the waste places to be glad and the desert to blossom as the rose.

"And so," said the old minister, his voice faltering and his hands trembling as they rested on Cecil's bowed head, " so we give him into Thine own hand and send him forth into the wilderness. Thou only knowest what is before him, whether it be a harvest of souls, or torture and death. But we know that, for the Christian, persecutions and trials are but stepping-stones leading to God ; yea, and that death itself is victory. And if he is faithful, we know that whatever his lot may be it will be glorious; that whatever the end may be, it will be but a door opening into the presence of the Most High."

Strong and triumphant rang the old man's tones, as he closed his prayer committing Cecil into the hands of God. To him, as he listened, it seemed as if the last tie that bound him to New England was severed, and he stood consecrated and anointed for his mission. When he raised his face, more than one of the onlookers thought of those words of the Book where it speaks of Stephen, — " And they saw his face as it had been the face of an angel."

A psalm was sung, the benediction given, and the solemn service was over. It was long, however, before the people left the house. They lingered around Cecil, bidding him farewell, for he was to go forth at dawn the next day upon his mission. They pressed his hand, some with warm words of sympathy, some silently and with wet eyes. Many affectionate words were said, for they had never known before how much they loved their pastor; and now he seemed no longer a pastor, but a martyr and a saint. More than one mother brought him her child to bless; others — strangers from a distance — lifted their children up, so that they could see him above the press, while they whispered to them that they must always remember that they had seen the good Mr. Grey, who was going far off into the west to tell the Indians about God.

Long afterward, when nearly all that generation had passed away and the storm of the Revolution was beginning to gather over the colonies, there were a few aged men still living who sometimes told how, when they were children, they had seen Cecil Grey bidding the people farewell at the old meeting-house ; and through all the lapse of years they remembered what a wonderful brightness was on his face, and how sweet and kind were his words to each as he bade them good-by forever.

CHAPTER V.

INTO TRACKLESS WILDS.

"I will depart," he said, " the hour is come,
And in the silence of yon sky I read
My fated message flashing."

EDWIN ARNOLD.

THE next morning Cecil rose early after a sleep-less night. On that day he was to go out from all that was sweet and precious in life and take the path into the wilderness. At first his heart sank within him ; then his strength of purpose revived, and he was resolute again.

He must go, and soon. The briefer the parting the briefer the pang. He had already bidden his friends good-by ; his parents were long since dead ; it only remained to part from the old Indian woman, his nurse in childhood, now his faithful house-keeper and the only inmate of his home.

He went to the kitchen, — for usually at this hour she was up and preparing breakfast. She was not there, and the room looked cold and cheerless in the gray dawn. He went to her door and knocked ; there was no response. He called her ; the room was as still as death. Alarmed, he opened the door ; no one was within ; she was gone, — had evidently been gone all night, for the bed was untouched.

He was pained and bewildered at this desertion, for only the day before he had given her a paper legally drawn up, securing to her the little property he possessed and making her independent for the rest of her life. She had taken it, listened in silence to the kindly expressions that accompanied the gift, and turned away without a word. Now she was gone; what could it mean?

Slowly he made the simple preparations that were needed for the journey — putting a little food, his Bible, and other necessaries into a kind of knapsack and strapping it upon his back. Then taking his staff, he went out from his home, never to return.

The sun was rising, the air was fresh and dewy, but his heart was sad. Yet through it ran a strange thrill of joy, a strange blending of pain and gladness.

"The parting is bitter, bitter almost unto death, but He will keep me," murmured the white lips, as he went down the walk.

The sound of voices fell on his ears, and he looked up. At the gate, awaiting him, was a group of his parishioners, who had come to look once more on the face of their pastor. One by whose bedside he had prayed in the hour of sickness; another, whom his counsel had saved when direly tempted; a little lame child, who loved him for his kindness; and an aged, dim-sighted woman, to whom he had often read the Scriptures.

He opened the gate and came out among them.

"God bless you, sir," said the old woman, "we wanted to see your bonny face again before you left us."

The little lame boy said nothing, but came up to Cecil, took his hand, and pressed it to his cheek in a manner more eloquent than words.

" Friends," said Cecil, in a faltering voice, " I thank you. It is very sweet to know that you care for me thus."

One by one they came and clasped his hand in tearful farewell. For each he had a loving word. It was an impressive scene, — the sorrow-stricken group, the pastor with his pale spiritual face full of calm resolve, and around them the solemn hush of morning.

When all had been spoken, the minister reverently uncovered his head ; the others did the same. " It is for the last time," he said ; " let us pray."

After a few earnest words commending them to the care of God, he drew his hand gently from the lame boy's cheek and rested it on his head in silent benediction. Then giving them one last look of unutterable love, a look they never forgot, —

" Good-by," he said softly, " God bless you all."

" Good-by, God bless *you*, sir," came back in answer ; and they saw his face no more.

One more farewell was yet to be said. The winding path led close by the country graveyard. He entered it and knelt by the side of the new-made grave. Upon the wooden headboard was inscribed the name of her who slept beneath, — " Ruth Grey."

He kissed the cold sod, his tears falling fast upon it.

" Forgive me," he whispered, as if the dull ear of death could hear. " Forgive me for everything wherein I failed you. Forgive me, and — Farewell."

Again he was on his way. At the entrance to the wood he saw a figure sitting on a rock beside the path. As he drew nearer he observed it was clad in Indian garb, and evidently awaited his coming. Who was it? Might it not be some chief, who, having heard of his intended mission, had come forth to meet him?

He hastened his steps. When he came nearer, he saw that it was only an Indian woman; a little closer, and to his inexpressible astonishment he recognized his old nurse.

" What does this mean?" he exclaimed. " What are you doing here, and in Indian garb, too?"

She rose to her feet with simple, natural dignity.

" It means," she said, " that I go with you. Was I not your nurse in childhood? Did I not carry you in my arms then, and has not your roof sheltered me since? Can I forsake him who is as my own child? My heart has twined around you too long to be torn away. Your path shall be my path; we go together."

It was in vain that Cecil protested, reasoned, argued.

" I have spoken," she said. " I will not turn back from my words while life is left me."

He would have pleaded longer, but she threw a light pack upon her back and went on into the forest. She had made her decision, and he knew she would adhere to it with the inflexible obstinacy of her race.

He could only follow her regretfully; and yet he could not but be grateful for her loyalty.

At the edge of the wood he paused and looked back. Before him lay the farms and orchards of the Puritans. Here and there a flock of sheep was being driven from the fold into the pasture, and a girl, bucket in hand, was taking her way to the milking shed. From each farmhouse a column of smoke rose

"*I* HAVE *spoken; I will not turn back from my words.*"

into the clear air. Over all shone the glory of the morning sun. It was civilization ; it was New England ; it was *home.*

For a moment, the scene seemed literally to lay hold of him and pull him back. For a moment, all the domestic feelings, all the refinement in his nature, rose up in revolt against the rude contact with barbarism before him. It seemed as if he could not go on, as if he must go back. He shook like a leaf with the mighty conflict.

" My God ! " he cried out, throwing up his arms with a despairing gesture, " must I give up everything, everything ? "

He felt his resolution giving way ; his gray eyes were dark and dilated with excitement and pain ; his long fingers twitched and quivered ; before he knew what he was doing, he was walking back toward the settlement.

That brought him to himself ; that re-awakened the latent energy and decision of his character.

" What ! shall I turn back from the very threshold of my work? God forgive me — never ! "

His delicate frame grew strong and hardy under the power of his indomitable spirit. Again his dauntless enthusiasm came back ; again he was the Apostle to the Indians.

One long last look, and he disappeared in the shadows of the wood, passing forever from the ken of the white man ; for only vague rumors floated back to the colonies from those mysterious wilds into which he had plunged. The strange and wondrous tale of his after-life New England never knew.

BOOK II.

THE OPENING OF THE DRAMA.

CHAPTER I.

SHALL THE GREAT COUNCIL BE HELD?

> The comet burns the wings of night,
> And dazzles elements and spheres;
> Then dies in beauty and a blaze of light
> Blown far through other years.
>
> JOAQUIN MILLER.

TWO hundred years ago — as near as we can estimate the time from the dim and shadowy legends that have come down to us — the confederacy of the Wauna or Columbia was one of the most powerful the New World has ever seen. It was apparently not inferior to that of the Six Nations, or to the more transitory leagues with which Tecumseh or Pontiac stayed for a moment the onward march of the white man. It was a union of the Indian tribes of Oregon and Washington, with the Willamettes at the head, against their great hereditary enemies, the Nootkas, the Shoshones, and the Spokanes.

Sonorous and picturesque was the language of the old Oregon Indians in telling the first white traders the story of the great alliance.

"Once, long before my father's time and before his father's time, all the tribes were as one tribe and the Willamettes were *tyee* [chief]. The Willamettes were strong and none could stand against them. The heart of the Willamette was battle and his hand was blood. When he lifted his arm in war, his enemy's lodge became ashes and his council silence and death.

"The war-trails of the Willamette went north and south and east, and there was no grass on them. He called the Chinook and Sound Indians, who were weak, his children, and the Yakima, Cayuse, and Wasco, who loved war, his brothers; but *he* was elder brother. And the Spokanes and the Shoshones might fast and cut themselves with thorns and knives, and dance the medicine dance, and drink the blood of horses, but nothing could make their hearts as strong as the hearts of the Willamettes; for the One up in the sky had told the old men and the dreamers that the Willamettes should be the strongest of all the tribes as long as the Bridge of the Gods should stand. That was their *tomanowos.*"

But whenever the white listener asked about this superstition of the bridge and the legend connected with it, the Indian would at once become uncommunicative, and say, " You can't understand," or more frequently, " I don't know." For the main difficulty in collecting these ancient tales — " old-man talk," as the Siwashes call them — was, that there was much superstition interwoven with them; and the Indians were so reticent about their religious beliefs, that if one was not exceedingly cautious, the lively, gesticulating talker of one moment was liable to become the personification of sullen obstinacy the next.

But if the listener was fortunate enough to strike the golden mean, being neither too anxious nor too indifferent, and if above all he had by the gift of bounteous *muck-a-muck* [food] touched the chord to which the savage heart always responds, the Indian might go on and tell in broken English or crude Chinook the strange, dark legend of the bridge, which is the subject of our tale.

At the time our story opens, this confederacy was at the height of its power. It was a rough-hewn, barbarian realm, the most heterogeneous, the most rudimentary of alliances. The exact manner of its union, its laws, its extent, and its origin are all involved in the darkness which everywhere covers the history of Indian Oregon, — a darkness into which our legend casts but a ray of light that makes the shadows seem the denser. It gives us, however, a glimpse of the diverse and squalid tribes that made up the confederacy. This included the " Canoe Indians " of the Sound and of the Oregon sea-coast, whose flat heads, greasy squat bodies, and crooked legs were in marked contrast with their skill and dexterity in managing their canoes and fish-spears ; the hardy Indians of the Willamette Valley and the Cascade Range ; and the bold, predatory riders of eastern Oregon and Washington, — buffalo hunters and horse tamers, passionately fond, long before the advent of the white man, of racing and gambling. It comprised also the Okanogans, who disposed of their dead by tying them upright to a tree ; the Yakimas, who buried them under cairns of stone ; the Klickitats, who swathed them like mummies and laid them in low, rude huts on the *mimaluse,* or " death islands " of the Columbia; the Chinooks, who stretched them in canoes with paddles and fishing implements by their side; and the Kalamaths, who burned them with the maddest saturnalia of dancing, howling, and leaping through the flames of the funeral pyre. Over sixty or seventy petty tribes stretched the wild empire, welded together by the pressure of common foes and held in the grasp of the hereditary war-chief of the Willamettes.

The chiefs of the Willamettes had gathered on Wappatto Island, from time immemorial the council-ground of the tribes. The white man has changed its name to "Sauvie's" Island; but its wonderful beauty is unchangeable. Lying at the mouth of the Willamette River and extending for many miles down the Columbia, rich in wide meadows and crystal lakes, its interior dotted with majestic oaks and its shores fringed with cottonwoods, around it the blue and sweeping rivers, the wooded hills, and the far white snow peaks, — it is the most picturesque spot in Oregon.

The chiefs were assembled in secret council, and only those of pure Willamette blood were present, for the question to be considered was not one to be known by even the most trusted ally.

All the confederated tribes beyond the Cascade Range were in a ferment of rebellion. One of the petty tribes of eastern Oregon had recently risen up against the Willamette supremacy; and after a short but bloody struggle, the insurrection had been put down and the rebels almost exterminated by the victorious Willamettes.

But it was known that the chief of the malcontents had passed from tribe to tribe before the struggle commenced, inciting them to revolt, and it was suspected that a secret league had been formed; though when matters came to a crisis, the confederates, afraid to face openly the fierce warriors of the Willamette, had stood sullenly back, giving assistance to neither side. It was evident, however, that a spirit of angry discontent was rife among them. Threatening language had been used by the restless chiefs beyond the mountains; braves had talked around the camp-fire of the freedom of the days before the yoke of the confederacy was known; and the gray old dreamers, with whom the *mimaluse tillicums* [dead people] talked, had said that the fall of the Willamettes was near at hand.

The sachems of the Willamettes, advised of everything, were met in council in the soft Oregon springtide. They were gathered under the cottonwood trees, not far from the bank of the Columbia. The air was fresh with the scent of the waters, and the young leaves were just putting forth on the " trees of council," whose branches swayed gently in the breeze. Beneath them, their bronze faces more swarthy still as the dancing sunbeams fell upon them through the moving boughs, thirty sachems sat in close semi-circle before their great war-chief, Multnomah.

It was a strange, a sombre assembly. The chiefs were for the most part tall, well-built men, warriors and hunters from their youth up. There was something fierce and haughty in their bearing, something menacing, violent, and lawless in their saturnine faces and black, glittering eyes. Most of them wore their hair long ; some plaited, others flowing loosely over their shoulders. Their ears were loaded with *hiagua* shells ; their dress was composed of buckskin leggings and moccasins, and a short robe of dressed skin that came from the shoulders to the knees, to which was added a kind of blanket woven of the wool of the mountain sheep, or an outer robe of skins or furs, stained various colors and always drawn close around the body when sitting or standing. Seated on rude mats of rushes, wrapped each in his outer blanket and doubly wrapped in Indian stoicism, the warriors were ranged before their chief.

His garb did not differ from that of the others, except that his blanket was of the richest fur known to the Indians, so doubled that the fur showed on either side. His bare arms were clasped each with a rough band of gold ; his hair was cut short, in sign of mourning for his favorite wife, and his neck was adorned with a collar of large bear-claws, showing he had accomplished that proudest of all achievements for the Indian, — the killing of a grizzly.

Until the last chief had entered the grove and taken his place in the semi-circle, Multnomah sat like a statue of stone. He leaned forward reclining on his bow, a fine unstrung weapon tipped with gold. He was about sixty years old, his form tall and stately, his brow high, his eyes black, overhung with shaggy gray eyebrows and piercing as an eagle's. His dark, grandly impassive face, with its imposing regularity of feature, showed a penetration that read everything, a reserve that revealed nothing, a dominating power that gave strength and command to every line. The lip, the brow, the very grip of the hand on the bow told of a despotic temper and an indomitable will. The glance that flashed out from this reserved and resolute face — sharp, searching, and imperious — may complete the portrait of Multnomah, the silent, the secret, the terrible.

When the last late-entering chief had taken his place, Multnomah rose and began to speak, using the royal language; for like the Cayuses and several other tribes of the Northwest, the Willamettes had two languages, — the common, for every-day use, and the royal, spoken only by the chiefs in council.

In grave, strong words he laid before them the troubles that threatened to break up the confederacy and his plan for meeting them. It was to send out runners calling a council of all the tribes, including the doubtful allies, and to try before them and execute the rebellious chief, who had been taken alive and was now reserved for the torture. Such a council, with the terrible warning of the rebel's death enacted before it, would awe the malcontents into submission or drive them into open revolt. Long enough had the allies spoken with two tongues; long enough had they smoked the peace-pipe with both the Willamettes and their enemies. They must come now to peace that should be peace, or to open war. The chief made no gestures, his voice did not vary its stern, deliberate accents from first to last; but there was an indefinable something in word and manner that told how his warlike soul thirsted for battle, how the iron resolution, the ferocity beneath his stoicism, burned with desire of vengeance.

There was perfect attention while he spoke, — not so much as a glance or a whisper aside. When he

had ceased and resumed his seat, silence reigned for
a little while.   Then Tla-wau-wau, chief of the Klac-
kamas, a sub-tribe of the Willamette, rose.   He laid
aside his outer robe, leaving bare his arms and shoulders, which were deeply scarred ; for Tla-wau-wau
was a mighty warrior, and as such commanded.   With
measured deliberation he spoke in the royal tongue.

"Tla-wau-wau has seen many winters, and his hair
is very gray.   Many times has he watched the grass
spring up and grow brown and wither, and the snows
come and go, and those things have brought him wisdom, and what he has seen of life and death has given
him strong thoughts.   It is not well to leap headlong
into a muddy stream, lest there be rocks under the
black water.   Shall we call the tribes to meet us here
on the island of council?   When they are all gathered together they are more numerous than we.   Is
it wise to call those that are stronger than ourselves
into our wigwam, when their hearts are bitter against
us?   Who knows what plots they might lay, or how
suddenly they might fall on us at night or in the day
when we were unprepared?   Can we trust them?
Does not the Klickitat's name mean 'he that steals
horses'?   The Yakima would smoke the peace-pipe
with the knife that was to stab you hid under his
blanket.   The Wasco's heart is a lie, and his tongue
is a trap.

"No, let us wait.   The tribes talk great swelling
words now and their hearts are hot, but if we wait,
the fire will die down and the words grow small.   Then
we can have a council and be knit together again.
Let us wait till another winter has come and gone ;
then let us meet in council, and the tribes will listen.

" Tla-wau-wau says, ' wait, and all will be well.' "

His earnest, emphatic words ended, the chief took his seat and resumed his former look of stolid indifference. A moment before he had been all animation, every glance and gesture eloquent with meaning; now he sat seemingly impassive and unconcerned.

There was another pause. It was so still that the rustling of the boughs overhead was startlingly distinct. Saving the restless glitter of black eyes, it was a tableau of stoicism. Then another spoke, advising caution, setting forth the danger of plunging into a contest with the allies. Speaker followed speaker in the same strain.

As they uttered the words counselling delay, the glance of the war-chief grew ever brighter, and his grip upon the bow on which he leaned grew harder. But the cold face did not relax a muscle. At length rose Mishlah the Cougar, chief of the Mollalies. His was one of the most singular faces there. His tangled hair fell around a sinister, bestial countenance, all scarred and seamed by wounds received in battle. His head was almost flat, running back from his eyebrows so obliquely that when he stood erect he seemed to have no forehead at all; while the back and lower part of his head showed an enormous development, — a development that was all animal. He knew nothing but battle, and was one of the most dreaded warriors of the Willamettes.

He spoke, — not in the royal language, as did the others, but in the common dialect, the only one of which he was master.

" My heart is as the heart of Multnomah. Mishlah is hungry for war. If the tribes that are our younger

brothers are faithful, they will come to the council
and smoke the pipe of peace with us; if they are
not, let us know it. Mishlah knows not what it is to
wait. You all talk words, words, words; and the
tribes laugh and say, 'The Willamettes have become women and sit in the lodge sewing moccasins
and are afraid to fight.' Send out the runners. Call
the council. Let us find who are our enemies; then
let us strike!"

The hands of the chief closed involuntarily as if
they clutched a weapon, and his voice rang harsh and
grating. The eyes of Multnomah flashed fire, and
the war-lust kindled for a moment on the dark faces
of the listeners.

Then rose the grotesque figure of an Indian, ancient, withered, with matted locks and haggard face,
who had just joined the council, gliding in noiselessly
from the neighboring wood. His cheek-bones were
unusually high, his lower lip thick and protruding, his
eyes deeply sunken, his face drawn, austere, and dismal beyond description. The mis-shapen, degraded
features repelled at first sight; but a second glance
revealed a great dim sadness in the eyes, a gloomy
foreboding on brow and lip that were weirdly fascinating, so sombre were they, so full of woe. There
was a wild dignity in his mien; and he wore the robe
of furs, though soiled and torn, that only the richest
chiefs were able to wear. Such was Tohomish, or
Pine Voice, chief of the Santiam tribe of the Willamettes, the most eloquent orator and potent medicine
or *tomanowos* man in the confederacy.

There was a perceptible movement of expectation,
a lighting up of faces as he arose, and a shadow of

anxiety swept over Multnomah's impassive features.
For this man's eloquence was wonderful, and his soft
magnetic tones could sway the passions of his hearers
to his will with a power that seemed more than human
to the superstitious Indians. Would he declare for
the council or against it; for peace or for war?

He threw back the tangled locks that hung over
his face, and spoke.

"Chiefs and warriors, who dwell in lodges and talk
with men, Tohomish, who dwells in caves and talks
with the dead, says greeting, and by him the dead
send greeting also."

His voice was wonderfully musical, thrilling, and
pathetic; and as he spoke the salutation from the
dead, a shudder went through the wild audience
before him, — through all but Multnomah, who
did not shrink nor drop his searching eyes from
the speaker's face. What cared he for the salutation of the living or the dead? Would this man
whose influence was so powerful declare for action
or delay?

"It has been long since Tohomish has stood in the
light of the sun and looked on the faces of his brothers or heard their voices. Other faces has he looked
upon and other voices has he heard. He has learned
the language of the birds and the trees, and has talked
with the People of Old who dwell in the serpent and
the cayote; and they have taught him their secrets.
But of late terrible things have come to Tohomish."

He paused, and the silence was breathless, for the
Indians looked on this man as a seer to whom the
future was as luminous as the past. But Multnomah's brow darkened; he felt that Tohomish also

was against him, and the soul of the warrior rose up stern and resentful against the prophet.

"A few suns ago, as I wandered in the forest by the Santiam, I heard the death-wail in the distance. I said, 'Some one is dead, and that is the cry of the mourners. I will go and lift up my voice with them.' But as I sought them up the hill and through the thickets the cry grew fainter and farther, till at last it died out amid distant rocks and crags. And then I knew that I had heard no human voice lamenting the dead, but that it was the Spirit Indian-of-the-Wood wailing for the living whose feet go down to the darkness and whose faces the sun shall soon see no more. Then my heart grew heavy and bitter, for I knew that woe had come to the Willamettes.

"I went to my den in the mountains, and sought to know of those that dwell in the night the meaning of this. I built the medicine-fire, I fasted, I refused to sleep. Day and night I kept the fire burning; day and night I danced the *tomanowos* dance around the flames, or leaped through them, singing the song that brings the *Spee-ough*, till at last the life went from my limbs and my head grew sick and everything was a whirl of fire. Then I knew that the power was on me, and I fell, and all grew black.

"I dreamed a dream.

"I stood by the death-trail that leads to the spirit-land. The souls of those who had just died were passing; and as I gazed, the wail I had heard in the forest came back, but nearer than before. And as the wail sounded, the throng on the death-trail grew thicker and their tread swifter. The warrior passed with his bow in his hand and his quiver swinging from his shoulder; the squaw followed with his food upon her back; the old tottered by. It was a whole people on the way to the spirit-land. But when I tried to see their faces, to know them, if they were Willamette or Shoshone or our brother tribes, I could not. But the wail grew ever louder and the dead grew ever thicker as they passed. Then it all faded out, and I slept. When I awoke, it was night; the fire had burned into ashes and the medicine wolf was howling on the hills. The voices that are in the air came to me and said, 'Go to the council and tell what you have seen;' but I refused, and went far into the wood to avoid them. But the voices would not let me rest, and my spirit burned within me, and I came. Beware of the great council. Send out no runners. Call not the tribes together. Voices and omens and dreams tell Tohomish of something terrible to come. The trees whisper it; it is in the air, in the waters. It has made my spirit bitter and heavy until my drink seems blood and my food has the taste of death. Warriors, Tohomish has shown his heart. His words are ended."

He resumed his seat and drew his robe about him, muffling the lower part of his face. The matted hair fell once more over his drooping brow and repulsive countenance, from which the light faded the moment he ceased to speak. Again the silence was profound. The Indians sat spell-bound, charmed by the mournful music of the prophet's voice and awed by the dread vision he had revealed. All the superstition within them was aroused. When Tohomish took his seat, every Indian was ready to oppose the calling of the council with all his might. Even Mishlah, as

superstitious as blood-thirsty, was startled and perplexed. The war-chief stood alone.

He knew it, but it only made his despotic will the
stronger. Against the opposition of the council and
the warning of Tohomish, against *tomanowos* and
Spee-ough, ominous as they were even to him, rose up
the instinct which was as much a part of him as life
itself, — the instinct to battle and to conquer. He
was resolved with all the grand strength of his nature
to bend the council to his will, and with more than
Indian subtility saw how it might be done.

He rose to his feet and stood for a moment in
silence, sweeping with his glance the circle of chiefs.
As he did so, the mere personality of the man began
to produce a reaction. For forty years he had been
the great war-chief of the tribes of the Wauna, and
had never known defeat. The ancient enemies of
his race dreaded him ; the wandering bands of the
prairies had carried his name far and wide ; and even
beyond the Rockies, Sioux and Pawnee had heard
rumors of the powerful chief by the Big River of the
West. He stood before them a huge, stern warrior,
himself a living assurance of victory and dominion. `

As was customary with Indian orators in preparing
the way for a special appeal, he began to recount the
deeds of the fathers, the valor of the ancient heroes
of the race. His stoicism fell from him as he half
spoke, half chanted the harangue. The passion that
was burning within him made his words like pictures,
so vivid they were, and thrilled his tones with electric
power. As he went on, the sullen faces of his hearers
grew animated ; the superstitious fears that Tohomish
had awakened fell from them. Again they were

warriors, and their blood kindled and their pulses throbbed to the words of their invincible leader. He saw it, and began to speak of the battles they themselves had fought and the victories they had gained. More than one dark cheek flushed darker and more than one hand moved unconsciously to the knife. He alluded to the recent war and to the rebellious tribe that had been destroyed.

" *That*," said he, " was the people Tohomish saw passing over the death-trail in his dream. What wonder that the thought of death should fill the air, when we have slain a whole people at a single blow ! Do we not know too that their spirits would try to frighten our dreamers with omens and bad *tomanowos ?* Was it not bad *tomanowos* that Tohomish saw ? It could not have come from the Great Spirit, for he spoke to our fathers and said that we should be strongest of all the tribes as long as the Bridge of the Gods should stand. Have the stones of that bridge begun to crumble, that our hearts should grow weak ? "

He then described the natural bridge which, as tradition and geology alike tell us, spanned at that time the Columbia at the Cascades. The Great Spirit, he declared, had spoken ; and as he had said, so it would be. Dreams and omens were mist and shadow, but the bridge was rock, and the word of the Great Spirit stood forever. On this tradition the chief dwelt with tremendous force, setting against the superstition that Tohomish had roused the still more powerful superstition of the bridge, — a superstition so interwoven with every thought and hope of the Willamettes that it had become a part of their character as a tribe.

And now when their martial enthusiasm and fatalistic courage were all aglow, when the recital of their fathers' deeds had stirred their blood and the portrayal of their own victories filled them again with the fierce joy of conflict, when the mountain of stone that arched the Columbia had risen before them in assurance of dominion as eternal as itself, — now, when in every eye gleamed desire of battle and every heart was aflame, the chief made (and it was characteristic of him) in one terse sentence his crowning appeal, —

"Chiefs, speak your heart. Shall the runners be sent out to call the council?"

There was a moment of intense silence. Then a low, deep murmur of consent came from the excited listeners; a half-smothered war-cry burst from the lips of Mishlah, and the victory was won.

One only sat silent and apart, his robe drawn close, his head bent down, seemingly oblivious of all around him, as if resigned to inevitable doom.

"To-morrow at dawn, while the light is yet young, the runners will go out. Let the chiefs meet here in the grove to hear the message given them to be carried to the tribes. The talk is ended."

CHAPTER II.

THE WAR-CHIEF AND THE SEER.

Cassandra's wild voice prophesying woe.
PHILIP BOURKE MARSTON.

THE war-chief left the grove as soon as he had dismissed the council. Tohomish went with him. For some distance they walked together, the one erect and majestic, the other gliding like a shadow by his side.

At length Multnomah stopped under a giant cotton-wood and looked sternly at Tohomish.

" You frightened the council to-day with bad *mim-aluse* [death] talk. Why did you do it? Why did you bring into a council of warriors dreams fit only for old men that lie sleeping in the sun by the door of the wigwam ? "

" I said what my eyes saw and my ears heard, and it was true."

" It cannot be true, for the Great Spirit has said that the Willamettes shall rule the tribes as long as the bridge shall stand ; and how can it fall when it is a mountain of stone ? "

A strange expression crossed Tohomish's sullen face.

" Multnomah, beware how you rest on the prophecy of the bridge. Lean not your hand on it, for it is as if you put it forth to lean it on a coiled rattle-snake."

"Your sayings are dark," replied the chief impatiently. " Speak plainly."

Tohomish shook his head, and the gloomy look habitual to him came back.

" I cannot.   Dreams and omens I can tell, but the secret of the bridge is the secret of the Great Spirit; and I cannot tell it lest he become angry and take from me my power of moving men with burning words."

" The secret of the Great Spirit !   What black thing is it you are hiding and covering up with words? Bring it forth into the light, that I may see it."

" No, it is my *tomanowos*.   Were I to tell it the gift of eloquence would go from me, the fire would die from my heart and the words from my lips, and my life would wither up within me."

Multnomah was silent.   Massive and commanding as was his character he was still an Indian, and the words of the seer had touched the latent superstition in his nature.   They referred to that strongest and most powerful of all the strange beliefs of the Oregon savages, — the spirit possession or devil worship of the *tomanowos*.

As soon as an Oregon Indian was old enough to aspire to a place among the braves, he was sent into the hills alone.   There he fasted, prayed, and danced, chanted the medicine-chant, and cut himself with knife or thorn till he fell exhausted to the ground.   Whatever he saw then, in waking delirium or feverish sleep, was the charm that was to control his future.   Be it bird or beast, dream or mystic revelation, it was his *totem* or *tomanowos*, and gave him strength, cunning, or swiftness, sometimes knowledge of the future, imparting to him its own characteristics. But *what* it was, its name or nature, was the one secret that must go with him to his grave. Woe unto him if he told the name of his *totem*. In that moment it would desert him, taking from him all strength and power, leaving him a shattered wreck, an outcast from camp and war-party.

"Multnomah says well that it is a black secret, but it is my *totem* and may not be told. For many winters Tohomish has carried it in his breast, till its poisoned sap has filled his heart with bitterness, till for him gladness and warmth have gone out of the light, laughter has grown a sob of pain, and sorrow and death have become what the feast, the battle, and the chase are to other men. It is the black secret, the secret of the coming trouble, that makes Tohomish's voice like the voice of a pine ; so that men say it has in it sweetness and mystery and haunting woe, moving the heart as no other can. And if he tells the secret, eloquence and life go with it. Shall Tohomish tell it? Will Multnomah listen while Tohomish shows what is to befall the bridge and the Willamettes in the time that is to come?"

The war-chief gazed at him earnestly. In that troubled, determined look, superstition struggled for a moment and then gave way to the invincible obstinacy of his resolve.

"No. Multnomah knows that his own heart is strong and will not fail him, come what may ; and that is all he cares to know. If you told me, the *tomanowos* would be angry, and drain your spirit

from you and cast you aside as the serpent casts its
skin.   And you must be the most eloquent of all at
the great council ; for there the arm of Multnomah
and the voice of Tohomish must bend the bad chiefs
before them."

His accents had the same undertone of arbitrary
will, of inflexible determination, that had been in
them when he spoke in the council.   Though the
shadows fell more and more ominous and threatening
across his path, to turn back did not occur to him.
The stubborn tenacity of the man could not let go his
settled purpose.

"Tohomish will be at the council and speak for
his chief and his tribe?" asked Multnomah, in a tone
that was half inquiry, half command ; for the seer
whose mysterious power as an orator gave him
so strong an influence over the Indians must be
there.

Tohomish's haggard and repulsive face had settled
back into the look of mournful apathy habitual to him.
He had not, since the council, attempted to change
the chief's decision by a single word, but seemed to
have resigned himself with true Indian fatalism to that
which was to come.

"Tohomish will go to the council," he said in
those soft and lingering accents, indescribably sweet
and sad, with which his degraded face contrasted so
strongly.   "Yes, he will go to the council, and his
voice shall bend and turn the hearts of men as never
before.   Strong will be the words that he shall say, for
with him it will be sunset and his voice will be heard
no more."

"Where will you go when the council is ended, that we shall see you no more?" asked Multnomah.

"On the death-trail to the spirit-land, — nor will I go alone," was the startling reply; and the seer glided noiselessly away and disappeared among the trees.

CHAPTER III.

WALLULAH.

Ne'er was seen
In art or nature, aught so passing sweet
As was the form that in its beauteous frame
Inclosed her, and is scattered now in dust.
CAREY: *Dante.*

MULTNOMAH passed on to seek the lodge of his daughter Wallulah, a half Asiatic, and the most beautiful woman in all the land of the Wauna.

Reader, would you know the tale of the fair oriental of whom was born the sweet beauty of Wallulah?

Eighteen years before the time of our story, an East Indian ship was wrecked on the Columbia bar, the crew and cargo falling into the hands of the Indians. Among the rescued was a young and exceedingly lovely woman, who was hospitably entertained by the chief of the tribe. He and his people were deeply impressed by the grace of the fair stranger, whose dainty beauty won for her the name of "Sea-Flower," because the sea, that is ever drifting weeds, had for once wafted a flower to the shore.

As she sat on the mat in the rude bark lodge, the stern chief softened his voice, trying to talk with her; the uncouth women gently stroked her long soft hair, and some of the bolder and more curious touched her white hands wonderingly, while the throng of dusky faces pressed close round the pale, sweet creature whose eyes looked at them with a deep, dumb woe they could not understand.

When she had become familiar with the Willamette tongue, she told them that she was the daughter of a chief far away across the great water, who ruled a country as broad as the land of the Wauna and far richer. He had sent her as a bride to the ruler of another land, with a fabulous dowry of jewels and a thousand gifts besides. But the ship that bore her and her splendid treasures had been turned from its course by a terrible storm. Day after day it was driven through a waste of blackness and foam, — the sails rent, the masts swept away, the shattered hulk hurled onward like a straw by the fury of the wind. When the tempest had spent itself, they found themselves in a strange sea under strange stars. Compass and chart were gone; they knew not where they were, and caught in some unknown current, they could only drift blindly on and on. Never sighting land, seeing naught but the everlasting sweep of wave and sky, it began to be whispered in terror that this ocean had no further shore, that they might sail on forever, seeing nothing but the boundless waters. At length, when the superstitious sailors began to talk of throwing their fair charge overboard as an offering to the gods, the blue peaks of the Coast Range rose out of the water, and the ever rain-freshened green of the Oregon forests dawned upon them. Then came the attempt to enter the Columbia, and the wreck on the bar.[1]

1 Shipwrecks of Asiatic vessels are not uncommon on the Pacific Coast, several having occurred during the present century, — notably that of a Japanese junk in 1833, from which three passengers were

Multnomah made the lovely princess his wife, and Sea-Flower showed the spirit of a queen. She tried to introduce among the Indians something of the refinement of her oriental home. From her the degraded medicine-men and dreamers caught a gleam of the majestic lore of Buddha ; to the chiefs-in-council she taught something of the grave, inexorable justice of the East, that seemed like a higher development of their own grim unwritten code. Her influence was very great, for she was naturally eloquent and of noble presence. More than one sachem felt the inspiration of better, purer thoughts than he had ever known before when the " war-chief's woman " spoke in council. Strange gatherings were those : blood-stained chiefs and savage warriors listening all intent to the sweetest of Indian tongues spoken in modulations that were music ; the wild heart of the empire stirred by the perfumed breath of a woman !

She had died three years before the events we have been narrating, and had left to her daughter the heritage of her refinement and her beauty.

saved at the hands of the Indians ; while the cases of beeswax that have been disinterred on the sea-coast, the oriental words that are found ingrafted in the native languages, and the Asiatic type of countenance shown by many of the natives, prove such wrecks to have been frequent in prehistoric times. One of the most romantic stories of the Oregon coast is that which the Indians tell of a buried treasure at Mount Nehalem, left there generations ago by shipwrecked men of strange garb and curious arms, — treasure which, like that of Captain Kidd, has been often sought but never found. There is also an Indian legend of a shipwrecked white man named Soto, and his comrades (See Mrs. Victor's " Oregon and Washington "), who lived long with the mid-Columbia Indians and then left them to seek some settlement of their own people in the south. All of these legends point to the not infrequent occurrence of such a wreck as our story describes.

Wallulah was the only child of the war-chief and his Asiatic wife, the sole heir of her father's sovereignty.

Two miles from the council grove, in the interior of the island, was Wallulah's lodge. The path that Multnomah took led through a pleasant sylvan lawn. The grass was green, and the air full of the scent of buds and flowers. Here and there a butterfly floated like a sunbeam through the woodland shadows, and a humming-bird darted in winged beauty from bloom to bloom. The lark's song came vibrating through the air, and in the more open spaces innumerable birds flew twittering in the sun. The dewy freshness, the exquisite softness of spring, was everywhere.

In the golden weather, through shadowed wood and sunny opening, the war-chief sought his daughter's lodge.

Suddenly a familiar sound attracted his attention, and he turned toward it. A few steps, and he came to the margin of a small lake. Several snow-white swans were floating on it; and near the edge of the water, but concealed from the swans by the tall reeds that grew along the shore, was his daughter, watching them.

She was attired in a simple dress of some oriental fabric. Her form was small and delicately moulded; her long black hair fell in rich masses about her shoulders; and her profile, turned toward him, was sweetly feminine. The Indian type showed plainly, but was softened with her mother's grace. Her face was sad, with large appealing eyes and mournful lips, and full of haunting loveliness; a face whose strange mournfulness was deepened by the splendor of its beauty; a face the like of which is rarely seen, but once seen can never be forgotten.

There was something despondent even in her pose, as she sat with her shoulders drooping slightly forward and her dark eyes fixed absently on the swans, watching them through the bending reeds. Now one uttered its note, and she listened, seeming to vibrate to the deep, plaintive cry; then she raised to her lips a flute that she held in her hands, and answered it with a perfect intonation, — an intonation that breathed the very spirit of the swan. So successful was the mimicry that the swans replied, thinking it the cry of a hidden mate; and again she softly, rhythmically responded.

" Wallulah ! " said the chief.

She sprang to her feet and turned toward him. Her dark face lighted with an expressive flash, her black eyes shone, her features glowed with joy and surprise. It was like the breaking forth of an inner illumination. There was now nothing of the Indian in her face.

" My father ! " she exclaimed, springing to him and kissing his hand, greeting him as her mother had taught her to do from childhood. " Welcome ! Were you searching for me ? "

" Yes, you were well hidden, but Multnomah is a good hunter and can always track the fawn to its covert," replied the chief, with the faint semblance of a smile. All that there was of gentleness in his nature came out when talking with his daughter.

" You have come from the council ? Are you not weary and hungry ? Come to the lodge, and let Wallulah give you food, and spread a mat for you to rest upon."

"No, I am hungry only to see Wallulah and hear her talk. Sit down on the log again." She seated herself, and her father stood beside her with an abstracted gaze, his hand stroking her long, soft tresses. He was thinking of the darker, richer tresses of another, whose proud, sad face and mournful eyes with their wistful meaning, so like Wallulah's own, he, a barbarian prince, could never understand.

Although, according to the superstitious custom of the Willamettes, he never spoke the name of Sea-Flower or alluded to her in any way, he loved his lost wife with a deep and unchanging affection. She had been a fair frail thing whose grace and refinement perplexed and fascinated him, moving him to unwonted tenderness and yearning. He had brought to her the spoils of the chase and of battle. The finest mat was braided for her lodge, the choicest skins and furs spread for her bed, and the chieftainess's string of *hiagua* shells and grizzly bear's claws had been put around her white neck by Multnomah's own hand. In spite of all this, she drooped and saddened year by year; the very hands that sought to cherish her seemed but to bruise; and she sickened and died, the delicate woman, in the arms of the iron war-chief, like a flower in the grasp of a mailed hand.

Why did she die? Why did she always seem so sad? Why did she so often steal away to weep over her child? Was not the best food hers, and the warm place by the lodge fire, and the softest bearskin to rest on; and was she not the wife of Multno-

mah, — the big chief's woman? Why then should
she droop and die like a winged bird that one tries
to tame by tying it to the wigwam stake and tossing
it food?

Often the old chief brooded over these questions,
but it was unknown to all, even to Wallulah. Only
his raven tresses, cut close year by year in sign of
perpetual mourning, told that he had not forgotten,
could never forget.

The swans had taken flight, and their long lingering
note sounded faint in the distance.

" You have frightened away my swans," said Wallulah, looking up at him smilingly.

A shadow crossed his brow.

" Wallulah," he said, and his voice had now the
stern ring habitual to it, " you waste your life with
the birds and trees and that thing of sweet sounds,"
— pointing to the flute. " Better be learning to think
on the things a war-chief's daughter should care for,
— the feast and the council, the war-parties and the
welcome to the braves when they come back to the
camp with the spoil."

The bright look died out of her face.

" You say those words so often," she replied sorrowfully, " and I try to obey, but cannot. War is
terrible to me."

His countenance grew harsher, his hand ceased to
stroke her hair.

" And has Multnomah, chief of the Willamettes
and war-chief of the Wauna, lived to hear his daughter say that war is terrible to her? Have you nothing of your father in you? Remember the tales of
the brave women of Multnomah's race, — the women

whose blood is in your veins. Remember that they spoke burning words in the council, and went forth with the men to battle, and came back with their own garments stained with blood. You shudder! Is it at the thought of blood?"

The old wistful look came back, the old sadness was on the beautiful face again. One could see now why it was there.

"My father," she said sorrowfully, "Wallulah has tried to love those things, but she cannot. She cannot change the heart the Great Spirit has given her. She cannot bring herself to be a woman of battle any more than she can sound a war-cry on her flute," and she lifted it as she spoke.

He took it into his own hands.

"It is this," he said, breaking down the sensitive girl in the same despotic way in which he bent the wills of warriors; "it is this that makes you weak. Is it a charm that draws the life from your heart? If so, it can be broken."

Another moment and the flute would have been broken in his ruthless hands and its fragments flung into the lake; but Wallulah, startled, caught it from him with a plaintive cry.

"It was my mother's. If you break it you will break my heart!"

The chief's angry features quivered at the mention of her mother, and he instantly released the flute. Wallulah clasped it to her bosom as if it represented in some way the mother she had lost, and her eyes filled with tears. Again her father's hand rested on her head, and she knew that he too was thinking of her mother. Her nature rose up in revolt against the

Indian custom which forbade talking of the dead. Oh, if she might only talk with her father about her mother, though it were but a few brief words ! Never since her mother's death had her name been mentioned between them. She lifted her eyes, pathetic with three years' hunger, to his. As their glances met, it seemed as if the veil that had been between their diverse natures was for a moment lifted, and they understood each other better than they ever had before. While his look imposed silence and sealed her lips as with a spoken command, there was a gleam of tenderness in it that said, " I understand, I too remember ; but it must not be spoken."

There came to her a sense of getting closer to her father's heart, even while his eyes held her back and bade her be silent.

At length the chief spoke, this time very gently.

" Now I shall talk to you not as to a girl but as to a woman. You are Multnomah's only child. When he dies there will be no one but you to take his place. Are your shoulders strong enough to bear the weight of power, the weight that crushes men? Can you break down revolt and read the hearts of plotters, — yes, and detect conspiracy when it is but a whisper in the air? Can you sway council and battle to your will as the warrior bends his bow? No ; it takes men, men strong of heart, to rule the races of the Wauna. Therefore there is but one way left me whereby the line of Multnomah may still be head of the confederacy when he is gone. I must wed you to a great warrior who can take my place when I am dead and shelter you with his strength. Then the name and the power of Multnomah will still live among the tribes, though Multnomah himself be crumbled into dust."

She made no reply, but sat looking confused and pained, by no means elated at the future he had described.

" Have you never thought of this, — that some time I must give you to a warrior?"

Her head drooped lower and her cheek faintly flushed.

" Sometimes."

" But you have chosen no one?"

" I do not know," she faltered.

Her father's hand still rested on her head, but there was an expression on his face that showed he would not hesitate to sacrifice her happiness to his ambition.

"You have chosen, then? Is he a chief? No, I will not ask that; the daughter of Multnomah could love no one but a chief. I have already selected a husband for you. Tear this other love from your heart and cast it aside."

The flush died out of her cheek, leaving it cold and ashen; and her fingers worked nervously with the flute in her lap.

He continued coldly, —

" The fame of your beauty has gone out through all the land. The chief of the Chopponish [1] has offered many horses for you, and the chief of the Spokanes, our ancient foes, has said there would be peace between us if I gave you to him. But I have promised you to another. Your marriage to him will knit the bravest tribe of the confederacy to us; he will take

---

[1] Indian name of the Nez Percés.

my place when I am dead, and our people will still be strong."

She made no reply. What could she do against her father's granite will? All the grace and mobility were gone from her face, and it was drooping and dull almost to impassiveness. She was only an Indian girl now, waiting to learn the name of him who was to be her master.

"What is the name of the one you love? Speak it once, then never speak it again."

"Snoqualmie, chief of the Cayuses," faltered her tremulous lips.

A quick change of expression came into the gaze that was bent on her.

"Now lift your head and meet your fate like the daughter of a chief. Do not let me see your face change while I tell you whom I have chosen."

She lifted her face in a tumult of fear and dread, and her eyes fastened pathetically on the chief.

"His name is —" she clasped her hands and her whole soul went out to her father in the mute supplication of her gaze — "the chief Snoqualmie, him of whom you have thought."

Her face was bewilderment itself for an instant; the next, the sudden light, the quick flash of expression which transfigured it in a moment of joy or surprise, came to her, and she raised his hand and kissed it. Was that all? Remember she had in her the deep, mute Indian nature that meets joy or anguish alike in silence. She had early learned to repress and control her emotions. Perhaps that was why she was so sad and brooding now.

" Where have you seen Snoqualmie ? " asked Multnomah. " Not in your father's lodge, surely, for when
strange chiefs came to him you always fled like a
frightened bird."

" Once only have I seen him," she replied, flushing
and confused. " He had come here alone to tell you
that some of the tribes were plotting against you. I
saw him as he went back through the wood to the
place where his canoe was drawn up on the bank of
the river. He was tall ; his black hair fell below his
shoulders ; and his look was very proud and strong.
His back was to the setting sun, and it shone around
him robing him with fire, and I thought he looked
like the Indian sun-god."

" I am glad it is pleasant for you to obey me. Now,
listen while I tell you what you must do as the wife
of Snoqualmie."

Stilling the sweet tumult in her breast, she tried hard
to listen while he told her of the plans, the treaties,
the friendships, and the enmities she must urge on
her husband, when he became war-chief and was carrying on her father's work ; and in part she understood, for her imagination was captivated by the
splendid though barbarian dream of empire he set
before her.

At length, as the sun was setting, one came to tell
Multnomah that a runner from a tribe beyond the
mountains had come to see him. Then her father
left her ; but Wallulah still sat on the mossy log, while
all the woodland was golden in the glory of sunset.

Her beloved flute was pressed close to her cheek,
and her face was bright and joyous ; she was thinking of Snoqualmie, the handsome stately chief whom

she had seen but once, but whose appearance, as she saw him then, had filled her girlish heart.

And all the time she knew not that this Snoqualmie, to whom she was to be given, was one of the most cruel and inhuman of men, terrible even to the grim warriors of the Wauna for his deeds of blood.

CHAPTER IV.

SENDING OUT THE RUNNERS.

Speed, Malise, speed ; the dun deer's hide
On fleeter foot was never tied ;
Herald of battle, fate and fear
Stretch around thy fleet career.

SCOTT.

A T early morning, the sachems had gathered in the council-grove, Multnomah on the seat of the war-chief, and twenty runners before him. They were the flower of the Willamette youth, every one of royal birth, handsome in shape and limb, fleet-footed as the deer. They were slender and sinewy in build, with aquiline features and sharp searching eyes.

Their garb was light. Leggins and moccasins had been laid aside ; even the *hiagua* shells were stripped from their ears. All stood nerved and eager for the race, waiting for the word that was to scatter them throughout the Indian empire, living thunderbolts bearing the summons of Multnomah.

The message had been given them, and they waited only to pledge themselves to its faithful delivery.

"You promise," said the chief, while his flashing glance read every messenger to the heart, "you promise that neither cougar nor cataract nor ambuscade shall deter you from the delivery of this summons ; that you will not turn back, though the spears of the enemy are thicker in your path than ferns along the Santiam? You promise that though you fall in death, the summons shall go on?"

The spokesman of the runners, the runner to the Chopponish, stepped forward. With gestures of perfect grace, and in a voice that rang like a silver trumpet, he repeated the ancient oath of the Willamettes, — the oath used by the Shoshones to-day.

"The earth hears us, the sun sees us. Shall we fail in fidelity to our chief?"

There was a pause. The distant cry of swans came from the river; the great trees of council rustled in the breeze. Multnomah rose from his seat, gripping the bow on which he leaned. Into that one moment he seemed gathering yet repressing all the fierceness of his passion, all the grandeur of his will. Far in the shade he saw Tohomish raise his hand imploringly, but the eyes of the orator sank once more under the glance of the war-chief.

"Go!"

An electric shock passed through all who heard; and except for the chiefs standing on its outskirts like sombre shadows, the grove was empty in a moment.

Beyond the waters that girdled the island, one runner took the trail to Puyallup, one the trail to Umatilla, one the path to Chelon, and one the path to Shasta; another departed toward the volcano-rent desert of Klamath, and still another toward the sea-washed shores of Puget Sound.

The irrevocable summons had gone forth; the council was inevitable, — the crisis must come.

Long did Multnomah and his chiefs sit in council

" *T*HE Earth hears us,
the Sun sees us."

that day. Resolute were the speeches that came from all, though many secretly regretted that they had allowed Multnomah's oratory to persuade them into declaring for the council: but there was no retreat.

Across hills and canyons sped the fleet runners, on to the huge bark lodges of Puget Sound, the fisheries of the Columbia, and the crowded race-courses of the Yakima. Into camps of wandering prairie tribes, where the lodges stood like a city to-day and were rolled up and strapped on the backs of horses to-morrow; into councils where sinister chiefs were talking low of war against the Willamettes; into wild midnight dances of plotting dreamers and medicine-men, — they came with the brief stern summons, and passed on to speak it to the tribes beyond.

BOOK III.

THE GATHERING OF THE TRIBES.

CHAPTER I.

THE BROKEN PEACE-PIPE.

My full defiance, hate, and scorn.
SCOTT.

IT is the day after the departure of the runners to call the great council, — eight years since Cecil Grey went out into the wilderness. Smoke is curling slowly upward from an Indian camp on the prairie not far from the Blue Mountains of eastern Oregon. Fifteen or twenty cone-shaped lodges, each made of mats stretched on a frame-work of poles, compose the village. It swarms with wolfish-looking dogs and dirty, unclad children. Heaps of refuse, heads and feet of game, lie decaying among the wigwams, tainting the air with their disgusting odor. Here and there an ancient withered specimen of humanity sits in the sun, absorbing its rays with a dull animal-like sense of enjoyment, and a group of warriors lie idly talking. Some of the squaws are preparing food, boiling it in water-tight willow baskets by filling them with water and putting in hot stones.[1] Horses are

---

[1] See Bancroft's "Native Races," vol. i., p. 270.

tethered near the lodges, and others are running loose on the prairie.

There are not many of them. The Indians have only scores now where a century later Lewis and Clark found thousands; and there are old men in the camp who can recall the time when the first horses ever seen among them were bought or stolen from the tribes to the south.

On every side the prairie sweeps away in long grassy swells and hollows, rolling off to the base of the Blue Mountains.

The camp has the sluggish aspect that an Indian camp always presents at noonday.

Suddenly a keen-sighted warrior points to a dim speck far over the prairie toward the land of the Bannocks. A white man would have scarcely noticed it; or if he had, would have thought it only some wandering deer or antelope. But the Indians, glancing at the moving object, have already recognized it as a horseman coming straight toward the camp.

Some messenger it is, doubtless, from the Bannocks. Once the whole camp would have rushed to arms at the approach of a rider from that direction, for the two tribes had been at bitter enmity; but of late the peace-pipe has been smoked between them, and the old feud is at an end. Still, the sight arouses considerable curiosity and much speculation as to the object of the visitor.

He is a good rider, his horse is fleet, and in less time than would have been thought possible reaches the camp. He gallops up, stops near the lodges that are farthest out, and springs lightly to the ground. He does not go on into the camp, but stands beside his horse till advances are made on the other side.

The dogs bark at him; his steed, a fiery black, tosses its head and paws the ground; he stands beside it immovably, and to all appearance is ready so to stand till sunset. Some of the warriors recognize him as one of the bravest of the Bannocks. He looks like a daring, resolute man, yet wary and self-contained.

After a while one of the Cayuse warriors (for this was a camp of the Cayuses) advanced toward him, and a grave salutation was exchanged. Then the Bannock said that he wanted to see the Cayuse chief, Snoqualmie, in the council-lodge, for the chief of the Bannocks had sent a " talk " to the Cayuses.

The warrior left him to speak with Snoqualmie. In a short time he returned, saying that the chief and the warriors had gone to the council-lodge and were ready to hear the " talk " that their brother, the chief of the Bannocks, had sent them. The messenger tied his horse by its lariat, or long hair-rope, to a bush, and followed the brave to the lodge.

It was a large wigwam in the centre of the village. A crowd of old men, women, and children had already gathered around the door. Within, on one side of the room, sat in three rows a semi-circle of braves, facing the chief, who sat on the opposite side. Near the door was a clear space where the messenger was to stand while speaking.

He entered, and the doorway behind him was immediately blocked up by the motley crowd excluded from the interior. Not a warrior in the council looked at him; even the chief, Snoqualmie, did not turn his head. The messenger advanced a few paces into the

room, stopped, and stood as impassive as the rest.
Then, when the demands of Indian stoicism had been
satisfied, Snoqualmie turned his face, a handsome but
treacherous and cruel face, upon the messenger.

"The warrior comes to speak the words of our
brother, the chief of the Bannocks ; he is welcome.
Shall we smoke the pipe of peace before we hear our
brother's words?"

The Bannock gazed steadily at Snoqualmie. In
that fierce and proud regard was something the
Cayuse could not fathom.

"Why should the peace-pipe be smoked?" he
asked. "Was it not smoked in the great council a
moon ago? Did not Snoqualmie say then that the
two tribes should henceforth be as one tribe, and that
the Bannocks should be the brethren of the Cayuses
forever?"

"Those were the words," replied the chief with
dignity. "Snoqualmie has not forgotten them."

All eyes were now turned on the messenger ; they
saw that something unexpected was coming. The
Bannock drew his form up to its full height, and his
resolute features expressed the bitterest scorn.

"Nor have the Bannocks forgotten. At the council you talked 'peace, peace.' Last night some of your
young men surprised a little camp of Bannocks, — a
few old men and boys who were watching horses, —
and slew them and ran off the horses. Is that your
peace? The Bannocks will have no such peace. *This*
is the word the chief of the Bannocks sends you!"

Holding up the peace-pipe that had been smoked
at the great council and afterward given to the medicine-men of the Bannocks as a pledge of Cayuse sin-

cerity, he broke the long slender stem twice, thrice, crushed the bowl in his fingers, and dashed the pieces at Snoqualmie's feet. It was a defiance, a contemptuous rejection of peace, a declaration of war more disdainful than any words could have made it.

Then, before they could recover from their astonishment, the Bannock turned and leaped through the crowd at the door, — for an instant's stay was death. Even as he leaped, Snoqualmie's tomahawk whizzed after him, and a dozen warriors were on their feet, weapon in hand. But the swift, wild drama had been played like lightning, and he was gone. Only, a brave who had tried to intercept his passage lay on the ground outside the lodge, stabbed to the heart. They rushed to the door in time to see him throw himself on his horse and dash off, looking back to give a yell of triumph and defiance.

In less time than it takes to describe it, the horses tethered near the lodges were mounted and twenty riders were in pursuit. But the Bannock was considerably in advance now, and the fine black horse he rode held its own nobly. Out over the prairie flew the pursuing Cayuses, yelling like demons, the fugitive turning now and then to utter a shout of derision.

Back at the lodges, the crowd of spectators looked on with excited comments.

" His horse is tired, ours are fresh ! " " They gain on him ! " " No, he is getting farther from them ! " " See, he throws away his blanket ! " " They are closer, closer ! " " No, no, his horse goes like a deer."

Out over the prairies, fleeting like the shadow of a hurrying cloud, passed the race, the black horse leading, the Cayuse riders close behind, their long hair outstreaming, their moccasins pressed against their horses' sides, their whips falling without mercy. Down a canyon they swept in pursuit and passed from the ken of the watchers at the camp, the black horse still in the van.

But it could not cope with the fresh horses of the Cayuses, and they gained steadily. At last the pursuers came within bowshot, but they did not shoot; the fugitive knew too well the reason why. Woe unto him if he fell alive into their hands! He leaned low along his horse's neck, chanting a weird refrain as if charming it to its utmost speed, and ever and anon looked back with that heart-shaking shout of defiance. But steadily his pursuers gained on him; and one, outstripping the rest, rode alongside and reached out to seize his rein. Even as he touched it, the Bannock's war-club swung in air and the Cayuse reeled dead from his saddle. A howl of rage burst from the others, a whoop of exultation from the fugitive.

But at length his horse's breath grew short and broken, he felt its body tremble as it ran, and his enemies closed in around him.

Thrice the war-club rose and fell, thrice was a saddle emptied; but all in vain. Quickly his horse was caught, he was dragged from the saddle and bound hand and foot.

He was thrown across a horse and brought back to the village. What a chorus of triumph went up from the camp, when it was seen that they were bringing him back! It was an ominous sound, with something of wolfish ferocity in it. But the Bannock only smiled grimly.

He is bound to a post, — a charred, bloodstained post to which others of his race have been bound before him. The women and children taunt him, jeer at him, strike him even. The warriors do not. They will presently do more than that. Some busy themselves building a fire near by; others bring pieces of flint, spear points, jagged fragments of rock, and heat them in it. The prisoner, dusty, torn, parched with thirst, and bleeding from many wounds, looks on with perfect indifference. Snoqualmie comes and gazes at him; the prisoner does not notice him, is seemingly unconscious of his presence.

By and by a band of hunters ride up from a long excursion. They have heard nothing of the trouble. With them is a young Bannock who is visiting the tribe. He rides up with his Cayuse comrades, laughing, gesticulating in a lively way. The jest dies on his lips when he recognizes the Bannock who is tied to the stake. Before he can even think of flight, he is dragged from his horse and bound, — his whilom comrades, as soon as they understand the situation, becoming his bitterest assailants.

For it is war again, war to the death between the tribes, until, two centuries later, both shall alike be crushed by the white man.

At length the preparations are complete, and the women and children, who have been swarming around and taunting the captives, are brushed aside like so many flies by the stern warriors. First, the young Bannock who has just come in is put where he must have a full view of the other. Neither speaks, but a glance passes between them that is like a mutual charge to die bravely. Snoqualmie comes and stands close by the prisoner and gives directions for the torture to begin.

The Bannock is stripped. The stone blades that have been in the fire are brought, all red and glowing with heat, and pressed against his bare flesh. It burns and hisses under the fiery torture, but the warrior only sneers.

"It does n't hurt; you can't hurt me. You are fools. You don't know how to torture." [1]

No refinement of cruelty could wring a complaint from him. It was in vain that they burned him, cut the flesh from his fingers, branded his cheek with the heated bowl of the pipe he had broken.

"Try it again," he said mockingly, while his flesh smoked. "I feel no pain. We torture your people a great deal better, for we make them cry out like little children."

More and more murderous and terrible grew the wrath of his tormentors, as this stream of vituperation fell on their ears. Again and again weapons were lifted to slay him, but Snoqualmie put them back.

"He can suffer more yet," he said; and the words were like a glimpse into the cold, merciless heart of the man. Other and fiercer tortures were devised by the chief, who stood over him, pointing out where and how the keenest pain could be given, the bitterest pang inflicted on that burned and broken body. At last it seemed no longer a man, but a bleeding, scorched, mutilated mass of flesh that hung to the stake; only the lips still breathed defiance and the eyes gleamed deathless hate. Looking upon one and

---

[1] See Ross Cox's "Adventures on the Columbia River" for a description of torture among the Columbia tribes.

another, he boasted of how he had slain their friends
and relatives. Many of his boasts were undoubtedly
false, but they were very bitter.

"It was by my arrow that you lost your eye," he
said to one; "I scalped your father," to another;
and every taunt provoked counter-taunts accompanied
with blows.

At length he looked at Snoqualmie, — a look so
ghastly, so disfigured, that it was like something seen
in a horrible dream.

"I took your sister prisoner last winter; you never
knew, — you thought she had wandered from home
and was lost in a storm. We put out her eyes, we
tore out her tongue, and then we told her to go out
in the snow and find food. Ah-h-h! you should have
seen her tears as she went out into the storm, and — "

The sentence was never finished. While the last
word lingered on his lips, his body sunk into a lifeless
heap under a terrific blow, and Snoqualmie put back
his blood-stained tomahawk into his belt.

"Shall we kill the other?" demanded the warriors,
gathering around the surviving Bannock, who had
been a stoical spectator of his companion's sufferings.
A ferocious clamor from the women and children
hailed the suggestion of new torture; they thronged
around the captive, the children struck him, the women
abused him, spat upon him even, but not a muscle
of his face quivered; he merely looked at them with
stolid indifference.

"Kill him, kill him!" "Stretch him on red hot
stones!" "We will make *him* cry!"

Snoqualmie hesitated. He wished to save this man
for another purpose, and yet the Indian blood-thirst

was on him; chief and warrior alike were drunken
with fury, mad with the lust of cruelty.

As he hesitated, a white man clad in the garb of
an Indian hunter pushed his way through the crowd.
Silence fell upon the throng; the clamor of the
women, the fierce questioning of the warriors ceased.
The personality of this man was so full of tenderness
and sympathy, so strong and commanding, that it impressed the most savage nature. Amid the silence, he
came and looked first at the dead body that yet hung
motionless from the stake, then sorrowfully, reproach-
fully, at the circle of faces around. An expression
half of sullen shame, half of defiance, crossed more
than one countenance as his glance fell upon it.

"Friends," said he, sadly, pointing at the dead,
"is this your peace with the Bannocks, — the peace
you prayed the Great Spirit to bless, the peace that
was to last forever?"

"The Bannocks sent back the peace-pipe by this
man, and he broke it and cast the pieces in our
teeth," answered one, stubbornly.

"And you slew him for it? Why not have sent
runners to his tribe asking why it was returned, and
demanding to know what wrong you had done, that
you might right it? Now there will be war. When
you lie down to sleep at night, the surprise may be
on you and massacre come while your eyes are heavy
with slumber; when you are gone on the buffalo
trail the tomahawk may fall on the women and children at home. Death will lurk for you in every thicket
and creep round every encampment. The Great
Spirit is angry because you have stained your hands
in blood without cause."

There was no reply. This white man, coming from far eastern lands lying they knew not where, who told them God had sent him to warn them to be better, had a singular influence over them. There was none of his hearers who did not dimly feel that he had done wrong in burning and scarring the poor mass of humanity before him, and that the Great Spirit was angry with him for it.

Back in the crowd, some of the children, young demons hungering for blood, began to clamor again for the death of the surviving Bannock. Cecil Grey looked at him pityingly.

"At least you can let him go."

There was no answer. Better impulses, better desires, were struggling in their degraded minds; but cruelty was deeply rooted within them, the vague shame and misgiving his words had roused was not so strong as the dark animalism of their natures.

Cecil turned to Snoqualmie.

"I saved your life once, will you not give me his?"

The chief regarded him coldly.

"Take it," he said after a pause. Cecil stooped over and untied the thongs that bound the captive, who rose to his feet amid a low angry murmur from those around. Snoqualmie silenced it with an imperious gesture. Then he turned to the young Bannock.

"Dog, one of a race of dogs! go back to your people and tell them what you have seen to-day. Tell them how we burned and tortured their messenger, and that we let you go only to tell the tale. Tell them, too, that Snoqualmie knows his sister died by their hand last winter, and that for every hair upon her head he will burn a Bannock warrior at the stake. Go, and be quick, lest my war-party overtake you on the trail."

The Bannock left without a word, taking the trail across the prairie toward the land of his tribe.

"The gift was given, but there was that given with it that made it bitter. And now may I bury this dead body?"

"It is only a Bannock; who cares what is done with it?" replied Snoqualmie. "But remember, my debt is paid. Ask of me no more gifts," and the chief turned abruptly away.

"Who will help me bury this man?" asked Cecil. No one replied; and he went alone and cut the thongs that bound the body to the stake. But as he stooped to raise it, a tall fine-looking man, a renegade from the Shoshones, who had taken no part in the torture, came forward to help him. Together they bore the corpse away from the camp to the hillside; together they hollowed out a shallow grave and stretched the body in it, covering it with earth and heaping stones on top, that the cayote might not disturb the last sleep of the dead.

When they returned to the camp, they found a war-party already in the saddle, with Snoqualmie at their head, ready to take the Bannock trail. But before they left the camp, a runner entered it with a summons from Multnomah calling them to the great council of the tribes on Wappatto Island, for which they must start on the morrow.

CHAPTER II.

ON THE WAY TO THE COUNCIL.

They arrived at the village of Wishram.
Irving : *Astoria.*

THE camp was all astir at dawn, for sunset must see them far on the way. They must first cross the prairies to the northward till they struck the Columbia, then take the great trail leading down it to the Willamette valley. It was a two days' journey at the least.

Squaws were preparing a hurried meal ; lodge-poles were being taken down and the mats that covered them rolled up and strapped on the backs of horses ; Indians, yelling and vociferating, were driving up bands of horses from which pack and riding ponies were to be selected ; unbroken animals were rearing and plunging beneath their first burdens, while mongrel curs ran barking at their heels. Here and there unskilful hands were throwing the lasso amid the jeers and laughter of the spectators. All was tumult and excitement.

At length they were under way. First rode the squaws, driving before them pack-horses and ponies, for the herds and entire movable property of the tribe accompanied it in all its marches. The squaws rode astride, like men, in the rude wooden saddles that one yet sees used by the wilder Indians of eastern

Oregon and Idaho, — very high, both before and behind, looking like exaggerated pack-saddles. A hair
rope, tied around the lower jaw of the horse, answered
for a bridle. To this must be added the quirt, a
short double-lashed whip fastened into a hollow and
curiously carved handle. The application of this
whip was so constant as to keep the right arm in con-
tinual motion ; so that even to-day on the frontier an
Indian rider can be distinguished from a white man,
at a distance, by the constant rising and falling of the
whip arm. With the squaws were the children, some
of whom, not over four, five, and six years of age, rode
alone on horseback, tied in the high saddles ; managing their steeds with instinctive skill, and when the
journey became fatiguing, going to sleep, secured by
their fastenings from falling off.

Next came the men, on the best horses, unencum-
bered by weight of any kind and armed with bow and
arrow. Here and there a lance pointed with flint, a
stone knife or hatchet, or a heavy war-club, hung at
the saddle ; but the bow and arrow constituted their
chief weapon.

The men formed a kind of rear-guard, protecting the
migrating tribe from any sudden assault on the part
of the Bannocks. There were perhaps two hundred
fighting-men in all. Snoqualmie was at their head,
and beside him rode the young Willamette runner
who had brought the summons from Multnomah the
day before. The Willamette was on horseback for
the first time in his life. The inland or prairie tribes
of eastern Oregon, coming as they did in contact with
tribes whose neighbors bordered on Mexico, had
owned horses for perhaps a generation ; but the sea-

board tribes owned very few, and there were tribes on Puget Sound and at the mouth of the Columbia who had never seen them. Even the Willamettes, sovereign tribe of the confederacy though they were, had but few horses.

This morning the young Willamette had bought a colt, giving for it a whole string of *hiagua* shells. It was a pretty, delicate thing, and he was proud of it, and had shown his pride by slitting its ears and cutting off its tail, as was the barbarous custom with many of the Indians. He sat on the little creature now; and loaded as it was with the double weight of himself and the heavy wooden saddle, it could hardly keep pace with the older and stronger horses.

In the rear of all rode Cecil Grey and the Shoshone renegade who had helped him bury the dead Bannock the evening before. Cecil's form was as slight and graceful in its Indian garb as in days gone by, and his face was still the handsome, sensitive face it had been eight years before. It was stronger now, more resolute and mature, and from long intercourse with the Indians there had come into it something grave and Indian-like ; but it only gave more of dignity to his mien. His brown beard swept his breast, and his face was bronzed ; but the lips quivered under the beard, and the cheek flushed and paled under the bronze.

What had he been doing in the eight years that had elapsed since he left his New England home? Let us listen to his story in his own words as he tells it to the Shoshone renegade by his side.

"I lived in a land far to the east, beside a great water. My people were white like myself. I was one of an order of men whom the Great Spirit had appointed to preach of goodness, mercy, and truth, and to explain to the people the sayings of a mighty book which he had given to the fathers, — a book that told how men should live in this world, and said that a beautiful place in the next would be given those who are good and true in this. But by and by the Great Spirit began to whisper to me of the Indians in the wilderness who knew nothing of the book or the hope within it, and a longing rose within me to go and tell them ; but there were ties that held me to my own people, and I knew not what to do. Death cut those ties ; and in my hour of grief there came to me a vision of a great bridge far in the west, and of Indians passing over it, and a voice spoke to me and bade me go and seek the land of the bridge, for the Great Spirit had a mission for me there ; and I went forth into the wilderness. I met many tribes and tarried with them, telling them of God. Many were evil and treated me harshly, others were kind and listened. Some loved me and wished me to abide always in their lodges and be one of them. But even while they spoke the Great Spirit whispered to me to go on, and an unrest rose within me, and I could not stay.

"So the years went by, and I wandered farther and farther to the west, across rivers and deserts, till I reached this tribe ; and they said that farther on, toward the land of the Willamettes, a great river flowed through the mountains, and across it was a bridge of stone built by the gods when the world was young. Then I knew that it was the bridge of my vision, and the unrest came back and I arose to go. But the tribe kept me, half as guest and half as prisoner, and would not let me depart ; until last night the runner came summoning them to the council. Now they go, taking me with them. I shall see the land of the bridge and perform the work the Great Spirit has given me to do."

The old grand enthusiasm shone in his look as he closed. The Shoshone regarded him with grave attention.

" What became of the book that told of God ? " he asked earnestly.

" A chief took it from me and burned it ; but its words were written on my heart, and they could not be destroyed."

They rode on for a time in silence. The way was rugged, the country a succession of canyons and ridges covered with green and waving grass but bare of trees. Behind them, the Blue Mountains were receding in the distance. To the west, Mt. Hood, the great white " Witch Mountain " of the Indians, towered over the prairie, streaking the sky with a long floating wreath of volcanic smoke. Before them, as they journeyed northward toward the Columbia, stretched out the endless prairie. Now they descended into a deep ravine, now they toiled up a steep hillside. The country literally rolled, undulating in immense ridges around and over which the long file of squaws and warriors, herds and pack-horses, wound like a serpent. From the bands ahead came shouts and outcries, — the sounds of rude merriment ; and above all the long-drawn intonation so familiar to those who have been much with Indian horsemen, — the endlessly repeated " ho-ha, ho-ha, ho-ha," a kind of crude riding-song.

After a while Cecil said, " I have told you the story of my life, will you not tell me the story of yours? "

" Yes," said the renegade, after a moment's thought ; " you have shown me your heart as if you were my brother. Now I will show you mine.

" I was a Shoshone warrior.[1] There was a girl in our village whom I had loved from childhood. We played together ; we talked of how, when I became a man and a warrior, she should become my wife ; she should keep my wigwam ; we would always love one another. She grew up, and the chief offered many horses for her. Her father took them. She became the chief's wife, and all my heart withered up. Everything grew dark. I sat in my wigwam or wandered in the forest, caring for nothing.

" When I met her, she turned her face aside, for was she not the wife of another? Yet I knew her heart hungered for me. The chief knew it too, and when he spoke to her a cloud was ever on his brow and sharp lightning on his tongue. But she was true. Whose lodge was as clean as his? The wood was always carried, the water at hand, the meat cooked. She searched the very thought that was in his heart to save him the trouble of speaking. He could never say, ' Why is it not done?' But her heart was mine, and he knew it ; and he treated her like a dog and not like a wife.

" Me too he tried to tread under foot. One day we assembled to hunt the buffalo. Our horses were all collected. Mine stood before my tent, and he came and took them away, saying that they were his. What could I do? He was a chief.

[1] See Bonneville's Adventures, chapters xiii. and xlviii.

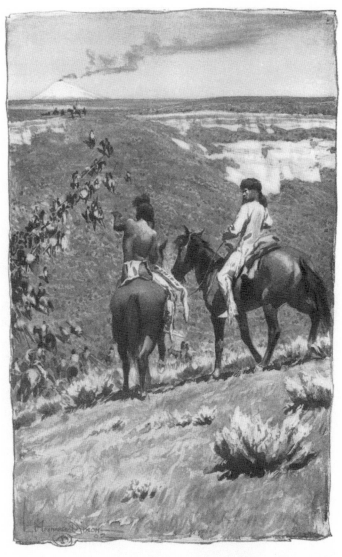

*T*HE Great "Witch Mountain" of the Indians.

" I came no more to the council, I shared no more in the hunt and the war-dance. I was unhorsed, degraded, dishonored. He told his wife what he had done, and when she wept he beat her.

" One evening I stood on a knoll overlooking the meadow where the horses were feeding; the chief's horses were there, and mine with them. I saw *him* walking among them. The sight maddened me ; my blood burned ; I leaped on him ; with two blows I laid him dead at my feet. I covered him with earth and strewed leaves over the place. Then I went to *her* and told her what I had done, and urged her to fly with me. She answered only with tears. I reminded her of all she had suffered, and told her I had done only what was just. I urged her again to fly. She only wept the more, and bade me go. My heart was heavy but my eyes were dry.

" ' It is well,' I said, ' I will go alone to the desert. None but the wild beasts of the wilderness will be with me. The seekers of blood will follow on my trail ; they may come on me while I am asleep and slay me, but you will be safe. I will go alone.'

" I turned to go. She sprang after me. ' No,' she cried, ' you shall not go alone. Wherever you go I will go : you shall never part from me.'

" While we were talking, one who had seen me slay the chief and had roused the camp, came with others. We heard their steps approaching the door, and knew that death came with them. We escaped at the back of the lodge, but they saw us and their arrows flew. She fell, and I caught her in my arms and fled into the wood. When we were safe I looked at her I carried, and she was dead. An arrow had pierced her heart. I buried her that night beneath a heap of stones, and fled to the Cayuses. That is my story."

"What will you do now?" asked Cecil, deeply touched.

"I shall live a man's life. I shall hunt and go on the war-trail, and say strong words in the council. And when my life is ended, when the sunset and the night come to me and I go forth into the darkness, I know I shall find her I love waiting for me beside the death-trail that leads to the spirit-land."

The tears came into Cecil's eyes.

"I too have known sorrow," he said, "and like you I am a wanderer from my own people. We are going together into an unknown land, knowing not what may befall us. Let us be friends."

And he held out his hand. The Indian took it, — awkwardly, as an Indian always takes the hand of a white man, but warmly, heartily.

"We are brothers," he said simply. And as Cecil rode on with the wild troop into the unknown world before him, he felt that there was one beside him who would be faithful, no matter what befell.

The long day wore on; the sun rose to the zenith and sunk, and still the Indians pushed forward. It was a long, forced march, and Cecil was terribly fatigued when at last one of the Indians told him that they were near a big river where they would camp for the night.

"One sun more," said the Indian, pointing to the sun now sinking in the west, "and you will see the Bridge of the Gods."

The news re-animated Cecil, and he hurried on. A

shout rose from the Indians in advance. He saw the head of the long train of horses and riders pause and look downward and the Indians at the rear gallop forward. Cecil and his friend followed and joined them.

"The river! the river!" cried the Indians, as they rode up. The scene below was one of gloomy but magnificent beauty. Beneath them opened an immense canyon, stupendous even in that land of canyons, — the great canyon of the Columbia. The walls were brown, destitute of verdure, sinking downward from their feet in yawning precipices or steep slopes. At the bottom, more than a thousand feet below, wound a wide blue river, the gathered waters of half a continent. Beneath them, the river plunged over a long low precipice with a roar that filled the canyon for miles. Farther on, the flat banks encroached upon the stream till it seemed narrowed to a silver thread among the jutting rocks. Still farther, it widened again, swept grandly around a bend in the distance, and passed from sight.

"*Tuum, tuum,*" said the Indians to Cecil, in tones that imitated the roar of the cataract. It was the "Tum" of Lewis and Clark, the "Tumwater" of more recent times; and the place below, where the compressed river wound like a silver thread among the flat black rocks, was the far-famed Dalles of the Columbia. It was superb, and yet there was something profoundly lonely and desolate about it, — the majestic river flowing on forever among barren rocks and crags, shut in by mountain and desert, wrapped in an awful solitude where from age to age scarce a sound was heard save the cry of wild beasts or wilder men.

"It is the very river of death and of desolation,"
thought Cecil. "It looks lonely, forsaken, as if no
eye had beheld it from the day of creation until now."

Looking again at the falls, he saw, what he had
not before noticed, a large camp of Indians on the
side nearest them. Glancing across the river, he
descried on a knoll on the opposite bank — what?
Houses! He could not believe his eyes; could it be
possible? Yes, they certainly were long, low houses,
roofed as the white man roofs his. A sudden wild
hope thrilled him; his brain grew dizzy. He turned
to one of the Indians.

"Who built those houses?" he exclaimed; "white
men like me?"

The other shook his head.

"No, Indians."

Cecil's heart died within him. "After all," he
murmured, "it was absurd to expect to find a settlement of white men here. How could I think that
any but Indians' had built those houses?"

Still, as they descended the steep zigzag pathway
leading down to the river, he could not help gazing
again and again at the buildings that so reminded
him of home.

It was Wishram, the ancient village of the falls,
whose brave and insolent inhabitants, more than a century later, were the dread of the early explorers and
fur traders of the Columbia. It was built at the last
and highest fishery on the Columbia, for the salmon
could not at that time ascend the river above the
falls. All the wandering tribes of the Upper Columbia came there to fish or to buy salmon of the Wishram fishers. There too the Indians of the Lower

Columbia and the Willamette met them, and bartered the *hiagua* shells, the dried berries, and *wappatto* of their country for the bear claws and buffalo robes of the interior. It was a rendezvous where buying, selling, gambling, dancing, feasting took the place of war and the chase ; though the ever burning enmities of the tribes sometimes flamed into deadly feuds and the fair-ground not infrequently became a field of battle.

The houses of Wishram were built of logs, the walls low, the lower half being below the surface of the ground, so that they were virtually half cellar. At a distance, the log walls and arched roofs gave them very much the appearance of a frontier town of the whites.

As they descended to the river-side, Cecil looked again and again at the village, so different from the skin or bark lodges of the Rocky Mountain tribes he had been with so long. But the broad and sweeping river flowed between, and his gaze told him little more than his first glance had done.

They were now approaching the camp. Some of the younger braves at the head of the Cayuse train dashed toward it, yelling and whooping in the wildest manner. Through the encampment rang an answering shout.

"The Cayuses ! the Cayuses ! and the white medicine-man ! "

The news spread like wildfire, and men came running from all directions to greet the latest arrivals. It was a scene of abject squalor that met Cecil's eyes as he rode with the others into the camp. Never had he seen among the Indian races aught so degraded as those Columbia River tribes.

The air was putrid with decaying fish ; the very skins and mats that covered the lodge-poles were black with rancid salmon and filth. Many of the men were nude ; most of the women wore only a short garment of skin or woven cedar bark about the waist, falling scarcely to the knees. The heads of many had been artificially flattened ; their faces were brutal ; their teeth worn to the gums with eating sanded salmon ; and here and there bleared and unsightly eyes showed the terrible prevalence of ophthalmia. Salmon were drying in the sun on platforms raised above the reach of dogs. Half-starved horses whose raw and bleeding mouths showed the effect of the hair-rope bridles, and whose projecting ribs showed their principal nutriment to be sage-brush and whip-lash, were picketed among the lodges. Cayote-like dogs and unclad children, shrill and impish, ran riot, fighting together for half-dried, half-decayed pieces of salmon. Prevailing over everything was the stench which is unique and unparalleled among the stenches of the earth, — the stench of an Indian camp at a Columbia fishery.[1]

Perhaps ten of the petty inland tribes had assembled there as their starting-point for the great council at Wappatto Island. All had heard rumors of the white man who had appeared among the tribes to the south saying that the Great Spirit had sent him to warn the Indians to become better, and all were anxious to see him. They pointed him out to one another as he rode up, — the man of graceful presence and delicate build ; they thronged around him, naked

[1] See Townsend's Narrative, pages 137, 138. Both Lewis and Clark and Ross Cox substantiate his description ; indeed, very much the same thing can be seen at the Tumwater Fishery to-day.

men and half-clad women, squalid, fierce as wild
beasts, and gazed wonderingly.

"It is he, the white man," they whispered among
themselves. "See the long beard." "See the white
hands." "Stand back, the Great Spirit sent him ; he
is strong *tomanowos ;* beware his anger."

Now the horses were unpacked and the lodges
pitched, under the eyes of the larger part of the
encampment, who watched everything with insatiable
curiosity, and stole all that they could lay their hands
on. Especially did they hang on every motion of
Cecil ; and he sank very much in·their estimation
when they found that he helped his servant, the old
Indian woman, put up his lodge.

"Ugh, he does squaw's work," was the ungracious
comment. After awhile, when the lodge was up and
Cecil lay weary and exhausted upon his mat within it,
a messenger entered and told him that the Indians
were all collected near the river bank and wished him
to come and give them the " talk " he had brought
from the Great Spirit.

Worn as he was, Cecil arose and went. It was in
the interval between sunset and dark. The sun still
shone on the cliffs above the great canyon, but in the
spaces below the shadows were deepening. On the
flat rocks near the bank of the river, and close by
the falls of Tumwater, the Indians were gathered to
the number of several hundred, awaiting him, — some
squatting, Indian fashion, on the ground, others
standing upright, looking taller than human in the
dusky light. Mingled with the debased tribes that
made up the larger part of the gathering, Cecil saw
here and there warriors of a bolder and superior race,

— Yakimas and Klickitats, clad in skins or wrapped in blankets woven of the wool of the mountain sheep.

Cecil stood before them and spoke, using the Willamette tongue, the language of common intercourse between the tribes, all of whom had different dialects. The audience listened in silence while he told them of the goodness and compassion of the Great Spirit; how it grieved him to see his children at war among themselves, and how he, Cecil, had been sent to warn them to forsake their sins and live better lives. Long familiarity with the Indians had imparted to him somewhat of their manner of thinking and speaking; his language had become picturesque with Indian imagery, and his style of oratory had acquired a tinge of Indian gravity. But the intense and vivid spirituality that had ever been the charm of his eloquence was in it still. There was something in his words that for the moment, and unconsciously to them, lifted his hearers to a higher plane. When he closed there was upon them that vague remorse, that dim desire to be better, that indefinable wistfulness, which his earnest, tender words never failed to arouse in his hearers.

When he lifted his hands at the close of his "talk," and prayed that the Great Spirit might pity them, that he might take away from them the black and wicked heart of war and hate and give them the new heart of peace and love, the silence was almost breathless, broken only by the unceasing roar of the falls and the solemn pleading of the missionary's voice.

He left them and returned through the deepening shadows to his lodge. There he flung himself on the couch of furs the old Indian woman had spread for him. Fatigued with the long ride of the day and the heavy draught his address had made on an overtaxed frame, he tried to sleep.

But he could not. The buildings of the town of Wishram across the river, so like the buildings of the white man, had awakened a thousand memories of home. Vivid pictures of his life in New England and in the cloisters of Magdalen came before his sleepless eyes. The longing for the refined and pleasant things that had filled his life rose strong and irrepressible within him. Such thoughts were never entirely absent from his mind, but at times they seemed to dominate him completely, driving him into a perfect fever of unrest and discontent. After tossing for hours on his couch, he arose and went out into the open air.

The stars were bright ; the moon flooded the wide canyon with lustre ; the towering walls rose dim and shadowy on either side of the river whose waters gleamed white in the moonlight ; the solemn roar of the falls filled the silence of the night.

Around him was the barbarian encampment, with here and there a fire burning and a group of warriors talking beside it. He walked forth among the lodges. Some were silent, save for the heavy breathing of the sleepers ; others were lighted up within, and he could hear the murmur of voices.

At one place he found around a large fire a crowd who were feasting, late as was the hour, and boasting of their exploits. He stood in the shadow a moment and listened. One of them concluded his tale by springing to his feet, advancing a few paces from the circle of firelight, and making a fierce speech to invisible foes.   Looking toward the land of the Shoshones, he denounced them with the utmost fury, dared them to face him, scorned them because they did not appear, and ended by shaking his tomahawk in their direction, amid the applause of his comrades.

Cecil passed on and reached the outer limit of the camp.   There, amid some large bowlders, he almost stumbled on a band of Indians engaged in some grisly ceremony.   He saw them, however, in time to escape observation and screen himself behind one of the rocks.

One of the Indians held a rattlesnake pinned to the ground with a forked stick.   Another held out a piece of liver to the snake and was provoking him to bite it.   Again and again the snake, quivering with fury and rattling savagely, plunged his fangs into the liver.   Several Indians stood looking on, with arrows in their hands.   At length, when the meat was thoroughly impregnated with the virus, the snake was released and allowed to crawl away.   Then they all dipped the points of their arrows in the poisoned liver,[1] carefully marking the shaft of each in order to distinguish it from those not poisoned.   None of them saw Cecil, and he left without being discovered.

Why did they wish to go to the council with poisoned arrows?

Further on, among the rocks and remote from the camp, he saw a great light and heard a loud hallooing. He went cautiously toward it.   He found a large fire in an open space, and perhaps thirty savages, stripped

[1] See Bancroft's *Native Races*, article " Columbians."   A bunch of arrows so poisoned is in the Museum of the Oregon State University at Eugene.

and painted, dancing around it, brandishing their weapons and chanting a kind of war-chant. On every face, as the firelight fell on it, was mad ferocity and lust of war. Near them lay the freshly killed body of a horse whose blood they had been drinking. Drunk with frenzy, drunk with blood, they danced and whirled in that wild saturnalia till Cecil grew dizzy with the sight.[1]

He made his way back to the camp and sought his lodge. He heard the wolves howling on the hills, and a dark presentiment of evil crept over him.

"It is not to council that these men are going, but to war," he murmured, as he threw himself on his couch. "God help me to be faithful, whatever comes! God help me to keep my life and my words filled with his spirit, so that these savage men may be drawn to him and made better, and my mission be fulfilled! I can never hope to see the face of white man again, but I can live and die faithful to the last."

So thinking, a sweet and restful peace came to him, and he fell asleep. And even while he thought how impossible it was for him ever to reach the land of the white man again, an English exploring-ship lay at anchor at Yaquina Bay, only two days' ride distant; and on it were some who had known and loved him in times gone by, but who had long since thought him lost in the wilderness forever.

---

[1] Irving's "Astoria," chap. xli.

CHAPTER III.

THE GREAT CAMP ON THE ISLAND.

Of different language, form and face,
A various race of men.
SCOTT.

" YOU say that we shall see the Bridge of the Gods
to-day? " asked Cecil of the young Willamette
runner the next morning. " Tell me about it; is it
high ? "

The young Willamette rose to his full height, arched
his right hand above his eyes, looked skyward with a
strained expression as if gazing up at an immense
height, and emitted a prolonged " ah-h-h ! "

That was all, but it was enough to bring the light
to Cecil's eyes and a sudden triumphant gladness to
his heart. At last he approached the land of his
vision, at last he should find the bridge whose wraith
had faded before him into the west eight years before !

The Cayuse band had started early that morning.
The chief Snoqualmie was impatient of delay, and
wished to be one of the earliest at the council; he
wanted to signalize himself in the approaching struggle
by his loyalty to Multnomah, whose daughter he was
to marry and whom he was to succeed as war-chief.

The women were in advance, driving the pack-
horses; Cecil rode behind them with the Shoshone
renegade and the young Willamette runner; while
Snoqualmie brought up the rear, looking sharply after

stragglers, — for some of his young men were very much inclined to linger at the rendezvous and indulge in a little gambling and horse-racing with the other bands, who were not to start till later in the day.

The young Willamette still rode the pretty little pony whose ears and tail he had so barbarously mutilated. It reeled under him from sheer weakness, so young was it and so worn by the journey of the day before. In vain did Cecil expostulate. With true Indian obtuseness and brutality, the Willamette refused to see why he should be merciful to a horse.

"Suppose he rode me, what would *he* care? Now I ride him, what do I care? Suppose he die, plenty more *hiagua* shells, plenty more horses."

After which logical answer he plied the whip harder than ever, making the pony keep up with the stronger and abler horses of the other riders. The long train of squaws and warriors wound on down the trail by the river-side. In a little while Wishram and Tumwater passed from sight. The wind began to blow; the ever drifting sand of the Columbia came sifting in their faces. They passed the Dalles of the Columbia; and the river that, as seen from the heights the evening before, wound like a silver thread among the rocks, was found to be a compressed torrent that rushed foaming along the narrow passage, — literally, as it has been described, "a river turned on edge."

There too they passed the camp of the Wascos, who were preparing to start, but suspended their preparations at the approach of the cavalcade and stood along the path eager to see the white man. Cecil noticed that as they descended the river the language of the local tribes became more guttural, and the custom of flattening the head prevailed more and more.[1]

Below, the scenery was less barren; the river entered the Cascade Range, and the steep banks, along which wound the trail, grew dark with pines, relieved here and there with brighter verdure. They saw bands of Indians on the opposite shore, descending the trail along that side on the way to the council. Many were on foot, though some horses were among them. They were Indians of the nine tribes of the Klickitat, and as yet had but few horses. A century later they owned thousands. Indian women never accompanied war-parties; and Cecil noticed that some of the bands were composed entirely of men, which gave them the appearance of going to war. It had an ominous and doubtful look.

At the Wau-coma (place of cottonwoods), the modern Hood River, they found the tribe that inhabited that beautiful valley already on the march, and the two bands mingled and went on together. The Wau-comas seemed to be peaceably inclined, for their women were with them.

A short distance below the Wau-coma, the young Willamette's horse, urged till it could go no farther, fell beneath him. The blood gushed from its nostrils; in a few moments it was dead. The Willamette extricated himself from it. "A bad horse, *cultus* [no good] !" he said, beating it with his whip. After venting his anger on it in that way, he strode forward on foot.

And now Cecil was all expectation, on the alert for the first sight of the bridge.

[1] Lewis and Clark. See also Irving's "Astoria."

"Shall we see it soon?" he asked the young Willamette.

"When the sun is there, we shall see it," replied the Indian, pointing to the zenith. The sun still lacked several hours of noon, and Cecil had to restrain his impatience as best he could.

Just then an incident occurred that for the time effectually obliterated all thought of the bridge, and made him a powerful enemy where he least desired one.

At a narrow place in the trail, the loose horses that were being driven at the head of the column became frightened and ran back upon their drivers. In a moment, squaws, pack-horses, and ponies were all mingled together. The squaws tried in vain to restore order; it seemed as if there was going to be a general stampede. The men dashed up from the rear, Snoqualmie and Cecil among them. Cecil's old nurse happened to be in Snoqualmie's way. The horse she rode was slow and obstinate; and when she attempted to turn aside to let Snoqualmie pass he would not obey the rein, and the chief's way was blocked. To Snoqualmie an old Indian woman was little more than a dog, and he raised his whip and struck her across the face.

Like a flash, Cecil caught the chief's rein and lifted his own whip. An instant more, and the lash would have fallen across the Indian's face; but he remembered that he was a missionary, that he was violating his own precepts of forgiveness in the presence of those whom he hoped to convert.

The blow did not fall; he grappled with his anger and held it back; but Snoqualmie received from him a look of scorn so withering, that it seemed when

Cecil's flashing eyes met his own as if he had been struck, and he grasped his tomahawk. Cecil released the rein and turned away without a word. Snoqual-mie seemed for a moment to deliberate within him-self; then he let go his weapon and passed on. Order was restored and the march resumed.

"You are strong," said the Shoshone renegade to Cecil. He had seen the whole of the little drama. "You are strong; you held your anger down, but your eyes struck him as if he were a dog."

Cecil made no reply, but rode on thinking that he had made an enemy. He regretted what had hap-pened; and yet, when he recalled the insult, his blood burned and he half regretted that the blow had not been given. So, absorbed in painful thought, he rode on, till a murmur passing down the line roused him.

"The bridge! The bridge!"

He looked up hastily, his whole frame responding to the cry. There it was before him, and only a short distance away, — a great natural bridge, a rugged ridge of stone, pierced with a wide arched tunnel through which the waters flowed, extending across the river. It was covered with stunted pine and underbrush growing in every nook and crevice; and on it were Indian horsemen with plumed hair and rude lances. It was the bridge of the Wauna, the Bridge of the Gods, the bridge he had seen in his vision eight years before.

For a moment his brain reeled, everything seemed shadowy and unreal, and he half expected to see the bridge melt, like the vision, into mist before his eyes.

Like one in a dream, he rode with the others to the place where the path turned abruptly and led

over the bridge to the northern bank of the Columbia. Like one in a dream he listened, while the
young Willamette told him in a low tone that this
bridge had been built by the gods when the world
was young, that it was the *tomanowos* of the Willamettes, that while it stood they would be strongest of
all the tribes, and that if it fell they would fall with
it. As they crossed it, he noted how the great arch
rung to his horse's hoofs; he noted the bushes growing low down to the tunnel's edge; he noted how
majestic was the current as it swept into the vast dark
opening below, how stately the trees on either bank.
Then the trail turned down the river-bank again
toward the Willamette, and the dense fir forest shut
out the mysterious bridge from Cecil's backward gaze.

Solemnity and awe came to him. He had seen the
bridge of his vision; he had in truth been divinely
called to his work. He felt that the sight of the
bridge was both the visible seal of God upon his
mission and a sign that its accomplishment was close
at hand. He bowed his head involuntarily, as in the
presence of the Most High. He felt that he rode to
his destiny, that for him all things converged and cul-
minated at the great council.

They had not advanced far into the wood ere the
whole train came to a sudden halt. Riding forward,
Cecil found a band of horsemen awaiting them. They
were Klickitats, mounted on good ponies; neither
women nor pack-horses were with tnem; they were
armed and painted, and their stern and menacing
aspect was more like that of men who were on the
war-trail than of men who were riding to a "peace-
talk."

The Cayuses halted a short distance away. Snoqualmie rode forward and met the Klickitat chief in the space between the two bands. A few words passed, fierce and questioning on the part of the Klickitat, guarded and reserved on the part of the Cayuse. Then the Klickitat seemed to suggest something at which the Cayuse shook his head indignantly. The other instantly wheeled his horse, rode back to his band, and apparently reported what Snoqualmie had said; for they all set up a taunting shout, and after flinging derisive words and gestures at the Cayuses, turned around and dashed at full gallop down the trail, leaving the Cayuses covered with a cloud of dust.

And then Cecil knew that the spectacle meant war.

The air grew softer and more moist as they descended the western slope of the Cascade Range. The pines gave way to forests of fir, the underwood became denser, and ferns grew thick along the trail. It had rained the night before, and the boughs and bushes hung heavy with pendant drops. Now and then an Indian rider, brushing against some vine or maple or low swaying bough, brought down upon himself a drenching shower. The disgusted " ugh ! " of the victim and the laughter of the others would bring a smile to even Cecil's lips.

And so approaching the sea, they entered the great, wooded, rainy valley of the lower Columbia. It was like a different world from the desert sands and prairies of the upper Columbia. It seemed as if they were entering a land of perpetual spring. They passed through groves of spreading oaks; they skirted lowlands purple with blooming *camas;* they crossed prairies where the grass waved rank and high, and sunny banks where the strawberries were ripening in scarlet masses. And ever and anon they caught sight of a far snow peak lifted above the endless reach of forest, and through openings in the trees caught glimpses of the Columbia spreading wide and beautiful between densely wooded shores whose bending foliage was literally washed by the waters.

At length, as the sun was setting, they emerged from the wood upon a wide and level beach. Before them swept the Columbia, broader and grander than at any previous view, steadily widening as it neared the sea. Opposite them, another river, not as large as the Columbia, but still a great river, flowed into it.

" Willamette," said the young runner, pointing to this new river. " Wappatto Island," he added, indicating a magnificent prospect of wood and meadow that lay just below the mouth of the Willamette down along the Columbia. Cecil could not see the channel that separated it from the mainland on the other side, and to him it seemed, not an island, but a part of the opposite shore.

Around them on the beach were groups of Indians, representatives of various petty tribes who had not yet passed to the island of council. Horses were tethered to the driftwood strewed along the beach ; packs and saddles were heaped on the banks awaiting the canoes that were to carry them over. Across the river, Cecil could see upon the island scattered bands of ponies feeding and many Indians passing to and fro. Innumerable lodges showed among the trees. The river was dotted with canoes. Never before had he beheld so large an encampment, not even among

the Six Nations or the Sioux. It seemed as if all
the tribes of Puget Sound and the Columbia were
there.

As they halted on the bank, a little canoe came
skimming over the water like a bird. It bore a messenger from Multnomah, who had seen the Cayuses as
soon as they emerged on the beach.

"Send your packs over in canoes, swim your
horses, camp on the island," was the laconic message.
Evidently, in view of the coming struggle, Multnomah
wanted the loyal Cayuses close at hand.

In a little while the horses were stripped of their
packs, which were heaped in the canoes that had followed the messenger, and the crossing began. A hair
rope was put around the neck of a horse, and the end
given to a man in a canoe. The canoe was then pad-
dled out into the stream, and the horse partly pulled,
partly pushed into the river. The others after much
beating followed their leader ; and in a little while a
long line of half submerged horses and riders was
struggling across the river, while the loaded canoes
brought up the rear. The rapid current swept them
downward, and they landed on the opposite bank at
a point far below that from which they started.

On the bank of the Columbia, near Morgan's Lake,
an old gnarled cottonwood still marks the ancient
landing-place ; and traces remain of the historic trail
which led up from the river-bank into the interior of
the island, — a trail traversed perhaps for centuries, —
the great Indian road from the upper Columbia to the
Willamette valley.

The bank was black with people crowding out to
see the latest arrivals. It was a thronging multitude

of dusky faces and diverse costumes. The Nootka with his tattooed face was there, clad in his woollen blanket, his gigantic form pushing aside the short Chinook of the lower Columbia, with his crooked legs, his half-naked body glistening with grease, his slit nose and ears loaded with *hiagua* shells. Choppunish women, clad in garments of buckskin carefully whitened with clay, looked with scorn on the women of the Cowlitz and Clatsop tribes, whose only dress was a fringe of cedar bark hanging from the waist. The abject Siawash of Puget Sound, attired in a scanty patch-work of rabbit and woodrat skin, stood beside the lordly Yakima, who wore deerskin robe and leggins. And among them all, conscious of his supremacy, moved the keen and imperious Willamette.

They all gazed wonderingly at Cecil, " the white man," the " long beard," the " man that came from the Great Spirit," the " *shaman* of strong magic," — for rumors of Cecil and his mission had spread from tribe to tribe.

Though accustomed to savage sights, this seemed to Cecil the most savage of all. Flat heads and round heads ; faces scarred, tattooed, and painted ; faces as wild as beasts' ; faces proud and haughty, degraded and debased ; hair cut close to the head, tangled, matted, clogged with filth, carefully smoothed and braided, — every phase of barbarism in its most blood-thirsty ferocity, its most abject squalor, met his glance as he looked around him. It seemed like some wild phantasmagoria, some weird and wondrous dream ; and the discord of tongues, the confusion of dialects, completed the bewildering scene.

Through the surging crowd they found their

way to the place where their lodges were to be pitched.

On the morrow the great council was to begin, — the council that to the passions of that mob of savages might be as the torch to dry brushwood. On the morrow Multnomah would try and would condemn to death a rebel chief in the presence of the very ones who were in secret league with him ; and the setting sun would see the Willamette power supreme and undisputed, or the confederacy would be broken forever in the death-grapple of the tribes.

CHAPTER IV.

AN INDIAN TRIAL.

Like flame within the naked hand
His body bore his burning heart.

DANTE ROSSETTI.

WAPPATTO Island had seen many gatherings of
the tribes, but never before had it seen so
large an assembly as on the opening day of the council. The great cottonwoods of the council-grove
waved over an audience of sachems and warriors
the like of which the oldest living Indian could not
remember.

No weapons were to be seen, for Multnomah had
commanded that all arms be left that day in the
lodges. But the dissatisfied Indians had come with
weapons hidden under their robes of deer or wolf
skin, which no one should have known better than
Multnomah. Had he taken any precautions against
surprise? Evidently not. A large body of Willamette warriors, muffled in their blankets, lounged carelessly around the grove, with not a weapon visible
among them; behind them thronged the vast and
motley assemblage of doubtful allies; and back of
them, on the outskirts of the crowd, were the faithful
Cayuses, unarmed like the Willamettes. Had Multnomah's wonderful astuteness failed him now when it
was never needed more?

He was on the council-seat, a stone covered with furs; the Willamette sachems sat in their places facing him; and mats were spread for the chiefs of the tributaries.   On a bearskin before the stern war-chief lay a peace-pipe and a tomahawk; and to the Indians, accustomed to signs and symbols, the two had a grim significance.

One by one the chiefs entered the circle and took their seats on the mats provided for them.   Those who were friendly to Multnomah first laid presents before him; those who were not, took their places without offering him either gift or salutation.   Mult-nomah, however, seemed unconscious of any neglect.

The chief of a Klamath tribe offered him a bril-liantly dyed blanket; another, a finely fringed quiver, full of arrows; another, a long and massive string of *hiagua* shells.   Each laid his gift before Multnomah and took his seat in silence.

The chief of the Chopponish presented him with a fine horse, the best belonging to his tribe.   Multno-mah accepted it, and a slave led it away.   Then came Snoqualmie, bringing with him Cecil Grey.   The chief's hour of vengeance was at hand.

" Behold the white man from the land where the sun rises, the white *shaman* of whom all the tribes have heard.   He is thine.   Let him be the white slave of Multnomah.   All the chiefs have slaves, but who will have a white slave like Multnomah? "

Cecil saw the abyss of slavery yawning before him, and grew pale to the lips.   His heart sank within him; then the resolute purpose that never failed him in time of peril returned; he lifted his head and met Multnomah's gaze with dignity.   The war-chief bent on him the glance which read men to the heart.

"The white stranger has been a chief among his own people," he said to Cecil, more in the manner of one asserting a fact than asking a question.

"I have often spoken to my people in the gatherings to hear the word of the Great Spirit."

Again the keen, inscrutable gaze of the great chief seemed to probe his being to its core; again the calm, grave stranger met it without shrinking. The instinct, so common among savage races, of in some way *knowing* what a man is, of intuitively grasping his true merit, was possessed by Multnomah in a large degree; and the royalty in his nature instinctively recognized the royalty in Cecil's.

"The white guest who comes into the land of Multnomah shall be to him as a guest; the chief should still be chief in any land. White stranger, Multnomah gives you welcome; sit down among the chiefs."

Cecil took his place among them with all the composure he could command, well knowing that he who would be influential among the Indians must seem to be unmoved by any change of fortune. He felt, however, not only the joy of personal deliverance, but mingled with it came the glad, triumphant thought that he had now a voice in the deliberations of the chiefs; it was a grand door opened for Indian evangelization. As for Snoqualmie, his face was as impassive as granite. One would have said that Cecil's victory was to him a matter of no moment at all. But under the guise of indifference his anger burned fierce and deadly, — not against Multnomah but against Cecil.

The last chief had taken his place in the council. There was a long, ceremonious pause. Then Multnomah arose. He looked over the council, upon the stern faces of the Willamettes and the loyal tributaries, upon the sullen faces of the malcontents, upon the fierce and lowering multitude beyond. Over the throng he looked, and felt as one feels who stands on the brink of a volcano ; yet his strong voice never rang stronger, the grand old chief never looked more a chief than then.

"He is every inch a king," thought Cecil. The chief spoke in the common Willamette language, at that time the medium of intercourse between the tribes as the Chinook is now. The royal tongue was not used in a mixed council.

"Warriors and chiefs, Multnomah gives you welcome. He spreads the buffalo-robe." He made the Indian gesture of welcome, opening his hands to them with a backward and downward gesture, as of one spreading a robe. "To the warriors Multnomah says, ' The grass upon my prairies is green for your horses ; behold the wood, the water, the game ; they are yours.' To the chiefs he says, ' The mat is spread for you in my own lodge and the meat is cooked.' The hearts of the Willamettes change not as the winters go by, and your welcome is the same as of old. Word came to us that the tribes were angry and had spoken bitter things against the Willamettes ; yes, that they longed for the confederacy to be broken and the old days to come again when tribe was divided against tribe and the Shoshones and Spokanes trampled upon you all. But Multnomah trusted his allies ; for had they not smoked the peace-pipe with him and gone with him on the war-trail? So he stopped his ears and would not listen, but let those rumors go past him like thistle-down upon the wind.

"Warriors, Multnomah has shown his heart. What say you? Shall the peace-pipe be lighted and the talk begin?"

He resumed his seat. All eyes turned to where the peace-pipe and the tomahawk lay side by side before the council. Multnomah seemed waiting for them to choose between the two.

Then Snoqualmie, the bravest and most loyal of the tributaries, spoke.

"Let the peace-pipe be lighted; we come not for strife, but to be knit together."

The angry malcontents in the council only frowned and drew their blankets closer around them. Tohomish the seer, as the oldest chief and most renowned medicine-man present, came forward and lighted the pipe, — a long, thin piece of carving in black stone, the workmanship of the Nootkas or Hydahs, who made the more elaborate pipes used by the Indians of the Columbia River.

Muttering some mystical incantation, he waved it to the east and the west, to the north and the south; and when the charm was complete, gave it to Multnomah, who smoked it and passed it to Snoqualmie. From chief to chief it circled around the whole council, but among them were those who sat with eyes fixed moodily on the ground and would not so much as touch or look at it. As the pipe passed round there was a subdued murmur and movement in the multitude, a low threatening clamor, as yet held in check by awe of Multnomah and dread of the Willamette warriors.   But the war-chief seemed unconscious that any had refused the pipe.   He now arose and said, —

"The pipe is smoked.   Are not our hearts as one? Is there not perfect trust between us?   Now let us talk.   First of all, Multnomah desires wise words from his brethren.   Last winter one of the tribes rose up against Multnomah, saying that he should no longer be elder brother and war-chief of the tribes.   But the rebels were beaten and all of them slain save the chief, who was reserved to be tried before you.   You in your wisdom shall decide what shall be done with the warrior who has rebelled against his chief and stained his hands with the blood of his brethren."

Two Willamette braves then entered the circle, bringing with them one whose hands were tied behind him, whose form was emaciated with hunger and disease, but whose carriage was erect and haughty. Behind came a squaw, following him into the very presence of Multnomah, as if resolved to share his fortunes to the last.   It was his wife.   She was instantly thrust back and driven with brutal blows from the council.   But she lingered on the outskirts of the crowd, watching and waiting with mute, sullen fidelity the outcome of the trial.   No one looked at her, no one cared for her; even her husband's sympathizers jostled the poor shrinking form aside, — for she was only a squaw, while he was a great brave.

He looked a great brave, standing there before Multnomah and the chiefs with a dignity in his mien that no reverse could crush, no torture could destroy. Haggard, starved, bound, his eyes gleamed deathless and unconquerable hate on council and war-chief alike.

There were dark and menacing looks among the mal-contents; in the captive they saw personified their own loss of freedom and the hated domination of the Willamettes.

"Speak! You that were a chief, you whose people sleep in the dust, — what have you to say in your defence? The tribes are met together, and the chiefs sit here to listen and to judge."

The rebel sachem drew himself up proudly and fixed his flashing eyes on Multnomah.

"The tongue of Multnomah is a trap. I am brought not to be tried but to be condemned and slain, that the tribes may see it and be afraid. No one knows this better that Multnomah. Yet I will speak while I still live, and stand here in the sun; for I go out into the darkness, and the earth will cover my face, and my voice shall be heard no more among men.

"Why should the Willamettes rule the other tribes? Are they better than we? The Great Spirit gave us freedom, and who may make himself master and take it away?

"I was chief of a tribe; we dwelt in the land the Great Spirit gave our fathers; their bones were in it; it was ours. But the Willamettes said to us, 'We are your elder brethren, you must help us. Come, go with us to fight the Shoshones.' Our young men went, for the Willamettes were strong and we could not refuse them. Many were slain, and the women wailed despairingly. The Willamettes hunted on our hunting-grounds and dug the *camas* on our prairies, so that there was not enough for us; and when winter came, our children cried for food. Then the runners of the Willamettes came to us through the snow, saying, 'Come and join the war-party that goes to fight the Bannocks.'

"But our hearts burned within us and we replied, 'Our hunting-grounds and our food you have taken; will you have our lives also? Go back and tell your chief that if we must fight, we will fight him and not the Bannocks.' Then the Willamettes came upon us and we fought them, for their tyranny was so heavy that we could not breathe under it and death had become better than life. But they were the stronger, and when did the heart of a Willamette feel pity? To-day I only am left, to say these words for my race.

"Who made the Willamettes masters over us? The Great Spirit gave us freedom, and none may take it away. Was it not well to fight? Yes; free my hands and give me back my people from the cairns and the death-huts, and we will fight again! I go to my death, but the words I have spoken will live. The hearts of those listening here will treasure them up; they will be told around the lodge-fires and repeated in the war-dance. The words I speak will go out among the tribes, and no man can destroy them. Yes, they go out words, but they will come back arrows and war in the day of vengeance when the tribes shall rise against the oppressor.

"I have spoken, my words are done."

He stood erect and motionless. The wrath and disdain passed from his features, and stoicism settled over them like a mask of stone. Multnomah's cold regard had not faltered a moment under the chief's invective. No denunciation could shake that iron self-control.

The rebellious chiefs interchanged meaning glances ; the throng of malcontents outside the grove pressed closer upon the ring of Willamette warriors, who were still standing or squatting idly around it. More than one weapon could be seen among them in defiance of the war-chief's prohibition ; and the presage of a terrible storm darkened on those grim, wild faces. The more peaceably disposed bands began to draw themselves apart. An ominous silence crept through the crowd as they felt the crisis approaching.

But Multnomah saw nothing, and the circle of Willamette warriors were stolidly indifferent.

" Can they not see that the tribes are on the verge of revolt ? " thought Cecil, anxiously, fearing a bloody massacre.

" You have heard the words of the rebel. What have you to say ? Let the white man speak first, as he was the last to join us."

Cecil rose and pictured in the common Willamette tongue, with which he had familiarized himself during his long stay with the Cayuses, the terrible results of disunion, the desolating consequences of war, — tribe clashing against tribe and their common enemies trampling on them all. Even those who were on the verge of insurrection listened reverently to the " white wizard," who had drawn wisdom from the Great Spirit ; but it did not shake their purpose. Their own dreamers had talked with the Great Spirit too, in trance and vision, and had promised them victory over the Willamettes.

Tohomish followed ; and Cecil, who had known some of the finest orators in Europe, listened in amazement to a voice the most musical he had ever heard. He looked in wonder on the repulsive features that seemed so much at variance with those melodious intonations. Tohomish pleaded for union and for the death of the rebel. It seemed for a moment as if his soft, persuasive accents would win the day, but it was only for a moment ; the spell was broken the instant he ceased. Then Snoqualmie spoke. One by one, the great sachems of the Willamettes gave their voices for death. Many of the friendly allies did not give their decision at all, but said to Multnomah, —

"You speak for us ; your word shall be our word."

When the dissatisfied chiefs were asked for their counsel, the sullen reply was given, —

"I have no tongue to-day ; " or " I do not know."

Multnomah seemed not to notice their answers. Only those who knew him best saw a gleam kindling in his eyes that told of a terrible vengeance drawing near. The captive waited passively, seeming neither to see nor hear.

At length all had spoken or had an opportunity to speak, and Multnomah rose to give the final decision. Beyond the circle of Willamettes, who were still indifferent and unconcerned, the discontented bands had thrown aside all concealment, and stood with bared weapons in their hands ; all murmurs had ceased ; there was a deathlike silence in the dense mob, which seemed gathering itself together for a forward rush, — the commencement of a fearful massacre.

Behind it were the friendly Cayuses, but not a weapon could be seen among them. The chief saw all ; saw too that his enemies only waited for him to pronounce sentence upon the captive, — that that was the preconcerted signal for attack. Now among some of the tribes sentence was pronounced not by word but by gesture; there was the gesture for acquittal, the gesture for condemnation.

Multnomah lifted his right hand. There was breathless suspense. What would it be? Fixing his eyes on the armed malcontents who were waiting to spring, he clinched his hand and made a downward gesture, as if striking a blow. It was the death-signal, the death-sentence.

In an instant a deafening shout rang through the grove, and the bloodthirsty mob surged forward to the massacre.

Then, so suddenly that it blended with and seemed a part of the same shout, the dreaded Willamette war-cry shook the earth. Quick as thought, the Willamettes who had been lounging so idly around the grove were on their feet, their blankets thrown aside, the weapons that had been concealed under them ready in their hands. A wall of indomitable warriors had leaped up around the grove. At the same moment, the Cayuses in the rear bared their weapons and shouted back the Willamette war-cry.

The rebels were staggered. The trap was sprung on them before they knew that there was a trap. Those in front shrank back from the iron warriors of Multnomah, those in the rear wavered before the fierce Cayuses. They paused, a swaying flood of humanity, caught between two lines of rock.

CHAPTER V.

SENTENCED TO THE WOLF-DEATH.

The other, great of soul, changed not
Countenance stern.
DANTE.

IN that momentary pause Multnomah did something
that showed the cold disdainfulness of his character as nothing else could have done. He had given
the death-sign ; he had not yet told how or when death
was to be inflicted. He gave the sentence *now*, as if
in utter scorn of the battle-cloud that hung quivering,
ready to burst.

"He would have torn the confederacy to pieces ;
let him be left bound in the wood of the wolves, and
torn limb from limb by them as he would have rent
the tribes asunder."

The two warriors who had brought the criminal
into the council came forward, flung a covering over
his head and face, and led him away. Perhaps no
custom of the northwestern Indians was more sombre
than this, — the covering of the culprit's eyes from
the time of his sentence till his death. Never again
were those eyes to behold the sun.

Then, and not till then, did Multnomah turn his
gaze on the malcontents, who stood, desperate but
hesitating, hemmed in by the Willamettes and the
Cayuses.

"You have chosen the tomahawk instead of the peace-pipe. Shall Multnomah choose the tomahawk also? Know you not that Multnomah holds your lives in his hand, and that he can crush you like an egg-shell if he chooses?"

The war-chief lifted his arm as he spoke, and slowly closed his fingers till his hand was clinched. The eyes of Willamette and tributary alike hung on those slowly closing fingers, with their own strained on their tomahawks. That was half the death-signal! Would he give the other half, — the downward gesture? The baffled rebels tasted all the bitterness of death in that agonizing suspense. They felt that their lives were literally in his grasp; and so the stern autocrat wished them to feel, for he knew it was a lesson they would never forget.

At length he spoke.

"Drop your weapons and Multnomah will forget what he has seen, and all will be well. Strike but a blow, and not one of you will ever go back over the trail to his home."

Then he turned to the chiefs, and there was that in his tones which told them to expect no mercy.

"How comes it that your braves lift their tomahawks against Multnomah in his own council and on his own land? Speak! chiefs must answer for their people."

There was sullen silence for a little time; then one of them muttered that it was the young men; their blood was hot, they were rash, and the chiefs could not control them.

"Can you not control your young men? Then you are not fit to be chiefs, and are chiefs no longer."

He gave a signal to certain of the Willamettes who had come up behind the rebellious leaders, as they stood confused and hesitating in the council. They were seized and their hands bound ere they could defend themselves; indeed, they made no effort to do so, but submitted doggedly.

"Take them down the Wauna in the sea-canoes and sell them as slaves to the Nootkas who hunt seal along the coast. Their people shall see their faces no more. Slaves in the ice-land of the North shall they live and die."

The swarthy cheeks of the captives grew ashen, and a shudder went through that trapped and surrounded mob of malcontents. Indian slavery was always terrible; but to be slaves to the brutal Indians of the north, starved, beaten, mutilated, chilled, and benumbed in a land of perpetual frost; to perish at last in the bleak snow and winter of almost arctic coasts, — that was a fate worse than the torture-stake.

Dreadful as it was, not a chief asked for mercy. Silently they went with their captors out of the grove and down the bank to the river's edge. A large sea-canoe, manned by Chinook paddlers, was floating at the beach. They quickly embarked, the paddles dipped, the canoe glided out into the current and down the stream. In a few moments the cotton-wood along the river's edge hid it from sight, and the rebels were forever beyond the hope of rescue.

Swift and merciless had the vengeance of Multno-mah fallen, and the insurrection had been crushed at a blow. It had taken but a moment, and it had all passed under the eyes of the malcontents, who were still surrounded by the loyal warriors.

When the canoe had disappeared and the gaze of that startled and awed multitude came back to Multnomah, he made a gesture of dismissal. The lines drew aside and the rebels were free.

While they were still bewildered and uncertain what to do, Multnomah instantly and with consummate address called the attention of the council to other things, thereby apparently assuming that the trouble was ended and giving the malcontents to understand that no further punishment was intended. Sullenly, reluctantly, they seemed to accept the situation, and no further indications of revolt were seen that day.

Popular young men, the bravest of their several tribes, were appointed by Multnomah to fill the vacant chieftainships ; and that did much toward allaying the discontent. Moreover, some troubles between different tribes of the confederacy, which had been referred to him for arbitration, were decided with rare sagacity. At length the council ended for the day, the star of the Willamettes still in the ascendant, the revolt seemingly subdued.

So the first great crisis passed.

That evening a little band of Willamette warriors led the rebel sachem, still bound and blindfolded, down to the river's bank, where a canoe lay waiting them. His wife followed and tried to enter it with him, as if determined to share his fortunes to the very last ; but the guard thrust her rudely away, and started the canoe. As it moved away she caught the prow wildly, despairingly, as if she could not let her warrior go. One of the guards struck her hands brutally with his paddle, and she released her hold. The boat glided out into the river. Not a word of farewell had passed between the condemned man and his wife, for each disdained to show emotion in the presence of the enemy. She remained on the bank looking after him, mute and despondent, — a forlorn creature clothed in rags and emaciated with hunger, an outcast from all the tribes. She might have been regarded as a symbolic figure representing woman among the Indians, as she stood there with her bruised hands, throbbing with pain where the cruel blow had fallen, hanging, in sullen scorn of pain, uncared for by her side. So she stood watching the canoe glide down the river, till it was swallowed up in the gathering shadows of evening.

The canoe dropped down the river to a lonely point on the northern shore, a place much frequented by wolves. There, many miles below the encampment on the island, they disembarked and took the captive into the wood. He walked among them with a firm and even tread ; there was no sign of flinching, though he must have known that his hour was close at hand. They bound him prostrate at the foot of an oak, tying him to the hard, tough roots that ran over the ground like a network, and from which the earth had been washed away, so that thongs could be passed around them.

Head and foot they bound him, drawing the raw-hide thongs so tight that they sank into the flesh, and knotting them, till no effort possible to him could have disentangled him. It was on his lips to ask them to leave one arm free, so that he might at least die fighting, though it were with but one naked hand.

But he hated them too much to ask even that small favor, and so submitted in disdainful silence.

The warriors all went back to the canoe, except one, an old hunter, famed for his skill in imitating every cry of bird or beast. Standing beside the bound and prostrate man, he sent forth into the forest the cry of a wolf. It rang in a thousand echoes and died away, evoking no response. He listened a moment with bated breath, but could hear nothing but the deep heart-beat of the man at his feet. Another cry, with its myriad echoes, was followed by the oppressive sense of stillness that succeeds an outcry in a lonely wood. Then came a faint, a far-off sound, the answer of a wolf to a supposed mate. The Indian replied, and the answer sounded nearer; then another blended with it, as the pack began to gather. Again the Indian gave the cry, wild and wolfish, as only a barbarian, half-beast by virtue of his own nature, could have uttered it. An awful chorus of barking and howling burst through the forest as the wolves came on, eager for blood.

The Indian turned and rejoined his comrades at the canoe. They pushed out into the river, but held the boat in the current by an occasional paddle-stroke, and waited listening. Back at the foot of the tree the captive strained every nerve and muscle in one mighty effort to break the cords that bound him; but it was useless, and he lay back with set teeth and rigid muscles, while his eyes sought in vain through their thick covering to see the approach of his foes. Presently a fierce outburst of howls and snarls told the listeners that the wolves had found their prey. They lingered and listened a little longer, but no sound or

cry was heard to tell of the last agony under those
rending fangs; the chief died in silence. Then the
paddles were dipped again in the water, and the canoe
glided up the river to the camp.

When they reached the shore they found the rebel's
wife awaiting them in the place where they had left
her. She asked no questions; she only came close
and looked at their faces in the dusk, and read there
the thing she sought to know. Then she went silently
away. In a little while the Indian wail for the dead
was sounding through the forest.

"What is that?" asked the groups around the
camp-fires.

"The rebel chief's wife wailing the death-wail for
her husband," was the low reply; and in that way
the tribes knew that the sentence had been carried
out. Many bands were there, of many languages, but
all knew what that death-wail meant the instant it
fell upon their ears. Multnomah heard it as he sat
in council with his chiefs, and there was something
in it that shook even his iron heart; for all the wilder,
more superstitious elements of the Indians thrilled to
two things, — the war-cry and the death-wail. He
dismissed his chiefs and went to his lodge. On the
way he encountered Tohomish, lurking, as was his
wont, under the shadow of the trees.

"What think you now, Tohomish, you who love
darkness and shadow, what think you? Is not the
arm of the Willamette strong? Has it not put down
revolt to-day, and held the tribes together?"

The Pine Voice looked at him sorrowfully.

"The vision I told in the council has come back
to me again. The cry of woe I heard far off then is

nearer now, and the throng on the death-trail passes
thicker and swifter. That which covered their faces
is lifted, and their faces are the faces of Willamettes, and Multnomah is among them. The time is
close at hand."

"Say this before our enemies, and, strong *tomanowos* though you are, you die!" said the chief, laying
his hand on his tomahawk. But the seer was gone,
and Multnomah stood alone among the trees.

Every evening at dusk, the widow of the rebel
sachem went out into the woods near the camp and
wailed her dead. Every night that wild, desolate
lament was lifted and rang through the great encampment, — a cry that was accusation, defiance, and
lament; and even Multnomah dared not silence her,
for among the Indians a woman lamenting her dead
was sacred. So, while Multnomah labored and plot-
ted for union by day, that mournful cry raised the
spirit of wrath and rebellion by night. And thus the
dead liberator was half avenged.

BOOK IV.

THE LOVE TALE.

CHAPTER I.

THE INDIAN TOWN.

The bare ground with hoarie mosse bestrowed
Must be their bed ; their pillow was unsowed
And the frutes of the forrest was their feast.
The Faërie Queene.

NEVER before had there come to Cecil so grand an opportunity for disseminating gospel truth. The work of half a lifetime might be done in a few days.

"The tribes are all gathered together in one encampment, and I can talk with them all, tell them of God, of the beauty of heaven and of the only Way. Then, when they disperse, they will carry my teaching in every direction, and so it will be scattered throughout all this wild land."

This was the thought that came to Cecil when he awoke on the morning after the trial. Now was the time to work! Now was the time for every element of argument, persuasion, and enthusiasm to be exerted to the utmost.

Earnestly did he pray that morning, kneeling in his lodge beside his couch of furs, that God would be with and help him. And as he prayed, warm and glowing was the love and tenderness that filled his heart. When the day was a little more advanced, he entered upon his work. The camp was astir with life ; nearly all had finished their morning meal, and the various employments and diversions of the day were begun. Each tribe or band had pitched its lodges apart, though not far from the others. It was not so much an encampment as a group of many encampments, and the whole made up a scattered town of huts and wigwams.

A precarious and uncertain quiet had succeeded the agitation of the day before. Multnomah's energy had awed the malcontents into temporary submission, and the different bands were mingling freely with one another ; though here and there a chief or warrior looked on contemptuously, standing moodily apart, wrapped in his blanket. Now and then when a Willamette passed a group who were talking and gesticulating animatedly they would become silent all at once till the representative of the dreaded race was out of hearing, when a storm of indignant gutterals would burst forth ; but there were no other indications of hostility.

Groups were strolling from place to place observing curiously the habits and customs of other tribes ; the common Willamette tongue, precursor of the more modern Chinook jargon, furnishing a means of intercourse. Everywhere Cecil found talk, barter, diversion. It was a rude caricature of civilization, the picture of society in its infancy, the rough dramatization of that phase through which every race passes in its evolution from barbarism.

At one place, a hunter from the interior was barter-
ing furs for *hiagua* shells to a native of the sea-coast.
At another, a brave skilled in wood-work had his stock
of bows and arrows spread out before him, and an admiring crowd were standing around looking on. But
the taciturn brave sat coolly polishing and staining his
arrows as if he were totally unconscious of spectators,
until the magical word " buy " was mentioned, when
he at once awoke to life and drove a bargain in bow
and quiver *versus* dried berries and " ickters " that
would have done credit to a Yankee.

At one place sat an old warrior from the upper
Columbia, making arrow-heads, chipping off the little
scales of flint with infinite patience, literally *wearing*
the stone into the requisite shape. Beside him lay a
small pack of flints brought from beyond the mountains, for such stone was rarely found along the lower
Columbia. Squaws sat in front of their wigwams sewing mats, — carefully sorting the rushes, putting big
ends with little ends, piercing each with a bodkin, and
sewing them all together with a long bone needle
threaded with buckskin or sinew. Others were weav-
ing that water-tight wickerwork which was, perhaps,
the highest art to which the Oregon Indians ever
attained. Here a band of Indians were cooking,
feasting, laughing, shouting around a huge sturgeon
captured the night before. There a circle of gamblers
were playing " hand," — passing a small stick secretly
from hand to hand and guessing whose hand contained
it, — singing as they played that monotonous " ho-ha,
ho-ha, ho-ha," which was the inseparable accompani-
ment of dancing, gambling, and horseback riding.

Among them all Cecil moved with the calm dignity

he had acquired from long intercourse with the Indians. Wherever he went there was silence and respect, for was he not the great white medicine-man? Gambling circles paused in the swift passage of the stick and the monotone of the chant to look and to comment; buyers and sellers stopped to gaze and to question; children who had been building miniature wigwams of sticks or floating bark canoes in the puddles, ran away at his approach and took shelter in the thickets, watching him with twinkling black eyes.

Wherever there was opportunity, he stopped and talked, scattering seed-thoughts in the dark minds of the Indians. Wherever he paused a crowd would gather; whenever he entered a wigwam a throng collected at the door.

Let us glance for a moment into the domestic life of the Indians as Cecil saw it that morning.

He enters one of the large bark huts of the Willamette Indians, a long, low building, capable of sheltering sixty or seventy persons. The part around the door is painted to represent a man's face, and the entrance is through the mouth. Within, he finds a spacious room perhaps eighty or a hundred feet long by twenty wide, with rows of rude bunks rising tier above tier on either side. In the centre are the stones and ashes of the hearth; above is an aperture in the roof for the escape of smoke; around the hearth mats are spread to sit upon; the bare ground, hard and trodden, forms the only floor, and the roof is made of boards that have been split out with mallet and wedges.

Cecil enters and stands a moment in silence; then

the head of the house advances and welcomes him. The best mat is spread for him to sit upon; food is brought, — pounded fish, nuts, and berries, and a kind of bread made of roots cooked, crushed together, and cut in slices when cold. All this is served on a wooden platter, and he must eat whether hungry or not; for to refuse would be the grossest affront that could be offered a Willamette host, especially if it were presented by his own hands. The highest honor that a western Oregon Indian could do his guest was to wait on him instead of letting his squaw do it. The Indian host stands beside Cecil and says, in good-humored hospitality, " Eat, eat much," nor is he quite pleased if he thinks that his visitor slights the offered food. When the guest can be no longer persuaded to eat more, the food is removed, the platter is washed in water, and dried with a wisp of twisted grass ; a small treasure of tobacco is produced from a little buckskin pocket and a part of it carefully mixed with dried leaves ;[1] the pipe is filled and smoked. Then, and not till then, may the Indian host listen to the talk of the white man.

So it was in lodge after lodge ; he must first eat, be it ever so little. Two centuries later, the Methodist and Congregational missionaries found themselves confronted with the same oppressive hospitality among the Rocky Mountain Indians.[2] Nay, they need not visit a wigwam ; let them but stroll abroad through the village, and if they were popular and the camp was well supplied with buffalo-meat, messengers would come with appalling frequency, bearing the laconic

[1] Lewis and Clark.
[2] See Parkman's " Oregon Trail , " also, Parker's work on Oregon.

invitation, " Come and eat ; " and the missionary
must go, or give offence, even though he had already
gone to half a dozen wigwams on the same errand.
There is a grim humor in a missionary's eating fresh
buffalo-meat in the cause of religion until he is
like to burst, and yet heroically going forth to choke
down a few mouthfuls more, lest he offend some
dusky convert.

At one house Cecil witnessed a painful yet comical
scene. The Willamettes were polygamists, each brave
having as many wives as he was able to buy ; and
Cecil was in a lodge where the brother of the head
man of that lodge brought home his second wife. At
the entrance of the second wife, all gay in Indian
finery, the first did not manifest the sisterly spirit
proper for the occasion. After sitting awhile in sullen
silence, she arose and began to kick the fire about,
accompanying that performance with gutteral excla-
mations addressed to no one in particular ; she struck
the dog, which chanced to be in the way, sending it
yelping from the wigwam ; and then, having worked
herself into a rage, began to scold her husband, who
listened grimly but said nothing. At last she turned
on her new-found sister, struck her, and began to lay
rending hands on the finery that their mutual husband
had given her. That was instantly resented ; and in
a few moments the squaws were rolling on the floor,
biting, scratching, and pulling each other's hair with
the fury of devils incarnate. The dogs, attracted by
the tumult, ran in and began to bark at them ; the
Indians outside the hut gathered at the door, looking
in and laughing ; the husband contemplated them as
they rolled fighting at his feet, and then looked at

Cecil. It was undoubtedly trying to Indian dignity, but the warrior sustained his admirably. " Bad, very bad," was the only comment he allowed himself to make. Cecil took his leave, and the brave kept up his air of indifference until the white man had gone. Then he quietly selected a cudgel from the heap of fire-wood by the doorway, and in a short time peace reigned in the wigwam.

In a lodge not far away, Cecil witnessed another scene yet more barbarous than this. He found a little blind boy sitting on the ground near the fire, surrounded by a quantity of fish-bones which he had been picking. He was made a subject for the taunting jibes and laughter of a number of men and women squatting around him. His mother sat by in the most cruel apathy and unconcern, and only smiled when Cecil expressed commiseration for her unfortunate and peculiarly unhappy child. It had been neglected and seemed almost starved. Those around apparently took pleasure in tormenting it and rendering it miserable, and vied with each other in applying to it insulting and degrading epithets. The little articles that Cecil gave to it, in the hope that the Indians seeing him manifest an interest in it would treat it more tenderly, it put to its mouth eagerly; but not finding them eatable, it threw them aside in disgust. Cecil turned away sick at heart. Worn, already weary, this last sight was intolerable ; and he went out into the woods, away from the camp.

But as he walked along he seemed to see the child again, so vividly had it impressed his imagination. It rose before him in the wood, when the noise of the camp lay far behind ; it seemed to turn its sightless eyes upon him and reach out its emaciated arms as if appealing for help.[1]

Out in the wood he came across an Indian sitting on a log, his face buried in his hands, his attitude indicating sickness or despondency. He looked up as Cecil approached. It was the young Willamette runner who had been his companion on the journey down the Columbia. His face was haggard ; he was evidently very sick. The missionary stopped and tried to talk with him, but could evoke little response, except that he did not want to talk, and that he wanted to be left alone. He seemed so moody and irritable that Cecil thought it best to leave him. His experience was that talking with a sick Indian was very much like stirring up a wounded rattlesnake. So he left the runner and went on into the forest, seeking the solitude without which he could scarcely have lived amid the degrading barbarism around him. His spirit required frequent communion with God and Nature, else he would have died of weariness and sickness of heart.

Wandering listlessly, he went on further and further from the camp, never dreaming of what lay before him, or of the wild sweet destiny to which that dim Indian trail was leading him through the shadowy wood.

[1] See Townsend's Narrative, pages 182-183.

CHAPTER II.

THE WHITE WOMAN IN THE WOOD.

I seek a sail that never looms from out the purple haze
At rosy dawn, or fading eve, or in the noontide's blaze.
CELIA THAXTER.

CECIL walked listlessly on through the wood. He was worn out by the day's efforts, though it was as yet but the middle of the afternoon. There was a feeling of exhaustion in his lungs, a fluttering pain about his heart, the result of years of over-work upon a delicate frame. With this feeling of physical weakness came always the fear that his strength might give way ere his work was done. Nor was this all. In these times of depression, the longing to see again the faces of his friends, to have again the sweet graceful things of the life that was forever closed to him, rushed over him in a bitter flood.

The trail led him to the bank of the Columbia, some distance below the encampment. He looked out over the blue river sweeping majestically on, the white snow-peaks, the canyons deep in the shadows of afternoon, the dense forest beyond the river extending away to the unknown and silent North as far as his eyes could reach.

" It is wonderful, wonderful ! " he thought. " But I would give it all to look upon one white face."

So musing, he passed on down the bank of the river. He was now perhaps two miles from the camp and seemingly in complete solitude. After a little the path turned away from the beach and led toward the interior. As he entered the woodland he came upon several Indian sentinels who lay, bow in hand, beside the path. They sprang up, as if to intercept his passage ; but seeing that it was the white *shaman* whom Multnomah had honored, and who had sat at the council with the great sachems, they let him go on. Cecil indistinctly remembered having heard from some of the Indians that this part of the island was strictly guarded ; he had forgotten why. So absorbed was he in his gloomy reflections that he did not stop to question the sentinels, but went on, not thinking that he might be treading on forbidden ground. By and by the path emerged from the wood upon a little prairie ; the cottonwoods shut out the Indians from him, and he was again alone. The sunshine lay warm and golden on the little meadow, and he strolled forward mechanically, thinking how like it was to some of the sylvan lawns of his own New England forests. Again the shade of trees fell over the path. He looked up, his mind full of New England memories, and saw something that made his heart stand still. For there, not far from him, stood a girl clad in soft flowing drapery, the dress of a white woman. In Massachusetts a woman's dress would have been the last thing Cecil would have noticed. Now, so long accustomed to the Indian squaws' rough garments of skin or plaited bark, the sight of that graceful woven cloth sent through him an indescribable thrill.

He went on, his eager eyes drinking in the welcome sight, yet scarcely believing what he saw.

She had not yet observed him. The profile of her half-averted face was very sweet and feminine; her form was rounded, and her hair fell in long black ringlets to the shoulders. He was in the presence of a young and beautiful woman, — a white woman! All this he noted at a glance; noted, too, the drooping lashes, the wistful lines about the lips, the mournful expression that shadowed the beauty of her face.

Who was she? Where could she have come from?

She heard the approaching footsteps and turned toward him. Absolute bewilderment was on her face for a moment, and then it glowed with light and joy. Her dark, sad eyes sparkled. She was radiant, as if some great, long-looked for happiness had come to her. She came eagerly toward him, holding out her hands in impetuous welcome; saying something in a language he did not understand, but which he felt could not be Indian, so refined and pleasing were the tones.

He answered he knew not what, in his own tongue, and she paused perplexed. Then he spoke again, this time in Willamette.

She shrank back involuntarily.

"That language?" she replied in the same tongue, but with a tremor of disappointment in her voice. "I thought you were of my mother's race and spoke her language. But you *are* white, like her people?"

She had given him both her hands, and he stood holding them; looking down into her eager, lifted face, where a great hope and a great doubt in mingled light and shadow strove together.

" I am a white man.   I came from a land far to
the East.   But who are you, and how came you
here ? "

She did not seem to hear the last words, only the
first.

" No, no," she protested eagerly, " you came not
from the East but from the West, the land across the
sea that my mother came from in the ship that was
wrecked."   And she withdrew one hand and pointed
toward the wooded range beyond which lay the
Pacific.

He shook his head.   " No, there are white people
in those lands too, but I never saw them.   I came
from the East," he said, beginning to surmise that
she must be an Asiatic.   She drew away the hand
that he still held in his, and her eyes filled with
tears.

" I thought you were one of my mother's people,"
she murmured ; and he felt that the pang of an exceeding disappointment was filling her heart.

" Who are you ? " he asked gently.

" The daughter of Multnomah."

Cecil remembered now what he had heard of the
dead white wife of Multnomah, and of her daughter,
who, it was understood among the tribes, was to be
given to Snoqualmie.   He noticed, too, for the first
time the trace of the Indian in her expression, as the
light faded from it and it settled back into the
despondent look habitual to it.   All that was chival-
rous in his nature went out to the fair young creature ; all his being responded to the sting of her
disappointment.

" I am not what you hoped I was, but your face is

like the face of the women of my own land. Shall we
not be friends?"

She looked up wistfully at the handsome and noble
countenance above her, so different from the stolid
visages she had known so long.

"Yes; you are not Indian."

In that one expression she unconsciously told
Cecil how her sensitive nature shrank from the barbarism around her; how the tastes and aspirations
she had inherited from her mother reached out for
better and higher things.

In a little while they were seated on a grassy bank
in the shade of the trees, talking together. She bade
him tell her of his people. She listened intently; the
bright, beautiful look came back as she heard the tale.

"They are kind to women, instead of making
them mere burden-bearers; they have pleasant
homes; they dwell in cities? Then they are like
my mother's people."

"They are gentle, kind, humane. They have all
the arts that light up life and make it beautiful, — not
like the tribes of this grim, bloodstained land."

"*This* land!" Her face darkened and she lifted
her hand in a quick, repelling gesture. "This land
is a grave. The clouds lie black and heavy on the
spirit that longs for the sunlight and cannot reach it."
She turned to him again. "Go on, your words are
music."

He continued, and she listened till the story of
his country and his wanderings was done. When he
ended, she drew a glad, deep breath; her eyes were
sparkling with joy.

"I am content," she said, in a voice in which there

was a deep heart-thrill of happiness. "Since my mother died I have been alone, all alone ; and I longed, oh so often, for some one who talked and felt as she did to come to me, and now you have come. I sat cold and shivering in the night a long time, but the light and warmth have come at last. Truly, Allah is good ! "

"Allah ! "

"Yes ; he was my mother's God, as the Great Spirit is my father's."

"They are both names for the same All Father," replied Cecil. "They mean the same thing, even as the sun is called by many names by many tribes, yet there is but the one sun."

"Then I am glad. It is good to learn that both prayed to the one God, though they did not know it. But my mother taught me to use the name of Allah, and not the other. And while my father and the tribes call me by my Indian name, 'Wallulah,' she gave me another, a secret name, that I was never to forget."

"What is it ? "

"I have never told it, but I will tell you, for you can understand."

And she gave him a singularly melodious name, of a character entirely different from any he had ever heard, but which he guessed to be Arabic or Hindu.

"It means, 'She who watches for the morning.' My mother told me never to forget it, and to remember that I was not to let myself grow to be like the Indians, but to pray to Allah, and to watch and hope, and that sometime the morning would come and I would be saved from the things around me. And now you have come and the dawn comes with you."

Her glad, thankful glance met his ; the latent grace and mobility of her nature, all roused and vivid under his influence, transfigured her face, making it delicately lovely. A great pang of longing surged through him.

" Oh," he thought, " had I not become a missionary, I might have met and loved some one like her ! I might have filled my life with much that is now gone from it forever ! "

For eight years he had seen only the faces of savage women and still more savage men ; for eight years his life had been steeped in bitterness, and all that was tender or romantic in his nature had been cramped, as in iron fetters, by the coarseness and stolidity around him. Now, after all that dreary time, he met one who had the beauty and the refinement of his own race. Was it any wonder that her glance, the touch of her dress or hair, the soft tones of her voice, had for him an indescribable charm? Was it any wonder that his heart went out to her in a yearning tenderness that although not love was dangerously akin to it?

He was startled at the sweet and burning tumult of emotion she was kindling within him. What was he thinking of? He must shake these feelings off, or leave her. Leave her ! The gloom of the savagery that awaited him at the camp grew tenfold blacker than ever. All the light earth held for him seemed gathered into the presence of this dark-eyed girl who sat talking so musically, so happily, by his side.

" I must go," he forced himself to say at length. " The sun is almost down."

" Must you go so soon ? "

" I will come again if you wish."

" But you must not go yet ; wait till the sun reaches the mountain-tops yonder.   I want you to tell me more about your own land."

So he lingered and talked while the sun sank lower and lower in the west.   It seemed to him that it had never gone down so fast before.

" I must go now," he said, rising as the sun's red disk sank behind the mountains.

" It is not late ; see, the sun is shining yet on the brow of the snow mountains."

Both looked at the peaks that towered grandly in the light of the sunken sun while all the world below lay in shadow.   Together they watched the mighty miracle of the afterglow on Mount Tacoma, the soft rose-flush that transfigured the mountain till it grew transparent, delicate, wonderful.

" That is what my life is now, — since you have brought the light to the 'watcher for the morning ; ' " and she looked up at him with a bright, trustful smile.

" Alas ? " thought Cecil, " it is not the light of morning but of sunset."

Slowly the radiance faded, the rose tint passed ; the mountain grew white and cold under their gaze, like the face of death.   Wallulah shuddered as if it were a prophecy.

" You will come back to-morrow ? " she said, looking at him with her large, appealing eyes.

" I will come," he said.

" It will seem long till your return, yet I have lived so many years waiting for that which has come at last that I have learned to be patient."

"Ask God to help you in your hours of loneliness and they will not seem so long and dark," said Cecil, whose soul was one tumultuous self-reproach that he had let the time go by without telling her more of God.

"Ah!" she said in a strange, wistful way, "I have prayed to him so much, but he could not fill *all* my heart. I wanted so to touch a hand and look on a face like my mother's. But God has sent you, and so I know he must be good."

They parted, and he went back to the camp.

"Is my mission a failure?" he thought, as he walked along, clinching his hands in furious anger with himself. "Why do I let a girl's beauty move me thus, and she the promised wife of another? How dare I think of aught beside the work God has sent me here to do? Oh, the shame and guilt of such weakness! I will be faithful. I will never look upon her face again!"

He emerged from the wood into the camp; its multitudinous sounds were all around him, and never had the coarseness and savagery of Indian life seemed so repellent as now, when he came back to it with his mind full of Wallulah's grace and loveliness. It was harsh discord after music.

Stripped and painted barbarians were hallooing, feasting, dancing; the whole camp was alive with boisterous hilarity, the result of a day of good fellowship. Mothers were calling their children in the dusk and young men were sportively answering, "Here I am, mother." Here and there, Indians who had been feasting all day lay like gorged anacondas beside the remnant of their meal; others, who had been gambling, were talking loudly of the results of the game.

Through it all the white man walked with swift footsteps, looking neither to the right nor the left, till he gained his lodge. He flung himself on his bed and lay there, his fingers strained together convulsively, his nerves throbbing with pain; vainly struggling with regret, vainly repeating to himself that he cared nothing for love and home, that he had put all those things from him, that he was engrossed now only in his work.

"Never, never! It can never be."

And the English exploring-ship in Yaquina Bay was to weigh anchor on the morrow, and sail up nearer along the unknown coast. The Indians had all deserted the sea-board for the council. Would Cecil hear? Would any one see the sail and bring the news?

" *I* WILL kill him!"

CHAPTER III.

CECIL AND THE WAR-CHIEF.

Children of the sun, with whom revenge is virtue.
YOUNG.

O N the next day came the races, the great diversion of the Indians. Each tribe ran only one horse, — the best it had. There were thirty tribes or bands, each with its choicest racer on the track. The Puget Sound and lower Columbia Indians, being destitute of horses, were not represented. There had been races every day on a small scale, but they were only private trials of speed, while to-day was the great day of racing for all the tribes, the day when the head chiefs ran their horses.

The competition was close, but Snoqualmie the Cayuse won the day. He rode the fine black horse he had taken from the Bannock he had tortured to death. Multnomah and the chiefs were present, and the victory was won under the eyes of all the tribes. The haughty, insolent Cayuse felt that he had gained a splendid success. Only, as in the elation of victory his glance swept over the crowd, he met the sad, unapplauding gaze of Cecil, and it made his ever burning resentment grow hotter still.

" I hate that man," he thought. " I tried to thrust him down into slavery, and Multnomah made him a chief. My heart tells me that he is an enemy. I hate him. I will kill him."

"Poor Wallulah!" Cecil was thinking. "What a terrible future is before her as the wife of that inhuman torturer of men!"

And his sympathies went out to the lonely girl, the golden thread of whose life was to be interwoven with the bloodstained warp and woof of Snoqualmie's. But he tried hard not to think of her; he strove resolutely that day to absorb himself in his work, and the effort was not unsuccessful.

After the races were over, a solemn council was held in the grove and some important questions discussed and decided. Cecil took part, endeavoring in a quiet way to set before the chiefs a higher ideal of justice and mercy than their own. He was heard with grave attention, and saw that more than one chief seemed impressed by his words. Only Snoqualmie was sullen and inattentive, and Mishlah the Cougar was watchful and suspicious.

After the council was over Cecil went to his lodge. On the way he found the young Willamette runner sitting on a log by the path, looking even more woebegone than he had the day before. Cecil stopped to inquire how he was.

" *Cultus* [bad]," was grunted in response.

"Did you see the races?"

"Races bad. What do I care?"

"I hope you will be better soon."

"Yes, better or worse by and by. What do I care?"

"Can I do anything for you?"

"Yes."

"What is it?"

"Go."

And he dropped his hand upon his knees, doubled himself together, and refused to say another word. As Cecil turned to go he found Multnomah standing close by, watching him.

"Come," said the stern despot, briefly. "I want to talk with you."

He led the way back through the noisy encampment to the now deserted grove of council. Everything there was quiet and solitary; the thick circle of trees hid them from the camp, though its various sounds floated faintly to them. They were quite alone. Multnomah seated himself on the stone covered with furs, that was his place in the council. Cecil remained standing before him, wondering what was on his mind. Was the war-chief aware of his interview with Wallulah? If so, what then? Multnomah fixed on him the gaze which few men met without shrinking.

"Tell me," he said, while it seemed to Cecil as if that eagle glance read every secret of his innermost heart, "tell me where your land is, and why you left it, and the reason for your coming among us. Keep no thought covered, for Multnomah will see it if you do."

Cecil's eye kindled, his cheek flushed. Wallulah was forgotten; his mission, and his mission only, was remembered. He stood before one who held over the many tribes of the Wauna the authority of a prince; if *he* could but be won for Christ, what vast results might follow!

He told it all, — the story of his home and his work, his call of God to go to the Indians, his long wanderings, the message he had to deliver, how it had been received by some and rejected by many; now he was here, a messenger sent by the Great Spirit to tell the tribes of the Wauna the true way of life. He told it all, and never had he been so eloquent. It was a striking contrast, the grim Indian sitting there leaning on his bow, his sharp, treacherous gaze bent like a bird of prey on the delicately moulded man pleading before him.

He listened till Cecil began to talk of love and forgiveness as duties enjoined by the Great Spirit. Then he spoke abruptly.

" When you stood up in the council the day the bad chief was tried, and told of the weakness and the wars that would come if the confederacy was broken up, you talked wisely and like a great chief and warrior; now you talk like a woman. Love! forgiveness! " He repeated the words, looking at Cecil with a kind of wondering scorn, as if he could not comprehend such weakness in one who looked like a brave man. " War and hate are the life of the Indian. They are the strength of his heart. Take them away, and you drain the blood from his veins; you break his spirit; he becomes a squaw."

" But my people love and forgive, yet they are not squaws. They are brave and hardy in battle; their towns are great; their country is like a garden."

And he told Multnomah of the laws, the towns, the schools, the settled habits and industry of New England. The chief listened with growing impatience. At length he threw his arm up with an indescribable gesture of freedom, like a man rejecting a fetter.

" How can they breathe, shut in, bound down like that? How can they live, so tied and burdened?"

" Is not that better than tribe forever warring against tribe? Is it not better to live like men than to lurk in dens and feed on roots like beasts? Yet we will fight, too; the white man does not love war, but he will go to battle when his cause is just and war must be."

" So will the deer and the cayote fight when they can flee no longer. The Indian loves battle. He loves to seek out his enemy, to grapple with him, and to tread him down. That is a man's life ! "

There was a wild grandeur in the chief's tone. All the tameless spirit of his race seemed to speak through him, the spirit that has met defeat and extermination rather than bow its neck to the yoke of civilization. Cecil realized that on the iron fibre of the war-chief's nature his pleading made no impression whatever, and his heart sank within him.

Again he tried to speak of the ways of peace, but the chief checked him impatiently.

" That is talk for squaws and old men. Multnomah does not understand it. Talk like a man, if you wish him to listen. Multnomah does not forgive; Multnomah wants no peace with his enemies. If they are weak he tramples on them and makes them slaves; if they are strong he fights them. When the Shoshones take from Multnomah, he takes from them; if they give him war he gives them war; if they torture one Willamette at the stake, Multnomah stretches two Shoshones upon red-hot stones. Multnomah gives hate for hate and war for war. This is the law the Great Spirit has given the Indian. What law he has given the white man, Multnomah knows not nor cares ! "

Baffled in his attempt, Cecil resorted to another

line of persuasion.   He set before Multnomah the arts, the intelligence, the splendor of the white race.

" The Indian has his laws and customs, and that is well ; but why not council with the white people, even as chiefs council together?   Send an embassy to ask that wise white men be sent you, so that you may learn of their arts and laws ; and what seems wise and good you can accept, what seems not so can be set aside.   I know the ways that lead back to the land of the white man ; I myself would lead the embassy."

It was a noble conception, — that of making a treaty between this magnificent Indian confederacy and New England for the purpose of introducing civilization and religion ; and for a moment he lost sight of the insurmountable obstacles in the way.

" No," replied the chief, " neither alone nor as leader of a peace party will your feet ever tread again the path that leads back to the land of the white man. We want not upon our shoulders the burden of his arts and laws.   We want not his teachers to tell us how to be women.   If the white man wants us, let him find his way over the desert and through the mountains, and we will grapple with him and see which is the strongest."

So saying, the war-chief rose and left him.

" He says that I shall never be allowed to go back," thought Cecil, with a bitter consciousness of defeat. "Then my mission ends here in the land of the Bridge, even as I have so often dreamed that it would. So be it ; I shall work the harder now that I see the end approaching.   I shall gather the chiefs in my own lodge this evening and preach to them."

While he was forming his resolution, there came the recollection that Wallulah would look for him, would be expecting him to come to her.

"I cannot," he thought, though he yearned to go to her. "I cannot go; I must be faithful to my mission."

Many chiefs came that night to his lodge; among them, to his surprise, Tohomish the seer. Long and animated was Cecil's talk; beautiful and full of spiritual fervor were the words in which he pointed them to a better life. Tohomish was impassive, listening in his usual brooding way. The others seemed interested; but when he was done they all rose up and went away without a word, — all except the Shoshone renegade who had helped him bury the dead Bannock. He came to Cecil before leaving the lodge.

"Sometime," he said, "when it will be easier for me to be good than it is now, I will try to live the life you talked about to-night."

Then he turned and went out before Cecil could reply.

"There is one at least seeking to get nearer God," thought Cecil, joyfully. After awhile his enthusiasm faded away, and he remembered how anxiously Wallulah must have waited for him, and how bitterly she must have been disappointed. Her face, pale and stained with tears, rose plainly before him. A deep remorse filled his heart.

"Poor child! I am the first white person she has seen since her mother died; no wonder she longs for my presence! I must go to her to-morrow. After all, there is no danger of my caring for her. To me my work is all in all."

CHAPTER IV.

ARCHERY AND GAMBLING.

To gambling they are no less passionately addicted in the interior than on the coast. — BANCROFT: *Native Races.*

THE next morning came the archery games. The best marksmen of each tribe contended together under the eyes of Multnomah, and Snoqualmie the Cayuse won the day.

These diversions were beginning to produce the result that the politic chief had intended they should. Better feeling was springing up. The spirit of discontent that had been rife was disappearing. Every day good-fellowship grew more and more between the Willamettes and their allies. Every day Snoqualmie the Cayuse became more popular among the tribes, and already he was second in influence to none but Multnomah himself.

The great war-chief had triumphed over every obstacle ; and he waited now only for the last day of the council, when his daughter should be given to Snoqualmie and the chiefs should recognize him as the future head of the confederacy.

Knowing this, the sight of Snoqualmie's successful archery was almost intolerable to Cecil, and he turned away from the place where the games were held.

" I will seek the young Willamette who is sick,"

he said to himself. "Then this evening I will go and visit Wallulah."

The thought sent the blood coursing warmly through his veins, but he chided himself for it. "It is but duty, I go to her only as a missionary," he repeated to himself over and over again.

He went to the lodge of the young Willamette and asked for him.

"He is not here," the father of the youth told him. "He is in the sweat-house. He is sick this morning, *hieu* sick."

And the old man emphasized the *hieu* [much], with a prolonged intonation and a comprehensive gesture as if the young man were very sick indeed. To the sweat-house went Cecil forthwith. He found it to be a little arched hut, made by sticking the ends of bent willow-wands into the ground and covering them over with skins, leaving only a small opening for entrance. When a sick person wished to take one of those "sweat baths" so common among the Indians, stones were heated red hot and put within the hut, and water was poured on them. The invalid, stripped to the skin, entered, the opening was closed behind him, and he was left to steam in the vapors.

When Cecil came up, the steam was pouring between the overlapping edges of the skins, and he could hear the young Willamette inside, chanting a low monotonous song, an endlessly repeated invocation to his *totem* to make him well. How he could sing or even breathe in that stifling atmosphere was a mystery to Cecil.

By and by the Willamette raised the flap that hung over the entrance and crawled out, hot, steaming, perspiring at every pore. He rushed with unsteady footsteps down to the river, only a few yards away, and plunged into the cold water. After repeatedly immersing himself, he waded back to the shore and lay down to dry in the sun. The shock to his nervous system of plunging from a hot steam-bath into ice-cold water fresh from the snow peaks of the north had roused all his latent vitality. He had recovered enough to be sullen and resentful to Cecil when he came up ; and after vainly trying to talk with or help him, the missionary left him.

It is characteristic of the Indian, perhaps of most half-animal races, that their moral conduct depends on physical feeling. Like the animal, they are good-humored, even sportive, when all is well ; like the animal, they are sluggish and unreasoning in time of sickness.

Cecil went back to the camp. He found that the archery games were over, and that a great day of gambling had begun. He was astonished at the eagerness with which all the Indians flung themselves into it. Multnomah alone took no part, and Tohomish, visible only at the council, was not there. But with those two exceptions, chiefs, warriors, all flung themselves headlong into the game.

First, some of the leading chiefs played at " hand," and each tribe backed its chief. Furs, skins, weapons, all manner of Indian wealth was heaped in piles behind the gamblers, constituting the stakes ; and they were divided among the tribes of the winners, — each player representing a tribe, and his winnings going, not to himself, but to his people. This rule applied, of course, only to the great public games ; in private games of " hand " each successful player kept his own spoils.

Amid the monotonous chant that always accompanied gambling, the two polished bits of bone (the winning one marked, the other not) were passed secretly from hand to hand. The bets were made as to who held the marked stick and in which hand, then a show of hands was made and the game was lost and won.

From " hand " they passed to *ahikia*, a game like that of dice, played with figured beaver teeth or disks of ivory, which were tossed up, everything depending on the combination of figures presented in their fall. It was played recklessly. The Indians were carried away by excitement. They bet anything and everything they had. Wealthy chiefs staked their all on the turn of the ivory disks, and some were beggared, some enriched. Cecil noticed in particular Mishlah the Cougar, chief of the Molallies. He was like a man intoxicated. His huge bestial face was all ablaze with excitement, his eyes were glowing like coals. He had scarcely enough intellect to understand the game, but enough combativeness to fling himself into it body and soul. He bet his horses and lost them ; he bet his slaves and lost again ; he bet his lodges, with their rude furnishings of mat and fur, and lost once more. Maddened, furious, like a lion in the toils, the desperate savage staked his wives and children on the throw of the *ahikia*, and they were swept from him into perpetual slavery.

Then he rose up and glared upon his opponents, with his tomahawk clinched in his hand, — as if feeling dimly that he had been wronged, thirsting for vengeance, ready to strike, yet not knowing upon whom the blow should fall. There was death in his look, and the chiefs shrunk from him, when his eyes met Multnomah's, who was looking on ; and the war-chief checked and awed him with his cold glance, as a tamer of beasts might subdue a rebellious tiger. Then the Molallie turned and went away, raging, desperate, a chief still, but a chief without lodge or wife or slave.

The sight was painful to Cecil, and he too went away while the game was at its height. Drawn by an influence that he could not resist, he took the trail that led down the bank of the river to the retreat of Wallulah.

CHAPTER V.

A DEAD QUEEN'S JEWELS.

For round about the walls yclothed were
With goodly arras of great maiesty,
Woven with golde and silke so close and nere
That the rich metall lurked privily.

The Faërie Queene.

H E found the sentinels by the pathway half reluctant to let him pass, but they did not forbid
him. Evidently it was only their awe of him as the
" Great White Prophet," to whom Multnomah had
added the dignity of an Indian sachem, that overcame their scruples. It was with a sense of doing
wrong that he went on. " If Multnomah knew," he
thought, " what would he do?" And brave as Cecil
was, he shuddered, thinking how deadly the wrath
of the war-chief would be, if he knew of these secret
visits to his daughter.

" It is an abuse of hospitality; it is clandestine,
wrong," he thought bitterly. " And yet she is lonely,
she needs me, and I must go to her; but I will never
go again."

Where he had met her before, he found her waiting
for him now, a small, graceful figure, standing in the
shadow of the wood. She heard his footsteps before
he saw her, and the melancholy features were transfigured with joy. She stood hesitating a moment like

some shy creature of the forest, then sprang eagerly forward to meet him.

"I knew you were coming!" she cried rapturously. "I felt your approach long before I heard your footsteps."

"How is that?" said Cecil, holding her hands and looking down into her radiant eyes. Something of the wild Indian mysticism flashed in them as she replied :

"I cannot tell; I knew it! my spirit heard your steps long before my ears could catch the sound. But oh!" she cried in sudden transition, her face darkening, her eyes growing large and pathetic, "why did you not come yesterday? I so longed for you and you did not come. It seemed as if the day would never end. I thought that perhaps the Indians had killed you; I thought it might be that I should never see you again ; and all the world grew dark as night, I felt so terribly alone. Promise me you will never stay away so long again!"

"Never!" exclaimed Cecil, on the impulse of the moment. An instant later he would have given the world to have recalled the word.

"I am so glad!" she cried, clapping her hands in girlish delight; and he could not pain her by an explanation.

"After a while I will tell her how impossible it is for me to come again," he thought. "I cannot tell her now." And he seized upon every word and look of the lovely unconscious girl, with a hunger of heart born of eight years' starvation.

"Now you must come with me to my lodge ; you are my guest, and I shall entertain you. I want you to look at my treasures."

Cecil went with her, wondering if they would meet Multnomah at her lodge, and if so, what he would say. He felt that he was doing wrong, yet so sweet was it to be in her presence, so much did her beauty fill the mighty craving of his nature, that it was not possible for him to tear himself away.

Some fifteen minutes' walk brought them to Wallulah's lodge. It was a large building, made of bark set upright against a frame-work of poles, and roofed with cedar boards, — in its external appearance like all Willamette lodges. Several Indian girls, neatly dressed and of more than ordinary intelligence, were busied in various employments about the yard. They looked in surprise at the white man and their mistress, but said nothing. The two entered the lodge. Cecil muttered an exclamation of amazement as he crossed the threshold.

The interior was a glow of color, a bower of richness. Silken tapestries draped and concealed the bark walls ; the floor of trodden earth was covered with a superbly figured carpet. It was like the hall of some Asiatic palace. Cecil looked at Wallulah, and her eyes sparkled with merriment at his bewildered expression. " I knew you would be astonished," she cried. " Is not this as fair as anything in your own land ? No, wait till I show you another room ! "

She led the way to an inner apartment, drew back the tapestry that hung over the doorway, and bade him enter.

Never, not even at St. James or at Versailles, had he seen such magnificence. The rich many-hued products of Oriental looms covered the rough walls ; the carpet was like a cushion ; mirrors sparkling with gems reflected his figure; luxurious divans invited to repose. Everywhere his eye met graceful draperies and artistically blended colors. Silk and gold combined to make up a scene that was like a dream of fable. Cecil's dazzled eyes wandered over all this splendor, then came back to Wallulah's face again.

" I have seen nothing like this in my own land, not even in the King's palace. How came such beautiful things here among the Indians?"

" They were saved from the vessel that was wrecked. They were my mother's, and she had them arranged thus. This was her lodge. It is mine now. I have never entered any other. I have never been inside an Indian wigwam. My mother forbade it, for fear that I might grow like the savage occupants."

Cecil knew now how she had preserved her grace and refinement amid her fierce and squalid surroundings. Again her face changed and the wistful look came back. Her wild delicate nature seemed to change every moment, to break out in a hundred varying impulses.

" I love beautiful things," she said, drawing a fold of tapestry against her cheek. " They seem half human. I love to be among them and feel their influence. These were my mother's, and it seems as if part of her life was in them. Sometimes, after she died, I used to shut my eyes and put my cheek against the soft hangings and try to think it was the touch of her hand; or I would read from her favorite poets and try to think that I heard her repeating them to me again!"

" Read!" exclaimed Cecil; " then you have books?"

" Oh, yes, I will show you all my treasures."

She went into another apartment and returned with a velvet case and a richly enchased casket. She opened the case and took out several rolls of parchment.

" Here they are, my dear old friends, that have told me so many beautiful things."

Cecil unrolled them with a scholar's tenderness. Their touch thrilled him ; it was touching again some familiar hand parted from years ago. The parchments were covered with strange characters, in a language entirely unknown to him. The initial letters were splendidly illuminated, the margins ornamented with elaborate designs. Cecil gazed on the scrolls, as one who loves music but who is ignorant of its technicalities might look at a sonata of Beethoven or an opera of Wagner, and be moved by its suggested melodies.

" I cannot read it," he said a little sadly.

" Sometime I will teach you," she replied ; " and you shall teach me your own language, and we will talk in it instead of this wretched Indian tongue."

" Tell me something about it now," asked Cecil, still gazing at the unknown lines.

" Not now, there is so much else to talk about ; but I will to-morrow."

To-morrow ! The word pierced him like a knife. For him, a missionary among barbarians, for her, the betrothed of a savage chief, the morrow could bring only parting and woe ; the sweet, fleeting present was all they could hope for. For them there could be no to-morrow. Wallulah, however, did not observe his dejection. She had opened the casket, and now placed it between them as they sat together on the divan. One by one, she took out the contents and displayed them. A magnificent necklace of diamonds, another of pearls ; rings, brooches, jewelled bracelets, flashed their splendor on him. Totally ignorant of their great value, she showed them only with a true woman's love of beautiful things, showed them as artlessly as if they were but pretty shells or flowers.

"Are they not bright?" she would say, holding them up to catch the light. "How they sparkle!"

One she took up a little reluctantly. It was an opal, a very fine one. She held it out, turning it in the light, so that he might see the splendid jewel glow and pale.

"Is it not lovely?" she said ; "like sun-tints on the snow. But my mother said that in her land it is called the stone of misfortune. It is beautiful, but it brings trouble with it."

He saw her fingers tremble nervously as they held it, and she dropped it from them hurriedly into the casket, as if it were some bright poisonous thing she dreaded to touch.

After a while, when Cecil had sufficiently admired the stones, she put them back into the casket and took it and the parchments away. She came back with her flute, and seating herself, looked at him closely.

"You are sad ; there are heavy thoughts on your mind. How is that? He who brings me sunshine must not carry a shadow on his own brow. Why are you troubled?"

The trouble was that he realized now, and was compelled to acknowledge to himself, that he loved this gentle, clinging girl, with a passionate love ; that he yearned to take her in his arms and shelter her from the terrible savagery before her ; and that he felt it could not, must not be.

"It is but little," he replied. "Every heart has its burden, and perhaps I have mine. It is the lot of man."

She looked at him with a vague uneasiness ; her susceptible nature responded dimly to the tumultuous emotions that he was trying by force of will to shut up in his own heart.

"Trouble? Oh, do I not know how bitter it is ! Tell me, what do your people do when they have trouble? Do they cut off their hair and blacken their faces, as the Indians do, when they lose one they love ?"

"No, they would scorn to do anything so degrading. He is counted bravest who makes the least display of grief and yet always cherishes a tender remembrance of the dead."

"So would I. My mother forbade me to cut off my hair or blacken my face when she died, and so I did not, though some of the Indians thought me bad for not doing so. And your people are not afraid to talk of the dead? "

"Most certainly not. Why should we be? We know that they are in a better world, and their memories are dear to us. It is very sweet sometimes to talk of them."

"But the Willamettes never talk of their dead, for fear they may hear their names spoken and come back. Why should they dread their coming back? Ah, if my mother only *would* come back ! How I used to long and pray for it !"

Cecil began to talk to her about the love and goodness of God. If he could only see her sheltered in the Divine compassion, he could trust her to slip from him into the unknown darkness of her future. She listened earnestly.

"Your words are good," she said in her quaint phraseology; "and if trouble comes to me again I shall remember them. But I am very happy now."

The warmth and thankfulness of her glance sent through him a great thrill of blended joy and pain.

"You forget," he said, forcing himself to be calm, "that you are soon to leave your home and become the wife of Snoqualmie."

Wallulah raised her hand as if to ward off a blow, her features quivering with pain. She tried to reply, but for an instant the words faltered on her lips. He saw it, and a fierce delight leaped up in his heart. "She does not love him, it is I whom she cares for," he thought; and then he thrust the thought down in indignant self-reproach.

"I do not care for Snoqualmie; I once thought I did, but — "

She hesitated, the quick color flushed her face; for the first time she seemed in part, though not altogether, aware of why she had changed.

For an instant Cecil felt as if he must speak; but the consequences rose before him while the words were almost on his lips. If he spoke and won her love, Multnomah would force her into a marriage with Snoqualmie just the same; and if the iron despot were to consent and give her to Cecil, the result would be a bloody war with Snoqualmie.

"I cannot, I must not," thought Cecil. He rose

to his feet ; his one impulse was to get away, to fight out the battle with himself. Wallulah grew pale.

"You are going?" she said, rising also. "Something in your face tells me you are not coming back," and she looked at him with strained, sad, wistful eyes.

He stood hesitating, torn by conflicting emotions, not knowing what to do.

"If you do not come back, I shall die," she said simply.

As they stood thus, her flute slipped from her relaxed fingers and fell upon the floor. He picked it up and gave it to her, partly through the born instinct of the gentleman, which no familiarity with barbarism can entirely crush out, partly through the tendency in time of intense mental strain to relieve the mind by doing any little thing.

She took it, lifted it to her lips, and, still looking at him, began to play. The melody, strange, untaught, artless as the song of a wood-bird, was infinitely sorrowful and full of longing. Her very life seemed to breathe through the music in fathomless yearning. Cecil understood the plea, and the tears rushed unbidden into his eyes. All his heart went out to her in pitying tenderness and love ; and yet he dared not trust himself to speak.

"Promise to come back," said the music, while her dark eyes met his ; "promise to come back. You are my one friend, my light, my all ; do not leave me to perish in the dark. I shall die without you, I shall die, I shall die ! "

Could any man resist the appeal? Could Cecil, of all men, thrilling through all his sensitive and ardent

nature to the music, thrilling still more to a mighty
and resistless love?

"I will come back," he said, and parted from her;
he dared not trust himself to say another word. But
the parting was not so abrupt as to prevent his seeing
the swift breaking-forth of light upon the melancholy
face that was becoming so beautiful to him and so
dear.

CHAPTER VI.

THE TWILIGHT TALE.

That eve I spoke those words again,
And then she hearkened what I said.
DANTE ROSSETTI.

THE next day the Indians had a great hunt. A circle of men on foot and on horseback was drawn around a large tract of forest on the western side of the Willamette River. Gradually, with much shouting, hallooing, and beating of bushes, the circle closed upon the game within it, like the folds of a mighty serpent.

There was a prodigious slaughter, a mad scene of butchery, in which the Indians exulted like fiends. Late in the afternoon they returned to camp, stained with blood and loaded with the spoils of the chase. Snoqualmie distinguished himself by killing a large bear, and its claws, newly severed and bleeding, were added to his already ample necklace of similar trophies.

Cecil remained in the almost deserted camp. He tried in vain to talk with the few chiefs who had not gone out to join in the hunt. Missionary work was utterly impossible that day. Wallulah and the problem of his love filled his thoughts. His mind, aroused and burning, searched and analyzed the question upon every side.

Should he tell Multnomah of Snoqualmie's cruelty, representing his unfitness to be the husband of the gentle Wallulah?

To the stern war-chief that very cruelty would be an argument in Snoqualmie's favor. Should he himself become a suitor for her hand? He knew full well that Multnomah would reject him with disdain; or, were he to consent, it would involve the Willamettes in a war with the haughty and vindictive Cayuse. Finally, should he attempt to fly with her to some other land? Impossible. All the tribes of the northwest were held in the iron grip of Multnomah. They could never escape; and even if they could, the good he had done among the Indians, the good he hoped would grow from generation to generation, would be all destroyed if it were told among them that he who claimed to come to them with a message from God had ended by stealing the chief's daughter. And had he a right to love any one? — had he a right to love at all? God had sent him to do a work among the Indians; was it not wicked for him to so much as look either to the right or to the left till that work was done?

Amid this maze of perplexities, his tense, agonized soul sought in vain for some solution, some conclusion. At times he sat in his lodge and brooded over these things till he seemed wrought up almost to madness, till his form trembled with excitement, and the old pain at his heart grew sharp and deadly.

Then again, trying to shake it off, he went out among the few Indians who were left in the camp and attempted to do missionary work; but enthusiasm was lacking, the glow and tenderness was gone from his words, the grand devotion that had inspired him so long failed him at last. He was no longer a saintly apostle to the Indians; he was only a human lover, torn by stormy human doubts and fears.

Even the Indians felt that some intangible change had come over him, and as they listened their hearts no longer responded to his eloquence; they felt somehow that the life was gone from his words. He saw it too, and it gave him a keen pang.

He realized that the energy and concentration of his character was gone, that a girl's beauty had drawn him aside from the mission on which God had sent him.

" I will go and see her. I will, without letting her know that I love her, give her to understand my position and her own. She shall see how impossible it is for us ever to be aught to each other. And I shall urge her to cling to God and walk in the path he has appointed for her, while I go on in mine."

So thinking, he left his lodge that evening and took the path to Wallulah's home.

Some distance from the encampment he met an Indian funeral procession. The young Willamette runner had died that morning, and now they were bearing him to the river, down which a canoe was to waft the body and the mourners to the nearest *mimaluse* island. The corpse was swathed in skins and tied around with thongs; the father bore it on his shoulder, for the dead had been but a slender lad. Behind them came the mother and a few Indian women. As they passed, the father chanted a rude lament.

" Oh, Mox-mox, my son, why did you go away and

leave our wigwam empty? You were not weak nor sickly, and your life was young. Why did you go? Oh, Mox-mox, dead, dead, dead!"

Then the women took up the doleful refrain, —

"Oh, Mox-mox, dead, dead, dead!"

Then the old man again, —

"Oh, Mox-mox, the sun was warm and food was plenty, yet you went away; and when we reach out for you, you are not there. Oh Mox-mox, dead, dead, dead!"

Then the women again, —

"Oh, Mox-mox, dead, dead, dead!"

And so it went on, till they were embarked and the canoe bore them from sight and hearing. Down on some *mimaluse* island or rocky point, they would stretch the corpse out in a canoe, with the bow and arrows and fishing spear used in life beside it; then turn over it another canoe like a cover, and so leave the dead to his long sleep.

The sight gave an added bitterness to Cecil's meditations.

"After all," he thought, "life is so short, — a shadow fleeting onward to the night, — and love is so sweet! Why not open my heart to the bliss it brings? The black ending comes so soon! Why not fling all thought of consequences to the winds, and gather into my arms the love that is offered me? why not know its warmth and thrill for one golden moment, even though that moment ends in death?"

The blood rushed wildly through his veins, but he resolutely put down the temptation. No, he would be faithful, he would not allow himself even to think of such a thing.

Reluctantly, as before, the sentinels made way for him, and he went on through the wood to the trysting-place, for such it had come to be. She was waiting. But there was no longer the glad illumination of face, the glad springing forward to meet him. She advanced shyly, a delicate color in her cheek, a tremulous grace in her manner, that he had not observed before; the consciousness of love had come to her and made her a woman. Never had she seemed so fair to Cecil; yet his resolution did not falter.

"I have come, you see, — come to tell you that I can come no more, and to talk with you about your future."

Her face grew very pale.

"Are you going away?" she asked sorrowfully, "and shall I never see you again?"

"I cannot come back," he replied gently. The sight of her suffering cut him to the heart.

"It has been much to see you," he continued, while she stood before him, looking downward, without reply. "It has been like meeting one of my own people. I shall never forget you."

She raised her head and strove to answer, but the words died on her lips. How he loathed himself, talking so smoothly to her while he hungered to take her in his arms and tell her how he loved her!

Again he spoke.

"I hope you will be happy with Snoqualmie, and — "

She lifted her eyes with a sudden light flashing in their black depths.

"Do you want me to hate him? Never speak his name to me again!"

" He is to be your husband ; nay, it is the wish of your father, and the great sachems approve it."

" Can the sachems put love in my heart? Can the sachems make my heart receive him as its lord? Ah, this bitter custom of the father giving his daughter to whomsoever he will, as if she were a dog ! And your lips sanction it ! "

Her eyes were full of tears. Scarcely realizing what he did, he tried to take her hand. The slender fingers shrank from his and were drawn away.

" I do not sanction it, it is a bitter custom ; but it is to be, and I only wished to smooth your pathway. I want to say or do something that will help you when I am gone."

" Do you know what it would be for me to be an Indian's wife? To cut the wood, and carry the water, and prepare the food, — that would be sweet to do for one I loved. But to toil amid dirt and filth for a savage whom I could only abhor, to feel myself growing coarse and squalid with my surround-ings, — I could not live ! "

She shuddered as she spoke, as if the very thought was horrible.

" You hate this degraded Indian life as much as I do, and yet it is the life you would push me into," she continued, in a tone of mournful heart-broken reproach. It stung him keenly.

" It is not the life I would push you into. God knows I would give my life to take one thorn from yours." The mad longing within him rushed into his voice in spite of himself, making it thrill with a passionate tenderness that brought the color back into her pallid cheek. " But I cannot remain," he went on, "I dare not; all that I can do is to say something that may help you in the future."

She looked at him with dilated eyes full of pain and bewilderment.

"I have no future if you go away. Why must you go? What will be left me after you are gone? Think how long I was here alone after my mother died, with no one to understand me, no one to talk to. Then you came, and I was happy. It was like light shining in the darkness; now it goes out and I can never hope again. Why must you go away and leave Wallulah in the dark?"

There was a childlike plaintiveness and simplicity in her tone; and she came close to him, looking up in his face with wistful, pleading eyes, the beautiful face wan and drawn with bewilderment and pain, yet never so beautiful as now.

Cecil felt the unspeakable cruelty of his attitude toward her, and his face grew white as death in an awful struggle between love and duty. But he felt that he must leave her or be disloyal to his God.

"I do not wish to go away. But God has called me to a great work, and I must do it. I dare not turn aside. You cannot know how dear your presence is to me, or how bitter it is for me to part from you. But our parting must be, else the work I have done among the tribes will be scattered to the winds and the curse of God will be on me as a false and fallen prophet."

He spoke with a kind of fierceness, striving blindly to battle down the mad longing within, and his tones had a harshness that he was too agitated to notice. She drew back involuntarily. There came into her face a dignity he had never seen before. She was but a recluse and a girl, but she was of royal lineage by right of both her parents, and his words had roused a spirit worthy the daughter of Multnomah.

"Am I a weight on you? Are you afraid I will bring a curse upon you? Do not fear, I shall no longer ask you to stay. Wallulah shall take herself out of your life."

She gave him a look full of despair, as if seeing all hope go from her forever; then she said simply, "Farewell," and turned away.

But in spite of her dignity there was an anguish written on her sweet pale face that he could not resist. All his strength of resolve, all his conviction of duty, crumbled into dust as she turned away; and he was conscious only that he loved her, that he could not let her go.

How it happened he never knew, but she was clasped in his arms, his kisses were falling on brow and cheek in a passionate outburst that could be kept back no longer. At first, she trembled in his arms and shrank away from him; then she nestled close, as if sheltering herself in the love that was hers at last. After awhile she lifted a face over which a shadow of pain yet lingered.

"But you said I would bring you a curse; you feared — "

He stopped her with a caress.

"Even curses would be sweet if they came through you. Forget what I said, remember only that I love you!"

And she was content.

Around them the twilight darkened into night; the

hours came and went unheeded by these two, wrapped in that golden love-dream which for a moment brings Eden back again to this gray old earth, all desolate as it is with centuries of woe and tears.

But while they talked there was on him a vague dread, an indefinable misgiving, a feeling that he was disloyal to his mission, disloyal to her; that their love could have but one ending, and that a dark one.

Still he strove hard to forget everything, to shut out all the world, — drinking to the full the bliss of the present, blinding his eyes to the pain of the future.

But after they parted, when her presence was withdrawn and he was alone, he felt like a man faithless and dishonored; like a prophet who had bartered the salvation of the people to whom he had been sent, in exchange for a woman's kisses, which could bring him only disgrace and death.

As he went back to the camp in the stillness of midnight, he was startled by a distant roar, and saw through the tree-tops flames bursting from the far-off crater of Mount Hood. The volcano was beginning one of its periodical outbursts. But to Cecil's mind, imbued with the gloomy supernaturalism of early New England, and unconsciously to himself, tinged in later years with the superstition of the Indians among whom he had lived so long, that ominous roar, those flames leaping up into the black skies of night, seemed a sign of the wrath of God.

CHAPTER VII.

ORATOR AGAINST ORATOR.

The gravity, fixed attention, and decorum of these sons of the forest was calculated to make for them a most favorable impression. — GRAY : *History of Oregon.*

THE next day all the Indians were gathered around the council grove. Multnomah presided, and every sachem was in his place.

There was to be a trial of eloquence, — a tourney of orators, to see which tribe had the best. Only one, the most eloquent of each tribe, was to speak; and Multnomah was to decide who was victor. The mother of Wallulah had introduced the custom, and it had become popular among the Indians.

Cecil was in his place among the chiefs, with worn face and abstracted air; Snoqualmie was present, with hawk-like glance and imperious mien ; there was Mish-lah, with his sullen and brutal features; there, too, wrapped closely in his robe of fur, sat Tohomish, brooding, gloomy, — the wild empire's mightiest master of eloquence, and yet the most repulsive figure of them all.

The Indians were strangely quiet that morning; the hush of a superstitious awe was upon them. The smoking mountains, Hood and Adams as the white man calls them, Au-poo-tah and Au-ka-ken in the Indian tongue, were becoming active of late. The previous night flame had been seen bursting from the top of Mount Hood and thick black smoke still puffed upward from it, and on Mount Adams rested a heavy cloud of volcanic vapors. Were the mountains angry? Aged men told how in the old time there had been a terrible outburst of flame and ashes from Mount Hood ; a rain of fire and stones had fallen over all the Willamette valley ; the very earth had trembled at the great mountain's wrath.

As the lower animals feel in the air the signs of a coming storm, so these savages felt, by some kindred intuition, that a mysterious convulsion of Nature was at hand. They talked in low tones, they were subdued in manner ; any one coming suddenly upon them would have been impressed by the air of uneasiness and apprehension that everywhere prevailed. But the chiefs were stoical, and Multnomah impassive as ever.

Could it have been that the stormy influences at work in Nature lent energy to the orators that day? They were unusually animated, at least for Indians, though a white man would have found them intolerably bombastic. Each speech was a boastful eulogy of the speaker's tribe, and an exaggerated account of the wonderful exploits of its warriors.

This was rather dangerous ground ; for all the tribes had been at enmity in days gone by, and some of their most renowned victories had been won over each other. Every one took it in good part, however, except Mishlah. When We-math, chief of the Klamaths, recounting the exploits of his race, told how in ancient times they had lorded it over the Mollalies, Mishlah glared at him as if tempted to leap upon him and strike him down. Fortunately the orator passed on to other things, and the wrath of the Mollalie chief gradually cooled.

Then came Cecil. It was a grand opening. He could speak of his own people, of their ancient savagery and present splendor, and show how the gospel of love and justice had been the cause of their elevation. Then would come the appeal to the Indians to accept this faith as their own and share in its uplifting power. It was a magnificent opportunity, the opportunity of a life-time.

But the mental conflict he had just passed through had rent his mind like a volcanic upheaval. It possessed no longer the intense concentration which had been the source of its strength. Tenderness, benevolence, missionary zeal, were still there, but no longer sovereign. Other passions divided his heart ; a hopeless and burning love consumed his being.

He spoke, but the fire was gone from his delivery and the vividness from his imagination. His eloquence was not what it had been ; his heart was no longer in his work, and his oration was a failure.

Even the Indians noticed that something was lacking in his oratory, and it no longer moved them as it had done. Cecil realized it, and strove to speak with more energy, but in vain ; he could not arouse himself ; and it was with a consciousness of failure that he brought his speech to a close and resumed his seat.

To a man of his morbid conscientiousness only one conclusion was possible.

" God sent me to proclaim salvation to these children of darkness," he thought, " and I have turned aside to fill my heart with a woman's love. His wrath is on me. He has taken his spirit from me. I am a thing rejected and accursed, and this people will go down to death because I have failed in my mission."

While he sat absorbed in these bitter, self-accusing thoughts, the speaking went on. Wau-ca-cus the Klickitat made a strong " talk," picturesque in Indian metaphor, full of energy. But the chief that followed surpassed him. Orator caught fire from orator; thoughts not unworthy a civilized audience were struck out by the intensity of the emulation; speakers rose to heights which they had never reached before, which they were destined never to reach again. In listening to and admiring their champions, the tribes forgot the smoking mountains and the feeling of apprehension that had oppressed them. At length Snoqualmie made a speech breathing his own daring spirit in every word. It went immeasurably beyond the others; it was the climax of all the darkly splendid eloquence of the day.

No, not of all. From his place among the chiefs rose a small and emaciated figure; the blanket that had muffled his face was thrown aside, and the tribes looked on the mis-shapen and degraded features of Tohomish the Pine Voice. He stood silent at first, his eyes bent on the ground, like a man in a trance. For a moment the spectators forgot the wonderful eloquence of the man in his ignoble appearance. What could he do against Wau-ca-cus the Klickitat and Snoqualmie the Cayuse, whose sonorous utterances still rang in their ears, whose majestic presence still filled their minds !

" The Willamettes are beaten at last, — the Willamette speakers can no more be called the best," was the one exultant thought of the allies, and the Willa-

mettes trembled for the fame of their orators. Back
in the shadow of the cottonwoods, an old Willamette
warrior put an arrow on the string and bent his bow
unseen on Tohomish.

" He cannot beat them, and it shall never be said
that Tohomish failed," he muttered. At that moment,
even as death hung over him, the orator's voice was
heard beginning his " talk ; " and the warrior's hand
fell, the bent bow was relaxed, the arrow dropped
from the string. For with the first accents of that soft
and lingering voice the tribes were thrilled as with the
beginning of music.

The orator's head was still bent down, his manner
abstracted ; he spoke of the legends and the glories of
the Willamette tribe, but spoke of them as if that tribe
belonged to the past, as if it had perished from the
earth, and he was telling the tale of a great dead race.
His tones were melodious but indescribably mournful.
When at length he lifted his face, his eyes shone with
a misty light, and his brutal features were illuminated
with a weird enthusiasm. A shudder went through
the vast and motley assembly. No boastful rant was
this, but a majestic story of the past, the story of a
nation gone forever. It was the death-song of the
Willamettes, solemnly rendered by the last and greatest
orator of the race.

At length he spoke of Multnomah and of the power
of the confederacy in his time, but spoke of it as of old
time, seen dimly through the lapse of years. Then,
when as it seemed he was about to go on and tell how
this power came to fall, he hesitated ; the words faltered on his lips ; he suddenly broke off, took his
seat, and drew his robe again over his face.

"*IT was the Death-song of the Willamettes.*"

The effect was indescribable. The portentous nature of the whole speech needed only that last touch of mystery. It sent through every heart a wild and awesome thrill, as at the shadow of approaching destiny.

The multitude were silent ; the spell of the prophet's lofty and mournful eloquence still lingered over them. Multnomah rose. With him rested the decision as to who was the greatest orator. But the proud old war-chief knew that all felt that Tohomish had far surpassed his competitors, and he was resolved that not his lips but the voice of the tribes should proclaim their choice.

"Multnomah was to decide who has spoken best, but he leaves the decision with you. You have heard them all. Declare who is the greatest, and your word shall be Multnomah's word."

There was an instant's silence ; then in a murmur like the rush of the sea came back the voice of the multitude.

"Tohomish ! Tohomish ! he is greatest !"

" He is greatest," said Multnomah. But Tohomish, sitting there dejectedly, seemed neither to see nor hear.

"To-morrow," said the war-chief, "while the sun is new, the chiefs will meet in council and the great talk shall be ended. And after it ends, Multnomah's daughter will be given to Snoqualmie, and Multnomah will bestow a rich *potlatch* [a giving of gifts] on the people. And then all will be done."

The gathering broke up. Gradually, as the Indians gazed on the smoking mountains, the excitement produced by the oratory they had just heard wore off.

Only Tohomish's sombre eloquence, so darkly in unison with the menacing aspect of Nature, yet lingered in every mind. They were frightened and startled, apprehensive of something to come. Legends, superstitious lore of by-gone time connected with the " smoking mountains," were repeated that afternoon wherever little groups of Indians had met together. Through all these gathered tribes ran a dread yet indefinable whisper of apprehension, like the first low rustle of the leaves that foreruns the coming storm.

Over the valley Mount Adams towered, wrapped in dusky cloud ; and from Mount Hood streamed intermittent bursts of smoke and gleams of fire that grew plainer as the twilight fell. Louder, as the hush of evening deepened, came the sullen roar from the crater of Mount Hood. Below the crater, the icefields that had glistened in unbroken whiteness the previous day were now furrowed with wide black streaks, from which the vapor of melting snow and burning lava ascended in dense wreaths. Men wiser than these ignorant savages would have said that some terrible convulsion was at hand.

Multnomah's announcement in the council was a dreadful blow to Cecil, though he had expected it. His first thought was of a personal appeal to the chief, but one glance at the iron features of the autocrat told him that it would be a hopeless undertaking. No appeal could turn Multnomah from his purpose. For Cecil, such an undertaking might be death ; it certainly would be contemptuous refusal, and would call down on Wallulah the terrible wrath before which the bravest sachem quailed.

Cecil left the grove with the other chiefs and found his way to his lodge. There he flung himself down on his face upon his couch of furs. The Indian woman, his old nurse, who still clung to him, was absent, and for some time he was alone. After a while the flap that hung over the entrance was lifted, and some one came in with the noiseless tread of the Indian. Cecil, lying in a maze of bitter thought, became aware of the presence of another, and raised his head. The Shoshone renegade stood beside him. His gaze rested compassionately on Cecil's sad, worn face.

" What is it ? " he asked. " Your words were slow and heavy to-day. There was a weight on your spirit ; what is it ? You said that we were friends, so I came to ask if I could help."

" You are good, and like a brother," replied Cecil, gently, " but I cannot tell you my trouble. Yet this much I can tell, " — and he sat upon the couch, his whole frame trembling with excitement. " I have sinned a grievous sin, therefore the Great Spirit took away the words from my lips to-day. My heart has become evil, and God has punished me."

It was a relief to his over-burdened conscience to say those harsh things of himself, yet the relief was bitter. Over the bronzed face of the Indian came an expression of deep pity.

" The white man tears himself with his own claws like a wounded beast, but it does not give him peace. Has he done evil ? Then let him remember what he has so often told the Indians : ' Forsake evil, turn from sin, and the Great Spirit will forgive.' Let my white brother do this, and it will be well with him."

He gazed at Cecil an instant longer; then, with a forbearance that more civilized men do not always show, he left the lodge without another word.

But what he said had its effect. Through Cecil's veins leaped the impulse of a sudden resolve, — a resolve that was both triumph and agony. He fell on his knees beside the couch.

" Thou hast shown me my duty by the lips of the Indian, and I will perform it. I will tear this forbidden love from my heart. Father, help me. Once before I resolved to do this and failed. Help me that I fail not now. Give me strength. Give me the mastery over the flesh, O God! Help me to put this temptation from me. Help me to fulfil my mission."

The struggle was long and doubtful, but the victory was won at last. When Cecil arose from his knees, there was the same set and resolute look upon his face that was there the morning he entered the wilderness, leaving friends and home behind him forever, — the look that some martyr of old might have worn, putting from him the clinging arms of wife or child, going forth to the dungeon and the stake.

" It is done," murmured the white lips. " I have put her from me. My mission to the Indians alone fills my heart. But God help her! God help her!"

For the hardest part of it all was that he sacrificed her as well as himself.

" It must be," he thought; " I must give her up. I will go now and tell her; then I will never look upon her face again. But oh! what will become of her?"

And his long fingers were clinched as in acutest pain. But his sensitive nerves, his intense susceptibilities were held in abeyance by a will that, once roused, was strong even unto death.

He went out. It was dark. Away to the east Mount Hood lifted its blazing crater into the heavens like a gigantic torch, and the roar of the eruption came deep and hoarse through the stillness of night. Once, twice, it seemed to Cecil that the ground trembled slightly under his feet. The Indians were huddled in groups watching the burning crest of the volcano. As the far-off flickering light fell on their faces, it showed them to be full of abject fear.

" It is like the end of the world," thought Cecil. "Would that it were; then she and I might die together."

He left the camp and took the trail through the wood to the trysting-place; for, late as it was, he knew that she awaited him.

CHAPTER VIII.

IN THE DARK.

There is not one upon life's weariest way,
Who is weary as I am weary of all but death.
                                        SWINBURNE.

THE grim sentinels by the pathway, who had been
so reluctant to let Cecil pass the day before, were
still more reluctant this evening. One of them planted
himself in the trail directly in front of Cecil, and did
not offer to let him go on, but stood sullenly blocking
the way. Cecil touched the warrior's arm and bade
him stand aside. For an instant it seemed that he
would refuse, but his superstitious respect for the white
tomanowos overcame his obstinacy, — and he stepped
unwillingly back.

But as Cecil went on he felt, and felt rightly, that
they would not let him pass again, — that the last act,
be it what it might, in his love drama, was drawing
to a close.

A few moments' walk, and he saw in the dark the
little figure awaiting him under the trees. She came
slowly forward to meet him. He saw that her face
was very pale, her eyes large and full of woe. She
gave him her hands ; they felt like ice. He bent over
her and kissed her with quivering lips.

" Poor child," he said, putting his arms around her
slender form and drawing it close in his embrace,

"how can I ever tell you what I have to tell you to-night!'"

She did not respond to his caress. At length, looking up in a lifeless, stricken way, she spoke in a mechanical voice, a voice that did not sound like her own, —

"I know it already. My father came and told me that to-morrow I must — " She shuddered; her voice broke; then she threw her arms around his neck and clung to him passionately. "But they can never tear me away from you; never, never!"

How could he tell her that he came to put her away from him, that he came to bid her farewell? He clasped her the tighter in his arms. For an instant his mind swept all the chances of flight with her, only to realize their utter hopelessness; then he remembered that even to think of such a thing was treachery to the resolves he had just made. He shook from head to foot with stormy emotion.

She lifted her head from his breast, where it was pillowed.

"Let us get horses or a canoe, and fly to-night to the desert or the sea, — anywhere, anywhere, only to be away from here! Let us take the trail you came on, and find our way to your people."

"Alas," replied Cecil, "how could we escape? Every tribe, far and near, is tributary to your father. The runners would rouse them as soon as we were missed. The swiftest riders would be on our trail; ambuscades would lurk for us in every thicket; we could never escape; and even if we should, a whole continent swarming with wild tribes lies between us and my land."

She looked at him in anguish, with dim eyes, and her arms slipped from around his neck.

"Do you no longer love Wallulah? Something tells me that you would not wish to fly with me, even if we could escape. There is something you have not told me."

Clasping her closely to him, he told her how he felt it was the will of God that they must part. God had sent him on a sacred mission, and he dared not turn aside. Either her love or the redemption of the tribes of the Wauna must be given up; and for their sake love must be sacrificed.

"To-day God took away the words from my lips and the spirit from my heart. My soul was lead. I felt like one accursed. Then it came to me that it was because I turned aside from my mission to love you. We must part. Our ways diverge. I must walk my own pathway alone wheresoever it leads me. God commands, and I must obey."

The old rapt look came back, the old set, determined expression which showed that that delicate organization could grow as strong as granite in its power to endure.

Wallulah shrank away from him, and strove to free herself from his embrace.

"Let me go," she said, in a low, stifled tone. "Oh, if I could only die!"

But he held her close, almost crushing the delicate form against his breast. She felt his heart beat deeply and painfully against her own, and in some way it came to her that every throb was agony, that he was in the extremity of mental and physical suffering.

"God help me!" he said; "how can I give you up?"

She realized by woman's intuition that his whole soul was wrung with pain, with an agony darker and bitterer than her own; and the exceeding greatness of his suffering gave her strength. A sudden revulsion of feeling affected her. She looked up at him with infinite tenderness.

"I wish I could take all the pain away from you and bear it myself."

"It is God's will; we must submit to it."

"His will!" Her voice was full of rebellion. "Why does he give us such bitter suffering? Does n't he care? I thought once that God was good, but it is all dark now."

"Hush, you must not think so. After all, it will be only a little while till we meet in heaven, and there no one can take you from me."

"Heaven is so far off. The present is all that I can see, and it is as black as death. Death! it would be sweet to die now with your arms around me; but to *live* year after year with him! How can I go to him, now that I have known you? How can I bear his presence, his touch?"

She shuddered there in Cecil's arms. All her being shrunk in repugnance at the thought of Snoqualmie.

"Thank God for death!" said Cecil, brokenly.

"It is so long to wait," she murmured, "and I am so young and strong."

His kisses fell on cheek and brow. She drew down his head and put her cheek against his and clung to him as if she would never let him go.

It was a strange scene, the mournful parting of the lovers in the gloom of the forest and the night. To the east, through the black net-work of leaves and branches, a dull red glow marked the crater of Mount Hood, and its intermittent roar came to them through the silence. It was a night of mystery and horror, — a fitting night for their tragedy of love and woe. The gloom and terror of their surroundings seemed to throw a supernatural shadow over their farewell.

"The burning mountain is angry to-night," said Wallulah, at last. "Would that it might cover us up with its ashes and stones, as the Indians say it once did two lovers back in the old time."

"Alas, death never comes to those who wish for it. When the grace and sweetness are all fled from our lives, and we would be glad to lie down in the grave and be at rest, then it is that we must go on living. Now I must go. The longer we delay our parting the harder it will be."

"Not yet, not yet !" cried Wallulah. "Think how long I must be alone, — always alone until I die."

"God help us !" said Cecil, setting his teeth. "I will dash my mission to the winds and fly with you. What if God does forsake us, and our souls are lost ! I would rather be in the outer darkness with you than in heaven without you."

His resolution had given way at last. But in such cases, is it not always the woman that is strongest?

"No," she said, "you told me that your God would forsake you if you did. It must not be."

She withdrew herself from his arms and stood looking at him. He saw in the moonlight that her pale tear-stained face had upon it a sorrowful resignation, a mournful strength, born of very hopelessness.

"God keep you, Wallulah !" murmured Cecil, brokenly. "If I could only feel that he would shelter and shield you!"

"That may be as it will," replied the sweet, patient lips. "I do not know. I shut my eyes to the future. I only want to take myself away from you, so that your God will not be angry with you. Up there," she said, pointing, "I will meet you sometime and be with you forever. God will not be angry then. Now farewell."

He advanced with outstretched arms. She motioned him back.

"It will make it harder," she said.

For a moment she looked into his eyes, her own dark, dilated, full of love and sadness; for a moment all that was within him thrilled to the passionate, yearning tenderness of her gaze; then she turned and went away without a word.

He could not bear to see her go, and yet he knew it must end thus; he dared not follow her or call her back. But so intense was his desire for her to return, so vehemently did his life cry out after her, that for an instant it seemed to him he *had* called out, "Come back! come back!" The cry rose to his lips; but he set his teeth and held it back. They *must* part; was it not God's will? The old pain at his heart returned, a faintness was on him, and he reeled to the ground.

Could it be that her spirit felt that unuttered cry, and that it brought her back? Be this as it may, while he was recovering from his deadly swoon he dimly felt her presence beside him, and the soft cool touch of her fingers on his brow. Then — or did he imagine it? — her lips, cold as those of the dead, touched his own. But when consciousness entirely returned, he was alone in the forest.

Blind, dizzy, staggering with weakness, he found his way to the camp. Suddenly, as he drew near it, he felt the earth sway and move beneath him like a living thing. He caught hold of a tree to escape being thrown to the ground. There came an awful burst of flame from Mount Hood. Burning cinders and scoria lit up the eastern horizon like a fountain of fire. Then down from the great canyon of the Columbia, from the heart of the Cascade Range, broke a mighty thundering sound, as if half a mountain had fallen. Drowning for a moment the roar of the volcano, the deep echo rolled from crag to crag, from hill to hill. A wild chorus of outcries rang from the startled camp, — the fierce, wild cry of many tribes mad with fear yet breathing forth tremulous defiance, the cry of human dread mingling with the last echoes of that mysterious crash.

CHAPTER IX.

QUESTIONING THE DEAD.

Then he said : " Cold lips and breast without breath,
Is there no voice, no language of death ? "

EDWIN ARNOLD.

WHILE Cecil was on his way that evening to seek Wallulah, a canoe with but a single occupant was dropping down the Columbia toward one of the many *mimaluse*, or death-islands, that are washed by its waters.

An Indian is always stealthy, but there was an almost more than Indian stealthiness about this canoe-man's movements. Noiselessly, as the twilight deepened into darkness, the canoe glided out of a secluded cove not far from the camp ; noiselessly the paddle dipped into the water, and the canoe passed like a shadow into the night.

On the rocky *mimaluse* island, some distance below the mouth of the Willamette, the Indian landed and drew his boat up on the beach. He looked around for a moment, glanced at the red glow that lit the far-off crest of Mount Hood, then turned and went up the pathway to the ancient burial hut.

Who was it that had dared to visit the island of the dead after dark ? The bravest warriors were not capable of such temerity. Old men told how, away back in the past, some braves had ventured upon the island after nightfall, and had paid the awful forfeit. They were struck by unseen hands. Weapons that had lain for years beside the decaying corpses of forgotten warriors wounded them in the dark. Fleeing to their canoes in swiftest fear, they found the shadowy pursuit was swifter still, and were overtaken and struck down, while the whole island rung with mocking laughter. One only escaped, plunging all torn and bruised into the river and swimming to the farther shore. When he looked back, the island was covered with moving lights, and the shrill echo of fiendish mirth came to him across the water. His companions were never seen again. A little while afterward the dogs barked all night around his lodge, and in the morning he was found lying dead upon his couch, his face ghastly and drawn with fear, as if at some frightful apparition.

"He disturbed the *mimaluse tillicums* [dead people], and they came for him," said the old medicine men, as they looked at him.

Since then, no one had been on the island except in the daytime. Little bands of mourners had brought hither the swathed bodies of their dead, laid them in the burial hut, lifted the wail over them, and left upon the first approach of evening.

Who, then, was this, — the first for generations to set foot on the *mimaluse illahee* after dark?

It could be but one, the only one among all the tribes who would have dared to come, and to come alone, — Multnomah, the war-chief, who knew not what it was to fear the living or the dead.

Startled by the outburst of the great smoking mountains, which always presaged woe to the Willamettes, perplexed by Tohomish's mysterious hints of some impending calamity, weighed down by a dread presentiment, he came that night on a strange and superstitious errand.

On the upper part of the island, above reach of high water, the burial hut loomed dark and still in the moonlight as the chief approached it.

Some of the Willamettes, like the Chinooks, practised canoe burial, but the greater part laid their dead in huts, as did also the Klickitats and the Cascades.

The war-chief entered the hut. The rude boards that covered the roof were broken and decayed. The moonlight shone through many openings, lighting up the interior with a dim and ghostly radiance. There, swathed in crumbling cerements, ghastly in shrunken flesh and protruding bone, lay the dead of the line of Multnomah, — the chiefs of the blood royal who had ruled the Willamettes for many generations. The giant bones of warriors rested beside the more delicate skeletons of their women, or the skeletons, slenderer still, of little children of the ancient race. The warrior's bow lay beside him with rotting string ; the child's playthings were still clasped in fleshless fingers ; beside the squaw's skull the ear-pendants of *hiagua* shells lay where they had fallen from the crumbling flesh years before.

Near the door, and where the slanting moonbeams fell full upon it, was the last who had been borne to the death hut, the mother of Wallulah. Six years before Multnomah had brought her body, — brought it alone, with no eye to behold his grief; and since then no human tread had disturbed the royal burial-place.

He came now and looked down upon the body. It had been tightly swathed, fold upon fold, in some oriental fabric ; and the wrappings, stiffened by time, still showed what had once been a rare symmetry of form. The face was covered with a linen cloth, yellow now through age and fitting like a mask to the features. The chief knelt down and drew away the face-cloth. The countenance, though shrunken, was almost perfectly preserved. Indeed, so well preserved were many of the corpses the first white settlers found on these *mimaluse* islands as to cause at one time a belief that the Indians had some secret process of embalming their dead. There was no such process, however, — nothing save the antiseptic properties of the ocean breeze which daily fanned the burial islands of the lower Columbia.

Lovely indeed must the mother of Wallulah have been in her life. Withered as her features were, there was a delicate beauty in them still, — in the graceful brow, the regular profile, the exquisitely chiselled chin. Around the shoulders and the small shapely head her hair had grown in rich luxuriant masses.

The chief gazed long on the shrunken yet beautiful face. His iron features grew soft, as none but Wallulah had ever seen them grow. He touched gently the hair of his dead wife, and put it back from her brow with a wistful, caressing tenderness. He had never understood her ; she had always been a mystery to him ; the harsh savagery of his nature had never been able to enter into or comprehend the refined grace of hers ; but he had loved her with all the fierce, tenacious, secretive power of his being, a power that neither time nor death could change. Now he spoke to her, his low tones sounding weird in that house of the dead, — a strange place for words of love.

"My woman, — mine yet, for death itself cannot take from Multnomah that which is his own; my bird that came from the sea and made its nest for a little while in the heart of Multnomah and then flew away and left it empty, — I have been hungry to see you, to touch your hair and look upon your face again. Now I am here, and it is sweet to be with you, but the heart of Multnomah listens to hear you speak."

He still went on stroking her hair softly, reverently. It seemed the only caress of which he was capable, but it had in it a stern and mournful tenderness.

"Speak to me! The dead talk to the *tomanowos* men and the dreamers. You are mine; talk to me; I am in need. The shadow of something terrible to come is over the Willamette. The smoking mountains are angry; the dreamers see only bad signs; there are black things before Multnomah, and he cannot see what they are. Tell me, — the dead are wise and know that which comes, — what is this unknown evil which threatens me and mine?"

He looked down at her with intense craving, intense desire, as if his imperious will could reanimate that silent clay and force to the mute lips the words he so desired. But the still lips moved not, and the face lay cold under his burning and commanding gaze. The chief leaned closer over her; he called her name aloud, — something that the Willamette Indians rarely did, for they believed that if the names of the dead were spoken, even in conversation, it would bring them back; so they alluded to their lost ones only indirectly, and always reluctantly and with fear.

"Come back!" said he, repeating the name he had not spoken for six years. "You are my own, you are my woman. Hear me, speak to me, you whom I love; you who, living or dead, are still the wife of Multnomah."

No expression flitted over the changeless calm of the face beneath him: no sound came back to his straining ears except the low intermittent roar of the far-off volcano.

A sorrowful look crossed his face. As has been said, there was an indefinable something always between them, which perhaps must ever be between those of diverse race. It had been the one mystery that puzzled him while she was living, and it seemed to glide, viewless yet impenetrable, between them now. He rose to his feet.

"It comes between us again," he thought, looking down at her mournfully. "It pushed me back when she was living, and made me feel that I stood outside her heart even while my arms were around her. It comes between us now and will not let her speak. If it was only something I could see and grapple with!"

And the fierce warrior felt his blood kindle within him, that not only death but something still more mysterious and incomprehensible should separate him from the one he loved. He turned sadly away and passed on to the interior of the hut. As he gazed on the crumbling relics of humanity around him, the wonted look of command came back to his brow. These *should* obey; by iron strength of will and mystic charm he would sway them to his bidding. The withered lips of death, or spirit voices, should tell him what he wished to know. Abjectly superstitious as was the idea it involved, there was yet something grand in his savage despotic grasp after power that, dominating all he knew of earth, sought to bend to his will even the spirit-land.

The chief believed that the departed could talk to him if they would ; for did they not talk to the medicine men and the dreamers ? If so, why not to him, the great chief, the master of all the tribes of the Wauna ?

He knelt down, and began to sway his body back and forth after the manner of the Nootka *shamans*, and to chant a long, low, monotonous song, in which the names of the dead who lay there were repeated over and over again.

" Kamyah, Tlesco, Che-aqah, come back ! come back and tell me the secret, the black secret, the death secret, the woe that is to come. Winelah, Sic-mish, Tlaquatin, the land is dark with signs and omens ; the hearts of men are heavy with dread ; the dreamers say that the end is come for Multnomah and his race. Is it true ? Come and tell me. I wait, I listen, I speak your names ; come back, come back ! "

Tohomish himself would not have dared to repeat those names in the charnel hut, lest those whom he invoked should spring upon him and tear him to pieces. No more potent or more perilous charm was known to the Indians.

Ever as Multnomah chanted, the sullen roar of the volcano came like an undertone and filled the pauses of the wild incantation. And as he went on, it seemed to the chief that the air grew thick with ghostly presences. There was a sense of breathing life all around him. He felt that others, many others, were with him; yet he saw nothing. When he paused for some voice, some whisper of reply, this sense of hyper-physical perception became so acute that he could almost *see*, almost *hear*, in the thick blackness and the silence; yet no answer came.

Again he resumed his mystic incantation, putting all the force of his nature into the effort, until it seemed that even those shadowy things of the night must yield to his blended entreaty and command. But there came no response. Thick and thronging the viewless presences seemed to gather, to look, and to listen; but no reply came to his ears, and no sight met his eyes save the swathed corpses and the white-gleaming bones on which the shifting moon-beams fell.

Multnomah rose to his feet, baffled, thwarted, all his soul glowing with anger that he should be so scorned.

"Why is this?" said his stern voice in the silence. "You come, but you give no reply; you look, you listen, but you make no sound. Answer me, you who know the future; tell me this secret!"

Still no response. Yet the air seemed full of dense, magnetic life, of muffled heart-beats, of voiceless, un-responsive, uncommunicative forms that he could almost touch.

For perhaps the first time in his life the war-chief found himself set at naught. His form grew erect; his eyes gleamed with the terrible wrath which the tribes dreaded as they dreaded the wrath of the Great Spirit.

" *C* OME *back! Come back!* "

"Do you mock Multnomah? Am I not war-chief of the Willamettes? Though you dwell in shadow and your bodies are dust, you are Willamettes, and I am still your chief. Give up your secret! If the Great Spirit has sealed your lips so that you cannot speak, give me a sign that will tell me. Answer by word or sign; I say it, — I, Multnomah, your chief and master."

Silence again. The roar of the volcano had ceased; and an ominous stillness brooded over Nature, as if all things held their breath, anticipating some mighty and imminent catastrophe. Multnomah's hands were clinched, and his strong face had on it now a fierceness of command that no eye had ever seen before. His indomitable will reached out to lay hold of those unseen presences and compel them to reply.

A moment of strained, commanding expectation : then the answer came ; the sign was given. The earth shook beneath him till he staggered, almost fell ; the hut creaked and swayed like a storm-driven wreck ; and through the crevices on the side toward Mount Hood came a blinding burst of flame. Down from the great gap in the Cascade Range through which flows the Columbia rolled the far-off thundering crash which had so startled Cecil and appalled the tribes. Then, tenfold louder than before, came again the roar of the volcano.

Too well Multnomah knew what had gone down in that crash ; too well did he read the sign that had been given. For a moment it seemed as if all the strength of his heart had broken with that which had fallen ; then the proud dignity of his character reasserted itself, even in the face of doom.

" It has come at last, as the wise men of old said it would. The end is at hand ; the Willamettes pass like a shadow from the earth. The Great Spirit has forsaken us, our *tomanowos* has failed us. But my own heart fails me not, and my own arm is strong. Like a war-chief will I meet that which is to come. Multnomah falls, but he falls as the Bridge has fallen, with a crash that will shake the earth, with a ruin that shall crush all beneath him even as he goes down."

Turning away, his eyes fell on the body of his wife as he passed toward the door. Aroused and desperate as he was, he stopped an instant and looked down at her with a long, lingering look, a look that seemed to say, " I shall meet you ere many suns. Death and ruin but give you back to me the sooner. There will be nothing between us then ; I shall understand you at last."

Then he drew his robe close around him, and went out into the night.

BOOK V.

THE SHADOW OF THE END.

CHAPTER I.

THE HAND OF THE GREAT SPIRIT.

" We view as one who hath an evil sight,"
He answered, " plainly objects far remote."
                              CAREY: *Dante.*

THE night came to an end at last, — a night not
soon forgotten by the Oregon Indians, and
destined to be remembered in tale and *tomanowos*
lore long after that generation had passed away.
The sky was thick with clouds; the atmosphere was
heavy with smoke, which, dense and low-hanging in
the still weather, shut out the entire horizon. The
volcano was invisible in the smoky air, but its low
mutterings came to them from time to time.

The chiefs met early in the grove of council.
Multnomah's countenance told nothing of the night
before, but almost all the rest showed something yet
of superstitious fear. Mishlah's face was haggard,
his air startled and uneasy, like that of some forest
animal that had been terribly frightened; and even
Snoqualmie looked worn. But the greatest change of
all was in Tohomish. His face was as ghastly as that

of a corpse, and he came into the council walking in a dull lifeless way, as if hardly aware of what he was doing. Those nearest to him shrank away, whispering to one another that the seer looked like a dead man.

Cecil came last. The severe mental conflict of the past night had told almost fatally on a frame already worn out by years of toil and sickness. His cheek was pale, his eye hollow, his step slow and faltering, like one whose flame of life is burning very low. The pain at his heart, always worse in times of exhaustion, was sharp and piercing.

He looked agitated and restless; he had tried hard to give Wallulah into the hands of God and feel that she was safe, but he could not. For himself he had no thought; but his whole soul was wrung with pain for her. By virtue of his own keen sympathies, he anticipated and felt all that the years had in store for her, — the loneliness, the heartache, the trying to care for one she loathed; until he shrank from her desolate and hopeless future as if it had been his own. All his soul went out to her in yearning tenderness, in passionate desire to shield her and to take away her burden.

But his resolution never wavered. Below the ebb and flow of feeling, the decision to make their separation final was as unchanging as granite. He could not bear to look upon her face again; he could not bear to see her wedded to Snoqualmie. He intended to make one last appeal to the Indians this morning to accept the gospel of peace; then he would leave the council before Wallulah was brought to it. So he sat there now, waiting for the " talk " to begin.

The bands gathered around the grove were smaller than usual. Many had fled from the valley at dawn to escape from the dreaded vicinity of the smoking mountains ; many hundreds remained, but they were awed and frightened. No war could have appalled them as they were appalled by the shaking of the solid earth under their feet. All the abject superstition of their natures was roused. They looked like men who felt themselves caught in the grasp of some supernatural power.

Multnomah opened the council by saying that two runners had arrived with news that morning ; the one from the sea-coast, the other from up the Columbia. They would come before the council and tell the news they had brought.

The runner from the upper Columbia spoke first. He had come thirty miles since dawn. He seemed unnerved and fearful, like one about to announce some unheard-of calamity. The most stoical bent forward eagerly to hear.

" The Great Spirit has shaken the earth, and the Bridge of the Gods has fallen ! "

There was the silence of amazement ; then through the tribes passed in many tongues the wild and wondering murmur, " The Bridge of the Gods has fallen ! The Bridge of the Gods has fallen ! " With it, too, went the recollection of the ancient prophecy that when the Bridge fell the power of the Willamettes would also fall. Now the Bridge was broken, and the dominion of the Willamettes was broken forever with it. At another time the slumbering jealousy of the tribes would have burst forth in terrific vengeance on the doomed race. But they were dejected and afraid. In the fall of the Bridge they saw the hand of the Great Spirit, a visitation of God. And so Willamette and tributary alike heard the news with fear and apprehension. Only Multnomah, who knew the message before it was spoken, listened with his wonted composure.

"It is well," he said, with more than Indian duplicity; "the daughter of Multnomah is to become the wife of Snoqualmie the Cayuse, and the new line that commences with their children will give new chiefs to head the confederacy of the Wauna. The old gives way to the new. That is the sign that the Great Spirit gives in the fall of the Bridge. Think you it means that the war-strength is gone from us, that we shall no longer prevail in battle? No, no! who thinks it?"

The proud old sachem rose to his feet; his giant form towered over the multitude, and every eye fell before the haughty and scornful glance that swept council and audience like a challenge to battle.

"Is there a chief here that thinks it? Let him step out, let him grapple with Multnomah in the death-grapple, and see. Is there a tribe that thinks it? We reach out our arms to them; we are ready. Let them meet us in battle now, to-day, and know if our hearts have become the hearts of women. Will you come? We will give you dark and bloody proof that our tomahawks are still sharp and our arms are strong."

He stood with outstretched arms, from which the robe of fur had fallen back. A thrill of dread went through the assembly at the grim defiance; then Snoqualmie spoke.

" The heart of all the tribes is as the heart of Multnomah. Let there be peace."

The chief resumed his seat. His force of will had wrung one last victory from fate itself. Instantly, and with consummate address, Multnomah preoccupied the attention of the council before anything could be said or done to impair the effect of his challenge. He bade the other runner, the one from the sea-coast, deliver his message.

It was, in effect, this : —

A large canoe, with great white wings like a bird, had come gliding over the waters to the coast near the mouth of the Wauna. Whence it came no one could tell ; but its crew were pale of skin like the great white *shaman* there in the council, and seemed of his race. Some of them came ashore in a small canoe to trade with the Indians, but trouble rose between them and there was a battle. The strangers slew many Indians with their magic, darting fire at them from long black tubes. Then they escaped to the great canoe, which spread its wings and passed away from sight into the sea. Many of the Indians were killed, but none of the pale-faced intruders. Now the band who had suffered demanded that the white man of whom they had heard — the white chief at the council — be put to death to pay the blood-debt.

All eyes turned on Cecil, and he felt that his hour was come. Weak, exhausted in body and mind, wearied almost to death, a sudden and awful peril was on him. For a moment his heart sank, his brain grew dizzy. How *could* he meet this emergency? All his soul went out to God with a dumb prayer for help, with an overwhelming sense of weakness. Then he heard Multnomah speaking to him in cold, hard tones.

"The white man has heard the words of the runner. What has he to say why his life should not pay the blood-debt?"

Cecil rose to his feet. With one last effort he put Wallulah, himself, his mission, into the hands of God; with one last effort he forced himself to speak.

Men of nervous temperament, like Cecil, can bring out of an exhausted body an energy, an outburst of final and intense effort, of which those of stronger physique do not seem capable. But it drains the remaining vital forces, and the reaction is terrible. Was it this flaming-up of the almost burned-out embers of life that animated Cecil now? Or was it the Divine Strength coming to him in answer to prayer? Be this as it may, when he opened his lips to speak, all the power of his consecration came back; physical weakness and mental anxiety left him; he felt that Wallulah was safe in the arms of the Infinite Compassion; he felt his love for the Indians, his deep yearning to help them, to bring them to God, rekindling within him; and never had he been more grandly the Apostle to the Indians than now.

In passionate tenderness, in burning appeal, in living force and power of delivery, it was the supreme effort of his life. He did not plead for himself; he ignored, put aside, forgot his own personal danger; but he set before his hearers the wickedness of their own system of retaliation and revenge; he showed them how it overshadowed their lives and lay like a deadening weight on their better natures. The horror, the cruelty, the brute animalism of the blood-thirst, the war-lust, was set over against the love and forgiveness to which the Great Spirit called them.

The hearts of the Indians were shaken within them. The barbarism which was the outcome of centuries of strife and revenge, the dark and cumulative growth of ages, was stirred to its core by the strong and tender eloquence of this one man. As he spoke, there came to all those swarthy listeners, in dim beauty, a glimpse of a better life; there came to them a moment's fleeting revelation of something above their own vindictiveness and ferocity. That vague longing, that indefinable wistfulness which he had so often seen on the faces of his savage audiences was on nearly every face when he closed.

As he took his seat, the tide of inspiration went from him, and a deadly faintness came over him. It seemed as if in that awful reaction the last spark of vitality was dying out; but somehow, through it all, he felt at peace with God and man. A great quiet was upon him; he was anxious for nothing, he cared for nothing, he simply rested as on the living presence of the Father.

Upon the sweet and lingering spell of his closing words came Multnomah's tones in stern contrast.

"What is the word of the council? Shall the white man live or die?"

Snoqualmie was on his feet in an instant.

"Blood for blood. Let the white man die at the torture-stake."

One by one the chiefs gave their voice for death. Shaken for but a moment, the ancient inherited barbarism which was their very life reasserted itself, and

they could decide no other way. One, two, three of
the sachems gave no answer, but sat in silence. They
were men whose hearts had been touched before by
Cecil, and who were already desiring the better life.
They could not condemn their teacher.

At length it came to Tohomish. He arose. His
face, always repulsive, was pallid now in the extreme.
The swathed corpses on *mimaluse* island looked not
more sunken and ghastly.

He essayed to speak ; thrice the words faltered on
his lips ; and when at last he spoke, it was in a weary,
lifeless way. His tones startled the audience like an
electric shock. The marvellous power and sweetness
were gone from his voice ; its accents were discordant,
uncertain. Could the death's head before them be
that of Tohomish? Could those harsh and broken
tones be those of the Pine Voice? He seemed like
a man whose animal life still survived, but whose soul
was dead.

What he said at first had no relation to the matter
before the council. Every Indian had his *tomanowos* appointed him by the Great Spirit from his birth,
and that *tomanowos* was the strength of his life. Its
influence grew with his growth ; the roots of his being
were fed in it ; it imparted its characteristics to him.
But the name and nature of his *tomanowos* was the
one secret that must go with him to the grave. If it
was told, the charm was lost and the *tomanowos* deserted him.

Tohomish's *tomanowos* was the Bridge and the fore-
knowledge of its fall : a black secret that had darkened
his whole life, and imparted the strange and mournful
mystery to his eloquence. Now that the Bridge was

fallen, the strength was gone from Tohomish's heart, the music from his words.

"Tohomish has no voice now," he continued ; " he is as one dead. He desires to say only this, then his words shall be heard no more among men. The fall of the Bridge is a sign that not only the Willa- mettes but all the tribes of the Wauna shall fall and pass away. Another people shall take our place, another race shall reign in our stead, and the Indian shall be forgotten, or remembered only as a dim memory of the past.

" And who are they who bring us our doom? Look on the face of the white wanderer there ; listen to the story of your brethren slain at the sea-coast by the white men in the canoe, and you will know. They come ; they that are stronger, and push us out into the dark. The white wanderer talks of peace ; but the Great Spirit has put death between the Indian and the white man, and where he has put death there can be no peace.

" Slay the white man as the white race will slay your children in the time that is to come. Peace? love? There can be only war and hate. Striking back blow for blow like a wounded rattlesnake, shall the red man pass ; and when the bones of the last Indian of the Wauna lie bleaching on the prairie far from the *mimaluse* island of his fathers, then there will be peace.

" Tohomish has spoken ; his words are ended, and ended forever."

The harsh, disjointed tones ceased. All eyes fell again on Cecil, the representative of the race by which the Willamettes were doomed. The wrath of all those hundreds, the vengeance of all those gathered tribes of the Wauna, the hatred of the whole people he had come to save, seemed to rise up and fall upon him, the frail invalid with the sharp pain throbbing at his heart.

But that strange peace was on him still, and his eyes, dilated and brilliant in the extremity of physical pain, met those lowering brows with a look of exceeding pity.

Multnomah rose to pronounce sentence. For him there could be but one decision, and he gave it, — the clinched hand, the downward gesture, that said, "There is death between us. We will slay as we shall be slain."

Cecil was on his feet, though it seemed as if he must fall within the moment. He fought down the pain that pierced his heart like a knife ; he gathered the last resources of an exhausted frame for one more effort. The executioners sprang forward with the covering for his eyes that was to shut out the light forever. His glance, his gesture held them back ; they paused irresolutely, even in the presence of Multnomah ; weak as Cecil was, he was the great white *tomanowos* still, and they dared not touch him. There was a pause, an intense silence.

" I gave up all to come and tell you of God, and you have condemned me to die at the torture-stake," said the soft, low voice, sending through their stern hearts its thrill and pathos for the last time. " But you shall not bring this blood-stain upon your souls. The hand of the Great Spirit is on me ; he takes me to himself. Remember — what I have said. The Great Spirit loves you. Pray — forgive — be at peace. Remember —"

The quiver of agonizing pain disturbed the gentleness of his look; he reeled, and sank to the ground. For a moment the slight form shuddered convulsively and the hands were clinched; then the struggle ceased and a wonderful brightness shone upon his face. His lips murmured something in his own tongue, something into which came the name of Wallulah and the name of God. Then his eyes grew dim and he lay very still. Only the expression of perfect peace still rested on the face. Sachems and warriors gazed in awe upon the beauty, grand in death, of the one whom the Great Spirit had taken from them. Perhaps the iron heart of the war-chief was the only one that did not feel remorse and self-reproach.

Ere the silence was broken, an old Indian woman came forward from the crowd into the circle of chiefs. She looked neither to the right nor to the left, but advanced among the warrior-sachems, into whose presence no woman had dared intrude herself, and bent over the dead. She lifted the wasted body in her arms and bore it away, with shut lips and downcast eyes, asking no permission, saying no word. The charm that had been around the white *shaman* in life seemed to invest her with its power; for grim chieftains made way, the crowd opened to let her pass, and even Multnomah looked on in silence.

That afternoon, a little band of Indians were assembled in Cecil's lodge. Some of them were already converts; some were only awakened and impressed; but all were men who loved him.

They were gathered, men of huge frame, around a dead body that lay upon a cougar skin. Their faces were sad, their manner was solemn. In the corner sat an aged squaw, her face resting in her hands, her long gray hair falling dishevelled about her shoulders. In that heart-broken attitude she had sat ever since bringing Cecil to the hut. She did not weep or sob, but sat motionless, in stoical, dumb despair.

Around the dead the Indians stood or sat in silence, each waiting for the other to say what was in the hearts of all. At length the Shoshone renegade, who had so loved Cecil, spoke.

"Our white brother is gone from us, but the Great Spirit lives and dies not. Let us turn from blood and sin and walk in the way our brother showed us. He said, 'Remember;' and shall we forget? I choose now, while he can hear me, before he is laid in the cold ground. I put away from me the old heart of hate and revenge. I ask the Great Spirit to give me the new heart of love and peace. I have chosen."

One by one each told his resolve, the swarthy faces lighting up, the stern lips saying unwonted words of love. Dim and misty, the dawn had come to them; reaching out in the dark, they had got hold of the hand of God and felt that he was a Father. One would have said that their dead teacher lying there heard their vows, so calm and full of peace was the white still face.

That night the first beams of the rising moon fell on a new-made grave under the cottonwoods, not far from the bank of the river. Beneath it, silent in the last sleep, lay the student whose graceful presence had been the pride of far-off Magdalen, the pastor whose memory still lingered in New England, the evangelist whose burning words had thrilled the tribes of the wilderness like the words of some prophet of old.

Beside the grave crouched the old Indian woman, alone and forsaken in her despair, — the one mourner out of all for whom his life had been given.

No, not the only one ; for a tall warrior enters the grove ; the Shoshone renegade bends over her and touches her gently on the shoulder.

" Come," he says kindly, " our horses are saddled ; we take the trail up the Wauna to-night, I and my friends. We will fly from this fated valley ere the wrath of the Great Spirit falls upon it. Beyond the mountains I will seek a new home with the Spokanes or the Okanogans. Come ; my home shall be your home, because you cared for him that is gone."

She shook her head and pointed to the grave.

" My heart is there ; my life is buried with him. I cannot go."

Again he urged her.

" No, no," she replied, with Indian stubbornness ; " I cannot leave him. Was I not like his mother? How can I go and leave him for others? The roots of the old tree grow not in new soil. If it is pulled up it dies."

" Come with me," said the savage, with a gentleness born of his new faith. " Be *my* mother. We will talk of him ; you shall tell me of him and his God. Come, the horses wait."

Again she shook her head ; then fell forward on the grave, her arms thrown out, as if to clasp it in her embrace. He tried to lift her ; her head fell back, and she lay relaxed and motionless in his arms.

Another grave was made by Cecil's ; and the little band rode through the mountain pass that night, toward the country of the Okanogans, without her.

And that same night, an English exploring vessel far out at sea sailed southward, leaving behind the unknown shores of Oregon, — her crew never dreaming how near they had been to finding the lost wanderer, Cecil Grey.

CHAPTER II.

THE MARRIAGE AND THE BREAKING UP.

Remembering love and all the dead delight,
And all that time was sweet with for a space.
SWINBURNE.

AFTER Cecil had been borne from the council-grove, the Indians, rousing themselves from the spell of the strange scene they had just witnessed, looked around for Tohomish the seer. He was gone. No one could remember seeing him go, yet he was missing from his accustomed place, and never was he seen or heard of more. Upon his fate, lost in the common ruin that engulfed his race, the legend casts no ray of light. It is certain that the fall of the Bridge, with which his life was interwoven, had a disastrous effect upon him, and as he said, that the strength of his life was broken. It is probable that the orator-seer, feeling within himself that his power was gone, crept away into the forest to die. Perhaps, had they searched for him, they would have found him lying lifeless upon the leaves in some dense thicket or at the foot of some lonely crag.

Whatever his fate, the Indians never looked upon his face again.

Multnomah made no comment on the death of Cecil, or on the prophecy of Tohomish, so much at variance with his own interpretation of the fall of the

Bridge. Whatever he had to say was evidently held in reserve for the closing talk with which he would soon dismiss the council.

"You shall see Multnomah's daughter given to Snoqualmie, and then Multnomah will open his hand and make you rich."

So said the war-chief; and a runner was dispatched with a summons to Wallulah. In a little while a band of Indian girls was seen approaching the grove. Surrounded by the maidens, as if they were a guard of honor, came Wallulah, all unconscious of the tragedy that had just been enacted.

Among the chiefs they passed, and stopped before Multnomah. As they paused, Wallulah looked around for Cecil in one quick glance ; then, not seeing him, she cast down her eyes despondingly. Multnomah rose and beckoned Snoqualmie to him. He came forward and stood beside the war-chief. The Indian girls stepped back a little, in involuntary awe of the two great sachems, and left Wallulah standing alone before them.

Her face wore a patient look, as of one who is very worn and weary, tired of the burdens of life, yet going forward without hope, without thought even, to other and still heavier burdens. She was clad in a soft oriental fabric ; her hair fell in luxuriant tresses upon her shoulders ; her flute hung at her belt by a slender chain of gold.

There was something unspeakably sad and heartbroken in her appearance, as she stood there, a listless, dejected figure, before those two grim warriors, awaiting her doom.

Multnomah took her hand ; the fingers of the other

were clasped around her beloved flute, pressing it
closely, as if seeking help from its mute companion-
ship. The chief gave her hand into Snoqualmie's; a
shudder passed through her as she felt his touch, and
she trembled from head to foot; then she controlled
herself by a strong effort. Snoqualmie's fierce black
eyes searched her face, as if looking through and
through her, and she flushed faintly under their
penetrating gaze.

"She is yours," said the war-chief. "Be kind to
her, for though she is your wife she is the daughter
of Multnomah." So much did the Indian say for
love of his child, wondering at her strange, sad look,
and feeling vaguely that she was unhappy. She tried
to withdraw her fingers from Snoqualmie's clasp the
moment her father was done speaking. He held
them tightly, however, and bending over her, spoke
in a low tone.

"My band starts for home at mid-day. Be ready
to go when I send for you."

She looked up with startled, piteous eyes.

"To-day?" she asked in a choked voice.

"To-day," came the abrupt reply; too low for the
others to hear, yet harsh enough to sting her through
and through. "Do you think Snoqualmie goes back
to his *illahee* and leaves his woman behind?"

Her spirit kindled in resentment. Never had the
chief's daughter been spoken to so harshly; then all
at once it came to her that he *knew*, — that he must
have followed Cecil and witnessed one of their last
interviews. Jealous, revengeful, the Indian was her
master now. She grew pale to the lips. He released
her hand, and she shrank away from him, and left the

council with her maidens. No one had heard the
few half-whispered words that passed between them,
but those who stood nearest noticed the deadly pallor
that came over her face while Snoqualmie was speaking. Multnomah saw it, and Snoqualmie caught from
him a glance that chilled even his haughty nature, —
a glance that said, " Beware; she is the war-chief's
daughter."

But even if he had known all, Multnomah would
have sacrificed her. His plans must be carried out,
even though her heart be crushed.

Now followed the *potlatch*, — the giving of gifts.
At a signal from the war-chief, his slaves appeared,
laden with presents. Large heaps of rich furs and
skins were laid on the ground near the chiefs. The
finest of bows and arrows, with gaily decorated quivers
and store of bow-strings, were brought. Untold treasure of *hiagua* shells, money as well as ornament to
the Oregon Indians, was poured out upon the ground,
and lay glistening in the sun in bright-colored masses.
To the Indians they represented vast and splendid
wealth. Multnomah was the richest of all the Indians of the Wauna; and the gifts displayed were the
spoil of many wars, treasures garnered during forty
years of sovereignty.

And now they were all given away. The chief
kept back nothing, except some cases of oriental
fabrics that had been saved from the wreck when
Wallulah's mother was cast upon the shore. Well
would it have been for him and his race had they
been given too; for, little as they dreamed it, the
fate of the Willamettes lay sealed up in those unopened cases of silk and damask.

Again and again the slaves of Multnomah added their burdens to the heaps, and went back for more, till a murmur of wonder rose among the crowd. His riches seemed exhaustless. At length, however, all was brought. The chief stood up, and, opening his hands to them in the Indian gesture for giving, said, —

"There is all that was Multnomah's; it is yours; your hands are full now and mine are empty."

The chiefs and warriors rose up gravely and went among the heaps of treasure; each selecting from furs and skins, arms and *hiagua* shells, that which he desired. There was no unseemly haste or snatching; a quiet decorum prevailed among them. The women and children were excluded from sharing in these gifts, but provisions — dried meats and berries, and bread of *camas* or Wappatto root — were thrown among them on the outskirts of the crowd where they were gathered. And unlike the men, they scrambled for it like hungry animals; save where here and there the wife or daughter of a chief stood looking disdainfully on the food and those who snatched at it.

Such giving of gifts, or *potlatches*, are still known among the Indians. On Puget Sound and the Okanogan, one occasionally hears of some rich Indian making a great *potlatch*, — giving away all his possessions, and gaining nothing but a reputation for disdain of wealth, a reputation which only Indian stoicism would crave. Multnomah's object was not that so much as to make, before the dispersal of the tribes, a last and most favorable impression.

When the presents were all divided, the chiefs resumed their places to hear the last speech of Multnomah, — the speech that closed the council.

It was a masterpiece of dignity, subtility, and command. The prophecy of Tohomish was evaded, the fall of the Bridge wrested into an omen propitious to the Willamettes; and at last his hearers found themselves believing as he wished them to believe, without knowing how or why, so strongly did the overmastering personality of Multnomah penetrate and sway their lesser natures. He particularly dwelt on the idea that they were all knit together now and were as one race. Yet through the smooth words ran a latent threat, a covert warning of the result of any revolt against his authority based on what plotting dreamers might say of the fall of the Bridge, — a half-expressed menace, like the gleam of a sword half drawn from the scabbard. And he closed by announcing that ere another spring the young men of all the tribes would go on the war-path against the Shoshones and come back loaded with spoil. And so, kindling the hatred of the chiefs against the common enemy, Multnomah closed the great council.

In a little while the camp was all astir with preparation for departure. Lodges were being taken down, the mats that covered them rolled up and packed on the backs of horses; all was bustle and tumult. Troop after troop crossed the river and took the trail toward the upper Columbia.

But when the bands passed from under the personal influence of Multnomah, they talked of the ominous things that had just happened; they said to each other that the Great Spirit had forsaken the Willamettes, and that when they came into the valley again it would be to plunder and to slay. Multnomah had stayed the tide but for a moment. The fall of the ancient *tomanowos* of the Willamettes had a tremendous significance to the restless tributaries, and already the confederacy of the Wauna was crumbling like a rope of sand. Those tribes would meet no more in peace on the island of council.

CHAPTER III.

AT THE CASCADES.

Wails on the wind, fades out the sunset quite,
And in my heart and on the earth is night.
PHILIP BOURKE MARSTON.

THE main body of Snoqualmie's followers crossed to the north bank of the Columbia and took the trail leading up the river toward the inland prairies. But Snoqualmie and Wallulah went by canoe as far as the now ruined Bridge of the Gods. There were three canoes in their train. Snoqualmie and Wallulah occupied the first; the other two were laden with the rich things that had once made her lodge so beautiful. It stood all bare and deserted now, the splendor stripped from its rough bark walls even as love and hope had been reft from the heart of its mistress. Tapestries, divans, carpets, mirrors, were heaped in the canoes like spoil torn from the enemy.

The farewell between Wallulah and her father had been sorrowful. It was remembered afterward, by those who were witnesses of it, that the war-chief had shown a tenderness unusual with him, that he had seemed reluctant to part with his daughter, and that she had clung to him, pale and tearful, as if he were her last hope on earth.

When Snoqualmie took her hand to lead her away, she shuddered, withdrew her fingers from his clasp, and walked alone to the canoe. He entered after her; the canoe-men dipped their paddles into the water, and the vessel glided away from the island.

She sat reclining on a heap of furs, her elbows sunk in them, her cheek resting on her hand, her eyes turned back toward her island home. Between it and her the expanse of waters grew ever broader, and the trail the canoe left behind it sparkled in a thousand silvery ripples. The island, with its green prairies and its stately woods, receded fast. She felt as she looked back as if everything was slipping away from her. Lonely as her life had been before Cecil came into it, she had still had her music and her beautiful rooms in the bark lodge; and they seemed infinitely sweet and precious now as she recalled them. Oh, if she could only have them back again! And those interviews with Cecil. How love and grief shook the little figure as she thought! How loathingly she shrunk from the presence of the barbarian at her side! And all the time the island receded farther and farther in the distance, and the canoe glided forward like a merciless fate bearing her on and on toward the savagery of the inland desert.

Snoqualmie sat watching her with glittering, triumphant eyes. To him she was no more than some lovely animal of which he had become the owner; and ownership of course brought with it the right to tantalize and to torture. A malicious smile crossed his lips as he saw how sorrowfully her gaze rested on her old home.

" Look forward," he said, " not back ; look forward to your life with Snoqualmie and to the lodge that awaits you in the land of the Cayuses."

She started, and her face flushed painfully; then without looking at him she replied, —

"Wallulah loves her home, and leaving it saddens her."

A sparkle of vindictive delight came into his eyes.

"Do the women of the Willamette feel sad when they go to live with their husbands? It is not so with the Cayuse women. They are glad; *they* care for the one they belong to. They love to sit in the sun at the door of the wigwam and say to the other women, 'My man is brave; he leads the war party; he has many scalps at his belt. Who is brave like my man?'"

Wallulah shuddered. He saw it, and the sparkle of malice in his eyes flashed into sudden anger.

"Does the young squaw tremble at these things? Then she must get used to them. She must learn to bring wood and water for Snoqualmie's lodge, too. She must learn to wait on him as an Indian's wife ought. The old wrinkled squaws, who are good for nothing but to be beasts of burden, shall teach her."

There came before her a picture of the ancient withered hags, the burden-bearers, the human vampires of the Indian camps, the vile in word and deed, the first to cry for the blood of captives, the most eager to give taunts and blows to the helpless; were they to be her associates, her teachers? Involuntarily she lifted her hand, as if to push from her a future so dreadful.

"Wallulah will bring the wood and the water. Wallulah will work. The old women need not teach her."

"That is well. But one thing more you must

learn ; and that is to hold up your head and not look like a drooping captive. Smile, laugh, be gay. Snoqualmie will have no clouded face, no bent head in his lodge."

She looked at him imploringly. The huge form, the swarthy face, seemed to dominate her, to crush her down with their barbarian strength and ferocity. She dropped her eyes again, and lay there on the furs like some frightened bird shrinking from the glance of a hawk.

" I will work ; I will bear burdens," she repeated, in a trembling tone. " But I cannot smile and laugh when my heart is heavy."

He watched her with a half angry, half malicious regard, a regard that seemed ruthlessly probing into every secret of her nature.

She knew somehow that he was aware of her love for Cecil, and she dreaded lest he should taunt her with it. Anything but that. He knew it, and held it back as his last and most cruel blow. Over his bronzed face flitted no expression of pity. She was to him like some delicate wounded creature of the forest, that it was a pleasure to torture. So he had often treated a maimed bird or fawn, — tantalizing it, delighted by its fluttering and its pain, till the lust of torture was gratified and the death-blow was given.

He sat regarding her with a sneering, malicious look for a little while ; then he said, —

" It is hard to smile on Snoqualmie ; but the white man whom you met in the wood, it was not so with him. It was easy to smile and look glad at him, but it is hard to do so for Snoqualmie."

Wallulah shrunk as if he had struck her a blow;
then she looked at him desperately, pleadingly.

"Do not say such cruel things. I will be a faithful wife to you. I will never see the white man
again."

The sneering malice in his eyes gave way to the
gleam of exultant anger.

"Faithful! You knew you were to be my woman
when you let him put his arms around you and say
soft things to you. Faithful! You would leave
Snoqualmie for him now, could it be so. But you
say well that you will never see him again."

She gazed at him in terror.

"What do you mean? Has anything happened to
him? Have they harmed him?"

Over the chief's face came the murderous expression that was there when he slew the Bannock warrior at the torture stake.

"Harmed him! Do you think that he could meet
you alone and say sweet things to you and caress
you, — you who were the same as my squaw, — and I
not harm him? He is dead; I slew him."

False though it was, in so far as Snoqualmie claimed
to have himself slain Cecil, it was thoroughly in keeping with Indian character. White captives were often
told, "I killed your brother," or, "This is your husband's scalp," when perhaps the person spoken of
was alive and well.

"Dead!"

He threw his tomahawk at her feet.

"His blood is on it. You are Snoqualmie's squaw;
wash it off."

Dead, dead, her lover was dead! That was all she

could grasp. Snoqualmie's insulting command passed unheeded. She sat looking at the Indian with bright, dazed eyes that saw nothing. All the world seemed blotted out.

"I tell you that he is dead, and I slew him. Are you asleep that you stare at me so? Awaken and do as I bid you; wash your lover's blood off my tomahawk."

At first she had been stunned by the terrible shock, and she could realize only that Cecil was dead. Now it came to her, dimly at first, then like a flash of fire, that Snoqualmie had slain him. All her spirit leaped up in uncontrollable hatred. For once, she was the war-chief's daughter. She drew her skirts away from the tomahawk in unutterable horror; her eyes blazed into Snoqualmie's a defiance and scorn before which his own sunk for the instant.

"You killed him! I hate you. I will never be your wife. You have thrown the tomahawk between us; it shall be between us forever. Murderer! You have killed the one I love. Yes, I loved him; and I hate you and will hate you till I die."

The passion in her voice thrilled even the canoe-men, and their paddle strokes fell confusedly for an instant, though they did not understand; for both Wallulah and Snoqualmie had spoken in the royal tongue of the Willamettes. He sat abashed for an instant, taken utterly by surprise.

Then the wild impulse of defiance passed, and the awful sense of bereavement came back like the falling of darkness over a sinking flame. Cecil was gone from her, gone for all time. The world seemed unreal, empty. She sunk among the furs like one

stricken down. Snoqualmie, recovering from his momentary rebuff, heaped bitter epithets and scornful
words upon her; but she neither saw nor heard,
and lay with wide, bright, staring eyes. Her seeming indifference maddened him still more, and he
hurled at her the fiercest abuse. She looked at him
vaguely. He saw that she did not even know what
he was saying, and relapsed into sullen silence. She
lay mute and still, with a strained expression of pain
in her eyes. The canoe sped swiftly on.

One desolating thought repeated itself again and
again, — the thought of hopeless and irreparable loss.
By it past and present were blotted out. By and
by, when she awoke from the stupor of despair and
realized her future, destined to be passed with the
murderer of her lover, what then? But now she was
stunned with the shock of a grief that was mercy
compared with the awakening that must come.

They were in the heart of the Cascade Mountains,
and a low deep roar began to reach their ears, rousing
and startling all but Wallulah. It was the sound of
the cascades, of the new cataract formed by the fall
of the Great Bridge. Rounding a bend in the river
they came in sight of it. The mighty arch, the long
low mountain of stone, had fallen in, damming up the
waters of the Columbia, which were pouring over the
sunken mass in an ever-increasing volume. Above,
the river, raised by the enormous dam, had spread
out like a lake, almost submerging the trees that still
stood along the former bank. Below the new falls
the river was comparatively shallow, its rocky bed
half exposed by the sudden stoppage of the waters.

The Indians gazed with superstitious awe on the

vast barrier over which the white and foaming waters were pouring. The unwonted roar of the falls, a roar that seemed to increase every moment as the swelling waters rushed over the rocks; the sight of the wreck of the mysterious bridge, foreshadowing the direst calamities, — all this awed the wild children of the desert. They approached the falls slowly and cautiously.

A brief command from Snoqualmie, and they landed on the northern side of the river, not far from the foot of the falls. There they must disembark, and the canoes be carried around the falls on the shoulders of Indians and launched above.

The roar of the Cascades roused Wallulah from her stupor. She stepped ashore and looked in dazed wonder on the strange new world around her. Snoqualmie told her briefly that she must walk up the bank to the place where the canoe was to be launched again above the falls. She listened mutely, and started to go. But the way was steep and rocky; the bank was strewn with the débris of the ruined bridge; and she was unused to such exertion. Snoqualmie saw her stumble and almost fall. It moved him to a sudden and unwonted pity, and he sprang forward to help her. She pushed his hand from her as if it had been the touch of a serpent, and went on alone. His eyes flashed: for all this the reckoning should come, and soon; woe unto her when it came.

The rough rocks bruised her delicately shod feet, the steep ascent took away her breath. Again and again she felt as if she must fall; but the bitter scorn and loathing that Snoqualmie's touch had kindled gave her strength, and at last she completed the ascent.

Above the falls and close to them, she sat down upon a rock ; a slight, drooping figure, whose dejected pose told of a broken heart.

Before her, almost at her feet, the pent-up river was widened to a vast flood. Here and there a half-submerged pine lifted its crown above it ; the surface was ruffled by the wind, and white-crested waves were rolling among the green tree-tops. She looked with indifference upon the scene. She had not heard that the Bridge had fallen, and was, of course, ignorant of these new cascades ; and they did not impress her as being strange.

Her whole life was broken up ; all the world appeared shattered by the blow that had fallen on her, and nothing could startle her now. She felt dimly that some stupendous catastrophe had taken place ; yet it did not appear unnatural. A strange sense of unreality possessed her ; everything seemed an illusion, as if she were a shadow in a land of shadows. The thought came to her that she was dead, and that her spirit was passing over the dim ghost trail to the shadow-land. She tried to shake off the fancy, but all was so vague and dreamlike that she hardly knew where or what she was ; yet over it all brooded the consciousness of dull, heavy, torturing pain, like the dumb agony that comes to us in fevered sleep, burdening our dreams with a black oppressing weight of horror.

Her hand, hanging listlessly at her side, touched her flute, which was still suspended from her belt by the golden chain. She raised it to her lips, but only a faint inharmonious note came from it. The music seemed gone from the flute, as hope was gone from her heart. To her overwrought nerves, it was the last omen of all. The flute dropped from her fingers; she covered her face with her hands, and the hot tears coursed slowly down her cheeks.

Some one spoke to her, not ungently, and she looked up. One of the canoe-men stood beside her. He pointed to the canoe, now launched near by. Snoqualmie was still below, at the foot of the falls, superintending the removal of the other.

Slowly and wearily she entered the waiting canoe and resumed her seat. The Indian paddlers took their places. They told her that the chief Snoqualmie had bidden them take her on without him. He would follow in the other canoe. It was a relief to be free from his presence, if only for a little while; and the sadness on her face lightened for a moment when they told her.

A few quick paddle-strokes, and the boat shot out into the current above the cascades and then glided forward. No, *not* forward. The canoe-men, unfamiliar with the new cataract, had launched their vessel too close to the falls; and the mighty current was drawing it back. A cry of horror burst from their lips as they realized their danger, and their paddles were dashed into the water with frenzied violence. The canoe hung quivering through all its slender length between the desperate strokes that impelled it forward and the tremendous suction that drew it down. Had they been closer to the bank, they might have saved themselves; but they were too far out in the current. They felt the canoe slipping back in spite of their frantic efforts, slowly at first, then more swiftly; and they knew there was no hope.

.The paddles fell from their hands. One boatman leaped from the canoe with the desperate idea of swimming ashore, but the current instantly swept him under and out of sight; the other sat motionless in his place, awaiting the end with Indian stolidity.

The canoe was swept like a leaf to the verge of the fall and downward into a gulf of mist and spray. As it trembled on the edge of the cataract, and its horrors opened beneath her, Wallulah realized her doom for the first time; and in the moment she realized it, it was upon her. There was a quick terror, a dreamlike glimpse of white plunging waters, a deafening roar, a sudden terrible shock as the canoe was splintered on the rocks at the foot of the fall; then all things were swallowed up in blackness, a blackness that was death.

Below the falls, strong swimmers, leaping into the water, brought the dead to land. Beneath a pine-tree that grew close by the great Columbia trail and not far from the falls, the bodies were laid. The daughter of Multnomah lay in rude state upon a fawn-skin; while at her feet were extended the brawny forms of the two canoe-men who had died with her, and who, according to Indian mythology, were to be her slaves in the Land of the Hereafter. Her face was very lovely, but its mournfulness remained. Her flute, broken in the shock that had killed her, was still attached to her belt. The Indians had placed her hand at her side, resting upon the flute; and they noticed in superstitious wonder that the cold fingers seemed to half close around it, as if they would clasp it lovingly, even in death. Indian women knelt beside her, fanning her face with fragrant boughs of pine. Troop after troop, returning over the trail to their homes, stopped to hear the tale, and to gaze at the dead face that was so wonderfully beautiful yet so sad.

All day long the bands gathered; each stopping, none passing indifferently by. At length, when evening came and the shadow of the wood fell long and cool, the burials began. A shallow grave was scooped at Wallulah's feet for the bodies of the two canoemen. Then chiefs — for they only might bury Multnomah's daughter — entombed her in a cairn; being Upper Columbia Indians, they buried her, after the manner of their people, under a heap of stone. Rocks and bowlders were built around and over her body, yet without touching it, until the sad dead face was shut out from view. And still the stones were piled above her; higher and higher rose the great rock-heap, till a mighty cairn marked the last resting-place of Wallulah. And all the time the women lifted the death-wail, and Snoqualmie stood looking on with folded arms and sullen baffled brow. At length the work was done. The wail ceased; the gathering broke up, and the sachems and their bands rode away, Snoqualmie and his troop departing with them.

Only the roar of the cascades broke the silence, as night fell on the wild forest and the lonely river. The pine-tree beside the trail swayed its branches in the wind with a low soft murmur, as if lulling the sorrow-worn sleeper beneath it into still deeper repose. And she lay very still in the great cairn, — the sweet and beautiful dead, — with the grim warriors stretched at her feet, stern guardians of a slumber never to be broken.

CHAPTER IV.

MULTNOMAH'S DEATH-CANOE.

> Gazing alone
> To him are wild shadows shown,
> Deep under deep unknown.
>
> DANTE ROSSETTI.

IF Multnomah was grieved at his daughter's death, if his heart sunk at the unforeseen and terrible blow that left his empire without an heir and withered all his hopes, no one knew it; no eye beheld his woe. Silent he had ever been, and he was silent to the last. The grand, strong face only grew grander, stronger, as the shadows darkened around him; the unconquerable will only grew the fiercer and the more unflinching. But ere the moon that shone first on Wallulah's new-made cairn had rounded to the full, there was that upon him before which even his will bowed and gave way, — death, swift and mysterious. And it came in this wise.

We have told how at the great *potlatch* he gave away his all, even to the bear-skins from his couch, reserving only those cases of Asiatic textures never yet opened, — all that now remained of the richly laden ship of the Orient wrecked long ago upon his coast. They were opened now. His bed was covered with the magnificent fabrics; they were thrown carelessly over the rude walls and seats, half-trailing on the floor; exquisite folds of velvet and damask swept the leaves and dust, — so that all men might see how rich the chief still was, though he had given away so much. And with his ostentation was mixed a secret pride and tenderness that his dead wife had indirectly given him this wealth. The war-chief's woman had brought him these treasures out of the sea ; and now that he had given away his all, even to the bare poles of his lodge, she filled it with fine things and made him rich again, — she who had been sleeping for years in the death-hut on *mimaluse* island. Those treasures, ere the vessel that carried them was wrecked, had been sent as a present from one oriental prince to another. Could it be that they had been purposely impregnated with disease, so that while the prince that sent them seemed to bestow a graceful gift, he was in reality taking a treacherous and terrible revenge? Such things were not infrequent in Asiatic history; and even the history of Europe, in the middle ages, tells us of poisoned masks, of gloves and scarfs charged with disease.

Certain it is that shortly after the cases were opened, a strange and fatal disease broke out among Multnomah's attendants. The howling of medicine-men rang all day long in the royal lodge ; each day saw swathed corpses borne out to the funeral pyre or *mimaluse* island. And no concoction of herbs, — however skilfully compounded with stone mortar and pestle, — no incantation of medicine-men or steaming atmosphere of sweat-house, could stay the mortality.

At length Multnomah caught the disease. It seemed strange to the Indians that the war-chief should sicken, that Multnomah should show any of the weaknesses of common flesh and blood ; yet so it was. But while the body yielded to the inroad of disease, the spirit that for almost half a century had bent beneath it the tribes of the Wauna never faltered. He lay for days upon his couch, his system wasting with the plague, his veins burning with fever, holding death off only by might of will. He touched no remedies, for he felt them to be useless ; he refused the incantations of the medicine-men ; alone and in his own strength the war-chief contended with his last enemy.

All over the Willamette Valley, through camp and fishery, ran the whisper that Multnomah was dying ; and the hearts of the Indians sunk within them. Beyond the mountains the whisper passed to the allied tribes, once more ripe for revolt, and the news rang among them like a trumpet call ; it was of itself a signal for rebellion. The fall of the magic Bridge, the death of Wallulah, and the fatal illness of Multnomah had sealed the doom of the Willamettes. The chiefs stayed their followers only till they knew that he was dead. But the grand old war-chief seemed determined that he would not die. He struggled with disease ; he crushed down his sufferings ; he fought death with the same silent, indomitable tenacity with which he had overthrown the obstacles of life.

In all his wasting agony he was the war-chief still, and held his subjects in his grip. To the tribes that were about to rebel he sent messages, short, abrupt, but terrible in their threat of vengeance, — messages that shook and awed the chiefs and pushed back invasion. To the last, the great chief overawed the tribes ; the generation that had grown up under the shadow of his tyranny, even when they knew he was dying, still obeyed him.

At length, one summer evening a few weeks after the burial of Wallulah, there burst forth from the war-chief's lodge that peculiar wail which was lifted only for the death of one of the royal blood. No need to ask who it was, for only *one* remained of the ancient line that had so long ruled the Willamettes; and for him, the last of his race, was the wail lifted. It was re-echoed by the inmates of the surrounding lodges; it rang, foreboding, mournful, through the encampment on Wappatto Island.

Soon, runners were seen departing in every direction to bear the fatal news throughout the valley. Twilight fell on them; the stars came out; the moon rose and sunk; but the runners sped on, from camp to camp, from village to village. Wherever there was a cluster of Willamette lodges, by forest, river, or sea, the tale was told, the wail was lifted. So all that night the death-wail passed through the valley of the Willamette; and in the morning the trails were thronged with bands of Indians journeying for the last time to the isle of council, to attend the obsequies of their chief, and consult as to the choice of one to take his place.

The pestilence that had so ravaged the household of Multnomah was spread widely now; and every band as it departed from the camp left death behind it, — aye, took death with it; for in each company were those whose haggard, sickly faces told of disease, and in more than one were those so weakened that they lagged behind and fell at last beside the trail to die.

The weather was very murky. It was one of the smoky summers of Oregon, like that of the memorable year 1849, when the smoke of wide-spread forest fires hung dense and blinding over Western Oregon for days, and it seemed to the white settlers as if they were never to breathe the clear air or see the sky again. But even that, the historic "smoky time" of the white pioneers, was scarcely equal to the smoky period of more than a century and a half before. The forest fires were raging with unusual fury; Mount Hood was still in course of eruption; and all the valley was wrapped in settled cloud. Through the thick atmosphere the tall firs loomed like spectres, while the far-off roar of flames in the forest and the intermittent sounds of the volcano came weirdly to the Indians as they passed on their mournful way. What wonder that the distant sounds seemed to them wild voices in the air, prophecying woe; and objects in the forest, half seen through the smoke, grotesque forms attending them as they marched! And when the bands had all gathered on the island, the shuddering Indians told of dim and shadowy phantoms that had followed and preceded them all the way; and of gigantic shapes in the likeness of men that had loomed through the smoke, warning them back with outstretched arms. Ominous and unknown cries had come to them through the gloom; and the spirits of the dead had seemed to marshal them on their way, or to oppose their coming, — they knew not which.

So, all day long, troop after troop crossed the river to the island, emerging like shadows from the smoke that seemed to wrap the world, — each with its sickly faces, showing the terrible spread of the pestilence;

_M_ULTOMAH'S _Death-canoe._

each helping to swell the great horror that brooded
over all, with its tale of the sick and dead at home,
and the wild things seen on the way. Band after band
the tribes gathered, and when the sun went down the
war-chief's obsequies took place.

It was a strange funeral that they gave Multnomah,
yet it was in keeping with the dark, grand life he had
lived.

A large canoe was filled with pitch and with pine-
knots, — the most inflammable materials an Oregon
forest could furnish. Upon them was heaped all that
was left of the chief's riches, all the silks and velvets
that remained of the cargo of the shipwrecked vessel
lost upon the coast long before. And finally, upon
the splendid heap of textures, upon the laces and the
damasks of the East, was laid the dead body of Multnomah, dressed in buckskin; his moccasins on his
feet, his tomahawk and his pipe by his side, as became a chief starting on his last journey.

Then as night came on, and the smoky air darkened into deepest gloom, the canoe was taken out
into the main current of the Columbia, and fire was
set to the dry knots that made up the funeral pyre.
In an instant the contents of the canoe were in a
blaze, and it was set adrift in the current. Down the
river it floated, lighting the night with leaping flames.
On the shore, the assembled tribe watched it in silence, mute, dejected, as they saw their great chief
borne from them forever. Promontory and dusky
fir, gleaming water and level beach, were brought into
startling relief against the background of night, as the
burning vessel neared them ; then sank into shadow as
it passed onward. Overhead, the playing tongues of

fire reddened the smoke that hung dense over the water, and made it assume distorted and fantastic shapes, which moved and writhed in the wavering light, and to the Indians seemed spectres of the dead, hovering over the canoe, reaching out their arms to receive the soul of Multnomah.

"It is the dead people come for him," the Willamettes whispered to one another, as they stood upon the bank, watching the canoe drift farther and farther from them, with the wild play of light and shadow over it. Down the river, like some giant torch that was to light the war-chief along the shadowy ways of death, passed the burning canoe. Rounding a wooded point, it blazed a moment brilliantly beside it, and as it drifted to the farther side, outlined the intervening trees with fire, till every branch was clearly relieved against a flaming background; then, passing slowly on beyond the point, the light waned gradually, and at last faded quite away.

And not till then was a sound heard among the silent and impassive throng on the river-bank. But when the burning canoe had vanished utterly, when black and starless night fell again on wood and water, the death-wail burst from the Indians with one impulse and one voice, — a people's cry for its lost chief, a great tribe's lament for the strength and glory that had drifted from it, never to return.

Among a superstitious race, every fact becomes mingled more or less with fable; every occurrence, charged with fantastic meanings. And there sprang up among the Indians, no one could tell how, a prophecy that some night when the Willamettes were in their direst need, a great light would be seen moving on the waters of the Columbia, and the war-chief would come back in a canoe of fire to lead them to victory as of old.

Dire and awful grew their need as the days went on ; swift and sweeping was the end. Long did the few survivors of his race watch and wait for his return, — but never more came back Multnomah to his own.

CHAPTER V.

AS WAS WRIT IN THE BOOK OF FATE.

A land of old upheaven from the abyss
By fire, to sink into the abyss again,
Where fragments of forgotten peoples dwelt.
                                        TENNYSON.

AND now our tale draws to a close. There remains but to tell how the last council was held
on Wappatto Island; how Mishlah the Cougar, chief
of the Mollalies, died; and how the prophecy of the
Bridge was fulfilled.

The morning after the obsequies of Multnomah,
the chiefs met in the grove where the great council
of the tribes had been held only a few weeks before.
The leaves, which had been green and glossy then,
were turning yellow and sickly now in the close hot
weather. All Nature seemed full of decay.

The chiefs were grouped before the vacant seat of
Multnomah; and the Willamette tribe, gathered from
canyon and prairie and fishery, looked on, sole spectators of the proceedings, — for none of the allies
were present. The ravages of the pestilence had been
terrible. Many warriors were missing from the spectators; many chiefs were absent from the council.
And there were some present from whom the others
shrunk away, whose hot breath and livid faces showed

that they too were stricken with the plague. There were emaciated Indians among the audience, whose gaunt forms and hollow eyes told that they had dragged themselves to the council-grove to die. The wailing of the women at the camp, lamenting those just dead ; the howling of the medicine-men in the distance, performing their incantations over the sick ; the mysterious sounds that came from the burning forest and the volcano, — all these were heard. Round the council the smoke folded thick and dark, veiling the sun, and shutting out the light of heaven and the mercy of the Great Spirit.

The chiefs sat long in silence, each waiting for the other to speak. At length arose a stately warrior famous among the Willamettes for wisdom and prudence.

" We perish," said the chief, " we melt away before the breath of the pestilence, like snow before the breath of the warm spring wind. And while we die of disease in our lodges, war gathers against us beyond the ranges. Even now the bands of our enemies may be descending the mountains, and the tomahawk may smite what the disease has spared. What is to be done? What say the wise chiefs of the Willamettes? Multnomah's seat is empty : shall we choose another war-chief? "

A pale and ghastly chief rose to reply. It was evident that he was in the last extremity of disease.

" Shall we choose another war-chief to sit in Multnomah's place? We may ; but will he be Multnomah? The glory of the Willamettes is dead ! Talk no more of war, when our war-strength is gone from us. The Bridge is fallen, the Great Spirit is against us. Let those who are to live talk of war. It is time for us to learn how to die."

He sunk flushed and exhausted upon the ground. Then rose an aged chief, so old that it seemed as if a century of time had passed over him. His hair was a dirty gray, his eyes dull and sunken, his face withered. He supported himself with tremulous bony hands upon his staff. His voice was feeble, and seemed like an echo from the long-perished past.

" I am old, the oldest of all the Willamettes. I have seen so many winters that no man can count them. I knew Multnomah's father. I went forth to battle with his father's father; and even before that I knew others, warriors of a forgotten time. Or do I dream? I know not. The weight of the time that I have lived is very heavy, and my mind sinks under it. My form is bowed with the burden of winters. Warriors, I have seen many councils, many troubles, but never a trouble like this. Of what use is your council? Can the words of wise men stay disease? Can the edge of the tomahawk turn back sickness? Can you fight against the Great Spirit? He sent the white man to tell us of our sins and warn us to be better, and you closed your ears and would not listen. Nay, you would have slain him had not the Great Spirit taken him away. These things would not have come upon us had you listened to the white *shaman*. You have offended the Great Spirit, and he has broken the Bridge and sent disease upon us; and all that your wisdom may devise can avail naught to stay his wrath. You can but cover your faces in silence, and die."

For a moment the council was very still. The

memory of the white wanderer, his strong and tender eloquence, his fearless denunciation, his loving and passionate appeal, was on them all. *Was* the Great Spirit angry with them because they had rejected him?

"Who talks of dying?" said a fierce warrior, starting to his feet. "Leave that to women and sick men! Shall we stay here to perish while life is yet strong within us? The valley is shadowed with death; the air is disease; an awful sickness wastes the people; our enemies rush in upon us. Shall we then lie down like dogs and wait for death? No. Let us leave this land; let us take our women and children, and fly. Let us seek a new home beyond the Klamath and the Shasta, in the South Land, where the sun is always warm, and the grass is always green, and the cold never comes. The spirits are against us here, and to stay is to perish. Let us seek a new home, where the spirits are not angry; even as our fathers in the time that is far back left their old home in the ice country of the Nootkas and came hither. I have spoken."

His daring words kindled a moment's animation in the despondent audience; then the ceaseless wailing of the women and the panting of the sick chiefs in the council filled the silence, and their hearts sank within them again.

"My brother is brave," said the grave chief who had opened the council, "but are his words wise? Many of our warriors are dead, many are sick, and Multnomah is gone. The Willamettes are weak; it is bitter to the lips to say it, but it is true. Our enemies are strong. All the tribes who were once with us are against us. The passes are kept by many warriors; and could we fight our way through them to another land, the sickness would go with us. Why fly from the disease here, to die with it in some far-off land?"

"We cannot leave our own land," said a dreamer, or medicine-man. "The Great Spirit gave it to us, the bones of our fathers are in it. It is *our* land," he repeated with touching emphasis. "The Willamette cannot leave his old home, though the world is breaking up all around him. The bones of our people are here. Our brothers lie in the death-huts on *mimaluse* island; — how can we leave them? Here is the place where we must live; here, if death comes, must we die!"

A murmur of assent came from the listeners. It voiced the decision of the council. With stubborn Indian fatalism, they would await the end; fighting the rebels if attacked, and sullenly facing the disease if unmolested. Now a voice was heard that never had been heard in accents of despair, — a voice that was still fierce and warlike in its resentment of the course the council was taking. It was the voice of Mishlah the Cougar, chief of the Mollalies. He, too, had the plague, and had just reached the grove, walking with slow and tottering steps, unlike the Mishlah of other days. But his eyes glittered with all the old ferocity that had given him the name of Cougar. Alas, he was but a dying cougar now.

"Shall we stay here to die?" thundered the wild chief, as he stood leaning on his stick, his sunken eyes sweeping the assembly with a glance of fire. "Shall we stand and tremble till the pestilence slays us all with its arrows, even as a herd of deer, driven into a deep gulch and surrounded, stand till they are shot down by the hunters? Shall we stay in our lodges, and die without lifting a hand? Shall disease burn out the life of our warriors, when they might fall in battle? No! Let us slay the women and children, cross the mountains, and die fighting the rebels! Is it not better to fall in battle like warriors than to perish of disease like dogs?"

The chief looked from face to face, but saw no responsive flash in the eyes that met his own. The settled apathy of despair was on every countenance. Then the medicine-man answered, —

" *You* could never cross the mountains, even if we did this thing. Your breath is hot with disease; the mark of death is on your face; the snake of the pestilence has bitten you. If we went out to battle, you would fall by the wayside to die. Your time is short. To-day you die."

The grim Mollalie met the speaker's glance, and for a moment wavered. He felt within himself that the words were true, that the plague had sapped his life, that his hour was near at hand. Then his hesitation passed, and he lifted his head with scornful defiance.

"So be it! Mishlah accepts his doom. Come, you that were once the warriors of Multnomah, but whose hearts are become the hearts of women; come and learn from a Mollalie how to die!"

Again his glance swept the circle of chiefs as if summoning them to follow him, — then, with weak and staggering footsteps, he left the grove; and it was as if the last hope of the Willamettes went with him. The dense atmosphere of smoke soon shut his form from view. Silence fell on the council. The hearts of the Indians were dead within them. Amid their portentous surroundings, — the appalling signs of the wrath of the Great Spirit, — the fatal apathy which is the curse of their race crept over them.

Then rose the medicine-man, wild priest of a wild and debasing superstition, reverenced as one through whom the dead spoke to the living.

" Break up your council !" he said with fearful look and gesture. " Councils are for those who expect to live ! and you ! — the dead call you to them. Choose no chief, for who will be left for him to rule? You talk of plans for the future. Would you know what that future will be ? I will show you ; listen ! " He flung up his hand as if imposing silence ; and, taken by surprise, they listened eagerly, expecting to hear some supernatural voice or message prophetic of the future. On their strained hearing fell only the labored breathing of the sick chiefs in the council, the ominous muttering of the far-off volcano, and loud and shrill above all the desolate cry of the women wailing their dead.

" You hear it? That death-wail tells all the future holds for you. Before yonder red shadow of a sun " — pointing to the sun, which shone dimly through the smoke — " shall set, the bravest of the Mollalies will be dead. Before the moon wanes to its close, the Willamette race will have passed away. Think you Multnomah's seat is empty? The Pestilence sits in Multnomah's place, and you will all wither in his hot and poisonous breath. Break up your council. Go to your lodges. The sun of the Willamettes is set,

and the night is upon us. Our wars are done ; our
glory is ended. We are but a tale that old men tell
around the camp-fire, a handful of red dust gathered
from *mimaluse* island, — dust that once was man.
Go, you that are as the dead leaves of autumn ; go,
whirled into everlasting darkness before the wind
of the wrath of the Great Spirit ! "

He flung out his arms with a wild gesture, as if he
held all their lives and threw them forth like dead
leaves to be scattered upon the winds. Then he
turned away and left the grove. The crowd of warriors who had been looking on broke up and went
away, and the chiefs began to leave the council, each
muffled in his blanket. The grave and stately sachem
who had opened the council tried for a little while to
stay the fatal breaking up, but in vain. And when he
saw that he could do nothing, he too left the grove,
wrapped in stoical pride, sullenly resigned to whatever was to come.

And so the last council ended, in hopeless apathy,
in stubborn indecision, — indecision in everything
save the recognition that a doom was on them against
which it was useless to struggle.

And Mishlah ? He returned to his lodge, painted
his face as if he were going to battle, and then went
out to a grove near the place where the war-dances of
the tribe were held. His braves followed him ; others
joined them ; all watched eagerly, knowing that the
end was close at hand, and wondering how he would
die.

He laid aside his blanket, exposing his stripped
body ; and with his eagle plume in his hair and his
stone tomahawk in his hand, began to dance the war-

dance of his tribe and to chant the song of the battles he had fought.

At first his utterance was broken and indistinct, his step feeble. But as he went on his voice rang clearer and stronger; his step grew quicker and firmer. Half reciting, half chanting, he continued the wild tale of blood, dancing faster and faster, haranguing louder and louder, until he became a flame of barbaric excitement, until he leaped and whirled in the very madness of raging passion, — the Indian war-frenzy.

But it could not last long. His breath came quick and short; his words grew inarticulate; his eyes gleamed like coals of fire; his feet faltered in the dance. With a final effort he brandished and flung his tomahawk, uttering as he did so a last war-cry, which thrilled all who heard it as of old when he led them in battle. The tomahawk sunk to the head in a neighboring tree, the handle breaking off short with the violence of the shock; and the chief fell back — dead.

Thus passed the soul of the fierce Mollalie. For years afterward, the tomahawk remained where it had sunk in the tree, sole monument of Mishlah. His bones lay unburied beneath, wasted by wind and rain, till there was left only a narrow strip of red earth, with the grass springing rankly around it, to show where the body had been. And the few survivors of the tribe who lingered in the valley were wont to point to the tomahawk imbedded in the tree, and tell the tale of the warrior and how he died.

Why dwell longer on scenes so terrible? Besides, there is but little more to tell. The faithless allies made a raid on the valley; but the shrouding atmosphere of smoke and the frightful rumors they heard of the great plague appalled them, and they retreated. The pestilence protected the Willamettes. The Black Death that the medicine-men saw sitting in Multnomah's place turned back the tide of invasion better than the war-chief himself could have done.

Through the hot months of summer the mortality continued. The valley was swept as with the besom of destruction, and the drama of a people's death was enacted with a thousand variations of horror. When spring came, the invaders entered the valley once more. They found it deserted, with the exception of a few wretched bands, sole survivors of a mighty race. They rode through villages where the decaying mats hung in tatters from the half-bare skeleton-like wigwam poles, where the ashes had been cold for months at the camp-fires; they rode by fisheries where spear and net were rotting beside the canoe upon the beach. And the dead — the dead lay everywhere : in the lodges, beside the fisheries, along the trail where they had been stricken down while trying to escape, — everywhere were the ghastly and repulsive forms.

The spirit of the few survivors was broken, and they made little resistance to the invaders. Mongrel bands from the interior and the coast settled in the valley after the lapse of years ; and, mixing with the surviving Willamettes, produced the degenerate race our own pioneers found there at their coming. These hybrids were, within the memory of the white man, overrun and conquered by the Yakimas, who subjugated all the Indians upon Wappatto Island and around the mouth of the Willamette in the early part of the present century. Later on, the Yakimas were driven back by the whites; so that there have been three conquests of the lower Willamette Valley since the fall of the ancient race, — two Indian conquests before the white.

The once musical language of the Willamettes has degenerated into the uncouth Chinook, and the blood of the ancient race flows mixed and debased in the veins of abject and squalid descendants; but the story of the mighty bridge that once spanned the Columbia at the Cascades is still told by the Oregon Indians. Mingled with much of fable, overlaid with myth and superstition, it is nevertheless one of the historic legends of the Columbia, and as such will never be forgotten.

One word more of Cecil Gray, and our tale is done.

The Shoshone renegade, who resolved at Cecil's death to become a Christian, found his way with a few followers to the Flat-Heads, and settled among that tribe. He told them of what he had learned from Cecil, — of the Way of Peace; and the wise men of the tribe pondered his sayings in their hearts. The Shoshone lived and died among them; but from generation to generation the tradition of the white man's God was handed down, till in 1832 four Flat-Heads were sent by the tribe to St. Louis, to ask that teachers be given them to tell them about God.

Every student of history knows how that appeal stirred the heart of the East, and caused the sending out of the first missionaries to Oregon; and from the movement then inaugurated have since sprung all the missions to the Indians of the West.

Thus he who gave his life for the Indians, and died seemingly in vain, sowed seed that sprung up and bore a harvest long after his death. And to-day, two centuries since his body was laid in the lonely grave on Wappatto Island, thousands of Indians are the better for his having lived. No true, noble life can be said to have been lived in vain. Defeated and beaten though it may seem to have been, there has gone out from it an influence for the better that has helped in some degree to lighten the great heartache and bitterness of the world. Truth, goodness, and self-sacrifice are never beaten, — no, not by death itself. The example and the influence of such things is deathless, and lives after the individual is gone, flowing on forever in the broad life of humanity.

I write these last lines on Sauvie's Island — the Wappatto of the Indians, — sitting upon the bank of the river, beneath the gnarled and ancient cotton-wood that still marks the spot where the old Columbia trail led up from the water to the interior of the island. Stately and beautiful are the far snow-peaks and the sweeping forests. The woods are rich in the colors of an Oregon autumn. The white wappatto blooms along the marshes, its roots ungathered, the dusky hands that once reaped the harvest long crumbled into dust. Blue and majestic in the sunlight flows the Columbia, river of many names, — the Wauna and Wemath of the Indians, the St. Roque of the Spaniards, the Oregon of poetry, — always vast and grand, always flowing placidly to the sea. Steam-boats of the present; batteaux of the fur traders; ships, Grey's and Vancouver's, of discovery; Indian canoes of the old unknown time, — the stately river has seen them all come and go, and yet holds its way past forest and promontory, still beautiful and unchanging. Generation after generation, daring hunter, ardent discoverer, silent Indian, — all the shadowy peoples of the past have sailed its waters as we sail them, have lived perplexed and haunted by mystery as we live, have gone out into the Great Darkness with hearts full of wistful doubt and questioning, as we go ; and still the river holds its course, bright, beautiful, inscrutable. It stays ; *we go.* Is there anything *beyond* the darkness into which generation follows generation and race follows race ? Surely there is an after-life, where light and peace shall come to all who, however defeated, have tried to be true and loyal ; where the burden shall be lifted and the heartache shall cease ; where all the love and hope that slipped away from us here shall be given back to us again, and given back forever.

Via crucis, via lucis.

THE END.

'A superbly written book, *The Eitingons* is much more than a family history, for the author has a deep knowledge of the cultural and political context, whether of twentieth-century America or the Soviet Union, in which they lived. It stands as an intimate portrait of a world that seems far removed from our own.'

Observer

'Unlike the hordes of amateur historians who have mobbed the world's libraries over the past decade on the theory that reconstructing lineage equates to personal discovery, Wilmers is up to something that commands general attention.'

New Yorker

'*The Eitingons* is a riveting history of the twentieth century. It deals with war, displacement, murder, espionage, the Jewish diaspora and psychoanalysis. It explains Trotsky's assassination, the growth of Freud's teachings, the importance of the fur trade, the uses of money and the lure of the past. There is a lightness and a truthfulness in the narrative that makes you turn every page with pure fascination.'

Colm Tóibín

'Wilmers' adventures in digging through [the Eitingons'] lost world makes Mary-Kay one of the book's most intriguing characters.'

Harper's

'Like characters in some Russian Jewish Stalinist Freudian capitalist twentieth-century fairy tale, the Eitingons are larger than life, their fates bitter and all too human.'

New York Times

'Wilmers pieces together what she can of the shadowy life of Leonid Eitingon, a high-level KGB killer . . . and looks for clues that her grandfather's cousin Max, a protégé of Freud in Berlin, and Motty, a New York fur trader, were also working for Stalin. What emerges is a fascinating story of family secrets and silences.'

New Statesman

'Well researched, bold, and revealing, Wilmers's book transforms a series of dark family secrets into an illuminating experience for anybody brave enough to delve into the enigma of family history.'

Publishers Weekly

'Compelling . . . [Wilmers] has produced a deeply researched family chronicle, which bears only a trace resemblance to the memoirs that dominate the book industry.'

Barnes and Noble Review

'An extraordinary memoir . . . Wilmers has turned the raw material of her family into literature.'

Sunday Telegraph

'Wilmers is a true scholar of these times and a sophisticated narrator.'

Daily Telegraph

'A truly fascinating family history, almost epic in its tracing back and forth across the Atlantic, and full of what heights human beings can reach, as well as the depths.'

Herald (Scotland)

Mary-Kay Wilmers is the editor of the *London Review of Books*, the largest-selling literary publication in Europe. She has written for the *Listener*, *TLS* and *New Yorker*.

The Eitingons
A Twentieth-Century Story

MARY-KAY WILMERS

VERSO
London • New York

Verso
UK: 6 Meard Street, London W1F 0EG
US: 20 Jay Street, Suite 1010, Brooklyn, NY 11201
www.versobooks.com

Verso is the imprint of New Left Books

ISBN-13: 978-1-84467-900-3

Library of Congress Cataloging-in-Publication Data
A catalog record for this book is available from the Library of Congress

Typeset by Hewer Text UK Ltd, Edinburgh
Printed in the US by Maple Vail

For Sam and Will
and in memory of
my parents

Contents

CONTENTS

Acknowledgements

It would be shaming to spell out how indebted I am both to Perry Anderson and to Jeremy Harding; without their help and encouragement the end of this project would still be several years off. And without Nadia Pokornaya's enthusiasm and Theodore Draper's generosity it would never have got off the ground. Many others, mainly Eitingons and near-Eitingons, not all of them still alive, talked to me about the Eitingon family in its various branches when the idea of a book was still a long way down the road: the two Galia Eitingons, Mark Eitingon, Mary Eitingon, Svetlana Eitingon, Vladimir Eitingon, Nikolai Khokhlov, Tatiana Kozlova, Boris Makliarsky, Lussia Neumann, Liza Pikielny, Evgenia Puzirova, Nina Rustanovich, Elena Sinelnikov-Muryleva, Anatoli Sudoplatov, Lee Thompson and last, but very far from least, the incomparable Zoya Zarubina. Joanna Biggs, Yoram Gorlizki, Lidija Haas, Ian Jackman, Paul Laity, John Lanchester, Dorothea McEwan, Jean McNicol, Andrew O'Hagan, Philip Oltermann, Nikita Petrov and Inigo Thomas variously pushed me along, guided my research, corrected my facts, improved my sentences. Tim Binyon, Oxana Poberejnaia and Tony Wood translated tedious stretches of Soviet-speak. Tariq Ali, Olena Bagno, Antony Beevor, Jenny Carr, Sheila Fitzpatrick, Harriet Garland, Mary Hope, Andrei Kishtimov, Yonatan Mendel, Marie

José Minassian, Vladimir Nikitin, Adam Phillips, Elaine Robson-Scott, Yuri Slezkine, Christopher Turner, Luba Vinogradova, Susan Watkins and Gaby Wood were all crucial at one moment or another. Finally, I'm grateful to everyone at Faber who has eased *The Eitingons* along the road to publication, principally my editor, Henry Volans, and David Watkins, and to my colleagues at the *London Review of Books*, individually and collectively, for their patience and their willingness to do things that I should have been doing myself and for not groaning as much as I would have done in their place.

Note on the Soviet Secret Service

The Soviet Secret Service had many different designations in the course of its history. These are the main ones.

1917–22	Cheka: Extraordinary Commission to Combat Counter-Revolution and Sabotage
1922–3	GPU/NKVD: State Political Administration/People's Commissariat for Internal Affairs
1923–34	OGPU: Unified State Political Administration
1934–43	NKVD as above
1943–6	NKGB: People's Commissariat for State Security
1946–53	MGB: Ministry of State Security
1953–4	MVD: Ministry of Internal Affairs
1954–91	KGB: Committee for State Security

When no specific historical period is intended I have referred generically to the GPU before the Second World War, and the KGB after it. Cheka was how Leonid and his colleagues mostly referred to it.

The table is adapted from Pavel Sudoplatov's *Special Tasks: The Memoirs of an Unwanted Witness – A Soviet Spymaster*.

The Eitingon Families

Mordecai (died 1880), Max's grandfather
Chaim (1857–1932), Max's father
Max had one brother, Waldemar, and two sisters, Fanny and Esther.

Mordecai, his grandfather
Itsak Leib (dates unknown), his father
Motty was the youngest of four brothers, Max (a different Max), Boris (my grandfather, died 1932), Naum (Boris's twin, died 1964). He also had four sisters.

There were also two Eitingon uncles, his father's brothers, one of whom was Monya's father.

Motty married Chaim's daughter Fanny and had two daughters. His second wife was Bess and they had a son, Tommy.

Boris (my grandfather) had three daughters: Niuta, Lola and Cesia – Cesia was my mother.

Boris (died 1915), his grandfather
Isaak (died 1912), his father
Leonid had two sisters, Sonia and Sima, and a younger brother, Izya.

Leonid had four children:
Vladimir (born 1918), his mother was Anna Shulman
Svetlana (1927, died a few years ago), her mother was Olga Naumova
Leonid (Lonya, born 1941) and Musa (born 1943), their mother was Musa Malinovskaya

His stepdaughter, Zoya Zarubina, was born in 1920. Her mother was Olga Naumova, her father Vasily Zarubin.

General Sudoplatov was Leonid's boss. Anatoli, the general's son, co-wrote his father's memoirs with him.

Eduard Sharapov is Leonid's biographer.

Part One

Embarrassment

When I was fifteen my mother told me that nobody liked me. 'Mats does,' I replied defiantly. Mats was my father's sister and my mother had mixed feelings about her.

Eighteen months older than my father, a consultant physician at a London teaching hospital, and unmarried, Mats was the supreme authority in my father's family: the person whose advice everyone sought and who could never be wrong. It was part of her thing to like and understand 'the young', as she used to call us, and I thought then, as I thought later, that she had a special feeling for me.

When Mats died my cousins – her other brother's children – and I divided up her belongings. The day was uneventful – no quarrels, no feuds – and there would be nothing to report were it not for a shaming action of mine. One of my cousins and I both wanted the same little mahogany box that had stood on a table by her front door. It was his turn to choose and he took the box.

Some minutes later, when he was out of the room, I opened the box and removed the letters that I knew were in it: they were the reason I'd wanted the box in the first place. At the end of the day, when we were getting ready to go home, my cousin picked up the box that was now his and saw that the letters had gone.

I confessed – obviously. What else could I do? But I was mortified, mortified as I had been when an Oxford landlady accused me of stealing her silver teaspoons (I hadn't) and before that when my biology teacher accused me of copying my best friend's homework (I had and I hadn't: she just told me what to say). It turned out that my cousin too had only been interested in the box for the sake of the letters, but one way or another – his better character perhaps – I got to keep both.

There were many reasons why I wanted the letters. I wanted them out of fondness for Mats and interest in her life. But I also wanted them because I thought they might shed light on my paternal great-grandfather's arrival in England from Germany in the late nineteenth century. And if there was nothing about that, there might be something about the Eitingons, or about me. What makes this story a story is that for all my eagerness to get hold of the letters (as well as letters to Mats, there were letters from her, addressed to her own aunt, a maiden aunt of the previous generation), and for all my faith in Mats's feelings for me, it turned out, when I came to read them, that in each one she had something disheartening to say about either my face or my character. I was spoiled, I wasn't 'at all pretty', my cousins (them again) were so much nicer than me.

Why do people keep letters? To begin with, when I'd wanted to justify nosing about in my mother's attic, I thought that anyone who kept their letters did it with a latecoming reader or readers in mind. It was a pleasing notion, or at any rate one that suited my purpose, but it's far more likely that people hang onto the letters they get for the same reason that they hang onto photographs – out of a need or a wish to memorialise themselves. Or because they don't want to discard their past or more generally to cut their lives short. But when they're dead? Is it more appropriate for those who inherit the letters along with the clothes and the furniture to read them or put them in the bin? Burning letters has something grand and criminal about it. Putting them out with the rubbish may seem merely disrespectful. But maybe less disrespectful than reading them.

So what to do? Safeguarding letters – our parents', our grandparents' – is one thing. Reading them is something else. You think you're interested in their story, only to discover that mainly you're obsessed with your own. And what goes for letters probably goes for every kind of rummaging in other people's lives, whether you're related to them or not. Perhaps there's a case for letting things lie, and being spared the worry about whose story you are really trying to tell and who gave you permission to tell it.

Mexico

At the villa in Coyoacán where in August 1940 Trotsky was murdered, there are two cats: a ginger one called Trotsky and a black one named after his murderer, Ramón Mercader. Or there were when I visited. The villa has for many years been a museum, and for a while visitors could wander about as they pleased: they could lie down on Trotsky's bed or sit where he was sitting when Mercader struck him with the most famous murder weapon in modern history. Now the rooms where he'd been living with his wife and grandson for the previous year and a bit are protected by a glass partition running along the corridor at waist height. The partition is 'alarmed' and every time a visitor leans over it, which most visitors inadvertently do, the alarm goes off. The walls of the main bedroom, still spattered with holes, mark a first, failed, assault in May 1940, and on the floor of the study where, three months later, Mercader got his man, the bloodstains look as if they've been rubbed into the stone.

Out in the yard, a red flag flies at half-mast over the Old Man and his wife Natalya's grave – a nine-foot slab of concrete with a hammer and sickle and Trotsky's name carved into it. The yard isn't big, but there's room for several tropical trees and some very large cacti. With the bougainvillea in bloom, the two cats nestling against each other in the spring sun, it seems quite idyllic. Only the sound of the alarm reminds you that in Trotsky's day this was less a villa than a fortress, that the tower in the corner looking out on the street was a real watchtower, not a place for Trotsky's grandson to play, that visitors were barred and most of Trotsky's entourage carried guns: that, in short, an emissary from Stalin was at all times expected.

Mercader struck Trotsky's head with the broad end of the ice-pick. Trotsky cried out ('a long, endlessly long "aaaa"', as Mercader remembered it), stood up, bit Mercader's hand, was pushed to the ground, got back up on his feet. Seizing whatever was to hand – books, inkpot, a dictaphone – he threw it at his assailant, before wrenching the ice-pick from him and finally staggering back, his face covered in blood, his blue eyes, Natalya said, 'glittering', his spectacles gone. Though they'd been living in anticipation of this moment for more than a decade, the rest of Trotsky's household didn't immediately understand what was happening, and three or four minutes went by before they came running into the study, fell on Mercader and began to beat him with the butts of their revolvers. At that point Mercader lost his nerve. 'They made me do it,' he shouted. 'They've got my mother.' It was his only moment of weakness and no one knew what he meant.

Natalya, seeing that Mercader's life was in danger, asked her husband what was to be done with him. 'Tell the boys not to kill him,' he said. And then said it again: 'No, no, he must not be killed.' Trotsky wanted Mercader to live so that he could tell the world on whose orders he'd been sent. But Mercader spent twenty years in a Mexican jail, six in solitary confinement, and in that time never let on that he'd acted on the Kremlin's instructions, pretending throughout that he was a follower of Trotsky's who'd lost faith in the Old Man.

Trotsky died the next day in hospital in Mexico City. Stalin, he'd said in 1936, sought not to strike 'at his opponent's ideas but at his skull'.

Had Trotsky died straight away and in silence Mercader would have escaped. That, at any rate, had been the plan. A car was waiting close to the villa, its engine running. Inside it were Mercader's mother, Caridad Mercader del Río, and the Soviet agent in charge of the operation. They heard Trotsky's 'aaaa', heard the screams and cries and sounds of running feet inside the villa, realised that something had gone wrong and drove off. Other accounts say they were waiting in different cars, but that doesn't change anything.

Pravda announced Trotsky's death three days later, on 24 August. He died, the paper said, 'from a fractured skull, received in an attempt on his life by one of his closest circle'. Stalin had been waiting – or, more precisely, preparing – for this moment for a very long time.

It seems strange now that Stalin didn't give the order to do away with Trotsky much sooner. But he was always more mindful of public opinion, both inside and outside the Soviet Union, than we imagine, and although he soon regretted sending Trotsky abroad, where it was difficult to curb his activity, it wasn't until the approach of the Second World War that he decided that the need to be rid of him was paramount.

In the meantime, wherever Trotsky went during the twelve and a half years of his exile, Stalin's men watched him; they watched at close quarters or at a distance; and they watched all day, every day. They intercepted his letters, infiltrated his household, raided his premises, murdered both his sons and picked off his acolytes one by one, as the need arose. He had been ruthless himself, and many people believed there was no reason to feel sorry for him now that his circumstances had so drastically changed. Trotsky was often enraged and always frustrated by the circumstances of his exile, but however relentlessly Stalin pursued him he remained sublimely defiant.

He wasn't sent abroad straight away. In those early days of Stalin's rule internal exile was the habitual punishment, and at the end of January 1928 Trotsky was taken to Alma-Ata, a town of earthquakes and floods, blizzards and heatwaves, in a far corner of Kazakhstan. He wasn't altogether displeased to get away from the Kremlin, and he and Natalya made the best of their new lives. 'A fine thing in Alma-Ata', she would later write,

> was the snow, white, clean, and dry. As there was very little walking or driving it kept its freshness all winter long. In the spring it yielded to red poppies. Such a lot of them – like gigantic carpets! The steppes glowed red for miles around. In the summer there were apples – the famous Alma-Ata variety, huge and also red. The town had no central waterworks, no lights, and no paved roads. In the bazaar in the centre of the town, the Kirghizes sat in the mud at the doorsteps of their shops, warming themselves in the sun and searching their bodies for vermin. Malaria was rampant. There was also pestilence, and during the summer months an extraordinary number of mad dogs. The newspapers reported many cases of leprosy in this region. In spite of all this,

we spent a good summer . . . The orchard was fragrant
with the ripe apples and pears; bees and wasps were
buzzing. We were making preserves.

While Natalya made jam, Trotsky did what he always
did: worked most of the day; kept in touch with his colleagues in the Opposition, even those who were in prison
(eight thousand of his supporters were arrested, deported
and jailed in that year alone); read, studied, dictated letters, issued directives. He liked hunting and sometimes in
the evenings went for walks in the nearby mountains with
a dog and a gun. His elder son, Lev Sedov (Lyova), was
there too, assisting his father, and to begin with it seemed
that he would also have the help of his 'secretariat': young
men who travelled to Alma-Ata in his wake. But each one
in turn was arrested, sent back to Moscow and in time disappeared. Local people kept away, even if they were sympathetic: Stalin had eyes everywhere.

In October Trotsky stopped getting letters: 'We are
under a postal blockade,' Natalya wrote to a friend. Even
there, in the far reaches of the Soviet empire, Trotsky was
getting too much attention; and on 20 January 1929, after
some last-minute shilly-shallying on Stalin's part, he was
told to pack his bags in readiness for another move. Two
days later, accompanied by his wife and son, he left Alma-
Ata still not knowing where he was headed. That, he was
informed, would be made clear in the course of the journey – the truth being that Stalin still didn't know where to
send him.

The train carrying them back to western Russia spent
twelve days in a siding – 'sunk in a coma', as Trotsky put
it – before the matter was resolved. The winter was the

harshest anyone could remember, and as the engine rolled backwards and forwards over the rails to keep the wheels from freezing, Trotsky read Anatole France and played chess with his family – his younger son, Sergei, had been allowed to visit the others en route. They didn't know where they were and nobody was allowed to leave the train, but once a day the engine and one carriage travelled to a nearby town to fetch the family's midday meal and a copy of *Pravda*. The paper was filled with attacks on Trotsky and reports of arrests among his followers.

He had hoped to be sent to Germany, but no German visa was forthcoming. Turkey, Trotsky was told, was the only country that would have him. And maybe this was true. He suspected, however, that Stalin had his own, more malevolent reasons for favouring Turkey; that Kemal Atatürk, Turkey's president, would be ready to do Stalin's bidding, whatever that turned out to be. He felt sure of it, though Kemal would deny it and later he himself would be more sanguine. On the other hand, Constantinople had been an assembly point for the remnants of the White Guard defeated at Trotsky's hands in the recent Civil War: perhaps they could be counted on to act as Stalin's proxies and finish him off.

The train travelled south, arriving in Odessa – the city of Trotsky's childhood, the place where he'd begun his revolutionary career – on 10 February. From there Sergei went back to Moscow to resume his studies – and would in time disappear. Accompanied by Lyova, Trotsky and Natalya were rushed to the harbour and, guarded by soldiers who a few years before had been under Trotsky's command, boarded the *Ilyich*. Apart from two of Stalin's agents there were no other passengers. The ship left

Odessa at dead of night in a gale. The Black Sea was frozen; and for the first sixty miles an icebreaker went ahead of them, forcing a passage.

They reached Constantinople two days later and were taken straight to the Soviet Consulate, where they were greeted as honoured guests. The agent who, ten years later, would be waiting outside the villa in Coyoacán to drive Trotsky's assassin away from the scene of his crime, arrived in Constantinople around the same time. His name was Leonid Eitingon. He was a relative of mine.

CHAPTER 3

HMS *Aquitania*

My parents met in December 1935, between Le Havre and New York. My mother was playing ping-pong; my father asked if she would give him a game. The ship on which they were travelling, the *Aquitania*, was the most luxurious, most extravagant of the transatlantic liners – with a Palladian Lounge and staterooms 'in the manner of Queen Anne'. Delivered in April 1914, it survived both world wars, remained in service for thirty-six years and probably represents the best investment Cunard ever made. A good omen perhaps.

My father was English; and though not English through and through, very 'English' in the manner of the day: tall, thin and a bit stiff. He worked for a multinational company based in Brussels and was on his way to the States on business. My more sophisticated, more flirtatious mother, at twenty-eight a rueful divorcee, was returning to New York after a visit to Moscow in the company of her uncle. Sixty years later, I heard her tell someone as if it were still fresh in her mind that my father hadn't thought to ask for her phone number at the end of the voyage: she'd been the one to make sure they would see each other again.

She'd come to the States eight or nine years before with her now discarded first husband, who was also her cousin. Born Cecilia Eitingon, she became Mrs Eitingon – 'Mrs E.' in my father's letters to his parents. The family was

Russian; they came from Orsha, Shklov and Mogilev, towns along the River Dnieper, in what used to be called Belorussia and is now independent Belarus. They were variously called Eitingon and Eitingen: an indication perhaps that they had come to Belorussia from Ettingen in Bavaria. The name is unusual, and it may be that all Eitingons belong to the same family. By now there were several sets living in the US, most of them close relatives of my mother's, and, like her, naturalised American citizens.

My strait-laced paternal grandparents seem not to have been pleased when my father met and fell in love with my mother. What had Mrs Eitingon been doing in Moscow, they wanted to know. It wasn't a normal place to go for a holiday. How could my father be sure that she wasn't in the pay of the Soviets? Mrs E., my father said in reply, was 'a very nice, quiet, normal and intelligent person' who 'spends her time doing sculpture as a hobby'. The answer, as often with my father, was a little naïve: spies wouldn't be spies if they couldn't pass themselves off as very nice people who did sculpture as a hobby.

It was after reading another of my father's letters that I realised how suspicious my grandparents had been. Did they really think my mother was a spy? Evidently so, since he felt obliged to tell them that she was 'no more in the pay of the Soviet government' than he was. Perhaps, he said, they would be reassured to know that they could find out a good deal about her – or at any rate her family – in the Standard Statistics, where they would discover that the Eitingons were 'the biggest fur dealers and dyers of fur in the world'. And 'of course they do a good deal of business with Russia'.

The letters were in a box in my mother's attic: methodical bundles, one for each year from the early 1930s to the late 1940s, by which time we were living in Belgium and it was easier for my father to speak to his parents on the phone. Each bundle was held together with a dark brown rubber band and labelled 'Charlie's Letters' in my grandmother's Germanic handwriting. As I undid them I began to worry that I was the one who was spying – or at the very least 'snooping', to use one of the words in my mother's plentiful vocabulary of disparagement.

My grandparents may not have been satisfied with my father's description of Mrs E., but it soon becomes evident from his letters that he and my mother were having a very good time together. They danced at the French Casino, they danced up in Harlem, they danced on the roof of the Waldorf-Astoria: 'You see life is pretty gay,' he wrote to his parents in February. In November, back on the *Aquitania*, travelling this time in the other direction, he writes to my mother about his memories of the previous journey and 'the table from which you used to smile coyly across at me when you came tripping in to dinner'.

On 15 June 1937 they got married at Paddington Register Office. Mats and my grandfather's brother (known as Uncle) were the witnesses. They had a wedding breakfast – *What was that?* I used to wonder – at Uncle's house in Connaught Square and then set off for Switzerland, where my father's parents were already on holiday. I don't know why they decided to get married in London, or to spend their honeymoon with my grandparents, but unlike my mother, my father was very close to his family, and because by one sleight or another what he wanted always turned out to be 'more convenient', he tended to get his own way.

I looked up my parents' wedding day in my grandfather's diary. 'Julia very depressed,' he had noted. He was a short, neat man with a tall wife (Julia) and three tall children. Authoritarian, set in his ways, disinclined to show human feeling, he used his diary mainly to record the weather and who he had written to that day. This was one of very few occasions when my grandmother's name was mentioned. If she was gloomy it isn't surprising. Why would she not have been on the day her favourite child got married? There were so many things for this severe German woman and her curmudgeonly husband to hold against their new high-living daughter-in-law: that she was Russian, that she was sexy, that she'd been married before, that unlike their own daughter she had no profession. However hard my mother tried to win favour in subsequent years, she was never considered a real member of my father's family – for one thing, winning favour wasn't what was wanted. They weren't – my grandmother might have said – that sort of people.

My paternal grandfather had come to England from Augsburg as a boy in the late 1870s; my grandmother, who was very much younger than him, nearly thirty years later. They were distant cousins and the marriage would have been arranged by well-meaning relatives. To my mother they both seemed forbiddingly English, despite their strong German accents. Many German Jewish refugees of the old sort were like that: more resolutely English than the English themselves. My father, who left England for good when he left Cambridge in 1930, was a more glamorous kind of Englishman; right up to the time of his death in 1980, he looked and sounded like someone whose life had been spent in a play by Noël Coward. He was calm and unassailable and seemingly suave. He didn't smoke through a cigarette holder, though he did sometimes smoke, and although he had a silk dressing-gown he only wore it at dressing-gown times of day. In every other way he was perfect for the part. 'A tall good-looking Englishman with a lordly air and a raffish glint in his eye' was how the *New Yorker* described him in the course of an article about his firm's difficult dealings with General Franco. Even now I am pleased when someone who didn't know him catches sight of him in a photograph, as if his being so good-looking were an achievement of mine.

As a young child in the 1940s I lived in the States, in a world filled with Eitingons, who in my mind compared very unfavourably with my father's family – whom I hadn't yet met. The Eitingons were excitable and cried far too often and asked unnecessary questions that troubled me for weeks – even years – such as which of my parents I preferred or whose death I would mind more. They weren't tall and glamorous like my father and their English wasn't good: they had heavy Russian accents, mixed up their tenses and did something funny with the definite article. My father, as I saw it, spoke perfect English with a perfect English accent. He also worried about his family in England who were living through the Blitz. Nothing as serious as that, I was certain, could have happened to the Eitingons.

In my imagination I was already English. My brother was much better at being American than I was, and I punished him for it by ostentatiously sweeping the floor with the American flag. Another thing I could do to annoy him was to tell people that his birthday was on 20 April – the same day as Hitler's – though that was riskier because, not surprisingly, he minded much more.

In *The Adventures of Augie March*, the hero, on a visit to Mexico City, where he hopes to see Trotsky, says of the great revolutionary: 'What it was about him that stirred me up was the instant impression he gave – no matter about the old heap he rode in or the peculiarity of his retinue – of navigation by the great stars, of the highest considerations, of being fit to speak the most important human words and universal terms.' This is in marked contrast with Augie March himself, who, as he describes it, is 'reduced to . . . sculling on the shallow bay, crawling from one clam-rake to the next'. I've been to Mexico City and I've read *My Life*, Trotsky's 'attempt at an autobiography', and Isaac Deutscher's biography, but when I reach for universal terms and try to say something about the history of the twentieth century I find that instead I've gone back to my childhood and to the fact – once so important – that my brother and Hitler were both born on 20 April.

CHAPTER 4

Objectivity

'Eto fakt?' ('Are you sure?')

'Eto fakt.' ('No, it's true.')

My father didn't like it when my mother talked to her relatives on the phone. Although he was good at languages and spoke several without any trouble, he had no interest in learning Russian. A question of snobbery perhaps, but, more likely, of pride and his own dignity. For all the forty years of his marriage the only Russian words that he knew were the usual pair, *do svidania* and *spasibo*, and that all-important word, *fakt*. He thought it very appropriate and very amusing that Russian has no word of its own for the incontestable units of what he cherished most deeply: 'objective reality'.

He valued rationality and everyone agreed that he was a very reasonable person. But 'reasonable' isn't the same as 'rational', and like most people who think of themselves as rational, my father took it for granted that objective reality was coterminous with his own thinking. The problem for me was that my belief in him was so extreme that it wasn't until after he died that I began to see myself as having something that could be described as my own way of thinking and realised that it was different from his. One consequence of this very late rebellion is that I now regard even the words 'objective' and 'objectivity' as instruments of oppression, as scarcely more than a way of saying: 'I'm right and you're wrong.'

But can you, logically, dismiss objectivity and at the same time recognise its lack? I think not. What to do? On the one hand, my father who saw 'things as they are'. On the other, my mother who never saw things the same way twice. 'Listen to the snake,' she used to say when, as a child, I pointed out that what she was saying today was the opposite of what she'd said yesterday. After my father's death, when I was able to see her character more clearly, it seemed that 'postmodern' was the only epithet that could adequately describe a character of such radical volatility.

Unswayed by his own emotions, my father, without realising it, was overpowered by my mother's, and too much a positivist to see how wayward her influence could be. Not given to intimacies, he relied on her to take care of all necessary human transactions. 'Your mother's wonderful with people,' he would say, confusing charm, of which she had a great deal, with understanding, which she had only intermittently and never when either his interest or hers was at stake. In a sense, perhaps, my parents weren't all that different from each other: his reasons and her feelings were equally incontestable. What neither of them left room for was uncertainty.

For that reason I doubt that my father would have seen the point of this story, where little is known for sure and the evidence I have been able to find is often thin and even more often contradictory. As for my mother, I've never known anyone with so little interest in the past – her own or anyone else's – but she had at times a highly attractive recklessness and it led her at first to enter into the spirit of the enterprise. Then she changed her mind and told me that I must drop the whole thing. What had been a good idea became a bad idea overnight. As always with her, there were no intermediate stages, no transition. Someone, I imagine, told her that they didn't like what I was doing, and snapping from one mode to another, she adopted that person's sentiments as if they had been hers all along.

The relationship between my father and the Eitingons didn't turn out well. He'd been quite taken with them at first. The letters he wrote to his parents make that plain. But after a time what he would have seen as their disorderliness got to him, their disorderliness with money especially. In the first place some of the older Eitingons were gamblers and my father didn't like that. One or two of their schemes, it's true, had been grandiose and irresponsible – and many people lost money as a result. But how would he have accounted for the fact that he consistently gambled – my word, not his – on the stock market? What – apart from success – was the difference? In his terms the answer would have been obvious: everything he did was based on an assessment of the facts – his were risks it was 'rational' to take.

In May 1939 my Eitingon grandmother left Poland for Brazil, where she lived until her death in the early 1970s. For much of that time my father supported her; he was therefore irritated to be reminded, as from time to time he was, that much of the money he sent was lost playing at cards. 'Can't we pay for her to have lessons?' he implored, though he must have known that poker, which she went on playing into her nineties, wasn't the same as bridge.

More seriously, he fell at one point for the hyperbolic claims of one of my Eitingon great-uncles and lost substantial sums of money – his own and, more embarrassingly, that of the firm for which he worked. That was in 1946. I can't remember now (if I knew then) what other economies were made, but it's the only time I remember seeing my father doing things in the kitchen – washing up, for example. (His ways were so princely that I sometimes used to amuse myself trying to imagine him going into a butcher's shop to ask for a couple of chops.)

There was obviously a difference of temperament between him and the Eitingons. They probably thought he was arrogant and rather cold; and no doubt, seen from their point of view, he was precisely that. In fact, like most of the members of his own family, he was both shy and self-assured, and it isn't necessarily a winning combination. What he must have loved in my mother, among other things, was the fact that she was always so fiercely present, so lacking in social diffidence, so seemingly convinced of her own feelings (and so wholehearted in her support for him). In these respects she wasn't different from other Eitingons, but he forgave her what he recoiled from in them: the tears, the exaggerations, the lack, as he would have said, of common sense.

My brother and I had far more trouble with her than with him, but although he was more willing to listen to our troubles it was unknown for him to take our side in a quarrel. 'You're lucky', my mother used to say, 'to have the example of a happy marriage like your father's and mine.' But I was more often than not exasperated with my parents' happy marriage: exasperated above all with what Philip Roth in a different context calls 'the tyranny of the we and its we-talk and everything that the we wants to pile on your head'.

'We thought . . .' 'Your father and I . . .' 'We would like . . .' 'We decided . . .' 'Your father agrees with me . . .'

Had my father lived longer, 'we' would long since have persuaded me to drop the idea of writing about the Eitingons. If the story was interesting, 'we' would have said, if it was worth someone's while to look into it and write about it, then someone surely would: someone who was qualified to write about it, an expert – a historian.

CHAPTER 5

Languages

No wars, no revolutions, no civil unrest or military coups, no famines or tidal waves: nothing extreme anywhere I've lived. In my mind I would have preferred a more demanding slot. The years between the end of the Second World War and the fall of the Berlin Wall gave women like me plenty of things to think about, and, for some, ideologies around which to organise their lives, but little to put up with, unless you include fear of the Bomb – and even that seemed to be a thing that came and went.

The counterpane I had on my bed as a young child – we were living in a place called Shippan Point on Long Island Sound – had a map of the world on it. In the evening, after my parents had said good night and gone back downstairs, I'd turn on the light and rearrange the world. Suppose Columbus hadn't discovered America, and suppose the Indians were still living in their tepees; suppose Marco Polo hadn't yet been to China; suppose Jesus hadn't been crucified, Abel hadn't been killed, Eve hadn't bitten into the apple; where in all those cases would we be? Suppose the dinosaurs re-roamed the earth, where would we be then? Such exciting thoughts and so sad that nothing could make them happen, that everything was now settled.

But many things have changed, and a twenty-first-century map on a child's bedspread would look very different from the one I had. Old countries have re-emerged, old cities recovered their former names; even in Europe new countries have appeared for the first time. Slovenia, Slovakia, Belarus: they haven't got the new-born splendour that the Andes had when Pizarro came upon them, but the maps have been redrawn, and even on the shallow bay it's in order to make some response.

I first got a sense that the world order was changing in June 1989, five months before the fall of the Berlin Wall, when footage of a Soviet rail accident was shown on the evening news – I mean on the *Nine O'Clock News* in London. It was an unusually bad accident: close to six hundred people died, and I can see the train now, stuck – sunk in a coma, Trotsky would have said – in flat, dry, yellowish countryside, somewhere near Ufa, in the east of the USSR. The striking thing (from my point of view) was that the footage had been made available to Western viewers. Before, if there had been an accident in the Soviet Union we read about it in the newspaper: we didn't see it on our television screens. No one claimed that what was happening now was an important moment in television history or international relations; there was no fanfare, just that train appearing out of nowhere in the corner of my sitting-room.

I had known some Russian in my twenties: now I decided it was time to learn it again.

My mother had wanted to teach us when we were still living in the States but the offer had always been resisted. It's a tricky business allowing other people to put their words into one's mouth, one's mother especially. But in 1947, when I was nine, my father was summoned back to company headquarters in Brussels, and we left the US and the strenuous monoglottism of American life. Suddenly and surprisingly, speaking English was no longer enough. In fact, it seemed provincial, even laughable. My father had studied French and German at Cambridge; he'd lived in Brussels for several years in the early 1930s; his French, as I saw it, was perfect. My poor mother, who spoke many languages fluently but not French, struggled for a few years and then got the hang of it. Eager as always to avoid being told what to say, I was in equal measure anxious to know it and reluctant to let anyone teach me. I picked it up soon enough and for several years French was the language in which I thought, went to school, talked to my friends. By the time I came to England, an uncertain fourteen-year-old schoolgirl, it was clear to me that languages offered my best chance of getting by.

Dimly perceiving a future as an interpreter at the UN, I decided when I got into Oxford that it would be sensible to know some Russian after all. 'Is there anyone here who has never done any Russian?' the head of the department, a tall, dark-suited émigré, asked would-be first-year students. I put my hand up. He walked over to where I was sitting, bent over me in an émigré sort of way and asked me in Russian a question I only half-understood. It could do no harm to say in reply that my mother was Russian. Three years later, I had my degree and not long afterwards lost interest in reading or speaking any language other than English.

Far from leading to the UN, language-hopping kept me at home, obsessively attending to other people's English words – washing them, ironing them, preparing them for publication. A very different form of ventriloquism from the kind I'd expected to practise in the sleek UN headquarters on First Avenue, but ventriloquism nonetheless. There's a theory that bilingual children develop at an earlier age a sense of how languages work and what they are for. And maybe that describes my case or maybe I owe my editorial pernicketiness to the embarrassment I used to feel at the mistakes my mother made.

Villains in movies spoke English with a Russian accent; so did Peter Ustinov; so did my mother (my friends found it very charming). But in the days of the Cold War you never heard anyone speak Russian in the ordinary way of things, in the street, in a shop, on the bus. Glasnost changed that: Russian railway accidents on the evening news were followed by Russian-speakers on *Newsnight*. I didn't like the fact that I couldn't understand them. So I met Nadia, who in those days barely spoke English.

In the Soviet Union, which they left in September 1989, Nadia had been a scriptwriter and Volodya, her husband, a dentist; he now practises in London and Moscow and keeps her in the manner to which many Russian women have always subliminally been accustomed. But when they first arrived here Nadia gave Russian lessons. She and I didn't do grammar: I was certain I'd be much slower to grasp it the second time round and didn't want to have to face up to that fact. So she told me about her life and I told her about mine. Then I told her about the Eitingons: the American Eitingons and their putative relatives behind the Iron Curtain.

CHAPTER 6

Cold War

At the beginning of 1988, the last year of the Cold War, the *New York Times* published an article headed 'Intellectuals and Assassins: Annals of Stalin's Killerati'.* Fingered among others were two friends, Pablo Neruda and David Siqueiros, the Chilean poet and the Mexican painter, both Communists; Siqueiros was involved in an earlier attempt to assassinate Trotsky, Neruda in helping Siqueiros to obtain a Chilean visa when he had to leave Mexico. But its two principal protagonists were called Eitingon. One was Trotsky's stalker, Leonid Eitingon. The other – a bolt from the blue – was Max, my grandfather's cousin, a close friend and colleague of Freud's.

Stephen Schwartz, the author of the piece, had set out to show how deeply involved Western intellectuals were in Stalin's nastiest moments. 'When Stalin's men sought agents for the most depraved and most criminal tasks,' he wrote, 'they found them not among brutes of the underworld, but among sensitive and cultivated people in the highest levels of intellectual society – poets and psychiatrists who became conspirators and spies.' Leonid Eitingon was Stalin's man –

---

* It appeared in the *Times Book Review* on 24 January. Theodore Draper's response was published in the *New York Review of Books* for 14 April and Stephen Schwartz's response to that in a letter to the *New York Review* for 16 June. A number of other letters on the subject of the Eitingons were published in both places around those dates.

that was obvious – but in Schwartz's reckoning sensitive, cultivated Max was Leonid's agent in Freudian camouflage.

If you set aside Schwartz's more lurid suggestions – that Max conspired with the Nazis, and through them was responsible for Stalin's decision to purge his generals in the run-up to the Second World War – the notion isn't entirely far-fetched even now, and it certainly wouldn't have seemed so if you'd been a Russian émigré living in Paris in the late 1930s.

In December 1938 a Russian singer, Nadezhda Plevitskaya, 'the nightingale of Kursk', was tried by a court in Paris for the part she had played in the kidnapping the previous year of an elderly White Russian general. She was married to another, younger Russian general who was probably working for the Soviets, and since he vanished a few hours after the first general disappeared it was assumed that he was responsible for the kidnapping. What was harder to work out was Plevitskaya's role in it all. Was she, as some people said, her husband's 'evil genius'? Or was she an innocent woman, dumped in the shit by a careless husband?

And what about Max? Why had his name come up in the course of her trial? A doctor, a psychoanalyst, what part had he played? He was, or had been, rich, very rich, but why would he have given money, and on a regular basis, to Plevitskaya and her husband? Plevitskaya said simply that he was her friend and her patron – that he'd dressed her 'from top to toe'. In the local press, émigré or French, any interpretation was possible. 'As for the celebrated Maecenas,' one newspaper would speculate, 'he was nothing more than a senior Soviet official, responsible for turning the furs requisitioned in Siberia into cash abroad, on behalf of the government.' Was Max, 'the celebrated Maecenas', in fact a Soviet agent? Was he acting on behalf of Leonid, described by Schwartz as 'the KGB's outstanding expert in operations against Russian anti-Communist exiles'? Did he set the operation up? By which Schwartz meant: did he pay for it?

All the Eitingons whom I knew, the members of my mother's immediate and not-so-immediate family, had once been rich, as Max was rich. They had all had a share in the same pot of gold. The money, as was the case with many Russian Jews, came from the fur trade: the Eitingon family, so one of them would boast, had been fur traders for three hundred years. The business, once in the hands of Max's father, was now in the charge of his cousin. This Eitingon was called Motty and he was my mother's uncle, the one with whom she was travelling from Moscow – Moscow! – to the US when she met my father over that game of ping-pong somewhere between Le Havre and New York.

Max Eitingon (1881–1943), Motty Eitingon (1885–1956), Leonid Eitingon (1899–1981): they were men of their times.

I was already aware of Leonid Eitingon's existence and I knew he'd been involved in Trotsky's assassination, and once or twice, when the occasion arose, I'd mentioned that I might have a connection with him. At the same time I knew that my family didn't think, or want to think, that this Leonid had anything to do with them: in fact they didn't accept that he was an Eitingon at all. One explanation I'd heard was that a Soviet citizen had come to

Moscow from the provinces sometime after the Revolution, and, needing a place to live, had borrowed the Eitingon name together with a flat the Eitingons had vacated in 1918. And if it didn't happen then maybe it had happened thirty years earlier, when Max Eitingon's father left Russia and a family quite unconnected with the Eitingons changed its name in order to establish a right to his property. 'Eitingon', they believed, had been a name that went with a flat: a flag of convenience for a very bad man. Few people in those Cold War days would have readily accepted having a KGB general as a relative; and if it doesn't seem so terrible now, imagine what it would have been like in the last days of the Second World War to have to accept that your uncle, say, had been a general in the SS or a concentration camp attendant. For many people there was no distinction.

I mentioned Leonid now to my mother's sister Lola, who said, testily: 'My family is the family I know. Others may have the same name but that's all.' My mother wasn't interested and said nothing. Her cousins wanted nothing to do with it. For the time being, 'Leonid Eitingon' was a confection where my family was concerned: a figment of the Soviet imagination or merely the imagination of Stephen Schwartz.

And yet, and yet. The next time I saw Lola – she lived in Brazil and came to Europe infrequently – it seemed she'd found a place in the family into which this supernumerary might fit. Her mother, she told me, my grandmother, a woman much given to grudges ('très rancunière'), had complained into her old age that my long since dead grandfather had once allowed a younger brother of his, a boy on the run, to stay in their house; that the boy had brought with him bundles of illicit (i.e. revolutionary) tracts and that he'd left some of them under his bed when he finally went on his way. As far as I know, my grandfather's only younger brother was my mother's Uncle Motty and it can't have been him, but the Russian for 'cousin' is *dvoiurodny brat* (literally, 'a brother related through his grandparents'), and a mistake Russians commonly make is to say 'brother' when they mean 'cousin'. Later on, when Lola's memory was failing, she denied the whole story and perhaps it wasn't true, but I made a note of her words as she spoke them and so know for sure what she said. Of course there's nothing to prove that Leonid was the brother or cousin in question, but it can't be ruled out.

As for Max, wherever among my relatives I asked I got this sort of answer: 'An absolute sweetie.'* In the photographs of Freud surrounded by his acolytes, Max is the one with spectacles and a moustache, the one of whom one might say: 'Who's that funny little man at the back? Should I have heard of him?'

In 1907 as a young doctor Max had come to Vienna to sit at Freud's feet; 'He was the first one to come to me,' Freud would later say, meaning the first one to come to him from abroad, and he was grateful for it. And not only that: Max remained loyal to Freud all his life, unlike many of Freud's other colleagues (Schwartz, unimpressed, calls him 'Freud's factotum'). Finally, he was very generous and Freud was grateful to him for that too.

---

* When I see him now in family photographs I'm reminded of Motty's son Tommy, with whom, as a small child, I considered myself in love largely because he was fond of me and, like me, fond of lamb chops. 'You only like lamb chops because Tommy does,' my brother would say, hitting the same note of disparagement as my mother when she said: 'You're not really left-handed – you're just trying to be like your brother.'

Motty, the undisputed head of the clan, was a more troubling figure for my family, someone in whom they had all made a large emotional investment and who with time sold that investment short. My mother had once adored him (he was the Eitingon to whom she spoke most days on the phone) and my father, too, though amused by his un-English ways, had consistently sung his praises in the letters he wrote to his parents. How could he not? Motty was a man of great wealth and great charm – until, that is, his luck ran out and with it his wealth and much of his charm. In that way and several others, all too like his near-namesake, Uncle Morty, in his friend Clifford Odets's play *Awake and Sing!*

Motty liked to be busy and to make deals, and money made it possible for him to make deals on a very grand scale. So it was that in 1926, for example, he signed a contract with the Soviet government for the purchase of an impressive eight million dollars' worth of fur for export to the United States. Such deals were not possible unless you had very good contacts inside the Soviet Union, and Motty had excellent contacts. So the question has to be asked: was Leonid one of them? And what favours would Motty have had to do in return? Schwartz doesn't mention Motty by name in the article but merely says that Leonid 'used as a cover business operations for the Soviet Fur Trust'. And though I don't know that he got that kind of cover I do know that he asked for it.

Cold War paranoia was still flourishing in the late 1980s, and the excitement caused by the appearance of 'Intellectuals and Assassins' wasn't quick to die down. In April the *New York Review of Books* published a rejoinder by the historian Theodore Draper. Entitled 'The Mystery of Max Eitingon', it was both an exasperated refutation of Schwartz and a diligent defence of Max. If what Schwartz said was true, Draper wrote, 'Max Eitingon is one of the most remarkable cases on record of a double life or personality.'

Left-wing apostates of one kind or another played a crucial part in the intellectual Cold War, people who had seen for themselves, or in themselves, what they didn't like about the Soviet system. And they tended to tell the most vivid tales. Schwartz comes from a family of Russian Jewish immigrants – many of them Communists, as he was in his younger days. By 1988 he was, in his own words, 'horribly disillusioned', and the case he makes against Max Eitingon connects with that disillusionment. But Draper too had been well to the left in his younger days: did his decision to investigate Schwartz's claims have something to do with that experience, with his own memories of the passion with which lies were told on both sides in the war between the West and the Soviet Union?

Provoked by Draper, Schwartz had another go at the Eitingons, this time in a letter to the *New York Review* stating quite clearly his belief that Motty, Max and Leonid were working together for the Soviet government: 'I do not believe', he wrote, 'that the Eitingon companies' relationship to the Soviet Union was an innocent one; I believe they provided business cover for GPU operations, and that the explanations of Dr Eitingon to his psychoanalytic colleagues' – about the ups and downs of the family fortune – 'were fabricated to hide a decision about allocation of funds by his Soviet masters.'

Might that be right? Can it be, as Schwartz suggests,

that Max was his own kind of double agent: Stalin's man as well as Freud's? Or should we go with Draper and dismiss the possibility of any connection at all between Max and the agencies of the Soviet state? And what about Motty? Schwartz doesn't believe that the relationship between Motty's companies and the Soviet Union was an innocent one. But might there be degrees of innocence just as there are degrees of complicity? Finally, Draper says there is 'no Leonid Eitingon in any known branch of the family'. But it isn't something he is able to prove.

Neither Communist nor anti-Communist, captivated by the left but never quite of the left, I'd like to say that I've set out to find the truth (but I'm not sure there will be a truth) or to avenge my family's honour (in whose eyes?) or to shine the light of freedom into the dark spaces of the twentieth century. But if that can't be done, if I can't manage these things, I can at least try to do these three men the justice of describing their lives as far as it's been possible for me to know them.

With Nadia's encouragement, I started making phone calls. Until the mid-1990s there were no telephone directories in the former Soviet Union, but if you were in the country and dialled 09 and were lucky enough to get through to the operator there was a good chance that you would get the number you were hoping for. A friend of Nadia's in Moscow dialled 09, and a number showed up for a family of Eitingons living on Varshavsky Chossay.

I had my text in front of me, dictated by Nadia, and I still have it now, in a yellow spiral notebook from Ryman. This, more or less, is what I said: 'Is that the Eitingons' flat? My name is Mary-Kay Wilmers. I am ringing from

London. Is it all right for you to speak to me? My mother's name is Eitingon and we are trying to put together a family tree but all the Eitingons we know live in the West. I know I had a relative in Moscow. He was called Leonid. Do you know someone of that name? Is he related to you?'

The first time I rang I spoke to Leonid's daughter-in-law (Galia), the second time to his granddaughter (Little Galia). I thought it would be proper to speak to his son, Lonya (a diminutive of Leonid), but every time I rang, Lonya was out. Clearly he didn't want any trouble from nosy relatives (or non-relatives) in the West.

Leonid, I would soon learn, had four children, plus a stepdaughter. I already knew that he had died in 1981. (Nadia had made enquiries of her own.) What I discovered now was that his family were happy both to acknowledge the fact of his existence and to use his ('our') name. It was all so much easier, so much more open than I'd expected. A drop of poison in my coffee, or on the tip of an umbrella, an electric shock delivered there and then down the phone line: I thought I was taking great risks in making these phone calls and instead found myself exchanging pleasantries with two women called Galia.

I'm exaggerating, of course. I didn't really believe that my life was in danger, but the psychological conventions of the Cold War were still in place and I was impressed with my own boldness in choosing to speak on the phone with the family of a high-level KGB functionary who was also a high-level killer. And a relative of mine.

CHAPTER 7

The Pale

In February 1893 a passport was issued to Chaim Eitingon, a merchant resident in the town of Orsha in what was then the Russian province of Mogilev, now part of independent Belarus. Six months later a similar passport was issued in his wife's name. Max Eitingon was their son. He was twelve in 1893.

The information about the passport comes from documents kept at the State Archives in Minsk. Although I got it in 1992, six months after the Soviet Union was dissolved, I wasn't allowed to know the name of the resourceful young Russian who went into the archives to look for it. I met him on several occasions, had meals with him in Moscow and in London, but I knew him only as Igor. An academic, or perhaps a research student, he had a useful relationship with a politician who for a time was a serious contender for high office. He would, for example, get the politician's car fixed, take his wife to the airport or find him a new battery for his radio. The politician might pay him for this or he might make it possible for him to earn some money elsewhere – e.g. by getting access to an archive that was supposed to be shut. The young man wouldn't have said why he wanted to see the archive: he might have told a fib – in a society where people lied habitually it wasn't a big deal – or he might not have said anything. The politician wouldn't in any case have cared very much. Academics, especially those who didn't teach, weren't well paid, and it was normal for a bright young man to assess what talents he had and market himself accordingly.

Whatever the exact procedure, the young man said something to the politician and I got a miscellaneous collection of data on the Eitingon family from the Belarus archive. If the politician were to succeed in his bid for power, I would get more – or so I was led to understand. For a while things looked good, but in the end it didn't work out.

Chaim Eitingon – Efim in Russian, Charles when he once visited the United States – was the founder of the family fortune. He was also my mother's great-uncle. He was there when she married her first husband in great pomp at the Hotel Adlon in Berlin in 1928, and can be seen, his pinched disapproving face just behind his wife's, less pinched but equally disapproving, in the one photograph my mother kept as a record of the event. My poor mother, no one could say she looked happy: she was only twenty-one, she hadn't wanted to get married and neither the ornate setting nor the many members of the Eitingon clan who turned out for the occasion made up for that.

Until the 1720s there had effectively been no Jews in the Russian Empire. But in the early 18th century as first Peter the Great, then Catherine expanded their territory westward, the empire gradually came to include a large Jewish population, the largest in the world. Privileged Jews – successful merchants, university graduates, the very wealthy – were allowed (on and off) to live in the cities of Inner Russia, principally Moscow and St Petersburg. But the vast majority went on living where they'd always lived. Or, to put it differently, were confined to the territory largely made up of present-day Belarus, most of Lithuania, much of Poland and some of the Ukraine, and formalised as the Pale of Jewish Settlement in 1791, when members of the Moscow merchant class protested against an influx of Jewish merchants from the provinces. In tsarist Russia there were no legal rights, no laws that applied equally to everyone, and no groups that weren't discriminated against. No one, with the exception of the tsar, was free to move around the country as they might have wished.

Chaim's father, my great-great-grandfather, was called Mordecai. He had four sons and four daughters by two wives and died in 1880.* Like Chaim, Mordecai was a merchant – in other words, a trader – and like many of his descendants what he traded was fur, buying pelts or skins from Jewish pedlars and exporting them to larger Jewish enterprises further west. He travelled more than I'd expected. In the only set of documents I possess – they come from the Leipzig City Archive – he and his wife are listed as Austrian citizens, and although it's clear that he continued to live mainly in Russia it's possible that sometime after 1867, when a new, more liberal Austrian constitution came into force, he established a trading post and with it a domicile in Buchach in eastern Galicia, roughly forty miles from the Russian border, since the same documents indicate that Chaim and his family had lived in Buchach for a time and that they too had Austrian nationality. Chaim is

* It wasn't so in my mother's day, but it seems that no one now knows which were the half- and which the full brothers. My guess is that Chaim and my great-grandfather, Itsak Leib, who fathered nine children and died young (young for dying), shared the same mother.

even said to have done military service in the Austro-Hungarian army, though I wonder – such were the Eitingon ways – whether he didn't make a donation to charity instead. These were men who knew how to get what they wanted and it certainly made sense for them to have Austrian passports: the Habsburg authorities imposed heavy tariffs on foreign goods passing through their territory, and Austrian anti-Semitism was much less active than its Russian counterpart in those years. If there was going to be more trouble in Russia, as there inevitably would be, better to be an Austrian citizen.

Whatever their citizenship, the lives Mordecai and his family led were Jewish lives and the language they spoke was Yiddish, effectively the Jewish language. It was quite usual for Russian Jews of Mordecai's generation – let's say he was born in 1825 – to be unable to speak Russian, let alone read it, though the little evidence I have suggests that his children could speak it at least. In the last decade of the nineteenth century only 1 per cent of Jews living in the Russian Empire described Russian as their first language.

Yet most of the Eitingons I knew, my mother's and grandmother's generations, spoke to each other in Russian, or in a few instances Polish; and it was pretty much taken for granted that they could speak and read German and English and in some cases French. Motty's daughter Lee told me not long ago that her mother, Chaim's daughter Fanny, who was seven years old when she left Russia, didn't even speak Russian, which I find hard to believe. But in the social hierarchy of languages German came first. That at least was the position until 1939, when events and, in time, fashion turned it the other way about.

My mother, who was born in 1907, not only didn't

speak Yiddish: she claimed not to have any memory of its being spoken. There were a few Yiddish phrases that she and my father regularly used – *goyim naches*, for example, designated the sort of daft thing a Gentile might do – but that's quite usual in Jewish families, however assimilated. It may be that, consciously or not, she wanted to forget any Yiddish she'd heard in her childhood, thereby marking the distance between the life she'd led with my father and the life, if not of her parents, then of her grandparents. What's interesting is that the changeover from a monoglot population despised because so inward-looking to a race of polyglots distrusted because so cosmopolitan seems to have taken not more than two generations.

In 1893, when the passports were issued, Chaim Eitingon was thirty-five. His wife was a few years younger and appears, as was often the case, to have been a relative of his mother's, which may explain why the couple look so alike – a humourless, fastidious pair. They had four children. Max was the eldest. The only one I knew was Lee's mother, Fanny, Motty's by then long since discarded first wife. Great-Aunt Fanny in my day was an old lady with a long straight nose, like her father's, who in my eyes was more impressive than the other New York Eitingons by virtue of being tall as well as being deaf and therefore unlikely to join a conversation.

Most of the documents I have been able to find suggest that Chaim was already well-off in 1893, though my mother used to tell me that her father and his twin brother (Chaim's nephews) were so poor in their youth that they slept on tables in the tailor's shop where they were apprenticed. I wonder. A contemporary of hers, one of her many cousins, said that they had all grown up in a 'golden ghetto'. Either one of them could have been misremembering. It wouldn't have been unlike my mother, who in later life wasn't poor, to have claimed great poverty on her father's behalf, and not unlike her cousin to have claimed great wealth, at least in the past where wealth tends to have a glow and a romance that it lacks in the present. On the other hand, they were talking about different generations so both might (just) have been right. One of the Soviet Eitingons, when I eventually got to know them, told me that his family had a cottage in the grounds of the enormous house in which my family lived. Everyone thinks what it suits them to think and it suits me to point out the inconsistencies: 'snake-speak', my mother might have called it.

Chaim had started out in the fur business at the age of seventeen, when he left the family home for Moscow. Not many young Jews were permitted to learn the ins and outs of their trade in the city, which suggests that Mordecai too was a gifted businessman who one way or another had been appointed (or had paid to be appointed) by the Imperial Court to the first or second merchants' guild. It wasn't an everyday thing. In 1852, out of 99,088 Jews living in the province of Mogilev, 2,672 were merchants, and of these five belonged to the second guild.

Chaim prospered, and in 1882, before he was twenty-five, he had founded his own wholesale fur business in Moscow. That, too, was a privilege: not many Jews were formally allowed to register as merchants in the cities of Inner Russia, and in the last decades of the nineteenth century the authorities were not inclined to bend the rules in anyone's favour.

CHAPTER 8

Anti-Semitism

Tsar Alexander II, a reasonably tolerant man, was assassinated early in 1881. Though the Jews weren't thought to be immediately responsible for his death, in most Russian minds they were very much part of the calamity that had befallen their country. 'These Yids make themselves too loathsome to Russians,' the new tsar, Alexander III, remarked; and the pogroms that followed his father's death lasted from 1881 until 1884. 'So long as they continue to exploit Christians this hatred will not diminish,' he warned, and he was right in the sense that the 'disturbances', i.e. the pogroms, were uncommonly violent and uncommonly prolonged. But the response of the Jewish population was more surprising. The old habit of self-abasement, the willingness to accept whatever God or the host nation decreed, gave way to a new determination to take matters into their own hands – either by leaving the country or by opposing the regime.

There is no record of the number of Jews who left Russia between 1881 and the First World War. But in 1880 an estimated eight thousand Jewish immigrants were registered at American points of entry; by 1890 the figure had risen to over forty thousand; a new crackdown in 1891 saw the Jews expelled from Moscow, and by the following year the figure had risen to seventy-six thousand. There are no exact figures for the countries of Western Europe, but the increase everywhere was substantial. Most of those who left Russia were poor. Hard-working, conservative Chaim, already a successful businessman, was prudent.

Prudent enough, or smart or quick or lucky enough, to open an office in Leipzig in 1891 and make Leipzig his headquarters. (He also negotiated with one of the Rothschilds to buy a stretch of land on the east bank of the Jordan, though the sale didn't in the end go through.) Leipzig was a pre-eminent centre of the European fur trade, and as Chaim's enterprise grew it became increasingly sensible for him to expand from there. Moving from one country to another wasn't in any case a difficult thing to do – or not if you had money. 'The frontiers', Stefan Zweig said of late nineteenth-century Europe, 'were nothing but symbolic lines that one crossed with as little thought as one crosses the Greenwich Meridian.' Having made his move Chaim would stay put. After twenty years he would apply for German citizenship and then change his mind, remaining an Austrian domiciled in Leipzig for the rest of his life. It was in the Austro-Hungarian army that his son Max would serve as a doctor in the First World War.

I visited Leipzig at the beginning of 1999, when the visual markers of the transition from Stalinism to the global market were still much in evidence: on the one hand, the bleak concrete spaces of the GDR; on the other, neon figures on the skyline marking the ups and downs of the dollar and the brand-new euro for punters to follow late into the night. The tourist shops – and there were lots of them – made what money they could out of the demise of the old world order, not only with books of photographs showing

the proud city of 1939 and its ruins in 1945, but, more
camply, with racks of retro postcards made of laminated
GDR exit and entry permits and restaurant menus.

I had once, very briefly, crossed Checkpoint Charlie,
but other than that had never been to what was East
Germany, and arrived in Leipzig with a suitable sense of
historical occasion. Leipzig/Halle Airport was new, white
and hardly used, with only the smell of a place where people still habitually smoked to indicate that this was a public space that hadn't long been part of the West. The road
to the city, like many in Eastern Europe, was wide and
empty, the countryside itself very flat, very bare.

It was February and the ground was covered in a hard
layer of snow. There were a few post-Stalinist settlements
here and there along the road; a few very new-looking factories, and in the distance clumps, or sometimes a wood,
of tall, thin trees. I tried to imagine what arriving here
might have been like for Chaim and his family and the
best I could do was to dress them in boots and long coats
and, even more inappropriately, give them a cart on which
to have dragged their belongings through Eastern Europe
until eventually they emerged through the trees and into
my life. It was a very brief fantasy: I knew perfectly well
that they would have travelled by train in some comfort in
their own compartment (or two compartments: one for
the children and one for the adults) and, if they were travelling overnight, with their own linen sheets to put on the
beds.

I'd heard from my mother that somewhere in the world
the Eitingons had a street named after them. But she was
vague about it and in those days I hadn't been keen to
know more. However, a cousin and contemporary of hers

whom I'd recently visited in New York knew all about it: indeed, in August 1992 she'd visited Leipzig as a guest of the mayor for the official reopening of the Eitingon-Krankenhaus, Saxony's first Jewish hospital. The street, too, the cousin said, was now once again known as Eitingonstrasse – re-re-named from Nazi times when it had been called Adolf-Hitler-Strasse.

I had been pleased at the idea of Eitingonstrasse becoming Adolf-Hitler-Strasse: it would, I thought, give some oomph to my story – though I knew it was likely that the old lady was just trying to give more oomph to hers. In the airport bookshop I consulted three different guidebooks as well as a map: nowhere was an Eitingon-strasse or hospital listed. I was amused by the thought that the old lady had been fibbing, but it didn't justify a flight to Leipzig.

The street, when I eventually found it, wasn't exactly a wide tree-lined avenue fit to honour the Führer or a boulevard to compare with the Karl-Marx-Allee of Honecker's Berlin: it was a dingy half-street that ran between the front of the hospital and the side of a 1950s football stadium, before petering out at the city cleaning works. It can't ever have been much of a street, though a contemporary account describes the hospital as 'situated in one of the best parts of Leipzig'. The building itself is hand-some – sober in a German-Jewish way. In its original gar-den setting it must have looked as it was intended to look – like a sanatorium, a *Stubenkrankenhaus*. Today it has more the appearance of a charitable institution whose donor was a serious but not a wasteful citizen. Originally advertised as having forty-four beds in 'third class', twenty-seven in 'second', eight in 'first', with no more than seven beds in any ward and everywhere the most advanced medical equipment, it had been intended for the widows and daughters of businessmen – it wasn't, in other words, a hospital for paupers, not even Jewish paupers. Though open to patients of all religions, the catering was 'strictly kosher'.

In December 1939 the army settled into the hospital, taking over all its advanced medical equipment, while the Jewish patients and staff were bundled off to a nursing home on the city's outskirts. Later a house would be bought with Eitingon money and turned into a replacement hospital of sorts, cut off by a high fence from the neighbouring town. From there deportations proper began in January 1942. In August 1943 the last remaining doctor, Otto Michael, was sent to Theresienstadt. He too now has a street to his name.

Leipzig, someone in Leipzig told me, is the 'town with the most landmarks in Europe'. Hard to know how to measure these things, but Bach was the city's musical director for more than twenty-five years, Goethe studied at Leipzig University, Schiller lived there, Wagner was born there and the Gewandhaus orchestra plays there. The world's first daily paper was published in Leipzig in 1650. But from the early Middle Ages until the mid-nineteenth century, it was probably more widely known for its trade fairs than anything else. In Soviet times the Eastern Bloc equivalent of the Frankfurt Book Fair was held in Leipzig, and even now it's evident as soon as you get off the plane that fairs are an essential part of the city's business.

Wagner called it a 'Jewish metropolis' but it was never a city friendly to Jews: for nearly 250 years the Dukes of

Saxony banned them from living anywhere in their territory. Jewish merchants nevertheless came to the fairs in
prodigious numbers, despite the financial penalties the
Saxon and Leipzig authorities chose to impose on them. In
1840 at the Easter Fair alone there were three-and-a-half
thousand Jewish visitors, mostly fur dealers from Austria,
Poland and Russia. They lodged, as Jewish visitors to the
fairs had always done, on the Brühl, a long street in the
centre of the city that would, in due course, become synonymous with the fur trade, and held religious services in
their rooms. The city, acknowledging its dependence on
them ('an important trade for Leipzig and Saxony is exclusively in the hands of these people'*), was resigned to their
presence, but it wasn't until 1837, when the fairs were
beginning to lose their attraction, that permission was
given for a synagogue to be built. If Chaim chose to make
this not altogether amiable city his headquarters it would
only have been because of its importance to the fur trade.

Migration, even for him, can't have been easy. German
Jews, like their English and French counterparts, had
embarked on the road to assimilation: they tended not to
speak Yiddish, or even know Hebrew; the form of religion
they practised was liberal rather than Orthodox; their intellectual interests secular rather than traditional; their dress
no different from anyone else's. These emancipated Jews
didn't just look down on the new arrivals: they didn't want
them there at all. Yet between 1880 and 1910 the percentage of foreign Jews in the city rose from 10 to 68 per cent.

Chaim and his wife didn't dress in the old Eastern
European way, and they spoke German as well as Yiddish,

* From an 1832 report addressed to the Leipzig City Police by the local
chamber of commerce (Handlungs-Deputirten und Kramermeister).

but unlike most of the younger members of their family they were Orthodox Jews. And that would have been a problem. In Leipzig all the Jewish community's institutions were liberal: Orthodox Jews were allowed to attend liberal services if they accepted the presence of an organ; they were allowed to send their children to religious instruction provided the children were bare-headed; they could be buried in the Jewish cemetery, but the cemetery didn't have a section reserved for Orthodox burials. The Kingdom of Saxony had never been especially enlightened in its attitude to foreigners and in that respect things hadn't changed since the creation of the Reich. In Prussia, for example, it was possible for foreigners to establish their own communities and organisations. Not so in Saxony.

That may have been one reason why between 1913 and 1915 Chaim made strenuous (if unavailing) efforts to become a naturalised German citizen. By then things were beginning to change. The law prohibiting ritual slaughter had been revoked in 1910. In 1917 an Orthodox rabbi was appointed. Five years later, the first Orthodox synagogue was officially opened; it was the second-largest synagogue in Leipzig, with seats for 1,200 people. The man who made it possible, who bought the land on which it was built, gave the money for its construction and chose the architect, was Chaim. According to contemporary reports it was a magnificent building: simple on the outside, 'like the Alhambra' inside. It served as the communal Orthodox synagogue until its destruction on Kristallnacht, in November 1938.

The new synagogue was unusually well managed: 'The board in charge of running the synagogue knew about the carelessness with which Eastern Jews in general behaved in their places of worship and were determined not to allow this to happen,' Adolf Diamant reported in his chronicle of Jewish life in Leipzig. Chaim was a scary man, as I imagine him. 'Your father visited me, looking very healthy and rejuvenated, and monosyllabic and impatient as, I assume, is in his nature,' Freud wrote to Chaim's son Max in 1920.

The Leipzig fur trade had its Masonic customs as well as its hierarchies, and in time Chaim would reach the very top, becoming a 'King of the Brühl'. Beside the kings – there might be more than one – there were twenty-five or thirty 'dukes' and 'counts', making up the fur-trading aristocracy: toffs who arrived on the Brühl every weekday morning in their own cars or horse-drawn carriages, ate in their own restaurants, met in their own coffee-houses, pursued their business by phone or telegram in their own offices, and generally had nothing to do with the lower ranks, the former travelling salesmen or pedlars milling about on the street below. There were a few Gentile fur traders but not many (the languages spoken on the Brühl were German and Yiddish), and on Friday afternoons as the sun started to set the merchants and the big shots all went home for the Sabbath. Once a handsome monument to nineteenth-century mercantilism, the Brühl when I visited had the dishevelled look of a street newly introduced to late capitalism. The back entrance of a Marriott Hotel occupied the space at No. 37, where Chaim's offices stood.

By the time Chaim was established in Leipzig several other members of the family had addresses there too. That was how Jewish enterprise worked – 'the larger the business, the larger the family', in the words of the historian Yuri

Slezkine. It's no wonder the Eitingons were known early on as the 'Rothschilds of Leipzig'. I have a list of the flats where they lived, or stayed when they were in town: they are all within a few streets of each other, in the most expensive part of the city, just off the Rosenthal, Leipzig's nicest park. The buildings are solid, classy, ornate, with stucco façades. Each one is four storeys high with one flat to each floor: flats with high ceilings and parquet floors and in some cases a ballroom. They were built at the end of the century, in uniform rows taking up a whole street without any shops or breaks of any kind to distract the eye from the suggestion of ease. It could well have been these streets my mother's cousin had in mind when she spoke of growing up in a 'golden ghetto'. ('We never talked about money,' she said on another occasion, 'because we had so much of it.') It isn't a place where I would have wanted to be, and I can easily imagine myself imprisoned there, a morose child of whom something lively had been expected.

The place where Chaim lived was an altogether different order of dwelling, one which it cost him 340,000 DM to build (say, a million pounds today) – just a little bit more than his three-yearly tax average, which came to 310,000 DM. 'Oh wow,' the taxi driver said as we came up to a large *Jugendstil* villa painted white with cream ornaments, a turret at the gable end and beside the top windows columns ending in palm-trees. It had a garden rather than grounds, but the garden in those days was large enough to house a 'pavilion' in which other members of the family might live, or stay for a time. Opposite is a girls' school built in 1907; at one end of the road is the Rosenthal, at the other the Gohliser Schlösschen, Leipzig's only castle. The zoo is near by. The street that runs along the bottom is called Poets' Way. Everything, it seems, is designed to promote a sense of well-being – except the street's present name, Lumumbastrasse, with its reminder of more recent distress and more advanced forms of prejudice. In the days of the GDR the house was a foreign students' residence; when I visited, it was being done up to be let. The city council, mindful of its landmarks, had decided that some parts of the house couldn't be altered. 'Mr Eitingon's apartment', I was told, 'is still as it was.'

Mr Eitingon died in 1932, three years after his wife. They were buried together in the new Jewish cemetery, where Orthodox rites could be performed. Their grave is larger by far than any of those near by; like the others, it is made of black marble and in Art Deco mode. Chaim's obituaries spoke first about the causes he had supported ('There was hardly an area where he did not give help'), his astounding generosity ('He was famous even outside Germany for his philanthropy'), his 'great commercial gifts', his 'conscientiousness' and his 'modesty'. Writing in the 1960s, Wilhelm Harmelin, whose family had been involved in the Leipzig fur trade, remembered Chaim as a 'reserved, almost shy' man 'whose face told of the suffering and compassion of Russian Jewry'. I must be projecting when I look at photographs and see it as pinched and disapproving.

Between 1926 and 1928 Chaim's firm, Ch. Eitingon Aktiengesellschaft, then the leading German fur wholesaler, had an annual turnover of twenty-five million marks, which strictly translates as seventy-two million dollars in 2008, a figure that hardly seems to do justice to the splendour of Chaim's achievement. He had by then retired, but the business he built up was the basis of Motty's fortune and of Max's largesse – and the source of the money that Leonid Eitingon would in time hope to use to facilitate the purposes of the Soviet state.

CHAPTER 9

1917

My mother and her sisters were in Moscow when the Revolution broke out. They'd been there, in a flat on Armiansky Pereulok, since 1914. Before that they'd been living in Poland, but when a house at the end of their street was hit by a German shell my grandparents decided they'd be better off in Moscow. 'What did you do during the Revolution?' I asked my Aunt Lola. 'We played cards,' she replied. 'The children in one room, the grown-ups in another.' My grandfather had been a textile manufacturer in Lodz until the war and would be again after it. 'How did he support himself and his family in Moscow?' I asked. 'He did business,' Lola said firmly. 'What sort of business?' 'Buying and selling,' she replied. 'Buying and selling what?' 'Whatever he could find a market for.'

Once again I had a picture of pedlars in long coats. And once again the picture was wrong. It's true that, like pedlars, the Eitingons spent their lives in search of ways to make money, but they were businessmen with large ambitions, merchants, factory owners. My grandfather and his twin, Motty's middle brothers, had moved to Lodz, 'the Manchester of Eastern Europe', at the end of the previous century to see what business they could do in this rapidly industrialising city. Many Russian Jews made the same journey but few prospered as the Eitingons did. In time they would have charge of the largest textile enterprise in the city.

As for the Moscow Fur Trading Company, it was said to have had thirty-two branches in Russia and a further seventeen throughout the world in its pre-Revolutionary heyday. My great-great-grandfather Mordecai's descendants had been doing well. Even the women. My mother's Aunt Bertha, for example, a qualified dentist, had a practice on the Arbat – and no street in Moscow was more fashionable.

With time, a dozen or so of Chaim's nephews, great-nephews and nephews by marriage were working for the family firm in different parts of the world, and Chaim's generosity towards them, his apparent willingness to give them their head, had a lot to do with his success. His younger son, Waldemar, Max's brother, had stayed in the fur business and in 1912 moved to New York, where he founded W. Eitingon & Co., a subsidiary of the Leipzig firm. A different Max Eitingon became a partner of Chaim's in Leipzig. But it was Chaim's nephew Motty who would before long become a whizz among fur dealers, a star far outshining his uncle.

Motty began, his obituary said, by 'sweeping out his uncle's office' in Leipzig. He'd arrived there in May 1902, at the age of seventeen, from Orsha, where he was born. In 1909 he married Fanny, Chaim's daughter – whatever his feelings, a smart move. He was approachable and good fun and everyone liked to be with him. I can imagine him going out with the hunters and trappers (though that's probably far-fetched), just as I can imagine him playing cards with the children as well as the grown-ups in Armiansky Pereulok and bringing presents at a time when anyone else would have thought there were no presents to be had. He wasn't reticent like Chaim, and unlike Chaim he didn't have the sadness of all the Russias in his face: like many Eitingons, he was a man of very great charm with a friendly face and eyes full of promises.

Charm. Once when I was quite young – six or seven perhaps – my father said to me that my mother and my brother were very charming, but that he and I were different. He said it because I was upset and he was trying to make me feel better, but it was no help at all. He didn't need to be charming: as I saw him then, and think of him now, he was Gary Cooper. But however much I wanted to be, I wasn't Margaret O'Brien, the small girl with bright brown eyes in *Meet Me in St Louis*; and even today when I remember the remark I can feel quite downcast.

In June 1918 Motty was arrested in Moscow. Though he had a 'right of abode' in Leipzig, he had spent the war years in Russia. The entry and exit records in Leipzig have him travelling to Moscow in July 1914, after which there is no evidence that he crossed a border again until October 1918.

He was arrested together with my grandfather, Boris, and their cousin 'Monya' (Solomon), who would be Motty's faithful colleague to a bitter end. Someone in the family suggested that Motty had been charged with 'international capitalism' – which seems to me exact and inexact enough to fit the bill. Giving an account of himself to New York Customs officials the following year, he told Sergeant Robert Morris, who made a note of what he said to pass on to his superior, who passed it on to the War Department, that the reason he'd been arrested was that 'he might break the law' – which law isn't specified. Talking to the FBI many years later, Motty mentioned that some documents had been confiscated: to do, he said, with dealings with the American Embassy at weekends when the banks were shut.* But surely it was enough that he was known – widely known – to be a very successful fur dealer, a man with gold in his pockets. As for the others, there is no record of what they were charged with – being in his company perhaps.

The three men were taken to the Butyrka prison and placed in a cell alongside three former ministers in the tsar's government, who, Motty told the FBI, were 'taken out one morning and shot'. Clearly their lives had nothing to offer the new regime. But international capitalists even then – or then especially – had their uses. 'You can do anything with the Bolsheviki if you have money,' Motty would later tell the *New York Times*. Half a million roubles was the price first asked for his release. (His companions were thought to be worth a mere two thousand roubles.) Then he was told one hundred thousand would do. The three of them talked it over and decided it would be prudent to pay the larger amount. Afterwards Motty recalled the figure as being the equivalent of eighty-five thousand dollars. I'm not sure whether that was more or less than he was worth, as ransoms went in the early Bolshevik days.

In any event, they were set free. But the following evening (we would by now be in late August) Motty learned from a sympathetic informer that he was about to be arrested again, and that the ransom would be much

* Although the US wouldn't formally recognise the Soviet regime for another fifteen years, the embassy wasn't boarded up until September 1919.

higher this time, perhaps double – which is when he left town. From all this one thing is certain: he was already known to be rich.

My grandfather left Moscow for Kiev immediately after his release. In Lola's words, he hoped to find something to do there. I'm not sure where Monya went. As for Motty, in one family story he got away, with his mother, two of his sisters and a niece, as part of a Swedish ballet troupe. In another there were no dancing girls, and his mother and sisters travelled without him to Finland. In Lola's version Motty went on his own to Stockholm: she didn't remember a ballet troupe. In one of Motty's own accounts, this one given to Sergeant Morris, the customs official with whom he parlayed his entry into the US, he went first to Kiev, where he stayed for six months, then to Poland, then to Germany, and from there to Sweden. In another, which he told much later (on this occasion to the FBI), he and Monya went directly to Minsk, which was in German hands at the time, and made their way together to Stockholm, I think via Leipzig. In any event, in May 1919 he boarded the SS *Stockholm* at Gothenburg and disembarked in New York. I relay this itinerary in its confusing, unreliable detail because I'm fascinated by the facility, both psychological and geopolitical, with which these people kept moving about.

Lola and her mother and sisters, meanwhile, stayed out of harm's way in Minsk. My grandfather didn't find anything to do in Kiev, and the family returned to the house in Lodz that they'd left in 1914 when the shell landed in their street. My mother remembered only the train journey back to Poland and a group of passengers flicking lice backwards and forwards at each other as a game or a kind of flirtation. It's the only moment of her childhood – she would have been eleven – I'd ever heard her describe, and that was after she'd had an operation, before the effects of the morphine wore off.

At the end of June 1920 Motty again set sail for New York, followed three months later by his family. Waldemar had done well with the New York business, but in 1919, six years after setting it up, he died of septicaemia. For all I know, Motty and Waldemar were fond of one another and Motty was extremely upset to hear the news. But maybe they weren't such good friends and maybe Waldemar's death was simply and uncomplicatedly Motty's good fortune. In any event, Motty would now move to New York and take over the American branch of the company, which would be called Eitingon Schild, and for a time Eitingon Schild seemed to take over the world.

Although there would be many more trips to Europe and he didn't give up his flat in Leipzig until the end of 1931, he would now spend most of his time in New York and before long become an American citizen.*

* From now on the greater part of the information in all the chapters to do with Motty comes from the *New York Times*.

Part Two

CHAPTER 10

New York

In 1920 Motty was thirty-five: the age Chaim was when he left Russia. He wasn't modest like Chaim. When he went to Europe in the summer, he travelled with his own horses and a man to look after them, while Fanny, his wife, was rumoured never to go anywhere without a white horse. He was the big man, the man in charge, the boss. He liked to look after people, and when things didn't go well, which they often didn't – 'You know in this family there were so many rifts, so many stories about money,' an Eitingon widow, a contemporary of my mother's, said to me some years ago in New York – he was always the person who minded most, who had tried hardest, who was most misunderstood. Motty's daughter Lee once told me that she saw her father as Prince Myshkin, which struck me as a long shot. Now I'm not so sure. He wasn't naïve in the manner of Prince Myshkin – he was too worldly for that – but he was so strongly persuaded of his own good intentions that he could hardly bring himself to think that he'd done anything wrong; and that is a kind of innocence as well as a trick. 'When anyone berated him,' *Women's Wear Daily* reported after his death, 'he generally put his arms around their shoulders affectionately.'

It took him no time at all to make his mark in America. By the mid-1920s, he was said by the labour historian

Philip Foner to be 'the wealthiest fur importer' in the country, with many manufacturers dependent on the credit he extended them. The distance between him and the rest had something to do with his knowledge of Russian fur ('I consider that Mr Motty Eitingon knows more about Russian furs than any man in this country,' a rival American dealer would say of him) and everything to do with the arrangements he made with the Soviet government and its agencies.

When he was arrested in Moscow in 1918 it was for a reason: people knew who he was and had some idea of what he was worth. Not an exact idea or they wouldn't have tried out two different sums, but good enough. The Eitingons were well known in the Russian fur trade; Motty in particular had been travelling between Moscow and Leipzig since he began working for Chaim at the start of the century. At the same time he must have been busy making what new friends he could. Many of the old guard, the private dealers and manufacturers, no doubt disappeared in the course of the Revolution, but others remained in one guise or another or reappeared with new designations: people with whom he hoped in future to be able to do business. Alexander Tyranovsky, for example, was a future head of the Soviet Fur Trust. Motty would tell the FBI that he came from a 'fine and wealthy family' and was spared persecution because he'd furnished Lenin and Stalin with funds in the early days – which must be a clue as to how things were done ('You can do anything with the Bolsheviki if you have money'). It's likely that Motty guessed how fierce competition in the trade would be once things settled down. Did he perhaps hope to let the new government know that he was sympathetic to their cause?

In 1920 the Soviet economy was at a virtual standstill after six years of war. In the period of War Communism during and immediately after the Civil War, arms and black propaganda were the only forms of trade on the official agenda. Not until the need for foreign currency became urgent would arrangements be made to export what could be exported – which principally was fur. In the meantime desperate American dealers begged their government to put pressure on the Soviet bureaucracy. ('I can't make out how it is that a rotten government, in my estimation, like the Soviet crowd can dictate to us and close our Americans out of Siberia because of some whim while we allow their subjects to do business in competition with American firms right in our own home,' a New York furrier wrote to the US Secretary of Commerce in 1924.)

Like other international dealers, Motty fell back on northern China – Harbin in particular. There is no record of his travelling to China once he'd settled in New York, but his connections must have been quite good: Eitingon Schild and its later incarnation, Motty Eitingon Inc., had some sort of operation and a handful of employees in Harbin for many years, and these were still of interest to the FBI as late as 1947.

Communism, Lloyd George told a meeting of the Allied Supreme Council in January 1920, would disappear the 'moment trade was established with Russia'. As he explained to the House of Commons, 'Commerce has a sobering influence in its operations. The simple sums in addition and subtraction which it inculcates soon dispose of wild theories.' Some of Lenin's colleagues feared he was right. But to most it was clear that something had to be done to revive the economy. The New Economic Policy – NEP – was announced by Lenin in March 1921 at the Tenth Party Congress; it was an attempt to get things going again by reintroducing an element of private enterprise into the system. And a first step was to get hold of some hard cash. In the words of Armand Hammer, the celebrated oilman and wheeler-dealer, 'The Soviets know how useless their money is.' It was a state of affairs both Hammer and Motty were quick to turn to their advantage.

The first Soviet trade agreement with a capitalist country was signed in London the same month. It was an occasion of some significance. With Britain regarded by the Soviet leaders as the greatest of the world powers, and diplomatic relations with any Western country still some way off, a trade agreement with the UK, as Leonid Krasin, the Soviet Commissar for Foreign Trade, pointed out, was of 'decisive importance'. Krasin didn't have the support of all of his colleagues. Nor did Lloyd George. When Krasin met the Cabinet in Downing Street at the start of the talks, Lord Curzon, then Foreign Secretary, refused to accept his outstretched hand. 'Curzon! Be a gentleman!' Lloyd George snapped. 'Did you shake hands with the hairy baboon?' Churchill, who stayed away from the meeting, is reported to have asked.

In fact, Arcos, the All-Russian Co-operative Society, the first Soviet overseas import–export organisation, had been registered with offices in Moorgate on 11 June 1920, nearly a year before the terms of the trade agreement were settled. Amtorg, the US equivalent, wouldn't come into existence for another three and a half years. Formally

Arcos was a 'private' British company, but its status was more complicated than that. It was an organ of the Soviet government, but it also acted as a commercial enterprise out for its own interest, if necessary at the expense of other Soviet agencies. Although it came into existence some months before the New Economic Policy was officially announced, it was, like NEP itself, a product of Lenin's decision to allow some 'breathing space' to the Revolution. After Lenin's death in 1924 the NEP experiment began to lose momentum, but the search for export earnings never really let up.

In this context restoration of the immensely lucrative fur trade was a priority. How could it not be? Russia had no cash and, without Russian fur, the foreign dealers were cut off from their richest resource. The result was fierce competition both between dealers outside the USSR and among the various Soviet trade organisations anxious to secure a share of the earnings. The man put in charge of reviving the fur industry was another friend of Motty's, an economist called Artur Stashevsky.

When Arcos began trading, Motty had a man on the spot: his Eitingon cousin Monya, who'd been arrested alongside him in Moscow. Monya was now in charge of the English branch of the Eitingon empire: the Moscow Fur Trading Company (London), with offices at 62 Queen Street in the City. Stripped of his Russian citizenship, Monya would be registered with the Home Office as a Czech subject living in Golders Green with an English wife.* It was, I assume, with Monya's assistance that

* In 1936 Monya applied to the Home Office to become a British subject. It isn't evident from the papers, now stored in the National Archives in Kew, whether the application was granted. However, an entry for 1958

Motty entered into relations with Arcos: relations that put him in a delicate position a few years later when the company premises were raided by British police.

A collection of Soviet documents shows Motty steaming ahead of his competitors and making a private arrangement with Arcos in August 1923.* The Soviets were wary, but not too wary, of him, and when an agreement was reached it stipulated that Arcos and Eitingon Schild would each put 150,000 dollars into an account with Henry Schroeder in London, for transfer to Russia – with Eitingon Schild then advancing Arcos up to seven hundred thousand dollars more at any one time, and 2.7 million in total (thirty-three million dollars, roughly, in today's currency), to buy furs which would be marketed by Arcos in England and else-where (mainly America) by Eitingon Schild. Only Arcos would be allowed direct operations in Russia itself. Profits would be split fifty–fifty.

Motty was careful to inform the US Secretary of State of his deal with Arcos, and to point out the benefit the US would derive from it: 'Pursuant to this agreement,' he wrote in a letter dated November, 'between five and ten million dollars' worth of furs which were formerly sold by Arcos

---

indicates that he was then an American citizen: certainly he was living in the States by the time I was old enough to distinguish one adult from another – I assume he'd gone there just before the start of the war. In the PRO catalogue the file was until very recently said to be closed for a hundred years – such was the paranoia of the Cold War – but no difficulties were made when I asked to see it in 2005. All I learned from it is that Monya made a number of business trips to Peshawar, in search of lamb-skins I imagine.

* The documents, from the Commissariat of Foreign Trade (NKVT), consist of an inventory of materials concerning the relations between various Soviet authorities and Eitingon Schild & Co. for the years 1923–6.

Ltd in London will now be sold through us here in New York.' Various details still had to be sorted out, however, and for that the general manager of Arcos in London, Mr Alexander Kviatkovsky, needed a US visa (the immediate reason for the letter). 'Mr Kviatkovsky', Motty now said reassuringly, had been 'a merchant and businessman of the highest standing' before the Revolution, 'being probably the leading capitalist in Siberia'. Alexander Tyranovsky, Alexander Kviatkovsky, Motty Eitingon: all three were important players in the pre-Revolutionary fur industry who soon learned to adapt to Russia's changed circumstances. In the event, and for reasons thought to be connected with the US government's reluctance to recognise the Soviet Union, Siberia's leading capitalist was unable to make the journey.

In reporting the deal, *Women's Wear* (so called before it became *Women's Wear Daily*) stressed the fact that Eitingon Schild would be allowed to bring 'unlimited' quantities of fur out of Russia without having to pay the 60 per cent licence duty which the Moscow government required of 'ordinary concessionaires'. Did that mean, their reporter wondered, that the fur would be sold for 'reasonable profits only'? No, Motty replied: selling the fur 'at ridiculously low prices' wouldn't be fair to his competitors. And it wouldn't have been fair to Arcos either, since profits had to be shared with them. Motty didn't quite say that, but he insisted that the arrangement was quite simple and wholly above board: 'We will pay for our purchases in Russia by cash, receive furs therefor, and Arcos will share in the profits. This is the only arrangement ever contemplated.'

Like everything involving foreign currency, fur concessions were determined at high political levels in the USSR – and in that sense were probably useful to all three governments concerned, the US as well as the British, if only as a means of communication. Chicherin, the Foreign Minister, Pyatakov, the Deputy Head of State Planning, and Krasin, the Commissar for Foreign Trade, were all involved in the transactions surrounding the Eitingon accords. The NKVD, too, would sooner or later have noticed, or been told, what was going on. The negotiations hadn't been straightforward – the Soviets were more interested in bank loans than joint ventures – but the Eitingon firm, Arcos said, had proved its seriousness as a partner by prompt payment of the money due under the agreement and by its general spirit of co-operation ('co-operative' was one of Motty's modes: thirty years later the FBI would remark on how co-operative he was under questioning).

Besides, the management of Arcos argued, the terms of the accords were much more favourable to the USSR than the terms agreed with other foreign companies, so the effect would be to exert pressure on these rivals to moderate their demands. Among the greedy foreign companies cited was one with which Motty had entered into agreement around the same time to buy Soviet furs, at a lower price presumably than the price Arcos offered. It was a very Motty-ish move.

At some point not long before the arrangement with Arcos, Motty made an agreement with a man called Otto Shulhof that appeared very promising. Shulhof, once the Commissioner of the Port Authority in New York, was now a dress manufacturer and had good connections with Russian dealers and carriers, and maybe with other officials of the new regime – customs officials, for example. Shulhof believed he could win approval for a fur contract from the Soviet government; and after lengthy discussions with Motty it was decided that he should go to Moscow on behalf of an Eitingon Schild subsidiary in Leipzig. In the event of a deal being struck he would be entitled to 10 per cent of the profits.

Early in 1923 he travelled to Moscow and won Krasin's approval for the scheme, as well, he said, as Lenin's and Trotsky's. He was going about the laborious task of collecting the other signatures he needed from the relevant Soviet authorities, and the way he told it later, had only two more to go when he learned that Motty had pulled out and signed the contract with Arcos instead – which would eventually bring in 2.5 million dollars profit, not through the Leipzig subsidiary, but direct to Eitingon Schild in New York.

Shulhof was beside himself; and when he met Motty in Berlin not long after the Arcos deal was signed accused him of being a double-crosser. Motty promised that Shulhof would get his cut; just that it would come out of the Arcos deal. Shulhof sulked and remonstrated, then, seizing his disadvantage, pressed Motty for a loan of ten thousand dollars to see his own sideline – a caviar concession – to a happy conclusion. Motty obliged, but Shulhof left Berlin with the sense that he'd been done down; and in due course, when his percentage was not forthcoming, he started legal proceedings.

As it happens, however, my collection of Soviet documents suggests that the various trade commissars decided to drop Shulhof for their own reasons. Why, in that case, did Shulhof blame Motty? The answer no doubt is that Motty would have said or done whatever was needed to make things go his way regardless of Shulhof; that he'd pushed Shulhof aside, dealt behind his back, used his connections and possibly offered the Soviets more blandishments than we know of. Whatever Motty's precise fault, the quarrel with Shulhof – or rather Shulhof's quarrel with him – dragged on for years.

Shulhof's indisposition would have seemed to Motty a trifling matter as he struggled to keep ahead of the game. If he was doing better than other dealers, it was in part thanks to the geographical spread of the Eitingon interests, which allowed him to deal through agents or subsidiaries spread over much of the world.* But it also had to do with his certainty that everything would work out the way he wanted it to. He was quite unusually persuasive (everyone has always said that of him) and he was up to a point sympathetic to the Soviet Union – though it isn't clear from the things he said of it, and the things that were said about him, where that point lay. What is clear is that he had a closer relationship with the men in charge of the Soviet fur trade than anyone else and a better sense of Soviet needs, as well as a greater willingness to meet them. Whether that involved side-benefits for the Soviet state – a helping hand for Leonid, for example, then or later – is another question. Fur concessions were very lucrative and any foreign businessman who wanted to stay ahead of his rivals might one way or another have been temptable.

As different trade agencies came into being, lobbied for advantage using whatever current argument about foreign capital – for or against – was fashionable, quarrelled with their rivals and disappeared, Motty kept his head, moving

* A Home Office report lists branches of Eitingon Schild in London, Moscow, Paris, Leipzig, Brussels and Montreal, and agencies in China, Japan, India and Persia.

from commissar to commissar to suit his own require-
ments while seeming to suit theirs. When in 1924 the
Deputy Trade Commissar declared that he was opposed
to joint ventures – straightforward contracts for sale and
supply were preferable – Motty graciously accepted a
lower percentage profit and stricter limits on the firm's
activities inside Russia. The following year there seems to
have been trouble brewing, and by the summer of 1926
Arcos and Eitingon were in dispute about payments that
had or hadn't been made, and a criminal investigation
into the Eitingon–Arcos accords had been launched by the
Soviet prosecutor's office. Motty's strategy, as always,
was to sit tight. (In a last, stylish letter to Arcos dated 17
July, he said that he'd received a cable from his London
office about a demand for immediate payment, but he was
on holiday, undergoing a cure in Leipzig, and couldn't
break it to come to London, though he would be happy to
travel to Paris for a conference with Arcos there.) By now
a different agency had got the upper hand over Arcos in
the USSR and Motty was reconsidering his alliances. In
fact, he had already won the most valuable contract of his
career.

Motty's great coup was announced with very little ceremony. An AP wire datelined Moscow, 26 January 1926
appeared in the *New York Times* the following day: 'The
Eitingon Schild company of New York City signed a contract with the Soviet government today for the purchase
of eight million dollars' worth of fur for export to
America.'

As Motty told the story in the 1950s, it was the
Russians who made the approach to him, in the form of an

offer from the Soviet Fur Trust. Eitingon Schild could acquire skins to the value of eight million dollars if it was prepared to put a few million up front – 5.6 million if Motty remembered correctly. It was the kind of sum that could do justice to a man's compass – and his ability to act on the world.

One of the strongest impressions he retained about the deal, when he came to look back on it, was that it had brought immense benefits to Russian trappers and hunters. The Soviet government, it seems, had recently taken over the operation of the Siberian fur industry and had increased hunters' pay, 'as a means', so it was said, 'of stimulating further interest' – the money for it, according to the *New York Times*, largely taking the form of a credit from Wall Street via the Harbin branch of the International Banking Corporation. The hunters too were people Motty would have known from a former life, and he liked the idea of Eitingon Schild vitalising the northern wastes.

Still, the investment was a risk, and although risk wasn't something Motty always recognised, he purchased two million dollars' worth of insurance from Lloyd's and brought in five other companies in New York to handle 50 per cent of the furs for a share of the liability. He also notified the Department of Commerce of his intentions, as he had of the Arcos deal three years earlier. If doubts were cast on his loyalty he could – and in due course would – point out that he'd kept Washington well informed. He had connections there as he had connections in the Soviet Union, and not only with people involved in the fur trade – Maxim Litvinov, for example, at that stage Deputy Commissar for Foreign Affairs, and a future ambassador to Washington, was a friend of his – and there is no reason to suppose that he didn't carry messages backwards and forwards between the two sides. Or that he didn't have other ways of helping the US government as well as the Soviet regime – both of whose support he both needed and got.

Why did the Russians award him the contract? Motty later attributed it to their grasp of 'high finance'. Fur, after all, was one of the highest export earners at their disposal and by treating with Motty, rather than a European fur dealer, they would acquire the dollars they needed not only to pay for their imports but to finance their various foreign operations – the kind Leonid would take charge of. That was obvious enough. Less obvious – at any rate Motty didn't talk about it – was the role of the family's Polish operation, run by the Eitingon twins, Naum (who was in charge) and Boris (my grandfather), but financed wholly or in part by Eitingon Schild. The Polish historian Kazimierz Badziak notes:

> In July 1925 the USSR's trading organisation in Poland bought new winter cotton goods worth 500,000 dollars from the Eitingons . . . In November 1925 a Russian delegation bought 200,000 dollars' worth of textiles from the Eitingons . . . The Eitingon company was at the top of the list of companies to have established steady import–export relations with its Soviet partner.

These goods weren't paid for in dollars, which were hard for the Soviets to come by: they were paid for in fur.

The Russians, I imagine, had a better understanding of the breadth of the Eitingon empire than the Department of Commerce. And they must also have known that Eitingon Schild would have to assure the success of its undertaking by stimulating the American market. They were right about that. By the end of 1925 American women were buying more Siberian furs than the rest of the world combined.

Motty's name was now beginning to appear on lists of donors to charitable causes, with a company gift of forty thousand dollars to the Fur Club charity chest and a personal gift, as one of thirty or so 'guarantors', to the Schola Cantorum, a large choral group put together before the war at Mahler's suggestion. He subscribed fifteen thousand dollars to the United Jewish Campaign, and a further five thousand for the training of Jewish parents in 'health awareness in Palestine'. His name could also be found on the list of governors of the National Association of the Fur Industry.

But he didn't always put up a good show. When his brother-in-law (and cousin) Waldemar died in 1919 Motty had been an executor of his will. Four and a half years later, in 1924, the *New York Times* reported that a lawyer named Isidor Gainsburg, *ad litem* guardian of one of Waldemar's daughters, was taking Motty to court on the grounds that he'd undervalued Waldemar's assets – the company's stock of furs in Europe and Russia – with a view to a purchase on behalf of the new management. Gainsburg believed that Waldemar's assets at the time of his death amounted to about 2.4 million dollars. It had come as a shock to the family when Motty reckoned the value of the estate at 922,246 dollars. However benign Motty could appear, however much my mother loved him, this was the kind of episode that cast a shadow over his magnanimity. I don't know how the issue was settled, but

I notice that May Eitingon, Waldemar's widow, is listed among the members of the board of Eitingon Schild; perhaps Motty put his arms around her shoulders and resolved the quarrel that way.

The Union

In February 1926, a few days after the announcement of Motty's eight-million-dollar coup, the fur workers' union came out on strike. The garment workers' unions in New York had been riven by ideological differences for some years (in 1920, newly arrived from Europe, Motty himself had intervened to settle a strike). On the face of it the struggle had already been won, resoundingly, by the 'communistic' left, but whoever was in the losing position fought a constant guerrilla campaign against the prevailing tendency – which kept the unions in a state of violent instability for most of the 1920s. This new dispute would harden the differences between left and right and show how institutionally – which is to say, criminally – anti-Communist the AFL, the American Federation of Labor, a trade-union congress of sorts, had become.

The strike itself was about working conditions, shorter hours in particular, and received very little publicity until the clashes between strikers and strike-breakers became difficult to ignore. The main representative of the fur workers was Ben Gold, a dashing and capable Communist in his late twenties, born in Bessarabia. Like most first-generation immigrants, Gold had left none of his political baggage at home and was by this time the manager of the New York Furriers' Joint Board, a council of fur workers' unions whose jurisdiction covered all of New

York City; he was also head of the strike committee.

In June it was announced out of the blue that there was an offer on the table. The strikers, about 1,200 of them, had been out for seventeen weeks when an agreement was formally reached; and the streets around Penn Station – the announcement was due to be made at the hotel over the road – were jammed with thousands of fur workers anxious to hear the good news.

Immediately rumours began circulating about a wizard intermediary who'd brought the dispute to an end. 'Motty Eitingon, president of the Eitingon Schild Company Inc.,' the New York Times reported on 11 June, 'was said to be largely responsible for the settlement of the strike. Mr Eitingon, who had hitherto taken no part in the negotiations, returned from Europe a few days ago and interested himself in an effort to end the long drawn battle.'* The story hinted at long hours, small hours and backroom deals. 'Mr Eitingon spent most of Wednesday night with Mr Gold, and the early morning hours yesterday with Mr Weinstein . . . At seven o'clock yesterday morning, it appeared that he was on the verge of success.'

'Mr Weinstein' was probably William Weinstone, a senior Workers' Party organiser from Detroit who'd been active in the dispute. Nobody was in any doubt about the identity of Ben Gold, which left Motty looking either like a man with a genius for reconciling enemies or an influential fellow-traveller, perhaps even a card-carrying Communist,

---

* In The Fur and Leather Workers Union (1950), Philip Foner reports that many of the more moderate manufacturers had been cabling Motty in Europe, 'beseeching' him to return and 'force' the leaders of the Association of Fur Manufacturers to 'settle the strike'. The cables, Foner writes, 'told him that they were "ruined if he did not come back"'.

who could call off a strike with a snap of his fingers. Though the industry had something to thank Motty for (the strike had cost it nearly thirty million dollars), management circles were bound to favour the latter view. What the union made of him is harder to say. The strike had been expensive for them too. When you added in legal fees, the total cost of the dispute was in the region of 850,000 dollars and the union ended the year with more than three hundred thousand dollars of unpaid debt. Maybe there was a sense of relief all round – but maybe Motty's intervention was seen as a necessary step in a process that would enable the fur workers to fight another day.

It occurs to me that Motty and Gold did a deal of some kind that allowed the union to recover part of its costs. Neither Motty nor his colleagues at the Soviet Fur Trust would have wanted to encourage more stoppages, but something – some money, some sweetener – may have been needed to get Gold on side. In any case there was no end of corruption and semi-corruption, and allegations of both, including a number from the AFL, who had a report into the strike ready by the beginning of 1927.

Once the report had been read by the executive council, the AFL publicity machine started up: the strike was a Communist racket; Party loyalists had filled the shop floors with young Communists who weren't fur workers at all, ensuring that employees of twenty or thirty years' standing were shown the door; gangs of hardliners had intimidated non-strikers and their families, sometimes even beaten them up. A passage of the report, which was leaked but not officially released, alleged a system of bribery designed to keep the police on the side of the strikers. To that end inspectors were 'paid' 250 dollars a week;

captains, 150 to a hundred; lieutenants, fifty; detectives, between fifteen and ten; patrolmen, from five to fifty.

Within days street battles between Communists and AFL men were raging in the fur district around West 30th Street. By the end of January 1927 William Green, the head of the AFL, was swearing to carry the battle to the Communists, 'until they are beaten to their knees'. Matters were not much better than they'd been during the strike itself when the fur workers were manning the picket lines.

Attention now focused on Motty. 'Manager Gold', according to a *New York Times* report of the findings, 'is charged . . . with having carried on secret negotiations with a wealthy Russian fur importer named Eitingon, who has a Soviet fur concession of about $8,000,000 a year.' It was further alleged (or rather stated), the *Times* man told his readers, 'that the final agreement entered into was forced by Eitingon'.

The AFL executive council recommended that 'the Government inquire into trade relations between any of the fur importers of the United States and the Soviet Government' and authorised the assiduous Green, a dog whose leash had got longer during the seventeen-week strike, to prevail on 'the proper authorities' to 'inquire into the activities of any and all Russian trade associations or combinations acting within the US as well as to have the State Department' – to which the AFL would shortly belong in all but name – 'inquire into the activities of the communistic groups, their friends, sympathisers and Russian concessionaire seekers, in order to determine the extent to which these influences are at work.' Matthew Woll, Green's vice-president, put it better. 'Our government', he asserted, 'has winked with one eye and been asleep with the other, while the agents of Moscow have come upon us.'

Motty protested that Eitingon Schild, like several other US companies, had 'contracts to buy merchandise from Russian institutions' but had 'never had a concession from Russia'; that neither he nor his firm had any other connection with the Soviet government and, more persuasively, that the US government 'has been aware of the contents of every contract we have closed with Russian institutions'. Motty's statement was sent to Herbert Hoover for his consideration. Hoover's department confirmed that everything he had said was 'correct' and that the Department of Commerce had indeed been 'fully informed' of Eitingon Schild's transactions with the Soviet government. Motty's caution, the care he took to keep Washington on side, was now paying off.

Norvin Lindheim, a vice-president of Eitingon Schild, issued another, haughtier reply on the firm's behalf. 'Having long since reconciled itself to the fact that Mr Eitingon spent six weeks in a Soviet jail in 1918 because he was a capitalist, and that he and his family suffered the loss of five million dollars as a result of the Soviet Revolution and were forced to flee from Russia, the company', Lindheim wrote, 'is optimistic enough to believe that it will be able to bear up under the news which we have just received that we are a seat of Communism in the United States.' It was a reasonable enough story to tell but it wasn't likely to satisfy Green and Co. 'It is rather difficult to believe that officials of the American Federation of Labor can be so credulous as to lend their authority to so gross a slander,' Lindheim continued. Then, to prove that in helping to settle the strike Motty had acted 'only for the best interests of the trade', he produced a statement signed by several fur-trade dignitaries and big shots, saying, in the words of the *New York Times*, 'that they had urged Mr Eitingon to mediate in the strike and they regarded any criticism of him as uncalled for'.

Motty had something sharper up his sleeve. With the left and right at one another's throats in the fur district and the press gunning for 'Russian concessionaires', he announced in February 1927 that he'd been asked to pay a sum of money in order to have his name removed from the report of the AFL investigative committee. He was careful not to associate the blackmail with any named individual, but even mentioning the possibility was enough to confirm the low opinion anyone in doubt ought by now to have had of the AFL and its culture: a point Motty pressed home by telling journalists that he was confident the organisation itself was beyond reproach.

Woll informed the press that he would be writing to Motty demanding the name of the person who'd approached him. But Motty had already taken the precaution of making a statement in writing about the incident and having it witnessed by a circuit court judge. His own business was concluded. When Woll said it was Motty's 'duty as a citizen' to disclose the name of the person who'd contacted him Motty declined; the AFL used his reticence to cast doubt on his integrity, but by the spring, the argument had faded away.

In the fur industry things were beginning to go the AFL's way. Within weeks of the tiff with Motty, it had engineered the expulsion of Ben Gold and another twenty-two left-wing union delegates from the Central Trades and Labor Council and prevailed on the International Fur

Workers Union to dissolve the Joint Board, which had been the powerhouse of the left in the New York area.

The Joint Board leadership had no intention of complying with the International Fur Workers' edicts. The Communist rank and file evinced a pent-up anger, which took the form of constant, low-level agitation, in the workplace and on the streets of the fur district. The police waded into a major fracas in March and, to shouts of 'Cossacks!', made a point of drubbing the Communists. Eleven Joint Board loyalists were arrested. By the beginning of April, the left looked badly placed, as the Associated Fur Manufacturers and the AFL signed an agreement to recognise the International Fur Workers and cease dealing with the Joint Board, now officially defunct.

Motty would not have underestimated Gold's tenacity or the strength of his following. He must therefore have looked on in the knowledge that there was more to come.

By 1927, US business with the Soviet Union was not, by and large, a vexed subject, as long as you weren't making as much money as Motty was. The press liked to emphasise the volume of trade with a regime that the US didn't recognise: a mortal enemy and precursor of the 'rogue state'. In 1926, according to the *Wall Street Journal*, 13.5 million dollars' worth of exports left the Soviet Union for the US, while nearly forty-six million dollars' worth of goods went the other way. With or without Motty's business, Amtorg, the commercial organisation set up by the Soviet government to handle its trade with the US and provide a cover for its own agents, was turning out to be a vital clearing house between the two countries.* In 1927 it tripled the value of its orders on the previous year and, despite Motty's direct deal with Moscow, it kept up a lively trade in Russian furs, punctuated by occasional bargain-basement oddities, which it hastened to advertise wherever it could: twenty thousand barrels of cement, for example, 'just arrived in New York; can sell at very cheap prices if disposed of immediately'.

In May that year, for reasons that will become clear, the British police raided the Arcos premises in London. The raid had no effect on Motty's business prospects: he'd moved on the previous year. But there would be repercussions in New York, and one of them, as far as Motty was concerned, was to increase the suspicion that people who dealt with Arcos might not be above board.

The raid itself was rather a grand show, with 'road breakers' tearing down the concrete walls of the building and the brick walls of the rooms inside. It took the police eight hours using 'the very latest in safe-cutting apparatus' to break into the safes, and three lorries were needed to

* Amtorg came into being in January 1924. Eighteen months later, its first president, Isaiah Khurgin, and his colleague Ephraim Skliansky drowned in a boating accident on Long Lake in upstate New York. Skliansky, the *New York Times* notes, had been 'a close friend' of Trotsky's: in fact he was Trotsky's deputy, his 'devoted assistant', according to Deutscher, when Trotsky was War Commissar, and eventually removed from his post by Stalin and Co. It's tempting to think that his death wasn't an accident. But in the summer of 1925 the killings hadn't yet begun, and it's likely that the boat overturned and that neither man knew how to swim. The *Times* in an obituary of Khurgin remarked that he would 'no doubt have been the first to recognise the grotesque humour of his end – that a man who had survived twenty years of revolution should drown at the age of 37 in a sheltered lake of the Adirondacks'.

cart away all the 'suspicious' papers and parcels. In America the Associated Press reported – sounding a little shocked – that 'women were searched and employees assaulted' by the police. The Foreign Office, however, was confident that the operation had been 'carried out in the best tradition of the British police'.

In Moscow thirty thousand demonstrators carrying banners ridiculing the British Foreign Secretary, Austen Chamberlain, marched on the embassy compound with a band at their head. 'Flaming orations' were delivered from the balcony of the headquarters of the Comintern and the Soviet news agency spoke of a flood of 'telegrams' to the Party, inveighing against the 'insolence of the British Conservative brigands' and describing the British as 'cultivated barbarians'.

In the event, little of any interest was discovered – the 'crucial document' the authorities were hoping to find didn't show up in the first instance, and for a week or two it wasn't even clear what it was, but more damaging evidence of Soviet espionage in the armed forces was uncovered by military intelligence around the same time, and the anti-Soviet feeling that had been running high in the Tory Party ever since the General Strike was about to be satisfied. Baldwin addressed the House of Commons on Empire Day, a fortnight after the raid. Every single MP was present, while 'thirty members of the House of Lords, the ambassadors of Germany, Japan and the USA and press representatives of eight nations sat in the Galleries waiting to hear what he said'. Or so the *Financial Times* reported, adding in bold type: 'Hardly once since that day in 1914 when the opening of the Great War was announced had excitement been so intense.' Three days later the Soviet chargé d'affaires was given his marching orders. At last – as the Tories saw it – the links with Russia built by Labour in 1924 could be cut. When the diplomatic mission left from Victoria Station in June sympathisers stood on the concourse singing 'The Red Flag'.

One of the casualties of the affair was a pending loan of ten million pounds from the Midland Bank to the Soviet government, which, the Labour opposition said, would have created more than five thousand jobs in Britain's most depressed industries. General dismay about the dangers of isolationism hardened criticism of the raid. Lloyd George spoke eloquently against the diplomatic break, reminding the House that no government was innocent of espionage and wondering how on earth relations with the Soviet Union would be resumed. 'What are you waiting for?' he asked the government. 'The Romanovs?'

Motty would have been aware that with Arcos marginalised, a good deal of Soviet trade would now come the way of the US. At the same time he would have had concerns about the increase in anti-Soviet sentiment. The British had transmitted whatever material they'd found in the Arcos offices to Washington, and the AFL, among others, tried to make the most of it. In an announcement at the end of May, Matthew Woll claimed that the name of a lawyer acting for the Joint Board during the fur strike had turned up on one of the documents seized in London. It wouldn't be long before Amtorg came under suspicion as a front for Soviet ambitions in the Americas. In the interim, the right-wing union leaders still had Ben Gold to deal with.

In June the Joint Board called a lightning strike on the grounds that management, having signed the agreement with the AFL, were in breach of contract with the Board.

Management replied that the Joint Board was a thing of the past. The strike nevertheless meant disruption, and it was a chance for the AFL to try to go in for the kill. Instructions were issued to affiliates to prepare a counter-picket. William Green accused the left of 'terrorisation', and the police, rattled by the prospect of daily clashes if AFL thugs were deployed, moved in on the Joint Board loyalists, arresting about 150 men. The strike continued. Ten days later, police arrested seven AFL men for assaulting pickets with iron bars. A statement by the strikers accused the Federation of having 'hired the most depraved elements of the underworld, armed them, paid them and turned them loose upon the strikers and their sympathisers'.

The dangerous mood in the fur district was briefly intensified by the impending execution after a dubious trial of the Boston anarchists Sacco and Vanzetti. In Union Square on 7 July the Sacco–Vanzetti Liberation Committee held a rally, with ten thousand or more attending. The meeting might have gone off peacefully, but then Ben Gold was spotted in the crowd and a reckless faction began calling for him to speak. Gold held back, and the organisers breathed a sigh of relief that turned rapidly into an outright refusal to have him on the podium. The riot that followed was eventually subdued by the police.

Two weeks later, at the Coney Island Stadium, the New York Symphony Orchestra performed a benefit concert for the pickets. According to the press, the twenty thousand-capacity auditorium was full. The evening featured a performance of 'The Ride of the Valkyries' and a speech by Ben Gold, 'the long haired and youthful leader', as the *New York Times* had called him in its coverage of the

Union Square riot. There was no mention of a donation from Motty, although it was the kind of event he enjoyed.

As Christmas approached, it was announced that the charity chest for the fur workers had raised nearly half a million dollars. The largest contributor was Motty, who'd pledged twenty-five thousand through the company and fifteen thousand personally. There is no knowing what, if anything, he gave to Ben Gold and the rank-and-file loyalists of the Joint Board or donated to the various benefit events organised in their defence. Meanwhile the committee the AFL had formed to oversee the 'reorganisation' of the fur workers announced with confidence at the end of January 1928 that it had achieved the 'complete elimination of Communists from the fur workers' union'.

It had taken some time for Otto Shulhof to try to get even with Motty for his humiliation in Moscow but in the winter of 1927 his case came to court. In the interim he'd doubled his claim against Motty from one to two million dollars, arguing that the deal he nearly clinched with the Russians would have earned him one hundred thousand a year – a figure he based on Motty's profits of 1.5 million dollars from the first year of the deal with Arcos.

Motty's choice of lawyer said a lot about his liberal left inclinations and perhaps about the circles he moved in. Arthur Garfield Hays was a successful attorney-at-law, with many wealthy clients, who nonetheless had a weakness for fighting injustices. His most famous brief was probably the Scopes Monkey Trial, where he seconded Clarence Darrow in Scopes's defence (John Scopes, a high school teacher, was charged in Tennessee in 1925 with teaching Darwinian evolution). At the time he took on

Motty he was conducting a battle of his own in the courts against the accusation that he was a Communist and conspiring against the US government. He was eventually awarded twenty-five thousand dollars in damages. Five years later, he volunteered his services for the defence of the men accused of torching the Reichstag. In 1935, flamboyantly, he would liken the oath of allegiance required of New York State schoolteachers to the Nazi salute.

Motty's defence was jobbing work for Garfield Hays, except for the fact that Motty had an exotic past which linked him with the Bolsheviks – details of his arrest and the exit fee he'd paid emerged during the trial. There was also the ever-present, low-key scandal that he'd made a fortune out of Soviet Russia. But the evidence soon came down to the nitty-gritty of Eitingon Schild earnings, and it transpired that Shulhof's sense of the company's first-year profits from the Arcos deal was about right. Motty had an answer to this, as he had to everything. The original Arcos contract was for a year only; when it was renewed, the terms were less favourable to Eitingon Schild, which was entitled to a far smaller share of the profits and had to advance a larger sum than it did the previous year.

So where was the evidence? Motty was unable to produce the original agreements with Arcos because they'd been returned, he said, to his London offices. Under cross-examination, the defendant didn't look good. Shulhof's caviar loan had come under discussion, and it emerged that he'd repaid it. But then, at some point, Motty had tried to appease Shulhof with a cheque for 3,250 dollars – representing 1 per cent of the total profits on the Arcos deal – and Shulhof had judiciously returned it. Motty claimed that he'd never promised Shulhof 10 per cent of

THE UNION

the profits in the first place. The jury was undecided and its members discharged. The next phase, deferred to the following year, would be arbitration, and failing a solution there, the Appeal Court.

In February 1928 Eitingon Schild, now described by the *New York Times* as the 'dominant skin dealer of the industry', acquired Kruskal, 'the largest coat jobber' – that's to say, wholesale merchant – 'in the fur trade'. It was the second acquisition of a big American company: the first had taken place two years earlier, at the end of 1925, when Motty had bought up two fur receivers in St Louis. At the same time he formalised Eitingon Schild's takeover of his brothers' company in Poland. With the acquisition of Kruskal, Eitingon Schild had control of a major wholesale outlet for finished garments and a direct connection with the high street. Within the next few years, its corporate structure would become gradually more opaque.

Not long after the Kruskal deal, an issue of Eitingon Schild stock worth five million dollars was announced by Goldman Sachs. The idea was to increase the company's working capital. Its prospects looked as good as they had two years earlier and Motty was in generous spirits. Four days after the share issue, the Co-operative Committee of Big Sisters convened at the Ritz-Carlton to raise money for the reclamation of young women, who were spending too much time, said one of the Big Sisters, in speakeasies and 'other questionable resorts': the problem, evidently, was that 'mechanised industry gives them more time for play'. Motty pledged one thousand dollars to the drive. He was in buoyant mood.

No one could have foreseen the trouble that lay ahead.

Quite why Eitingon Schild got into difficulty might be hard even for a business historian to make out. There were a lot of things in play, including Motty's character, I suppose, though this remains largely hidden behind the gradual evolution through impressive year-on-year losses and capital reorganisations to the point at which Eitingon Schild in effect ceased trading. In my own head I find it puzzling that he should have reached the peak of his career and achieved the extent of his scope in the 1920s when he still seemed such a grand figure to me in the 1940s. How much had it to do with the way he was? He wasn't, his daughter said, 'very reflective' – which will turn out to be a bit of an understatement. How much was it a matter of bad luck? Or, to put it differently, historical circumstance? Or the recession in Poland? How much a matter of carelessness or over-extendedness? It's also difficult, because of his elusiveness and charm and magnificence, to know whether he understood what tough times lay ahead when Eitingon Schild began to show signs of slipping.

In the autumn of 1928 he visited England, and travelled in Holland, France and Germany – in October he was in Berlin, with some two hundred other members of the Eitingon clan, for my mother's first wedding. Early the following year, he made preparations for another tour, which would take in Poland. The *Wall Street Journal* reported Eitingon Schild profits of 2.1 million dollars for 1928 (and balanced assets and liabilities of 25.7 million). When the Crash came in the autumn of 1929, 'the fur market had its most violent decline in history', *Time* reported, 'average drops ranging from 30 to 50 per cent'. Yet it seemed to strike the retail fur trade a glancing blow – nothing more – perhaps because when the rich are ruined, they are never quite finished; perhaps, more realistically, because the trade opted for dramatic price cuts. As Christmas approached, one feature-writer puffed mink and Persian lamb to the high-street consumer, on the grounds that they 'solve the problem of a coat for wear with many frocks'. The piece continued: 'One may shop, lunch, tea and dine – even go on to dance – in a mink coat and be correctly clad.' Whatever the mood of the retailers, Eitingon Schild – which now had a stake in retail – creaked audibly under the weight of events.

Motty ascribed the company's difficulties to low pricing. The Crash, he said, had caused 'one of the most drastic and rapid declines in prices of skins in the history of the fur industry', as indeed it had. But just how bad had things got? In February 1930, in a letter to shareholders, he announced a net loss for the previous year of 2.4 million dollars. Not surprisingly, he had a solution. A number of the directors and board members would donate their Eitingon Schild stock to the company to offset the inventory write-offs occasioned by the price collapse. Another result of the donation, he said, would be to create a surplus of about 1.8 million dollars which would be used to put the company back on its feet. Prospects for 1930 – would Motty, or any CEO, have said otherwise? – were 'promising'. The next six months' trading produced profits of 218,000 dollars, less than one-fifth of the figure achieved in the same period – before the Crash – in 1929. By the end of a year that turned out not to be so promising after all, Eitingon Schild had taken a loss of more than a million dollars.

CHAPTER 12

Moscow

In May 1991, six months after speaking to the two Galias for the first time and failing to speak to Leonid's son, I went to Moscow to meet my putative relatives. Looking now at my notebooks, I see that before leaving London I had prepared a long list of phrases – compliments of one kind or another – with which I hoped to disguise my curiosity. I would refer to Leonid as *nash dyadya* (literally, 'our uncle') and speak of his *yarkaya litchnost* (his 'outstanding character') and so on. In the event I couldn't manage any of it. I'm a bad actress and it's probably just as well.

I'd been to Moscow once before, as a student in the late Fifties. The occasion was the second leg of an exchange between Oxford and Moscow universities intended to be an annual event but never repeated. The authorities in Oxford hadn't wanted me to go, but there were so few women students in those days, and so very many fewer doing Russian, that faced with choosing between a nice dreamy girl who was inclined to take her shoes off in the rain and me in some new-found green eye make-up they decided reluctantly – and not without informing me – that I was the less hazardous choice. We had a good time on the boat from Tilbury to Leningrad, where they opened the Hermitage for us; and in Moscow I did my best, putting a brave face on the fact that the more highly regarded stu-

dents went on the sly to visit Pasternak and instead travelled several stops on the Metro to look at some heavy
machinery, out of a feeling – what possessed me? – that I
should acknowledge what the Soviets did well.

But it was difficult being there. How, for instance,
could I decline to eat the meatballs we were given for
breakfast under the eye of the pinstriped Master of
Pembroke College? You might think you'd have to be very
neurotic to find that a problem, but before long my not
eating my breakfast meatballs led to my being taken to the
women's ward of a Moscow hospital – and you can imagine what the Master of Pembroke made of that.*

Thirty-five years later, Moscow was still a scary,
uncomfortable place. Things have changed a lot since
then, but in 1991 if you were in the centre of town and
wanted to sit down you had to take a trip on the Metro;
there were no distractions, no cafés, no shops, nothing to
break up what Colin Thubron called the 'desolate simili-
tude' of the buildings. The city was still too big, the roads
still too wide ('the least democratic roads on earth' –
Thubron again), and the drivers unbelievably heedless.
Most people, on the street, on the bus, on the Metro,
would have been just as pleased if you hadn't come to their
country. Not because they saw you as the enemy or the
former enemy or the enemy all over again: they seemed not
to see you at all. No one in the street looked at anyone
else, at least not in the eye. Doors slammed in your face; if
you tried to buy something, the assistant barked; if you

---

* The Russian 'students' who came to Oxford weren't students at all, but
teachers for the most part, with a sprinkling of KGB minders. It's only just
occurred to me that the Master of Pembroke had probably come with us
to Moscow to act as our MI6 minder.

asked someone the way, they didn't answer or answered over their shoulder, walking away. Halfway along the street where I was staying there was a patch of mud and a puddle that seemed unlikely to drain: someone had put a plank across it – in the circumstances, it seemed an outstanding civic gesture.

I didn't think it would be prudent to let Leonid's family know that the flat I was staying in belonged to a foreign correspondent, and made things far more difficult for myself by ringing them from call boxes – one of the surprising facts of late Soviet Russia (as of late capitalist America) is that the phone boxes always worked – and not giving them a number where they could ring me. A well-heeled woman in her fifties, I was masquerading as Nancy Drew. It was embarrassing and so too was my mission. In the eighteen years since I made that trip there have been innumerable books by Jewish men and women describing their return to the towns and villages in Eastern Europe which their families had been obliged to leave in the run-up to the Second World War. But where they wanted to make sense of their own history or to honour the memory of their grandparents I was bringing some beads in exchange for a story.

The Soviet 'defeat' in the Cold War was another difficulty. I'd somehow persuaded myself that Lonya and his family would think I'd come to gloat – or if not that, to take advantage of their new situation. But when I look back now on those first encounters it's quite evident that in their eyes my presence and the fall of the Soviet regime were unrelated matters. Or, to be more precise, I was just another thing the change had thrown up. But then I also thought they would be bitter about the disappearance of the old regime, yet none of Leonid's family whom I met on that occasion seems to have been at all sorry to see it go.

The two Galias lived quite a way from the centre of town in a two-room flat with four locks on the front door and a mass of pom-poms on each wall; on a later visit I counted twenty-eight lacquered spoons on the walls of their kitchen – itself no bigger than a cupboard. As in all the other Moscow flats that I visited in the immediate post-Soviet years there was every mod con apart from space and a lock on the lavatory door: three TVs, two videos, every kind of kitchen appliance, leather sofas and chairs and alcohol of every denomination. The two Galias are nice-looking women; one was then in her forties, her daughter not quite twenty, both blondes with the help of a bottle of bleach. Lonya was less evidently likeable: a middle-aged man with a commendable paunch who found my presence so hard to accept that I'd been there an hour at least before he so much as looked at me. When he did it was to ask me how people feel about the KGB in my country. 'Is it', he said, 'as I feel about the CIA? That it's the number one enemy?'

It was 9 May the day I saw them, the forty-sixth anniversary of the end of the war. (Russia celebrates its victory over the Germans a day later than the rest of Europe.) VE Day, *Den Pobedy*, had been Leonid's favourite holiday; and the family, I was told, not quite truthfully, had always spent it together. (Leonid, who was taken ill at the end of April 1981, died regretting that he wouldn't live long enough to commemorate the Soviet victory one more time.) At the two Galias' the occasion was celebrated with a great deal of food, laid out and eaten in no particular order: pizza, chicken, fish, caviar, crab salad (those dismaying tasteless sticks), other salads, bread, chocolate cake, meringues, slices of orange, vodka, champagne, brandy and Fanta. And between every mouthful, or so it seemed, another toast was proposed, but no one chin-chinned with me and no one spoke of the victory as a shared victory, nor was there any mention of friendship between nations. It might not have been like that had I said my lines and generally managed my part a bit better: but I felt like an intruder, I was an intruder – and that, I was quite certain, was how they saw me. At the same time they were much less reluctant to talk about Dyadya Leonid than I was to ask about him.

I was lucky, I realised later, to have stumbled on the two Galias. For one thing, they didn't see themselves as keepers of Dyadya Leonid's shrine. 'We're not Party people,' the older one told me quite early on. And some of the father's shortcomings had, it later turned out, been handed down to his son – which might not have disposed the two women to admire the old man. No doubt one reason they were as nice to me as they were was that they saw me as their passport to high times in the West: something I didn't quite manage – or not to their satisfaction. I arranged for them to come to London; did the necessary paperwork and paid their fare, but the tacky hotel near the *London Review* office, more Euston than Bloomsbury, was a terrible letdown. Not that they said anything, but they didn't need to.

It was one of the many ironies of the end of the Cold War that if you were in your own eyes a 'generous' Westerner, you imagined that anyone coming to visit from

Eastern Europe would be dazzled by everything they saw
– and very grateful for whatever you gave them. But that
wasn't how it worked. Surviving for years under a despotic regime, living in a place where you have to queue for
every potato, doesn't make you more humble, as we
seemed to think it should, or nicer or better than anyone
else. And if you spent a good part of your life fantasising
about Western abundance it only made you more resentful
of the moral and economic rationing to which you were
likely to be subjected once you were within physical reach
of Bond Street or the King's Road.

Six months later, when I was in Moscow again, hoping to
learn something about Dyadya Leonid's career, I was told
that the KGB now had a press office. The idea of the KGB
wanting to put its best foot forward was rather appealing.
(Around the same time, in London, I'd had reason to ring
the very recently unbanned ANC. 'ANC. How can I help
you?' said the person who answered the phone. That too
was surprising in a world-historical way.) The press office
was sufficiently like a press office to have both a listed
phone number and no one in the office to pick up the
phone.

I gave up and went into town, hoping that some way of
making contact would occur to me. It was three o'clock in
the afternoon and already getting dark. I wandered
around, past the rows of women standing outside Detsky
Mir, the children's store, cradling one or two old toys that
they were hoping to sell. There was nowhere to sit, so I
bought a pie from a stall to eat in the street and then wandered some more. The bronze figure of Felix Dzerzhinsky,
Leonid's protector, for thirty years an inspiration to the

resourceful men and women of the KGB, had been removed from its plinth outside the Lubianka.

I circled the immense neo-baroque building, put up in the late nineteenth century by the All-Russia Insurance Company, but headquarters of the Russian secret service in all its Soviet and post-Soviet incarnations since 1918. I noted its many humanly discouraging features – the endless façade, the heavy bars on the windows – and decided to go in. I'd seen a BBC correspondent do it on television: why shouldn't I? I walked up the steps to the tall double doors and knocked politely, as if outside the headmaster's study. No one answered. The BBC man hadn't bothered to knock: I took hold of one of the handles, put my shoulder up against the panelling and pushed the door open.

A Bond analogy might seem to be called for, but Ealing Comedy is more appropriate. A U2 pilot 'violating' Soviet airspace for the first time would not have been more excited than I was. The Cold War had gone on for forty years and I had spent most of my life under its tutelage. I even remembered its beginnings in odd bits and pieces: FDR at Yalta and then his death; Ana Pauker's brutal face on the front page of every newspaper when Romania turned Communist in 1947; my father coming into the restaurant where my mother and I were waiting for him with news of the Communist takeover of Czechoslovakia in 1948. Now the war was nearly but not quite over and here I was kicking in the door of its last saloon.

The door opened into a sort of sentry box on either side of which was a wooden platform, a bit like an alcove, and on each platform, facing one another, stood a young soldier, rifle at the ready. They didn't greet me but they didn't point their rifles either. They knew everything was different now that Yeltsin was effectively in power and the KGB had a press office. But they were flustered, uncertain how to proceed. My excitement held.

A bell was rung and a middle-aged man in civilian clothes came to ask my purpose. He wasn't especially friendly: it was nearly five o'clock, he said – closing time at the Lubianka these days. Grudgingly, he agreed to call his colleague. 'Igor Prelin – Mr Prelin – he is efficient in this problem.' (The getting to see the archive problem.) Relieved and disappointed, I realised I wouldn't be spending the night in a cell.

Someone took me down a long, sombre corridor smelling of furniture polish, into a lecture theatre. Maybe it was Mr Prelin himself who escorted me, tall, handsome Mr Prelin in his geometrically patterned jersey. But it was an odd place to choose, since we sat in the auditorium chatting as though we were waiting for a lecture to start while it was Prelin who really gave the lecture in his guarded sort of way.

He had nothing to say about Leonid – except that there was nothing to say. Someone else had been making enquiries about him and had gone away empty-handed. But maybe he only said that to wind me up and make sure that I didn't lose interest, because whatever else he did, Mr Prelin, like many of his colleagues, would soon be in the business of selling, leasing out or otherwise exploiting the KGB archives. Hence, no doubt, the need for a KGB press office. The next time I met him I realised I'd put him on to a good thing.

In his more active days Mr Prelin, it turned out, had been stationed in Guinea-Bissau and Angola; and he was happy enough to talk about that, to tell me, indeed, that he'd been standing right next to Amílcar Cabral, the

Guinean nationalist, when he was shot and that he'd arranged for Agostinho Neto, the president of Angola, to be flown out of Luanda for surgery in the USSR when Neto had cancer. Since Neto didn't recover from the surgery I wondered whether Mr Prelin was in some sense responsible for his – or Cabral's – death. (And if so, why was he boasting about it?) I didn't press the point but instead asked for the address of the Africa Institute (titular head: Anatoli Gromyko, son of the Foreign Minister who had always said 'no'). 'Why should I know?' Mr Prelin replied. 'I'm not a scholar, I'm a spy.'

CHAPTER 13

Family

To the Eitingons in the former Soviet Union the possibility of relatives in the West was a far trickier subject than the fall of the old regime. Other Eitingons, in Leningrad and further east, had from time to time got in touch with them, they told me, but they hadn't been interested. Like my Eitingons in America, the only Eitingons they'd been willing to acknowledge were their own. Now they wanted to know about these American Eitingons and then again they didn't; they wanted to be part of a larger family and they didn't; they wanted to be connected with the rich furrier and they didn't; they wanted to see themselves as poor relations and they didn't. One thing was clear: their reluctance to claim any connection was matched by an equal reluctance to wave the connection away.

Leonid Alexandrovich Eitingon, to give him his full KGB name, was born Naum Isaakovich Eitingon on 23 November 1899. Like Max, he was born in Mogilev on the River Dnieper, one of the longest, widest and least sung rivers in Europe. There had been Jews living in the town since the sixteenth century, and by the time of the 1897 Census they made up nearly half of a total population of over forty thousand. Thirty kilometres upriver was Shklov (77 per cent Jewish and described as a shtetl) and forty kilometres north of Shklov was Orsha (56 per cent Jewish). It was from these three places that the Eitingons variously set out to remake their lives – or, in Leonid's case, the world.

I visited the two Galias in May 1991. Ten years later I spent a few days in Belarus. I wanted to see what it looked like. In tsarist times Mogilev was the capital of the Belorussian province of the same name. The Soviets made Minsk the capital of the new Belorussian Republic; and Minsk is now the capital of independent Belarus. In 2001 Belarus was a country few people in the West had heard of and in which, it seemed at first, no one lived. Minsk Airport, unlit and coated in grey marble, was to all intents and purposes deserted: there appeared not to be more than three or four flights a day. The roads between the towns are wide but hardly anyone was using them. In seven hours of driving I saw no cyclists, no private cars, no towns even: just woods, endless tall thin woods of pine and birch trees, a few clearings, a few people making their way on foot from one distant settlement to the next, a number of khaki lorries with the state's initials branded on them, and here and there a collective farm, not abandoned but not peopled either. Belarus was then and still is a dictatorship, a country loosely modelled on the USSR.

Napoleon's army marched through the region on its way back from Moscow; one of the Galias even showed me a reference to an Eitingon, a schoolteacher, who'd taken part in the war of 1812. The army fell apart as it tried to cross the Berezina not far from the point where the road between Minsk and Mogilev along which I was driving traverses the river. It was for some nebulous rea-son – a memory of *War and Peace* perhaps – an exciting thought. In the autumn of 1915 Nicholas II moved his military command to Mogilev from St Petersburg with heaven knows what hope for a change in his fortunes (perhaps his bad luck came from using a synagogue to stable his horses); but his fortunes didn't change and in November 1917 the Bolsheviks took control of the city. By the time the war ended, however, the Germans occupied all the territory of present-day Belarus to the west of Mogilev, and for several months in 1918 Mogilev itself. In 1941 the Germans returned, with devastating consequences for the whole region but for the Jews above all: 90 per cent of Belorussian Jews – some eight hundred thousand people – disappeared. And it was here, in 1944, that Leonid would take part in a large-scale sting behind the German lines.

Now an immensely tall angel of victory looks over the edge of the ravine alongside which Mogilev is built; it's a Soviet angel but more graceful, less thickly set than most monuments to Soviet military achievement. Near by are the tsar's former headquarters, Russian baroque buildings in the process of restoration. I spent a day looking for signs of Mogilev's former Jewish life and found a few here and there, among the faded green, yellow, pink and orange stucco buildings, many of which had probably once belonged to Jews. (The synagogue that had been requisitioned by the tsar's horses was now a sports centre.) Jews, I was told, didn't like the wooden houses in which most Russians lived, calling them 'stick-houses', and as soon as they could afford to they built stone ones, preferably on two storeys, either to let or to accommodate their own extended families.

I stumbled on a young American Jewish 'missionary' (my word) whose 'organisation' (his word) had sent him to Mogilev to revive what there was to revive of the town's former Jewish life. He had just been conducting a service – maybe because it was Passover – and three old men, in their eighties, came out of his house: a tall thin one in a black suit with a full row of silver teeth to match the row of medals on his jacket and two shorter, rounder ones. They all smiled and shook my hand; and then the two shorter ones took each other's arm and walked off with the thin one by their side.

The 1897 Census shows several sets of Eitingons living in one or other of the three towns. But the Census is known to be unreliable, and the Eitingon data are almost impossible to make sense of. The pool of first names, and therefore of patronymics, is so restricted you can't tell whether the person you are looking for is the young one or the middle-aged one, married or single, dead or alive, real or a creature of your imagination. Russian and Hebrew names are used interchangeably and with little regard for the difference between Mordukh, Movshov and Matus – that's to say, Mordecai, Moses and Max. The 1897 Census is a revision of the 1874 Census, which adds a further layer of complication. But most discouraging of all is the absence, in many cases, of any correlation between age and date of birth; Mordukh Itskov Eitingon, for example, the Mordecai I take to be my mother's father's father's father, is said to have been born in 1872 and yet to be sixty-two years old in 1897.

When the Census was completed Mogilev, Orsha and Shklov were all small towns whose Jewish inhabitants lived in close proximity to each other. In the eighteenth century Shklov had been a centre of Jewish enlightenment, staunchly opposed to the Hasidim – among whose sins was praying 'with great madness' – but 150 years later, bypassed by the new railway, it was a shtetl in decline, with a handsome town hall, a marketplace, an onion dome, several synagogues, and a collection of streets in which numerous sets of Eitingons were living, often in the same house. It is inconceivable that Leonid's family and Motty's and Max's didn't know each other: indeed, that the three of them weren't cousins, however many removes separated Max and Motty from Leonid.

Leonid was the eldest of the four children of Isaak Eitingon, who in most accounts that I've seen spent his working life at the head office of a paper factory just outside Shklov, founded in the nineteenth century by the tsar's Minister of Roads. The factory, renamed Spartak when it was taken over by the Soviets, was still there when I visited – a string of dilapidated buildings running along a disused railway line. In its Soviet heyday it made 75 per cent of the country's cigarette paper and employed 1,200 people; in the post-Soviet doldrums it recycled old cardboard and employed less than half that number, but it was still Shklov's biggest employer. Reborn today, thanks to a large government investment, it is set to produce fifty million rolls of toilet paper a year.

In the newly renovated city museum in Mogilev a large and vigorous Socialist Realist painting, divided like a medieval triptych, records different aspects of the people's discontent in the years leading up to the Revolution. One section shows a strike at the paper factory in May 1908. The label suggests that this wasn't a fictional strike, yet there is no mention of it either in a history of the factory that the manager showed me or in the official accounts of himself and his family that Leonid had to produce at significant moments in his career. Can it have been a strike that should have happened but didn't? Was Leonid's father on the wrong side? It's a small and irritating puzzle.

Leonid's elder son, Vladimir, a professor of economics, takes a dim view of his grandfather, describing him as a thoughtless, superficial man who worked, not at the paper factory, but first as a book-keeper for the 'rich Eitingons' and later as a travelling salesman. No one, it seemed, was very interested in this man. Zoya, Leonid's stepdaughter, who was close to Leonid (closer than anyone, she would say), generally brushes aside any reference to the Eitingon family. So when I ask about Leonid's father, she just says: 'No one talked about him.' I did, however, hear it said that Isaak had been very handsome and that Leonid had inherited his good looks (more of those later). And everyone agrees – children and grandchildren as well as the documents – that Isaak died around 1910, when he was in his mid-thirties, probably of a perforated ulcer and probably in St Petersburg.

Boris Israelovich Eitingon, Leonid's grandfather, Isaak's father, was a private notary: 'just a clerk', in the words of the unimpressible Vladimir; 'an honourable man and not wealthy', in Leonid's more generous version. He was evidently something of an intellectual – a private library is recorded – and according to Vladimir he founded a political circle sympathetic to the Narodniks, the pre-Revolutionary populists, with whom Leonid as a young boy was involved.

There are different accounts of what happened to Leonid and his family after Isaak's and then Boris's deaths – Boris died in 1915. It was Vladimir who claimed that they ended up in a cottage on the rich Eitingons' estate. Most of the others say that until their grandfather's death they lived in his house, 'one of the best houses in Shklov', with six bedrooms and an orchard, and that when he died they returned to Mogilev, where they lived with their maternal grandmother. They also say that after the Revolution the house was requisitioned ('nationalised' is their word) and turned into a kindergarten. Another variant has it that the house was occupied by the Gestapo during the Second World War and then given to the kindergarten by Leonid and his younger brother Isaak.

Later in his life, when Leonid got into trouble, a questionnaire was sent to the NKVD in Mogilev to check up on what he'd said about his grandfather's house and its orchard. No one remembered Leonid – if he was in trouble it was as well not to have known him – but several middle-aged men remembered being chased out of the orchard for stealing the old man's apples.

There aren't many Jews left in Shklov. The Nazis rounded them up and shot them; and of the few who got away most left for Israel in the 1970s. Still, the current manager of the paper factory was Jewish: he hadn't yet been born when his pregnant mother made her way on her own to the Urals. A Jewish woman I spoke to had been pushed out of a first-floor window at the back of the house by her father as the Nazis approached. The rest of her family, parents and brothers and sisters, were taken outside, ordered to sit in a circle with their neighbours, and shot. She was eleven. Now her husband was dying in the room in which we talked. He coughed and sometimes groaned or seemed to fall asleep, but when she asked him a question – 'Isaak, do you remember . . .' – he was always able to answer. I wondered whether, like her, he'd been a schoolteacher but she said no, he was a hairdresser. I don't know why that seems significant: maybe because she was so admirable and the occasion so solemn it was a relief to discover that he hadn't been a poet or a philosopher – or a rabbi.

The centre of Shklov was looking trim, almost manicured, but the cluster of streets – Dneprovskaya, Shkolnaya, Potchtovaya, Proboinaya – in which the Eitingons had lived was evidently not thought to deserve such attention. In most of the side streets the tarmac lost heart before the row of houses came to an end, and there were hens and geese and cockerels running and pecking about in the dirt as the streets made their way down to the bank of the Dnieper. On one street a man with a horse and a bucket was drawing water from a well. Only two or three stone buildings remained – one of them a synagogue – and none was habitable. For the rest it was wooden houses, some painted, some not.

The kindergarten was still there, more or less where it was supposed to be, and the building that housed it was easily big enough for six bedrooms. An old lady who stopped by said that she'd heard a Jewish family had lived there, and if you took out the slides and the sandpits there'd be room for the orchard that's also mentioned in the record. And, best of all, there was another, smaller caretaker's house at the back of the playground. It was a new house, but there's no reason why it shouldn't have been built on the site of an old one. In a perverse sort of way it would please me to think that some of my mother's relatives might even have lived in the caretaker's cottage at the bottom of Leonid's grandfather's orchard.

No one else among Leonid's relations appeared to know anything about a cottage on the rich Eitingons' estate, but they all knew that there'd been Eitingons in the West who had a lot of money. One of them had heard that Leonid's grandfather helped a young Eitingon orphan emigrate to the States, where he'd married the boss's daughter and in that way founded the Eitingon fortune. And it's true that an Eitingon orphan is mentioned in the 1897 Census and that Motty (who wasn't an orphan) did marry the boss's daughter. They didn't say these things because they wanted to claim that the money was theirs – not at all; and they certainly weren't pleased that, thanks to what was termed the 'Leipzig connection', they'd been described as millionaires in one of Moscow's 'scurrilous' post-Soviet newspapers. Like good Soviet citizens, most of them found money quite vulgar while not being wholly indifferent to it. As for Max, they had never heard of him and had no interest in hearing about him now. Had I described him as a famous doctor – or, even better, a scientist – they might have felt differently. Their world wasn't one in which Freud's name cut much ice.

Both Isaak and his father played their part in Shklov's civic life. Isaak was on the board of the local savings society; he was a member of the campaign to bring middle-school education to Shklov; and was entitled – i.e. had the funds and the status – to be in charge of one of the local voluntary fire brigades. In 1904 there were pogroms in Mogilev; and in Orsha in 1905 thirty people died when local 'peasants', supported by the police, went on the rampage. There were no troubles that I know of in Shklov, where Isaak commanded a small self-defence group.

Isaak's father was the agent for a number of Moscow and St Petersburg insurance companies and a member of the municipal tax office. What strikes me is that there is no mention of 'my' Eitingons being engaged in any local activity. Shklov, Orsha, Mogilev: these are the places where their wives live and their children are born – the men, the Census records, are 'away in Moscow making money'. Leonid's less prosperous, more civic-minded relatives are at home earning a living. They haven't yet made it to Moscow.

CHAPTER 14

Bandits

'My childhood ended with my father's death,' Leonid said in one of his 'autobiographies'. Leonid was eleven when his father died and perhaps it gave him a head start in life, a chance to exercise his will from an early age.*

Most Soviet citizens had to produce 'autobiographies', formal accounts of themselves, several times in the course of their career. In every case it had to be done with care and a certain artfulness. You had to know which were the right credentials and how to balance self-justification and self-criticism; and you had to figure out in advance how your words could be twisted by someone who had power over you and didn't wish you well, while at the same time preparing yourself for the fact that your words were liable to be twisted whatever you said.

I have copies of autobiographies Leonid wrote in 1942 and 1946 (the second in his own confident, intelligent handwriting).

They are interesting for the account they give of the first phase of his working life, when he was a young man chasing 'bandits' – i.e. counter-revolutionaries and uncooperative peasants – on Soviet territory during the Civil War, and for what one can deduce from the list of his medals

* Most of what I know of Leonid's early career comes either from his autobiographies or from the State Archive of Public Organisations in the Gomel region, i.e. the former Party Archives.

and the dates they were awarded. From 1925, when Soviet Intelligence first sent him abroad, until the Second World War nothing that he did is spelled out, none of his assignments is specified. 'At the end of 1925,' he writes, 'I was transferred to the International Department of OGPU and I have continued in this line of work until the present day.'

Автобиография
Члена ВКП(б) Эйтингона
Наума Исаковича
п/б № 3035365

Родился в ноябре 1899 года в гор. Могилеве. Отец мой был служащим, всю свою трудовую жизнь служил в конторе на Шкловской бумаж-ной фабрике (впоследствии эта ф-ка называлась «Спартак») и умер в 19.. году. После его смерти моя мать осталась с четырьмя детьми, из них я был старшим. С этого ....

A man in his line of work couldn't reveal what he'd been up to, but at the same time he had to make it plain that what he did was of the greatest national importance. Thus he'd be expected to list the medals he'd been awarded but on no account to reveal what he'd done to earn them. And that still hasn't changed. All sorts of beans have been spilled, most of them in the early 1990s and in exchange for dollars, but the code persists.

'My childhood ended with my father's death' was, I imagine, a form of words since it was his grandfather's death, five years later, that altered the family's material circumstances. Altered them so drastically according to Vladimir that the sixteen-year-old Leonid had to get a job cleaning lavatories. But Leonid says nothing in his auto-biographies about cleaning lavatories. Much of his short pre-Revolutionary career was taken up with teaching and compiling statistics in a local government office. All he had to his credit as a member of the new proletariat was a spell humping sand and washing gravestones for a local cement factory. Leonid's elder sister became a doctor, the younger (eventually) an engineer, his brother a chemist. It may be that he was telling the truth when he said that he had to leave school early in order to feed his family; but it's just as likely that the reason he left school early was that he wanted to.

He was a tall and handsome young man who did as he pleased and got the most out of life, a contemporary was later to say; a show-off, his mother complained. As a teenager he'd been not a Bolshevik but a member of the more fiery Socialist Revolutionary Party, something he is always careful to mention in his autobiographies before adding: 'It was the only political mistake I made in my whole life.' The SR, descendants of his grandfather's Narodniki, were rivals of the Bolsheviks, and among the peasants especially, far more popular. They weren't Marxists, weren't interested in the industrial proletariat, at least not to begin with, and, believers in direct action, had a number of prominent assassinations to their name. I'm not sure I believe Leonid when he says he was only in the party a few months and never played an active part in it.

Playing an active part was, after all, what the young (and old) Leonid liked most of all. The Civil War soon gave him his chance. In January 1919, with the German occupiers at last out of the country and the cement factory shut down for the winter, he found more congenial work with the committee in charge of food provision (Gubprodkom: Provincial Provisions Committee). He and his friends rampaged up and down the countryside with the 'supplies squads' (*prodotriad*) requisitioning food, suppressing any attempted sabotage on the part of the kulaks and generally liquidating every form of anti-Soviet activity. 'Rampaged' is my word: the others – 'requisitioning', 'suppressing', 'liquidating' – are all ones Leonid used in his autobiographies. I don't think he was free to liquidate and suppress as he pleased: 'they used us to liquidate kulak sabotage' is the way he puts it, which suggests that other people were in charge. But still the passage gives one a good idea of how exhilarating those years must have been for a young man eager to defend the Revolution and do battle with its enemies; and a good idea, too, given what we know of those years, of how brutal he could be.

His misfortune was to understand too quickly what needed to be done. After a few months he was promoted to a desk job; from there he was sent to Moscow to take a course at the Soviet of Workers' Co-operatives (where he learned about Marxism and, in his words, 'started to look at things differently'); and when the course was finished he was asked to stay on to train other young recruits. It wasn't what he wanted to do and extricating himself was difficult, but he got his own way and before long was back in Belorussia doing what he enjoyed most: pursuing the enemy.

In May 1920 he joined the Cheka – he wasn't yet twenty-one. The provincial capital had been evacuated from Mogilev to Gomel the previous year, making the official designation of the body he now worked for the Gomgubcheka – or Gubcheka for short (*guberniya*: 'province'). The whole province, he wrote in his autobiography, was 'teeming' with bandits, and he spent most of 1921 helping to clear them out. Sometimes, he added, 'I went out myself with the troops.'

For the people in the middle it was a savage business. The Bolsheviks had few supporters in the countryside and were largely dependent on their ability to inspire fear. To make matters worse, many of the early Chekists were no older than Leonid and, like him, given to dangerous displays of bravura. Thus in October 1921, Leonid was wounded in the leg. The doctor, fearing gangrene, told him the leg would have to be amputated: Leonid took out his Mauser, pointed it at the doctor and said he would shoot anyone who tried to remove it. No one did. Leonid's children told me the story the first time I met them: they wanted me to know from the start what sort of person he was.

(The leg healed and he didn't even develop a limp. Or not until much later. The most you could say, Vladimir told me when I got to know them all better, was that he had 'a special way of walking, with one shoulder a bit higher than the other'. It was 'sort of charming', Vladimir said, 'like something that might appeal to one in a woman'.)

Most of the 'bandits' were peasants who either refused to comply with the supplies squads' demand that they hand over their produce or were resisting attempts to conscript them into the Red Army. Resisting conscription, like desertion, was a capital offence. But since it was in any case within the powers of the Cheka to administer justice as it saw fit, refusing to hand over food, or having no food to hand over, might end almost as badly. According to the historian Geoffrey Hosking,

> a 'supplies squad' would arrive in a village, take over the largest house, evict the 'kulak' who lived in it, and instruct all the villagers to deliver a pre-set quota of produce. Those who did not or could not comply were subject to searches, which might involve the ripping up of floorboards and the destruction of furniture, followed, if they proved fruitless, by beatings and arrests. Similarly, armed roadblocks were set up, and checkpoints at railway stations, where peasants taking produce to market were searched and in effect robbed.

Recalcitrant peasants who managed to evade the attentions of the army as well as the supplies squads fled into the forest, where they joined up with others like them and formed armed bands that it was the task of the local Cheka to track down.

Towards the end of 1920 an official review of the Gomgubcheka concluded despairingly that 'a Gubcheka does not exist in Gomel'. The staff, the inspector noted, were mediocre, illiterate, ignorant and ineffective ('Comrade Bezpalo sits in his office thinking for long periods of time'). It was 'essential' to curtail 'counter-revolutionary efforts on the economic front' – i.e. to deal with the unwillingness of the peasants to hand over their food – yet no one in the Gubcheka was 'even aware of who the enemies were'. Only one man seemed to know what he should be doing; and that was Comrade Eitingon – 'a bright spot in the ranks of the functionaries'.

In January 1921 Comrade Eitingon was promoted to director of the Secret Operations Department, making him third in the Gomgubcheka chain of command. His salary was 8,800 roubles – roughly two thousand roubles more than the next in rank and four thousand more than the majority of his fellow Gubchekists, of whom there seem to have been at that time around 250. In April Nikolai Vollenberg, as chairman of the Gubcheka, reported on the organisation's achievements ('Informing in the town has been well set up: there are 300 informers') and failings (lack of staff mainly: 'In the Secret Operations Department the only worker is Comrade Eitingon, who is not in a position to get to grips with all the work without assistants').

As the son of a railway mechanic Vollenberg didn't have to worry about his class origins. Leonid did. And on 20 October 1921 – as part, it would appear, of a general purge – the Gomel Provincial Review Committee resolved to remove his Party membership. There were several reasons: his 'bourgeois background', a lack of 'proletarian psychology and discipline', a lack too of 'the humility befitting a private in the Communist Army' and – this sounds very plausible – his 'commissar-like mannerisms'. The committee didn't disagree that there was in him 'a loyalty to the Party's interests and a readiness to suffer for them'; and a month later the order expelling him from the Party was rescinded. The stated reason this time was the wound he'd received 'in the struggle against banditry' (the business of his leg) and his 'forthcoming departure for the Bashkir region'.

Another version of the story, a different document, suggests that Leonid's departure for Bashkiria was itself a reprimand: that Vollenberg and he were sent to Central Asia as a result of a botched operation in Gomel which they'd dreamed up. Short of competent men to deal with the bandits, the two of them had the idea of releasing from jail a former Party member and Civil War veteran, one Rudominsky, and using him to sweep out a group of bandits in the west of the province. But once more at liberty, Rudominsky found banditry more attractive and set about robbing and killing the local population. There were complaints, and Vollenberg despatched Leonid to sort things out. Leonid tracked him down all right but instead of sorting things out – which would have meant arresting, if not killing him – Leonid sat down and got drunk with him.

An 'accident' in the course of the evening was, in this version, the cause of the wound in his leg. It wasn't a proud moment. It made the Cheka look foolish in the eyes of the local population; it put Leonid out of action for two months; and, to make matters worse, Rudominsky got away, taking with him a large sum of money, several sacks of revolvers and, in one account, a harem of women. No wonder Leonid threatened to shoot the doctor (if he did): a show of proletarian humility wouldn't have brought back his self-respect.

In the event Leonid and Vollenberg were lucky to escape to Bashkiria, the present-day Bashkortostan, with nothing worse than a black mark on their reputations. There they would set about liquidating a new set of bandits.

The word 'bandit' (*bandit*) as it is used in Russian encompasses many categories of human behaviour. In the years when the Revolution was fighting for its survival, the Soviets were determined to impose their discipline on the countryside, and the job was done in large measure by the Cheka's young and far from squeamish recruits, many of them not even Party members. But highwaymen like Rudominsky or roving bands of kulaks were relatively minor concerns: the real threat, as the Bolsheviks perceived it, came from abroad, from émigré organisations – which in Soviet eyes were synonymous with émigré conspiracy.

In 1921 the conspirator they feared most was Boris Savinkov, 'arch-terrorist', 'arch-fiend', 'arch-murderer', 'arch-conspirator', 'arch-revolutionary' and 'arch-desperado', as *Time* magazine would describe him. And arch-fantasist. A former Socialist Revolutionary terrorist (he had organised the assassination of Vyacheslav Plehve, the tsar's Minister of the Interior, in 1904) and later Deputy Minister of War in Kerensky's government, he sided with the enemy in the Russian–Polish War of 1920, and while claiming to have been invited to join the Soviet government, had formed a new organisation in Paris dedicated to overthrowing the Bolshevik regime. With that in mind he had put in place a network of agents to collect intelligence inside Russia and encourage discontent wherever they found it. 'When all is said and done, and with all the stains and tarnishes there be, few men tried more, gave more, dared more and suffered more for the Russian people,' Churchill would say of him, bamboozled by his own eloquence and Savinkov's wayward zeal.

The Soviet response was an elaborate hoax known as Operation Sindikat. In late 1920 or early 1921 one of Leonid's colleagues in Gomel visited Savinkov at his headquarters in Warsaw pretending to belong to an anti-Bolshevik underground, infiltrated his organisation and eventually lured Savinkov back onto Soviet territory, where he was arrested and died, pushed down a stairwell inside the Lubianka. Such was Soviet pride in the operation that several decades later the spot where he was pushed was still being pointed out to young KGB recruits, Oleg Gordievsky among them.

The agent provocateur himself, Pavel Selyaninov, a legendary figure in the Soviet secret service, was known as 'Alexander Opperput' – an uncharacteristically clumsy alias derived from the words *operatsiya* ('operation') and *putat* ('confuse'). Because his cover had to be preserved – deception, however cunning, was never something the Soviets owned up to – it was reported in due course that Opperput too had been arrested. So diligent was the hoax that Leonid was later praised for taking part in his arrest. Neither Savinkov nor Opperput is mentioned in the documents I have from the archive in Gomel: the operation was too important – an affair of state, not a local matter. Or in Leonid's autobiographies. Letting on that you knew things other people didn't know – that you knew who was there when Trotsky was killed, to take the obvious example – could cost you your life. 'In our family', Leonid's stepdaughter often says, 'we didn't talk about such things.' It wasn't simply that Leonid was mindful of what might get him or his family into trouble: he had a mafioso's sense of propriety about what could be talked about and what couldn't.

Attached to Leonid's 1946 autobiography is a letter from General Pavel Sudoplatov, Leonid's boss at the time, recommending him for promotion. 'Major General Comrade Eitingon', Sudoplatov wrote, 'personally took part in the arrest of Savinkov's emissary Opperput and in liquidating the Savinkov organisation in Gomel.' Did Sudoplatov know that Opperput was a fiction; did Leonid?

*

In the early 1990s the fierce General Sudoplatov, now in his eighties, was living in Moscow with his son and daughter-in-law. The first time I visited him, handsome Mr Prelin from the Lubianka was there too, with a crew and a camera: he was making a film about the general's life. Which didn't sit very well with what he'd said when I met him in the Lubianka and he'd told me to forget about Leonid: there was no material. That Leonid's family, who'd set up my visit, spoke of the general so respectfully was one reason it was hard not to be nervous in his presence. (I remembered how I used to feel accompanying my father when he went to visit his boss.) But obviously that wasn't all: there was the part Sudoplatov had played in world history – the deaths he had caused, the crimes he hadn't been afraid to commit – and there was the fact that he addressed me at all times as if addressing the General Assembly of the UN with his shoe in his hand.

A year or two later the general published his own kill-and-tell memoir, *Special Tasks: The Memoirs of an Unwanted Witness*. Although Leonid's family thought the book vulgar – or at any rate 'unnecessary' – as well as inaccurate, Sudoplatov writes very admiringly of Leonid as a man of great resourcefulness and intelligence and a real fighter (*boevik*). In his account, Leonid's time in Gomel didn't end with a reprimand. On the contrary. The posting to Bashkiria – he was sent 'to enforce discipline in the area' – was a reward, not a punishment. In fact it was Dzerzhinsky himself who sent him there. (In another version of Leonid's career Dzerzhinsky's intervention occurs two years later in a different context – we'll come to it in a moment.) As for the wound in his leg, that, according to

Sudoplatov, happened in Bashkiria: in a Lermontovian moment he 'was slashed in the leg by a sabre'.

There is no need to believe the general's book, but what about his letter? Or the documents from the archive in Gomel? Or Leonid's autobiographies? Or indeed the dependably post-Soviet, i.e. pro-Soviet, biography of Leonid by Eduard Sharapov that came out in 2003, sub-titled *Stalin's Avenging Sword*? And if so much is con-cealed at this stage of Leonid's career, when nothing much hangs on his actions, how much trickier will it be later on?

One more incident from Leonid's days in Gomel. In the early 1990s, when it was newly the fashion, or newly pos-sible, to make connections between one's own history and that of the USSR, an old man called Meir Zhitnitsky, then living in Israel but in his youth briefly married or 'married' to Leonid's sister Sima, recalled his connection with the Eitingon family in an interview in April 1991 in the Israeli newspaper *Maariv*. Recalled in particular an occasion when Leonid rounded up a number of the town's prosper-ous citizens – most of them Jews – kept them for a while in the cellar of the local Cheka, then took them to an aban-doned railway station and shot them. It's a horrible story but probably true, given the place and the time, Leonid's revolutionary zeal and the accuracy of the rest of Zhitnitsky's testimony.

When news reached Leonid's mother of what he had done, she repudiated him in the local synagogue, so Zhitnitsky reports, tearing her clothes ('rending her gar-ments') to signal that he was no longer her son. It wasn't only that he had killed a great many Jews, and that she suspected some of her own relatives were among them: it was also a matter of honour – in our family, she said, there has never before been an executioner. In time Leonid's brother and sisters persuaded her to stop thinking about the railway station and what had happened there; and when Leonid was preparing to go to China, his next assignment, she moved to Moscow to live in his flat. Her daughters and their families eventually joined her there. Leonid would never be more than an occasional visitor.

A zealous young Bolshevik, you could say, was showing his true worth by killing these rich people regardless of their race or provenance or the possibility of their being related to him. As chairman of a provincial Cheka during the Civil War, Berezin, in Anatoli Rybakov's novel *Children of the Arbat*, had 'regarded his work in the Cheka as his revolutionary duty': he'd 'applied the Red terror', as Rybakov puts it, though he'd also released a number of 'luckless liberals or terrified bourgeois'. Leonid, too, had 'applied the Red terror', but he was younger than Berezin and perhaps for that reason more single-minded in pursuit of his revolutionary duty.

A small observation about the word 'liquidate', which hardly seems to belong in the Russian language, though liquidation was much practised in Russian history. It was a word my mother often used, as in 'I see you've decided to liquidate that friend' or 'that dress'.

CHAPTER 15

China

At the end of 1925, Leonid was sent to China. He was twenty-six and it was his first foreign posting. Known now in Moscow as 'Leonid Alexandrovich Eitingon', he became 'Leonid Alexandrovich Naumov' in China, a name he would still be using in the spring of 1929 when he arrived in Constantinople to keep an eye on Trotsky. The initial change from Jewish Naum to Soviet Leonid had presumably been intended to make him sound less obviously Jewish – though if that is the case it's odd that he didn't, like Trotsky (whose real name was Bronstein), or many of his Jewish colleagues in the Cheka, change his surname to something more obviously Russian. Naum is such an unambiguously Jewish first name that simply appending a Russian suffix might be thought insufficient: a (characteristically) defiant gesture, or at least an indication that he wasn't worried about being Jewish, or ashamed of it. (Another, quite different possibility is that he knew – or knew of – another Naum Isaakovich Eitingon, my grandfather's twin brother, and didn't want to risk any confusion, but I'm not sure that would have deterred him.)

Most other Jewish operatives are still known by their aliases – Mikhail Borodin, for instance, Leonid's colleague in China, whose real name was Gruzenberg, or Alexander Orlov, his colleague in Spain, whose real name was Feldbin – but there are very few written occasions when

Leonid's surname isn't 'Eitingon'. His mother sometimes called him 'Nakhke', the diminutive of Naum, and in his 'autobiographies', as on his gravestone, he is 'Naum Isaakovich'. Everywhere else that I've encountered him he is 'Leonid'. Everywhere except in the present. Western Sovietologists and post-Soviet historians consistently refer to him as 'N. I. Eitingon'. Thus the full title of Sharapov's biography is *Naum Eitingon: Stalin's Avenging Sword*.

Leonid was posted to the Far East, General Sudoplatov writes in his memoir, because 'his distant European relatives declined his request to provide him with recommendations, papers, and money for travel and cover for operational work in Western Europe'. It's just possible that in the early days of the Soviet Union, before Stalinism took hold, someone in Leonid's position could have had that sort of contact with relatives in the West, especially if – and it's a large if – those relatives had their own friendly dealings with the Soviet Union. In other words, it may be that Motty was asked and that he declined. Or even that he was asked and didn't decline: Leonid would spend many years in Western Europe and six months or more in the US. On the other hand, Motty had interests in China: maybe that was what Sudoplatov was trying not to say.

Five pages later, Sudoplatov refers to the discussion of the Eitingon family in the American press and asserts that Leonid 'never contacted' any of the Eitingons cited in either the *New York Times* or the *New York Review of Books*. Every intelligence agent has a duty to disinform, which must be liberating when you're writing an account of your life; disinformation is a very postmodern thing: it allows you to have your cake and eat it.

The switch to overseas operations marked a decisive change in Leonid's trajectory. There were thousands of Chekists by the end of the Civil War: only a tiny handful were assigned to external duties. His linguistic abilities may have had something to do with it. Or – just possibly – the extended Eitingon network. Or – more plausibly – his native intelligence and (for better or worse) his temperament. In 1923, after a year in Bashkiria, he had been summoned to Moscow and assigned first to OGPU's eastern department, then to its international department. A colleague of Sharapov's, the historian Ilya Kuznetsov, writing in the *Journal of Slavic Military Studies* in March 2001, suggests that this was the occasion on which the great Dzerzhinsky intervened – there could be no greater honour – and secured Leonid a place at the General Staff Academy (the future Frunze Academy), in whose eastern department he would study 'strategy and tactics together with future marshals of the Soviet Union', as Sudoplatov enviously puts it. He might have been even more envious had he known that Leonid stood alongside those future marshals to form the guard of honour at Lenin's funeral. If he did – it's stated quite clearly in one of my more reliable documents, but no member of Leonid's family has ever mentioned it.

If anyone asked him a question about his past, Leonid, who wasn't a talkative man, used to say: 'My secrets aren't mine. They belong to the state.' And many of those secrets, I don't doubt, died with the state. Which is a roundabout way of saying that I know what was happening in China in the early 1920s and why a Chekist like Leonid would have been sent there, but sometimes even the most elementary things elude me. None of the many books I've consulted – apart from Sudoplatov's memoir and Sharapov's biography – mentions his presence in China. Either he was too insignificant or, as his family would have it, too good at his job.

'Did you mainly live in Beijing or Harbin?' I asked Leonid's daughter Svetlana, who was born in China.

'Harbin,' she said, confidently.

'No, in Beijing and Shanghai. They weren't in Harbin,' her half-brother Vladimir, who wasn't with them in China, interjected.

Svetlana, miffed: 'You'd have to ask Zoya about that.' (Zoya – Leonid's stepdaughter – was living in China with her mother before Leonid even arrived in the country and remembers it quite well.)

Vladimir: 'Zoya only remembers one thing. How she dropped her mother's urine sample on the tram and cried: "What shall I say to Mummy?"'

The first congress of what was to become the Chinese Communist Party met in Shanghai's French Concession in the summer of 1921. Twelve delegates attended (Mao was one), representing maybe fifty committed Communists. The first Soviet 'residency' was up and running in Beijing before the end of the year, and a network of agents and residencies in other towns quickly followed. China, Lenin had said in 1913, is 'a land of seething political activity, the scene of a virile social movement and of a democratic upsurge': it was now up to the Bolshevik regime to keep the agitation going.

At the beginning things moved swiftly. By 1923 the USSR had formed an alliance with Sun Yatsen, the leader of the Kuomintang, the Nationalist Party as it came to be known: a 'bourgeois' grouping in Moscow's eyes but the only quasi-revolutionary force in the country. The Communist Party in 1923 was too small and inexperienced to take on the burden of Moscow's expectations. Even Sun, however promising an ally, controlled only the province of Guangdong in the south of the country. What he did have, however, was charisma and a determination to raise an army that would reunite China, ridding it both of the warlords who controlled the north, including Beijing, and the imperial powers, British mainly but also French and German, whose headquarters were Shanghai.

In October the Comintern sent its most illustrious agent, Mikhail Borodin ('the father of Red China', Sudoplatov would call him), to Canton to work with the Kuomintang (KMT). To Sun, Borodin was a saviour, the man who would rescue his revolution as Lafayette had rescued the American Revolution. A deal was struck: Sun would not only allow the Chinese Communists to combine in a United Front with the Kuomintang, he would entrust the KMT's political organisation to Borodin, and in exchange his army would receive military training and arms from the Soviet Union with the prospect of launching a Northern Expedition to take Beijing from the warlords, part of whose fiefdom it had become. In the period from 1924 to 1927 up to 135 Soviet military advisers were working in China.

The understanding with Sun was a very big affair for the Soviet leadership. Revolution had failed in Germany and the rest of Europe. In China the Communist movement was growing rapidly and was now – against its own better judgement – nested within a radical nationalist movement that had every prospect of taking control of the

CHINA

country. For the next two years – 1924–5 – Borodin and his Soviet colleagues set about creating a National Revolutionary Army, disciplined and ideologically motivated. To this end a military academy was set up at Whampoa, an island off Guangdong, under the formal command of Chiang Kaishek, Sun's right-hand man.

In the event Sun didn't wait until his force was ready to light out for Beijing. Perhaps because he knew he was dying, he accepted an invitation from one of the northern generals to attend a conference in the capital, where he died in March 1925. Chiang Kaishek was his successor.

When Leonid arrived in Shanghai at the end of 1925 it was China's liveliest city, the most elegant and one of the most squalid, the most modern and the most bohemian. The French lived in their Concession, protected by their own, Indo-Chinese police force; the Anglo-Saxons lived and ruled in the International Settlement guarded by the Shanghai Municipal Police, a force modelled on the Met and commanded largely by the British with large numbers of Sikhs and others working under them. In both cases it was like living at home: only better. 'In the matter of mellow creature comforts, of savoury fleshpots deftly served, no Croesus of America, North or South, can ever hope to attain the comfortable heights and depths that Shanghai takes for granted,' the (London) *Times* reported. Governed on the one hand by the imperial powers and on the other by the local warlord, the city, it used to be said, consisted of a narrow layer of heaven on a thick slice of hell.

Shanghai was also the country's financial and industrial centre and its busiest port; it contained half of China's factories and its largest working-class population. In late

1924 and early 1925 it was hit by a depression and as the factories closed, the trade unions flourished. In such a situation the KMT and the Communists were bound to prosper – membership of the Communist Party increased from around 130 in 1922 to sixty thousand in 1927. In May 1925 Chinese workers protesting against the closure of a Japanese textile mill were fired on by Japanese guards; one worker was killed. Two weeks later students and workers came together to demonstrate against the Japanese action in particular and foreign domination generally. The British commander of the Shanghai Municipal Police lost his nerve and ordered his men to fire. Twelve Chinese were killed. There were anti-imperialist demonstrations in twenty-eight Chinese cities and, by early June, seventy-four thousand workers were on strike in Shanghai. With both the KMT and the Communists playing their part, the strike continued until September. The British saw in it the hand of the Bolsheviks but that was true only up to a point.

If, as I imagine, Leonid's main purpose in being there was recruitment, he must have found many willing volunteers among the angry and disaffected Chinese population. His arrival in the city coincided with that of Iakov Minsky, the head of the Shanghai residency, posing as the Soviet vice-consul with Leonid as his deputy. The trick was to avoid taking on as agents those whose affiliations had already been made public or whose sympathies anyone could guess at – or who were simply too hot-headed. In time Leonid would be praised – this is something that comes up again and again – for the skill with which he set up networks of agents, and although this was his first real go at it, I doubt whether even then he was lacking in confidence. 'At the time,' Sharapov reports, 'the staff of over-seas residencies were afforded a large degree of freedom in recruiting networks of agents, and residents had the right to confirm newly acquired agents without co-ordinating with Moscow' – a state of affairs very much to Leonid's liking.

Just as important to the Soviets as angry and disaffected Chinese, but more troubling, were the émigré communities who might at any given moment be conspiring against the Soviet Union. Of the thirty thousand Europeans living in international enclaves in China nearly twenty thousand were Russians, refugees from the Civil War or from unrest in Manchuria. After 1920 they ceased to enjoy extraterritorial privileges, setting them apart from other Europeans. Some cut their losses and took Chinese citizenship; others applied for Soviet passports with no apparent intention of returning to the Soviet Union. There were successful doctors and lawyers, entrepreneurs and policemen among them, and some who were merely rich, but there were also many who had come looking for jobs and, not finding them, drifted instead into the mercenary professions, selling their services as soldiers and body-guards and more or less straightforward prostitutes, or selling their souls to Leonid and his colleagues. It was one of the things Leonid did best: identifying those émigrés who would be likely to act as informers in their own com-munities.

The Northern Expedition was finally launched by Chiang Kaishek in July 1926. Some three months later, the United Front reached the Yangtze at Wuhan in the centre of the country. There the left and right factions of the KMT split up. The expedition had picked up a lot of popular support in the course of its advance, leaving the right mistrustful and the left overjoyed. So while the left, denouncing Chiang Kaishek as a despot, decided to set up its own provisional government in Wuhan, Chiang determined to carry on east towards Nanjing and Shanghai.

In Shanghai meanwhile there was renewed agitation by the unions, and a few days before Chiang's arrival in the city the workers overthrew the old administration and took control. Their leaders, flush with success and mistrustful of Chiang, appealed to Moscow to be allowed to detach the Party from the KMT. Moscow refused. The fall of Shanghai was a great victory and the Soviet Union celebrated it as such while unaccountably giving Chiang the credit for it. Stalin, it's said, was anxious above all that the occasion be seen as a vindication of the alliance with the KMT, which Trotsky had opposed from the start.

On 12 April Chiang showed his hand. Strongholds of the left were stormed, and the order went out to execute not only all the Communists in the city but anyone who could be accused of being in league with them. In all between five and ten thousand people died and the rising effectively delivered Shanghai into Chiang's hands. Stalin had once said that Chiang should be 'squeezed like a lemon and then thrown away'. Instead, the Chinese Communist Party was almost annihilated.

The Russian adventure in China was virtually over. Nine months of KMT repression, abortive Communist revolts and further arrests and executions followed, causing great disillusionment. Membership of the Party dropped from sixty thousand in May 1927 to fewer than ten thousand the following year. It would be back, its base not among the urban proletariat but in the countryside, under Mao. In the meantime Sino-Soviet relations sharply deteriorated.

Stalin had been proved wrong: the compact with the KMT turned out to have been a terrible mistake, as Trotsky had predicted. Angry and humiliated, angry above all at having been publicly humiliated, he lost little time in demanding Trotsky's exclusion from the Party's Central Committee – it wouldn't be long before he demanded his expulsion from the Party itself. The episode effectively marked the end of the notion of world revolution as Lenin had conceived it.

Leonid wasn't in Shanghai when these things happened. Sometime early in 1926, he left Shanghai for Harbin, in the far north-east of the country, another Chinese city that wasn't altogether Chinese. It was there that the resourceful young Zoya and her mother came into his life.

The following spring the three of them, now a family, were in Beijing, China's nominal capital – Leonid's daughter Svetlana was born in the American hospital there. 'Was Leonid the resident in Beijing?' I asked Zoya. 'I'm sure he was,' she replied, and then added, 'but don't ask me' – which I take to mean 'don't quote me'. In the brief and reticent memoir she published in the US in 1999 she says only that Leonid 'had a special assignment in Beijing'.* Later still she told me that he was the assistant military attaché. But titles like that – 'military attaché', 'vice-consul', 'third secretary' – are almost invariably meaningless, or meaningful only in the sense that they denote a spy.

On 6 April 1927, six days before Chiang Kaishek gave the

* The book, *Inside Russia: The Life and Times of Zoya Zarubina*, is presented as a biography by Inez Cope Jeffery, but consists of interviews with Zoya, some in quotation marks, some written up in the third person.

order to round up the Communists in Shanghai, the Soviet Embassy in Beijing was raided. Like Shanghai, the capital had been a centre of Soviet activity, spying principally, and the foreign powers (the 'Powers') agreed with the Manchurian warlord Zhang Zuolin – known as the 'Old Marshal' – that it was time to make a stand. The Beijing Metropolitan Police entered the embassy quarter, and with diplomats from several Western countries looking on approvingly from an upstairs window in the Dutch Embassy, the men forced their way into the Soviet Embassy compound.

A number of arrests were made: of Chinese Communists found sheltering in the building, among them the Party's co-founder and leading theoretician, and of Russian 'students of Chinese', as Zoya described them to me – 'KGB probably,' she added, 'but they were our friends.' (Whether they already knew or were studying Chinese is an interesting question.) They were lined up, she said, with their hands tied behind their backs, and just as she was rushing to say goodbye to them before they were led away – Zoya always moves at speed – she heard that Leonid was looking for her. She found him standing in a narrow alleyway between the buildings. Speaking to her 'in French', he asked her to go to their apartment to fetch the revolver he'd hidden in a drawer. 'Can you imagine?' she said. 'I was seven. It was the first job I did for him.' I wish now that I'd asked her what use Leonid found for the gun. Not that she'd have told me.

Meanwhile, in the office of the military attaché – Leonid's office? – the staff set about burning their files. But the fire had scarcely taken hold when Zhang Zuolin's men climbed onto the roof of the building, lowered a hose down the chimney, extinguished the fire and gathered up seven truckloads of damp files that the fire had scarcely touched.

That night the women and children slept in the embassy ballroom. The compound, Zoya said, was flooded; the intruders, she explained, had broken the pipes: nearly eighty years later, she was still careful not to mention the fire.

At almost every level the raid was a serious blow. In those days the Cheka and its successors often found it easier to penetrate European diplomatic missions outside Europe; and in the very early days, easiest of all were the embassies in Beijing. The events of 6 April revealed the extent of the Soviet infiltration. The British, in particular, not only recovered a number of highly secret documents (now comfortably lodged in the National Archives in Kew): they found out who among their staff was working for the Soviets and, more important, were confirmed in their suspicion that Arcos was the centre of Soviet espionage in the UK. The British government authorised the spectacular raid on its London offices the following month.

For the Soviets there was only one consolation: they had shown the enemy what their 'tradecraft' was capable of. But that could hardly make up for the wealth of detail that the raid had uncovered, from the codes they used to the names of their agents, to larger stratagems (officers were instructed 'not to shrink from any measures, even including looting and massacres', when promoting conflict between the Chinese population and Westerners), to guidance on agent management.*

The instructions about looting and massacring were no

---

* Christopher Andrew and Oleg Gordievsky cite these instructions in their book *KGB: The Inside Story*, pp. 111 and 88; these documents too can be found in what used to be the Public Record Office and is now the National Archives in Kew.

doubt issued in Moscow, and may well have applied only to Soviet military intelligence, but I wonder about the more mundane advice; about this, for example, on the correct relationship between a recruit and the officer in charge of him:

> On no account should the agent have any chance to suspect that he is supplying us with valuable material for which as soon as an opportunity occurs he may bargain with us. On the contrary, we must always point out to him that we are waiting for something more important from him, and if we pay him extra it is only because we hope he will be more successful in the future.

Was it standard issue? It wouldn't have been written by Leonid – he was only in Beijing for a short while after all – but it's not difficult to read it in his voice: the tone accords so well with the crushing common sense-cum-cynicism he would display throughout his career.

Russia virtually broke off relations with the Beijing government after 6 April. In the south the Chinese Communist Party – at Stalin's instigation – revolted against both wings of the KMT; and made a brief attempt to set up a commune in Canton that ended in catastrophe. In July the exodus of Soviet personnel began, from Borodin downwards. It was a hazardous journey: the KMT had no interest in Borodin's returning safely to Moscow, and Sudoplatov credits Leonid with smuggling him and other Bolshevik advisers out of the country and across the Gobi Desert to Ulan Bator. By December Chiang Kaishek had ordered Soviet consulates closed in all the areas he controlled.

*

Zoya and her mother had already been living in China for a few years when they first met Leonid in Harbin. As far as I can tell, he'd come to the city from Shanghai to serve as the new 'vice-consul'. Zoya's father, Vasily Zarubin, was a colleague of Leonid's and when he was recalled to Moscow, Zoya stayed on in Harbin with her mother, Olga Naumova, a Chekist too, though of a more modest, clerical sort.* It was Zoya, as she proudly recalls, who introduced her mother to Leonid. She had been playing in the lobby of the hotel where all the Soviet 'diplomats' stayed when one of the 'comrades' came up to her and said: 'I want you to meet Dyadya Leonid. He has just arrived and will stay here too.' Later that day she presented him to her mother. They took to each other immediately: 'It was love at first sight'; it was 'a forest fire'.

The story has its peculiarities. Olga, it seems, was still planning to return to Moscow. Why, in that case, had she not gone back with Zarubin? Why, as it turned out, did she need new documents? Documents that Leonid brought to her room, dangled in front of her and then tore up to indicate that she wouldn't be going back to Moscow after all but staying in China with him. According to some, she had learned that Zarubin had a new 'wife' in Moscow and decided not to go back; according to others, Leonid had

* Olga's last name is a puzzle. She seems to have been Olga Vasileva when Leonid met her, but Zarubin's first name was Vasily and it's likely that 'Vasileva' was derived from that. In every printed source connected with Leonid she is referred to as 'Naumova', which is also the name on her gravestone, but if she was Vasileva because of Zarubin she is just as likely to have been Naumova because of Leonid – unless of course Leonid chose the name Naumov because of her. Either way and whatever the truth, it's a pity that she should be known only as an appendage of one or other of her 'husbands' – with neither of whom she was very happy.

already prised her away from Zarubin in Moscow, before any of them went to Harbin; some even suggest that Leonid was ordered to 'marry' her by his bosses. What's endlessly interesting and endlessly frustrating about the business of Leonid's life is that every anecdote from the trivially personal to the mega-political exists in more than one version, and you can never be sure of the story you're trying to tell.

Zoya says nothing about the new vice-consul's duties. When her father was there he'd been expected to 'help' Russian citizens living or stranded in Harbin 'fill out the necessary papers for repatriation'. That sounds gentlemanly: I wonder how many were executed once they were back in the Soviet Union.

Situated in the central Manchurian plain in the far northeast of China, Harbin had been a small fishing village on the southern bank of the River Songhua (*haerbin*: a Manchu word meaning 'where the fishing nets are dried') until the last decade of the nineteenth century. Then, in the general scramble for profit and influence on the East Asian mainland (a time known in Chinese history as 'the mad rush to divide the melon'), Russia acquired the right to build, first, a railway line running west to east across Manchuria that would be known as the Chinese Eastern Railroad (CER), and later a southern branch to go as far as the Russian naval base at Port Arthur. By the turn of the century the place where the fishing nets are dried had become the 'wild, wooden boom town' where the two railway lines intersected – the 'Chicago of the Far East'.

The common enemy then, as it would be later, was Japan. Both in tsarist times and in Soviet, monitoring and blocking Japanese expansionist designs in Manchuria was a primary Russian concern. It was China's defeat by the Japanese in 1895 that had led to the signing of a treaty with Russia, of which the railway concession was a major part, and Russia's defeat ten years later in the Russo-Japanese War, fought largely over control of the railway, that led to the southern spur being ceded to Japan. Nicholas II had dreamed of a 'Yellow Russia' that would keep Japan out of Manchuria for good. As with most of his dreams there had never been much chance of its being fulfilled. But the Soviets would not be much more successful.

The CER, and with it Harbin itself, remained in Russian hands, at least until the Revolution. Russian citizens were tried in Russian courts; order was maintained by tsarist forces. Thanks to the CER, Russian children went to Russian schools and institutes of higher learning. There were Russian churches, Russian theatres, a Russian symphony orchestra, a Russian opera company, Russian newspapers and Russian toffs. A huge icon hung in the Central Railway Station; the main street was graciously named 'Kitaiskaya', which is Russian for 'Chinese'.

With a few exceptions the two communities met only during the working day, conducting whatever business they had with each other in a lingua franca known as *Moia-tvoia* ('Mine and yours'). The Chinese, tucked away in their own quarters on the other side of the track, provided most of the workforce; and although Harbin was more cosmopolitan than most Russian cities, and far more tolerant, very few Chinese were allowed to live among the Russians. A single marriage between a Russian man and a Chinese woman was recorded in the entire pre-Revolutionary period.

The Bolsheviks seized power in Harbin on 12 December 1917: on 26 December, the Chinese, backed by Harbin's Western consulates and fiercely anti-Bolshevik railway employees, booted them out, forestalled a Japanese takeover and took charge. Not that that simplified anything. The question of who ran Harbin was even more complicated after the Revolution than it had been before. For the next decade and a half the Western powers (including the US), White Russians, Chinese warlords, Japanese agents and Soviet infiltrators battled and intrigued in the area, taking and losing charge in rapid succession. For Moscow the priority was to keep control of the CER, a far shorter route to Vladivostok than the line running north through Russian territory, and fend off Japanese seizure of it for as long as it could.

When Leonid came to Harbin the CER was more or less under Soviet control, with an assertive new general manager who had got the better of the local White Russians if not of Zhang Zuolin, the Old Marshal, whose home territory this was and who, sympathetic to the Japanese, continued to contest Soviet domination of the railway, sometimes by harassing its representatives, sometimes in more open conflict. In January 1926, for example, the Soviet managers of the railway were arrested by the Old Marshal because they refused to transport his troops on credit. They weren't held for long and it wasn't an unusual occurrence; obtaining their release was part of Leonid's remit.

In 1917, at the outbreak of the Revolution, there had been some thirty-four thousand Russians living in Harbin: by the end of the Civil War, the number had risen to 120,000 out of a population of just under half a million. To begin with, the new arrivals ate pheasant and caviar (much cheaper than it had been in Petrograd), went to the opera, complained about the servants, about the funds that should have reached them from the liquidation of the family business in the USSR but never came and never would, about the Jews and the Bolsheviks destroying their country.

But then attitudes hardened among both the Russians and the Chinese. Chinese nationalism took an aggressive, xenophobic turn, while non-Chinese, feeling more threatened than they did elsewhere in China, complained of Chinese 'barbarism' and the 'yellow peril'. From being a 'haven of tolerance', the city turned into a stronghold of Russian Fascism. The new exiles, observers complained, were stubbornly uninterested in anything to do with China. Which isn't hard to believe: so many lived their lives in their own heads, fantasising magic wands that would sweep the Bolsheviks away. 'The more successful a Russian is, the less he is likely even to speak Chinese,' Owen Lattimore, visiting Harbin in the late 1920s, would report with contempt.*

Gradually, however, as their money ran out, the new

* I try to imagine what my mother, who lived most of her life in a kind of exile, would have made of such an existence and whether she would have learned, or tried to learn, Chinese. Had I asked she would have tushed me away. To someone else she might have said she'd never felt part of any of the places where she'd lived, including Eastern Europe, though she'd liked being a young woman in New York and living in Switzerland as an old lady. It's true that she was always quick to learn the local language, but I wonder if that isn't a way of keeping yourself to yourself, of not allowing other people into your locker. I don't think that my parents, who travelled incessantly, ever went anywhere where neither of them could speak the language – or at least read the newspaper.

arrivals did what everyone else did in Harbin – got jobs, opened restaurants and shops, bought and sold opium, resumed their professions or fell into despair. But even among those who seemed to adapt to their new circumstances, most continued to dream of return; and it was the intensity of that dream, coupled with what appeared to be a native inability to believe in the reality of anything that wasn't Russian, that made it easy for Leonid and his kind to ensnare them – to sweet-talk some of them back to 'the motherland' (and thus out of its enemies' reach) with talk of the 'proud', 'constructive' lives they might live there and to persuade others to give up on their old friends and join the Soviet cause. Vyacheslav Pentkovsky, for example, an associate of Leonid's, had been an officer in the tsar's navy: he was now a Chinese-speaker (and Chinese citizen) who worked in the law courts in Harbin and passed on 'important information' to the Soviets. The more people you recruited the better an agent you were considered to be, which is one reason the pre-war emigration was always at sixes and sevens: you could never be certain which of your friends was also your enemy. In some sense the two sides believed the same thing: believed, that is, that militant followers of Grand Duke Nikolai or Grand Duke Cyril really might cross the border, rally their supporters and restore the Romanovs to their throne.

Like Paris or Constantinople, Harbin teemed with émigré organisations. Every aspiration, every route back to Russia had its own outfit, each one deeply, and in some cases murderously, suspicious of the others. 'Pink and reddish, green and whitish, they were all waiting for the Bolsheviks to fall so that they could go back to Russia and resume the feuds that the October Revolution had interrupted,' Grand Duke

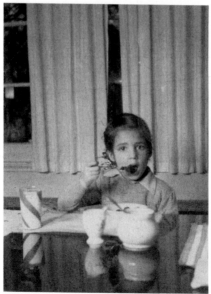

1 From left: Cesia, Niuta and Lola before World War I. Their mother is
wearing the black hat
2 MK, Stamford, Connecticut, 1942

3 Ernst and Julia Wilmers, *c.*1900
4 Charlie and Mats as teenagers in the 1920s

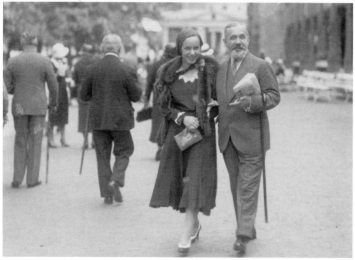

5 Julia Wilmers and her children in the 1930s
6 Cesia and her father in the 1920s

Polizeidirektion in Wien.

Herren-Fahrer-

Führer-Schein

welchem hiemit die Bewilligung zur selb-
ständigen Führung von Kraftwagen mit
Explosionsmotor erteilt wird.

Wien, am

Unterschrift des Inhabers: Trocken-
                                   Stempel.

7 & 8 Cesia's driving licence, Vienna, 1927
9 Cesia and Charlie on their honeymoon

10 Cesia in the 1940s
11 MK, second from left, in Moscow, 1958. The two girls on the right were
Russian; the men were Oxford undergraduates

12 Chaim and his daughter Fanny
13 Motty as a young man
14 The Eitingon tomb in Leipzig

15 Ben Gold addresses his followers (© *Bettmann/CORBIS*)

16 Motty in the 1940s

Alexander, a cousin of Nicholas II, remarked, no doubt with some satisfaction. It's tempting to represent the White Russians as they've been represented in the West ever since 1917, as charming and hopeless, the women in floaty white dresses, the men in bow ties and pointed beards looking like Chekhov and philosophising a bit. But many, we know, wore black shirts rather than bow ties, and were tougher, more racist, more brutal than that. In an atmosphere of counter-revolutionary terror Leonid and his colleagues imagined, and they weren't always wrong, that the Whites and the Japanese were in a conspiracy together, that the Japanese were offering the émigrés help and protection, creating a nest of vipers that would have to be dealt with.

One of Leonid's agents, a man after his own heart, known as 'Osipov', worked as a chauffeur for the Japanese police and then in the political section of the Japanese police force that was concerned with the Soviets. In 1929, with the help of 'Osipov', Leonid and his staff managed to fob the Japanese off with 'documents' suggesting that twenty Russian agents working for the Japanese had applied in secret to have their Soviet citizenship restored. The plot worked; the Japanese were fooled and duly executed the men. That was the kind of ruse Leonid enjoyed: we'll see it in practice again in Spain in the late 1930s and in Belorussia during the Second World War.

In the letter he wrote in 1946 recommending him for promotion Sudoplatov speaks of Leonid's 'resounding success in demoralising White émigré organisations in China'. Many of his 'resounding' successes, I would guess, were in luring would-be counter-revolutionaries back onto Soviet territory and having them disappear once they got there. He had played a small part in Operation Sindikat, the operation that lured Boris Savinkov back onto Soviet territory; he probably already knew then how these things were done.

In the late spring of 1928 KMT armies were poised to take Beijing. Zhang Zuolin saw that he didn't stand much of a chance, had no strong feelings about Beijing in any case, and evacuated the city. On 3 June a convoy of twenty cars brought him to Beijing's railway station to start his journey back to Mukden, his Manchurian capital, on an armoured train. A military band played and he entered his private carriage smiling broadly. As the carriage passed under a bridge on the outskirts of Mukden an explosion brought down a span of masonry. The Old Marshal died a few hours later. Standard accounts blame his death on rogue Japanese officers wanting to push Tokyo into a more aggressive policy in Manchuria. If that was the case, they chose the wrong target. Zhang Zuolin's son, the Young Marshal, who succeeded him, was rather less willing than his father to do Japan's bidding.

Leonid's biographer has a different account of the Old Marshal's death. According to him, Leonid had evidence that the Japanese were indeed plotting to set up a puppet regime in Manchuria, and since Soviet interests were threatened, there is, as he puts it, a 'version' of events which holds that the decision to liquidate the Old Marshal was taken in Moscow; the ruse had been to time the explosion in such a way that it happened on a section of the railway guarded by Japanese. The rogue officers in that account were simply fall-guys, Leonid's dupes. Of course it would be all the more to his credit if Leonid and his men were in fact guilty and their guilt never discovered. Indeed, as far as Leonid was concerned that would be a perfect outcome.

The killing of Zhang Zuolin has been much written about, yet Sharapov's 'version' has so far made little headway. 'A version exists,' Sharapov says: does that mean the Soviets were responsible and no one wants to own up? Or, more plausibly, that at some point in the past someone wanted to be thought responsible but wasn't? The fact that the Young Marshal was more independent of the Japanese than his father was neither here nor there, it seems: it adds an element of implausibility to both accounts.

The Old Marshal's death, whoever was responsible for it, made little difference to the situation in Manchuria as far as Leonid was concerned. On 27 May 1929 Zhang Zuolin's former comrade-in-arms Zhang Jinghui surrounded the Soviet Consulate in Harbin, seized documents belonging to the military attaché, arrested a number of Chinese Communists and thirty-nine 'consular' employees and demanded that the Soviets stop spreading Communism in the region. 'We were not worried overmuch about the attaché's papers,' a former colleague of Leonid's, Georgi Agabekov, would later explain, 'for, as in the case of the famous Zinoviev letter, we could assert any document of a compromising character to be a forgery.' Even so, the authorities in Moscow were said to be 'furious' with the attaché for not managing to destroy his papers before the raiders could get their hands on them.

Not long after that, Leonid was recalled to Moscow.

In October 1928 Chiang Kaishek proclaimed a new Nationalist government in Nanjing, theoretically in control of all of China and accepted as such by all foreign powers, including the USSR. In practice large parts of the country remained under local warlords as before, only now making formal submission to Nanjing.

Four years later the Japanese seized control of the whole of Manchuria, setting up the puppet state of Manchukuo. Moscow meanwhile clung onto its ownership of the CER for three more years, then sold its stake to Japan. The upheaval that followed was enormous; fifty thousand former employees of the railway migrated back to Russia; thirty thousand were shot during the Great Terror of 1937. But that wasn't the end of it. The Soviet Union's first condition for entering the war against Japan in 1945 was that the railway be handed back. Only when Mao came to power four years later did Russia finally accept joint control with China. In 1952 all rights were at last transferred to the People's Republic.

CHAPTER 16

Constantinople

In 1929 Leonid was sent to Constantinople. He was accompanied by his family: Olga and the two girls, Zoya, his stepdaughter, and Svetlana, his daughter. He was just thirty, 'an elegant, well-dressed young man' in the words of his one-time colleague Georgi Agabekov. There can't have been many Soviet officials, in those early days or later, to whom those epithets would have applied. Indeed, Leonid himself in later years was known to complain of the low standard of dress among the Soviet *agentura*: anyone, he said, could spot an NKVD man on the streets of Western Europe 'prancing along in his blue serge suit with its square shoulders – made to order by some Russian émigré tailor in the Latin Quarter. He struts down the Champs-Elysées for the special delight of French counter-intelligence, and deludes himself that he's a second Colonel Lawrence.'*

To judge from his photographs, I wouldn't call Leonid good-looking or elegant, but he had very dark eyes and thick, pitch-black hair, and as a young man, he was arrogant and saturnine and knew how to cut a dash. His look, people said, was quite fierce, and everything I know about him suggests that he was always a frightening figure; a deep scar acquired later on – a hunting accident, it was said – would make him seem more frightening still. He was

* Nikolai Khokhlov, *In the Name of Conscience: The Testament of a Soviet Secret Agent*.

good at his job and good above all at getting what he wanted, so that when people say, as many have, how charming he was, they don't mean that he had the kind of charm that's always there, even when it isn't needed; what they mean is that many women fell for him. He wasn't gregarious and didn't like large gatherings, but his presence in a room wasn't ignored. And certainly he cared about his appearance.

He wasn't yet – if he ever was – Trotsky's designated stalker. It may have been a matter of chance – nothing more – that he was there at the start and at the end of the chase. But none of the files that I've had access to makes that clear: it was in the nature of Soviet bureaucracy to require that everything be documented and nothing divulged. Leonid's biographer, writing seventy years later, could have made a connection if there was one to make but he says nothing, mentioning only that the ship that brought Trotsky across the Black Sea was also the one that carried the mail between the residency and Moscow. Only Zoya in her memoir takes her chances and says that she 'definitely learned that Leonid's assignment in Turkey was to catch up with Trotsky'.

Still using the name 'Naumov', Leonid had come to Turkey as the agent in residence, the *rezident* stationed in the Soviet Consulate in the guise of an attaché. Agents coming into a country to do a specific job or living there under a false identity were known as 'illegals' and in theory they had no connection with the embassy. But in the early years of the Soviet Union these arrangements were quite fluid. Agabekov, for example, had had a desk job in Moscow but was now in Constantinople as an illegal, sent under commercial cover to run a Soviet company selling bicycles.

Older and more experienced than Leonid, Agabekov, an Armenian, was also less attached to the Soviet cause. Not long after Leonid's arrival in Constantinople he defected and the following year published the first of two semi-autobiographical accounts of Soviet intelligence. In Belgium in 1938 the *agentura* caught up with him. He was lured to Paris, and there an NKVD hitman, a former officer in the Turkish army, 'our assassin' (in Sudoplatov's proud words), stabbed him, put his body in a suitcase and dumped it in the sea. Whether Leonid recruited the Turk, whether he arranged that particular death, I can't say for sure. But two things are certain: Paris was on his beat in those years and murder was always part of his remit.

In the second book Agabekov describes a late-night meeting in his flat in Constantinople with Leonid and the former *rezident* in Greece, a man called Molotkovsky, recently arrived from Moscow. Molotkovsky was 'pensive': Leonid 'more interested in the gramophone which he wound up from time to time'. Molotkovsky wanted Leonid to take over the agency network in Greece – 'the people running the show in Moscow are bureaucrats rather than Chekists and are letting valuable sources go.' Leonid's response was surprisingly nonchalant: 'It's all the same to me. If you want I'll go to Greece . . . I'm not scared of failure . . . I have to say I'm fed up with all this work . . . As soon as I go back to Moscow, I'll stop working for OGPU, I'll go away somewhere.'

It's an extraordinary remark to have made, especially at a time when, Agabekov reports, the bosses in Moscow were more than usually concerned with the 'mental attitudes' of their agents, 'when the least suspicion was enough to cause this or that collaborator of OGPU to be relieved of his duties'. Later on it would always be so: Trotsky's exile, far from providing relief, had only ex-acerbated Stalin's paranoia. Not that the bravado that enabled Leonid to make the remark – the *je-m'en-foutisme* – is at all out of character. As for failure . . . well, he had had a notable failure in Harbin and no one had punished him for it. One of the mysteries of Leonid's career is that he failed two or three times, yet each time was forgiven when others lost their lives for less serious offences. Or is the conversation with Agabekov a trick? Is he more (that's to say, less) straightforwardly trying to smoke Agabekov out?

It was also in his character never to be fazed, and with equal nonchalance he added the agency in Greece to his responsibilities.

Three months later Agabekov defected:

> On Thursday 19 June I boarded the steamer *Tadla*, bound for Marseille. Only yesterday I had a meeting with Eitingon-Naumov, who told me that Moscow was surprised by my long silence and demanded I send materials. I promised to meet him on Saturday and give him some post for Moscow. Today I am already on the steamer. A few more minutes, and it's goodbye to Istanbul,* with your beautiful shores and everything I have lived here in these last nine months. On Saturday evening, when Naumov will be waiting for me on the Galata Bridge with post for Moscow, I will already be in Naples.

---

* 'Constantinople' gradually gave way to 'Istanbul' in the early years of the last century. In March 1930 an act was passed requiring foreigners to adopt 'Istanbul' as the city's sole designation.

As the ship approached Piraeus he threw his revolver into the sea.

Trotsky and Natalya stayed at the consulate in Constantinople, looked after and spied on, until the end of February. A few members of the consular staff were sufficiently on their side to warn them against agents of the European powers operating in the city. They said nothing about the Soviet agents milling around under a variety of real and assumed names.

In due course they moved, first to a hotel, then to a dilapidated villa on the island of Prinkipo in the Sea of Marmara, where once the emperors of Byzantium had locked up their rivals. The journey by steamer from Constantinople took an hour and a half, making it a good place for Trotsky to shelter from the attentions of his enemies. 'Here we were reasonably safe,' Natalya wrote after his death, 'all the more so because the place was almost uninhabited during a large part of the year.' Isaac Deutscher, Trotsky's biographer, speaks of the 'cobwebbed squalor' of the house they had rented from an impoverished pasha, but Natalya remembered it as 'a beautiful place, spacious, peaceful . . . bathed in golden sunlight', with the waves 'lapping the shore a few steps from our home'. Less sentimentally, Trotsky's American friend Max Eastman, shocked at the general absence of amenities, described the 'red-cliffed island' as crouching in the Sea of Marmara 'like a prehistoric animal drinking'.

With the exception of a short visit to Copenhagen, they remained on Prinkipo for more than four years. They didn't dislike it, but they didn't want to be there, didn't want to be so far away from the rest of the political world or within such easy reach of both Stalin's men and the vengeful White emigration. 'They sat there all the time as in a waiting-room on a pier, looking out for the ship that would take them away,' Deutscher wrote. Trotsky made strenuous efforts to persuade other countries to have him: Germany first of all, then Britain, France, Czechoslovakia, Holland. Each one turned him down. 'Trotsky whose frown meted death to thousands, sits disconsolate, a bundle of old rags, stranded on the shores of the Black Sea,' Churchill noted with glee.*

Constantinople in 1929 was like Casablanca in the movie, a city governed by the politics of the black market; a place where loyalties were bought and conspiracies hatched; where people might be overheard conversing with each other in any European or Middle Eastern language and no one would think it surprising; where 'services' were rendered and throats were slit, and absinthe was drunk because it was 'so cooling'; a place, as Eric Ambler describes it, where it was easy to buy drugs or, for a bit more cash, hire an assassin. A place, in short, where Leonid could go about his business without fear of upsetting the authorities or running out of hired hands.

Most of the nationalist movements and political dissidents in the south and east of the USSR – in Kazakhstan, Armenia, Georgia, Azerbaijan – had offices, or cells, in the city and these were easily penetrated. 'OGPU', Agabekov

* That was in 1929 in *John O'London's Weekly*. Eight years later, when Trotsky had moved on and the essay, originally entitled 'The Ogre of Europe', was retitled 'Leon Trotsky, alias Bronstein' and included in *Great Contemporaries*, the wording was changed to 'sits disconsolate – a skin of malice stranded for a time on the shores of the Black Sea'.

wrote, 'managed to get hold of the correspondence of all these groups, and therefore knew how little danger they posed to Soviet power.' And if OGPU needed to know more it was always possible, in the unhappy aftermath of the Russian Civil War, to promise something – money or a change of circumstances – in exchange for information about what was going on in one or other of the Soviet Union's distant domains, or nearer home.

This is how it might work. The Armenian Patriarch in Echmiadzin wanted to make one of his clergymen in Constantinople – a certain Basmachyan – a bishop and to that end summoned him to Yerevan (capital of Soviet Armenia) to be consecrated. Basmachyan, Agabekov reports, applied for a visa, Leonid got wind of it, instructed the Soviet consul to refuse to issue one and told his men to sound Basmachyan out: if he engaged on his return to Constantinople as bishop to 'render certain services to OGPU' he would get not only a visa but 'every help toward his elevation to the episcopate'. 'Burning with the desire to become a bishop', Basmachyan 'agreed to everything'.

With the Turks themselves the Soviet government, and by extension Soviet Intelligence, maintained the most 'courteous' relations while at the same time intercepting and decoding Turkish telegrams on the sly. There were many reasons to keep things sweet. Trotsky obviously was one. Another was the hope that in return the Turks would close their eyes to Soviet intrigue in the Middle East: in Syria and Palestine, for example, where Leonid was a frequent visitor. Then there was the fact that the Turkish government enjoyed diplomatic relations with the many countries that didn't recognise the Soviet Union; and because security in many foreign embassies was haphazard, Soviet agents seem to have had little trouble suborning their staff. The military attaché at the French Embassy kept his Soviet colleagues posted about the situation on the Turkish border with Syria; a member of staff at the Japanese Embassy allowed professional safebreakers from Moscow to break into the strongroom he was supposed to be guarding.

Turkey was an information hub for the Soviets, and thanks in large part to its proximity to the Soviet Union, information gathered there was treated differently from information gathered elsewhere. A courier shuttled backwards and forwards to Odessa on the *Ilyich* carrying with him whatever purloined material was to hand in the form of undeveloped film; if he was in danger of being searched or attacked all he had to do was open the box and expose the film.

The Turkish government meanwhile, though friendly enough to allow the Turkish police to swap information with Soviet Intelligence, was yet not so friendly as to bow to Stalin's pressure to put Trotsky behind bars. (Trotsky had been responsible for getting arms to Kemal when Kemal needed them. 'Fellow soldiers don't forget such things,' Trotsky said, more confident now than he had been on his arrival in Turkey.) And because the Turks were on good terms with both parties there's no knowing whether a Turkish gendarme standing guard at the gate of the villa where Trotsky and Natalya were staying reported to his own commanding officer or to Leonid or to both.

Trotsky himself made no fuss about things of that kind. Asked whether he wasn't afraid that OGPU might lay a trap for him when he was out sailing or fishing, he replied that once OGPU decided to destroy him there wouldn't be anything he could do about it and in the meantime he saw no reason why he should be his own jailer.

In the event Kemal didn't lock Trotsky up and the White Russian émigrés didn't exact their revenge. The danger had a more familiar source and it didn't touch Trotsky directly – not yet. Again he worked prodigiously. *My Life*, *History of the Russian Revolution* and *The Stalin School of Falsification* were written and published between 1929 and 1932; and according to Natalya, Trotsky supervised their translation into French, English and German 'down to the last comma'. Together with Lev Sedov, he edited the *Opposition Bulletin*, most of which he himself wrote, organised his following and kept up, to the extent that OGPU allowed, with dissident Communists all over the world.

That he was able to do so much was in some degree thanks to the overlapping troupe of assistants and bodyguards which would from now on accompany him wherever he went. They were loyal supporters and they had an uncomfortable time of it. Trotsky's qualities tended towards the heroic, but he was also implacable. 'The guard', one of the young men, Jean van Heijenoort, subsequently wrote, 'was exhausting . . . To be awakened at two in the morning in order to take a turn of duty is hard to endure when it goes on month after month.'* Trotsky was high-handed with his entourage; he had the ways of a martinet and could be quite petulant (if his lunch wasn't on the table on the dot of one o'clock, he would go back to his study and refuse to come back again until suppertime) as well as sarcastic.

There were visitors, naturally. From the Soviet Union as

---

* Jean van Heijenoort, *With Trotsky in Exile: From Prinkipo to Coyoacán.*

well as the West, though many (maybe most) of the former eventually turned out to be colleagues of Leonid's: 'A Latvian Franck stayed at Prinkipo for five months,' Natalya would write. 'Later we learned that he was an informer of the Russian Secret Service.' Agabekov refers to a former officer, retained by the Soviets, who had known Trotsky's family in Moscow and repeatedly visited him in Turkey 'under the privilege of old friendship'. There were countless others, some pretending to be supporters of Trotsky, some pretending not to be.

The saddest case is that of Yakov Blumkin. Intelligent, adventurous, according to Natalya 'something of a poet', he'd been a member of the Cheka from its earliest days and was famous for the assassination – against Dzerzhinsky's orders – of the German ambassador Count Mirbach in 1918. (It was in large measure thanks to Trotsky that he escaped execution.) The story of his undoing is told in many versions, but it seems that in the summer of 1929, stationed like Leonid in Constantinople but still widely known to be a devoted follower of Trotsky, he made the mistake of paying the Old Man what was intended to be a secret visit. The mistake was compounded when he agreed to pass a message from Trotsky to Karl Radek, a former secretary of the Comintern, now a non-person in Moscow. For that he was arrested, charged with treason and executed – 'the first party member on whom capital punishment was inflicted for an inner party offence', Deutscher points out.

Blumkin wasn't arrested straight away: a fellow agent, Lisa Gorskaya, was instructed to 'abandon bourgeois prejudices' with a view to uncovering the exact extent of his collaboration with Trotsky. Lisa Gorskaya, a consummate agent and a handsome woman, known to American

Intelligence, a CIA operative once told me, as 'Lisa Big Hands and Big Feet', soon afterwards married Vasily Zarubin, now the OGPU *rezident* in Berlin, thereby becoming, in a roundabout way, a relative of Leonid's – his stepdaughter Zoya's stepmother, to be precise.

From the time of his expulsion from the Soviet Union in 1929 until his death in Mexico in 1940, Trotsky never missed a chance to broadcast Stalin's errors to the widest possible audience, to make him look stupid or villainous, to show him up as Lenin's betrayer not his heir. Yet Stalin made no moves. Fear of what the world might say, as well as reluctance to face what was likely to be Trotsky's immense posthumous popularity, may have played a part, but above all the Old Guard remembered what happened to the Jacobins once they started killing their leaders.

In the meantime it was of course useful to Stalin to know who Trotsky's supporters were and what they were up to, and how, if necessary, they could be got rid of; and the best way to find that out was through Trotsky himself. Hence Blumkin's fate and hence, more straightforwardly, the succession of Kremlin envoys who arrived on Prinkipo claiming to be in search of a job as Trotsky's secretary or bodyguard, and the supporters who turned out not to be supporters at all. 'The shadowy figure of the *agent provocateur* was to follow Trotsky like a curse,' Deutscher wrote in *The Prophet Outcast*.

In the night of 1 March 1931 there was a fire at the villa on Prinkipo. 'Along with the house, everything we had with us and on us also burned,' Trotsky wrote to a colleague in Paris. 'Everything, from our hats to our boots went up in smoke, including my entire library, although by

chance my archive was saved, or at least the most important part of it.' There was an investigation; witnesses were
cross-examined; but nothing was found: no evidence of
the fire having natural causes and no evidence that it
didn't. The household moved into a nearby hotel and
Trotsky 'laid out his manuscripts on the table, called the
stenographer, and began to dictate a chapter of his book',
a secretary noted admiringly.

'One day we read in the papers that there was a fire on
the island of Prinkipo where Trotsky lived,' Zoya recalls in
her short post-Soviet memoir. She doesn't say that Leonid
had a part in it but again she doesn't say that he didn't.
There are many ways of suggesting things while keeping
them dark and it's one of the things that spies are meant
to be good at. A few years before her memoir was published I suggested to Zoya that Stalin's men, Leonid or the
military, could have got Trotsky at any time of Stalin's
choosing. She disagreed while telling me that Leonid had
nearly got him in Turkey when the house was set fire to.
Was the fire supposed to have killed Trotsky after all? Or
was it just a bit of showmanship, a flexing of muscles, a
reminder that Stalin could strike whenever he wanted to?
That seems too wasteful. I imagine its purpose may have
been more straightforward: to interfere one way or another with his work, perhaps even to destroy the archive
which in the event was the one thing that was saved.

'Trotsky left the country, and very shortly after that',
Zoya continues, 'Leonid took us back to Moscow.' But
Trotsky didn't leave the country until July 1933. Leonid
was the one who left in 1931. That doesn't, however,
mean that he lost interest in Trotsky.

CHAPTER 17

Vienna

Max Eitingon was born in Mogilev in June 1881. He was Chaim's eldest child. Waldemar, who died young (and opportunely for Motty) in New York, was his brother and Fanny, who married Motty, his sister; another sister was called Esther. He made his way west with his family in the 1890s, becoming, like the others, an Austrian citizen in the course of the journey. He had trouble at school – because of a bad stammer, it was said – and not having taken the Abitur, the final school-leaving exams, was unable to enrol officially at any university. However, he was interested in all intellectual matters, philosophy especially, and took courses at Wittenberg, Heidelberg and Marburg before registering to study medicine at Leipzig in 1902.

In December 1906 Max wrote to Freud.* He was by now a 'sub-assistant' at the Burghölzli Psychiatric Clinic in Zurich, where Bleuler presided and Jung also worked, and where psychoanalysis was already being practised. He wasn't at the end of his medical studies yet – that would take him in all nine and a half years – but he had read Freud's *Studies in Hysteria*, the account of Anna O, published in 1895, and wanted, he told Freud, to refer a patient to him for treatment, a young Russian woman, a probable hysteric. He was in no doubt, he told Freud, that her symptoms – she

---

* The correspondence between Max and Freud, edited by Michael Schröter, was published in 2004.

had many – were 'sexually determined'. When Freud suggested that one of his students might take the woman on, Max was insistent: 'I really would like to see you yourself, Herr Professor, take charge of the treatment.' He was always like that: modest but very determined.

Four weeks later Max accompanied his patient on the journey from Zurich to Vienna. 'You were the first to come to the lonely one,' Freud was to write to him: the first foreigner, the first messenger, the first emissary, the first swallow. It was a momentous thing: 'a new beginning in the history of the psychoanalytic movement', Sidney Pomer, a younger colleague would write many years later. 'And you will be the last to leave,' Freud had added.

Every Wednesday evening Freud and his acolytes – there were eleven at the start of 1907 – gathered to discuss Freud's work around an oblong table in the waiting room at 19 Berggasse.* Max spent two weeks in Vienna and was there for the meetings of 23 and 30 January, his heart, he would report, pounding as he entered the room. But he wasn't shy about speaking out and there were some prickly exchanges, a consequence of differences of view between Zurich and Vienna.

About the ostensible patient, meanwhile, the young Russian woman, the putative hysteric who provided the excuse for Max to come to Vienna, we know only that she wasn't considered a suitable case for treatment. Max, on the other hand, being intelligent, educated and psychoanalytically inclined, was very suitable. And so began the first ever training analysis.

* Among them, Adler and Otto Rank are the only names that are well(ish) known today, in part perhaps because they would both eventually break with Freud.

It wasn't a formal affair in the way orthodox Freudian analysis is today; Max didn't even lie down on the famous couch in Freud's study. Instead he accompanied Freud on long walks through the city. I had imagined the two of them, strolling, pausing, arguing, shrugging, gesticulating, as they wandered along a footpath in the Vienna Woods, a picture of refugees on Hampstead Heath in the 1940s and 1950s in my head. Not a bit of it. The two Jewish doctors in their long winter overcoats marched at a lick through the streets of Vienna, Max, in my fantasies, trying hard to keep up with the flow of Freud's thoughts. 'I remember the swift pace and rapid spate of speech on such walks,' Ernest Jones, Freud's first biographer in English, wrote of his own experience a year later.

From the correspondence between Max and Freud it's evident that Max's tendency to prevaricate, his dithering – Freud referred to it as his 'provisos' – was a major preoccupation of his analysis. Who knows what, psychoanalytically, lay behind it. But in the real world it wouldn't be implausible to talk about Max's money. He was a rich young man – the only psychoanalyst in the world, it was later said, with a private income – and he didn't have to make up his mind. Not everyone wished him well on those grounds, and back in Zurich some people suggested that the reason Max travelled to Vienna before anyone else was that he was the only one who could afford the train fare. That said, Jung himself was in Vienna less than a month later.

In due course, and with Jung's help, Max finished his thesis – 'The Effect of Epileptic Attacks on Mental Association' – and finally completed his studies. That bit of dithering was now done with: his papers were in order

– he was in every official way a psychiatrist. But of course he didn't need to set up in practice immediately.

Knowing your own mind: it's surprising how difficult it can be; and if you feel you don't know yourself and therefore don't know what or who you want, it must be overwhelming when something you realise you do want suddenly comes into view. It can organise your entire life. That, I imagine, is what happened to Max when he met Freud. In fact it had probably been set in train by the experience of reading the *Studies in Hysteria*. Hence his bold – boorish – insistence that Freud, rather than one of his students, see the young Russian woman he brought to Vienna.

Another example. At least once, in 1909, and maybe also in 1908, Max returned to Vienna to resume his walking analysis. And in the autumn of 1907, nine months after his first visit to Vienna, he met Freud in Florence. Max liked to holiday and he liked to visit the sites of European high culture, as did Freud, so the meeting may have been accidental, but it probably wasn't. And when Freud moved on to Rome so, too, did Max, who spent four hours with Freud, once more on foot, before making his way back to Florence. As Jung unamiably, and unfairly, put it, Max had 'parlayed' his way into an 'excursion' with Freud. When Max wanted to be somewhere nothing stood in his way.

Jung, so the story went, was jealous of Max: jealous, I suppose, of his financial ease, but jealous also of the affection that Freud had for him. Jung's esteem for the great man may have been short-lived but he'd been as excited to meet him as Max had been. ('Anyone who knows your science has eaten of the tree of paradise and attained vision,' he said to Freud a few months after meeting him.) 'An impotent gasbag' was how Jung described Max in a letter to Freud, fit only to be a member of the Russian Duma. But then he thought about it again and conceded that 'impotent' wasn't the right word. Women were another area where Max dithered and another reason Jung envied him: envied him, as he put it, 'the uninhibited abreaction of the polygamous instinct', by which Jung meant that while dithering between one woman and another, Max ensured himself a good time – with both? – and didn't worry unduly about it.

In November 1909, his studies finished, Max moved to Berlin to join Karl Abraham who, like him, had been working in Zurich with Bleuler and Jung, and who would in time become Freud's ablest and most dependable follower. The 'provisos' were still a problem. 'I am cleaning up the last scraps of my "provisos",' Max wrote to Freud in September 1910. 'Hurry up, time is passing,' Freud wrote to him in November 1911. It also bothered Freud that his patient didn't report on himself with any regularity. 'I beg, once again, for your forgiveness if you find my silence objectionable,' Max, a recalcitrant supplicant, wrote in the letter of September 1910.

The polygamous instincts, too, were still troubling: 'Dear Herr Doctor,' Freud wrote from the Hotel Milano in Rome later that month, 'I was told that a man with a lady had asked after me. If that man was you you are at least not without company, which in fact you hardly ever are.' (Strange that the two men were again in Rome at the same time. Had Max 'parlayed' another encounter?)

Slowly, slowly, Max redeemed himself. He didn't publish enough, Freud told him, which was a pity because

Freud thought highly of the one paper he produced, a critique of Jung entitled 'On the Subconscious in Jung and Its Turn to the Ethical' – i.e. to the explicitly Christian. But he did set up practice, occasionally asking Freud to refer patients to him. At the same time – whether in gratitude or because he was determined that Freud should share his admiration – he bombarded him with volume upon volume of Dostoevsky's collected work. 'For three days', Freud wrote, 'it has been raining Dostoevsky here; every day there is at least one parcel; 14 volumes and one small supplementary edition have already found their way.' 'An oversized present', Freud called it, as many of Max's presents were: I didn't properly understand the meaning of the phrase 'generous to a fault' until Max came into my life. 'There's something truly Jewish about this,' Freud would say about his present-giving on another occasion.

Equally (or more) momentous, at the end of August 1912 Max got engaged. 'Dear Herr Professor,' he wrote to Freud, 'As you have on so many occasions offered the friendliest proof of your interest in me, I would now like to make a very personal announcement to you. I have recently got engaged – to a Russian woman – and I am planning to get married in around three or four months' time.' Unfortunately Freud didn't much like Russians – 'savages' was a word he applied to them – and to anyone reading the correspondence between Max and Freud it's clear that Freud didn't much like Max's wife.

The Russian woman, Mirra Raigorodsky, had been an actress – at the Moscow Art Theatre, it's said – and if, as family legend suggests, Max's mother hadn't wanted him to marry her that may explain why. But she was also four years older than Max, and that too may have been held against her, and, worse, she'd been married before and had a child or even two children, but these, it seems, weren't subjects she was willing to talk about, even with Max. Whatever the reason, she was coolly welcomed by her mother-in-law. (My Aunt Lola called her 'a pest'.) But there is no indication that Max reported these things to Freud, psychoanalytically relevant though they may have been: he was always loyal to his wife and guarded in what he told Freud.

A more intriguing hypothesis is that Max, so much more enigmatic than his gasbag reputation suggests, had also been married before. That at any rate is what Theodore Draper was told in the late 1980s after the publication in the *New York Review of Books* of 'The Mystery of Max Eitingon'. The art historian Meyer Schapiro, so Draper was told, had been friends with this wife, another art historian, for more than forty years, although interestingly, as far as I know, no one told Draper her name. Still, Max was interested in art history: maybe she was the companion who went with him to call on Freud at the Hotel Milano in Rome in September 1910. Who knows? There's married and 'married' after all.

Mirra was pretty, 'exquisite, tiny and a great charmer', according to another of Max's nieces, who obviously didn't agree with Lola; and cat-like in the only photograph I have of her, dressed in complex layers of oriental shawls against the background of an oriental garden. Freud complained that she had no interest in the things that Max was interested in – i.e. psychoanalysis. But Max was interested in many things – Russian things mainly: Russian philosophy, Russian music and crucially, as it would turn out, Russian folk songs – that Freud himself had no time for, and these were interests Mirra shared.

Mirra was spoiled in the way of pretty women who marry rich husbands, especially when there are no children, and was in equal measure fragile and demanding. Her physical health was poor; this comes up regularly in Max's correspondence; and her mental health quite shaky. (Max to Freud, Berlin, 11 November 1920: 'Her chronic gall bladder and liver problems of course remain, but her tempestuous reaction to her physical condition has calmed down.' Max to Freud, Merano, 14 January 1921: 'Luckily Mirra's regaining of strength coincides with the subduing of extreme alertness.')

That same month Max told Freud that he'd just discovered that Mirra's father, to whom she'd been close, had died the previous May; but he didn't tell Mirra for another nine months – her health, he said, was too precarious. The effect on her of the news, when he eventually divulged it, was as 'devastating' as he'd expected. But more disconcerting is the revelation of how well Max could keep a secret. It's something worth keeping in mind.

Max had wanted to have children but for whatever reason, connected or not connected to Mirra's frailty, it wasn't possible, as he reported despondently, and psychoanalytically, to Freud: 'May I, dear Professor, tell you something about myself? A depression with a strong feeling of insufficiency, from which I suffered immensely last year, and again briefly but sharply on my return at the end of the war, is directly tied to a narcissistic ailment: that we may never have children.' Whether or not to make up for it, they would live and holiday in style, and if Mirra took advantage of Max's wealth, so more high-mindedly did Freud himself. 'Does an old woman like her really need a box with a hundred pairs of shoes?' Freud harrumphed to Arnold Zweig, but we don't know what Mirra said about him.

I would like to be able to say something here about Max's money, which played such a large part in his life, and in the life of everyone around him, but all I know is that he had a lot of it. Until, in the late 1920s, with rising inflation and the collapse of the fur market, he had less. Whether the money came in the form of an allowance from his father, or later from Motty, or of shares in the fur company in Leipzig or New York, or the textile company in Poland, I have no idea. But it seems as if for most of his life all he had to do was to shake the money tree and watch the moidores come down.

'Fortuitous circumstances have meant that there has always been very little friction between my aims and the reality of my life,' he would write to Freud in 1922, assuring him that a gift which Freud had categorised as a 'sacrifice' was not a sacrifice at all. His family, Max explained, 'replaces its lack of understanding for my efforts with a considerable and unambiguous sympathy for my personality and what I do'. Perplexingly, nothing that Max at any point said suggests that he worried that the reason Freud was so nice to him had to do with his money. I'm not saying it did and I'm not saying it didn't: only that the effect on other people of his great wealth seems to have been something Max didn't take into account.

When the First World War broke out Max enlisted in the Austrian army as a captain in the medical corps. He was stationed for the most part in different hospitals in northern Hungary, what is now eastern Slovakia, where he treated the victims of 'war neuroses'. He seemed to enjoy the work without the customary prevarication. Wartime perhaps suited him. 'Eitingon is dedicating himself body and soul to the hospital section, which he seems to be leading in an exemplary fashion,' their colleague in psychoanalysis the Hungarian Sándor Ferenczi reported to Freud. It was as if he'd been woken up by the war, made aware for the first time of the world outside his own head and of a place in it that he might occupy.

Not that he'd entirely got over his habit of doing things by halves. Of being in one place and another place at the same time. 'Dr Eitingon just called that he got sick in Kassa and is going to Karlsbad,' Ferenczi wrote to Freud in March 1916 – most probably, 23 March. The 25th and 26th Max spent with Freud in Vienna, so his illness can't have been that debilitating; he was in Karlsbad until 21 April and in Leipzig until the end of the first week in May. He was the director of the psychiatric observation section at the garrison hospital, the psychiatrist who interviewed the patients on their way in, to determine what was wrong with them, and on their way out, to see if they were cured. Was it normal for a doctor to take a six-week holiday in the middle of a war? Am I being too judgemental?

The answer probably is yes. Forty years later, after Max's death, a collection of tributes to him was published privately in Jerusalem, a volume entitled *Max Eitingon: In Memoriam*. The most interesting, the only one that's at all personal, describes Max *in situ* at the garrison hospital in Kassa (now Kosice in Slovakia) in 1915. The German theatre director Adolf Lantz – he would become quite a well-known film-maker after the war – was waiting for his final medical exam before enrolling in the Austro-Hungarian army. Things were not going well for him; his uniform was in tatters, he couldn't speak Hungarian and when he caught sight of his face in a mirror he didn't immediately recognise himself. 'Then', he writes,

> there strode through the waiting room a senior doctor in a white overall and carrying a stethoscope. As he passed he happened to look in my direction. He stopped and for a moment he looked at me searchingly through his gold-rimmed spectacles. 'Do you by any chance come from Berlin?' he asked. I said I did. 'Aren't you Lantz, the theatre director?' I said I was. 'My name is Eitingon. I saw your photograph in a newspaper once. I can't remember whether it was the *Weltspiegel* or the *Berliner Tageblatt*. That's how I knew you.'

The photograph had appeared more than three years previously. Lantz was amazed. A memory for faces can be useful in all sorts of contexts. I don't know about Leonid, but his stepdaughter Zoya's memory of the people she had come across, however glancingly, was prodigious. On the other hand, Max, we know, was stagestruck, and that may explain this particular feat. He invited Lantz to have supper with him that night in his flat and Lantz, like many others, was overwhelmed by Max's benevolence: 'kindness and a keen wish to help me radiated out of him.'

Lantz became Max's secretary and for the next two years followed him to different postings. It was his job to write up the reports that Max dictated from his notes late into the night. Again Lantz is full of praise: Max was so patient, so hard-working, so thorough, so meticulous; his reports were 'like little works of art'. Finally, it appears that Max, like Leonid, is supposed – in Max's case supposed by Lantz – to have been able to speak, or to get by in, thirteen languages. The Eitingons were polyglots in the old Jewish way, but thirteen languages . . . My mother was an Eitingon of that sort, but six was as many as she had need for.

Max would turn out to be an unusually capable administrator and I assume that Ferenczi had that talent in mind when he said that Max was 'leading the hospital in exemplary fashion'. But in other letters from this time Ferenczi also writes about Max's 'great successes' in the few analyses he has taken on and the 'brilliant results he has achieved with hypnosis'. I mention this because some of Max's colleagues – Sándor Radó and Ernest Jones, in particular – were always inclined to disparage both his intellectual gifts and his contribution to the practice of psychoanalysis. Yet even Ernest Jones mentions the 'excellent practical work' of the Continental analysts Abraham, Ferenczi and Eitingon, and the impression it made 'if not on the general medical public, at least on the high-ranking army medical officers'. Institutionally, the war had done psychoanalysis no harm.

On the contrary. 'The war neuroses demonstrated the Freudian mechanisms in the plainest manner even to the blindest and most bigoted,' Max himself was to write a few years later: towards the end of the war, he reported, there had been a real prospect of 'psycho-analytic treatment centres for neurotics' being set up in the Austro-Hungarian army.* It didn't happen – when the war was over the Austro-Hungarian army no longer existed – but psychoanalysis now had a foothold in many psychiatric clinics. Even Freud, always the most pessimistic, had to

---

* *International Journal of Psycho-Analysis*, Vol. IV, 1923.

concede that psychoanalysis had lately been granted a measure of official recognition, not only in Central Europe, but in Britain and America too, and by the military of all people. In time many, in Central Europe especially, would dismiss it as 'the Jewish science', but not yet.

In October 1919 Freud invited Max to join the inner sanctum of psychoanalysis, the secret Psychoanalytic Committee. There could be no greater honour. In 1912, the year the committee was formed, there had been two defections from the Freudian camp and Jung's was looming: the committee's brief, explicitly stated, would be to watch over Freud's domain in the way that the Paladins had watched over Charlemagne's. In other words, to guard against further heresy. Abraham, Jones, Ferenczi, Hanns Sachs and Otto Rank were the original members, each of them in possession of an antique Greek intaglio from Freud's collection mounted in a gold ring. Max would take the place intended for Anton von Freund, a rich brewer and a friend of psychoanalysis who was dying. Inevitably there were those who complained that a rich man had been invited to succeed another rich man for the usual reason.

Freud just about acknowledged as much. 'Personal friendship' but also gratitude – 'the feeling of being indebted to you in many ways' – lay behind the invitation, he wrote to Max. To which Max could only reply that whatever he had given Freud – 'small gifts that are really not worth mentioning' – could never equal his own 'inextinguishable and ever-growing' feeling of being indebted to Freud. It wouldn't be right to say that what mattered most in their friendship was that Max was generous and Freud was grateful, but it was the currency in which the relationship was expressed.

Or rather gifts, of money or of things, were the currency in which Max most often expressed his feelings.

Three years later, and with even more cause to be grateful, Freud wrote Max a letter in which he described the course of their relationship as it had evolved, in his words, 'from friendship to sonship'. On the face of it a momentous declaration, it also suggests – or suggests to me – that there was something too ingratiating, even abject about Max's attitude to Freud. Freud's daughter Anna, who had a soft spot for Max, was even, some said, though I find it hard to believe, in love with him, spoke of Max's 'over-goodness' and distrusted it. But Freud's view was robust. At first, he wrote, he'd been wary of Max's efforts to get close to him – all those volumes of Dostoevsky – but now he was ready to accept what he knew from their walks together in Vienna: 'From my ambulant analysis I am familiar with the conditions of your love, and I know that you have never managed to free yourself from them.' Max, it seems, needed to make the 'sacrifices' on which Freud had come to depend and from now on Freud would no longer cavil: 'Things will always continue as they have up to now: I need something and you will endeavour to get hold of it. It is a destiny of your own choosing.'

At the end of the war Max had returned to Berlin, where he and the frail Mirra remained despite the unrest ('We are gradually getting used to the revolution,' he assured Freud). He deplored the 'ghastly end of the tribunal pair Liebknecht–Luxemburg' and dreaded the 'approaching chaos', the moment, as he put it, when everything will take place under 'the unrestrained dictate of the pleasure principle', but in the event he and Mirra weathered the storm.

The Bolsheviks are mentioned in his letters, sometimes fearfully – he worries about Mirra's family in the Soviet Union – but are neither praised nor excoriated. Nothing that I've seen suggests an attachment either to the Soviet enterprise or to its enemies. If Max had sympathies for one side or the other he kept them to himself. The world of secular politics doesn't seem to have been something he talked about.

He was a Zionist, committed, unlike Freud, to the idea of a Jewish homeland in Palestine. From which it followed that he believed in his tribe and, if he didn't exactly believe in its God, he didn't, again unlike Freud, go so far as not to believe in him. 'In him was deeply ingrained the devotion to those related to him, the reverence for tradition, and the genuine piety characteristic of the old patriarchal Jewish family,' his colleague Sidney Pomer said of him after his death. Ernest Jones, who had every reason to resent Max as Freud's protégé (Max was the only member of the committee whom Freud addressed by his first name), suggested that a biblical attitude to Freud's writing had prevented Max from doing any thinking of his own, which is perceptive but not fair: Max may have had a Talmudic reverence for Freud's utterances but he also had his own thoughts and was quite capable of disagreeing with Freud, however little he enjoyed doing so. And one of the main things he and Freud disagreed about was Judaism.

It's impossible to imagine Freud without his Jewishness, but he wasn't devoted to it in the way that Max was. He had no thought of going to Palestine ('that tragically mad land', as he described it to Arnold Zweig, that 'has never produced anything but . . . presumptuous attempts to overcome the outer world of appearance by the inner world of wishful thinking'), though with time, and the rise of Hitler, quite a few psychoanalysts were to make their way there. Max, on the other hand, had had dreams of the biblical landscape since his childhood and the time when his father had nearly bought a piece of land on the east bank of the Jordan. The purchase was eventually cancelled but the memory didn't go away, and Max paid his first visit to Palestine in 1910 – evidently a more intrepid young man than his hesitant ways and careful demeanour would suggest. When he moved to Berlin from Zurich after finishing his studies his plan was to stay in the city for a year and then move to Palestine, where he had thoughts, already as a student, of establishing an institute of psychoanalysis.

CHAPTER 18

Berlin

It's just as well that Max didn't go back to Jerusalem then. Weimar Germany was a good time for psychoanalysis – possibly the best there has been – and also for Max, who moved unexpectedly, but thanks to his talents as well as his cash, into its vanguard.

In due course psychoanalysis would become a financial transaction: the analyst listens and the analysand pays. The paying indeed is considered to be crucial. In the heyday of Central European social democracy, in Weimar Berlin as in Red Vienna, it wasn't like that. 'The poor man', Freud said in Budapest in September 1918, 'should have just as much right to assistance for his mind as he now has to the life-saving help offered by surgery.' He was addressing the Fifth International Congress of Psychoanalysis. What was required, he told the assembled analysts, were free walk-in clinics 'so that men who would otherwise give way to drink, women who have nearly succumbed under the burden of their privations, children for whom there is no choice but running wild or neurosis, may be made capable, by analysis, of resistance and efficient work'.

The Berlin Poliklinik opened on 14 February 1920.* Its

---

* The mistakes, misinterpretations and bad judgements are mine, but I wouldn't have been able to write about the Poliklinik and the role that Max played there had it not been for Elizabeth Ann Danto's pioneering work *Freud's Free Clinics: Psychoanalysis and Social Justice, 1918–38*.

opening ceremony lasted all day: a Beethoven piano sonata was performed, and some Chopin, some Schubert and some Schoenberg; there was a reading from Rilke's *Book of Hours* by the analyst Ernst Simmel; and, to close the festivities, Karl Abraham gave a paper on 'The Rise of the Poliklinik from the Unconscious'. The only person who didn't speak was the person who would pay for it and would run it. Guess who? Modest Max.

The idea for the clinic wasn't new: Max and Karl Abraham had begun to draw up plans for a training institute with an outpatient facility attached to it in 1909–10, when they formed the all-important German Psychoanalytic Society (DPG) as a branch of the International Psychoanalytic Association (IPA) – like the early Bolsheviks and other revolutionaries, the early analysts regulated their lives with formal bodies known by their initials. The Vienna Ambulatorium, organised along the same lines, opened in 1922 and in the next few years a dozen co-operative mental clinics came into being in cities from Zagreb to London, 'expressions', as Elizabeth Danto puts it, 'of Freud's social conscience'. It's a long time since anyone has spoken of Freud's social conscience in a psychoanalytic context, but as his address to the analysts assembled in Budapest makes clear, it was very much in evidence in 1918.

'Behind all Freud's psychoanalytic projects lay an interesting tension between psychological theory and therapeutic practice,' Danto explains. 'Whereas his theory aimed to be ahistorical, a de facto science, Freud's clinical *practice* conformed to the social democratic political ideology that prevailed in post-World War One Vienna.' As Vienna changed, so did the terms of psychoanalysis. Now all too often in the public mind a mere alternative to scientology, psychoanalysis in those days saw itself and was often seen as a branch of public health.

Treatment, Danto reports, was available to the unemployed, to factory workers, students, domestic servants, labourers – everyone, children as well as adults. They might see trainees and they might see established physicians. 'The broad-mindedness of interwar political culture', Danto writes, 'set a tone that allowed people from frankly opposite social worlds to meet in a psychoanalyst's waiting room. Even among analysts who outwardly avoided politics' – Max, I'm sure, was one of them – 'a practice at a free clinic implicitly reflected a civic commitment to human welfare.' But it also reflected something larger if equally characteristic of the time. 'Revolutionism', the analyst Helene Deutsch would write in *Confrontations with Myself*, was 'a spirit of reform . . . [that] can never be defined simply through its social application; it is an attribute of individuals who are drawn to everything that is newly formed, newly won, newly achieved.'

From now on Max would be at the centre of everything psychoanalytic – the Poliklinik, the Berlin Psychoanalytic Committee, the publishing house, which he financed and which was always in need of more money, the *Zeitschrift* (or *Bulletin*) – until in 1926 he became president of the International Psychoanalytic Association.

At the same time there was always something a little to one side about him, as if he didn't quite fit in. Were he English one might call it a class difference. It starts with his appearance. Danto describes him as 'a small round-faced man with short, dark hair parted carefully to the side, a neatly trimmed moustache, and a bemused air'. None of the other early analysts that I have seen in photographs looks in any way like Rimbaud, say, or Augustus John; you wouldn't easily mistake them for gun-runners or even painters, but they don't, as Danto describes Max, wear 'impeccably tailored' suits; and they may have a hair or two out of place, their appearance may even be tousled, dishevelled, unkempt; and they may sometimes look at the camera with a wild or worried or anxious expression rather than an air of perfect calm and eau de Cologne. Behind that exterior it would be possible to think Max had a secret life.

And if one were thinking along those lines, Max's disappearances, his habit of downing tools for two, sometimes three months at a time, his holidays in the south, could easily be seen as confirmation. Thus on 10 December 1920 he tells Freud that he's going to Merano for six weeks. On 11 February he's still there, on the 15th he's in Milan, on the 25th he's in Paris. In the autumn of 1922 he travelled from Paris to London to discuss psychoanalytic business with Ernest Jones; he returned to Paris and from there went to Palermo and in the middle of December to Taormina and Selinunte, where he stayed until 31 December, when he began his return journey, via Rome and Florence, arriving back in Berlin on 27 January. And so on, year on year.

At first I told myself that these were – or might be – journeys made on Leonid's instructions. Then I had second thoughts as I began to realise the extent to which health was a preoccupation of the early analysts; most letters to Freud contain an account of someone's – the letter-writer's, his wife's or his colleague's – physical symptoms. And health for the inter-war middle class – I'd have said rich but the analysts weren't rich – necessitated travel. (When I used to complain to my mother about the boring places, in Switzerland mainly, where we spent our summer holidays she told me that I was very lucky that I didn't have to drag myself – her expression – behind her as she had behind her mother on the trek from Karlsbad to Marienbad and back.) On the other hand, what better pretext for a meeting with Leonid than Mirra's need to spend time in the south?

Max's absences – a rich man's privilege – were resented by his colleagues (even Freud had occasion to remark on them) and may explain, or in part explain, why some of his colleagues were determined to take a dim view of his intellectual talents. He just wasn't, they said, an original thinker, though his 'philosophical' understanding of psychoanalysis was good enough, and almost everyone, however malicious, agreed that he was (as Danto puts it) a masterful administrator. And of course he wasn't just rich: he was staggeringly rich and staggeringly generous. (The psychoanalyst Karen Horney's daughter called him 'der Rosenmax' because he never came to visit without bringing flowers.) Together with Abraham and Ernst Simmel he had worked out in detail how a clinic open to the public should function; and when the time came he put up the money: twenty thousand marks, according to Danto, with further subventions as necessary.

I should mention at this point – it will come up again – the name of Alexander Etkind, the author in the 1990s of *Eros of the Impossible*, a history of psychoanalysis in Russia, a man with an unusual ability to romance the facts and still be taken seriously. In his book Etkind proposes –

it's a gargoyle scenario – that the money was put up not by Max himself but by the Soviet government through Max in a bid to control the psychoanalytic movement. Of course the money was there thanks by and large to the Soviet fur trade, but Etkind has something quite different in mind: an ambition on Trotsky's part to control the international psychoanalytic movement. Poor Max: Trotsky's, Stalin's, Freud's – whose was he?

Meanwhile he also found the location for the clinic, a suite of five rooms in a residential building on Potsdamer Strasse in the centre of Berlin, and commissioned Freud's son Ernst, who had studied architecture with Adolf Loos in Vienna, to design its Modernist interior. 'Ernst', Danto writes, 'modified his father's luxuriantly adorned analytic couch, stripped it of ornamentation, and streamlined its shape to produce the model most frequently used today.'

A plaque on the door promised free psychoanalytic consultations from 9 to 11.30 a.m. every weekday except Wednesday. Max was in charge of these (Danto: 'It was always Eitingon who determined the patients' course of treatment and matched them with their analysts'), as he'd been in charge of the initial interviews in Kassa. Three hundred and fifty members of the public applied for treatment in the first year; some walked in off the street, others were recommended by their friends or their doctors. Within a month twenty adult analyses had been started; four months later a child treatment programme was under way.

At the end of ten years three farmers, 173 'bureaucrats' (this was Prussia) and 562 people who gave no profession, or had none to give, had been treated. In between the farmers and those of no fixed profession were domestic servants, academics, factory workers, shopkeepers, a bandleader, a general's daughter, a niece of the chief minister of state, a very influential politician (unnamed) and almost every other sort of person you can think of. Only the aristocracy appears to be missing, but maybe they came into the category of those with no jobs to list – or, like the truly well-off, saw their analysts elsewhere for which privilege they paid the usual fees. 'As time went on,' Max reported of an initial set of statistics put together for the Seventh International Psychoanalytic Congress (held in Berlin in September 1922), 'the proletarian element diminished, while the "intelligentsia" and the lower middle class began to preponderate.'

Max and his colleague Otto Fenichel were determined collectors of figures and compilers of statistics, and by 1930 patients had been classified according to gender (women far outnumbered men), age (thirty to forty mainly), diagnosis (obsessional neurosis among men was the most frequent), length of treatment (most often three to six months) and outcome (generally speaking, 'condition improved'). What lay behind all this statistical activity was the drive for efficiency – how to fit more patients into the day – and a wish to confirm, in their own eyes and in those of the world, that psychoanalysis was as important as somatic medicine to a just, well-run and healthy society.

Although everyone involved with the clinic made some financial contribution, directly or indirectly, by accepting lower fees, or no fee at all, by giving up their time, by their ungrudging (for the most part) dedication, nothing would have been possible without Max and his money – which was generally known but never made public. As for the patients, those who could pay paid as much or as little as they thought they could afford, the rest didn't pay at all.* No one was stopped from paying, in other words, but (with luck) no one got out of paying who shouldn't have done. Max, with what Danto calls 'his characteristic mix of diplomacy and ruthlessness', saw to that. To his colleagues in Berlin and elsewhere who were troubled by the notion of a fee-less analysis Max replied that, on the contrary, the position of the analyst was 'very considerably strengthened' by the fact that he had no material interest in the patient. There were several reasons for that, most of which had to do with shaming the patient out of his neuroses.

The clinic's patients were all treated in the same way – same doctors, same rooms, same couches – for as long as their condition required. There could be no question of those who paid most getting the most experienced analyst or – as happened elsewhere – of non-paying patients being relegated to trainee analysts. If it sounds Utopian now that is our loss, not because therapy, the contemporary version of psychoanalysis, though in many places freely available, is a watered-down form of the original practice (it may be all the more effective for that), but because the social enthusiasm of Weimar Germany lasted so briefly.

Hitler's attempted putsch in 1923 cast its shadow but those who weren't minded to join him contrived (almost) to ignore him for another eight or nine years. In any case the clinic – by 1924 reborn as an 'institute' to emphasise its greater role in the training of analysts – thrived. In 1928 it

---

* Patients' fees accounted for roughly 10 per cent of the clinic's receipts. General funds from the Berlin Psychoanalytic Society (the membership fee was quite steep), more modest private donations and Max made up the rest.

was reckoned that 110 non-fee-paying analyses took place every day in Potsdamer Strasse, and that wasn't counting training analyses – Max again was in charge of the training programme, which he not only administered but in large part devised. Psychoanalysis no longer had any need to be defensive. Not only was it more widely accepted with every year that passed: among the avant-garde it was as fashionable as Mahler or Schoenberg – or Marx for that matter – and debated with the same intensity.

Of the analysts themselves, a majority were on the left (didn't believe in God, did believe in the possibility of human progress) – the middling, Marxisant left. The Communist left wasn't interested. 'My own approach was that of a straitlaced German Communist,' Hede Massing, a Communist spy turned informer, was to write in *This Deception*, a memoir of her spying days. 'Psychoanalysis to us in Germany was a snobbish bourgeois intellectual pastime.' More enlightened, less straitlaced Communists in the 1920s and 1930s – Trotsky is the outstanding example – were likely to be drawn to Adlerian analysis, which put more stress than Freud did on social causation.

Trotsky's troubled elder daughter, Zinaida – who, it so happens, had been staying with him on Prinkipo when the fire that Leonid started broke out – was sent to Berlin by her father in the autumn of 1931 to seek psychoanalytic assistance. I once hoped that Max might have been the doctor she saw. In fact it was the Adlerian Arthur Kronfeld. (Trotsky and Adler, friends from before the Revolution, used to play chess together in Vienna.) Unfortunately the analysis didn't take. More interested in politics than in her own mind, she spoke angrily of being 'stuck in the swinishness of psychoanalysis'; and in

January 1933, the turmoil in her head echoing the turmoil in the streets, she gassed herself.

Quite a number of institute analysts – Simmel and Fenichel are the outstanding examples – sought to extend the sociopolitical reach of psychoanalysis and in some cases to link up with the Frankfurt School. But here again Max was on his own. Uninterested as far as one can tell in his colleagues' political activities, he remained devoted to the Russian émigré philosopher Lev Shestov, a Judaeo-Christian existentialist. He even tried to interest Freud in him, and although there were aspects of Shestov's thinking that might have persuaded Freud that he was worth taking seriously, Freud would have none of it: 'You cannot imagine', he wrote to Max, 'how alien these philosophical contortions appear to me. The only satisfaction they give me is that I take no part in this pitiable waste of intellectual energy.' Max wasn't in the least discouraged, and carried on worshipping both his heroes.

Freud, the father figure, was the more public idol but Shestov's preoccupations – his concern with such matters as God, freedom, immortality, etc. – were close to Max's heart, however much Freud mocked them. Shestov too was a friend as well as a hero and was ceremoniously received at Max's house in prosperous Dahlem on the outskirts of Berlin, where the Eitingons held – some said and some complained – a Russian salon. The Berlin avant-garde had no particular liking for the Russian *ancien régime*, and German Jews no great respect for Russian Jews, so the 'salon' was yet another thing that set Max apart from the other analysts. Yet to the extent that the 'salon' was a salon it was more cosmopolitan than specifically Russian. Pirandello, for example, was often a guest. But so was Nadezhda Plevitskaya, 'the nightingale of Kursk', 'the Russian songbird', and her husband, the general Nikolai Vladimirovich Skoblin. Max's hospitality provided the occasion for Lou Andreas-Salomé to hear Plevitskaya give one of her 'unforgettably wonderful' concerts and for Plevitskaya to kneel at Lev Shestov's feet.

Alexander Etkind, full of hypotheses, thinks that Leonid and even Trotsky may have joined Pirandello at Max's dinner table – picture the two of them, Trotsky and Leonid, arriving at the same time on Max's doorstep – but whatever secret allegiances Max may have had, I find it hard to believe that Trotsky ever came to supper at his house. As for Leonid, it's imaginable – but only just – and not on the same evening as the Kierkegaardian Shestov.

'We've tried out Hotel Eitingon for you, and it was a superb experience,' Anna Freud wrote to her father in 1922. 'Whatever you want, you can have.'

> Stacks of space; peace and quiet or company depending on what you need; solitude or being together with the family; you can have your meals brought to you if you want; warm and cold baths and showers at any time of day; they'll sort out travel tickets for you . . . even early morning departures take place with ease and absolute punctuality . . . Then when you leave you get provisions for your journey, chocolate, and not even the chance to pay for your car.

So much niceness might, I imagine, put one's capacity to respond to the test.

The food too was 'marvellous', so Joan Riviere, then a trainee analyst visiting Berlin for the Psychoanalytic

Congress in 1922, reported to her family in England. Max, she said, had 'surprising good taste' (for a Jew, for an analyst?): 'a private house, so unusual looking into a garden at the back – with glassed-in balcony – but all very new and grand, in beautiful modern taste – wonderful paintings, panelling, Chinese wallpaper and influence on furniture, beautiful bookshelves, pictures, rugs, objets d'art – and marvellous *food*.'*

Alix Strachey, another English analytic candidate with a Bloomsbury connection and the attendant snobbery, was also surprised to find that Max's house wasn't as vulgar as it might have been: 'I suspect the man of having taste,' she wrote to her husband, James, Freud's chief English translator. 'It was heavenly to lean back & look at rows & rows of bookshelves, & well-arranged furniture & thick carpets & 2 or 3 almost passable pictures.' But she wasn't carried away, adding: 'I daresay all this is comparative.'

Only the grandest Swiss hotel could have matched the comforts Hotel Eitingon provided. Plevitskaya and her husband, who stayed with the Eitingons for a time, had two rooms and a bathroom to themselves and their own entrance. Not only that: Max commissioned the Russian writer Ivan Lukash, Nabokov's friend (the original of the writer Bubnov in Nabokov's novel *Glory*), to help Plevitskaya with her memoirs and then paid for the printing.

Everyone who knew him agreed, as they acknowledged in the volume of tributes published after his death, that Max was a highly cultured man: 'a true heir of the nineteenth century as represented by Marx, Darwin and Freud'; 'not only had he read most of the works of the

* Cited in Brenda Maddox: *Freud's Wizard*.

world's greatest writers, he could quote important pas-
sages from them with the greatest ease'; 'a man whose
delight in artistic work was itself an unceasing work of
art'; a connoisseur of art who had paintings by both
Rembrandt and Kandinsky in his house; the owner of a
large library who when he emigrated to Palestine took
only his books with him; while his wife, 'who was his
equal in artistry and elegance, joined him in many intellectual pursuits'.

On Christmas Day 1925 a calamity occurred. The faithful,
optimistic Abraham, Freud's 'rock of bronze', died. He
was forty-eight. Max took over the running of the clinic in
absentia – he was in Sicily and didn't intend to come back
until March – but a more important post, the presidency
of the International Psychoanalytic Association, remained
to be filled. Max had been the association's secretary and
would normally have succeeded Abraham as president.
'We have owed him this honour for a long time,' Freud
wrote to Jones on 30 December, but the situation wasn't
straightforward: 'His ailing wife,' Freud complained
(again), 'takes up too much of his time. Of what use to us
is an absent president?'* On his return from Sicily, and for
all Freud's misgivings, Max was offered and accepted the
honour. Awareness of his money may well have come into
it, especially in those inflationary times, but Freud won't
have overlooked Max's loyalty or his capacities as an

---

* How to cover for Max's absences seems to have been one of the
Poliklinik's first priorities. Already in a *Rundbrief* (circular letter) of 12
December 1920 Abraham was assuring anxious colleagues that volunteers
from the Berlin Psychoanalytic Society would 'oversee the Poliklinik as
Eitingon's stand-in during his trips'.

organiser. 'From then on', Jones reports, he 'developed a high sense of responsibility, which was to many somewhat of a surprise.'

I don't know what Max said to Freud to persuade him that he could do the job, but his absences didn't get any shorter. On the other hand, it's evident from the little that is known about him outside Jones's and Sándor Radó's accounts that he was far more capable and authoritative than those two wanted to concede. An 'enlightened despot', Anna Freud called him. He may not have had much worldly presence but after Abraham's death he was the man in charge at the clinic and, from early 1930, in the German Psychoanalytic Society itself. He was, if you like, a company man and, importantly, less vain than his better-known colleagues.

Being Freud's favourite had its advantages and its disadvantages. Everyone had cause to be grateful, yet – or for that reason – he wasn't much liked. Danto tells us that 'not all the psychoanalysts were sympathetic to his politics or convinced of his personal charm'. That he was too conservative for many of his colleagues – too much Shestov, too little Adorno – isn't hard to see. But how ironic then that he should be the one eventually accused of working for the Soviet government. As for his charm, some saw it, some didn't. My mother's cousin Lee called him 'an absolute sweetie'. Her cousin Lussia said he was the only member of the Eitingon family who had no charm at all. Ernest Jones wasn't swayed by it, but Jones was 'a mean son of a bitch', in the words of the nicely named American psychoanalyst Smiley Blanton.

Even Freud, who loved Max above all others, could be harsh (but Freud could always be harsh); in 1937 he wrote to Max's friend Arnold Zweig: 'Our friend does like to help others with money or other favours, but somehow he manages to arrange things in such a way that he doesn't get much recognition for this, and his protégés soon distance themselves from him . . . All in all he doesn't get on with people very well – that is to say, there are signs of exaggerated charity, of mismanaged compensation.' Was he in some way emotionally handicapped – the sort of person who today is called 'autistic' – or was it just the way Freud made him seem?

'Inhibited' was the epithet most often applied to him by those of his colleagues who didn't much like him: too inhibited to be an effective analyst. Max, Sándor Radó said, was 'totally inhibited and without a trace of originality or scientific imagination'. Danto puts it more gently: 'He was not known for his clinical acumen.' Which is true in the sense that he didn't write many papers, though he wrote some, and didn't participate in many discussions, though he too had his doctrinal quarrel with Freud (the issue was lay analysis). But it was Max, together with Abraham, who had the vision of how a free clinic should be run and who ran it; who with his money made the clinic and the publishing house possible.

Yet very few of the studies of psychoanalysis that I've read even mention him and no one I've talked to who knows anything about psychoanalysis – my analyst, for example, who was herself analysed by Ernest Jones – has had anything to say about him. 'In a movement full of lively people Eitingon stood out for his lack of distinctiveness,' the historian of psychoanalysis Paul Roazen wrote in *Meeting Freud's Family*. And some years ago now Ernst Falzeder, a German historian of psychoanalysis, produced a diagram showing who the early analysts had analysed and who they'd been analysed by: Max wasn't on it. 'I haven't included Max Eitingon,' Falzeder told me when I asked after him. 'I haven't got much material about this very enigmatic figure in the history of psychoanalysis.'

In the 1980s I wrote about Freud in the guise of a review of Janet Malcolm's two books about American analysts, *Psychoanalysis: The Impossible Profession* and *In the Freud Archives*. In the course of it I mentioned that in a field where there was a lot of boasting no one seems to have boasted of having been analysed by my relative, Max Eitingon. I said it largely because I wanted to see whether I would get a response. I got two. This, from the philosopher Richard Rorty, was one of them:

> At least one analyst analysed by Eitingon boasted of it. She was Ellen Simon . . . I put in my six years on her couch, more or less constantly under the gaze of a photo of Eitingon which she had next to her chair. I was always hearing what Eitingon had said to her, what Freud had said to Eitingon etc. She thought the world of Eitingon and I had the feeling of being in an apostolic succession (analysed by somebody who had been analysed by somebody who had been analysed by Freud . . .). Though I never felt the temptation to go into the analysis business myself, I did think that my own analysis was a considerable success, so maybe your relative knew his onions.

Ellen Simon herself wrote about Max in the memorial volume published in Jerusalem after his death. Beginning with the statutory praise ('Everyone spoke of him with respect, love, admiration and reverence'), she went on to describe their first meeting. 'He came to meet me with out-stretched hand,' she wrote, 'as though we were two old friends.' She didn't let on that Max was her analyst, though the description makes most sense if we see him as an analyst putting a trainee analyst at their ease. She noted 'his extremely elastic, supple gait . . . his total concentration . . . the plastic quality of his voice . . . modulated and calm yet full of life and movement' and concluded that 'his understanding transcended normal human understanding'.

Max, it's true, didn't undertake many analyses: a man who mainly expressed himself by giving presents and drawing up timetables may have shied away from that degree of human contact, however ritualised; he may even, in his Russian way, have found the patients' suffering too hard to bear – but that's only a guess. More plausibly, his stammer, which seems never to have gone away, was a problem: who would choose to be analysed by a man with a stammer? Or, for whatever reason (that's precisely what we can't be sure of), he thought it was more important to be free to go to Taormina or Palermo or Leipzig, or wherever else he may have gone, whenever he wanted to and for however long. When one looks at the records of the clinic's activities that he attached such importance to and kept so meticulously it becomes evident that he also did less teaching than any of his senior colleagues – and only once, between April and June 1923, did he teach a course on his own. Was he busier as an analyst than I think? Too taken up with administration? Too shy? Too lazy? Too spoiled? Who can say?

Once in Jerusalem he seems to have engaged more directly with students. Two other contributors to the memorial volume besides Ellen Simon had training analyses with him in Palestine, and speak reverentially of his quasi-Buddhist ways. 'He was like a gardener tending his plants,' one said. 'He knew that a tree doesn't grow fast and that it will not produce fruit before its time.' The other one said the same, slightly differently: 'He let the slow man move slowly; he let the fast man run. He often seemed to move in two directions at the same time.' Two directions at the same time! How tempting – how novelettish – to suggest that he was doing the same: keeping up with Freud, keeping up with Stalin. Is it entirely implausible? One thing is certain: he was secretive enough.

As time went by and the clinic's activities – discussion groups, seminars, meetings, public lectures – multiplied and the number of analysts as well as of patients and trainee analysts increased, the space in Potsdamer Strasse became too cramped. In 1928 – thanks yet again to 'der Rosenmax' – the clinic moved to a larger set of rooms along the length of a balconied apartment building in leafy Wichmannstrasse. The opening, marked by a series of inaugural lectures, was less grand this time, but the move consolidated Berlin's claim to be considered the centre of psychoanalysis.

Then things began to go wrong. For Max, whose family was losing its money. And for the clinic, as the Nazis gained ground.

Part Three

CHAPTER 19

Sliding

Motty stayed at the National Hotel when he went to Moscow for the fur auctions. My mother told me that and told me that the hotel always kept the same room for him, which I used to think meant that no one was allowed to use it when Motty was not there. In those days the National looked out on the Alexandrovsky Gardens and some of the rooms on the top floor had a view of the Kremlin – a privilege for which you had to pay a bit more. The Lux and the Metropole were the hotels where visiting Western Communists were put up.

A cousin of Leonid's, an old lady called Reveka, remembered being taken by her mother to see Motty in his hotel sometime in the late 1920s. This was the first evidence I had that some of Leonid's family and some of mine had in fact met. In the late 1920s Motty was, we know, a very prosperous fur dealer. Fruma, Reveka's mother, was very poor. Most of her bits and pieces – wedding presents mainly – had already gone to Torgsin, the state pawn shop, and she didn't know what to do next. Maybe Motty would help her. But maybe he wouldn't. If she had Reveka with her he might find it hard to refuse.

Always ready to charm and be charmed, Motty was immediately taken by the child and told his partner to come down and see the *tsvetok* – 'the little flower' – that Fruma had been hiding from them all these years. Reveka squirmed. 'I wasn't pretty,' she said. 'I had nice hair and a nice complexion – that's all.'

Motty asked after Leonid's sisters, Sonia and Sima, and then said: 'A vash glavny Eitingon.' Your main man. 'Is he still a Chekist?'

'I don't know,' Fruma answered.

'That means he still is.'

'Then why ask?' she replied.

Motty took a hundred-dollar bill out of his pocket and gave it to Reveka, which embarrassed her even more. She didn't want the money and on the way home told her mother how angry with her she was for making her go to the hotel in the first place. 'You were just using me,' she said. 'You thought that if I came along you'd be more likely to get something from him.'

When they got home the hundred-dollar bill had gone. They turned out their pockets and turned them out again, and finally decided it must have been lost in the street as they walked back to their apartment. Some months later they moved to another flat. They were unpacking their things when suddenly, among the mess and the muddle, the banknote turned up. Reveka didn't remember how the money was spent, except that she got something she'd always wanted: a raspberry-coloured beret like the one Tatiana has in *Eugene Onegin*.

In May 1930, the head of the New York Police Department, Police Commissioner Whalen, went on the anti-Communist offensive in New York. Funds, he announced, were being channelled from the Soviet Union through Amtorg to Communists in the US, and he had documents to prove it. By July, a House Committee – an early incarnation of HUAC, the House Un-American Activities Committee – had been set up to investigate Communist activity in the US. Its chairman was Congressman Hamilton Fish Jr.

One of the first to appear before the Fish Committee was the AFL zealot Matthew Woll, who railed far and wide, but mainly against 'senior government officials' who saw to the issue of visas for subversives after being 'dined and wined by Communist agents'. Were it not for the AFL, he told the committee, the Communists 'would have made considerable progress in New York industries and would have had the dress, fur and other needle trades in their hands'.

John J. Leary, the labour editor of the *New York World*, assured the committee that the main conduit for Russian money was through US-based 'merchants' who had contracts with the Soviet government. The money these US businesses owed for goods, he explained, was not payable in Moscow but turned over to 'representatives' of the Soviet Union in America, who then allocated a proportion of the payments to American Communists and Communist causes. So what firms did Leary have in mind? Well, he could think of one or two right away, he said, including the Eitingon Schild Corporation, which had one of the biggest contracts with Moscow held by any American company.

Then there was the matter of the 1926 fur strike and its settlement. 'This strike', Leary reminded the committee, 'was finally settled by Matty [*sic*] Eitingon . . . It was settled overnight after many weeks of struggle. Mr Eitingon . . . returned from a visit to Russia and went into conference with the strike leaders. An immediate settlement followed. What the inference is I leave to the committee.'

That is probably the first time Motty's name was mentioned at a committee hearing. He'd have been in Europe at the time.

He must have read about the hearing in the press because he cabled Hamilton Fish in person: he wanted to appear before the committee, which had heard testimony he believed was misleading. 'If newspaper reports are correct,' he said in his telegram, 'your committee has been grossly misinformed concerning the activities of the Eitingon Schild Company and myself as its president. Earnestly request opportunity to lay the truth of the matter before you.' As far as I know, he was not invited to give evidence before the committee, which was winding up in any case.

I don't doubt that, like very many of his contemporaries, Motty was sympathetic to the Soviet government (and not only out of convenience) and I don't doubt that he advanced their cause in various ways – not all of them to do with cash. It's possible, for example, that he intervened in the fur strikes (there was another, smaller one in 1937), not just because he liked playing the big shot, or the workers' friend, or the industry's saviour, but because Moscow wanted him to. Of course it suited the Soviet Union, in the general way of things, to have a large and important union controlled by the left in whatever denomination, but a prolonged stoppage in the US fur industry didn't suit them at all. Who better than Motty to resolve that contradiction? In writing about the 1926 strike, Philip Foner tells his readers that Motty 'expressed amazement' when he discovered how little the fur workers earned (he thought it was about 125 dollars a week; in fact it was between twenty-eight and thirty). Clearly he hadn't studied the situation before launching himself into it. It was the same with his politics. If he was a fellow-traveller, which many people, Theodore Draper among them, have now said he probably was, it was a matter of temperament rather than anything more cogitated – and of the way things fell out.

Maybe, though, it's going too far to call him a fellow-traveller. My mother spent a lot of time with him between her marriages, in what we used to call, when we were growing up, her parlour pink days. Motty by then had a second wife with theatrical connections. They called themselves socialists (though not to the FBI) and their names come up from time to time in memoirs and biographies of the 1940s as patrons of left-wing causes, theatres especially. (They took my mother to the Group Theatre, and Clifford Odets, so she once said, had wanted to marry her.) 'Yesterday I met the furrier Moté Eitingon, precise equivalent of a Hampstead Russian Jew à l'américaine,' Isaiah Berlin would write to his parents in August 1940. The composer Marc Blitzstein was one of those whom Motty took in and looked after; and according to Eric Gordon, Blitzstein's biographer, Motty used to read *Das Kapital* in German in the evening, translating for his wife as he went along. On the other hand, what sort of socialist is it who has no idea how little the workers in his own industry earn? Was he, too, just a parlour pink at a time when it was a fashionable thing to be? After all, he never made any secret of his left-wing sympathies (although there were always those – my father among them – who thought them a little silly in someone apparently so rich): would he not have been more discreet if he'd had something more sinister than his business activities to hide?

The Fish Committee delivered its report to the House of Representatives in January 1931. It estimated that there were between five and six hundred thousand Communists in the United States, that the headquarters of the twenty national 'divisions' were in New York and that their goal was . . . well, it was the usual goal. Fish recommended that the Communist Party be outlawed, and members have their citizenship rescinded; that all 'alien' Communists be deported and all further naturalisations of known Communists blocked. Communist publications should be banned from the mail and interstate commerce laws should be tweaked to make the despatch of Communist periodicals and papers illegal. Very little, if any, of this was taken to heart by Congress. One member of the committee, John E. Nelson, issued an individual report calling for less 'hysteria' about Communism, which was best opposed by improving the conditions of American workers. As for Amtorg, the committee had found it impossible to show a conclusive link between the delegation and subversive activities in the US, even though they could confidently – and correctly – state that it was run by 'Communists and revolutionists'. The main NKVD man in New York, Gaik Ovakimian, known to the FBI as the 'wily Armenian', posed for nine years as an engineer with Amtorg.

A month later, in February 1931, Motty signed a contract for the purchase of fifty million dollars' worth of furs for sale in America and Europe. It was probably the largest contract of its kind that anyone in the trade had negotiated. Was it Motty's character, his optimism, that made this kind of deal possible? Or the seeming success of Eitingon Schild, despite the Crash and the company's losses in 1929 of almost 2.5 million dollars? Or his friendship with Maxim Litvinov, the new Soviet Foreign Minister, a more worldly figure than many Soviet functionaries? Who knows? Though there was probably less hoopla about the deal than there'd been about his coup in 1926, it had the makings of a profitable venture: Eitingon Schild would take ten million dollars' worth of furs every year for five years, and would be able to nominate which furs it wanted, to the value of eight million dollars. In 1928, on her twenty-first birthday, Motty had given my mother, his favourite niece, an ermine coat – which I still sometimes wear. But sable must have been the thing in the early 1930s, because Eitingon Schild immediately made it known that it would be taking all the sable the Russians had to offer.

'It is a part of the fascination of New York City', the *Saturday Evening Post* reported in July, 'that you may walk along a street as drab as West 30th, enter a warehouse, stumble in semi-darkness past mounds of sables, karakul and pony skins, and then abruptly be shown into an oak-panelled office with a turkey-red carpet and rich furnishings where men speak casually of $50,000,000 contracts.' Sitting at his desk (alas not described) was Motty (also, alas not described): 'I signed a five-year contract . . . with the Russians,' he told the reporter. 'We agreed not to take less than $10,000,000 worth a year. If prices go up', he continued, optimistic as always, 'the amount will be larger.' (Fifty million dollars in 1931 translates, roughly, into seven hundred million today.) Fatally perhaps, no provision was made for the possibility of prices going down.

The new deal had been negotiated in London via Arcos (transformed after the raid into a straightforward Soviet trading organisation) acting on behalf of the Pushno syndicate in Moscow that now dealt with all Soviet fur exports. When news of the agreement was released in the States, Motty had once more taken care to point out that the contract had been signed 'with the knowledge of the government at Washington'. Obviously he didn't have to tell them everything: only enough to make them think he'd told them everything, and in that he seems to have been very successful.

When a first valuable consignment of furs – 2.5 million dollars' worth – arrived in New York it's fair to assume that Motty had paid for some or all of it in advance. But on 10 March he and his directors announced that the company was in a difficult period. In private, Motty felt sure the new contract with the Russians would set things straight. In any case it was an exhilarating deal to have struck.

Eitingon Schild showed profits of 320,000 dollars in the first half of 1931 and thereafter began sliding irreversibly into loss. The Stock Exchange directed its members to give details of all recent sales and purchases of the shares to its Committee on Business Conduct, but no evidence of impropriety emerged. The company struggled affably along with mounting losses – 4.7 million dollars in 1932 – and yet there was Motty, at the fur auction in Leningrad in the summer of 1933, announcing price stability at home (he was sure that sales would hold up) and admiring the sheer volume of skins available to international buyers.

He was in Europe in November 1933 when Eitingon Schild announced a recapitalisation plan which would involve rejigging its debts with the banks, raising new loans, doing away with all its preferred shares and issuing

a uniform 'common stock'. It was a complicated arrangement – lacking in transparency, we would now say – that
involved giving another company in which Motty had an
interest, the Fur Companies Syndicate Inc., a de facto stake
in Eitingon Schild and thus a share of its profits. On the
face of it, this may have seemed a reasonable arrangement.
Yet within a few months there was rancour among a
minority of stockholders about the way the recapitalisation had been carried out. I imagine it looked to them as
though Motty had been careless with one company and
then called in another, in which he was intimately
involved, to take the profits which might have accrued to
the first if he'd only shown more circumspection as president. It looked, in other words, as though whatever went
under and whatever did not, Motty would emerge on top.

The following April the same minority baulked at a
proposal from Motty that Eitingon Schild should sell off
its holdings in the Lodz operation. To sell up a European
component of the empire when things in New York looked
so rocky seemed on the face of it unwise. It's true that the
whole capitalist world was in a slump and no country was
worse hit than Poland, but the Polish firm, though in debt
here and there, was still prospering. And then there was
the additional problem of the purchaser, for Motty intended to sell the operation to the Fur Companies
Syndicate Inc., in other words, at least partly to himself.
The minority also grumbled that the agreement between
Eitingon Schild and the Syndicate already entitled the latter to a high proportion of the recapitalised Eitingon profits: more than a million dollars, it appeared, at the time the
plan was mooted. Any vestige of enthusiasm for the proposal was swept away when disgruntled shareholders

learned that Motty's brother Naum, now running the Polish company on his own after the death of my grandfather, was also a participant in the Fur Companies Syndicate.

In fact when the deal was approved and Eitingon Schild's interests in Lodz were sold off for 3.5 million dollars, Motty had a plausible answer – he always did. He argued that a rival consortium had been bidding for the Lodz business on far less advantageous terms than he and his colleagues in the Fur Companies Syndicate were willing to offer. Eitingon Schild deals – and FCS deals for that matter – were always undertaken with the best interests of the shareholders in mind.

My great-uncle Naum was a rapacious businessman: the ugly capitalist among his colleagues in the textile industry in Lodz, feared and loathed by many of them.* In private life too he was quarrelsome, interested above all in money and in playing and winning at cards. My mother and her sisters detested him. They were adamant: he was 'a devil'. But for Motty, who expected always to be liked, Naum was the perfect partner. When I first learned that Leonid's real name was Naum – Naum Isaakovich even, just like my great-uncle – I had a moment of high excitement: alas they were not the same person.

Naum relocated to New York in the autumn of 1934. On his arrival he told the press that there was no better place in the world than Poland for a Jewish person to get along and get ahead. Relations between the regime and Poland's Jews were, he said, 'fair and most friendly'. He dismissed reports of Polish Jews being beaten by Fascist

* Kazimierz Badziak, 'Textile Concern of the Eitingon Family in the Second Republic' in *Lodz Yearbook*, Vol. 35.

gangs and – it's hard to believe – insisted that Nazi sympathisers in Poland were shipped off to concentration camps.
'There is therefore no reason', he declared, 'for American
Jewry to interfere.' A *Times* reporter relayed the final
words of wisdom to what Naum must have hoped would
be a supine American public: 'Economic conditions in
Poland are better than last year, said Mr Eitingon, and
business is increasing.' What Motty made of his brother I
don't know. If I have no memory of seeing them together
that doesn't mean much. But I'm told that when the
Eitingon empire finally collapsed Naum was the only one
who had any money salted away, and that, at any rate,
says something about him.

Motty had married his second wife, Bess, earlier that year
and set off with her on a three-month tour of Europe.
Beatrice Tepfer ('Pepper' in the FBI files) had not long
before emerged from a marriage to Paul Robeson's lawyer,
Robert Rockmore. The honeymoon tour included Poland –
where they may have seen for themselves the anti-Semitism
that Naum would dismiss a few months later – and the
Soviet Union, in which Bess, an excitable woman with
many connections among the show-business left, took a
lively interest. ('Excitable' doesn't do justice to Bess's lack
of calm. 'Hysterical' might suggest it, but she was nicer
than that, and in hard times more stoical. 'Hyperbolic' is
another possibility: Robeson, she told an interviewer, was
'flabbergastingly impressive' in one of his roles. The hyper-
bole was very nice if you were the person it referred to – no
one minds praise – but 'impossible' was the word Mats
would use, writing to her parents in 1938, as in 'I like
Motty very much. Bess of course is impossible.')

In my memories of our American life Motty was second only to my father in importance. He too was excitable (unlike my father), and he wasn't one for the everyday American world where men were home from the office at six for their first Martini. As I see him now he'd be wearing vaguely bohemian clothes – a navy blue shirt and a brown suit, for example. He and Bess when I knew them, or remember knowing them, lived in a large house in Hillcrest Park, which was part of Stamford, Connecticut: a house filled with people. It was more my brother's territory than mine – too many boys – and I didn't go there more than I had to. But we lived in the neighbourhood for a while – roughly 1941–4 – in the house on Shippan Point on Long Island Sound that I mentioned at the start: a house Motty had bought for his first wife when he left her. It was one of a sequence of houses and flats that we moved into and then out of within a few years. (I make it ten before I left home, at which point my parents more or less settled down.) It had a big garden that ran down from the front of the house, past the blue pines that my mother said were very special, stopped briefly to let the road go by and continued a long way down, past my mother's victory garden, to its own small stretch of beach. My mother wasn't much of a swimmer, but my father used to swim out until he was only a dot in the distance and once or twice, in a panic, I begged my mother to divorce him before he drowned.

Motty was restless and didn't like things to go on for too long; if he was telling you something he was liable to interrupt himself, saying 'story short', and jump straight to the conclusion. He needed his day to be busy and loved the telephone. Several of his sisters (he had six) lived near by and he was close to them, and to his first wife and his nephews and nieces; and when our parents were away he looked after my brother (I was shipped off to an aunt in Chicago) and reported on him regularly by telegram to my parents in Europe. He was keen, too, to be surrounded by interesting people with some claim on the world's attention, and when he travelled to Europe with my mother in 1935 they were accompanied, as my father put it (you could tell he was impressed), by 'the Russian ambassador at Washington'.

His ways were those of old Europe. He was a man for paying you compliments, giving you presents and sending you flowers ('Yesterday morning a huge bunch of gladioli arrived for me from Motty and all marvellously done up from a terrific florist,' Mats reported excitedly to her parents); attentive but not entirely relaxed or American in his manner, still less his speech ('He is very nice' – Mats to her parents again – 'only speaks in an atrocious accent'): face to face, one of the most likeable people you could meet. 'Generosity', *Time* magazine reported in 1930, 'is his outstanding characteristic.' 'He has a wonderful reputation everywhere,' my father was still writing to his parents at the beginning of 1940.

As with most people in his position, Motty's friends were for the most part, like him, first-generation immigrants, most of them Jewish and most of them from the Pale and places around it. I don't think he knew many assimilated 'Americans', let alone Gentiles.* Perhaps European immigrants of his age made freer use of their political education than their predecessors had. Many

* 'I must say,' my father reported to his parents not long after arriving in the US, 'it is amazing the way people invite you here, Jews and Christians alike, though each does so separately, of course.'

would have inclined to a socialist reading of the volatile places from which they or their parents had scrambled or been pushed. At any rate, a lively sociability and a convivial household were as important to him now, in his remarried life, as his standing in the industry.

He had a good deal of admiration for the arts, and many of his friends were artists – musicians and writers. He was drawn to people who did things that were different from anything he could do, and were admired for it, and to the sense of himself as a kind man, which he was until he wasn't, a benefactor, with money to dispense and bestow. He gave money to art and to artists but in his heyday he also supported most of the extensive Eitingon clan – 'That's how it is: everyone in the family participates,' my mother wrote to my father a few months before their marriage – or topped up the income of those who had money but not enough. (My brother remembers that Motty used to ask him to guess how much change he had in his pocket, promising to give him the lot if he guessed right.)

But if he went to the theatre and married Bess and was a friend of Clifford Odets and Lee Strasberg and Luise Rainer it's because the theatre was somewhere he wanted to be. And if Leopold Stokowski and Vladimir Horowitz and Nathan Milstein were more than acquaintances – the Eitingons, my father reported, 'are very much in the musical set' – it was because he liked classical music and had an understanding of it. It wasn't just a question of Bess's influence: he was supporting young musicians long before he met her.

In October 1927, for example, when it was announced that the young violinist Benno Rabinof would shortly make his debut at Carnegie Hall, the *New York Times* reported that for many years the boy from the East Side 'with a hunger for music' had been looked after by a guardian angel in the form of 'Motti Eitingon, a New York merchant, who was so convinced of his future that he took the financial cares off the family's shoulders'. Rabinof's mother was a seamstress, the *Times* reported, who sewed late into the night to raise the money for his violin lessons. On occasions like this it's not hard to see – or rather it's hard not to see – Motty as a money man with a soft heart in the old Hollywood mode.

CHAPTER 20

Friends

One of those Motty looked after was an Austrian writer, a recent arrival in the US, some ten years younger than him, by the name of Franz Hoellering.* I don't think Hoellering was Jewish – his father at any rate was a Catholic musician – but he was on the left, a known anti-Fascist and maybe a premature anti-Fascist, i.e. a Communist, or a former Communist. It was a relationship that, as far as I can tell, caused the FBI serious concern. As far as I can tell, because virtually every name in the FBI files is blacked out, which means that one has to guess – but it's not a wild guess: the biographical facts overlap fairly neatly – that Hoellering's is the name the marker pen has obscured.

He was a writer with a wide range and a decent reputation: in 1929 in Germany he'd written the script for a movie called *Katharina Knie*; he was for a time the *Nation*'s film critic (*Gone with the Wind* was 'a major event in the history of the industry but only a minor achievement in motion-picture art'); he published short stories in McCall's *Redbook*; was the author of at least

---

* 'An awfully nice fellow', according to my father, writing home in 1936; Kurt Weill, whom he met in the same year, was 'a very nice little fellow'. My father was often bland in that way. When he retired and began to read Proust he kept saying: 'He's a marvellous writer.' Snippily taxed by me with having nothing more interesting to say, he smiled and took no notice.

two novels, *The Defenders* (1941) and *Furlough* (1944); and back in Europe after the war he translated Tennessee Williams into German (he would also write the screen adaptation of the 1958 *Mädchen in Uniform*). Edmund Wilson, reviewing *For Whom the Bell Tolls* in the *New Republic*, compared Hemingway's method as a writer of 'novels of contemporary history' with that of 'André Malraux or Franz Hoellering'; and an official list of writers banned by Hitler runs 'Benes, Churchill, Koestler, Silone, Hoellering . . .' When America entered the war he became the head of the German Department of the New York Office of War Information.

Hoellering came to the States from Berlin, where he'd been the editor-in-chief of the Ullstein newspaper *B.Z. am Mittag* – Arthur Koestler was its foreign editor – until he was dismissed at the end of 1931 for criticising Hitler's use of Luftwaffe planes to fly around the country on his electoral campaigns. Walter Krivitsky, a high-level Soviet defector who had been the illegal *rezident* in the Netherlands, and so a former colleague of Leonid's, would later tell the FBI that Hoellering owed his job on the paper to OGPU, which may or may not be true – defectors are more given than most to seeing skulduggery everywhere. In Germany, however, Hoellering's dismissal was a cause célèbre: evidence of the moral bankruptcy of the Ullstein Press, 'the most scandalous capitulation there had so far been to National Socialism'. He came to the States via Prague, and Motty met him at a party in 1934 or 1935, given by a woman whose name, he told the FBI, he couldn't remember, a friend of a friend, a sculptor.

Motty liked Hoellering and since, as he also told the FBI in 1954, he was in those days very wealthy, and

Hoellering was strapped for cash ('in a poor financial position'), Motty and Bess gave him the use of the old stable, now renamed the 'studio', in the grounds of their house in Hillcrest Park while he tried to get a book written.* When summer came round and the book still wasn't finished, he stayed on: in fact it took two years to write the book, and the Hoellerings remained in Hillcrest Park before moving to the 'beach house' that went with our house on Shippan Point – which might explain why I have such a clear memory of Franz Hoellering's face and that of his wife, Marta, who was Czech and an actress and a friend of my mother's.

Krivitsky had put it about that Hoellering had been an OGPU agent of an unsatisfactory sort: weak and unaggressive, on the one hand; 'too highbrow and too much a freelancer', on the other; and, finally, anxious 'to get out of Communist control'. From the Soviet point of view he was a minor figure who'd become disaffected even before the Hitler–Stalin Pact. Motty, it seems, was unruffled by the whole business, telling the FBI that he knew from Hoellering that he'd been a Communist 'in his early life'. But it's obvious from Motty's FBI file – which I'll come to

---

* Edmund Wilson, a friend of Hoellering's, didn't think much of the place, noting in his diary for 14 February 1949: 'They had added a few flimsy rooms, decorated in very bad taste . . . Lamps in the living room, with stands of some green material which worried one both by their clumsiness and by the impossibility of working out whether they represented dolphins or human figures . . . two busts of Negroes, done by Bess, a man and a woman, the latter with rouge on the mouth and nails . . . two abominable paintings . . . Dark-stained bookcases above the radiators, dried up and warped miscellaneous books: a cheap old series of the English romantic poets mixed up with odds and ends of Soviet Marxist publications. Nevertheless,' he adds perplexingly, 'I liked the room.'

later – that his association with Hoellering preoccupied the American authorities a great deal.

For a couple of years the Eitingon place in Hillcrest Park had a separate postbox marked for Hoellering and this, it appears, is how the FBI came to be informed of his connection with Motty. But the FBI document also confirms, among other things, that the subject whose identity is blacked out had stories published in the *Redbook* and that he worked for a time at the Office of War Information. The evidence isn't conclusive: the man referred to but never named in the Eitingon files may not have been Hoellering, but I'd be surprised.

Whittaker Chambers at any rate – former Communist agent, turned virulent anti-Communist – didn't have any doubts about Hoellering's allegiance. Not that Chambers was given to doubts of that sort and not that I like to be in his company. But after Theodore Draper wrote about the Eitingons in the *New York Review of Books*, he got the following note from Mary McCarthy:

> I knew Motty Eitingon (slightly) in 2 contexts. The 2nd was through a Franz Hoellering, Vienna, ex Ullstein Press (actress wife), a friend of Edmund's [Wilson] who had been given a house on Eitingon's place in Stamford. I never much liked the Hoellerings. Then, some years later when Whittaker Chambers resurfaced, he asked to see Edmund, which he did, to tell him that Hoellering was an agent. H's reaction when tackled jestingly by Edmund was peculiar.

(There is no mention of the first context.)

Marc Blitzstein, too, was a beneficiary of Motty and Bess's hospitality in the 1930s and of their various outbuildings – in his case, the gardener's cottage. In time he would write a rumba that he called 'Chez Eitingon' describing the daily commotion at Hillcrest Park as ten or twenty people, relatives, servants and guests, went about their different business. He also had in common with Hoellering the kind of politics that would – and did – interest the FBI. A child prodigy, a student of Schoenberg and Nadia Boulanger, and in his younger days a composer of rebarbative polyphonal music, he was now (he said as much to HUAC) a Communist; he championed the work of Kurt Weill in the *New Masses*, wrote a play about Sacco and Vanzetti and become involved with Lee Strasberg's Group Theatre. In 1933, though gay, he married a relative of Bess's and was devastated when she died three years later. That summer, the summer of 1936, he spent at Hillcrest Park and while he was there wrote his most famous, anti-capitalist musical, *The Cradle Will Rock*, a dramatisation, loosely speaking, of the right to strike. Appalled, embarrassed but good-humoured, Bess recognised herself in the character of Mrs Mister, wife of the boss of Steeltown and confused patron of the arts.

As for Motty, he always enjoyed looking after people and whether he was or wasn't a fellow-traveller, or indeed a Soviet agent, he had no difficulty consorting with Communists.

Roosevelt had established diplomatic relations with the Soviet Union at the end of 1933 and New York was now becoming a terminal for goods moving between Russia and America. Goods but not comrades. In the spring of 1934, around the time Motty and Bess left for their honeymoon, a Soviet vessel put in at Pier 8 on 36th Street in Brooklyn. The arrival caused a stir, not only because the

Kim was the first Soviet ship to dock in the city since 1917, but because, as the press reported with some excitement, there was no obvious hierarchy of officers and crew on the *Kim*: the fo'c'sle, and the traditions of the fo'c'sle, were gone. But when a group of New York Communists went down to the pier to fraternise with the sailors, the crew shouted from the deck that they were damned if they'd have anything to do with 'American Reds'.

At home, however, it was becoming marginally harder for anti-Communism to forge ahead. Not that there wasn't such a thing as being un-American. Hamilton Fish seems to have ignored Motty's request to set things straight after the allegations made by Woll and Leary in 1930, and now Motty was summoned to appear before McCormack–Dickstein, a House special committee authorised to look into Nazi and 'other' propaganda in the US, under the general heading 'Un-American Activities'. Though the committee did try to address the Fascist plot against the FDR White House in which the Du Pont family, among other leaders of large corporations, was involved, it spent much of its time – indeed most – on the 'other' kind of menace, the category to which they suspected Motty belonged. It held hearings in six cities, arriving in New York in November 1934 and convening in the Supper Room of the Bar Association, a short walk uptown from the fur district. Motty appeared at an afternoon session and can only have testified for seven or eight minutes.

The transcript of the hearing is intriguing. John McCormack, who presided, begins the questioning. Motty supplies a few basic details about his affairs. McCormack asks: 'How long have you been in the business?' Motty answers: 'Thirty-three years.'

'You employ how many help?'

'In New York City about seventy,' Motty says: 'All told a few thousand.'

'Do you employ help elsewhere?'

Motty must like this question.

'All over the world. We have branches all over the world.'

McCormack comes aggressively to the point.

'You are not a member of the Communist Party?'

Motty: 'No.'

McCormack then wanted to know whether Motty had any Communist employees: he didn't; whether he contributed payments to any union, perhaps in the form of an unemployment fund: he didn't.

'Do you know Ben Gold?' McCormack asks.

Motty: 'Yes.'

'How long have you known him?'

'I only knew him in 1926. I have not seen him since.'

McCormack: 'You have not seen him since?'

'No.'

'How long did you know him before that?'

'I met him in 1926.'

'You have not seen him since 1926?'

'No I did not.'

There followed an odd exchange about whether or not the workforce at Eitingon Schild was unionised. They weren't, Motty said, because the company had no working men. 'We are in the dealing business.'

Which may, strictly speaking, have been true. By 1934 Motty was in so many departments of the fur trade, including finishing and dressing, that he must have had some working men and they must have been unionised. But they would have been employees of the subsidiary companies and the question was about Eitingon Schild.

On the other hand even in 1926 Eitingon Schild had a representative sitting in on the negotiations between management and the union before Motty rode to the rescue.

'Did you get any contracts with the Russian government?' McCormack asks.

'Yes.'

'What are they?'

Motty, I imagine, is more than happy to answer this question.

'We have all told about eighty-five million dollars of contracts.'

'Covering how many years?' McCormack asks.

'Since 1923.'

'During any of those years have you contributed to the Communist Party in the United States, directly or indirectly, in any way?'

'Never.'

There was then a brief discussion about how the contracts with the Russians were obtained, which Motty took as an opportunity to mention once more the personal insurance he'd taken out a decade earlier. Each time his company was about to close a contract, he told the committee, 'we went to Washington and we asked the advice of the Department of Commerce'.

McCormack's vice-chairman, Sam Dickstein, hadn't really believed Motty when he'd claimed to employ no unionised labour. He asked him whether he manufactured furs and Motty replied that no, he didn't, he was a dealer. 'We are importers of furs from all over the world.'

Dickstein asked if he'd ever had any trouble from members of 'the left wing of the Communist Party', by which he meant the Communist Party.

'No,' Motty replied. 'I never had any trouble. I suppose the reason you're asking these questions is that I met Ben Gold at the time when I think they had a strike. At that time the left-wing union' – Motty knew better than to muddle leftism and Communism – 'was in control of the business.'

'You mean', Dickstein says, sticking by his solecism, 'that the left wing of the Communist Party were controlling the fur industry, practically?'

'They were controlling it in 1926.'

Dickstein asked whether there were threats of violence from the Communists.

'No,' Motty replied, 'I would not say that. The question in 1926 was this: they wanted to have high wages for the hours that they worked.'

'At any rate,' Dickstein rejoined, 'there was some trouble between the left wing and the right wing.'

Motty was silent. Finally McCormack pitched in with more questions – the same questions in fact – about whether Motty had given money to any un-American organisation, and so on and on. 'Never.' Or to a union. 'Never.' And none of the money he'd got from his deals with the Soviet Union had gone to anybody else? (Amtorg was the unspoken subject of this question.) It had not.

A moment later Motty was excused.

He was in Europe again towards the end of 1935. It was on this occasion that he took my mother with him to Moscow – she was twenty-eight and not yet over her divorce: did she think no one else would ever want to marry her? She wasn't happy in Russia and soon left for Poland to visit her mother and sister Lola, who were still living in Lodz. My father met her on the return crossing:

'An Austrian Jewess, I should *guess* . . . she has asked me to ring her up in New York, where by the way she has a box at most of the concerts,' he reported back to London, then added, intriguingly: 'I can hear Dad suggesting that I may be called upon to play my cards well and Mum uttering warning notes, but she does not appear dangerous and I may add I am not as soft as I am supposed to be.' His parents may not have thought him tough enough with the girls, but his correspondence with my mother indicates that he had it all pretty much his own way.

In July Litvinov, to whom the FDR administration's recognition of the Soviet Union was widely attributed, signed a trade agreement with the Americans envisaging thirty million dollars' worth of Soviet purchases over the coming year. It was in many ways détente *avant la lettre*, which didn't do much for the AFL. That summer, the AFL-affiliated fur workers met in Toronto and voted for a united front with the left-wing furriers' union. William Green, the AFL president, could only huff and puff and threaten that any branch admitting Communists would have its charter withdrawn. The alliance went ahead and it put the Communists in a majority. It was only a matter of time before Ben Gold's star rose again.

Motty spent a few weeks in Europe at the beginning of 1937: Russia perhaps, Poland certainly, maybe London, maybe Paris; and if in Paris he probably met up with Max or even (who knows?) with Leonid, though I don't suppose they had much to do with each other – not socially at any rate – and if they did occasionally meet they wouldn't have wanted anyone to notice.

When he got back to New York the quarrel between

Eitingon Schild and the minority shareholders, which had been brewing since the recapitalisation, reached some sort of climax. The restive minority felt that the company's conversion of their preferred stock to common stock didn't reflect the value of their original holdings, which they'd gamely reckoned at 123 dollars a share. Three assessors appointed by the courts to make an independent estimate of the shares at the time the plan was approved now reported back. They felt that the company had been worth about 2.6 million dollars and on that basis announced the value of the preferred shares to have been about 55 dollars. The next step was to put the report before a judge for approval.

The dissident shareholders were chiefly at odds with Motty over the value of one of his subsidiaries – a partly owned subsidiary – known as the Fur Merchants' Sales Company, and over the valuation of a subsidiary of the subsidiary, wholly owned by Fur Merchants' Sales and therefore partly owned by Motty, the Laclede Real Estate Investment Co. It is typical of Motty that when he'd got his assets in a muddle, as he had in a major way with Eitingon Schild, and someone threatened to confiscate them, he'd try to claim they were worthless anyway and slip away with a few prize items hidden under his coat. This had been his strategy with Merchants and Laclede, which the assessors felt were worth two million or so but which Motty had insisted a few years earlier weren't worth much more than half a million. It seems that it's in the nature of fur dealers to depreciate the value of their inventory (and thus bury their profits and regulate their taxable income): maybe the habit died hard.

A few weeks after the corporate appraisal, the chief

assessor, Joseph McKee, put in for a larger fee than he'd
originally stipulated. He'd been at his wits' end, driven
mad almost, trying to get an elementary hold on the way
Eitingon Schild actually worked. Just how mad can perhaps be seen from his revised billing, based on the time it
had taken him to decipher the Eitingon books: he was now
putting in for 892 hours and three-quarters, owing to the
'intricacies', the *New York Times* reported, of 'company
and inter-company accounts'.

Apparently Motty's empire consisted of the ailing
Eitingon Schild and ten subsidiaries: two in New York,
five in St Louis, one in Leipzig, as well as the London outfit formally constituted five years earlier and run by
Monya, plus a residual company left over in Poland after
the sale of the Lodz business to the Fur Companies
Syndicate. I'm not even sure McKee felt he'd got to the
bottom of it by the time he delivered his report and put in
for his new fee: fifty thousand dollars. In June the court
that had appointed him awarded forty thousand.

Then there were the properties, some of them quite
large. In Palestine, in Brazil (land for a cotton plantation
to supply the mills in Lodz), in California, in Connecticut,
in New York (the first airport hotel at La Guardia), right
down to the 1939 World Trade Fair Parking Lot, which
appears to have been the only thing Motty had left at the
very end of his life. These are all alluded to, from time to
time, in passing, but when or how or why they were
acquired and then un-acquired I don't know.

The Cradle Will Rock, meanwhile, was in rehearsal with a
view to a private performance, hosted by Virgil Thomson,
for the head of the Federal Theater Project and a group of

Marc Blitzstein's admirers, including Orson Welles and the actor Howard da Silva. The performance went well and it was decided that the FTP would sponsor a run. It had the makings of a great success with John Houseman as the producer, Welles directing and da Silva, who was later blacklisted, playing the union organiser, Larry Foreman. One or two changes were in due course discussed and agreed on, notably the widowing of Ella Hammer, whose lover, Farmer Sickle, was struck from the score in order to avoid the obvious symbolism. The toning down came to nothing. The flagging spirits of the anti-Communists in Congress had revived after four years of Roosevelt. *The Cradle Will Rock* would not go into production after all. Or not under the auspices of the Project.

The cancellation, which took place a few days before the musical was due to open, was quite brutal, the sort of thing one could more easily imagine happening in Munich than New York. The theatre was locked up and placed under guard, the cast forbidden by their union to appear on stage. *The Cradle Will Rock* opened even so, on 16 June 1937 at the Venice Theater on Seventh Avenue. It was a famous occasion, famously described in his memoirs by John Houseman, its producer:

> The curtain rose on Marc Blitzstein sitting pale, tense, but calm, at our eviscerated piano . . . We could hear Marc's voice behind us setting the scene: Streetcorner, Steeltown, USA, followed by a short vamp that sounded harsh and tinny on our untuned upright. Then, a most amazing thing happened. Within a few seconds, Marc became aware that he was no longer singing alone. It took our handheld spotlight a few seconds to

locate the source of that second voice. It came from a stage right box in which a frail girl in a green dress was standing glassy-eyed and frozen with fear only half audible at first but gathering strength with every note . . . Our actors had been forbidden to appear onstage. There was no ruling against their appearing in the theatre. And that's what they did. They acted all over that house, improvising with amazing ingenuity. Spontaneously, unrehearsed, undirected, they played each scene in a different and unexpected part of that theatre. Between the seats, in the aisles, in stage boxes upper and lower, in the rear of the theatre, so that the audience sometimes had to turn and stand to see them . . . It was a most glorious evening and the cheering and the applause lasted so long that the stagehands demanded an hour's overtime.

I'm sure Motty and Bess were there. My mother wasn't: she was in London, where she'd got married the previous day. Show-business history being one of show-business's favourite subjects, a movie called *Cradle Will Rock*, about that night, was made by Tim Robbins sixty years later.

As for Franz Hoellering, here too the story hots up. Letting him stay at Hillcrest Park was not the only favour Motty did him: in 1937, according to the FBI files, he had funded him on a trip south of the border. In March that year, at Trotsky's instigation, his supporters set up an independent commission to investigate the charges made against him in Moscow. Its chairman was the American philosopher John Dewey. Because Trotsky wouldn't be allowed to enter the US the hearings were held in Mexico, in the house where

Trotsky was staying – not the one in which he would be murdered, but the Blue House belonging to Diego Rivera and Frida Kahlo. There were about fifty people present, of whom, thanks to Motty, Hoellering was one. Leonid was in Spain, and sometimes in France, around that time. Was Hoellering reporting to someone, and if so, to whom? The wily Armenian, Gaik Ovakimian, was working overtime on an early plan to assassinate Trotsky: might he have been Hoellering's New York contact?

The FBI contended that Hoellering 'took notes of all the proceedings' and wrote them up into a report to give to Motty 'so that he would know what was going on', as he'd been 'nice' enough to finance the trip 'as a present'. Krivitsky had a different, perhaps more plausible take on it. In his view Hoellering had been paid by the US Communist Party to report on the hearing to the Party in Moscow. 'The Communists', the FBI reports Krivitsky as saying, 'had to have someone at the hearing and it had been arranged through Motty Eitingon.' When Motty next saw him, Hoellering was 'bitterly anti-Stalin', so Motty told the FBI; and it wouldn't be very long before he'd assumed a more or less orthodox anti-Communist position.

The FBI investigated Motty in 1942 (briefly), 1945, 1946, 1947 and 1954. In 1945 he is said by 'a confidential informant' to have taken 'a considerable interest in the Trotsky hearings and to have told some of the members of the Dewey Commission that the Russian ambassador to the United States was interested in the hearing'. He is also supposed to have said 'that he regretted to see people as well known and as of good character as those on the commission becoming involved in it'. Why he made that remark, or what he meant by it, I can't decide. His gist seems to be that respectable people shouldn't have been messing about in the business of a disreputable state. But perhaps he was suggesting that outsiders had no right to interfere in the Soviet Union's affairs. This wouldn't have been a disgraceful point of view – plenty of people accepted the Moscow Trials without a murmur at the time. But wasn't he too smart to say that to the FBI, even (or especially) if it was the case that the 'Russian ambassador' had asked him to find someone to go to the hearings and that Hoellering had been present on the Soviet government's behalf?

In the 1954 transcript – by this time Hoellering, now a firm anti-Communist, has returned to (West) Germany – Motty says that Hoellering asked him to lend him the money for the trip to Mexico as he'd been asked to report on the hearings for an Austrian or Czech paper. The loan, he said, was never repaid. Finally, did Leonid have something to do with Hoellering's trip to Mexico? It's unlikely that he did and a little less unlikely that he didn't.

By rolling and readjusting, recapitalising, selling this or that, redescribing one thing as another thing, Motty had pulled Eitingon Schild out of its immediate difficulties. But the tide was running against the fur men by the end of 1937, and riding the depression was no longer just a case of a deft hand at the tiller. A seven-week labour dispute the following year made things no better, and the company's losses for 1938 were going on a million dollars.

Other dealers would soon see their fortunes revive with the war in Europe, and once America entered the field they began to do a brisk trade – there were so many orders from the military, including the linings of airmen's jackets and waterproofs for the infantry. But the demand in this case was for wolf pelts and sealskins, largely domestic and Canadian, a very different proposition from the luxury furs that Motty dealt in. The new business was no longer about enabling a woman to be 'correctly clad for all occasions'. Such occasions had included 'tea' and 'shopping', but no mention was made of war. In March 1939 my father told his parents that Motty had 'officially severed his connection with Eitingon Schild but had assured the Stock Exchange that he would be back any time there was a chance of their doing business again. At present it's not possible because they have no working capital and cannot raise any here because their assets are mainly tied up in Poland.'

In April Motty wrote to Monya in London: 'The only realistic opportunity at the moment is "parking space on the World Fair Grounds" and I hope that the money I will manage to earn there will ease my situation at least to an extent.' Things had reached a very low point if Motty was now considering an investment in parking.

Worried about Monya or worried about himself, he was anxious that Monya should come to the States as soon as possible. 'What about your plans and opportunities to get a visa to come here? . . . Only know this, my dear Moniusha: your future concerns me as much as my own.' At the same time, he wrote to Sam Kallin, one of the firm's management in London, who was about to be laid off, giving an anguished account of the misfortunes at head office. 'We have no capital for new business and all looks quite hopeless . . . As you can see, dear Sam, the troubles come from all directions . . . I am troubled by the thought of what will happen to you, for even I personally cannot at the moment see an opportunity to come to your help by any means, as I myself am going through the most difficult period of my life.'

The refrain of personal difficulty was one that Motty most often took up when he had to tell people why he was letting them down. Sam Kallin was now cast adrift, but Motty was still keen to get Monya out of range of the coming war. In another letter to him in April, there was more anguish, and more rather perfunctory soul-searching: 'Naturally I know that we must help the people who have been in our business for so long, but on the other hand I simply do not know what I can do. You cannot imagine what sort of problems we have here, how we care for every cent not to get stuck in the middle.'

When Motty wrote to Monya the following month, it seems to have been in response to a repeated request for cash. 'I received your letters of the 21st, 22nd and 25th of April. Today I am sending you £200 by telegraph' – a rough calculation makes that nine thousand pounds in the boom that preceded the crash of 2008. 'You can imagine how uncomfortable I feel about not having more money, but as you say yourself, "when a trouble comes, open up the gate for another as well."' Who Motty opened up the gate for is a moot point but Monya at least would very shortly be resettled in New York.

At the close of 1939, the *Wall Street Journal*, which had monitored the fortunes of Eitingon Schild in the same imperturbable tones for many years, felt that there might eventually be an improvement on the company's 1938 figures, although the fog of war made it hard to say with any certainty. Poland was a worry, no doubt about that, even if Motty had heard that the business was still running, in spite of coal shortages. By the following spring he had put in a claim, through the State Department, on his Polish assets – whose value he reckoned at two million dollars on the eve of the German invasion (say, thirty million today). The State Department, which had no way of checking, even if it wanted to, simply presented the claim to Berlin.

Meanwhile, Motty had come to an agreement with the renegade shareholders on at least one of their longstanding grievances. He'd offered to make a payment – or was it a repayment? (always hard to tell) – of one hundred thousand dollars to Eitingon Schild. Where the money was supposed to have come from is not clear. From the Fur Company Syndicate maybe, or possibly out of his own pocket, which was a notional source in almost all his dealings with the exception of bequests to charity. The offer, on the face of it, was a symbolic acknowledgement that the dissidents had a reasonable case when they argued that the syndicate had done too well out of the Eitingon recapitalisation, and in January 1939, with things looking disastrous for the firm by now, the court gave its approval to the settlement.

My mother and father tightened their belts: 'Motty's business not very brilliant at the moment so we are watching our expenses more closely.' Did they, I wonder, have shares in one or other of Motty's companies? There's no evidence to suggest it. In which case, I suppose, they received subventions from Motty on the grounds that the Eitingon business was the business of all the Eitingons. We know that Motty felt that he should support those who weren't able to look after themselves, but my parents didn't come into that category. Of all the Eitingons dotted about the world I can't think that my mother was one of the needier. On the other hand, the business in Lodz had belonged to her father as much as it belonged to Motty or Naum, and maybe that was the basis on which my parents received their remittance. In any case, as so often with Motty, he already had something else up his sleeve.

'Motty', my father reported in December 1939, 'has started some business with a very wealthy Russian and so they do more entertaining than they have done for some time.' And in January 1940: 'Motty asked me to tell you' – it was typical of Motty's familial manner that he should have wanted to reassure my father's parents – 'that his business was all right again and he's over all his worries.' If only. 'He is in very high spirits,' my father added, 'and it does one good to see him.' Then more ominously: 'The confidence people have in him is tremendous and they all want to go along with him.' That more than anything is what made Motty so dangerous.

In the spring of 1940 the Stock Exchange applied to the Securities and Exchange Commission to strike Eitingon Schild common stock – by then the only stock – from the list. The company's assets were now valued at three million dollars, but of this 2.4 million was tied up in Leipzig and Lodz, and subject to 'exchange restrictions' – which is to say, German restrictions. When independent accountants looked the situation over, they thought it best to ascribe no value to the European assets and, as a result, the company showed a capital deficiency. Eitingon Schild's annual report stated that it was no longer doing business in New York in any case. The stock was delisted in the summer. In one sense, events in Europe had dealt the killer blow. Yet it was fair to ask how on earth Eitingon Schild, once the greatest fur-dealing company in the world, was worth no more than six hundred thousand dollars, after its Polish and German plant had been removed from the reckoning. There is no obvious answer.

CHAPTER 21

Palestine

Max had taken the loss of his income well enough – better, more realistically than Motty. It was easier for him of course. He had no part in making the money, or in losing it. Still, one might have expected some of his sense of himself to have disappeared with his great wealth – but it didn't. 'We have gradually got used to the idea that one part of the fortune which used to be such a strong support of our existence has vanished altogether and that the remaining part has become at best questionable. But one doesn't get used just to the thoughts, but also to the bare facts,' he wrote to Freud in February 1932. Freud responded wistfully:

> Personal matters apart, I had always hoped that as a last resort you could have given your all-powerful brother-in-law a little nudge that would have led him to pour one of his money bags over our publishing house. It probably would have meant very little to him back then, but we didn't really have a claim on his attention, and you probably had good reasons for not giving him that nudge.

Freud seems to have forgotten that in 1920 Motty had given the publishing house five thousand dollars – more than fifty thousand in today's values.

Two months later Max had a mild stroke, and his left arm remained paralysed for a short time. On hearing from

Mirra that he was unwell, and thinking his ill-health must be connected to the loss of his money – Max had explained that 'personal allowances' in the Eitingon fortune had been reduced from a third to a quarter of the original amount and were due to cease altogether – Freud offered to put a thousand dollars 'at [his] disposal' to ease the situation. There is no indication that the offer was taken up.

Now, for the first time in his life, and in poorish health, Max had to think of earning his living. Max to Freud, 19 June 1932: 'We are still faced by the same question: what are we to live off? A question that might seem obvious, but one which I didn't come even close to considering until a few years ago.' The income from his practice had been in steady decline since 1930; now he was about to lose his second-to-last 'well-paying' patient and there were no new ones in prospect. 'Foreigners, who even in the past did not exactly travel the globe to attend my practice, will become even rarer in the future given the unstable political situation in Germany.'

Max wasn't destitute. He still went on holiday; he still had his house; he still sent cigars to Freud when they couldn't be had in Vienna; he still paid him visits. But he decided not to seek re-election as president of the International Association and, more seriously, he could no longer support the publishing house or the clinic: patients would have to pay more and members of the Berlin Psychoanalytic Society would have to contribute whatever they could to keep the clinic going. But not for long. Within a few years the clinic would suffer a change of ownership and the publishing house disappear altogether; the Central European psychoanalytic enterprise was about to be suspended.

*

At the end of January 1933 Hitler became chancellor. Two months later the Enabling Act was passed giving him complete control of the German state. That psychoanalysis as practised at the institute by Jewish analysts would no longer be tolerated was obvious. Or is obvious with hindsight. Max either saw things more clearly than Freud or was more alarmist. 'I want to be there until the last moment, eventually close it down myself if it has to be closed down at all, or else be there in person when someone else closes it down . . . I don't want to leave it under the command of anyone else in case the institute remained open and I, as a foreigner and a foreign doctor, couldn't actually work there myself,' he wrote to Freud a few days before the Act was passed.

Determined not to panic himself ('Austria is not given to German brutality'), Freud encouraged Max to hold out as long as he could while also reminding him that the institute wasn't legally his to close down. More rational, less apocalyptic than Max, he wanted it to be understood that if psychoanalysis was to survive in Germany the institute had to remain open whatever the circumstances. 'They might beat us,' he said in conclusion, 'but they can't beat psychoanalysis.'

At that point Max seemed to need no encouragement to stay at his post: he had already told his relatives in the US that he couldn't come to the States – his work wouldn't allow him to leave Berlin. Whether he was already in his head planning a different move is unclear.

In the event his resolve to go down with his ship was short-lived. On 8 April a decree was published requiring all medical organisations to aryanise their governing boards. Max wasn't an Aryan; he wasn't even German: he was Polish, the nationality he'd chosen at the break-up of the Austro-Hungarian Empire. There were two prominent Aryan doctors at the clinic, Carl Müller-Braunschweig and Felix Boehm, who was also Max's deputy as head of the German Psychoanalytic Society. Boehm, an ambitious man somewhat lacking in scruple, saw in the decree an opportunity for advancement.

On 11 April, three days after the decree was published, Max set out for a two-week holiday in Menton. Does that seem strange, like the holiday he took in the middle of the First World War? Or is it strange only with hindsight? Could he have had an assignation with Leonid? Or was it just that he didn't want to change his plans once he'd made them? Maybe he'd booked the hotel room and was now worried that he wouldn't get his money back if he cancelled. (How did those things work in the 1930s?) In any case Mirra, Freud uncharacteristically told Max, deserved a break.

Writing to Freud from Menton on 21 April Max was more businesslike. Felix Boehm by then had done what he could to bring his moment forward, scurrying between the Nazi authorities, in the hope of being told that the law insisted that he take Max's place, and Freud, in the hope of getting his blessing. 'Boehm's private reconnaissance into the lion's den was both an unnecessary and a dangerous step,' Max told Freud. 'Unnecessary' because Max had already given Boehm carte blanche to take over as head of the Berlin psychoanalytic enterprise in the event of the Nazi Party requiring it, and 'dangerous' because it would have the effect of inviting the Nazis' attention.

Max, meanwhile, had lost interest in outmanoeuvring the authorities: 'I want to emphasise again', he said to

Freud at the end of the same letter, 'that the things we owe our cause must not come into conflict with our Jewishness. In other words we must not for all our cleverness forget that we are upright people and things that are done without tact and in bad taste are unlikely to result in wise decisions (apologies for pointing out the obvious).' Freud – less protective of his Jewishness – wouldn't have put it like that but he'd meant something similar when he said in an earlier letter: 'I would like to issue a motto: no provocations but no concessions either.'

As things turned out the aryanising decree was found not to apply to them 'as theirs wasn't a standard medical organisation'. A general meeting was held on 6 May – behind closed curtains to shield the clinic's meeting room from the sight of Wichmannstrasse covered in swastikas – but no radical decisions were taken. It's thought that Max didn't resign from the clinic and the Society until 18 November, when he officially proposed Boehm and Müller-Braunschweig as the new directors.

On 13 June he spoke at Ferenczi's funeral; Freud, who wasn't there, read his speech and said again, as he'd said in the past, that it was a pity Max wrote so little when he wrote so well. In August Max went to see Freud in Vienna. On 7 September he saw his patients for the last time and the following day left for Palestine via Naples and Rome. He would stay there two months before returning to Berlin to resign from his official duties and pack up his things. He emigrated on the last day of the year.

Psychoanalysis was speedily aryanised. By 1936 the Jewish analysts were safely out of the country – Jones, who wasn't Jewish, was one of the last to break with the Nazis – and the institute had been renamed the Göring Institute after its new director, Hermann Göring's cousin, Matthias Göring. Those of Freud's books that remained in the clinic library were locked away in what Elizabeth Danto calls a 'poison cupboard'; and before too long, and to Göring's great joy, Jung, no friend of the Jews, had joined forces with the new enterprise. Boehm, eager to show his new masters how useful psychoanalysis could be to the Reich, assured them that he had 'never known psychoanalysis have a destructive effect on love of country'. His fellow Aryan turn-and-turn-again Müller-Braunschweig, not only a former colleague of Max's but a future head of the West German psychoanalytic organisation, was more gung-ho. 'Psychoanalysis', he said, 'works to remodel incapable weaklings into people who can cope with life, the inhibited into confident types, those divorced from reality into human beings who can look reality in the face, those enslaved by their instincts into masters.' If only. For the 'untreatable patient', the patient incapable of remodelling himself, there was a ready solution: euthanasia.*

Settling in Palestine was difficult. 'The reason behind my recent silence was that our move abroad has not been an entirely easy process during which bouts of depression are inevitable,' Max wrote to Freud in the summer of 1934. Though he visited Freud most years, he corresponded with him only rarely now: two letters and one telegram in 1935, three letters in 1936. But when it was put to him that he would be better off in the United States and Motty sent him a visa he brushed it all aside despite Mirra's 'begging

* Müller-Braunschweig's remarks are quoted in 'Psychoanalysis, Nazism and "Jewish Science" ' by S. Frosh in the *International Journal of Psychoanalysis*, No. 84 (2003).

him' to take up the offer. 'Dear friends,' he is supposed to have said to his new colleagues when they discovered that he might be about to leave, 'I'm a stubborn man. This is the place I've chosen and I'm not going to leave here until I'm carried out.' (*Eigensinnig* was the word he used, which can mean 'stubborn' and can mean 'selfish'.) As before, when Max knew what he wanted there were no provisos – no ingratiating gifts, no doing what Mirra wanted.

Once settled he seems to have done every Jewish thing. 'Every cultural Jewish activity drew him,' Sidney Pomer wrote in the 1960s. His new friends were writers and artists, as his old friends in Europe had been; he 'took over' – I'm not sure in what sense – the Jewish National Museum when 'the museum was struggling for its very life'; and when he died the director, praising him, as all his friends praised him, for his knowledge, his culture and his love of the arts, said: 'He was a man made to live art.' How much pleasure he got from the biblical landscape, how much interest he took in the country itself (its politics, for example) – all that is unclear. Maybe it was enough to know he was there.

He mentions riots in a letter to Freud ('Recently there were uprisings in Tiberias, and we had a victim in one of our newest settlements. It is not very nice'); and the schol-ar Lukasz Hirszowicz, when I spoke to him in the early 1990s, remembered that he'd gone to see Max on behalf of the League for Jewish–Arab Understanding in connection with the riots, but his only memory of the occasion was the voice of Max's secretary saying: 'Two Eastern European Jews [*zwei Ostjuden*] are here to see you.' Max advised Youth Aliya, the organisation that looked after young Jewish immigrants and trained some of their leaders. An

Israeli historian, Shmuel Dotan, writing in the wake of Stephen Schwartz, fingers Max as a member of the Palestinian CP, but it's unclear what evidence he has unless Max gave money to the Liga V, which Schwartz and others, correctly, call a Communist front organisation. But Liga V – League for Victory – was collecting money for the Soviet war effort and, as Walter Laqueur who has written extensively about Israeli and European history and was there at the time recalls, 'There was great pro-Soviet enthusiasm in Palestine after 1941 and just about everyone gave some money or sent ambulances.' For all the emotion associated with 'making aliya' – the 'return' to Palestine – I suspect that, as with the great majority of refugees from Hitler's Germany, the life Max led in Palestine was as close as geography allowed to the life he'd led in Berlin.

He stayed in touch with the analysts who had had to leave Europe; like an admiral keeping track of his ships, he had a world map in his study on which little flags marked the exact position of every Freudian analyst in exile. Several had only been able to leave Germany or Austria thanks to the affidavit of support he provided for them.

His main preoccupation – his main ostensible preoccupation – remained psychoanalysis. 'The history of psychoanalysis in Palestine begins with the emigration from Germany of Dr Max Eitingon,' Rafael Moses wrote in the *Journal of the American Academy of Psychoanalysis and Dynamic Psychiatry* in 1998. 'In everything, but particularly in matters of psychoanalytic politics, Eitingon is miles ahead of all the other colleagues who have emigrated to Palestine,' Otto Fenichel wrote in 1934 to his former colleagues now dispersed around the globe, and then added: 'We all know how he likes to make his moves in secret, but

1 Leonid in his prime

2 Leonid with his siblings
3 Leonid's father
4 Leonid's grandfather

5 Leonid as a young Bolshevik
6 Leonid, seated centre right, with fellow Chekisti

7 Sudoplatov in 1935
8 Zoya in 1943 before going to Tehran

9 Leonid with Olga (left), Vladimir and Zoya
10 Leonid with Zoya and her daughter, late 1940s

11 Alexander Orlov, US citizen, in 1972

12 Ramón Mercader
13 Sylvia Ageloff
14 Caridad Mercader in her seventies

15 Leonid in mufti
16 Leonid in old age

this time he is taking it to such an extreme that I wasn't even able to make out whether he had succeeded or not in his plan to open an institute at the University of Jerusalem.'

He hadn't: the university instead established a chair in general psychology. Freud, who was on the board of the university, was furious. Max, undeterred, set up his own institute. ('He did not argue about things,' his new colleague Daniel Dreyfuss writes in the memorial volume. 'He rendered his account to himself alone and did what he felt the future demanded of him.') The Palestine Institute of Psychoanalysis, modelled on the Berlin clinic and staffed by refugee analysts, offered both treatment and training.* But unlike the Berlin patients, the men and women seeking treatment here were likely to be the usual kind: middle-class Jewish neurotics. Meetings between analysts took place in German, and many analyses were carried out in a language in which neither analyst nor patient was fluent; sometimes, Jewishly, analyst and patient used different languages.

In May 1934, Max opened his own practice at 14 Balfour Street (now Max Eitingon House): a good address, I assumed, but I didn't know how good – No. 18 is the official residence of Israel's prime ministers.

Before long Max's holiday habit resumed. Every summer from 1935 to 1938 he spent in Europe, whether or not

---

* Today the Israel Institute of Psychoanalysis, named after Max, and situated on Disraeli Street in Talbiye, one of Jerusalem's nicest neighbourhoods, makes a point of the role it has played in Israel's wars, both in the IDF and in civil defence, bringing to mind, on the one hand, Max's successes with the casualties of shellshock in the First World War and, on the other, Boehm and Müller-Braunschweig's promise to turn out an army of fit and fighting patriots.

there was a psychoanalytic congress to attend. Where exactly he went and how long he spent in each place isn't clear; he visited Freud, he saw various members of his family, he spent time in Italy, he rented a villa outside Paris: but we have no precise details. Long holidays and a habit of secrecy: was there a connection?

CHAPTER 22

Songbird

On 20 September 1937 Max and Mirra caught a 6 a.m. train from Paris to Florence. At the Gare de Lyon to see them off – at that ungodly hour – were Mirra's friend Nadezhda Plevitskaya, 'the nightingale of Kursk', and her husband, General Skoblin.* Two days later, on 22 September, the most senior White Russian officer in Europe, Evgeny Karlovich Miller – General Miller – went missing in Paris. Skoblin and Plevitskaya were the main – the only – suspects in the case.

Mirra, disliking life in Palestine, had been in Paris since February, staying with her sister and her sister's husband, a man whose name will come up again, Leonid Raigorodsky. (Mirra, too, was called Raigorodsky, as far as we know: maybe her sister married a cousin, as my mother had done first time round.) I don't suppose there's anything significant in the fact that Mirra had been in Paris for five months without Max: her sister apparently needed looking after; her friends Skoblin and Plevitskaya lived near by; there were plenty of shoe shops. As Freud saw it, she was punishing Max for his refusal to move to the States.

Max had left Palestine in the third week of July and was with Freud in Vienna by the 27th. From there I'm not sure

---

* Theodore Draper seems not to have been entirely persuaded of the Eitingons' presence in Paris in the summer of 1937, but the publication of the Freud–Eitingon correspondence in 2004 confirms that they were indeed there and that they left for Florence on 20 September.

where he went. A reference in Plevitskaya's trial to a villa in Bois-le-Roi, a small town south of Paris, suggests that he and Mirra spent August and maybe part of September there. He probably wasn't all that well: he'd had that stroke five years before and would have a heart attack in 1938; his colleagues in Palestine in their tributes to him often refer to his poor health. Perhaps Mirra had joined him for a cure in Karlsbad or Marienbad. I doubt that we will ever know for sure.

In Paris – we do know this – in the days leading up to their departure for Florence they stayed at the George V, now a Four Seasons hotel, but always a place where rich people stayed – even, it seems, when they no longer had access to the money tree. Skoblin and Plevitskaya had a house in Ozoir-la-Ferrière, a suburb south-east of Paris favoured by Russian exiles, but spent part of the week not far from the George V, at the more modest – but not that modest – Hotel Pax on avenue Victor Hugo. They were a good-looking couple with an interesting past, but a few things were unclear about them – such as their political allegiance and their means of support.

On the night of 22/23 September Skoblin in his turn disappeared. Neither he nor General Miller would be seen in public again. The press was perplexed. 'While it would be reckless to suggest that Miller was the victim of right-wing extremists,' the *Manchester Guardian* commented on 25 September, 'it seems almost equally improbable that the Soviet could have any interest in kidnapping him.' *Poslednie Novosti*, one of two Russian-language papers in Paris, was more brutal: 'Who', it asked, 'would need the life of an elderly general, the head of an organisation the activity of which has declined greatly in recent years?'

General Miller's disappearance was the most notable thing that had happened in the world of the Russian emigration in several years: everyone knew about it, talked about it, had an opinion. It was both trite and fascinating. Six years later, in 1943, it was the subject of Nabokov's first story in English, 'The Assistant Producer', where it is told in the form of a trashy movie scenario; and seventy years later a movie was indeed made – Eric Rohmer's *Triple Agent*.

Miller and Skoblin, both distinguished veterans of the Civil War, belonged to the leading association of ex-tsarist officers, known by its initials as ROVS – Nabokov calls it the White Warriors' Union (WW for short). Miller was its head, Skoblin his deputy. Like all such associations, but more intensely than most, ROVS was feared, distrusted, infiltrated and obsessed over by the Soviets, though in truth it amounted to very little – 'but a sunset behind a cemetery' is how Nabokov wonderfully describes it. It had suffered a serious reverse in 1930 when Miller's predecessor, General Kutepov, was seized on a Paris street one winter morning, bundled into a taxi, driven to the coast and never heard from again. He died, we know now, on a ship taking him to the Soviet Union: the dose of chloroform used to overpower him proved too much for his weak heart.

'The Kutepov operation was to set an important precedent,' Christopher Andrew and Vasily Mitrokhin write. 'In the early and mid-1930s the chief Soviet foreign intelligence priority remained intelligence collection. During the later years of the decade, however, all other operations were to be subordinated to "special tasks".'* 'Special tasks' in my

---

* *The Mitrokhin Archive: The KGB in Europe and the West*, published in 1999, is by far the most sober and dependable account of Soviet espionage

mind – or at any rate in the place where I have my fantasies – meant Leonid. The Administration of Special Tasks was his department, and in the immediate post-Soviet period, when I was doing my researches and finding it hard to locate any trace of him, there was always someone to tell me what I wanted to hear: that he'd been right there at the heart of things. (If one of your characters is an assassin you'd just as soon he wasn't a minor one – a one-horse assassin.) Now it turns out that Kutepov's disappearance, and indeed that of General Miller, were the work of Leonid's colleague Yasha Serebriansky. Close but not close enough.

Traditionally the Soviet worry had been that these veterans' associations would find volunteers to enter Soviet territory, foment rebellion and sabotage the regime from inside the country. That had been the worry with Savinkov in the early 1920s and in Turkey a few years afterwards. But in the later 1930s as the German threat began to look more real, and the progress of the war in Spain less rosy, other scenarios may have seemed more alarming to the Soviet regime: was Miller negotiating with the Germans? Did he have information to pass on to them; did he know about the Soviet Union's own on-again, off-again flirtations with the Nazis? Did he have some connection with the Tukhachevsky business?* Was he plotting with Franco's people in Spain?

Any of these things are possible, just as it's possible that

---

and worse, and I owe it a considerable debt while not wishing to implicate it in any mistakes I may have made.

* Tukhachevsky was Stalin's most talented general, executed in 1937 along with eight of his fellow officers for – this was the official line – conspiring with the Germans. What Stalin really feared was that Tukhachevsky, a popular and outspoken man, might be in a position to overthrow him.

the regime was simply attending to its housework when it got rid of Miller. As tensions rose in Europe a few things needed tidying up, and one of them was the power, as the Soviets saw it, of the émigré organisations. Get Skoblin to do away with Miller and then do away with the witness. Was that what happened? Kill the leader and his deputy – decapitate the organisation?

General Miller left his house in Boulogne-sur-Seine at nine o'clock on the morning of 22 September, a Wednesday; an hour and a half later he was in his office at 29 rue du Colisée. At midday he summoned Colonel Kusonsky, the secretary of ROVS, told him he had a rendezvous at 12.30 – he didn't say where or with whom – and would be back after lunch. But before going out, and very unusually, he handed Kusonsky a sealed envelope to be opened in case he didn't return.

At 12.15 he left the building, coatless, hatless and wallet-less. The note, not opened until much later, read as follows:

> I have an appointment at 12.30 today with General Skoblin at the corner of rue Jasmin and rue Raffet. He is to take me to a rendezvous with two German officers, one a military attaché in a neighbouring country, Strohman, a colonel, the other, Herr Werner, who is attached to the local German Embassy. Both these men speak Russian well. It is possible this is a trap, and that is why I am leaving you this note.

Two things seem clear: Miller hadn't forgotten what happened to General Kutepov and he didn't trust Skoblin – General Golubkov in Nabokov's story, 'a very versatile spy'.

At 2.45 Kusonsky went home. Around five o'clock

247

he thought of ringing ROVS to see if Miller was back, but to do so he would have had to go out to a café, and so he didn't.

At eight o'clock Miller failed to show up for a meeting in the rue du Colisée. Half an hour later the caretaker rang his house: Miller hadn't been home all day. At nine Miller's wife wanted the police to be informed but was told it was too soon. At ten – what a time it took these people to get their act together: no wonder the Revolution overtook them – a message was sent to Kusonsky.

At 10.50 Kusonsky, back in the rue du Colisée, opened Miller's envelope and read out his note. It was a terrible moment, both for those who knew what Skoblin had been up to and those who didn't. Two men immediately set out for Ozoir-la-Ferrière in the hope of finding Skoblin at home, but at 2 a.m. his friend Matsylev found him in bed in the Hotel Pax. Brought to the rue du Colisée, he was shown Miller's note: 'Golubkov perused' – Nabokov wrote – 'and knew at once that all was lost.'

It was 2.15 when Kusonsky and Matsylev prepared to set out with Skoblin for the police station. But Kusonsky, seeming to have something on his mind, withdrew to another room for a moment, leaving Matsylev alone with Skoblin. Matsylev, a loyal friend, failed to notice that Skoblin had slipped out of the room. He was halfway down the stairs when Matsylev raised the alarm. All the old men, the colonels and the lesser generals, rushed out in pursuit. 'Hurriedly, clumsily,' Nabokov writes, 'they stomped down the ugly steps, and emerged, and stopped under a black drizzle, and looked this way and that, and then at each other again.' Skoblin had gone.

At 2.30 Kusonsky and his fellow soldiers finally made

it to the police station but had trouble explaining themselves to the police because their French was so bad.

Skoblin was seen one last time when he turned up at 2.45 at the house of fellow expatriates in Neuilly-sur-Seine; he told them he'd lost his wallet, asked for a hundred francs, got two hundred; drank a big glass of water and left. And that's it.

If the story was reported in the *Manchester Guardian* it must also have been reported in the Italian, German and Austrian press. Max's correspondence with Freud has been published; his correspondence with his friend the writer Arnold Zweig is available. Does it seem odd or merely Max-like that he didn't mention what had happened either to Freud or to Zweig? Was he guilty? Embarrassed? Did he not want to say that these people were his friends? Max visited Freud again in October, before returning to Palestine, but didn't say anything. Maybe he didn't want to confirm Freud in his view that all Russians were savages. Even stranger (or more Max-like), when, after his name had been in the papers, he finally wrote to Freud about the affair he told him – even gave the impression of believing it himself – that there was no evidence against Plevitskaya or indeed against Skoblin.

Meanwhile, Plevitskaya – Nabokov's name for her is 'La Slavska'. The police came to see her in her hotel room just before dawn. She'd been with her husband the entire day, she assured them: she could account for all his movements; and even when they weren't together – between twelve and two – they were together because she was at her dressmaker's and he was waiting for her outside in his car. But no, she didn't go out to check that he was still there.

She spent that day – the 23rd – wandering the streets, and in the evening called on her doctor. Anxious to stay out of trouble, he passed her on to Raigorodsky (whom she knew presumably through Mirra), but Raigorodsky too was anxious not to get into trouble. She stayed in his house that one night, and the following day he accompanied her to the Quai des Orfèvres, where, all the while protesting her innocence, she gave herself up. She was remanded in custody, accused of complicity in General Miller's abduction. If she heard again from her husband she didn't let on. 'One wonders', Nabokov writes, 'if in some way or other her husband . . . thought it safer to leave her in the lurch.'

Not that Skoblin was out of danger. Far from it. Once the youngest general in the tsar's army, now an unwanted servant of the NKVD, he met a colleague – Leonid perhaps – by pre-arrangement somewhere in France and travelled with him to Spain, where he succumbed to whatever nasty fate the NKVD thought appropriate. Skoblin's prey meanwhile travelled at great speed to Le Havre inside a large trunk, was loaded onto a Soviet ship and, dodging every maritime formality, reached Leningrad. There he was unloaded and taken to Moscow, where he was interrogated and eventually shot.

Le Figaro, among others, suspected collusion between the Soviet Embassy and the Sûreté Nationale. Miller's journey was smoother than it should have been; Skoblin's escape far too easy. To some it seemed likely that Marx Dormoy, the French Minister of the Interior, had called off the police and the coastguard. That would explain why when he was summoned to appear at Plevitskaya's trial he was somehow – and to the president of the tribunal very annoyingly – lost from sight. Whether he was being mindful of relations between the Front Populaire and the Soviet government or had something more sinister in mind isn't clear. Similar concerns were raised at the time of Kutepov's abduction, when it was thought that the police commissioner, the improbably named Charles Adolphe Faux-Pas Bidet, was in league with a Soviet agent.

In the Soviet Union reports of the incident were clearcut: Skoblin was working for the Germans. Puzzlingly, the story resurfaced in the USSR's dying days when former KGB agents and their hangers-on took the trouble to reconstruct Skoblin's past as a Soviet agent in novelette form. But these are difficult texts to read, the mixture of fact and romance, or information and disinformation, liable to induce feelings of panic in anyone looking for facts; and since they don't mention any members of the Eitingon family – in any way that I can make out – I've left them to one side, noting only the reluctance of the Soviet (and post-Soviet) secret service to let go of its past. A mixture no doubt of pride at its own prowess (how good we were at putting people into suitcases) and lingering infatuation with Plevitskaya.

Even Nabokov conceded that the real-life Plevitskaya, though 'a corny singer', had 'a fine voice'. She had sung with Chaliapin and recorded with Rachmaninov, who sometimes accompanied her when she sang in the States. (Motty, I assume, knew Rachmaninov: did he also know Plevitskaya?) The Russian emigration had always loved her; loved to see her on stage all dressed up in 'flowing draperies and jewelled headdress' or, more affectingly, 'in the short skirts of the Russian peasant'; loved her rich, masculine voice, loved to hear her sing the old songs – 'for when she sings folk songs she is the music,' the *New York World* reported in April 1927. 'For us,' one émigré sighed, 'she is, more than an artist, a memory of the beautiful stories and green meadows of Russia.'

She'd begun life in a convent, escaped to a travelling circus, married a Polish dancer (Edmond Plevitsky), moved to Moscow, sung in restaurants, and in 1909 was spotted at the autumn fair in Nizhny Novgorod, from where her career took off. She sang for the Romanovs and moved them to tears. 'The kind of people for whom music and sentiment are one . . . found in the tremendous sonorities of her voice both a nostalgic solace and a patriotic kick,' Nabokov said of La Slavska. Alexandre Benois, Diaghilev's set designer, was less cynical: Plevitskaya, he said, 'captivated all from the monarch down to the pettiest bourgeois, with her Russian beauty and the brilliance of her talent'. She sang for the troops in the First World War and when the Revolution came she sang for the Red Army, but one way or another ended up with the Whites, marrying Skoblin in Gallipoli in 1920, when she was thirty-six and he was twenty-seven.

They spent their married life on the émigré circuit, first in Berlin – Nabokov used to see them at parties – then in Paris. They had a house, they had a car; Plevitskaya, we know, was liable to spend several hours at her dressmaker's. How did they pay for it? Not with money Skoblin got from ROVS. That was a cause, not a job.

With Plevitskaya now in custody the police began their investigation. Documents were unearthed in Ozoir-la-Ferrière, in Miller's house in Boulogne-sur-Seine, at the headquarters of ROVS and in several other White Warrior haunts, official and unofficial. But since all the documents were in Russian and some in code, and since the translators may well have had agendas of their own, the French police couldn't be sure that they had an accurate fix on them. According to the *Times* of 22 October the material found in Ozoir made it clear that Skoblin 'compiled dossiers of all Russian organisations in France, whether tsarist, republican or Soviet', but without knowing what he did with the information it's hard to know what to blame him for.

The following February, their investigation completed, the police reported to the examining magistrate that none of the documents they'd collected shed any light on Miller's disappearance. The suspects – Kusonsky, Matsylev and others – were all questioned. Nothing came of the questioning. Some of Miller's fellow officers thought him too old and not up to the job; some wondered what had happened to the money that had been in the ROVS treasury; but Miller was a grand old man, the embodiment of the *ancien régime*, and the fact that he was old and useless was no reason to kill him.

Was policy the issue? Did someone want to pay Miller back for his unwillingness to send volunteers to fight the left in Spain? No, that didn't make sense: he'd never been against the idea. Could he have been killed by 'German Fascists'? Unlikely: only a sense that he owed it to the French not to sympathise with their enemy held him back from embracing the Fascist cause. Was the kidnapping the work of a foreign government, i.e. the Soviet Union? Miller wasn't important enough, it was said, which is odd given that half a dozen Russians, Red and White and none of them more 'important' than Miller, had been taken out in the previous few years.

Having excluded every other possibility, the police came to the obvious conclusion: Skoblin. Miller, they said, was no longer disposed to follow blindly where Skoblin led and the two men had fallen out over an operation to send emissaries into Soviet territory via Finland. It could have made sense: Miller sending in Whites and Skoblin ensuring that they were debriefed and shot, but these were areas the police didn't go into.

Still, it's clear, though never spelled out: the police knew Skoblin was guilty just as they knew that the money Plevitskaya earned from her concerts – the couple's only known source of income – was far from being enough to account for the high style in which they lived their lives. So, the police concluded quite reasonably, Skoblin must have had hidden resources. Where might they have come from? Alas it hadn't been possible to discover their source. They could hint at it, though, and they did, by citing a Colonel Fedosenko, who had accused Skoblin a few years before of working for the Soviets but hadn't been able to prove it and was dismissed from ROVS for his pains. Was that as far as the French government allowed them to go in saying the Soviet regime was responsible for the general's abduction?

About Plevitskaya they had no doubts: she was an intelligent woman, everyone said so, and she knew perfectly well what her (less intelligent) husband had been up to. Which was an odd thing to say given that they themselves precisely don't say what he was up to.

The police report is one of several documents relating to General Miller's abduction filed at Columbia University

in New York and the Hoover Institution in California.*
Taken together they confirm everything that's hinted at in
the police report: the subversive activities in Finland and
also the Baltic states (where Plevitskaya often went on
tour); Miller's sympathy for the Nationalists in Spain and
Hitler's party in Germany and his reluctance to get into
trouble with his French hosts by collaborating with either
of them. From the many rumours and malicious remarks
that the various sets of documents report, it's clear that
almost every Russian officer in Paris had his own secret
affiliation, his own business, his own allegiance, his own
lies to tell. Nabokov's White Warriors distrusted each
other even more than the early psychoanalysts distrusted
their colleagues, and with more reason. 'By an amusing
coincidence,' Nabokov writes in 'The Assistant Producer',
'a German press agency and a Soviet one laconically
stated that a pair of White Russian generals in Paris had
absconded with the White Army funds.'

Finally, try as the Soviets might to say that Skoblin was
acting on behalf of the Germans, it was everywhere else
assumed that he was an agent of the NKVD and had been
for a long time, that it was a question of money rather than
conviction, that on its behalf, or rather on its orders, he had
had Miller abducted, boxed up and returned to the Soviet
Union. And if he was guilty, Plevitskaya, because smarter
and a woman and a certain kind of woman, was even more
so. 'It is a constant rule in all countries,' the author of the
police report observed, 'that spies are recruited among

---

* To be more precise, the documents come from the Nicolaevsky
Collection at the Hoover Institution and the Filonenko Papers at
Columbia, which also holds Plevitskaya's prison diaries. All the documents
were very generously passed on to me by Theodore Draper.

women of the theatre, singers, dancers, stars and demi-mondaines.'

Rue de la Roquette in Paris, where Plevitskaya waited fourteen months in the women's prison for her trial to begin, is a long, unhappy street – the *voie funéraire* that leads from the Bastille via place Léon Blum to Père-Lachaise. In poor health, old, fat, abandoned by her friends – there is no suggestion that Max went to see her when he was in Paris for the 15th Congress of the International Psychoanalytic Association in 1938 – Plevitskaya had every reason to feel hard done by and filled six notebooks with recriminations and memories of happier times alternating with each other.

By the time her trial began, on 5 December 1938, she was hated. Only in recent years has her reputation recovered, rescued by post-Soviet nostalgia for the *ancien ancien régime*, her association (proven or unproven) with the NKVD now overlooked, her singing for the tsar memorialised. In the late 1930s it was not only the émigrés who'd taken against her: so had the French, whose sympathy for the Soviet way was fast disappearing in the wake of Stalin's purges. More to the point, the country was tired of playing host to NKVD derring-do; the killings and abductions on French territory had been going on for too long.

It was nonetheless a great moment when she entered the courtroom dressed like, of all things, a nun. The press rushed towards her, flashes popping, as the spectators craned forwards to see her in her novel outfit. The entrance of the Miller family, the general's wife (not his 'widow' because maybe he wasn't dead), his son and his brother aroused more sympathy, but less interest. Skoblin's guilt was scarcely doubted. But on whose behalf was he acting? And was Plevitskaya his accomplice or his evil genius? That by now was the leading question.

Some people in ROVS, the prosecutor said to her, considered Skoblin a double agent.

Plevitskaya: 'We were always Whites.'

Was she her husband's accomplice?

'I never involved myself with politics. We lived well precisely because I did not shove my nose into his business. We loved each other.'

Asked why in that case Skoblin abandoned her at the last minute, Plevitskaya burst into tears.

'You were a happy couple. Why isn't he here to defend you?'

'He probably doesn't know where I am,' she replied, shedding a few more tears.

It was a painful business. She'd been used to rapturous audiences: now her audience was unmoved, even exasperated. She spoke French reasonably well but in court pretended not to understand what was being said to her; and in her own speech reverted to the peasant Russian of her childhood.

The Skoblin couple, the president of the tribunal said, 'undoubtedly' had money from 'secret sources'.

Plevitskaya answered that she never did the accounts at home.

'You received money from Monsieur Eitingon. Who is he?'

'A very good friend, a psychiatrist. His wife is a former actress at the Moscow Art Theatre.'

(In *Le Figaro* she was reported as saying that *M. Oettingen, le généreux docteur extrémiste*, their friend, dressed her from head to toe *en tout bien tout honneur par admiration pour mon talent*. And the same sentiment, the paper reported, inspired *le généreux docteur* to lend her husband four thousand dollars. *M. Oettingen*'s generosities, a financial auditor advised the court, were *incontrôlables* – which means that they couldn't be verified, not that they were out of control, as I'd hoped.)

Asked about the nature of her relationship with Monsieur Eitingon, Plevitskaya said that she'd never sold herself. 'I didn't take money . . . But whether my husband received any money, that I don't know.'

Maître Ribet, counsel for the Miller family, pointed out that Plevitskaya had sworn to the police that she'd last seen Madame Eitingon 'in July 1937' and Max 'eight to ten months' before the kidnapping. Yet it had lately been established – by scrutinising the record of the phone calls they had made – that the Eitingons left Paris two days before the kidnapping of General Miller and that Skoblin and his wife had taken them to the station.

'Why did you lie?'

Perhaps, Plevitskaya replied, she hadn't understood the question at first, or maybe she'd forgotten. 'But now,' she said, 'I remember that we were with them the previous day, and in the morning we got up early to take them to the station. I have nothing to hide.'

Ribet: 'The first night after your husband ran away, you spent at the house of Eitingon's brother-in-law. Why was that?'

The reason, she said, wiping away another tear, was that she couldn't bear to spend the night in the place her husband had been taken from.

The first day of the trial ended and nothing was

resolved. From her answers it was clear that Plevitskaya was neither as innocent as she pretended nor as guilty as the majority of the people in the room wanted her to be, though everyone seemed to agree that she was 'a strong woman', 'the driving force behind her husband', as *Posledniye Novosti* put it. A lot now hung on a 'green Bible' from which she wouldn't be separated and that was supposed to contain, written on its first page in invisible ink, the key to the code in which Skoblin corresponded with his agents.

Plevitskaya: 'I had a Bible that I wanted to have with me in prison . . . But it wasn't green . . .'

Maître Filonenko for the defence said it was 'yellowish-green'.

'Yes,' Plevitskaya said, 'it was just yellow.'

Why the Bible was thought to have writing on it in invisible ink I don't know. Certainly no secret writing was found. Yet the prosecution, in the person of the nicely named Maître Flash, went on insisting that the key was invisibly there. If Plevitskaya was so determined to cling onto the Bible, he maintained, it was because she wanted to hide it from the authorities.

The Bible, it turns out, was given to her by Max, but was it Max the secret agent or Rosenmax the present-giver? He sent it from Palestine, Plevitskaya would write in her prison diary, together with a flask of holy water from the River Jordan and an icon of St Nicholas.

As the trial carried on, witnesses were called on Max's behalf. First his brother-in-law Leonid Raigorodsky, then the psychoanalyst René Laforgue. (Marie Bonaparte – psychoanalyst and Princesse de Grèce – sent a letter.) The two men said much the same things: that Max was a rich man, a scholar, a pupil of Professor Freud, and in the present matter 'as pure as snow'. Raigorodsky was more florid than Laforgue and made more of Max's wealth ('He is a very well-known psychiatrist worth many millions. I can name performers to whom he has given cheques for ten thousand francs'). The court briefly considered the possibility that Miller's body had been buried in the grounds of a villa in Bois-le-Roi rented by Max but quickly dismissed it.

'Didn't he buy Soviet furs?' Maître Flash asked.

'There are many Eitingons,' Raigorodsky said in reply. 'It's his cousin who trades in furs.' The implication here, and in every discussion of Max's wealth, was that all commercial dealings with the Soviet Union were of themselves suspect.

On 15 December Plevitskaya was convicted of complicity in the disappearance of General Miller and condemned to twenty years' hard labour. It was, everyone agreed, a vindictive sentence.

'No one kidnapped General Miller,' a reporter for a Communist newspaper was overheard telling two young women lawyers. 'He simply escaped from his old wife with a young girlfriend.'

Plevitskaya was transferred to the women's prison in Rennes and died there in 1940, the occupying Germans no kinder than the French had been. By then she had confided to the prison chaplain that Skoblin took part in the abduction of General Miller and that she had known this all along: she said nothing about her own involvement. Guilty or not guilty, guilty and not guilty, she had a very twentieth-century career.

*

And Max? Was he after all a Soviet agent? Was there room left in the life we know about for another, clandestine existence? The NKVD didn't like its people to show left-wing sympathies, or even much interest in politics, so there are no grounds there for believing him innocent. He was secretive, kept his own counsel and lived his life in separate compartments; his comings and goings were strictly his own business: meetings with Leonid could have been slipped unnoticed into his generous holiday schedules. Then his money: why did he have so much of it even when Motty had lost most of his? Is it too simple to suggest that when his father died in 1932 he still had money to leave him? Or should we take it that some of what he had came from the USSR, not through the fur but more directly, and that he knew how to dispense it in ways that would in turn benefit the Soviet Union? And not just by keeping Skoblin in cars and Plevitskaya in pretty frocks. Or should we take the simple option and say that his salient characteristic, his generosity, his need to give people things, in the end found him out?

In the diary she wrote before her trial, when she was still in prison in Paris, Plevitskaya devoted three pages of scribblings to 'friend Eitingon': '*Scholarly, rich.* What does he need Communists for?' (*Zachem emu Kommunisti?*) She mentions their fifteen-year friendship, his generosity towards artists, the help he gave her with her memoirs, the Bible and the holy water that he sent her from Jerusalem. 'So where', she asks again, 'is Communism?' Is she bluffing, trying to protect Max as well as herself? Or was her friend Mirra, about whom we know so little, the sleeper, and Max Mirra's alibi?

And what about Max's letters to Freud? Why did he

not mention the abduction when it happened? There could
be a sinister reason, but it could just be a question of manners, of not wanting to obtrude a story of his into other
people's lives. But even so it's hard to understand why he
told Freud that there was no evidence against her or her
husband and why, like Plevitskaya, he wanted to hide the
fact that he'd been in contact with his friends in the days
leading up to the kidnapping. Maybe he did after all have
something to hide.

Max to Freud, 5 December 1938: 'In November I got
very annoyed with a number of Parisian newspapers which
mentioned my name in a nonsensical and sensationalist
manner in relation to the trial of a famous Russian singer,
whom we did indeed know and liked, and whose husband,
a Russian general, had supposedly kidnapped another general . . .'

Max to Freud, 19 December 1938: 'They have built a
droll little character out of myself, my brother-in-law from
New York and some other mysterious ingredients . . . It
looks like the accused was given a heavy punishment in
spite of a seeming lack of clear evidence. What a terrible
story.'

Max to Freud, in response to Freud's questioning, 8
January 1939:

I got drawn into the Plevitskaya trial because the
accused woman had been asked in a preliminary interview what she had been living off all those years – they
had the suspicion that she was living far above her
means, an idea quite unjustified for those who really
knew her. She answered that she made a living through
concert tours, that her husband had a position as an

officer and that she had friends, including Dr Eitingon . . . who had helped her out. To a large extent this is true, particularly regarding the distant past, because Mirra and I have known the singer for 16 years and appreciated and loved her extraordinary talent for singing Russian folk songs. She would often visit us in Berlin, and we would always see her when we were in Paris. On the 22nd of September 1937 . . . a general von Miller mysteriously went missing. The following night the husband of the singer, General Skoblin, went missing too; he had organised the meeting . . . from which von Miller never returned. So they assumed that he was responsible for the unresolved abduction of von Miller, believed he was guilty, even though they hadn't found a trace of evidence. They assumed his wife was involved in the plot too and sentenced her to twenty years' hard labour without having to show any proof of their theory. It somehow felt like a political trial, like the Dreyfus trial . . . To be honest I have to say that the grotesque lies in the newspapers didn't annoy me very much. I only felt sorry for the accused Russian singer . . . The French jury . . . wanted to turn the case into a warning to those Russians who think they can get away with anything on French soil. And so they ended up judging in their own interest just like the first Russian jury in the Karamazov trial.

It's an upsetting letter, that last letter to Freud. Whatever one thinks of Plevitskaya's sentence it isn't true that there was no evidence against Skoblin or even his wife. And isn't it suspicious that Max, like Plevitskaya, didn't want to mention the fact that he left Paris two days

before the abduction and that Plevitskaya and Skoblin saw
him off at the station? Was he embarrassed by his own
foolishness? Anxious and sentimental about his friend? Or
was something more serious at stake?

Without that letter I would have been reasonably certain of Max's innocence. Now I'm more perplexed. It may
just be that I want to find a story where none exists.
Certainly none of Max's colleagues, as far as I can tell,
picked up on his connection with Plevitskaya (not even the
malicious Jones). Some of the recent books on the early
history of psychoanalysis refer, inevitably, to Stephen
Schwartz's argument, mostly to refute it, and, like them, I
want no part of it. It might have been possible to take that
sort of paranoid invective seriously at the height of the
Cold War, or even as it was coming to an end: now it
sounds slightly mad. At the same time I'm reasonably confident that had Theodore Draper known as much about
Max as it's possible to know now he would have been less
sure of his ground. On the one hand, there's Max the
impotent gasbag who, thanks to his money and his organ-
isational skills, set psychoanalysis on its feet. On the other,
there's Max the art lover, the embodiment of European
high culture, who secretly . . . No, probably not. But the
mystery remains and I don't see how it can go away.

Max died in Jerusalem in July 1943. Mirra died three years
later.

CHAPTER 23

Spain

These are some of the things that you can buy in the main food market in Valencia: sheep's heads with eyes, hens' eggs straight from the hen's belly, pigs' and calves' trotters fresh from the butcher's saw, condensed blood, coxcombs, tripe and meninges. You can, I imagine, find much the same things in any number of other towns in Europe and elsewhere, but Valencia is the only place that I have seen them. Leonid lived in the Hotel Inglés in Valencia during much of the Spanish Civil War and sometimes when I think of him there, I think of the food market and its distressing wares.

He was generally known as General Kotov, Leonid Alexandrovich Kotov, and his codename was Pierre. To some he posed as a military attaché, but officially he was the deputy chief of the NKVD in Spain and at the end the chief. 'The Spanish Republic', Eric Hobsbawm said sixty years later, 'remains the only political cause which, even in retrospect, appears as pure and compelling as it did in 1936.' Part of the reason, it seems fair to say, is that 'our side' lost. And Leonid was one of those who would eventually help it to lose.

Leonid's boss, Alexander Orlov – codename Shved, Party name Nikolsky, real name Feldbin – arrived in Spain in early September 1936, some six weeks after the war began. Leonid's stepdaughter, Zoya, dismisses Orlov as 'an ordinary military man' but he wasn't very ordinary, as we shall see. Leonid presumably got there around the same time.

Leonid, now thirty-seven, was accompanied by a different 'wife': Alexandra Kochergina (Shura), an officer in the GPU – 'an attractive brunette', as General Sudoplatov amiably remembers her. She worked in the visa section; and since everyone who came to Spain to join the International Brigades had to surrender their passport, I take it to mean that Kochergina was part of the team that recycled passports for future NKVD use: Ramón Mercader probably used one to travel to Mexico. Orlov's wife, too, had come to Spain and was living outside Valencia with their daughter. In July 1938 the Orlov family relocated to North America – I haven't used the word 'defected' because the issue is still vexed. That was when Leonid took charge.

Stalin had been slow to announce his intention to intervene on behalf of the Spanish Republic, but when he did it was in stirring terms. 'Liberation of Spain from the yoke of the fascist reactionaries is not the private concern of Spaniards alone, but the common cause of all progressive humanity,' he said in an open letter to Spanish Communists. No one today would be taken in by such high-sounding sentiments, but if Stalin had some sense of what he was expected to do and to say it was in part at least thanks to Trotsky, who within days of the war's beginning was denouncing him as the 'liquidator and traitor of the Spanish revolution' for his failure to take a stand.

Saving the Republic was never Stalin's paramount aim. He sent advisers and matériel (and pilots to fly the Soviet planes and crews to man the Soviet tanks), but he was preoccupied with thoughts of purging the Red Army and didn't commit troops: the International Brigades were mustered in their stead. The Republican army would be taken in hand by high-level Russian generals – more than four thousand Red Army non-combat personnel are thought to have been in Spain in a variety of guises – and members of the Comintern kept a firm grip on the thirty-five thousand international volunteers.

Yet by December 1936 there were already those like Gerald Brenan who were wondering whether Stalin's idea had been to save the Republic or destroy it. In post-Soviet Russia you can still hear it said that it all turned out for the best. In General Sudoplatov's proud words: 'The Spanish Republicans lost, but Stalin's men and women won.'

Materially, the intervention would cost Stalin little. The arrival of Russian tanks and aircraft in Spain coincided almost to the day with the departure for Odessa of 70 per cent of Spain's gold reserves, the fourth-largest in the world. It was Artur Stashevsky, the commercial attaché (one of Motty's Moscow friends), who suggested to Juan Negrín, then the Spanish Finance Minister, that the gold be sent to Russia for safekeeping, the theory being that it could be used to pay for Soviet weapons etc., and what was left re-exported to Spain whenever the Spanish government asked for it back.

Those at any rate were the terms of the agreement. The gold, worth between five and six hundred million dollars at 1936 values, travelled from Odessa to Moscow in an armoured train. When it arrived in the capital Stalin is supposed to have said that 'the Spaniards would no more see their gold again than see their own ears'. Later when the Spanish government – which by then was Franco's government – asked for the gold to be returned they were told that the gap between the five hundred tons of gold sent to Russia and the cost of the equipment sent to Spain was too small to be worth considering.

Twenty years later Orlov was to tell a US Senate Judiciary Committee that the 'gold operation' had been entrusted to him 'personally' by Stalin, but Orlov was a mysterious man, or a man of mystery who told good stories.* In the account he gave to the US Senate it took sixty Spanish sailors three nights to load the crates onto four Russian steamships, which then headed out into the Mediterranean from the port of Cartagena with an escort of Spanish warships. There was a discrepancy between the Spanish and the Russian tallies – 7,800 crates as against 7,900 – but Orlov thought it best not to point that out until he got to Russia and there no one was interested: Stalin, Orlov said, 'probably decided he could use a hundred boxes of gold'.

In 1937 Leonid and Orlov were both decorated, Orlov with the Order of Lenin, Leonid with the Order of the Red Banner: for the Spanish gold was the general assumption. For persuading Negrín and Largo Caballero, the prime minister, to give it up? For getting it safely to Moscow? The precise achievement is not spelled out. That's how it was with medals awarded to GPU personnel: the mission was secret – the medal compounded the mystery. The gold operation had, it's true, worked out well (especially if Stalin got the benefit of those extra boxes), but it's also possible that the medals were awarded for

* US Subcommittee to Investigate the Administration of the Internal Security Act. Testimony of Alexander Orlov, September 1955 and February 1957.

something more sinister that Orlov and Leonid had both been involved in.

In the early 1990s I met Leonid's son Vladimir in Galway. There is a business school attached to Galway University, and Vladimir was there with a view to setting up something similar at his university in Voronezh. I was there because he'd promised to talk to me about his father. In the immediate post-Soviet period it was usual to talk about public servants such as Leonid via their medals. I'd done it many times before, though never with Vladimir. 'Red Banner: Spain,' he began.

'For what in Spain?' I asked.

Vladimir: 'In every document it's written "for fulfilling a task". Let's say he was a senior adviser in the special services and he assisted in specific tasks.'

'Which tasks?'

Vladimir: 'Why do you need to know?'

'He believed that everything he did was for the good of his country,' I replied. 'One should be proud . . .'

Vladimir: 'Without doubt. But is pride necessarily connected with the need to specify?'

Without Russian assistance, without their generals, their 'advisers' and their weapons, it's unlikely that the Republic would have been able to repel the Nationalist assault on Madrid in November 1936. But if the capital was saved thanks to the Russians, it nonetheless remained under siege for another two and a half years, and as time went on there was less and less to be grateful to the Soviets for. The Spanish government and with it the Soviet Embassy moved to Valencia that autumn: Leonid shuttled between the two cities. Later, the embassy would move to Barcelona.

The NKVD was engaged from the outset in a war on two fronts: against Franco and the Nationalist forces and, increasingly as time went on, against the 'Trotskyists' among the Republicans and the International Brigades. The war against the Nationalists – the storied war, the war Hemingway wrote about – took the form largely of guerrilla action behind enemy lines. A group of fifty men (or men and women) might attack heavily guarded military installations (airfields, ammunition dumps) and if necessary fight their way out. Or a small group of nine or ten might dash into enemy territory, do what they had to do – cut supply lines, derail a train or blow up a bridge: think *For Whom the Bell Tolls* – and dash out. Had Robert Jordan ever existed, Stanley Payne points out, 'he would have been working for Orlov and the NKVD'. Or for Leonid, who was in charge of day-to-day operations as well as devising the overall strategy.

In fact – well, in Orlov's telling, or rather his biographer's – Leonid took Hemingway round one of the guerrilla training camps ('a small token of recognition for the extensive efforts Hemingway had expended for the Republican cause'), showed him 'every phase of the training' and organised 'a lunch that would tantalise even a gourmet chef'.* Hemingway, Orlov reports, 'was beside himself'. 'The Commies acted like a bunch of filthy swine in Spain,' Hemingway would say in subsequent years,† but at the time he admired their spirit and their discipline, and compared

---

* Edward P. Gazur, *Secret Assignment: The FBI's KGB General.*
† Quoted in José Luis Castillo-Puche, *Hemingway in Spain: A Personal Reminiscence.*

them very favourably with the 'horse thieves' in charge of the Republican forces. 'Horse thieves' is how Robert Jordan describes them. 'Was there ever a people whose leaders were as truly their enemies as this one?' he asks.

At first there were just two training camps: one in Madrid, the other at Benimamet near Valencia – the one Hemingway is supposed to have visited. 'Schools for saboteurs', Orlov called them. In 1957 he boasted to the US Senate that six schools for saboteurs had eventually been set up where foreign and Spanish Communists were taught how to reconnoitre behind enemy lines and sabotage enemy installations, 'arsenals, warships and things like that': the school in Barcelona alone, he said, had six hundred students. In his autobiography he claims that by October 1937 there were '3,200 regulars and 900 trainees in six guerrilla schools, and about 14,000 organised partisans on the territory of the enemy'. I wonder how many of these Leonid recruited for spying duty in the ranks of the NKVD.

The beauty of guerrilla warfare – in this instance at least – was the economies it afforded. Leonid didn't have to send his own men behind Fascist lines: he could contrive to send his other, undeclared enemy, the anarchists, instead. Thus when, in the dark days of the 1950s, he would be questioned about his friendship with the anarchist leader Juan García Oliver, he was able to reply that the relationship was entirely instrumental: he'd established a connection with García (he even made him a present of an American machine-gun) precisely in order to be in a position to direct anarchist forces behind Franco's lines.

*

Many people born too late have had wistful thoughts about the Spanish Civil War: first Madrid, then Barcelona was the place to be. Everyone agreed that it was intoxicating. 'All languages are spoken and there is an indescribable atmosphere of political enthusiasm, of enjoying the adventure of war . . . of absolute confidence in speedy success,' Franz Borkenau wrote in his diary in the summer of 1936. 'And everybody is friends with everybody in a minute.' By December it was evident that the fun was dissipating: that you had to be careful who you talked to and what you said; strangers were following you and some of your friends found themselves in jail for no reason they could have anticipated.

Above all, it was no longer safe in Republican-held territory to disagree with any aspect of Communist policy. Most of those non-Communists who wrote about their experience – Borkenau, Orwell, Gerald Brenan – are fierce about this. 'The Communists have got into the habit of denouncing as a Trotskyist everybody who disagrees with them about anything,' Borkenau would write the following year. And, he added, 'a Trotskyist, in Communist vocabulary, is synonymous with a man who deserves to be killed'. Orwell said the same. Martha Gellhorn took a different view: 'I am tired of explaining', she would later write, 'that the Spanish Republic was neither a collection of blood-slathering Reds nor a cat's paw of Russia.' But she wasn't right.

Leonid had his own kind of good time in Spain. Pretty dour at home, he loosened up here. The brandy, the music, the women, the sound of the balalaika at night in the camps: it was all to his liking. As the siege of Madrid dragged on most bars and restaurants closed, but at the Gaylord Hotel, where the Soviet high-ups entertained foreign journalists and each other, there was always enough vodka and caviar. He was a jolly fellow, Orlov said (Orlov evidently liked him), a rogue, a rascal, a lover of practical jokes. He learned Spanish and having, according to some, grown a beard to disguise the scar on his chin, was mistaken for a Spaniard, which was as it should be. A matter not just of official policy, of disguising from Russia's putative allies, Britain and France, the extent of the intervention: the Spaniards by and large resented the presence of so many alien and interfering Russians.

Then there is the matter of Caridad Mercader and her son. I'm not sure when he met them or how quickly he recruited them both into *los organos*, the organs of state security, but his relationship with Caridad has been a great preoccupation to historians.

Isaac Don Levine, the most lurid of Cold War historians, says of her that she was 'a woman who had plumbed all the depths of a wild and violent age'. Born in Cuba in 1892 to a liberal aristocratic father and brought to Spain as a young child, she married a minor Spanish nobleman at the age of sixteen, had five children, and 'having made life unbearable for her husband with her frivolities and hysteria', left him. That's Levine's story. Caridad's youngest son, Luis Mercader, reports in a biography of his brother Ramón that their father used to take Caridad to brothels and make her watch what went on there. And when that drove her mad, he put her in an asylum. From all this she emerged a member of the unruly left, part anarchist, part Communist, and after another rackety spell, spent mainly with sundry French Communists (she liked to tell people what Maurice Thorez, the eventual leader of the French Communist Party, looked like with no clothes on), she hurried back to Barcelona at the proclamation of the Republic in 1931.

Among the first to enlist in the Republican cause, she had made a name for herself by saving the Nationalist general Goded from the fury of the mob on the second day of the uprising. Wounded, she was despatched – by Leonid, I presume – to Mexico. Officially she was there to gather support for the Republic but she arrived not long after the Mexican president had agreed to give Trotsky asylum, and when a Catalan writer shouted out, 'Bitch, you've come to prepare Trotsky's assassination,' she replied rather carelessly: 'Who knows?' Whether or not that was her purpose, the knowledge of Mexico she acquired then would have stood her and Leonid in good stead later on.

That isn't something that appears to interest historians. The question on their mind is whether or not Leonid seduced her. From Robert Conquest (yes) to Walter Laqueur (no) to Hugh Thomas (yes) to Sudoplatov (no) there is scarcely anyone who holds back from giving his view. Leonid's family are adamant that there was no affair. One of his daughters told me early on that Caridad wasn't good-looking enough for her father, although every photograph, and there are many, shows a very handsome woman indeed. 'Why are they looking at you?' Luis Mercader once asked his mother. 'Because everybody has always looked at me,' she replied.

Ramón was her second son. In the first phase of the war he learned how to operate behind enemy lines; in the second, less heroic phase he was still at Leonid's side, training foreign volunteers to keep an eye on each other. David

Crook, for example, a young English Communist charged with monitoring Orwell's activities, received his instruction from him. Luis Mercader reports that Ramón worshipped Leonid. Once, Ramón told Luis, when Leonid sent a group of guerrillas behind enemy lines in Guadarrama and they had trouble getting back, Leonid climbed up on a tank and drove across the lines on his own to distract the enemy and allow his men to make their way back to safety. It would be fair to say in Leonid's favour that he didn't stand on ceremony. Or, as Sudoplatov puts it, 'He had none of the pretensions of a high-ranking bureaucrat.' He was, Luis remarks, *un tío enormemente capaz y valiente*. Or still more encomiastically: a *tipo humano verdaderamente excepcional* – 'truly exceptional'.

In the summer of 1937 Ramón left Spain for Moscow, where he remained until he unlearned to be Ramón Mercader, unlearned to speak Spanish or to think about Spain; and became instead Jacques Mornard, a Belgian playboy cum businessman, who spoke such perfect French and such fluent American English that it wouldn't occur to the friends he was about to acquire that he wasn't a native French speaker who had spent time in the States. Once that had been achieved he joined his mother who was waiting for him in Paris and in due course travelled to the States and then to Mexico on a Canadian passport in the name of Frank Jacson.

Trotsky set sail for Mexico in December 1936, around the time that Stalin's attention began to shift away from the wider European aspect of the conflict in Spain, the war against Franco and his backers, to his own war against the Spanish left: against the anarchists and the socialists but, above all, against the POUM, the party whose criticisms of Stalin were the most virulent. Since none of these groups took the Moscow line, they were all considered enemies, potential traitors, potential followers of Trotsky. The fact that the number of self-declared Trotskyists in Spain was exceedingly small was neither here nor there. Nor did it matter that Andrés Nin, the leader of the POUM, and once Trotsky's secretary, had broken with him. At the end of the year articles denouncing the POUM began to appear in Soviet newspapers.

Moscow had effectively taken the decision to rid the world of 'Trotskyists' three months earlier, when Yezhov took over as the People's Commissar for Internal Affairs, i.e. as head of the NKVD. By the new year the clean-up had spread to Spain. Where before Stalin had sought only to destabilise his Spanish enemies, he now wanted to see them liquidated, and the revolution suppressed. Communist appointees took over the Republican army while Orlov and Co. took over the Republic's secret police. The Russian ambassador, more a viceroy than a common or garden diplomat, so overstepped the mark that Largo Caballero, still (though only just) prime minister, kicked him out: 'Out you go, out!' he expostulated. 'You must learn, Señor Ambassador, that the Spaniards may be poor and need aid from abroad, but we are sufficiently proud not to accept that a foreign ambassador should try and impose his will on the head of the Spanish government.' The ambassador returned to Moscow and was shot.

Not only did the Communists dominate the various Republican police forces: they filled the prisons with their own enemies. More ominously, the NKVD had secret prisons of their own, where socialists, Republicans and anarchists were taken to be tortured or shot as spies or traitors. There was even a secret crematorium which made it possible for the NKVD to dispose of its victims without leaving any trace of their remains. The agent in charge of the crematorium was a twenty-seven-year-old Spanish Communist from Salamanca whom Leonid had recruited the previous year.

As the war against the Spanish left accelerated, a number of members of the non-Communist left from other countries, people sympathetic to the POUM, Trotskyists, real and imaginary, were brought to Spain to die. Spain was in that sense a useful dumping ground, easy to get to unobserved, by sea via Marseille or through the Pyrenees. Erwin Wolf, for example, another former secretary of Trotsky's, was murdered (under Leonid's direction), as was the Austrian socialist Kurt Landau. Some were got rid of not because they were enemies but because they knew too much or had failed to perform satisfactorily – and it wasn't always possible to know which reason applied. Mostly these people arrived in Spain from France, where the NKVD was well installed and where Leonid is known to have had many contacts, but in France it was difficult to lose people without attracting attention. In Spain it couldn't have been easier.

Most of Leonid's family – Vladimir is the exception – believed, or wanted to believe, that all his time in Spain had been spent fighting the Fascists. At any rate that's what they told me he did. The killings, they said, had been Trotsky's work. But when later on Leonid was recommended for promotion what counted was the effort he'd put into the struggle against the 'Trotskyists' and the part he'd played 'in a series of special operations'. 'How many people did Leonid liquidate in Spain?' handsome Mr Prelin, the PR man from the Lubianka, asked rhetorically and then answered his own question: 'Tens of agents, people suspected of betrayal. No one will speak about that because no one knows. In intelligence work nothing is ever fully open – witnesses lie too.' In Galway Vladimir told me that as a 'senior adviser in the special services' his father 'had helped them do what they had to do.' That, he said, vague as ever, is what he got his medal for.

On 3 May 1937 the Communists moved on the Barcelona telephone exchange, held by the anarchists since the day the war began. The fighting lasted five days – and several hundred people died in the course of it. There may have been some local provocation but if there was it was the excuse the Communists were waiting for. Insisting that the crisis had been caused by Nationalist agents among the anarchists and above all in the POUM (Orlov had forged documents to show that the party was 'a German-Francoist spy organisation'), they banned *La Batalla*, its newspaper, closed its headquarters in Barcelona and turned them into a prison for 'Trotskyists', disbanded its battalions at the front and arrested forty members of its central committee. Nin, one of the best-known people in the Spanish revolutionary movement and one of the most fierce in his denunciations of Stalin, was taken off separately, while his friends were placed in underground dungeons in Madrid and Barcelona – if the husbands couldn't be found the wives were taken in their place. Curiously, it's reported that García Oliver, Leonid's anarchist friend, now Spain's Minister of Justice, was in Moscow in April/May 1937; and every time he announced that it was time for him to return to Spain he was held up by yet another invitation to dine at the Savoy Hotel.*

Legalistic as always, or simply anxious to believe in their own righteousness, Nin's assailants were determined that he should confess to being a Fascist agent before they killed him. He refused and his death is in every account horrific even by the standards then current. When he was finally dead a group of German 'volunteers' got up in Gestapo uniform charged into the house where he'd been murdered to fake a rescue, leaving a few German banknotes behind to make it seem genuine.

The operation is credited to Orlov 'and his men'. Leonid's presence is never mentioned and I would like to think he wasn't there. But this was a crucial operation from the Soviet point of view, the culmination of twelve months of propaganda and persecution, so when Vladimir says that his father received the Order of the Red Banner for 'fulfilling a task' but won't say what the task was, it occurs to me to wonder whether assisting in the elimination of Nin rather than arranging the safe passage of Spain's gold was the 'specific' task in question. Stalin wouldn't have underestimated the value to the Soviet Union of Spain's gold reserves, and it's more likely that that was the action the medal rewarded. But news of Nin's death would have brought its own kind of pleasure.

The trial of Stalin's generals began in Moscow on 11 June 1937. In Spain there were no trials: foreigners and agents were murdered on the spot – shot in the back of the head most often – while Soviet officials were summoned to

* Walter Krivitsky, *I Was Stalin's Agent.*

Moscow and not heard from again. Antonov-Ovseenko, the consul-general in Barcelona; General Berzin, the head of the military mission (who'd once complained that Orlov and the NKVD were treating Spain as a colony not an ally); Stashevsky, who'd had the idea of shipping out the Spanish gold; Mikhail Koltsov, the *Pravda* correspondent: each of these had been the recipient of Stalin's gratitude and was subsequently recalled and murdered. 'Everyone felt the danger, everyone was actually trembling,' Orlov told the US Senate.

Orlov wasn't summoned until the following year. In the account he gave to the Senate there were two attempts to do away with him. First a telegram from Moscow informed him that the Nationalists were plotting something against him and twelve guards were on their way from Russia to protect him. Understanding the guards' real purpose, Orlov, as he put it, 'sent Eitingon to the front, to the German international brigade with an order to pick out ten guards who would be my personal body-guard'. Some months later a telegram came from Yezhov, commanding him to go to Antwerp for a conference on board a Soviet ship with someone – not named – whom he knew 'personally'. His staff, Leonid included, immediately understood the import of the telegram and mindful of the fate of Antonov-Ovseenko and the rest, Orlov made his way instead to Paris and from there to Canada and the United States.

The astonishing thing about Orlov's case is that he left the Service, to all intents and purposes defected, wrote a book – admittedly after Stalin's death, but Stalin had successors – called *The Secret History of Stalin's Crimes*, yet survived for another thirty-five years and died in his bed of natural causes. Not only that. Andrew and Mitrokhin report that for several years before his death the KGB tried to persuade him to return to a 'comfortable flat' and a 'generous pension' in Russia. The point being to show that he wasn't a defector – merely himself a victim of Stalin's crimes.

To Luis Mercader, Orlov was *un ruso muy simpático y muy alegre* (a cheery sort), but the historian Antony Beevor describes him as 'the most terrifying adviser to come to Spain'. He was short and fat with a small, unbecoming moustache and an explosive manner: physically less imposing than Leonid, less rugged, less ready to jump on a tank. Kirill Khenkin, an on-and-off official of the NKVD and a slippery raconteur, describes coming to Orlov's office in the Hotel Metropole in Valencia: 'I was amazed at how well-groomed he was. He had just shaved and doused himself with eau de Cologne. He was wearing morning dress: flannel trousers and a silk shirt without a tie. At his belt was a 7.65 Walther pistol in an open suede holster.' What really got to Khenkin, however, was 'the lavish breakfast wheeled in on a trolley by a white-coated servant' – and the fact that he was offered none of it.

That Orlov was well thought of even before he went to Spain is evident from his having been the *rezident* in London at a time when the UK was seen as the Soviet Union's main adversary (he was also, briefly, a minder for the illustrious British contingent, Burgess, Philby and Maclean). Of his time in Spain he later told the FBI that his position as NKVD chief 'made him the top Soviet official'; and every history of the Civil War that I've seen confirms his power and importance. But his most striking achievement was to have got out and survived to tell his story, or a version of it, in *Life* magazine a month after Stalin died.

As far as I know, he was the only intelligence operative whose decision to leave the service was determined not by moral repugnance, self-hatred or simple disillusionment but by a fine assessment of his own best interests. Which causes one only to wonder why his colleagues didn't see things the same way. Why did they believe that Stalin or Yezhov or their own local boss would believe them when they hadn't believed anyone else?*

Orlov knew that every other NKVD defector had sooner or later died a violent death at the hands of his colleagues. He secured his own survival by writing a letter to Yezhov warning him that he had deposited with his lawyer an account of everything he knew about Soviet espionage which would be made public should he in turn find himself the object of NKVD surveillance or should he learn that any harm had come to his remaining relatives in the USSR.† Orlov had had his fingers in many pies and he had no trouble reminding Stalin and Yezhov of that. His letter,

* 'Strange as it may seem,' Orlov wrote, 'the feeling of one's own innocence and the expectation of justice towards oneself happens to be strong in a person, even when he sees that justice is being rudely violated in respect of others. Many of the NKVD officers hoped that if they returned to the Soviet Union voluntarily, at a time when their comrades were being exterminated, they would have given Stalin the strongest proof of their loyalty to his regime, and he would do them no harm.'

† 'Of all the motives which kept NKVD officers from breaking with Moscow,' Orlov wrote in *The Secret History of Stalin's Crimes*, 'the most decisive was the fear of reprisals against their parents and other close relatives. All of them knew the extraordinary law introduced by Stalin on 8 June 1934, which decreed that if a man in military service fled abroad, his closest relatives were subject to deportation to the remotest regions of Siberia . . . if an officer of the NKVD fled the country or failed to return from a mission abroad his closest relatives were liable to imprisonment for ten years, and in those cases where the officer had disclosed state secrets, they were liable to the death penalty.'

astutely designed to trouble the two men, in its references to Trotsky especially, was backed up with a two-page appendix detailing the operations in which he had taken part in various countries.

There are different theories as to why the stratagem worked. The most straightforward, though least likely, is that Stalin couldn't find Orlov as he hopped from lodging to lodging. More interesting is the possibility that Orlov and Stalin were playing a game with each other. Or – more plausibly – that Orlov was playing a game with Stalin and that Stalin quite enjoyed it. Orlov, it seems, was and wasn't on Stalin's side. If he never revealed what the FBI considered 'significant information', thereby making it possible, as the NKVD's files record, for a number of agents to resume working for Moscow within a few months of his disappearance, it's because he could see the importance of keeping a few cards up his sleeve – there was no way of knowing when he might have to remind Stalin of his existence.

I asked Nikolai Khokhlov, a more straightforward defector living in the US, what he made of Orlov's disappearance. 'You should think about the psychological upheaval that people in a situation like that go through,' he said. 'For foreign intelligence services they are always traitors. Even when they are met with open arms. That is just a pretence. In reality it's almost a brotherhood between the intelligence officers, especially the high-ranking officers of the West and the East, and while they have to do their job and feud and go to the Cold War they think that somehow they are colleagues in a profession. So they don't have much sympathy for those who cross over. And Orlov knew that. So for him what Western intelligence thought of him was much less important than what Stalin would do. So he kept sending Stalin discreet and indiscreet messages to make him understand that he would tell only a small part of what he knew. And exceptionally Stalin got the message. In this sense Orlov was in-between. He didn't really come over to the West. He left and he had nowhere to go but where he went.'

The Soviet version was simpler. 'Do you remember Orlov?' I asked General Sudoplatov, the first time I met him, when handsome Mr Prelin was filming him in his flat.

'Of course, that bastard,' he replied. 'Traitor. Thief. He stole fifty thousand US dollars and escaped with it. That's how I remember him.'

Prelin: 'He wrote a lot of lies.'

Sudoplatov: 'Yes, he gave himself the title of general though he never was one.'

I don't know what Leonid thought. Orlov and he had a last brandy together on the eve of Orlov's departure, and as Orlov tells it, everything was understood between them and nothing was said. He left expecting Leonid to be recalled in his turn, and it's possible to guess but hard to know why he wasn't.

Franco celebrated the defeat of the Republic with a victory parade through Madrid in May 1939. Leonid had gone by then, taking care only that La Pasionaria and the few members of the Republican government whom the Russians still favoured got out safely too. You can catch a glimpse of him in Volume IV of the Soviet writer Ilya Ehrenburg's memoirs. It's late January 1939; the Russian Embassy in Barcelona has been evacuated and the files are being thrown onto a bonfire by Leonid and another comrade. Ehrenburg isn't fond of Leonid – 'the man who was known as Kotov filled me with a certain mistrust; he was neither a diplomat nor a soldier' – and feels that he is enjoying his task more than he should be, especially when he picks up one of Ehrenburg's books and remarks: 'I'd better cede the cremation rites to the author.'

Franco's revenge was fearsome – some two hundred thousand Republican prisoners were shot – and among Republicans feelings ran so high that a guerrilla war against him and his regime persisted throughout the 1940s and 1950s, while in every European army there was a substantial contingent of Republican refugees who'd chosen to rejoin the battle against the Axis powers. Many Spaniards who'd sought refuge in France joined the Resistance; others, Largo Caballero among them, were rounded up by the Vichy milice and sent to Germany as slave labour. A number of those who had worked alongside the NKVD in Spain, and therefore knew what the Russians had been up to, were summoned to Moscow in the course of the war and shot there and then. Others were taken in by Russia as ordinary refugees and would serve under Leonid in the partisan war against Hitler.

Leonid had always had plenty to do outside Spain. He was a more experienced traveller than Sudoplatov, and helped him zigzag his way back to Russia after an important assassination in Rotterdam in May 1938 (Sudoplatov, who was always very grateful for that, remembered Leonid in southern France dressed as 'an ordinary French street pedlar without a necktie, wearing his beret no matter how hot it was' – only the string of onions appears to be missing). In the late summer of that year he met Guy Burgess in

Paris. But as always there are a great many things that aren't known for sure: whether or not it was he who arranged for Skoblin to be murdered in Spain in 1937, or who masterminded the demise of his former colleague from Constantinople, Georgi Agabekov, at the hands of the unnamed Turk in Paris in 1938, or the death of Trotsky's German translator, Rudolf Klement, whose headless corpse was washed ashore on the banks of the Seine in August that year.

Klement, the designated secretary of the Fourth International, was murdered before the group's founding conference even took place.* Held in Paris that September, the conference was a tribute to the NKVD's organising skills. The secretary was already dead and the Russian section was represented by Mark Zborowski, the NKVD minder and probable killer of Trotsky's son Lev Sedov. At least the interpreter, a young American called Sylvia Ageloff, was a genuine follower of Trotsky, but she'd been targeted by the NKVD and somewhere outside the meeting room her new boyfriend was waiting for her to come out. He was the dashing Jacques Mornard, a.k.a. Ramón Mercader.

Ageloff wasn't glamorous and nothing in her life had led her to expect attentions such as Mornard lavished on her: the flowers and clothes that he bought her, the visits to nightclubs and restaurants to which he treated her and her friends. No one could make him out: who was he, what did he want, why did he hang out with a group of Trotskyites when he appeared not to know anything about Trotsky or the theory of permanent revolution? Sometimes it seemed that he was going to say something but then he

---

* The Fourth International was founded by Trotsky's supporters in opposition to the Comintern, the Third International.

thought better of it and didn't. He told them he'd been in the Belgian army but deserted out of boredom. Was he just an inoffensive young man, they wondered, an innocent, a playboy? No one was sure, but before setting off for the States, he said, alarmingly, to one of Ageloff's friends: 'Mon vieux, si tu savais ce que je vais faire maintenant.'

'When the Spanish Civil War ended,' Sudoplatov would write, 'there was no room left in the world for Trotsky.'

CHAPTER 24

Success

Trotsky had been living abroad for well over a decade when the Spanish Civil War ended. Stalin, you could say, had been patient. However constricted Trotsky's circumstances, however close the watch, he was still alive, still working, still missing no chance to denounce Stalin in print. But the international situation was now pressing, and Stalin wouldn't wait any longer.

Sudoplatov was given the order in March 1939. He had by now overtaken Leonid in the NKVD hierarchy. Though eight years younger, and never, as Leonid had been, a young star – Leonid was a captain with three stripes when Sudoplatov was only a lieutenant, an agent with a big reputation when Sudoplatov was still a young lad – he had stayed in Moscow steadily climbing the Party ladder, while Leonid was outside the country travelling from engagement to engagement. As Sudoplatov was to say, Leonid was a fighter, a *boevik*: 'He could take on an armed man.' On top of that, he was a graduate of the Frunze Academy and unlike Sudoplatov he had military experience, acquired first in the Civil War in Russia and lately in Spain. Sudoplatov was more diplomatic, smoother, better-looking. As Zoya put it, he 'loved to go and see the bosses': 'Idu k samomu,' he would say. Or: 'Ya poshel na tretii.' Or: 'Edu v Kreml.' ('I'm going to see Himself'; 'I went up to the third floor';*

* Stalin's private apartment was on the third floor of the Kremlin.

'I'm going to the Kremlin.') The memory sticks in her mind, or her throat.

Accompanied this time by the fearsome Beria, Sudoplatov entered the Kremlin building, took the stairs to the second floor and walked down the long wide carpeted corridor. He remembers the occasion in detail, as he does all his meetings with Stalin. 'I felt I could hear my heart beating when Beria opened the door and we entered a reception room so huge it made the three writing tables seem tiny.' Stalin got up, shook their hands and motioned them to sit down as he 'began to pace back and forth in his soft Georgian boots'.

Then he sat down opposite them and spoke. I doubt that he used the exact clichés that Sudoplatov puts in his mouth, but his meaning, as he came to the point, would have been clear: he'd had enough of Trotsky's vitriol, of his sway – of his existence. He wanted him dead: dead within a year, dead before war broke out, dead before there could be any question in anyone's mind of his return to the Soviet Union as the more competent war leader. And dead, finally, before he could finish writing the biography of Stalin he'd embarked on a few years before. It was (or may have been) 'the only occasion in history', General Volkogonov writes, 'when the sitter killed the painter before the work was done'.* Stalin more than most believed in the power of the single malevolent individual –

* A general in the Soviet army, later an adviser to President Yeltsin, and the author of biographies of Lenin, Stalin and Trotsky, written in quick succession in the late 1980s and early 1990s, Dmitri Volkogonov is much resented by more loyal post-Soviet historians, first because he gave himself access to archives no one else has had access to and second because of his 'ideological metamorphoses', as Leonid's biographer describes them – that's to say, his 'fiercely anti-Communist' views.

he was his own model – and though Trotsky may not have been as much of a threat to the Soviet Union as Hitler he compounded that threat a hundredfold. 'To build a major railroad bridge,' Stalin had said in an address to the Central Committee, 'thousands of people are needed. But to blow it up you only need a few' – and in his mind those few would be answering to Trotsky.

At least three thousand NKVD functionaries were liquidated between 1936 and 1938, the years of the Terror. Sixty per cent of those working inside the country for the NKVD's Foreign Department had been shot by the time Sudoplatov had his interview with Stalin – that's 275 out of a total of 450. Leonid's colleagues, the men and women who worked mainly abroad, were no luckier: 'After Trotskyists,' Andrew and Mitrokhin write, 'the largest number of "enemies of the people" pursued abroad by the NKVD during the Great Terror came from the ranks of its own foreign intelligence service.' (Leonid's biographer supplies a list of names, a sort of martyrology.)

Leonid himself was briefly placed under surveillance on his return from Spain in the spring of 1939 after two colleagues denounced him as an English spy. Sudoplatov too was fingered, and first threatened with expulsion from the Party, then entrusted by Stalin with Trotsky's assassination. Not a sinecure: two of his predecessors were shot for failing to get the job done.

Stalin had begun to speak about wanting Trotsky eliminated – 'bumped on the head' – in 1931 when Trotsky was still in Turkey and Leonid was on duty there. In January that year Trotsky's library was destroyed in the fire that mysteriously broke out in the house where he was living on

Prinkipo. Whether the fire was intended to destroy Trotsky himself or his archive, his ever-expanding dossier of Stalin's mistakes, is another question, as yet unresolved. Bumping on the head – at any rate bumping Trotsky on the head – was discussed only at the very highest level and wouldn't in 1931 have been entrusted to Leonid, still a relatively junior figure. It was Dzerzhinsky's first successor as head of state security, Vyacheslav Menzhinsky, and Menzhinsky's eventual successor, the terrifying Genrikh Yagoda, who are said to have travelled to Constantinople with assassination in mind – White émigrés would as usual be blamed – but nothing came of their visit and Trotsky moved on.

Plans were again made to kill him when he was hiding in France, his next port of call, and again came to nothing. Sergei Shpigelglas was in charge of the *agentura* there, and Yagoda instructed him to mobilise the entire station, but in June 1935 Trotsky left France for Norway unscathed, while Yagoda and Shpigelglas lost first their jobs, then their lives. Shpigelglas was shot as an enemy of the people in 1938; Yagoda was replaced by the even more terrifying Yezhov in 1936 and was tried and shot two years later, by which time Yezhov, the man who lent his name to the Terror, the Yezhovshchina, had in his turn been replaced by Beria. He would be shot a year later. By 1939, Volkogonov writes, Stalin was 'frantic'.

Entrusted with the job, Sudoplatov passed it on to Leonid. 'Bring in whoever you want,' Stalin had supposedly said, and Leonid didn't blench. 'For us,' Sudoplatov writes, 'enemies of the state were personal enemies.' Leonid's biographer makes the point that as a young man in Gomel when Trotsky was the head of the Red Army, and later at the military academy, Leonid might have met Trotsky and would certainly have looked up to him, but loyal Soviet citizens, and much more so loyal members of the NKVD, would long since have had to get used to these reversals, even learned to take them in their stride.

Leonid had spent several years in Spain, he'd introduced a number of Spaniards into the NKVD, not least Mercader, and he spoke Spanish, which Sudoplatov didn't. On his CV Leonid said he spoke it well and Orlov had said that his Spanish was 'flawless', but I wonder how well he actually spoke it: so well that he might be mistaken for a native or just well enough for no one to know that he was Russian? Might he on this assignment pass for a Mexican, or more plausibly a Spaniard? And if he wore a beret in France would he be wearing a sombrero in Mexico? And, finally, isn't it just as likely that Sudoplatov passed the job on to him because Leonid was the *boevik*, the man, as Andrew and Mitrokhin put it, with 'long experience of "special actions"', while Sudoplatov, so much more circumspect, was the one who kept in with the bosses? Still, I don't want to be unfair. Beria, Sudoplatov, Leonid, Mercader: that may have been the hierarchy but all four lives were on the line, Sudoplatov's as much as Leonid's.

Mexico had at first seemed a haven for Trotsky, the one country where officially he was welcome. The president, Lázaro Cárdenas, a sympathetic figure, a radical, though not a Communist either of Stalin's sort or of Trotsky's, had sent his own train to meet him at Tampico, when he arrived in the country as – Cárdenas insisted – the president's guest. The Communist Party, with many refugees from Spain among its members, was less keen to have him there and organised demonstrations in protest at his presence, but Cárdenas let him be, setting no restrictions on his activity, provided he didn't interfere in Mexico's domestic politics. Yet mindful of his own position, he took care never to meet Trotsky in person.

When Stalin summoned Sudoplatov to the Kremlin Trotsky had already been in Mexico for more than two years, and the surprising thing is that Stalin's patience had held out that long, his anxiety perhaps assuaged by all the proxy killings of the late 1930s. Not only were Trotsky's followers taken out one by one, so was anyone whom Stalin cared to call a follower – there were thousands of those – and so were his children, all four of them now dead, one certainly, one most probably, and two indirectly at Stalin's hand. One of the saddest things is to read in Deutscher's biography the account of his eldest son Lev Sedov's entrapment in Paris at the hands of the NKVD:

> He was, next to his father, the GPU's most important target. The feeling that he was being spied upon and that his mail was intercepted by a mysterious hand never left him. He feared that he would be kidnapped. He was lonely, defenceless, and completely dependent on the comradeship of the little band of Trotskyists around him . . . But within the narrow circle of his comrades he confided most of all in Mark Zborowski, a young and well-educated man, who had studied medicine and philosophy and who worked in the organisation under the pseudonym Etienne, helping to publish the *Bulletin* and sitting on a little Russian Committee supposed to deal with the Opposition in the USSR . . .

Such was his knack for dissimulation that he never incurred the slightest suspicion on the part of Lyova and Trotsky. And so complete was Lyova's trust in him that he held the key to Lyova's letter-box and collected the mail for him. The mysterious hand that 'intercepted' Lyova's correspondence was Etienne's. He was also in charge of the most confidential files of Trotsky's archives; he kept these in his own home.

Lyova had his appendix removed in a Russian émigré hospital in Paris in February 1938. After the operation he was fine, then suddenly he wasn't. A few months later Zborowski, the man generally held responsible for his death, was thinking of joining Trotsky's secretariat in Coyoacán.

From the Kremlin's point of view it would have been very useful. Or would have been in other circumstances. The complicating factor was Alexander Orlov, Leonid's former boss who'd jumped ship in Barcelona with a warning to Stalin of the knowledge he had and the use to which he could put it. Orlov's name comes up several times in Sudoplatov's account of the ill-starred chase after Trotsky, but whether as a genuine bogeyman or as an excuse it's sometimes hard to make out. What's certain is that sometime in 1938 Orlov – calling himself 'Stein' – wrote to Trotsky to advise him that his life was in danger.* 'Sometime' because accounts vary: it could have been May

---

* Fearful that the NKVD would trace the letter to him, Orlov took great care to disguise his identity, claiming that the warning had come to him from his 'nephew', an NKVD defector living in Japan. The defector, General Lushkov, was real enough, but he wasn't anyone's nephew, or at any rate not 'Stein's', and had never said anything about Trotsky.

(Volkogonov), the summer (Andrew and Mitrokhin) or December (Orlov's biographer). He wasn't sure where the danger would come from but mentioned two possibilities. The first was Lev Sedov's entourage in Paris and specifically someone called Mark. But Trotsky, who in any case wasn't much given to listening, knew Zborowski only as Etienne and paid little attention. In the end it didn't matter. Zborowski didn't go to Mexico. Either he was turned down by Trotsky's secretaries, warier of Etienne than Lyova had been ('When all is said and done Lyova's blindness toward Zborowski is still astonishing,' Jean van Heijenoort would write forty years later).* Or it had never been the plan. But Orlov wasn't fooling.

Not knowing Trotsky's address in Mexico, he asked – or 'Stein' asked – Trotsky to put a notice in the *Socialist Appeal*, a sympathetic New York paper, to indicate that he'd received the letter. Trotsky complied but, disbelieving and impatient, 'insisted' that 'Stein' go to the paper's

---

* Like many of his NKVD colleagues, Zborowski lived his double life with exemplary skill. After Lyova's death he became, almost unbelievably, Trotsky's main contact with his European supporters. 'While unobtrusively encouraging internecine warfare between the rival Trotskyite tendencies,' Andrew and Mitrokhin write, 'Zborowski impeccably maintained his own cover.' He fled to the US with the German invasion of France, and continued for a while to spy on Trotskyites there, while at the same time getting a job as a research assistant at Harvard. A spell in prison for perjury – denounced by Orlov, he'd denied working for the Soviets in the US – scarcely interrupted his smooth passage through American academia; he published two books, one of them, about life in the shtetl, much praised and often reprinted, and ended his life as director of the Pain Institute at Mount Zion Hospital in San Francisco. He died in 1990. That he was able to slip so easily, so much more easily than Orlov, from one life to another was due to the fact that he was, as it were, a freelance, a mere agent, while Orlov was an officer of the KGB.

offices and discuss the matter with 'Comrade Martin'. Orlov went to the paper's offices, identified 'Comrade Martin' from a distance but, put off by his 'swarthy looks', left the building without talking to him. When later he tried to contact Trotsky by phone from San Francisco Trotsky wouldn't take the call, having decided – he even laughed about it with Zborowski – that the whole 'Stein' thing was an NKVD provocation and a waste of his time. It was a serious mistake: the second possibility Orlov warned Trotsky against was 'agents provocateurs' coming to Mexico from Spain 'under the guise of Spanish Trotskyites'. Mercader fitted the bill perfectly.

The assassination was codenamed UTKA (Leonid's coinage). The word means 'duck' – 'sitting duck', we might think – but also 'disinformation', *canard*, and this, it seems, was the meaning intended: Trotsky as purveyor of slanders. Beria, Sudoplatov and Leonid considered which network of agents to use. Uncertainty about Orlov – and the beans he might spill – meant that they had no friends to call on inside Trotsky's household. Unaccountably, Beria suggested bringing Orlov himself into the picture, but Leonid demurred – he hadn't got on with him in Spain, though that isn't how Orlov remembered it, or pretended to remember it. In any case Beria, as Sudoplatov now reminded him, had said at the moment of Orlov's disappearance that there should be no further contact with him. There was some question of using Beria's own contacts in Western Europe – 'a string of Georgian princes' – but they too soon faded from view.

The plan was now settled, or nearly. There would be two groups, one to be known as HORSE, the other as

MOTHER, who would have no knowledge of each other's existence. The first centred on the Mexican painter (and loyal Stalinist) David Siqueiros, the other on Caridad Mercader and her son. Leonid, though more closely tied to the second, would be in charge of both. Siqueiros, like Mercader, had fought in Spain, and at the end of the war was, again like Mercader, kicking his heels – or getting instructions – in Paris before embarking for Mexico.

'Spare no expense,' Stalin had said, and when Sudoplatov worked out that setting the two operations in train would cost 'no less than three hundred thousand dollars', Leonid – his biographer reports – wondered whether use should be made of his family connections in the US.* A quid pro quo, Sharapov suggests: 'The Soviet authorities had granted Leonid's relatives substantial privileges at the fur auctions in Leningrad right up to 1948.' There is no mention of Leonid's relatives in the US in Sudoplatov's account or in Volkogonov's or in any other, and no sooner does Sharapov mention them than he drops the subject. Where and how, I wonder, is Motty referred to in Leonid's KGB file? What words are used and with what implication?

In June 1939, Leonid and Sudoplatov made their way to Paris to meet and assess the two groups. They started out on a train to Odessa; from there they went to Athens by boat; from Athens on a different boat, with different documents, to Marseille; and from Marseille by train to Paris. They wouldn't have wanted, I assume, to be taken for Russians, so what language did they speak to each

---

* Other sources suggest more modest amounts and some – Luis Mercader, for instance – far greater. I doubt whether anyone has had access to NKVD accounts.

other? Or did they not speak? In July Sudoplatov returned to the Soviet Union (route not specified) while Leonid stayed behind to coach Mercader and his mother in 'intelligence tradecraft': how to work a source, disguise one's appearance, recruit other agents – and crucially, in Ramón's case, sweet-talk Sylvia Ageloff. I don't know when Siqueiros went back to Mexico or who, if anyone, was responsible for his training.

In late August mother and son set sail for New York. For Leonid it was more complicated. He'd travelled in the past on all sorts of passports – very often Middle Eastern. This time he was a Pole and when, at the beginning of September, Hitler occupied Poland, he was stuck. As Sharapov puts it, 'Getting a visa to leave France, for a citizen of a state that was living its last days, was a problem.' His options – so we're told: can it be true? – were to be mobilised in the French army or interned as a foreigner. To which the only solution was the usual Soviet solution: disappearance. The Polish refugee obtained a fake residence permit, thanks to an Englishman who had connections with the French police, entered a psychiatric hospital – run by a Russian émigré doctor, a Red, I imagine – stayed there a month and re-emerged as a mentally ill Syrian Jew. The reason was simple: if you were mad you weren't allowed to serve in the army but you were allowed (encouraged?) to travel abroad. He arrived in New York a month later and in no time at all had set up an import–export company in Brooklyn, 'an area with a large Jewish population', Sharapov explains.

When I was a child, if someone was said to be in import-export it seemed to mean that no one knew exactly what they did but whatever it was it didn't amount to much. I now see why. There is no indication of what Leonid imported and exported – unless it was the money that Ramón needed to maintain his cover and pursue his courtship.

Leonid waited until November to make his first trip to Mexico. Like Trotsky, he kept away from the local Communists – other, of course, than those with whom he was conspiring. He reviewed his contacts and set up his camp – hid his documents and his money in the apartment of a Spanish refugee named Marta Meller whom he'd probably known, even recruited, even slept with in Spain – talked to Siqueiros, conferred with Caridad, and went back to New York, where he kept an eye on Ramón's relationship with Sylvia Ageloff, on occasion having supper at another table in the same restaurant, for example. The plot was inching ahead.

Ageloff had left Mercader in Paris when she went back to her family in New York in February 1939, and wouldn't see him again for another six months. Deutscher describes her as an intelligent woman, though plain (there would be other ways of saying that now), and is more interested in the fact that she'd been a student, at Columbia, of the Marxist philosopher and future anti-Communist Sidney Hook. Obviously that counted for little when she was swept off her feet by the handsome Mercader, though many things about him seemed odd to her and her friends, among them that although supposedly Belgian he didn't speak French with a Belgian accent. Then when she saw him again in New York in September that year, he was no longer the Belgian businessman-cum-playboy and bon viveur Jacques Mornard whom she'd known in Paris but, thanks to the magic powers of the NKVD, a Canadian businessman with interests in Mexico, implausibly called Frank Jacson (with the stress on the last syllable): the change of name, he said, was necessary if he was to avoid being drafted in the Belgian army. The good thing was that she could go on calling him Jacques without giving anything away.

In October Mercader left for Mexico City 'on business' (oil and sugar). On New Year's Day 1940 Sylvia joined him. They stayed together in Mercader's apartment in the Montejo Hotel and while Mercader bided his time Ageloff called on Trotsky in his house on the Avenida Viena. Her sister Ruth had been Trotsky's secretary in Mexico a few years before; she herself spoke Spanish, French and Russian as well as English: she was nice, she was useful, and, in herself, entirely trustworthy. For the next few months she would remain in Coyoacán working for Trotsky. Leonid, so Volkogonov reports, was delighted.

Mercader brought her to work every morning in his Buick Sedan and every evening he waited outside the house to pick her up and drive her home. On the one hand, the smooth young man, a bit spoiled, a bit too used to his treats, but modest and very helpful, unintrusive almost to a fault; on the other, the louche businessman who seemed to be entirely adrift in the world, with plenty of money and offices that didn't always turn out to be where he said they were. If he was dodgy, Trotsky's household concluded, at least it had nothing to do with politics.

At the end of March Ageloff returned to the States; she would be back in the summer. Before leaving she asked Mercader to promise that he wouldn't enter Trotsky's house in her absence. Was she suspicious? Maybe, but not necessarily given the aura that surrounded Trotsky and the endless danger to his life. But then one small thing led to another. She didn't hear from him for a couple of weeks. Was he all right?

Had he disappeared? Anxious, lovelorn, she asked one of Trotsky's household, Marguerite Rosmer, to get in touch with him, which Rosmer did: was perhaps pleased to do because, so it's said, she was sweet on him (it was hard not to be, he was so good-looking and so attentive); and then when Rosmer's husband had to be taken to hospital (nothing serious), it was quite natural to ask Mercader to drive him there in his Buick; and then to drive her to and from the hospital while her husband recovered. Mercader was becoming quite a familiar figure on the rim of the household and, maybe just as important, he was now able to report on the number of Trotsky's guards and the disposition of the villa's defences. Leonid will have been even more delighted.

In the early months of 1940 the Mexican Communist Party stepped up its attacks. 'Death to Trotsky, death to Trotsky': the cry punctuated every meeting. At the Party's congress in March the top leadership was purged on the grounds that it had been overtaken by Trotskyists. Documents arrived from Moscow that 'proved' the Old Man's 'treachery to the working class' and his links with German and British Intelligence; and as Volkogonov describes it, 'Notices were posted in the streets to the effect that Trotsky was organising a revolution in Mexico with the aim of establishing a Fascist dictatorship.' On May Day twenty thousand people marched through the city calling for Trotsky's expulsion.

Trotsky knew this hadn't happened by chance – that's to say, without ideological reinforcement from Moscow. Sinister characters were gathering in the city. One was Vittorio Vidali, an Italian Communist, known in Spain as Carlos Contreras, lover and possible executioner of the photographer Tina Modotti; another was Iosif Grigulevich, a mysterious figure, not often mentioned, whom Andrew and Mitrokhin describe as 'one of the most remarkable of all Soviet illegals' ('It is a measure of Grigulevich's skill . . . that though born a Lithuanian Jew he would be able to pass himself off at a later stage as a Costa Rican diplomat'). Both men are said – how can one know for sure? – to have played a part in the particularly horrible murder of Andrés Nin in Spain.

Trotsky summoned his guards to warn them that an attack was imminent. It came in the early hours of 24 May. Leonid gave the order, Grigulevich and Siqueiros led the assault.

Late in the evening of 23 May Siqueiros and some twenty of his followers, 'laughing and joking as if it were a feast day', put on a mixture of army and police uniforms, armed themselves with pistols and revolvers, and set out for the Avenida Viena. They had scaling ladders, firebombs, a saw and a machine-gun. They drove up to the villa just before 4 a.m. and unloaded. Grigulevich went up to the garage door, the only entrance to the house, and called the guard. A young American, Robert Sheldon Harte, was on duty there, as Grigulevich knew he would be. Harte unbolted the door.

Siqueiros and his men, 'animated', as Andrew and Mitrokhin put it, 'by an exuberant ideological mix of art, revolution, Stalinism and exhibitionism', burst into the house all guns firing. Natalya woke up first, then Trotsky; they realised after a moment that what they were hearing were gunshots (not fireworks, as Trotsky first thought), smelled the gunpowder, and slid to the floor. 'Clearly what we had always expected', Trotsky would say later, 'was now happening: we were under attack.' The would-be assassins, spraying Trotsky's and Natalya's bedroom with bullets from four directions (two doors, two windows), must have been sure they would get them: the Mexican police counted seventy-three bullet holes in the walls and doors alone. Splinters of glass flew into the room; plaster fell from the ceiling. Natalya shielded her husband as they crouched together in a corner of the room that the bullets somehow couldn't or didn't reach.

Then there was silence, then an explosion and a flash of light. Natalya lifted her head and saw the silhouette of a uniform standing in the doorway, 'the curve of a helmet, shining buttons, an elongated face'. The wearer raised his pistol, and fired repeatedly into the empty bed. Their grandson Seva, Zinaida's son, who was now living with them, called out, 'Dedushka' ('Grandfather'), then was silent. His bedroom was on fire. Was he dead, had he been kidnapped? At last they heard his voice coming from the patio, 'ringing out', Deutscher writes, 'like a staccato passage of music, bravely, joyously'. The raiders had run out of ammunition and left. Everyone was safe. Everyone apart from Harte, who was missing.

Harte's body was found a month later in the grounds of a farm outside Mexico City rented by two painters, Stalinists and friends of Siqueiros. Trotsky had liked him and insisted on a plaque being placed on the wall of the house 'in memory of Robert Sheldon Harte (1915–1940), murdered by Stalin'. To anyone who suggested that Harte had betrayed him, he replied that if that were the case 'he could have stabbed me on the quiet'. As often with Trotsky things were not so clear-cut. Young, a little naïve and uncertain whether to give his allegiance to Trotsky or Stalin (a portrait of Stalin hung on the wall of his apartment in New York), Harte seems to have thought that nothing more than a raid on Trotsky's archive was planned and is said to have been appalled when he understood what was happening.

Still, Trotsky was right. It was effectively Stalin who killed Harte. 'What were we supposed to do with him?' Grigulevich later asked a colleague, without wanting an answer. He couldn't stay on in Mexico to reveal to all and sundry what had happened and who had recruited him. 'After all,' Grigulevich continued, 'we would have had to hide him and then illegally take him out of Mexico. In a word, no end of trouble!' Besides, someone had to take the blame for the failure. 'Put yourself in Siqueiros's shoes,' Grigulevich concluded. 'He had telegrammed to Moscow that Bob Sheldon had betrayed them and that was why they shot into an empty bed. Moscow ordered us to shoot the traitor. Which is what we did.'

Siqueiros disappeared and the police, bemused by what had happened, by the fact that no one had even been hurt, let alone killed, in the raid, and disconcerted by Trotsky and Natalya's self-possession, took a while to be persuaded that Trotsky hadn't somehow staged the raid himself in order to discredit his opponents.* Unfazed, combative, un-

---

* Siqueiros wasn't arrested until well into the autumn. At his trial he insisted that the aim had been to destroy Trotsky's archive and administer a 'psychological shock' to the country that would make it easier finally to get Trotsky expelled. 'I never denied and still do not deny that formally, from the standpoint of the law, my participation in the attack on Trotsky's house was a crime,' he said later. 'For this I spent a long time in prison' – in fact a year – 'more than three years in exile, lost a large sum of money, paid in the form of bail, and was submitted to insulting attacks in the outside world.' In 1967 he was awarded the International Lenin Prize for 'strengthening peace among peoples'.

self-pitying, the Old Man followed the investigation with interest, appeared in court when necessary, identified Harte's body when it was found, and through it all carried on working as before.

The attack had taken place in the early hours of Friday morning. 'Fear and tequila', Grigulevich would say, though I don't know to whom, were responsible for its failure. On Sunday the bad news got through to Moscow via TASS, the Soviet news agency. Beria, 'beside himself', summoned Sudoplatov to his dacha ('he sent his car and driver for me'), but seemed not to know whom to blame. Sudoplatov, in his own account, was bland, placatory in response: no point, I imagine, in reminding Beria that he was the one who'd sent Grigulevich to Mexico to take the unruly Siqueiros in hand. The conversation was short: Beria was having lunch in his garden with the two men who would succeed him when his own turn came to be executed. Sudoplatov wasn't asked to stay.

Two days later Leonid's report arrived. Where Sudoplatov in his book blames the 'miners and peasants' who formed Siqueiros's team, Leonid blamed only himself ('Taking the entire responsibility for this nightmarish failure, I am prepared at your earliest demand to leave Mexico in order to receive the punishment due for such a failure') and promised that 'the error' would be 'corrected' in two to three weeks, though for that more money – between ten and fifteen thousand dollars – would be needed. What remains to me odd, indeed insoluble, is that they – all four of them: Stalin, Beria, Sudoplatov, Leonid – should have entrusted this key mission to such a wayward, volatile, un-Soviet figure as Siqueiros. Volkogonov in his book reports that Stalin raged at the failure of the operation. Sudoplatov in his retorts that Volkogonov was not in the room, so how could he know?

In Coyoacán new watchtowers were erected, the number of guards increased, the outside walls raised, the house itself sandbagged, and new armoured doors and steel shutters installed. 'This is not a home,' Trotsky said, 'it's a medieval prison.' Urged to go incognito to the States and live there in hiding, he refused: he wasn't going to spend the rest of his life skulking.

Mercader hadn't always been the assassin in waiting. The story is told that way because it's less embarrassing for the men in charge, and more dramatic. Or maybe – these things are so rarely clear – in the minds of Stalin and Beria, Sudoplatov and Leonid, Mercader was always the fallback killer, but not in his own: he believed he was getting to know the house for someone else's benefit, whoever that turned out to be. Still, he'd had experience of hand-to-hand combat in Spain – he knew how to do these things.

On 28 May Mercader came to the house to collect the Rosmers and drive them to the port in Veracruz: they were returning to France. While he waited he went to Seva's room, gave him a model glider and showed him how to work it. He was rewarded with an invitation to join the family at the breakfast table. It was four days after the raid and the first time that Mercader and Trotsky met face to face.

On 12 June he came round saying he was going back to New York 'on the orders of his boss' and left his car with the guards in case they wanted to use it.

He stayed in New York for a month; when he got back he didn't call at Avenida Viena for three weeks. He was not in a good mood. Had Leonid told him something he didn't want to hear? 'Usually robust and gay', Deutscher recounts, he returned from the States 'nervous and gloomy; his complexion was green and pale; his face twitched; his hands trembled. He spent most of his days in bed, silent, shut up in himself; refusing to talk to Sylvia.' When he did go out he said disconcerting things that people would afterwards brood over. He threatened to drive his car over a precipice, with friends of Trotsky's and Natalya's, Trotskyists from Minnesota, in the back; another time he boasted about his strength – he could 'split a huge ice-block with a single blow of an ice-pick'. He demonstrated his 'surgical skill' by carving a chicken with unusual dexterity, and later someone recalled that he said he'd known Rudolf Klement, whose body had been dismembered with similar 'surgical skill'. Looking at the fortifications in Coyoacán, he said they were worthless because 'in the next attack the GPU would use quite a different method'. Clearly he now knew what was expected of him.

Mercader, so I was told, never lost his affection for Leonid. Didn't – can that be right? – hold it against Leonid when Leonid warned him, as he must have done, that Caridad's life was at stake: why otherwise would Mercader have cried out, 'They've got my mother,' when Trotsky's guards set upon him? As for Mercader's own life, that wasn't much of an issue for Leonid. 'Mexico', he had assured Mercader (we know it from Volkogonov), 'is the ideal country for an act of vengeance. They don't even have the death penalty.' I wonder what 'even' is doing in that sentence.

At the end of July Mercader returned to his beat. On the 29th Natalya invited him and Sylvia to tea. They stayed for an hour while Natalya, who thought she sensed a wedding in prospect, talked to them about married life and that sort of thing.

On 1 August he drove Natalya and Sylvia on a shopping expedition.

On 8 August he came by with flowers and chocolates. He knew Trotsky was a keen climber and offered to take him on an expedition into the mountains. He was, he added, an experienced Alpinist. But he didn't push it.

On 11 August he came to collect Sylvia after dinner but on this occasion entered the house instead of waiting for her in his car.

On 17 August he arrived uninvited and told Trotsky he was preparing an article about ideological differences among his American followers – which was strange given how little interest he'd shown in politics of any kind – and wondered whether Trotsky would look over what he'd written. It was a hot day, yet he was wearing a dark suit and carrying a raincoat (he'd once boasted to Natalya that he never wore a coat even in winter). Throughout the interview he sat on Trotsky's writing table, with a commanding view of the Old Man's head inclined over the bogus typescript. This was the dress rehearsal.

Three days later he was back. He'd rewritten the article and hoped Trotsky would look at it again. As before his raincoat was draped over his arm, though there hadn't been any change in the weather. He looked poorly and both Trotsky and Natalya commented on it. Natalya offered him tea but he said his stomach was upset and asked for a glass of water instead. Grudgingly, Trotsky did what he felt he had to do – Mercader after all was Sylvia's boyfriend, practically her husband – and took him into his study. The ice-pick was out of sight under Mercader's raincoat. There was a knife in one pocket and a gun in the other.

Trotsky wasn't killed outright – either he moved his head or Mercader shut his eyes as he landed the blow – but died in hospital twenty-six hours later. At least he knew the identity of his killer and wouldn't have been wrong in surmising that Stalin had sent him.

Part Four

CHAPTER 25

Back on the Road

The FBI had first taken notice of Motty in the summer of 1942 when someone heard shooting at his place in Hillcrest Park. It appeared to be target practice, according to the Bureau's confidential informant, who saw two men and a woman firing off a Winchester or a Remington. It was an odd report and it's difficult to know what to make of it.

> On July 16, 1942 Confidential Informant[ ]by letter, fur-
> nished additional information, which indicated that he had
> seen two men and a woman with two guns firing at a temporary
> target set up against a slope of a hill on the EITINGON es-
> tate. These people fired from thirty to forty-five rounds
> with guns, one of which appeared to be a Winchester or Reming-
> ton pump, using .22 calibre shorts, and the other gun seemed
> to be some type of special target gun which shot twenty-two
> shorts.   ALL INFORMATION CONTAINED

Certainly it's hard to imagine Motty trying to fire a gun. What's more likely is that he had 'invited' a few Soviet citizens to stay in his house while he was away and in his absence his guests were doing the genuine American thing – having fun with a gun. Another local had already drawn the attention of the police to the fact that Motty, 'a Russian Jewish furrier', had been hosting parties, or possibly meetings, late at night, and that cars had been seen leaving the house at unusual hours. Theodore Draper told me he was certain that Motty 'was involved' with the Soviets. 'What would he have done?' I asked. 'He had a big house,' was the first thing Draper said in reply.

*

With the ending of the Hitler–Stalin Pact the Soviet Union was no longer so monstrous in the American imagination. Even Stalin was becoming the avuncular, heroic and astute figure that the Party had devised for domestic consumption. When Averell Harriman returned from Moscow in the autumn of 1941, having led a US delegation in tripartite talks with Britain and the Soviet Union, he couldn't stress enough how great the Leader was. The fur workers too were now in solidarity with their bosses against Fascism. That October, management and unions in New York raised one hundred thousand dollars in a matter of weeks for British and Soviet War Relief: one of the rare drives in which Motty's name didn't feature.

Things had seemed to go well in the fur industry at the start of the war. In 1940, the year Eitingon Schild went under, there'd been a rise in fur imports to the US. But 'foreign styling' was out, 'a thing of the past', the *New York Times* asserted. 'American furriers are on their own. And they say this is going to be one of the biggest seasons in years.' In 1942, a few months after Pearl Harbor, the *Wall Street Journal* declared that 'war has made New York City the fur capital of the world, replacing London'.

But it didn't work out as well as the optimists had hoped. First the prices went up. Then the industry went into a slump. It wasn't a case of shortages. Russia's entry into the war made little difference to the volume of skins being exported. Women and children continued trapping and large shipments of Russian furs left the Far East for the Pacific ports of America. Nor did the downturn have to do with the excise tax that was slapped on luxury fur in 1944. The same 20 per cent was levied on jewellery, but the jewellers' businesses did well. Nobody quite knows why the quality furriers took such a hit.

It was Motty who unexpectedly gave the disabled, war-weary market a fillip. According to *Fortune* magazine, a new company known as Motty Eitingon Inc., constituted in 1943, and Holt Renfrew, a major dealer in Montreal, were collaborating on a joint purchase of Russian fur.* By 1944 they had formed a syndicate to take what must have been some magnificent furs off Amtorg, beginning with a quantity of sables – seven thousand in all, for which the syndicate paid just under a million dollars, a bit of a bargain, even at the time.

The syndicate stimulated high street sales and reawakened the sense that it was good to be glamorous. It was an encouraging moment for a man who'd lately experienced a setback to his multimillion-dollar profile, if not to his irrepressible way of going about things.

I have a photo of Motty taken probably in the early 1940s, when we were living quite close to him at the house with blue pines on Shippan Point. He's wearing a short-sleeved linen shirt with two parallel rows of large white buttons, giving the effect of an apron, or a smock. He is sitting in a deckchair with his big hands around a ledger from which the edge of an airmail envelope is peeping out.

---

* It seems that the deal with Holt Renfrew dated back to the end of 1939, because on 12 January 1940 my father wrote to his parents: 'Motty called us last night from NY to tell us that he'd just made arrangements to do business with Holt Renfrew, the biggest fur people in Canada, and also two other parties, all of which will enable him to go ahead on a bigger scale again.' (Maybe one of the other 'parties' was a 'very wealthy Russian' enthusiastically mentioned by my father in a letter written the previous week.) 'Now', my father added, 'he will have enough working capital to go ahead again, and he was very happy over the confidence' – that again – 'these people showed him.'

He's smiling up at someone, the smile revealing a very good, large set of teeth and causing the eyes to pucker: it's the position of the lower eyelids, not the upper ones, that the smile seems to have changed. There is what must have been a trademark gleam in the eyes, something very endearing and . . . charming. Motty would have been in his late fifties and there isn't much hair to speak of. The face is in general big, the features also big, especially the nose and ears, and the overall effect is fairly irresistible. I've looked at this photo now and then, and come to feel that despite the frankness of expression and the openness of the face itself, this is a portrait of an unknowable person. I don't mean that something inconceivable was hidden away behind the affability – a long career in espionage, for instance, or murder, or adultery. Only that charm is a way for a person not to be there. It stands in for character, and once character has been off duty for a few years, it may abscond completely and let someone else sign the cheques or deal with the person at the door.

Sometime in 1943, at the height of the American–Soviet alliance and without any prompting from his neighbours, the FBI too began to feel that Motty had unsavoury connections. If you'd looked up his businesses in the Manhattan phone directory after the war – and after the virtual demise of Eitingon Schild – you would have discovered a bewildering array of trading names listed at the premises on West 30th Street, including the old company itself, which was kept in a state of dormancy. But there were also Motty Eitingon Inc. and Motty Eitingon & Co., and a third which was of special interest to the FBI: Eitingon, Gregory and Jaglom Inc.*

* After resigning from Eitingon Schild Motty became president of Eitingon-Gregory Inc., wholesalers and importers of skins. The company

George Gregory, the partner in this company, was a factor, I think – he lent money to fur dealers and fur manufacturers. His original name was Gregori Josefowitz, according to the FBI, 'a native of Lithuania', and he'd cropped up in connection with another of the Bureau's espionage inquiries, perhaps as a friend or acquaintance of still another person under scrutiny. This is very much how it went with the files, one name leading to another, as it does in the most mundane police investigation. So here was Motty's name next to Gregory's. Then, of course, there was Hoellering, and quite possibly Blitzstein ('quite possibly', because so many of the names are blacked out), and the fact that Motty and Bess were friends with Paul Robeson and his wife.

Within a year of Motty's case being 'originated', the Bureau had a sizeable file on the go. It would be closed and reopened several times but would change very little over the years. Quite the opposite: with Motty's files as with Leonid's, repetition is of the essence, and by reading them through, subjecting oneself to the tedium of the same story, or the same allegation, reiterated six or seven times, one begins to see American anti-Communism, and its Soviet counterpart, in a new light – as cults modelled on other cults, sacralised forms of words.

---

was constituted under New York laws in February 1940. Eitingon-Gregory merged with Gregory-Eitingon Factoring Corporation, formed under New York laws a day later, to form Eitingon, Gregory and Jaglom Trading Company in 1943. The merger was made in order to liquidate the business, and no sooner had it changed its name than it became inactive. Motty Eitingon Inc. had been established in the interim. In the spring of 1944 Motty became a director of Goldhill Processing, a New Jersey company whose headquarters were nonetheless where you'd have expected them to be, in Manhattan, on West 30th Street. In March 1945 a fire in the factory led to the closure of the company.

The Bureau put its investigation into a higher gear when Motty decided to travel to Latin America in the summer of 1945. In mid-July he arrived in Buenos Aires, where he planned to buy pelts, having travelled via Mexico City and Rio, and he would go back via Brazil, with a longer stopover to sort out the affairs of the cotton plantation set up before the war by my aunt Lola's husband at Motty's instigation. The Bureau's efforts to keep tabs on him were entirely pointless. Almost nothing of any significance happened, yet the trip was attended by a flurry of cable traffic between Washington, Miami and the embassies in Buenos Aires and Rio. His advent was signalled with frantic waving of arms – 'fur dealer . . . suspected of being a Russian agent', 'subject alleged to be paymaster of OGPU in US' etc., etc. – and reiterative jumping up and down, and before the trip was over, a directive went from Hoover's office to the FBI in Miami to the effect that Motty should be interrogated on his arrival in the US. It was also decided to sneak an agent in with him on the plane back to Miami.

The various reports of Motty's doings were collated within a few weeks of his return to New York. They were all uninformative and dull. The stay in Buenos Aires was especially stupefying. 'Subject made long-distance calls to Canada, New York and New Jersey.' Subject extended an invitation for friends to eat at his hotel. Subject refused invitations to go out to dinner – who was listening to his phone calls? – because he was too busy.

The report from Rio hadn't much more to say. Motty had been met at the airport by Aunt Lola's husband, Herman Pikielny, and a fur dealer who had a retail business in the city. He saw his sister Bertha, the former dentist with a practice on the Arbat, now married to Abram

Lekich, a former colleague of Motty's from Poland probably working for or with him in Brazil. He was trailed
from the airport to a hotel in Copacabana, and his activities were monitored in a desultory way: his taxis, his
lunches, his confirmation of the onward flight to Miami. It
was all a bit like a corporate accounts department running
a check on one of their managers' expense claims. It certainly lacked the whoosh of a respectable spy chase.

The agent who boarded Motty's flight for Miami insin-
uated his way into Motty's vicinity and they conversed.
Motty spoke about his daughter Lee, who was now in
Paris working as a correspondent for Time-Life. She'd
been hoping to travel to the Soviet Union for a piece of
reportage, but he doubted she'd get the accreditation and
felt the best approach would be for her to go unofficially
with him when he travelled to Moscow in the autumn. The
agent noted that Lee had covered an ILO conference in
London earlier in the year – before long there might have
to be a file on her. Apparently Motty evinced a 'definite
sympathy and admiration for Russia' but he would not be
drawn on the subject of Soviet policy.

At Miami Airport, his luggage was searched and his
address book combed. His wallet was turned inside out.
Nothing of a 'suspicious or derogatory nature' was found.
He was asked politely about his itinerary in South
America and in due course sent on his way. All he had to
say about politics was that he doubted the regime in
Argentina would last much longer. His passport identified
his height as 5'8"; it said he had grey eyes, dark brown
hair, an 'oval' face and a 'dark' complexion. Our man in
Rio said he was 5'6", thin and blond with blue eyes. Since
then, he had put on twenty-five pounds, at least according

to the description filed for Hoover's office by Miami. His hair was 'dark brown' and his eyes were once again grey. His complexion, however, was 'medium-sallow', as anyone's might be during an interview with the FBI, and he had grown by an inch or more. It was reported that he 'dresses conservatively, usually in grey' – why usually? – and that he was 'slightly round-shouldered and stooped'. He had, it was noted, 'a pleasant salesmanlike manner'.

The Bureau kept Motty's file 'active' through the early part of 1946, though the New York office, to whom it fell to enter odds and ends, found little to add. They discovered, for instance, that his salary in 1938 had been twenty-seven thousand dollars (say, four hundred thousand today) and that he'd recently moved to a ten-room apartment at 983 Park Avenue – we moved to an apartment on the same block not long afterwards. They sent an agent to the place where he'd been living before the move, on West 55th Street, and interviewed the super, who mentioned that Motty and Bess entertained a lot. It was felt that the Bureau should now go through Motty's garbage – this procedure was known as 'trash coverage' – in the Park Avenue block in case anything interesting turned up. A note was made to interview Lee and another figure at Time-Life, whom she'd certainly have come across in the course of her career: the wretched Whittaker Chambers, who was at that time managing editor of *Time*. Chambers, according to a note in the file, had already mentioned Motty once before, in passing, during an interview with the FBI about . . . the name is censored. I'm fairly sure it's Franz Hoellering.

By the spring, things had gone quiet and New York sent a memo to Hoover's office advising that it was probably pointless going through Motty's rubbish 'at the exclusive

1 Max

2 Mirra

3 The Psychoanalytic Committee: (standing, from left) Otto Rank, Karl
Abraham, Max, Ernest Jones; (seated, from left) Freud, Sándor Ferenczi, Hanns
Sachs (© *Bettmann/CORBIS*)
4 Max with Marie Bonaparte (left), Anna Freud and Ernest Jones, Paris 1938

5 Plevitskaya in her glory days

6 Plevitskaya in the dock

7 General Skoblin
8 General Miller

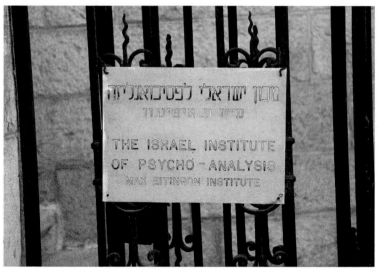

9 One of the shares that made it all possible
10 The gate at the Max Eitingon Institute in Jerusalem (© *Eyal Granit*)

11 The Freudian family romance: a section of Ernst Falzeder's diagram, revised to include Max to Freud's right (© *Ernst Falzeder*)

apartment house where the subject resides'. 'Inasmuch as no further leads are outstanding,' the last entry for 1946 reads, 'this case is being closed.'

By now Motty had come up with the notion that would put the Eitingon show back on the road. He was about to embark on a large-scale processing of sheep and lamb skins to produce what he called Bonmouton, elegant and plausible furs for the American mass market. The plant – a forty-acre site in Bristol, Pennsylvania – opened in February 1946. On the 13th my father wrote to tell his parents that a deal had been worked out between his boss and Motty, which allowed him – my father – a 10 per cent participation in his firm's very large investment. 'I have great hopes', he said, 'of it turning out very well financially.' I would have thought he'd be more level-headed until I read his letters and understood from them how beguiled by Motty he'd been.

Within a week or two of the plant's opening Motty Eitingon Inc. had raised the interest of the press.

'Fur coats for a large number of American women' was his goal, Motty told the *New York Times*. What he didn't say, and I don't know why – not glamorous enough perhaps, though suitably patriotic – is that he had a contract with the Air Force to supply the discarded sheep's wool for the linings of airmen's jackets. (Maybe he thought it better not to mention it because he also had a contract with the Soviet government to supply them with a million sheepskin coats, but maybe that was just an FBI rumour.) *Fortune*, always on the side of bigger business and not much interested in airmen's jackets, reported enthusiastically that Motty Eitingon had 'a new and mysterious process for making the

...outon is the magic word that makes normally calm women say

in May, they have to hurry down to their favorite store to order a

...mouton fur coat. For they know that Bonmouton is the new

era fur with the price modesty of mouton and the manners of a mink.

That although Bonmouton started life as a lamb, it has been

transformed by modern alchemy into a fur of ravishing beauty.

That Bonmouton has the sleekness of nutria...and the rich gleam

of beaver. That Bonmouton has been specially treated to resist the

matting effect of rain. And that the only trouble with Bonmouton is

that there just isn't quite enough to go around.

That's why they're standing in line for Bonmouton.

MOTTY EITINGON, INC., 224 West 30th Street, New York

(*Advertisement*)

skins of sheep and lamb look like the skins of much rarer animals'. The idea of shaving the wool off sheepskins and lambskins and treating the remaining pelts to make them look like something swankier wasn't entirely new. But 'Motty', as the reporter called him, cosying up to 'one of the shrewdest operators in the queerly assorted circles of the fur business', was convinced that 'his particular form of magic' was more effective than anything that had previously been tried:

> Motty expects to stir up the greatest demand that any one branch of the US fur trade has ever seen. He estimates that of some 40 million women who buy all varieties of coats each year, 15 million will take Bonmoutons and moutons – a mere seventy-five times the number now buying them. If all this more or less comes true, Motty is likely to crack the whole ingrown, sharp-dealing fur industry wide open – which might not be such a bad idea.

If all this more or less comes true.

Nothing was easier for Motty than thinking on a grand scale, and when he was quizzed about his decision to go for 'mass production methods' he was only too happy to explain. In November, he told *Fortune*, 'waggling a thin forefinger', he would be processing sixty thousand skins a week, which would be enough for more than half a million coats a year. The imagery of heavy plant may have been banal compared with the broad geographical sweep that he'd been used to, but he managed pretty well. 'Some indication of the scale of operations', he told the *Times*, 'will be found in the fact that a carload of salt per day will be used in processing operations and that normal production will require water at the rate of 1,800 gallons per minute. Two cars of coal per day will be required to supply steam.' At full capacity, he said, he'd be taking on about six or seven hundred staff. As for the sheep themselves, 'a high percentage of the skins would have to be imported' (hence the trip to Argentina): 'American sheep raisers cannot yet supply the quantities that will be required.' A titanic operation was under way.

At the same time he'd let it be known that he needed to travel to Europe in fairly short order. He was worried about his assets in Leipzig (about 750,000 dollars' worth), in Lodz, where he was invested, he'd said, to the tune of 6.4 million dollars, and in Britain, where he also had the remains of the company Monya used to look after. In Romania, apparently, the new government had frozen some Eitingon assets – one of Motty's brothers-in-law had managed a corner of the Eitingon textile empire there. There were a few debts to collect in Paris and he wanted to visit the Soviet Union to snap up some skins: he was still dealing in luxury furs when he could. This harmless conversation, or statement of intent, was later passed on to the FBI. Evidently Motty dropped in a few of the more spectacular figures – he mentioned, for instance, that since the 1920s he'd bought something between 150 and two hundred million dollars' worth of Russian furs.

I'm not sure if he made that trip to Europe. But he'd have had to be in New York for the Bonmouton presentation at the Waldorf-Astoria a few months later. The journalists were impressed by the show. 'The fur, which is lamb dyed and processed by Motty Eitingon, made an appearance in a variety of colours and styles for around-the-clock wear,' the *Times* correspondent wrote. Samples included a double-breasted overcoat in amber, 'French champagne' or 'hunting pink'. One of the couturiers had used the last colour for a short coat known as 'Pink Lady', to be 'worn over slacks or to cocktails'. My mother's Bonmouton was brown and I don't think she wore it to cocktails, preferring her mink for those occasions. She gave another brown one to Mats, who wasn't one for mink coats and didn't go to that many cocktail parties, but made do with her 'really wonderful moutoncoat' on all occasions: 'It is so light and soft and looks lovely,' she told her parents. 'Bonmouton is the new era fur with the price modesty of mouton and the manners of a mink,' it said in the Saul Steinberg ad.

Production, as far as anyone could tell, was going ahead in Bristol and orders were flooding in.

In mid-November the head of Amtorg was recalled to Moscow after a minor stir occasioned by the behaviour of the Russians living in the former J. P. Morgan mansion at Glen Cove. The property had been leased to the Soviet government for fifteen thousand dollars a year and was used to house some of Amtorg's staff. The trouble – and the protests – had begun in the summer when local residents were startled and offended, according to the *Times*, to see 'picnic refuse' left by the tenants on the terraces of the building. Word had also got round that the Russians were 'littering the broadloom carpets with empty milk bottles'. Apparently they'd used the ornamental lake – or was it the swimming pool? – to bathe 'in the nude in the ancient custom of dwellers along the Dnieper'. People were up in arms.

'Milk bottles' is curious: Russian overseas delegations weren't known for drinking milk. It was nonetheless embarrassing. 'There is no doubt', the *Times* remarked once things had settled down, 'that the Soviet representatives in this country are now acutely aware of publicity value and there is even less doubt that the Soviet Government resented the picture presented at that time of a "peasant" group cavorting bucolically on the landscaped lawns of the Morgan estate.' There were no complaints from the neighbours of the George Dupont Pratt estate, not far from Glen Cove, which the Russians actually purchased – the price was thought to be 120,000 dollars – to house the Soviet delegation to the infant United Nations, whose temporary headquarters were near by.

Motty was on reasonable terms with all the senior representatives of Amtorg. He told the FBI a few years later that he tried to keep a more or less fluent entertainment diary. Amtorg people and visiting Soviet officials were welcomed at one of his establishments at some point every year, or he would attend one of their regular functions. This was business the way it should be done; anything else would have seemed strange and ill-mannered.

CHAPTER 26

War

It took Leonid nearly a year to get back to Moscow from Coyoacán. As before, it was a circuitous journey and there are different accounts of where he stopped and for how long, but it seems that he went first to Cuba on an Iraqi passport, lay low for a time and re-emerged with a Bulgarian passport, which he used to travel to New York. In New York, according to Sudoplatov, he 'used his acquaintances in Jewish society to acquire new documents and passports'. From there he went to California to check up on two agents, Polish Jews, whom he'd planted in the early 1930s. (On that earlier occasion the main purpose of his trip had been to recruit Chinese and Japanese immigrants who might prove useful in the Far East.)

What name, I wonder, did he use in New York and was it always the same one? 'Eitingon' in any case would have been tricky. More interestingly, who were his Jewish acquaintances? Is it possible that they were also acquaintances of Motty's? It's always a little thrilling to think of Leonid walking down a street where I might have seen him – maybe because one's sense of one's childhood becomes so fixed later in life that to introduce a new character into it, however tangentially, is like beginning the novel all over again – and even more to imagine a meeting between him and Motty on a park bench in Brooklyn, Motty so smart and so charming, Leonid so smart and so gruff.

(Conspirators are always said to meet on park benches: did you in the old days, if you saw two men together on a bench, imagine that one was a spy and the other his pay-master?)

Caridad was still with him, and from California the two sailed east to Shanghai, took the train to Harbin and from there the Trans-Siberian Express to Moscow. At the end of May they arrived at the Kazan Station, where Sudoplatov was waiting on the platform to greet them. That day, or the next, the three of them were received by Beria in his office, and Leonid reported on his mission. On 17 June 1941, five days before Germany invaded the Soviet Union, Leonid and Caridad received the Order of Lenin, the highest Soviet order, from the president, Mikhail Kalinin. Of Leonid Stalin had said: 'As long as I live not a hair of his head shall be touched.'

Stalin had only just gone to bed when German bombers attacked Soviet airbases. It was 3.15 a.m. on Sunday, 22 June 1941. No one had been able to persuade him that there would be a German invasion. By four o'clock, when he was woken up, German special forces were cutting telephone lines along Russia's western frontier. More than 1,200 Russian aircraft, most of them on the ground, were lost by the end of the morning. In the first four months of the war the Soviets lost 2.3 million men.

On 27 June Stalin, appalled at these losses, 'abruptly stopped ruling', as Richard Overy puts it in *Russia's War*. He went to his dacha and remained there until 1 July, when he returned to the Kremlin. Two days later he made his first broadcast to the nation. 'Comrades! Citizens! Brothers and sisters!' he began – not a combination of words he'd ever used before. He called Russia's enemies 'fiends and cannibals', and made it clear that this was a patriotic war, 'a war of the entire Soviet people'. Zoya even now remembers the speech with enthusiasm. The country was won over.

On 5 July Leonid and Sudoplatov were put in charge of the NKVD's Administration for Special Tasks, also known as 'Yasha's Group' after Yakov Serebriansky, who'd been its head for more than ten years until he was deposed and arrested at the end of 1938. The first priority would be to defend the approaches to Moscow and then Moscow itself.

The department they were now in charge of was formed and re-formed, modelled, remodelled and redesignated two or three or four times, but in all its guises it specialised in the kinds of operation Leonid had always been concerned with: intelligence, illegal networks, disinformation, guerrilla warfare. And murder. 'We used to think that they sent people behind enemy lines to blow up bridges etc.,' one of my Moscow informants told me early on, 'but their most important activity behind lines was to kidnap Germans and Russian collaborators and bring them to Moscow to interrogate them and quite often to shoot them.'

So on the face of it, you could say, not very different from the French Resistance. Or is that unfair? The movies, by which I mean popular opinion (which includes my opinion), have been kind to the Resistance, and 'kind' is a large understatement: the myth of the Maquis is what many of us like best about the twentieth century. Leonid and Sudoplatov treated the Germans much as members of the French Resistance treated them, but also in much the same way as they treated every other perceived enemy of the Soviet state not only during the war but before it and after it. Stalin was right to see Trotsky as a threat, but he was a threat only to Stalin; and paranoid megalomania, though spellbinding in the movies, was responsible for the century's worst crimes.

Sudoplatov writes proudly of the war. 'This chapter in NKVD history', he says in his memoir, 'is the only one that was not officially rewritten, since its accomplishments stood on their merit and did not contain Stalinist crimes that had to be covered up.' And a few lines later, he adds with some bitterness that roughly five thousand books and articles on the war were published in the Soviet Union between 1945 and 1992 and in none of them is his name mentioned: 'Where my name was on a document,' he says, and for a minute or two it can seem quite poignant, 'only a series of dots appears.' At first he wasn't mentioned 'for security reasons' – Stalin's crimes – and then his name was excluded 'because I was a convicted criminal and an unwanted witness'. We can't know what Leonid would have said had he lived beyond the collapse of the Soviet Union, but Sudoplatov says on his behalf that 'the summit of his career was the struggle with the Fascists'.

Naturally Sudoplatov isn't being truthful when he says that the NKVD's wartime record didn't have to be doctored. It did. Not least in his own writing. Wars offer dictators opportunities for action, against the enemy but also against their own side, that in peacetime they can only dream of. It isn't just that tens of thousands of Soviet soldiers were executed for 'defeatism' by the NKVD. Entire nations, Chechens, Ingush, Kalmyks and several others whom Stalin chose to accuse of treachery, were transplanted from one part of the Soviet Union to another – their deportations arranged and supervised by the NKVD.

From the German point of view the war against the Soviet Union was to be a war of annihilation, a *Vernichtungskrieg* Hitler called it, in which the three main enemies of German civilisation, Jews, Bolsheviks and Slavs, would be exterminated. On 28 June Minsk was captured. On 16 July German armoured divisions took Smolensk, the last major city before Moscow. Sudoplatov and Leonid did their best to try to save Red Army units surrounded by Germans. I don't know what tricks, what diversionary activity, they might have resorted to, but before July was over the attempt was abandoned. By mid-September Kiev had fallen and Leningrad was encircled; it would remain under siege for nine hundred days. The battle for Moscow – Hitler's Operation Typhoon – began on 30 September to the south of the city and on 2 October to the north; it would end, Hitler prophesied, with Moscow razed to the ground, 'gouged from the earth', in the historian Catherine Merridale's phrase, and the space where it had been would be covered over with a huge artificial lake. 'The name Moscow', Hitler said, 'will disappear for ever.'

At the beginning of October, as bookshops in Berlin, certain of victory, began displaying Russian grammars in their windows for use by Russia's future occupiers, Stalin gave the order to begin evacuating his government to the city of Kuibyshev, the former Samara, five hundred miles to the east on the River Volga. In mid-October, the central offices of the NKVD were evacuated. Beria was still in the process of weeding out Stalin's supposed enemies from the Red Army's senior command – business left unfinished from the time of the Purges – and the most senior officers then being interrogated were taken to Kuibyshev; three hundred others, for whom there was no transport, were shot.

Leonid and his troops remained near by, in Moscow's northern suburbs. Charged with defending the city from its enemies outside and within, they planted mines and shot looters. 'It was absolutely necessary to establish order,' a former member of Omsbon, Sudoplatov's Special Motorised Brigade, would tell Merridale: he was keeping watch from the second floor of GUM, the department store facing Red Square, with orders to shoot anyone, potential looter or enemy.

Omsbon was the operational arm of the Administration for Special Tasks. Consisting of some twenty thousand men and women, it included eight hundred of the Soviet Union's leading athletes, several 'key' (Sudoplatov's word) members of the intelligentsia, political immigrants of all nationalities including 119 Spanish men and six women, as well as a small number of experienced NKVD officers, victims of the Purges now released from jail to fight another day – among them Yakov Serebriansky himself, the Yasha of Yasha's Group. 'To be enrolled was to be part of a select and glamorous elite,' Merridale writes. The incomparable Zoya, who was also a track-and-field champion, was unsurprisingly one of this elite. Leonid, who after his time in Spain had more experience of unconventional warfare than almost any of his compatriots, directed their training.

In September, at the start of the battle for Moscow, there were eight hundred thousand Russian soldiers between the German army and the capital: by 10 October, ninety thousand were left. With the leading German units only twelve miles away, Sudoplatov's men were laying mines at the railroad and subway stations, at the football stadium, along the road from the airport, at VIP dachas; even the Puppet Theatre which served as their own radio headquarters was set to be blown up.

Few believed that the Germans would be repelled and networks were established that would remain in Moscow under the expected occupation, gathering information, rattling the enemy and making life unbearable for everyone (by poisoning the water supply, for example); there was a plan to assassinate Hitler either when he came to Moscow to claim his victory (not that he was likely to make the journey) or elsewhere. Zoya was the NKVD liaison officer with the designated assassins. 'The assignment was not very pleasant,' she said to Antony Beevor when he was preparing his book about Olga Chekhova, who was to be part of the plot.

There was every reason for the NKVD to recruit Zoya. A twenty-one-year-old with a cool head, she had outstanding family connections, she was a linguist and she was – and is – very resourceful and very active: 'I was at the forefront everywhere.'* But she is modest, too, in her way, careful to indicate that she was part of a larger enterprise. 'Just a contact person', someone to take messages and drop letters (it wouldn't do, she said, to have a lot of men going in and out of the same apartment). As the anniversary of the October Revolution approached, she carried chairs from neighbouring theatres down into the Metro

---

* Driving with her through a featureless set of North London streets, I was surprised that she'd noticed that we'd gone round the block. (She was already in her eighties.) 'Listen,' she said, 'I used to be paid to notice that sort of thing, why should I have forgotten now?'

station on Mayakovsky Square so that the celebration could go ahead as it always had done on 7 November, despite the presence of German planes trying to breach Moscow's air defences. 'It worked very well because Stalin could get there by the underground from his headquarters.' The next day, 'sure enough', she writes in her memoir, the soldiers came out on parade: 'They literally went from Red Square via Gorky Street to the battle front.'

In the event Moscow wasn't occupied. As the German offensive petered out, Field Marshal von Bock noted in his diary: 'The Russians, who have destroyed almost all facilities on the main roads, have been able to obstruct our transport arrangements to such an extent that the Army Group no longer has what it needs to survive and to fight.' At the same time Stalin gave up trying to assassinate Hitler, fearing that without Hitler the Germans and the British might be drawn into an alliance against the Soviet Union. And Zoya wasn't invited to the ceremony on 7 November, she tells us in her memoir: Leonid described it to her. But Leonid wasn't there. He had already left Moscow on an 'important' – i.e. clandestine – mission.

He was to arrange the assassination of Franz von Papen, briefly German chancellor and now ambassador to Turkey. It was an assignment that could have had monumental consequences. Worried as always by the Soviet Union's vulnerability to the east, Stalin feared an alliance between Turkey and Germany that would lead to an invasion of the Caucasus. Killing von Papen, a powerful man in his own right and sympathetic to Turkey, would make such an alliance impossible and instead (with luck) provoke Hitler into a punitive attack on Turkey – provided of course it was believed that the Turkish government had arranged von Papen's death.

Another, more baroque notion in Stalin's head was that von Papen, an anti-Nazi Nazi, would effect an alliance with Britain (and Turkey) at Russia's expense. That possibility too would be closed off if von Papen were assassinated and Hitler believed that Turkey was responsible.

Leonid – now, as before in Turkey, called Leonid Naumov – was accompanied on this occasion not by Olga, Zoya's patient mother, or by the sad Kochergina, Olga's successor, who'd committed suicide sometime in the previous year, but by a new 'wife', Musa Malinovskaya, a pretty blonde champion *parachutistka* whom he'd met in Spain. Pretty and blonde enough to be the model for the figure of the parachutist in the Metro station at Revolution Square and pretty and blonde enough to be the mother of Leonid's two youngest children, themselves called Leonid and Musa, but not pretty and blonde enough for him to marry her. He stayed with her when he got back to Moscow the following August, perhaps because she was already pregnant, and remained with her until 1947, the year their second child was born.

It has occurred to me that the reason Leonid had so many 'wives' wasn't just that he was, as Andrew and Mitrokhin call him, 'one of the NKVD's most celebrated womanisers'. It could have been as much a strategic consideration: a couple would be less conspicuous in the eyes of Turkish or German or Mexican Intelligence and in practical terms less vulnerable. In a paragraph or two it will emerge that a hairdresser was part of the plot: did he do Malinovskaya's hair?

In the event the bomb went off too soon. The Bulgarian

assassin was still on the other side of the road from von Papen when it exploded in his hand. Von Papen and his wife were thrown to the ground. A few passers-by were injured and the Bulgarian was dead.

It happened at ten o'clock on the morning of 24 February 1942 on Atatürk Boulevard – Ankara's main street – as von Papen and his wife were making their way to the German Embassy. It was so public, so un-cloak-and-dagger that Leonid – I assume he was in charge – must have been very sure of his plan, but he was used to sneakier operations which left the operative room for manoeuvre. Here there was none and everything went wrong.

Von Papen wasn't dead. The identity of the assassin was quickly ascertained – the name of the hotel where he was staying appears to have been stamped on the heel of the shoe that was all that remained of him – and his accomplices were soon traced: a student called Abdurakhman and Suleiman the hairdresser. In court Abdurakhman squealed: in October 1941, he said, he'd been to the Soviet Embassy in Ankara with an offer to sell them documents relating to a plot to assassinate Stalin. Thrown out of there, he'd travelled to Istanbul, to try his luck at the Soviet Consulate. There he met with two officials, Kornilov and Pavlov, who were setting up the attempt on von Papen. It took very little time to persuade the Turkish authorities, and everyone else, that the attempted assassination had been a Soviet plot. Leonid had done really badly.

Pavlov and Kornilov were put on trial alongside Abdurakhman and Suleiman and at the end of April sentenced to twenty years in prison. Leonid was still in Ankara when the trial was going on – in what guise or disguise I don't know. He would later describe himself 'wandering around' the city and 'going for meals' in the company of a lawyer sent from Moscow to advise on the case.

'Wandering around', 'going for meals': my favourite moments in Leonid's story are the in-between, inconsequential ones. Leonid in prison and, unable to change his shirt every day, protecting his shirt collar with a strip of gauze or Olga cutting the labels out of his shirts so his girls wouldn't know which countries he'd visited. The downtime in an agent's day: how is it spent? Journalists waiting for the action to resume read thrillers: do the thrillers' real-life prototypes read them too? The most extraordinary times in the life of a man of action, the ones we know least about, are the most ordinary. Did he and Musa talk about Ankara – the architecture, the landscape, the food? I know from Leonid's family what he didn't talk about, and I know that he was generally quite silent, and when he did speak was often sarcastic: but I have no idea how an everyday conversation with Leonid might run.

The bungled assassination of von Papen is a curious episode in Leonid's career. He'd failed in his assignment ('I let a great failure happen') and Stalin and Beria were reportedly furious ('extremely displeased'). Yet he wasn't punished: Sudoplatov stood up for him, the biographer tells us (Sudoplatov and the biographer were friends). Nor did he appear to be remorseful: charged in due course with 'causing harm to the agency', he dismissed the accusation because it had not been his intention to do harm ('I only admit that in my practical activities I let a great failure happen'). One thing only counted as a mistake in his eyes: his early membership of the Socialist Revolutionary Party. On the other hand, he had let his colleagues Pavlov and

Kornilov down and he felt bad about it: but not that bad. He returned to Moscow in August 1942, in the company of the Soviet ambassador, bringing with him 'four suitcases full of sugar and other food products'. Clearly he didn't feel that prudence was called for.

His boss was more circumspect. 'Sudoplatov is an extremely careful man and always was,' Boris Makliarsky, the son of Leonid's colleague Mikhail Makliarsky, said to me one day. We were talking about the Second World War. 'When my father first asked him about von Papen and the failed assassination, Sudoplatov said: "I don't know anything about it."'

Makliarsky: 'But it's all in *Pravda*.'

Sudoplatov: 'I don't read *Pravda*.'

In February 1945, Turkey declared war on Germany. One way or another Stalin got what he wanted. Pavlov and Kornilov had been amnestied and allowed to return to the Soviet Union a few months before.

Leonid had been away from Moscow for seven or eight months. I assume that the failed assassination didn't take up all his time, that he did other things, had other assignments in the region – Iraq, Iran, Greece were countries he visited – and that whatever they were, whatever contacts he made or unmade (he said during his interrogation that he'd been in touch with members of the French Resistance), they worked out more satisfactorily than the killing of von Papen. Back in Moscow, he rejoined Sudoplatov, whose department had now been renamed the Fourth Administration – a new address for very familiar activities. Which is no doubt why, despite Soviet pride at what was achieved in the course of the war, it's oddly difficult to find out what precisely – *chto konkretno*, the Russians would say, 'what concretely' – Leonid was up to in those years.

One indication comes from Nikolai Khokhlov, the future defector, who in June 1941, a few weeks before war broke out, was beginning a tour of the Soviet Union with a vaudeville act. He was not yet twenty, and he whistled for a living; he was an 'artistic whistler'. Exempt from military service on grounds of bad eyesight, he abandoned the vaudeville act, volunteered for the defence of Moscow, and in due course found himself face to face with Leonid in a 'safe apartment' on Gorky Street: 'Sprawling in an armchair, heavy and motionless, the stranger silently drilled me with his little eyes for several seconds. Then, without rising, he stretched out his hand to me and said: "Sit down. How are your parachute jumps?"'

Khokhlov was later to write a memoir of those years, which he called *In the Name of Conscience*. The book makes Leonid seem rather gross by comparison with the handsome, courtly Sudoplatov. Gross perhaps, but redoubtable: 'many an intricate intelligence operation', the young Khokhlov was told by fellow operatives, had originated in Leonid's head. Boris Makliarsky spoke of Leonid's 'capacity to cast a spell on people to make them do what was necessary'. It's a nice way of putting it.

The assignment Leonid gave Khokhlov was to liquidate Wilhelm Kube, the 'butcher of Belorussia', in German-occupied Minsk. A year and a half was spent preparing him for the task, which would involve impersonating – effectively becoming – a German officer in a city occupied by the German army. Leonid had strong views about Soviet citizens operating undercover abroad: 'Languages can be learned at the institute. We're lousy with linguists.

But just try to send them abroad! From half a mile away you can tell it's a Russian.' German history, German culture, the German economy, German books, newspapers, news bulletins, songs: all that had to be inculcated. At a POW camp run by the NKVD the German inmates demonstrated parade routine, what to do on meeting a general, how to report to an officer, and other points of Prussian military etiquette. 'I took pictures', Khokhlov writes, 'showing the correct regulation distance from elbows to hips when standing at attention, the position of the head when making an about-face . . .' The French Resistants, whose sense of what they were up to was more theatrical, were less meticulous in preparing their interventions. Leonid, alert to what he saw as his compatriots' laziness, had his own Prussian approach.

A trial period at a different POW camp failed to give Khokhlov away: neither the prisoners nor their Russian guards had any idea that this German infantry officer supposedly captured at Stalingrad was in reality an artistic whistler from Moscow. The most difficult thing, Khokhlov said, wasn't remembering not to speak Russian so much as remembering not to understand it when he heard it spoken.

In August 1943 Khokhlov was dropped into Nazi-occupied Belorussia. For the next few weeks he would be Otto Witgenstein, a lieutenant in the German Secret Field Police on leave in Minsk. The gauleiter was duly killed – blown to bits by a bomb attached to the springs of his bed – and Operation Kube, Khokhlov would later say, was the 'most spectacular and successful feat' of his wartime career.

'The war completely changed my position in the NKVD,' Sudoplatov announced in his memoirs. He was now a man in charge of large numbers of other men. 'During the course of the war,' he writes, 'we placed 212 guerrilla detachments and units comprising 7,316 men to the rear of the enemy. We trained a thousand officers and technicians in sabotage for the Red Army. We also sent out 3,500 civilian saboteurs and agents.' And the result? In Sudoplatov's account: 137,000 German officers and soldiers annihilated, eighty-seven high-ranking German officials killed in individual terrorist operations, 2,045 Soviet collaborators liquidated. At the end of the war he would become a general – and Leonid a major-general. It was rare for NKVD men to be so honoured.

Even so, Andrew and Mitrokhin are unimpressed: 'Just as the KGB later sought to take refuge from the horrors of its Stalinist past by constructing a Leninist golden age of revolutionary purity, so it also sought to reinvent its record during the Great Patriotic War as one of selfless heroism – best exemplified by its role in special operations and partisan warfare behind enemy lines.' Between the Red Army, the regular forces of the NKVD, who functioned mainly as punishment squads, and the partisans, it's hard to know how or where Sudoplatov's Special Forces fitted in. They scarcely feature in Western histories of the war in the east, and the documents that I have say nothing; the archives are closed; even Zoya was silent. Sudoplatov's account may be reasonably accurate – I have read others that self-evidently aren't – but when he wrote it he was a vain old man who remembered things his way.

By the early summer of 1944 Field Marshal Ernst von Busch's Army Group Centre, stretched out around Minsk, was the only significant German force left on Soviet territory. The battle of Kursk the previous year had put paid to German hopes of victory; the siege of Leningrad had finally been lifted at the end of January; by May most of the Ukraine and the Crimea had been liberated. The campaign to drive the Germans out of Belorussia, which Stalin code-named Operation Bagration – General Bagration, one of the heroes of the war against Napoleon, was a fellow Georgian – began on 22 June, the third anniversary of the German invasion. Within days Minsk was retaken and the order given to press on into Poland.

Sudoplatov was summoned to the Kremlin on the eve of the offensive – 'I went up to the third floor.' Stalin was no longer pleased with his department; they didn't understand the realities of the war. Why hadn't they taken advantage of the enemy's desperation? Seized the opportunity to trick German high command into sending reinforcements – both more men and more stuff – that the Soviets could scoop up and use for their own purposes?

In that spirit a Soviet agent known to German military intelligence as 'Heine' sent out a message informing the Abwehr that scattered groups of German soldiers and officers in the Belorussian forest were trying to break through to the front line. This was on 19 August 1944. German high command saw no reason not to believe him. All the Soviets now had to do was to bring one such group into being, and that was easily done: an imaginary force consisting of a number of Soviet agents, NKVD officials and German prisoners of war was assembled near the River Berezina. A real-life lieutenant colonel, a POW called Heinrich Scherhorn, was their notional commander.

In fact Leonid was in charge, with (in Sudoplatov's account) a group of illustrious Chekists backing him up that included Mordvinov, the NKVD colonel who had been 'Pavlov' when Leonid was in Ankara (so no hard feelings), Yakov Serebriansky and Willie Fisher, who would later be known over much of the Western world as the Soviet spy 'Rudolf Abel', arrested in the US and exchanged for the U2 pilot Gary Powers in 1962.

When two German parachutists, sent by the local German HQ to establish contact with Scherhorn's beleaguered unit, were caught approaching the base, 'Heine' sent a message to the Abwehr in the names of the two men, confirming that contact had been made with the unit 'under Scherhorn's command'. The Abwehr checked Scherhorn's identity and in Sharapov's telling informed Hitler and Göring – no less – of the need to provide the detachment with assistance. A distribution point was set up, and over the course of the next months, food, technical supplies and munitions were dropped behind Soviet lines to give material support to the 'German group' in the forest. Men, too, were sent: combat troops and experienced saboteurs came from the SS, while the Abwehr despatched its own agents. Soviet counter-intelligence sent disinformation back to Germany under their names.

A small part of Operation Bagration, the adventure continued for nine months. At the end of March Scherhorn was informed that on Hitler's orders he'd been awarded the Iron Cross. On 5 May, a telegram arrived from the Abwehr announcing that 'owing to present circumstances' they were unable to provide further assistance. The war was lost. Or rather won.

Had Leonid lived beyond the fall of the Soviet Union, would he, like Sudoplatov, have boasted about the war and his part in it? 'In this administration,' he would tell his interrogators, 'I worked on the deployment of agents and saboteurs in the occupied territories of Belorussia and the Baltic states.' That's all. He was always circumspect, down to earth, uninterested in approximation. Did he, I wonder, enjoy the game or was he merely efficient?

Unlike Sudoplatov and many others among his colleagues, Leonid was a military man, a soldier, and, I think, proud of it. A provincial boy, he'd been chosen to attend the Frunze Academy. That was an honour. His family, we know, said that 9 May, the day the Soviet Union celebrated its victory over the Germans, was the holiday that meant most to him; and Sudoplatov was sure that what he achieved in the war meant more to him than anything else he had done. Would he have felt differently about planning the death of a German gauleiter like Kube, responsible (so it's said) for the deaths of fifty-five thousand Jews, from the way he felt about planning Trotsky's death? Did he feel that Trotsky was a worthier opponent? What about Agabekov, his old colleague from Constantinople: he defected, it's true, but he didn't, as far as I know, do anyone much harm. Did Leonid wholeheartedly feel that he deserved to die? Did he regret having to hire the Turkish killer (if he did)? Did he consider Kube a different order of enemy, one about whose death there was no need to have any misgivings?

Back in Moscow in the autumn of 1944, Nikolai Khokhlov was fêted by his friends and his bosses and summoned to the Kremlin to receive the Order of the War for the Motherland. At the same time he was hoping that once the motherland was secure he would be released from his duty to it – which was starting to make him uncomfortable.

Leonid and Sudoplatov, still his bosses, wouldn't hear of it. 'Your assignment is to go abroad, familiarise yourself with the new surroundings, and be ready – at a moment's notice – to move further on.' Invasion could come from any direction. 'We must be ready for everything,' they said; and sent him to Romania.

'Romania is an excellent school for an intelligence agent,' Sudoplatov remarked as they walked together in the city park in Bucharest:

'You will find here – and I hope be able to adopt – many details of life abroad that cannot be described in any textbooks or instructions. For the time being don't think about the length of your stay. You may be here half a year, perhaps much longer. Consider this country as a springboard. Learn the Romanian language thoroughly, make a minute study of the mode of living and the customs. Meet rather seldom with our comrades. Try to live completely independently. Open your own store, if this can help you. Buy an automobile. Check first to see if such actions conform with your cover story. Do not consider this as a period of idleness. I have big plans for you. Gather experience and assurance.'

Khokhlov spent two years in Bucharest in the guise of a Polish shopkeeper called Levandowski. In July 1947 Polish Levandowski took out Romanian citizenship, becoming Romanian Levandowski. (Khokhlov of course remained a Soviet citizen.) He was operating under the auspices of Bureau No. 1, whose purpose, he would later explain to a US congressional committee, was preparation for future war.

By September 1949 he'd made up his mind: he couldn't, in peacetime, go on working for an organisation whose purpose was to kill people, whether or not they were enemies or future enemies of the state. 'I request you to return me immediately to the Soviet Union and release me from further work in intelligence,' he wrote to his superiors with unusual boldness. Within days he was back in Moscow. 'An idle, monotonous period in a foreign country would become boring for any alert and energetic person,' Sudoplatov said sympathetically. Leonid was more menacing. 'Everything', he said, 'has limits, including our patience.'

CHAPTER 27

The Bomb

'Our scientists were better than America's. The American bomb was made by foreigners, by immigrants. Soviet scientists, Russian scientists built ours. And when the Americans and the British say we stole their plans they're lying. They want to hide their ignorance. They didn't have good enough physicists. They invited the Italian Fermi, the Hungarian Teller – that's how it was in America. We did it all ourselves, with our atomshiki.'

General Sudoplatov became more and more agitated. He was eighty-five, he had high blood pressure. 'Nichevo, nichevo,' his son kept saying. 'It's OK, it's OK.'

It wouldn't be right to say that Sudoplatov had a point when he made that speech, but he wasn't as wrong as I initially thought. US and UK nuclear research was always more advanced, but the dramatic progress that was made everywhere in the course of the 1930s was built on discoveries by scientists in several different countries – among them Germany and the Soviet Union. 'Nuclear physicists', in David Holloway's words, 'were the very model of an international scientific community.' That changed at the end of the decade as scientists began to see the military implications of nuclear fission. US and UK scientists went quiet, and from September 1939 no reference to the possibility of atomic bombs was allowed in the German press. All sorts of things held the Russians up – among them the time it took scientific journals from the West to arrive in the country – but Stalin's reluctance to worry about Germany in the run-up to the Second World War was crucial. Western nuclear physicists, by contrast, many of them Jewish refugees from Eastern and Central Europe, were all too alert to the possibility of a German nuclear bomb.

Having told me that the Soviet atomshiki had no need of Western physicists, Sudoplatov tells the readers of his memoir at the very start of a chapter on 'Atomic Spies' that the most important and celebrated nuclear physicists engaged in the Manhattan Project regularly shared their calculations and their findings with the Soviets. 'These claims, if true,' Thomas Powers wrote in the *New York Review of Books* in June 1994, 'would suggest a degree of Communist subversion of Western science and society beyond anything charged by anti-Communist zealots in the 1950s.'

'If true': but they aren't. No one has ever thought that Fermi and Szilard and Bohr shared their calculations with the Soviets. Oppenheimer, it's well known, had a Red period. And he is a more interesting case. He nearly joined the Party; his brother did join and so did many of his friends; he opposed the building of a hydrogen bomb, which was thought to be unpatriotic of him, on the grounds that its effect would be genocidal (Truman called him a 'crybaby'); he was complicated, secretive, happy to live in ambiguity – the sort of person an anti-Communist might detest – but there is no evidence, in the Venona decrypts* or elsewhere, to indicate that he passed on any secrets. In

---

* In 1946 the US Army Security Agency, with some assistance from British Intelligence, began decrypting wartime messages exchanged between the Centre in Moscow – i.e. KGB headquarters – and its American residencies.

fact Sudoplatov's claims are contradicted by a series of documents printed as an appendix in his own book.

The man who did most to help the Soviets, Klaus Fuchs, a German refugee and a naturalised British subject, seems to have interested Sudoplatov rather less than Oppenheimer and Co. Mystery even now makes Oppenheimer glamorous. No mystery or glamour attaches to Fuchs. With his identity revealed thanks to the Venona decrypts, he confessed in January 1950, was put on trial and found guilty. He'd begun working on TUBE ALLOYS, the British atomic bomb project, in 1941; and as soon as the Soviet Union entered the war sought out someone to whom he could pass on the information he already had. Two years later he moved to New York as part of the British team chosen to work on the Manhattan Project (ENORMOZ in NKVD-speak) and from there was transferred to Los Alamos. He wasn't the only one among his colleagues who believed that as allies the Soviets had a right to know what Britain and the US were working on. But he believed it more strongly than most of the rest.

In October 1944 another physicist at Los Alamos, Theodore Alvin Hall, took the decision to share his work with the Russians. An eighteen-year-old Harvard graduate when he arrived at Los Alamos, Hall was the youngest scientist there – and according to Andrew and Mitrokhin

---

The existence of the operation – eventually codenamed Venona – was kept from the public but also from the American government, for a time indeed from the CIA, for fear of leaks, or for reasons of inter-agency rivalry. The interception itself had come to an end in 1945, when a Soviet agent in the US army's Signal Intelligence Service alerted Moscow, but the process of decryption lasted for a further thirty-five years. It came to an end in 1980 and even then not all the codes had been cracked. The material, which led to a feast of name-naming, wasn't declassified until 1995.

'probably the youngest major spy of the 20th century'. Vaguer in his political sympathies than Fuchs, Hall strongly believed that for the United States to have a nuclear monopoly would put the whole world in danger. Though their motives in that sense were similar, neither Hall nor Fuchs had any idea of what the other was up to.

In July 1945 the US detonated a test bomb in the desert at Alamogordo. The Soviets knew the test was coming: Fuchs and Hall had each independently supplied the date for which the explosion was scheduled, but it wasn't until the *Enola Gay* dropped its bomb on Hiroshima three weeks later that Stalin and Beria all at once understood the strategic implications of nuclear weapons. For years they'd dragged their feet, doubting that it was possible to make a bomb (the Germans hadn't succeeded), distrustful of their own scientists (not understanding the science, they couldn't be sure they weren't being tricked); and besides the data from the US and the UK were so copious, so readily available: wasn't it all too good to be true? Now, suddenly realising that a mistake had been made, they set up a new directorate, Department S, under Sudoplatov with Leonid and two others as his deputies, to manage the atomic project and ordered their atomshiki to get a move on. In Stalin's eyes the scientists were to blame. Or so he said. 'If a child doesn't cry the mother can't know what he needs,' he told Igor Kurchatov, the Soviet Union's leading atomic scientist.

The first Soviet bomb was successfully tested four years later, on 29 August 1949, at the Semipalatinsk test site in Kazakhstan. It was the same 'Fat Man' bomb that Fuchs and Hall had described, the one tested at Alamogordo and used at Nagasaki: a plutonium bomb as opposed to the uranium bomb dropped at Hiroshima. Yet here again Sudoplatov hadn't been entirely wrong when he said that the atomshiki made their own bomb. It's true that they had a detailed blueprint, but they investigated every aspect of that blueprint down to the last detail. 'We have to learn ten times more than we need to know today,' one of Kurchatov's colleagues was to say. Fuchs and Hall brought the making of a Soviet bomb forward by a year or maybe two, taking the West completely by surprise – 'the failure to predict how quickly the Soviets would develop the Bomb was probably the greatest blunder of Western intelligence during the entire Cold War'* – but the main thing that had stood in its way was Stalin's paranoia, not the incompetence of Soviet physicists.

Fuchs and Hall were not the only scientists at Los Alamos to share their secrets with the Soviets but none of the others was as important, and fifty years later some of them are still known only by their Soviet codenames. Even Hall's name wasn't known to the public – or indeed to Sudoplatov – until the Venona transcripts were declassified in 1995. Until then it was thought that they had got almost all their information from Fuchs and, independently of Fuchs, from David Greenglass, Ethel Rosenberg's brother. Greenglass was a machinist. He entered the US army in 1943, was quickly promoted to technical sergeant and after a spell at the uranium-enrichment facility at Oak Ridge, Tennessee, was posted to the high-explosives laboratory at Los Alamos. Like the Rosenbergs, he was a Communist, and towards the end of 1944 he was recruited to work for the Soviets by Julius Rosenberg. 'My darling,' he wrote to his wife who'd acted as go-between,

* Gerard De Groot, *The Bomb: A Life*.

'I most certainly will be glad to be part of the community project that Julius and his friends have in mind.' Greenglass was far from being as useful to the Soviets as Fuchs and Hall, but until he left the army in 1946 he had data to pass on – notably about the high-explosive lens designed for use in implosion.

In June 1950 Greenglass was arrested for espionage. A zigzag trail had led from Fuchs to Fuchs's minder, Harry Gold, to Greenglass and the Rosenbergs. Everyone, it seems, was willing to spill the beans. Everyone except the Rosenbergs. As the day of their trial approached Greenglass insisted – insisted day after day for ten days – that his sister was innocent and then testified against both Ethel and Julius as part of an immunity agreement, claiming in Ethel's case that she had typed up the notes he had handed over to her husband, when in fact or in all probability they'd been typed up not by Ethel but by Ruth, Greenglass's wife. Both Greenglass and his wife changed their testimony to incriminate Ethel, and in exchange Ruth Greenglass, who had gone out of her way to encourage her husband to get as much information for the Russians as he could, was officially declared 'an unindicted co-conspirator' and lived the rest of her life in New York City under a new name.

More than half a dozen of Julius Rosenberg's closest friends had vanished immediately after Greenglass's arrest. The authorities concluded that he was the centre of a large spy ring and Venona confirmed it, or seemed to confirm it, or could be read as confirming it: he was 'the kingpin'. But because they couldn't use the Venona evidence they had to get him to confess in order to be able to roll up the whole network. And the way to get him to talk, as they saw it, was through his wife – 'Proceeding against his wife might serve as a lever in this matter,' J. Edgar Hoover, the head of the FBI, wrote to the US Attorney General. But the only evidence against Ethel was the notes she didn't type up. Or rather the notes she didn't type up were the only evidence that could be used: the interrogators knew from Venona that she'd acted as a lookout, ferried cash from Julius to her brother and back. But even in the early 1950s you didn't go to the electric chair for that. The couple were executed on 19 June 1953 because they wouldn't say they were guilty or name any names, because Ethel had seemed cold and distant in the courtroom and because some people wanted them to be. Their crime, the judge said, was 'worse than murder': 'Putting into the hands of the Russians the A-bomb years before our best scientists predicted Russia would perfect the bomb has already caused, in my opinion, the Communist aggression in Korea, with the resultant casualties exceeding 50,000 and who knows but that millions more innocent people may pay the price of your treason.'

Fuchs, by contrast, whose contribution to the development of Soviet nuclear science was so much greater, was sentenced to fourteen years in prison – the maximum sentence for spying for a friendly nation, which in 1950 the Soviet Union still was – and released after nine. He spent the rest of his life in East Germany, where he had a second career as a nuclear scientist. Hall was never charged. His career as a spy effectively ended in 1951 when he was questioned by the FBI, but the evidence against him came from the Venona decryptions, and it wasn't considered worth compromising the programme to make his name public. He eventually moved to Britain and worked at the Cavendish Laboratory in Cambridge. Harry Gold was sentenced to thirty years in prison; Greenglass to fifteen – and released after ten. 'As a spy who turned his family in, I don't care,' he told CBS in 2001. 'I sleep very well.'

Zoya was twenty-four or twenty-five – a good age for brain power – when she was asked to translate the documents that came to the Soviet Union from Los Alamos. She had already proved herself a loyal and proficient linguist at the Tehran Conference in 1943, then at Yalta in 1945. Her father, Vasily Zarubin, had been the senior NKVD officer in the US until the summer of 1944. Her stepfather was working in a nearby office. She was dependable: perhaps it hardly mattered that she didn't know any physics beyond what she had learned at school – the 'squiggles', as she called them, were the same in every language.

So she sat all day on her own with a scientific diction-ary in a room somewhere in or near Department S – assuming that Department S was a physical space, a series of rooms along a corridor – and translated the material that had come from Los Alamos. And when she'd finished for the day she would put all the documents in a big safe that stood waiting in the corner of the room and lock them securely away until she came back the next morning.

Except that she wasn't as good at physics as she should have been. ('Have you forgotten everything you learned at school?' Kurchatov asked her.) The work was taxing and very boring. 'All those particles . . .' she groans when the sub-ject is broached. 'I knew many of the words separately,' she says in her memoir, 'but when I put them together, they made no sense . . . It wasn't language – it was gobbledygook.' With time she improved, even the harsh Kurchatov thought so; and when in the 1960s she saw the film of *My Fair Lady* she compared herself, disarmingly, with Eliza Doolittle and

Kurchatov with Henry Higgins. Eventually the job was taken over by more expert translators; political prisoners, she suspected, released pro tem from the Gulag in the Urals or Central Asia: 'Their haunted look suggested suffering.'

Thomas Powers, committed to the view that there is scarcely a word of truth in what Sudoplatov has to say about the bomb, reports that soon after the publication of *Special Tasks* in April 1994 the Russian Foreign Intelligence Service, the successor to the KGB, 'issued a statement saying that, far from being in charge of atomic intelligence during the war, "Pavel Sudoplatov had access to atomic problems during a relatively brief period of time, a mere twelve months, from September 1945 to October 1946."' Leonid had said in the late 1940s that he was appointed to Department S 'in the second half of 1945' and by the end of 1946 had new work (with Sudoplatov) in a different directorate.

Which may explain why when you read about Soviet espionage in the United States in the late 1940s you find at most one or two mentions of Leonid's name. In 1930 there were four OGPU officers and four illegal agents in the US; by April 1941, there may have been as many as three or four hundred.* Thomas Powers speaks of 'an espionage

---

* 'By April 1941,' Andrew and Mitrokhin write, 'the total NKVD agent network in the United States numbered 221, of whom 49 were listed in NKVD statistics as "engineers" (probably a category which included a rather broad range of scientists).' But in the footnote attached to this passage they note that 'the Venona decrypts of NKVD wartime telegrams from the United States include the codenames of approximately 200 agents (about half of whom remain unidentified). Since these telegrams represent only a fraction of the wartime communications between the Centre and its American residencies, the total NKVD network must have been substantially larger.'

assault on the United States of stunning scope and alarming success'. Yet the most reliable history of the Venona project cites Leonid only in connection with an attempt to spring Mercader from his Mexican jail, which Leonid (under the codename TOM) directed and aborted from the Centre in 1944.* So that's no help.

Some of the espionage took place at a very high level, involving friends of Roosevelt's in the Treasury and the State Department, and there has never been any suggestion that Leonid (or Sudoplatov) had anything to do with them. But what about the buzz of activity around Los Alamos? Sharapov, Leonid's intermittently reliable biographer, reports that Leonid 'prepared' Willie Fisher (Rudolf Abel) for his assignment as an atomic spy in America. Which he may have done. But in Andrew and Mitrokhin's version Fisher's training, which began in 1946, was supervised by someone else, higher up the intelligence ladder. In that account he wasn't going to be one spy among many: he was to take charge of the whole American operation. Perhaps for that reason his training took a year, maybe two, and by the time he arrived in the States in 1948, Leonid was in another department, inching towards disaster.

Sudoplatov mentions the two Polish Jewish moles whom Leonid 'planted' in California at the beginning of the 1930s and checked up on in 1941 on his long way back from Coyoacán, one of them a dentist whose studies in Paris the OGPU had had to pay for. A year or so later, according to Sudoplatov, they became couriers in the network centred on Los Alamos, but that wouldn't have had

* John Earl Haynes and Harvey Klehr, *Venona: Decoding Soviet Espionage in America.*

anything much to do with Leonid, who in 1942 was busy with von Papen.

I had wondered whether the Polish moles were the same as the Cohens, who did play an important part in the Los Alamos network, Lona Cohen especially, but it's clear for many reasons that they weren't. On the other hand, Morris Cohen, Lona's husband, an American, a Communist and a volunteer in the Mackenzie-Papineau Battalion of the International Brigades, was recruited in Spain in April 1938. Might it have been Leonid who recruited him there? 'I was one of a group of various nationalities sent to a conspiratorial school in Barcelona,' Cohen is said to have written in his KGB autobiography, by which we assume – that's to say, Orlov's biographer assumes – he meant one of Orlov's 'schools for saboteurs'. So yes, if that is the case, maybe he was recruited by Leonid.

Lona Cohen, recruited by her husband, became an agent in 1941 and spent the last weeks of the war in New Mexico waiting for Theodore Hall to deliver the results of the Alamogordo test. When he finally handed them over she caught the train back to New York. Appalled to find military policemen on board searching passengers' luggage, she stuffed the documents inside a newspaper and gave it to a policeman to hold while she opened her bags for him to inspect. The policeman handed the paper back and went on to search the bags. This is the story as told by Andrew and Mitrokhin and it's a good one. In Sudoplatov's account a box of Kleenex substitutes for the newspaper: Lona Cohen arrives at the station late; can't find her ticket; gives the Kleenex to the conductor to hold while she rummages in her bag; and gets on the train having forgotten about the Kleenex. 'I felt it in my skin that the conductor would return the box of Kleenex,' Sudoplatov has her say to no one in particular. Hard to know what to make of the discrepancy, except that Sudoplatov, while praising Cohen's 'tradecraft', makes her sound like an archetypally silly woman. More of a womaniser, Leonid was less of a conventional chauvinist.

Lona Cohen had also acted as a courier for the Rosenbergs, and as soon as they were caught the Cohens decamped to Mexico, where they were looked after by a pair of Soviet agents, both of them members of the Spanish Communist Party in exile. Leonid by then was busy with dissident nationalists in the Baltic states and would have had nothing to do with any of this, but Spain . . . the bomb . . . Mexico. I imagine some tutelary involvement.

That wasn't the end of the Cohens' career. Whoever recruited Morris Cohen had recruited well. Back eventually in Moscow, they were renamed Helen and Peter Kroger and despatched to Britain using New Zealand passports. They were eventually caught (through no fault of their own), tried, and in 1961 sentenced to twenty years in prison. In 1969 they were exchanged for the British lecturer Gerald Brooke. Both died in Moscow in the 1990s and each was posthumously awarded the title of Hero of the Russian Federation by President Yeltsin. They are hardly mentioned in the Venona transcripts.

If – if – Leonid recruited the Cohens it showed exceptional judgement. Or intuition. Or something more: 'I saw him as a skilled chief of intelligence,' Sudoplatov was to say of his first encounter with Leonid. 'Therefore he was assigned to work with illegal persons – this was sacred in our business.' But maybe he was good at paperwork, too; he had done a lot of it in his early years in Gomel, even though he hadn't enjoyed it. Writing about Leonid in the *Journal of Slavic Military Studies*, Ilya Kuznetsov reports that 'he communicated closely with scientists in the USSR who were directly involved in Soviet nuclear projects'.* 'Liaison': maybe that's what he was doing. On at least one occasion, we know from Leonid's daughter Svetlana, the Kurchatovs and the Eitingons stayed in the same holiday home where 'our rooms were next to Kurchatov's and they were very busy discussing something'. Leonid had a 'terrific brain', his granddaughter said, and cited the fact that he'd read 'all the atomic textbooks' in preparation for this job, which probably means that he read Henry Smyth's *Atomic Energy for Military Purposes* in Zoya's Russian translation.† But for all that, it isn't easy to imagine Leonid in all his middle-aged bulk sitting at an office desk in the Lubianka day after day.

Building an atomic bomb was the kind of large-scale undertaking that the Stalinist economy was best suited to, but however much money Stalin was willing to spend, however many hundreds of thousands of workers he mobilised, it couldn't be done without a secure supply of

---

* Kuznetsov is an emeritus professor of history at Irkutsk State University but he says some funny things. For example, that Trotsky was initially sent abroad 'to replace the Soviet station chiefs in Turkey, Norway and France'.
† Subtitled 'Official Report on the Development of the Atomic Bomb under the Auspices of the US Government' and published in September 1945, the book, which is still in print, was officially intended, as the author's friendly preface puts it, for scientists 'who can understand such things and who can explain the potentialities of atomic bombs to their fellow citizens'. In the same friendly spirit the author left a few things out: 'sensitive' information he didn't think the Soviets should have.

decent-quality uranium. In 1943 the government had ordered one hundred metric tons of uranium metal: by August 1945 only one kilogram had been produced. No one had a clear idea of what could be obtained from Eastern Europe or any idea at all of the sorts of deposit there might be in the Soviet Union itself. And meanwhile the US and the UK were doing their best to ensure that the Russians wouldn't be able to buy uranium from any other country: by December 1945, the West controlled 97 per cent of the world's output of high-grade uranium.

In February 1945 – when the Soviet uranium panic was at its height – Sudoplatov's department had news from captured German documents of high-quality uranium ore in Bukovo in the Rhodope mountains of Bulgaria. This, at any rate, is the story that Sudoplatov tells and since it's the only part of Sudoplatov's atomic tale that Leonid's biographer more or less repeats, I'm almost inclined to believe it. A vast mining operation was set in train ('we assigned three hundred engineers from the Red Army with coal-mining experience'), supervised by the prime minister of Bulgaria, Georgi Dimitrov himself, and guarded against American spies and local saboteurs by troops from the NKVD. When a pair of American spies and their wives were detained at the site Leonid was flown in. What he did with them isn't clear; in the strange version told by Sharapov he tried to persuade them to change sides – it didn't work.

Bukovo's uranium deposits, though thin, were the initial source for the first Soviet reactor. The following year much larger deposits were found in the Urals. The Americans and the British – this is the story Sudoplatov tells – knew exactly how much or how little uranium was mined in Bulgaria and from that they could estimate how long it would take to produce a Soviet bomb. They knew nothing of the deposits in the Urals and the intention was that they shouldn't find out. Leonid's task was to 'create the story' that would persuade them that the Soviet Union had no other uranium source and thus wouldn't be able to produce a bomb for five or six years. Visiting delegations and local spies filled out the plot and, whatever the contribution of this particular sub-story, it's still a fact that the first Soviet bomb was exploded much earlier than the West expected – Fuchs himself was surprised – and in the general's own account at least, it contained Soviet uranium.

Finally, the Rosenbergs' phone number. I was having supper with Leonid's granddaughter in a café in Camden Town when she told me that the Rosenbergs' names were in his address book. Did Leonid know them? Did he in fact recruit them? Do secret agents have address books that they leave lying around?

Part Five

CHAPTER 28

The Fall

In April 1947, the FBI instructed that Motty be monitored again. The issue, as always, was 'Penetration and Possible Use of American Fur Industry by Soviet Agents'.

Out came all the old allegations, rehashed and enlarged on. A confidential informant felt that 'during the entire period of the war, Eitingon was always in a position to furnish the finest furs from Russia' and 'is very closely connected with the Amtorg corporation'. The same informant, paraphrased, went on to say: 'Subject is regarded by a majority of the Gentile fur dealers in the United States as very sympathetic to the Communist ideology . . . It is common gossip that he donates between fifty and one hundred thousand dollars annually to the Communist Party in the United States.' Another informant mentioned the Soviet contract for a million sheepskin coats. Another, or maybe the same, informant said that everyone in the industry knew Motty was 'an avowed Communist and contributes large sums of money to the Communist Party'. A third, however, told the Bureau he didn't think this was right. Motty was 'interested more in making money than in any political or ideological consideration'.

But by the spring of 1947 Motty wasn't making money. Within months of its launching the Bonmouton idea had begun to seem ill-conceived. There are several ways of explaining that: the advent of rayon (i.e. fake fur) is one, over-expansion another, over-extension (too much borrowing) a third. In the family it's also been said that he was 'too chummy' with the unions; that at the start of the Bonmouton deal he gave fur cutters, who were normally piece workers, contracts and hourly wages and when he went bust they made him honour the contracts. 'So they became creditors and got money we might have got.'

He'd filed for bankruptcy at the end of 1946. There was none of the pally 'Motty' in *Time* magazine's account of the downfall of 'the nation's largest single operator in furs'. Now it was plain 'Eitingon', to which was added a snide parenthesis for those who couldn't figure out how to pronounce his name: 'rhymes with biting gone'. Chapter XI bankruptcy allowed him to continue trading while the possibility of a reorganisation was debated by all the parties involved. For editors and journalists, it was the first case of a major fur company in financial difficulty since the war.

Just before Christmas the court ruled that Motty could remain in charge of the Bonmouton venture, which would continue to run while the mess was sorted out. The referee in bankruptcy – a kind of adjudicator appointed by the courts – said that he could find no signs of 'dishonesty or crookedness on the part of the debtor'. But the creditors' committee were taking a tough position. Having originally said that the salaries of Eitingon family members involved in the business should be reduced by a third, they now proposed to halve them. That included Naum and Monya, both of them vice-presidents. The Modern Industrial Bank, a creditor, wanted appraisers in to establish 'that we're not chasing a will-o'-the-wisp'. An inventory was taken: Motty had 2.6 million mouton skins in stock or on order and fifteen thousand assorted furs of other kinds. At the latest count, he had processed ninety thousand of the mouton skins.

In the New Year a trio of Motty's business acquaintances offered to put a million dollars into the company. And at the end of February a new plan was unveiled and met with provisional approval. There would be 1.5 million dollars in new capital; the company would be run by a creditors' committee with Motty participating.

By April three million dollars' worth of debt had been paid off or adjusted, a feat achieved by trading a good deal of future production against what was owed. Motty's non-business assets were pledged as security against the company's new loans, which had the effect of cheering up the creditors and boosting confidence in the company. The plan was to shift as many processed skins as possible – the target was forty-five thousand by the end of April. By the middle of the month fifteen thousand skins were on their way. Buyers were asked to make out two cheques, one to the creditors and another to the company, in what was roughly a fifty–fifty split.

Not long after the plan was confirmed, Motty's line – now rather a minor line – in luxury fur suffered a blow when disagreement arose about the shape of the 1947 season. The New Look required longer hemlines but no one could say how far they were going to go. A typical fur coat had been thirty-five inches the previous year: would it now be thirty-eight inches or forty-two, or even forty-five? No one could decide. The result was that retailers were waiting until the last possible moment before putting in orders, and manufacturers were feeling the pinch. But the word was that many fur dealers and manufacturers had made a fortune during the war years and the delay, like the post-war tumble in prices, was manageable for most of them. The obvious exception, as the *Wall Street Journal* pointed out, was Motty Eitingon Inc.

The New York branch of the FBI followed Motty's fortunes through the Chapter XI bankruptcy hearings with interest. Perhaps they were intrigued by the fact that he had run into difficulty for the second time in less than ten years. Had money been siphoned out of his companies to support pro-Soviet activities in the US? The suggestion was plausible. Yet when they went into it, the Bureau could find nothing to suggest that this was the case.

They nonetheless had an intelligent analysis of the Bonmouton fiasco. Motty had been buying and selling sheepskins since the latter part of the war and when he decided to go for a full-scale blitz on the mass market, he spent half a million dollars in advertising. The orders began piling up in the in-tray and peaked at about a hundred, with a value of fourteen million dollars. Before the Chapter XI petition, he'd received about half the value of the contracts in promissory notes from purchasers and these he'd used to raise short-term loans with a number of factors and banks. But time was against him and he couldn't meet the contracts when he needed to. The plant was new, and it had all been a bit of an experiment; the conversion of lambskins into desirable fashion garments was not a straightforward process, and there were hold-ups when batches turned out to be sub-standard. Over and above the advertising there'd been the outlay on premises – two million at least for the plant and an unknown but high figure for warehousing in Philadelphia, even though this was charged to one of the company's subsidiaries.

Somebody obviously thought that Motty had been deceitful about his borrowing and passed this information on to the FBI. Allegedly he played a clever game with the promissory notes he received from companies who'd put in orders. Like any ordinary dealer or manufacturer, he took them to banks and factors – that's to say, individuals or small groups who lent money, normally on a short term – as surety against a loan. But when the date fell due for the skins he was supposed to supply and hadn't, Motty went to the buyer and asked for an updated note. He would then take the renewal note to a different lender and raise a further loan, as if the renewal note were a first-time agreement to pay Motty Eitingon Inc. for a consignment of Bonmouton.

In due course, whatever was owed to him by interested buyers became a form of indebtedness, since he'd already raised all the money he could on the contracts and still hadn't delivered many of the skins. And where contracts had been met, several buyers felt that they'd taken delivery of a product which was far less impressive than they'd hoped. So much for 'French champagne' and 'hunting pink'.

The FBI kept the file open through 1947 as it became clear that the reorganisation plan was not going to work. By October the consortium of lenders, who should by now have had their 1.5 million dollars back, were drumming their fingers, and it was proving impossible to deliver to contract-holders at the rate required to keep the business from going under. The logistics hadn't been properly considered. Motty's Bonmouton scheme, his stab at a democratic fur, required production on a martial scale.

His supply lines had folded before he'd even managed to engage.

The business was now being run – or wound down – by a thirteen-man supervisory committee who felt it was pointless to continue along the lines of the Chapter XI plan. The United Shearling Company, a subsidiary but also a creditor (that was how Motty did things), might, it was thought, take the lead in a much-reduced operation that could survive the collapse of the present one. Shearling, as its name suggests, dealt in first fleeces – the first cut is the softest. As chairman of the United Shearling board, Motty was once more doing business with himself. He didn't resign until the following year, shortly after the Bonmouton debacle.

The Shearling scheme involved Motty Eitingon Inc. going for a bankruptcy proper, so that the company would no longer be struggling with the huge commitments it had made to a comparatively small number of buyers. The notion was to scatter the product across a much wider market. The bankruptcy adjudication could be filed with the plan for yet another relaunch, of a somewhat more modest enterprise. Notification of bankruptcy proceedings, accompanied by a new 'plan of arrangement', was duly given at the end of October. The plan was approved the following year, after Motty and the supervisory committee, who were still in charge of the company, found a buyer for the warehouses in Philadelphia. There was a new issue of preferred stock, and the company continued as debtor-in-possession until 1949, but I've no real sense of how it fared during those years.

At the time it got into difficulty, Motty Eitingon Inc. had at least four other subsidiaries besides United

Shearling: the Bristol Processing Corporation, which would be inactive by the early 1950s, if not before; the New Bristol Corporation, which had taken over from the Processing Corporation and was also inactive; the New Easton Corporation, an old tannery, also defunct; and Goldhill Trading, which became inactive a few months after it was formed in 1949. To acquire the warehouses in Philadelphia, Motty had also set up something called the United Shearling Realty Company. Once the warehouses were sold, the company became inactive. To survey Motty's empire in the early 1950s was like looking around the old shacks on the periphery of an exhausted gold mine. As for the parent company, by 1953 it was showing about sixty thousand dollars in hand, with a sales volume of 120,000 dollars and untenable long-term debt. Or that's how the FBI saw it the following year.

As the Cold War intensified Moscow thinned back its diplomatic commitments in the US; and with the Communist takeover of Prague in February 1948 trade between Russia and America went into steep decline. Ben Gold testified in the autumn to a House subcommittee on labour affairs that he was a member of the Party, and that he'd joined in the early 1920s.

The complexion of the New York unions was finally changing; the days of working men visiting the piers to salute the sailors on Soviet ships were done. Korea was probably decisive, and in the late summer of 1950, when the *Mauretania* docked in New York with a consignment of Russian furs, the longshoremen refused to unload it. 'We're practically at war with Russia now,' one of them told the press. The *Mauretania* returned to Le Havre with the furs, and in future shippers made sure they found ways around the anti-Communism of the American working man: one of them was relabelling, another was sending overland from Montreal, but the most reliable was probably bribery. When one such case came to court in 1952, it emerged that a group of longshoremen had been paid seventy thousand dollars to break the ban.

Fur nonetheless retained a privileged position in Soviet–American trade as import–export figures for other items fell away. Six million dollars' worth of Russian furs were contracted to go to the States for the 1949–50 season and in July 1950, forty American buyers were expected at the Leningrad fur auction. Whatever the name under which they were trading I feel reasonably certain that Motty or Monya or both were among them. The following year the Truman Administration banned fur imports from the Soviet Bloc and Communist China.

The FBI lost interest in Motty quite soon after they reopened the file in 1947. The problem was that there was very little new to say about him. Nothing, at any rate, but recycled gossip. Or recycled rebuttals – of which a number must have convinced them that they should back off for a time. Motty was a 'loyal American' though he couldn't afford 'to antagonise the Russians', said one source, and if he had made contributions to pro-Soviet organisations he'd probably have thought of them as 'a business investment rather than a furtherance of Soviet ideology'. Someone in New York told them he was just a speculator – 'gambler' might have been more appropriate – and that he entertained lavishly. An ill-informed source in San Francisco told them he'd never travelled to Russia to purchase furs direct but had gone through the demon intermediary Amtorg. Even the New York staff of the FBI might have smiled at this, the last entry for the year, as they closed the file a few weeks later, in the autumn of 1947.

In the spring of 1954 they decided to reopen it. They were in different territory to begin with, worrying about Jack Soble, a known Soviet agent, and his entourage, which may have included one of Motty's old associates, Alexandra Tillo. Tillo had helped Motty – maybe even saved his life – when he was detained by the Bolsheviks in Moscow in 1918. After his getaway, he'd brought her to the US as an employee of Eitingon Schild, telling Immigration that no one knew more about Russian furs. She'd travelled first class on the *Mauretania* from Cherbourg in the summer of 1922 and stayed with Motty for eight or nine years. Then, when she didn't get the promotion she felt she deserved, she'd left the company and settled in Beverly Hills.

Soble might have been a crucial link between Motty and Leonid, had any solid evidence emerged about a link to Tillo, since he had early on penetrated Trotsky's entourage and followed the great man to Prinkipo, posing as a friend and a colleague and, finally, someone with whom Trotsky couldn't agree. And if it were possible to run this early and remote connection with Trotsky together with the later, remote connection, in 1937, when Motty had funded Hoellering's trip to Mexico, it would look to the FBI, or anyone else, very much as if Motty and Leonid did on occasion act together. But to what end? Motty was no fool and unless he was all along the deeply unreadable figure that the FBI worried he might be, it seems unlikely that he would have colluded in the kind of intelligence work that led to the murder of traitors to the Revolution.

Whatever the contact between them – if there was any – Leonid would never have let Motty know the sort of thing that he did: he was far too professional, as he himself might have said. If Motty did help with money (hard currency) or cover he would have been given to think he was doing it in a very good – that is, respectable – cause. And if at the same time it was useful to him, so much the better. 'The subject', the FBI concluded, 'is not pro-Soviet but is a shrewd businessman who posed a pro-Soviet front to gain a choice position with the Russians in order to acquire Russian furs and make a fortune.' All things considered, that's surprisingly fair. Yet even more surprising – and in the circumstances providential – is the Bureau's failure to make any link at all with Leonid, given how many other tenuous associations were invoked to cast Motty as a traitor.

In 1991 I asked a CIA operative living in retirement in a suburb outside Washington DC what he knew about the Eitingons. He had a rough – very rough – idea of Leonid's career, formed in the course of his professional life, and vague notions of Motty ('Solly or Molly') and Max, probably derived from the recent articles in the *New York Times* and the *New York Review of Books*. Of Leonid, he said: 'A person who is capable of the amount of deception he was might well have used a Jewish background as a cover.' Of Solly or Molly that he might have used the fur trade as a cover. Maybe (though he didn't suggest it) Max used psychoanalysis as a cover. Maybe we all use our lives as cover, as Freud might have said, pointing up the connection between espionage and psychoanalysis. As for connections between Leonid and Solly, the CIA man ventured only that they may well have been parallel operations, as indeed they may have been – like those of the conscious and the unconscious mind.

In September Motty himself was interviewed. A dazzling performer, he enjoyed a good deal more leeway this time than he had when he'd given so little away to McCormack–Dickstein, or when he'd watched politely as his wallet was flipped open and shaken at the airport in Miami in 1945.

The early part of the interview allowed him to show off his man-of-the-world qualities to an impressive extent. He went back over the escape from the Bolsheviks, he talked about his talent for acquiring fur, he twirled a few big figures around and discussed some of his subsequent trips to Moscow with Monya. Which led the FBI to enquire about the kinds of friend he had in Russia.

Motty mentioned a couple of names, among them his old friend Artur Stashevsky, who stayed at the Fur Syndicate until 1936, when he was sent to Spain to 'manipulate the Spanish economy', as Krivitsky put it: in fact he was the man who first suggested sending Spain's gold reserves to Moscow for 'safekeeping'. The FBI reports that in January 1937, as Motty remembered it, 'he met Stashevsky on a street in Paris' and had dinner with him and that 'during dinner Stashevsky remarked that he did not agree to the way that the Soviet Government wanted many things done at the embassy' – he was the commercial attaché in Spain – 'and that in frequent cases he took chances and did things his own way'. Six months later, in June 1937 to be precise, Motty told the FBI, Stashevsky was executed. How Motty came by that information is a puzzle, or a clue: executions weren't much talked about in

Soviet times. Who was Motty's informant? 'Stashevsky's great mistake', Antony Beevor writes, 'was to have complained . . . about the vicious activities of the NKVD in Spain.'

Stashevsky would have known that General Kotov, the designation Leonid had used in Spain, was really called Eitingon, and maybe he mentioned his presence there to Motty. Or maybe Motty already knew. The FBI clearly didn't and Motty was careful to tell them that he'd found Stashevsky's dedication to the Party chilling: if Motty said something that Stashevsky couldn't go along with, 'expressed his non-Communist ideas', it seems that Stashevsky would look at him as though he had been ready 'to drink the blood from my veins'. (Was Leonid like that too?)

Amtorg came up, as it would have to, and Motty dutifully explained how little of his business with the Russians – around 10 per cent in all – had gone through the organisation and why it had been such a coup to get a contract direct with Moscow, because that way you went out there and what you saw was what you got. But yes, he had always kept some sort of social life going with the chairman of Amtorg and always entertained visiting officials of the Soviet Fur Syndicate when they were over.

He had never come under pressure, he said, to supply the Russians with intelligence. Only once or twice had they ever asked him to do anything that wasn't connected to the fur business. Amtorg had wanted to rent offices in the Empire State Building sometime in the 1930s, and had asked him to arrange a meeting with the former governor of New York, who had a financial interest in the building. Nothing had come of it. And in 1937 he was asked if he'd form a company, a sort of agency, that could buy machinery from the US on behalf of the Soviet Union. He'd been interested but no one followed up the offer.

Then there was the matter of Hoellering and what Krivitsky had said about him being an OGPU man and whether Motty had been doing the Russian ambassador a favour by funding Hoellering's trip to Mexico, since the ambassador was very interested to hear in detail how Trotsky performed, but strangely this isn't something the FBI mentioned to Motty. And of course there is no record to indicate whether Motty was surprised, or feigned surprise, at the implication that Hoellering was an agent. He'd known he was a Communist, he said again, and was able to account for his later disaffection – the Trotsky hearings had much to do with it.

Motty, who was keen to be helpful, told the FBI that Hoellering had been refused a passport after the war, even though he was by now an anti-Communist, and that when he'd submitted an anti-Communist article he'd written – for the *Nation*, he seemed to recall – to someone in the State Department the passport had been issued.

The conversation now turned to Ben Gold, whose career remained more or less undimmed despite several unsuccessful attempts to run for public office and a perjury case in which he was accused of falsely swearing that he was not a Communist. The union had kept an impressive membership under Gold, and a high profile. It was Gold – and implicitly the International Fur and Leather Workers – who'd presided over the march through New York in 1948 urging rapid recognition of the state of Israel, and it was Gold's colleagues in the union who'd aggressively invoked the Fifth Amendment when they were brought before the HUAC six months later.

Motty may have been a bit edgy on the subject of Ben Gold, but he held his ground. No, he said, they hadn't been personal friends, although he had 'on occasion lunched with Gold and his associates in connection with business' – though that isn't quite what he'd said earlier. But there was nothing political in it and, in response to another question, he assured his interrogators that 'no pressure was asserted on him by Gold, the Communists, or the Russians, to hire Communist Party members in his factories'. Besides, he didn't handle the hiring and firing in the workplace: this was done by his factory manager. Gold, he told them by way of reassurance, was 'strictly an American Communist' and believed in 'evolution not revolution'.

Finally money, and the old suspicion that Motty donated money – a great deal of it – where he shouldn't have. Did he, as 'common gossip' had it, give anything between fifty and a hundred thousand dollars a year to the Communist Party? The answer was no. He often gave away as much as 150,000 dollars a year to charity but never to the Communist Party 'of any country at any time'. Yes he had given maybe five hundred dollars in 1946 to the National Council of American–Soviet Friendship but he hadn't known that the organisation was 'Communist-controlled' and only later learned that it was on the list of organisations deemed subversive by the Attorney General. The point here was to warn Motty that he had been – and therefore remained – on shaky ground with his wayward generosity towards left-wing groups, and to leave no doubt in his mind that the Bureau was tracking him.

'Attendance at Soviet Embassy Affairs' was the next heading. He used to go to cocktail parties, Motty said, but not now any longer, though sometimes the hardy Monya went in his place. And then, at last, 'Subject's Sentiments Regarding Communism and the Soviet Union'. No, he said once more, he'd never been a Communist or given money to the Party, even though he sympathised with 'the Russian people'. He was most certainly against the Soviet regime and wished to disavow the 'Nazi-like methods used by the Russian hierarchy'. He had come to believe, he went on, that the Soviet Union meant to foment revolution worldwide, and possibly war. He was in favour of America preparing to meet the Soviet threat. And that was enough surely. 'Politically', the file states, 'the subject considers himself an anti-Communist liberal.' And then, something very much in his favour: 'But not a Socialist.'

The investigation was wound down in the same month. In December, as the file was prepared for despatch to Washington, the New York office added a few remarks to the effect that Motty had been a model interviewee. He was, the file says, 'co-operative and friendly' and 'did not hesitate to answer all questions asked of him'; in fact he 'volunteered much of the information disclosed throughout the interview'. It was noted that 'the co-operative attitude of Eitingon may well be of value to the Bureau' in subsequent inquiries.

One of the last pieces of information to go on record with the FBI about Motty takes the form of a memo from an employee in Los Angeles, filed as the final investigation was coming to a close. The memo drew Hoover's attention to an article in the *Saturday Evening Post*, an interview with Leonid's recently defected former colleague Nikolai Khokhlov written up as a first-person piece, in which Leonid was clearly referred to. It contains nothing of interest to later Eitingon-watchers, but you might have expected it to generate a new file on Motty, since it mentioned Leonid in connection with the murder of Trotsky. 'The foregoing is brought to the Bureau's attention', the employee wrote, 'merely to indicate the identical last name for General EITINGON and MOTTY EITINGON and the alleged apparent common interest in LEON TROTSKY.' Quite. 'It is not known', the memo went on, 'if Eitingon is a common Russian surname or if these two individuals could be related.' It was the best clue they had and they ignored it. Leonid, if not his colleagues, would, I'm sure, have done better.

> The foregoing is brought to the Bureau's attention merely to
> indicate the identical last name for General EITINGON and MOTTY EITINGON
> and the alleged apparent common interest in LEON TROTSKY. It is not
> known if EITINGON is a common Russian surname or if these two indivi-
> duals could be related, and the significance, if any, of these two
> similarities is not known.
>
> INDEXED-95   SE-22
> HHD:JAD

The file was closed and then reopened, because of a renewed FBI splurge on Soble, and once it closed again, at the end of 1954, there was nothing further on Motty – or not as far as I know – beyond a note two years later to say that he'd died.

I wonder whether they felt they'd been wasting their time. In 1954 Motty was approaching seventy and his days of quality espionage, if there'd been any, were done. We were now living in Brussels and when I last saw him, bringing his usual bunch of flowers for my mother, he seemed a sad and stooped old man. But perhaps I just saw him that way because my parents were no longer in love with him and that made him seem somehow divested in my eyes. As for the name, you'd think that in the hot days of the Cold War someone in the FBI would know what a common Russian surname looked like and if they didn't they'd have bothered to find out whether 'Eitingon' was a plausible candidate. Bothered, more to the point, to question Motty one more time. Khokhlov's article was published in November 1954. Motty had been brought in for questioning by the New York offices two months before.

That had been Motty's last performance. After the Bonmouton fiasco the world withdrew from him, and so gradually did the wider family, even Monya. One of Motty's letters written in 1951 makes this plain. A letter from Monya's wife, Louisa, has thrown Motty on the defensive. The issue is entitlement and I think Louisa must have been trying to get it straight with Motty how much of the company and family assets were Monya's – especially in the property deals that they'd done together. Her letter is lost, or at any rate I haven't seen it. But replying to Monya, Motty says: 'It makes me sad to think that you, Monya dear, could doubt that you would get what's due to you. And anything I promised I and my family would be responsible. I always appreciated all the help you gave me as my partner and sorry for all the trouble I caused you.'

Motty's memory, he tells Monya, isn't what it was and he can't find details of the various family members' share in the assets of Motty Eitingon Inc. Motty had always been terribly disorganised, one of the old ladies told me. Which, like a collapsing memory, could sometimes be useful.

Monya had watched the assets reinvested in property over the years and must have wondered, as Motty got older and conveniently vaguer and his troubles increased, whether he would see any return. In his private papers, or those which his son showed me, which are not extensive, there is a small ruled sheet with an entry in longhand that I suspect was written by Monya or Louisa. It's a jotted inventory of properties and monies of which whoever wrote it felt they ought to get a cut. I don't know what these properties were or how they'd been acquired, but they were obviously vivid and contentious in the mind of the person who wrote the note. Next comes: 'Profits in Europe, until taken over by M.E. Inc.' – a reference to the most successful period of Eitingon dealing, before the war. Underneath this list, in the same hand, the remark: 'Not a single dollar as partner.'

Finally, as an afterthought, at the right-hand margin, are listed 'Brazil, Palestine, Hillcrest', the three bracketed together as 'private'. Were they set down to serve as a reminder of something else worth bringing up when Motty was confronted, something to let him understand that Monya and Louisa knew he wasn't down to his last dime?

If Motty was left with some valuable bricks and mortar and a bit of land, he also had a kind of liquidity. He continued to dress mouton skins and trade in furs, though at very low levels now. But he was also deeply in debt. From a note he wrote in the summer of 1956, it looks as though the IRS or some other government department has taken possession of a property on Broadway against payment of about sixty thousand dollars in overdue tax. By now he was very unwell, and, in periods of delirium, spent a lot of time writing down figures and percentages in obscure notes, probably to Monya.

One of them, dated 6 July, suggests that he's recovering from some form of blood-poisoning: 'They discovered my virus and I am absolutely out of danger. The virus was in

my bloodstream and was responsible for the chills which
one day looked fatal.' In fact he had leukaemia but maybe
he wasn't told or maybe – more likely – he didn't want to
know. Didn't want to know, his daughter suggested,
'because he was in a trough'. I can see that it wasn't a good
place for his life to end. I wonder whether he thought that
when his health got better he would become a rich man all
over again.

The following day, he felt well enough to write a long
letter to Monya. It was a kind of apology and a kind of
self-exoneration, and confirms that they'd had a terrible
falling-out over money – 'accountings and payments',
Motty calls it. The details are too abstruse – and some of
the sums too petty – to make much sense of exactly what
was at stake, but it is an interesting document if only
because it shows how far Motty had fallen. 'My check
account', he writes about his relative destitution the previous year, when the row had really begun to get under way,
'was $58. Goldberg before going to Europe gave me $500.
Natel advanced me $150 a week. That is all what I had.
And from this I had to help Esther $150 a month, Natel
$100, so not to be in default. And with the exception of
the land in Israel nothing else, absolutely nothing, no
assets to pawn.'

The land he'd acquired in Palestine – now Israel – seems
to be valued at very little, and more trouble than it was
worth, though it turns out from the letter to Monya that
he'd already given it away, one-third to Naum for going
out there to tackle some legal hitch, and another third
against a loan of ten thousand dollars. The remainder, he
explained, was earmarked for his first wife: 'And because
I was not able to give Fanny anything, the family decided

that I am to give Fanny the last third of Israel property. Fanny was sick, frightened to death, and I had to agree to it.' He goes on: 'And so no cash value in my insurance which I dropped, no other asset, a sick boy and debts.' The sick boy was my cousin Tommy, the one I'd liked so much, who'd had a nervous breakdown when he was a student and never really recovered.

It's hard not to feel sorry for Motty. Ill, cashless, in debt, and nowhere to live – Naum had offered to pay for an apartment for him and Bess, when they'd finally run out of homes, and for a time they had the use of a friend's place. 'Left only', he wrote, 'the will to fight and the hope, that through patience I will make money again.' And yet, he said, and he was right, Monya didn't believe him, thought it was a trick, saw him still 'as the reach [rich] man, who still had cash value of 12,000 in insurance and a house, on which he could raise a mortgage'. 'And in one of those days,' Motty's letter continued, 'you came to my office, you got excited and you hallert [hollered] in full voice, "You are a kruck, I tell you are a kruck," and you ran away. This last remark, Monetzka, was hard to swallow, after 44 years of our co-operation.'

When Motty died three weeks later Monya was left with eight dollars in the bank and his life insurance. 'Mr Eitingon always played for big stakes,' *Women's Wear Daily* told its readers in an obituary notice. 'There were never, according to the people who knew him best, any little triumphs or little failures.'

Was he a traitor, a spy, a Communist – a committed Communist? I find it hard to believe. I think he liked to be connected to the right sort of people, conspicuous people and people with power – in Washington and in the

Kremlin – and he liked to do favours, especially favours that would turn out to be useful to him. 'Motty was very smart,' Theodore Draper said when we were talking about what he might or might not have done for the Soviet Union. If cash was needed or someone had to be put up for a few nights that was no problem. But he was also a snob and I doubt whether he would have gone out of his way for Leonid, formidable but inconspicuous, unless of course he was asked to by a more illustrious figure – an ambassador at Washington, for example. At some point when things were going badly for him it was suggested that there might be work for him in Milwaukee. 'I can't live in Milwaukee,' he said. 'I'm a man of the world.'

CHAPTER 29

Doctors' Plot

Not a hair of Leonid's head would ever be touched, Stalin had said, when he heard that Trotsky was dead. But in October 1951 Leonid was arrested. He would spend, in all, twelve years in jail.

He was arrested one late afternoon as he was returning from the Baltic states, where he'd spent the previous three months 'liquidating' – that's the official word – Lithuanian (Sudoplatov) or Latvian (Sharapov) nationalists. Zoya, who'd persuaded one of Beria's 'handsome bodyguards' to take her to Vnukovo Airport to meet him, watched his plane land and then wondered why, instead of stopping in the usual place, it carried on 'wheeling' to a far edge of the field. Leonid emerged, she ran out to him (her KGB rank entitled her to do that), and found him surrounded by 'military escorts'. Something wasn't right.

She went home and told her mother that Leonid had gone straight to his office. In the early hours of the morning 'they' knocked at the door, six or seven of them. They looked everywhere, went through every book, examined every photograph asking who each person was. They stayed until daylight but in Zoya's account the only things they found to take away were a portrait of Stalin she'd given Leonid on his fiftieth birthday and her photographs of 'Mr Churchill' and 'Mr Roosevelt', souvenirs of her time at Tehran and Yalta.

His being Jewish was the reason for his detention,

although the eventual charge was high treason, as it was with most victims of Stalin's paranoia. He was taken first to the Central Prison inside the Lubianka and either there, or later in Lefortovo jail, where political prisoners were held, treated quite brutally. He had been an imposing figure, in uniform especially, with the look of someone who was well fed and used to having his say. In no time at all he'd turned into an ordinary Soviet citizen, thinner, shakier, with a dismaying row of brown teeth.

A few months after the Soviet victory at Stalingrad in February 1943, the editor of *Krasnaya Zvezda*, the army newspaper, was told that he had too many Jews on his staff and would have to let some go. He was angry – the paper had already lost nine Jewish correspondents at the front – but he too was Jewish and it wasn't long before he in turn was replaced. The Bolsheviks had early on abolished the tsarist laws discriminating against Jews, replacing them with laws that prohibited anti-Semitism in every form. In 1931 Stalin had even likened anti-Semitism to cannibalism: 'Anti-Semitism', he told the Jewish Telegraphic Agency, 'is an extreme expression of racial chauvinism and as such the most dangerous survival of cannibalism.' Sometimes taboo, but never very far below the surface, anti-Semitism didn't take hold until the late 1930s.

Now, as Germany's defeat came to seem more certain, a wave of Russian nationalism swept the country and many Jews lost their jobs. There were those – Beria was one – who felt that the Jews were owed something since they had suffered more during the war but Stalin would have none of it: all Soviet citizens, he decreed, had suffered equally. Jews in prominent positions were especially vulnerable. 'To sit at the bottom was safer,' as one Soviet citizen put it.

'Leonid', Zoya once said, 'wasn't a Jew Jew.' And it's true that he didn't look particularly Jewish or observe any Jewish practices. If he abandoned 'Naum Isaakovich' in favour of 'Leonid Alexandrovich' he held on to the unmistakably Jewish 'Eitingon'. Of his 'wives' only the first, the one of whom we hear nothing further, Vladimir's mother, Anna Shulman, was Jewish, but the colleague to whom he was said to have been closest, and with whom he most often played cards, was the fully Jewish Leonid Raikhman, arrested at the same time as he was.

His mother, we know, set some store by her Jewishness. She was the daughter of a rabbi and marked the Jewish holidays as best she could. She knew Hebrew and read the Bible, as her grandchildren observed, from right to left. She didn't approve of Leonid's ways or his profession but she'd learned to keep her own counsel and when she felt well disposed towards him called him 'Nakhke'. He didn't later in life often go to see her and when he did had little to say to her – mainly he made his way through the matzos which she kept on top of a cupboard. He wasn't in any case her favourite child – that was his brother – and their relationship was quite uneasy.

There was a saying in the late 1940s: 'Call a Jew a cosmopolitan – that way no one can call you an anti-Semite.' The 'anti-cosmopolitan' campaign, which took over from the random sackings of the early 1940s, lasted from 1947 until Stalin's death in 1953. It began with editorials in *Pravda* denouncing excessive Jewish influence in the arts. In January 1948 the Jewish actor Solomon Mikhoels, recipient of both the Order of Lenin and the Stalin Prize, was executed – 'run over by a lorry in Minsk'. A few months beforehand he had said, 'Jews feel more physically secure in the Soviet Union than in any other country in the world,' but maybe he only said it because he didn't feel very secure.

Mikhoels was the chairman of the Jewish Anti-Fascist Committee, set up by the government in 1942 to generate support in the West for the Soviet war effort. The following year Stalin had sent him to the US to raise money and make friends. He met Chaplin and Chagall and Theodore Dreiser. There were fund-raising dinners and rallies all over the country. Fifty thousand people gathered in the Polo Grounds in New York, where, speaking in Yiddish, Mikhoels urged them to give their support to the Red Army. But what was good then – the Soviet press was ecstatic – was bad now.

Within a few months of Mikhoels's death the Jewish Anti-Fascist Committee was disbanded. There was no more talk of setting up a Jewish homeland in the Crimea – briefly seen as a way of currying favour with America. Instead there were warnings of an 'international Jewish bourgeois-nationalist organisation' plotting with the Americans, and possibly the British, to murder the Kremlin leadership and overthrow the Soviet government. The public understood well enough what was going on and many non-Jews divorced their Jewish spouses. In time ten members of the Jewish Anti-Fascist Committee were tried and executed, along with a Yiddish novelist and four Yiddish poets. 'How could you be a Soviet patriot with relatives all over the world?' one of them was asked by his interrogators. It was an important question. 'We know Jews,' Khrushchev said to a group of Polish Communists. 'They all have connections with the capitalist world because they all have relatives living abroad.'

In the 1920s it had been possible for Leonid to ask Motty for help. As far as we know he didn't get it: 'We know the sort of work he does,' Motty is supposed to have said. Nevertheless, as General Sudoplatov pointed out, the approach had been made ('His distant European relatives declined his request . . .'). Leonid's nieces, too, were aware of it. They knew because Leonid hadn't approached Motty himself: their mother, Leonid's sister Sonia, had gone to the National Hotel to talk to Motty on Leonid's behalf. There are several plausible reasons for that. Prudence is one: it could have been unwise for Leonid to be seen going into the hotel. Deniability is another: he may have wanted to be able to say truthfully that Motty and he had never met. It may be on the other hand that they had already met and failed to see eye to eye. And it may be that Leonid was quite simply too proud.

It's surprising that Sonia should have mentioned this to her daughters. In the postwar years even knowing the name of an American relative could be dangerous. In prison Leonid was asked by his interrogator: 'Which of your near or distant relatives lives abroad?'

'None of my relatives lives abroad.'

'Are you sure?'

'Absolutely sure.'

'It is, however, known that you have relatives in America. Please name them.'

'I know all my close relatives well, they all live in the USSR. Such distant relatives as I know don't live abroad.'

Whoever was questioning him was merely setting out the dossier: he was well aware of the fact that Leonid had relatives abroad and Leonid knew better than to deny it.

In 1948 when Israel came into existence things only got

worse. Stalin had supported the Jewish fighters against the British and been one of the first to recognise the Israeli state. But he didn't like to think of his subjects having divided loyalties – belonging to networks he might not know of – and before long the existence of Israel began to aggravate those anxieties. At the end of the summer of 1948 Golda Meir arrived in Moscow as the head of the first Israeli legation to the Kremlin. On Saturday 11 September a huge crowd came to welcome her outside Moscow's main synagogue. At Rosh Hashanah even larger crowds accompanied her through the streets shouting: 'Next year in Jerusalem.' That was when the Jewish Anti-Fascist Committee was eliminated – that's to say, liquidated. A Yiddish newspaper and Yiddish publishing house were closed down immediately. It was just a start.

The Doctors' Plot – 'an intricate network of cross-cutting purges'* – had its origin in the death of Stalin's cultural commissar, Andrei Zhdanov, at the end of August 1948. Although Stalin was happy finally to get Zhdanov out of the way, and although Zhdanov died of natural causes, it later emerged that his doctors had been remiss in their treatment of him. The doctors in question hadn't been Jewish but many others were, and another member of the Soviet elite who'd died a few years earlier had been treated by a Jewish doctor, Yakov Etinger, who was heard on a bug talking too frankly about Stalin. Viktor Abakumov, who was then head of the security service, but whom Stalin had had in his sights for a while, was considered to have been insufficiently zealous in dealing with Etinger.

* Yoram Gorlizki and Oleg Khlevniuk, *Cold Peace*.

And from there, very loosely, it became necessary to purge not only Jewish poets and intellectuals but Jewish doctors and the security service itself, which was nominally in charge of the purging, its Jewish officers especially – which is how Leonid got involved.

It's sometimes hard to see the sense of what Stalin was up to, but if his actions can seem baroque his aims were usually quite straightforward. To safeguard both his own power – more difficult now, given his age and failing health – and the prestige of the Soviet Union in the wider world, the two being almost always largely synonymous. So first of all there was the danger posed by 'the Zionist network' thanks to Israel's existence and the support it was getting from America. Then there was the local threat represented by Abakumov, whom Stalin had put in charge of the MGB, as the KGB was then called, the institution on which he depended to implement his wishes and take care of treacherous Jews (i.e. Jews *tout court*) inside the country. To make matters worse, Abakumov enjoyed Beria's support and Stalin by now was both eager to sideline Beria and afraid of him.

The strutting, unpopular Abakumov was purged before Leonid, his function as spearhead of the anti-cosmopolitan campaign taken by a more energetic – or, to use Sudoplatov's epithet, 'primitive' – anti-Semite, Mikhail Ryumin, 'the Midget', as Stalin not very affectionately called him. Ryumin began his new job the month Leonid was detained.

It was a Jewish colleague arrested before him who denounced Leonid as a 'Zionist plotter' along with his friend Raikhman and several others. But in their accounts of what happened to him Leonid's family are always inclined to make him the victim of a more singular fate. The first time we talked about it Zoya told me that Leonid was arrested on the grounds that as a linguist he would become Minister of Foreign Affairs in the new Jewish republic. I didn't ask why anyone would pick out Leonid, a blunt, sarcastic man not much interested in diplomacy, when there were many more suave Jewish linguists in the security service to choose from – though, come to think of it, suave diplomacy wasn't the kind the Soviets practised. On another occasion she might say it was because he knew about Trotsky's death or because someone much grander had taken against him. The story I heard from Leonid's nieces is more dashing, more in keeping with family myth. As they tell it, a 'bastard' who worked with Leonid made some anti-Semitic remarks. 'Leonid immediately put his gun on the table and said: "If you say that once more I shall shoot you."' And 'that', they said, 'was the man who informed on him'.

General Sudoplatov, a Gentile, describes Ryumin circling round Leonid, looking for ways to incriminate him. There were sinister connections, he told Sudoplatov, between Leonid and his doctor sister Sonia; and besides, he said, Sonia was refusing to treat non-Jewish patients. Every time Ryumin came up to him with another set of accusations Sudoplatov, in his own telling, saw him off with a brave cliché. 'As Communists we must evaluate people by what they do, not by the rumours that are spread about them,' he said he said – and he probably did because that was the way it was advisable to speak. Should he have been more forthright? Probably not. Ryumin had, after all, been appointed by Stalin on the understanding that he would flush out the 'Jewish nationalists' in the security service. It followed, at least for the time being, that all the Jews he rounded up were Jewish nationalists – i.e. traitors.

A few days after Leonid's arrest Sudoplatov met Abakumov's replacement as head of the MGB, Semyon Ignatiev, at a staff meeting. 'What do you think of Eitingon now?' the new boss asked him. 'I still remember my prompt reply,' Sudoplatov proudly reports in his memoir. '"My assessment of people and their deeds is always in agreement with the Party line," I said.' And the Party, as he saw it, 'eventually vindicated' him. Eventually vindicated him in the sense that Ryumin was eventually shot.

Leonid was in prison for seventeen months. In her memoir Zoya says it was Stalin himself who sent him there, as if it had been a personal matter between the two men. Certainly he wasn't arrested without Stalin's knowledge, but that's hardly the same thing. 'Of all the state institutions, Stalin devoted most of his time and attention to the punitive organs, which were in effect outside the state's control and under his personal supervision,' Dmitri Volkogonov, the old Soviet general turned chronicler of the regime, wrote in his biography of the Leader. Stalin regularly dictated the questions investigators put to suspects and routinely reviewed transcripts of the interrogations. It was, we are told, his favourite pastime.

I don't have a complete transcript of Leonid's interrogation, but I do have a heavily edited version of the five volumes in which its proceedings are recorded, the selection made and transcribed in 1991 by Igor, the young man in Moscow whose political connections made it possible for him to spend several days in the archives on my behalf. First he transcribed what he thought appropriate into numbered exercise books that he handed in for inspection every night as he left the building. Then at the end of the week he typed up what remained after the nightly inspections. Twenty-two pages of generously spaced A4 survived, which also included material from Leonid's autobiographies and other documents. I don't know on what principles Igor made his selection – a rough combination, I imagine, of what he thought I wanted to know and what the times would allow – just as I don't know for sure that someone else, a more powerful figure in this particular hierarchy, censored it. It isn't an orderly document: issues appear, disappear, reappear in no particular order.

Only answers are transcribed. With the exception of the exchange I quoted about Leonid's putative relatives in the West, the questions themselves are missing, giving the transcript the appearance of a series of loosely related fragments. In a different context they could be plot summaries for a sequence of stories about Soviet life. In the original the interrogator – there were different interrogators throughout his time in jail – wrote out both his questions and Leonid's answers, each one of which Leonid then signed off, just as he signed off every page.

His answers are adept and straightforward; he obviously had experience of this kind of situation and was careful not to say too much or to paint himself into a corner. He spoke modestly and to the point; there's no boasting, no showing off, no name-dropping; no 'I was there, I arranged Trotsky's death, who do you think you are to speak to me like that?' His interrogators, in the way of things, will have been less intelligent than he was, more limited in outlook, and probably just as frightened. Any reversal was possible after all: Leonid may have had to spend time in prison but Ryumin was shot.

The charge against Leonid was that he had 'nationalist sentiments' – i.e. wasn't convinced that all was well for the Jews in the USSR – and from there it was a small step to calling him a traitor. Compromising connections were the first line of attack. And most compromising of all in 1951 was the existence of relatives in the West, 'Zionists' especially. Other Jewish interrogations have long lists of uncles and brothers and sisters and cousins with 'Zionist tendencies' living outside the Soviet Union. But apart from the exchange I quoted, effectively a dead end, the only suggestion of a connection between Leonid and the Eitingons in the US comes from a disgraced (and long since executed) former colleague, who is quoted as saying that Leonid 'had relatives abroad, specifically in America. They are well-to-do furriers.' And the most interesting thing about that is that either Igor himself or someone with more authority thought it best not to allow me to see Leonid's response. All of this of course applies only to the transcript I have – heaven knows what Eitingons might be locked away in the KGB archive.

Friends and colleagues, too, were a liability. If they were Jewish and tainted, and most of Leonid's friends were Jewish and most Jews were tainted, so would he be. Thus a typical response to a question that didn't survive on my transcript: 'Meizerov Semyon Moiseevich: my long-time acquaintance and good friend. I first met him in Harbin, where he was the interpreter in our *rezidentura*. Later we both worked in the foreign department of OGPU. In 1939 or 1940 he was dismissed from the service. I often went hunting with him.'

In Stalin's eyes friendships were bad, suggesting as they did that friends might have other friends, and that together they might form a network – that's to say a conspiracy. So Leonid does well to give a straight answer: to say that he and Meizerov were friends and, as evidence of their friendship, that they went hunting together. Hunting, smoking, drinking: that's how the male members of the Soviet *nomenklatura* bonded.

Visiting each other's houses, having meals together – that was another potential trap and again Leonid is careful: 'Mikhail Borisovich Makliarsky is a former employee of the Ministry for State Security . . . We met not only in the course of our work but at each other's houses. In 1949 he invited me for dinner at his house to celebrate his winning the Stalin Prize for the script of his film *Secret Agent*. In the summer of 1950 he invited me for dinner again. He also visited me at my house on several occasions.'

To the extent that there was evidence against Leonid it came from colleagues who'd been arrested before him and had already confessed. His colleague Shvartsman, once Isaac Babel's interrogator, was one. As Leonid explained, 'At some point in 1950 Lev Leonidovich Shvartsman . . . came into my office and we exchanged views and we said that Jewish Chekists were being fired from their jobs . . . we even said that restrictions had allegedly been put on the number of Jews entering the universities. We didn't touch on other issues.'

Shvartsman, arrested three months before Leonid, had famously confessed to all sorts of misbehaviour – having sex with his son, for example – in the hope of being put under psychiatric observation. Leonid must have had that in mind when he acknowledged the 'nationalist' conversation but pointed out that it hadn't 'touched on other issues'.

Later on, invited to speak about himself rather than his friends or his colleagues, Leonid was more forthright and pugnacious. Yes he had 'started to have nationalistic moods' in 1950, as he saw his Jewish colleagues being dismissed from the service or transferred to 'the periphery'. And his own situation too was unsatisfactory – 'fragile' is the word he used. In fact he had nothing to do and his staff had nothing to do; the whole ministry was in a mess.

He was being careful but he also had something to say. Abakumov, his boss, was in prison, maybe dead – so it was safe if not mandatory to blame him for what had gone wrong. But Leonid took a riskier path and didn't entirely blame Abakumov. There had been several reorganisations of the security services in the late 1940s at the behest of Stalin himself – via Molotov – and Leonid was quite outspoken about these: 'I must note that the reason for the feebleness of the intelligence services has been the constant reorganisation.' In the past – i.e. in his heyday – the Cheka had had resounding successes: against the White Army, the Fourth International (the Trotskyists) and the Nazi occupation. Now nothing was happening, and whatever measures were undertaken were largely ineffectual. Men with experience were ignored, their place taken by young pups just out of school 'who don't know how to work in foreign conditions', and agents who had once had autonomy abroad were now no better than assistants to the local ambassador.

Why, he asks, has no one put their mind to turning a few American agents, for example? They aren't well paid: 'We could buy lots of them.' He may be part of an old guard now, still showing signs of being obsessed with the Trotskyist enemy, but one of the very striking things about Leonid is that under interrogation or in prison he never stopped thinking about how the job should be done.

CHAPTER 30

Stalin's Death

Stalin died on 5 March 1953. On 21 March Leonid was back home. Two officers escorted him to his flat; in Zoya's account they were standing behind him 'bearing all his decorations and medals' when her mother answered the door. Leonid had lost forty-two kilos in prison, and as Olga rushed to embrace him, they both lost their footing and fell into the arms of his escorts.*

Stalin had died in his dacha at Kuntsevo in the presence of his daughter, Svetlana, and eight members of his entourage, eight rivals in the struggle for the succession. Khrushchev and Beria were the principal contenders. Beria – the only one not to have wept at the old man's timely demise – was the first to leave the dacha. He quickly kissed the warm body and immediately called for his driver to take him to the Kremlin ('Khrustalev, the car': the phrase would not be forgotten). 'He's off to take power,' Mikoyan said to Khrushchev. He wasn't wrong. 'They were all terrified of Beria,' Svetlana noted as everyone in turn 'rushed for the door'. 'I wasn't just weeping for Stalin,' Khrushchev said in his memoirs. 'I was terribly worried about the future of the country. I already sensed that Beria

---

* A family story has it that one of the two escorting officers had taken part in Leonid's interrogation. When they reached the door of his flat the officer knelt at Leonid's feet to ask his forgiveness. This, I was told, would make an 'interesting story' for my book.

would start bossing everyone around and that this could be the beginning of the end.'

Beria was the longest-serving agent of Stalin's repressions and in his own right one of the Soviet regime's most hated figures. Ruthless even by Soviet standards, cruel, a womaniser, a rapist – an 'Oriental' like Stalin, it was generally said, when both men were safely dead and disgraced. (Beria was a Mingrelian.) 'When he came into the house,' Stalin's adopted son, Artyom Sergeev, recalled, 'he brought darkness with him.' But he was also among the most intelligent of Stalin's men and, when it suited him, as it did now, certainly the most enlightened. Leonid wasn't his protégé, but he'd worked with him well enough.

Beria had been out of favour with Stalin since the start of the 1950s. Now he was fully intending to make up for lost ground; and on the evening of the day Stalin died, he merged the whole intelligence complex (in those days still denominated the MGB) with the Ministry of Internal Affairs and appointed himself the new ministry's boss. The following day at six o'clock on the dot Sudoplatov got a call from Beria's secretary letting him know that Beria had gone home for the day: in Stalin's time ministry employees had to wait to go home until Stalin went to bed at three or four or five in the morning.* It was the first indication Sudoplatov had that things had changed at the top.

Unlike Stalin or Khrushchev Beria wasn't an anti-Semite. (Some people, Stalin among them, suspected him of being a 'secret Jew'.) And reluctant though he usually was to disagree with Stalin ('oleaginous' is a word that often

---

* 'Grandfather never went to bed before three or four in the morning,' Leonid's granddaughter said on one of the first occasions we met. 'Like Stalin?' I asked eagerly. 'Like Stalin,' she replied.

comes up), he hadn't been entirely convinced about the Doctors' Plot. Now he suddenly announced that the plot had never existed and exonerated all the alleged plotters.

I don't know what Leonid's feelings were when he heard the news of Stalin's death. He'd had to have a lot of faith to do the things he did: faith in himself, in the Party and, above all, in Stalin. But after everything he'd seen and everything he'd done, and everything that had been done to him, how much was left? What mattered now was getting back to work and doing the things he knew needed to be done. If Stalin had to die to make that possible so be it. It wouldn't have been difficult for him to think that Stalin had lost his bearings in old age. Zoya once said that Leonid had taught her that 'you have to blot some things out. If you don't you can't live, it's too much, and so he taught me: "Blot it out, blot it out."'

As a young man he'd been ambitious – it was all part of the derring-do – but later on he seems not to have been much concerned with his own advancement. It was the job that interested him and, beyond that, the larger idea – which Stalin still embodied. Sudoplatov and others say that in his later years Leonid became quite cynical. That by the end of his life he no longer had any faith in the Party – which was nothing more, he said, than a machine for running the country. 'We have not built socialism,' he is supposed to have told Zoya. But in 1953 he didn't say anything like that, and I don't imagine he thought it. The Revolution, the socialist idea, Stalin – whatever you call it – was still too powerful for such notions to be available to anyone who didn't have recourse to an alternative, equally powerful, usually Christian set of convictions. For now, despite Stalin's death and his own arrest and the seventeen months he'd spent in prison at great cost to his health, he still believed there was a job to be done.

Within days, maybe hours, of Stalin's death he wrote a letter to Malenkov from his prison cell. Malenkov, Beria's ally, was briefly the top man in the new collective leadership, and Leonid wanted to remind him who he was and what he'd done and, by implication, what he could do in the future. He went over the steps of his career, telling Malenkov, who probably already knew as much as he needed to know, that he'd given his life to fighting the enemies of the Soviet Union, 'foreign Trotskyists' in particular, and, at the last, the supreme Trotskyist himself. But in the past few years, he wrote, resurrecting the pre-war bogeymen, 'people connected with the Trotskyists' had been trying to get their own back on him. Did he really believe that? Or was there no one else whom it was safe to blame? No one now living and no one with close ties to anyone now living? And not Stalin of course – not yet, and as far as Leonid was concerned, not ever. 'I hope', he said mawkishly at the end (this was the letter's ostensible purpose), 'that the comrades who will be given the task of deciding my sentence will let me die the way I lived – as a soldier.' But release was what he had in mind – and believed he deserved.

In Zoya's account Beria had Leonid brought to his office so that he could inform him in person that he would be released and reinstated in his old job within a few days. 'My first thought', Zoya writes, 'is that Beria needed him very much for special covert operations.' Sudoplatov says nothing about Beria giving Leonid the good news in person, but he does say that Leonid was immediately asked whether he 'was willing to continue his service after his release'.

For the moment, however, Leonid wasn't quite the man he'd been. He had spent a good deal of his confinement in the isolation block of the Butyrka prison (Cell 20, for the record); he'd been deprived of sleep for long periods, had not known if it was day or night, and on occasion he'd been beaten. His health had been seriously impaired by prison food and stomach ulcers; twice he'd been taken to the prison hospital after vomiting blood. And so, in reply to the invitation, he said, in the incongruous English of Sudoplatov's translators, that for the moment 'he wasn't up to par' but would be happy in due course to return to his post.

Zoya likes to talk about Leonid's return from prison and the moment her mother threw herself at him in the presence of the 'two gentlemen escorts'. 'Anyway, you understand, la la la I was there,' she explained. ('La la la' is Zoya's way of saying 'and so on, like a novel', and is often accompanied by a fluid movement of the hands.) 'And immediately we assembled all the relatives.' This was one get-together about which Leonid wasn't grudging. The family, Leonid's nieces especially, noticed a change in his manner. He'd become gentler, less arrogant, less inclined to tell the children to go and play somewhere else. More sentimental too, they said: Ira might now be 'Irochka' and Lena 'Lenochka', which they'd never been before. He even got into the way of saying 'please' when he wanted something. 'Can you imagine what it was like to be a general in the NKVD? – how rich, what power he had in his hands,' Leonid's granddaughter said to me one day rather wistfully. She was overlooking the small mercies – the 'please's and 'thank you's and minor endearments – her family enjoyed when that power had been taken away.

That Leonid had reason to be grateful to his family may have had something to do with the improvement in his manners. At the time of his arrest he'd no longer been living with Musa, the blonde *parachutistka*, the mother of his youngest children, but he supported her, as he told his interrogators. Or rather, since he no longer had an income, his family did. 'I'll never know why that woman couldn't get a job,' Zoya often complains, which sounds reasonable, though there's some suggestion that Musa's health was bad. Zoya felt the responsibility and, still in her early thirties, a war widow (though she didn't mind that too much) and professionally in a difficult position after Leonid's arrest, she resented it: 'All that time I supported her and my mama didn't know. I felt I had to do that for him. I loved him, I adored him, I understood that he was a man, he was a revolutionary.' But Zoya wasn't the only family member to contribute to Musa's support: both Leonid's brother and his sister Sima were short of money as a result, but perhaps they didn't contribute as much as Zoya did – or just talked about it less.

Zoya had never met Musa 'when' – again it's a story Zoya likes to tell – 'two days after Leonid's arrest, the bell rings and up pops the little lady. "I am Musa," she said.' But Zoya had already figured that out: 'I don't know where or when but I'd seen a photograph of her and the two babies and I understood.' Anxious to protect her mother's feelings, she told Musa not to come to the flat again. Musa lived in the same building (a KGB perk, without doubt) as Zoya's father: Zoya would visit her there. The blonde *parachutistka* was never, it seems, treated as part of the family: it seems she didn't quite fit the bill.

Her daughter, Musa, a gymnast, was one of the guests at the tea-party the two Galias laid on for my first visit in 1991, as was her son, Leonid a.k.a. Lonya. 'We never told Leonid that Lonya worked in a shop,' Leonid's grand-daughter once told me. (He was a successful furniture salesman.) Evidently it wasn't the right sort of job for the son of a KGB general. Zoya and her half-sister Svetlana, a doctor; Svetlana and her half-brother Vladimir, first a Chekist, then an academic: they are the children who feature in Leonid's story. The other two are acknowledged, but they are a family apart. Once when Leonid was ill and needed a transfusion, it was Lonya's blood that they gave him: other than that no stories are told, nothing is said, about Leonid and his younger children, except that he was grateful to Zoya for looking after them.

When the family celebrations were over Leonid was taken to hospital, where his ulcers would be treated and his health generally restored. He wasn't the only former prisoner among the patients. Quite a few people of his rank and higher – a deputy minister, for example – were there too, so Zoya reports. She of course went to visit him in hospital: 'Mama wouldn't go – she was too emotional.' By May, fattened up and returned to par, he was back at Sudoplatov's side, eager as always to get on with the job. Former colleagues, I was told, admired him for that: both for his sheer willingness to go back to the same work after what had happened to him and for his ability to think about it in new ways. They'd been assigned a new department, a new Bureau for Special Tasks, but their remit was much as before: 'individual terror' – i.e. assassination and kidnapping – and sabotage directed at enemies of the Soviet state far and wide.

It seemed that now things were going Leonid's way. Beria was an energetic man, a man in that sense after his own heart. In the two months since Stalin died he had got rid of countless agency employees. According to one observer, 'hundreds of dismissed employees began to wander through other institutions seeking work' – simple dismissal was, I imagine, a novel experience. Some two hundred agents had been recalled from abroad, and nearly a hundred new appointments had been made. Killings and kidnappings would continue as before but at the same time old revanchist projects were dropped and more enlightened policies discussed if not yet put in train. For example, Stalin had set his heart on doing away with Tito: it was one of the last things he had discussed with Sudoplatov.* Beria, instead, had rapprochement in mind.

Nikolai Khokhlov, the former artistic whistler now a junior officer in the Bureau for Special Tasks, reports in his memoir that his two bosses were kept so busy 'writing projects and plans they did not leave their offices for days at a time'. Imagine Leonid's relief that after the dismal years of inaction he would at last be able to get on with his job as it needed to be got on with. But in the summer the Bureau for Special Tasks was closed down.

Given that Stalin had no interest in his succession, had designated no heirs and instituted no procedures for transferring power, it's surprising that the struggle to succeed him

---

* There'd been an attempt on Tito's life a month before Stalin died: the report bringing news of its failure seems to have been the last thing Stalin ever read.

wasn't more turbulent. On the one hand, Beria, on the other, Khrushchev; on the one hand, the State, on the other, the Party. Because Beria was the one everyone feared, the most ambitious, the most astute and, thanks to his control of the Ministry of State Security, the most powerful (every member of the Praesidium knew that Beria had a dossier on them), the others quickly united against him.

In March, directly after Stalin's death, his progress had seemed almost irresistible. The entire leadership, even the diehard Molotov, recognised that a degree of liberalisation was required, that in a situation where no one had complete authority, it was necessary both to streamline the way things were done and to take some interest in popular opinion. Of course everyone hoped that in the process they would improve their own position. But Beria was in a league of his own. He didn't just annul the Doctors' Plot, freeing its victims and imprisoning its instigators – while making plain to his colleagues the extent of Stalin's complicity. Within a few weeks of the Leader's death he had gone quite a way to de-Stalinising the security service, obtained the release of a million inmates of the Gulag ('Our cities', Sudoplatov complains in his memoir, 'were flooded with riff-raff'), got more goods into the shops and taken steps to liberalise the Soviet Union's relationship with the West. A workers' uprising in East Germany on 16 June proved the excuse his enemies were waiting for: the reforms had gone too far.

On 26 June he was arrested. When Sudoplatov got to work on the 27th he found that the portrait of Beria that had only recently been hung on the wall of the ante-room to his office had already been taken down.

Leonid immediately understood the precariousness of

his own situation. Beria had only just reinstated him: he was bound to be seen as Beria's man. 'Eitingon was more of a realist than I,' Sudoplatov reports in that I'm-only-a-naïve-Gentile mode he sometimes likes to adopt. 'He correctly sensed that the Jewish team recently reinstated in the ministry would be the first to go.' 'Why are you crying?' one of Leonid's nieces asked her mother when Stalin died. 'Because we won't see Dyadya Leonid again.' This, it turned out, was quite wrong. A few months later her mother was in a pioneer camp collecting raspberries when she heard on the radio that Beria had been arrested. She wouldn't see Leonid for another eleven years.

What happened to Beria after his arrest isn't entirely clear: either he was shot straight away and posthumously tried and found guilty; or he was allowed to go on living until a trial could take place, at the end of which he was found guilty and immediately executed. Either way he was the last Soviet leader to be shot. Not long afterwards, everyone who possessed a copy of the *Soviet Encyclopedia*, the Soviet equivalent of the *Encyclopedia Britannica*, got a letter instructing them to cut out the entry on Beria and replace it with a new one, enclosed with the letter, on the Bering Strait. The two entries were exactly the same length.

At the very end of his life, someone said, Leonid had a photograph of Stalin by his bed. I'm not sure that's true: it's the sort of thing it would be too tempting to make up ('That's an interesting story for your book'). But it isn't out of the question. 'It's too easy just to say they were assassins,' the son of one of Leonid's KGB colleagues warned me. 'They were believers.' Too easy, equally, just to say they were believers.

CHAPTER 31

In Vladimir

In the summer of 1953 Leonid arranged for Zoya to have a holiday on the Black Sea. Having a good time was another of the things she did well, and on her way home from the station, she stopped at a market and bought a fat celebratory watermelon. Five minutes later, as she approached the building at 2 Tchkalova, she realised there would be no celebrations. A number of cars were parked outside the entrance, and cars, especially when there were four or five of them huddled together, were almost always a bad sign. Inside she found strange men milling about in the lobby. She walked past them, said nothing, went upstairs, and as she crossed the threshold of the family flat, the fat watermelon still under her arm, discovered Leonid ready to be taken away all over again.

'I appreciate all that you did for the family,' he said to her on his way through the door, accompanied by ten secret service men. 'I hope you will keep it up.'

'Once again,' she writes, 'the family was left wondering why he was arrested.' But Leonid knew that Beria's arrest had made him vulnerable. And so did Zoya. 'Faithful service', as the faithful Sharapov writes, 'was no guarantee of a quiet life.'

Beria had been Leonid's boss since November 1938, when he took over from Yezhov as head of the NKVD. The two men weren't friends – they wouldn't, for example, have visited each other's houses. (Beria was fond of young women and Zoya, who was often summoned late at night to provide simultaneous translations of the Hollywood movies that he liked to watch, knew him better.) But it was Beria who was in overall charge of the Trotsky operation and it was Beria who set up the succession of 'special' departments that Sudoplatov headed with Leonid as his deputy; and although their focus, as well as their names and designations ('bureau', 'administration', 'department'), changed a few times between the German invasion in June 1941 and Beria's fall in June 1953, their function remained much the same. Whether the enemy was declared or undeclared, an individual or a collective, Leonid and Sudoplatov's business took place behind its back.

Between fifteen and twenty of Beria's men, or those whom it suited Khrushchev and the others to call Beria's men, Sudoplatov among them, were detained or lost their jobs in the late summer of 1953. Six of his closest associates were executed alongside him. The difficulty for the country's 'reformed' leadership had been to make Beria's disappearance seem consistent with the idea of a regime that was mending its ways. So Beria and his henchmen were treated in the old way, arrested and summarily executed as soon as a pretext became available, while Leonid and Sudoplatov were ceremonially put on trial for actions that were no more insalubrious than the manner of their boss's disposal.

The new regard for propriety opened the way for new sorts of illegality. The law said an investigation should last no longer than nine months, but Leonid waited four years in Butyrka prison while the case against him was looked into. Once Beria had been got rid of there was no longer any need to hurry. Leonid and Sudoplatov had no supporters in high places. Khrushchev was effectively in power and the old Stalinists were disappearing from view (Molotov, Malenkov and Kaganovich were dismissed in 1957). Leonid in any case had spent most of his life abroad and had few remaining connections inside the country. And if he and Sudoplatov weren't exactly Beria's men, they nonetheless provided proof of Beria's guilt – more later – which the new regime was pleased to have and to linger over.

To linger over and to dissociate itself from. Ivan Serov, for example, the new man in charge of the KGB, as it was now called, was one of Beria's former deputies. Why would he have wanted them back in their old jobs, breathing down his neck and with tales to tell? And he wasn't the only one. There was little that was new about the new men. Like Khrushchev they had made their way up through the system, and, centrally or tangentially, were implicated in the crimes of Stalin's regime. Leonid was doing himself a further disservice every time he sent a letter of advice to the Central Committee. Naturally he didn't see it that way.

He first wrote to the Central Committee protesting at the injustice of his situation in 1955. The letter is proud (important assignment in Mexico), truthful ('I have had nothing to do at all with Beria's crimes': Beria was charged with plotting to overthrow the Soviet state), sentimental ('In the event of my death I plead with you, in consideration of my many years of work for the state security organs, to provide a pension for my little boy Leonid and my little girl Musa'), and self-pitying ('If for some reason I am not to be trusted then I beg not to be forced to drag out my old age in prisons and prison sick bays but to be given a chance to die like a soldier the way I have lived all my life'). No matter. His situation didn't change.

In March 1957 he was finally charged with high treason. At his trial he chose to defend himself; or rather, having listened to the evidence against him, chose not to defend himself, saying at the end, in words cited in Sharapov's biography:

> You are judging me as Beria's man. But I wasn't his man. If I was anyone's, then consider me Dzerzhinsky's. But, more accurately, I am a man of the Party. I carried out the tasks the Party and the government assigned me. But I am not going to speak about them to you. I hold my life no more precious than the secrets the state has entrusted me with. And from your faces I can see that you have already decided. So I have nothing further to say.

Found guilty, he was sentenced to twelve years in prison. 'Have no illusions that some positive work that you and Eitingon did abroad many years ago will save you,' the procurator, Roman Rudenko, said to Sudoplatov, who was sentenced to fifteen years. Rudenko, Zoya told me, was 'a Ukrainian of the worst sort'.

The case against them centred on four murders, four deaths by poisoning, carried out in different towns inside the Soviet Union between 1946 and 1947. The only link between the victims – an American Communist called Isaiah Oggins, a Polish engineer, a Ukrainian 'nationalist', and a Catholic bishop with Ukrainian connections – was the poison used to kill them.* The laboratory that manufactured it was known as 'Lab-X', or 'Mairanovsky's Laboratory', after its director, Grigory Mairanovsky. Officially it was Laboratory No. 1 within the state security system, and from the 1930s to the 1950s it had rendered reliable service to the regime – and in that sense nothing distinguished these four murders from countless others, among them most probably that of Raoul Wallenberg. The immediate order came from Beria, but, Sudoplatov insisted, the original directive came from the 'government'; and in the case of the bishop it was the Ukrainian Khrushchev in particular who wanted him dead. Was another reason for their punishment that they knew too much about Khrushchev? 'No man, no problem,' handsome Mr Prelin had said, quoting Stalin, when asked why it had been necessary to kill Oggins. 'Mairanovsky went to the camp, gave him an injection and sent him into the next world. Then he came back and said he died of natural causes.' That was Mairanovsky's expertise: executing the designated enemy and making it look like death by natural causes.†

* Oggins, among many things, none of them so far quite clear, knew too much about the Gulag system (i.e. had several years' experience of it); the Polish engineer was called Samet and supposedly had more information than he should have had about Soviet submarines; Alexander Shumsky was the Ukrainian 'nationalist'; and Bishop Teodor Romzha was the head of the Catholic Church in Ruthenia (part of Soviet Ukraine since 1945).

† For a man like Stalin, who liked things to happen fast, Mairanovsky had been very useful, but that didn't of course stop Stalin from arresting him in 1951 – Mairanovsky was a Jew. Released in 1961, he returned to his KGB flat in Moscow, but when he applied for rehabilitation he was ordered to leave the city. Transferred to Makhachkala, the capital of Dagestan, he became the head of a biochemical laboratory there and died in the city three years later.

In August 1992, when facts like these were beginning to come out and the public in the former Soviet Union was still interested in them and sometimes shocked, *Moscow News* published a piece about the four murders and the part Sudoplatov and Leonid played in them. It wasn't surprising, the authors of the piece wrote, that Sudoplatov should have preferred to remain silent about these 'acts of terrorism'. But what about his present-day colleagues, they asked. 'The unwillingness to reveal the names of those responsible, the complete absence of official information on the laboratory of death, and the complete inaccessibility even today of the archives of the operative technical and reconnaissance directorates can mean only this: either the special services' bloody past is too dear to them, or this past is too closely connected with the present.' Fifteen years later the old techniques seem more reliable than ever. Ricin, incidentally, was Mairanovsky's poison of choice.

At the Centre activity slowed down for a short while after Beria and his colleagues' arrest, but there was no change of policy or of method – Lab-X had simply changed its name to Special Laboratory No. 12. In October 1953 Nikolai Khokhlov, now a recalcitrant intelligence officer, was dismayed but not surprised to find himself instructed to murder the leader of an émigré organisation based in West Germany, Georgi Okolovich – the first major assassination target of the post-Stalin era. There was some fussing over the method but 'cigarettes' and poison bullets were eventually chosen. A little crazy with the wish to escape to a morally less compromised life, Khokhlov went instead to Okolovich's house in Frankfurt, rang his doorbell and told him that the Soviet authorities had ordered his assassination; that he, Khokhlov, was in charge of it and that he hoped not to carry it out. In the event Okolovich didn't die but the CIA got Khokhlov, and more or less willingly – his family were still in Moscow – he defected to the US.

Three years later, in September 1957, when Khokhlov was back in Frankfurt for an anti-Communist conference, his old department put radioactive thallium in his coffee. Though he was very ill for several weeks, he survived to resume his anti-Soviet activity.

We met for the first time at the railway station in Frankfurt. He was now a retired professor of psychology at California State University with an interest in the paranormal. He was in his early seventies and not very well. He worried about our arrangements and the fact that he'd come wearing different clothes from those he told me he'd have on. This was in 1992 and he was on his way to Moscow. The reason he was keen to meet me was that I had talked to Sudoplatov about him and had a tape of our conversation. 'I only want to hear what he says about me,' Khokhlov told me straight away. He had a bit of a thing about Sudoplatov, who in the old days had been a father figure to him and whom he saw as a model intelligence officer. I think he expected him now to have come round to his way of thinking about the Soviet regime. But Sudoplatov remembered Khokhlov chiefly for his protracted attempt to leave the service – his 'snivelling', Sudoplatov ungraciously called it.

I saw Khokhlov again a few years later when I was in California. We'd agreed to meet in a supermarket car park in Pasadena (the places he lit on always had a flavour of the old-time KGB). By then I knew something that he didn't. In 1952 Sudoplatov had told him – Leonid was then in prison – that he would soon be going to Paris. 'It is a wonderful city,' Sudoplatov had said, 'but you will not have time to enjoy it. The agent whom you are going to meet has a good friend. A Russian émigré. Find out all you can about this friend. His mode of life, habits, where he usually dines, walks . . . above all try to see this man.' Then, after a pause: 'He bothers us very much this "friend", very much.' And another pause: 'He must be put away.' The mission was called off at the last minute without Khokhlov ever knowing whom he'd been supposed to assassinate. I now told him that his target would have been Alexander Kerensky. Khokhlov laughed and his wide blue eyes widened. It wasn't the importance of the mission that excited him as I first thought: he was laughing with pleasure and relief at not having had to go through with it.

In the summer of 1957 Leonid was transferred to the Central Prison in the ancient and illustrious city of Vladimir, 150 miles east of Moscow. The setting was incongruous. Vladimir had been the geographical centre of the Great Russian nation and from time to time its capital before the various Mongol invasions. Alexander Nevsky and Dmitri Donskoy, medieval Russia's heroic warrior rulers, were crowned there; Alexander Nevsky's body lay more or less undisturbed in the nearby monastery until Peter the Great ordered it to be moved to St Petersburg in the early eighteenth century. By the mid-twentieth century the town with its many churches was an officially licensed tourist attraction, a place where the sight of old women prostrating themselves in front of the altar of the Uspensky Cathedral might reassure foreigner visitors that the old

Russia of their imagination had not been entirely swept away.

When I visited the cathedral in 1958 in the company of the Master of Pembroke, services, however compromised and curtailed, were still being held there, and my relative Leonid was sitting out his sentence in the prison near by. Had his circumstances or mine been such that I knew of him and knew where he was, I would most probably not have been allowed to travel to the Soviet Union in the first place.

Nicholas II had started using the building to house political prisoners at the beginning of the century. Greville Wynne, the British businessman-cum-spy, spent some months there in the early 1960s. 'Vladimir', he said, 'is a special prison, specially bad.' But it was nothing like as bad for Leonid as it was for Greville Wynne – which suggests that prison life under Khrushchev was sufficiently like prison life everywhere for a native general to be treated with more respect than a foreign spy.

Greville Wynne's daily soup consisted chiefly of fish eyes and water; he was obliged to spend days at a time in his freezing cell without any clothes to wear; and his oil drum . . . I don't think I'll go on. Leonid was allowed letters and food parcels and visits once a month from his family; he had access to newspapers and to the prison library; and when he showed symptoms of what might have been (but turned out not to be) cancer of the colon Zoya waved her wand over a couple of high-ranking generals and with the help of Leonid's doctor sister Sonia arranged for a surgeon – 'a top surgeon, a Jewish surgeon' – to come from Moscow to operate on him. In the Soviet Union more than in most countries favours were a vital currency, and if Zoya was never shy of asking for one it's probably because she was often owed one.

Leonid's women had had no contact with him during the four years he spent in Butyrka awaiting trial. Like so many other Soviet women, they had gone every day or every week to the prison gate to make enquiries and to leave parcels of food and small amounts of money that they hoped would get through to him. Now it was all more straightforward but still they worried about him, suffered for him, quarrelled and competed over him:

Zoya: 'I used to assemble them all for their visits. Svetlana was delicate. Mother used to panic. I couldn't ask her to go by train so I had to find a car and petrol.'

Svetlana's daughter: 'My parents used to visit him in prison. Sometimes Zoya went but not often.'

In Vladimir Leonid regained his dignity. 'He behaved like a toff,' the mathematician R. I. Pimenov, a fellow prisoner, recalled with distaste. Pimenov was a dissident: he had no reason to like Leonid. Sudoplatov, who arrived in Vladimir the following year, speaks of 'a small, exclusive club of former NKVD leadership' with Leonid at its head. I can well imagine that. Excused manual labour because the authorities didn't want them to have contact with other prisoners, these disgraced Chekists played chess and perhaps dominoes too and sometimes one or other of them lost their cool and talked too much while Leonid and Sudoplatov, in Sudoplatov's account, 'simply listened' and were careful not to say anything they might later regret.

In prison or out of prison, at home smoking or out in the field, Leonid still believed, as he had done in his late teens, that he knew better than anyone how to deal with his country's enemies. But when he warned the government against allowing the 'refugees' from the Spanish Civil War to return home – 'They know too much' – the head of the KGB is supposed to have said: 'What's he doing that ugly face, let him just sit there.' And in Moscow, a contemporary remembered, people talked about 'that man who sat in prison worrying about the government that put him there and kept him there so many years'. But he and Sudoplatov carried on submitting 'operational proposals' for Khrushchev to consider. In the 1930s those who'd been arrested on no obvious grounds would say, 'I'm guilty,' and hope against all rational expectation that that would save them. In the 1950s there were other prisoners besides Leonid and Sudoplatov who wanted to show how useful they could still be. No Chekist would have forgotten the case of Yakov Serebriansky, arrested in 1938 and released in 1941 when war began because Stalin was suddenly made to see how valuable he might be.

So it was, as Sudoplatov writes, 'in an effort to attract attention to our appeal' that Leonid and he 'devised and wrote, for Khrushchev's consideration', a number of 'operational proposals'. One, which he describes in *Special Tasks*, was 'to establish a Soviet counterforce to President Kennedy's newly created Green Berets'. This initiative – rewarded with two kilograms of sugar – in time led to the formation of the group 'which stormed Amin's palace in Kabul in 1979, setting off the Afghan war'. (Well, that's his story, though it isn't clear that Afghanistan was worth two kilograms of sugar to the Soviets.) Their next suggestion – that contact be resumed with the Kurdish leader Mustafa Barzani so that he could act as a 'counterforce to the irascible Iraqi dictator General Abdul Karim Kassem'

– was rewarded with the right to receive more frequent food parcels.

Sudoplatov appealed more than forty times to the Supreme Court and the Procurator's Office to reconsider his case. Leonid, who had launched his own appeals but not in such numbers, had laughed at him; 'Laws and power struggles', he'd said, 'are incompatible.' Neither of them had any luck. As Zoya tells it, most members of the Central Committee were sympathetic, but Rudenko – the Ukrainian of the worst sort – wouldn't hear of it: 'So long as I'm alive,' he said of Leonid, 'he'll rot in jail.'

In 1963, a few days before he was due to have his operation, Leonid made one last pitch. 'It's quite possible', he began by telling Khrushchev to whom the letter was addressed, 'that this will be the last letter I send you.' His doctors, he said, were hopeful but he was old and weak and wanted only one thing before he died: to be reconciled with the Party to which he had given his life. So far it's not unlike a letter a delinquent husband might send his long-suffering wife. In the Soviet system, as in married life, the road from outrageous behaviour to outrageous abjection is always liable to be short.

Leonid was less given to abjection than most, however, and on this occasion he moved swiftly into a very different mode. First he listed the foreign countries in which he acted as either a legal or an illegal resident – China, Greece, France, Iran, Spain and the US. It isn't complete, but it was unlike Leonid to reveal even that much. Whether one should take it as a form of submission ('I'll tell you everything') or defiance ('I have a lot more experience than you have') is not entirely clear, but the rest of the letter suggests that more than anything he was furious at the way his life was being frittered away on the say-so of people who knew less than he did. He went on to remind Khrushchev that others ('hundreds and thousands' of them) were involved in the work he did, that members of the Politburo and the Central Committee – Khrushchev's is one of the few names he pertinently refrained from mentioning – knew what he was up to and on occasion provided technical assistance. What purpose, he then asked, was served by keeping him in prison? Was it to anyone's benefit when he still had ten years of active service in him? (He was sixty-four.) Finally, as if to prove it, he suggested to Khrushchev that he consider what should be done to take advantage of current unrest in China. It is an astonishing performance.

The chapter devoted to Leonid in Zoya's memoir is called 'The Years of Tragedy', and when I first knew her she often referred to her family's suffering while suggesting that I wouldn't be able to understand it. Russians more than most talk about their suffering, collective and individual, in their lives as in their fiction, but in her case it struck me as odd and out of character: she is such a vigorous woman. It was also, I thought, inappropriate, given the picture of Soviet life that I had in my head and how much more other Soviet families had suffered, some of them at Leonid's hands. With time these remarks stopped; and she was more likely to say, as she did now: 'My family did some ugly things but I understand why they did them.' And with time I began to see the difficulties that a Soviet high functionary brought in his train. Leonid, it's true, did many ugly things that a better man or a different man wouldn't have done. They were the reason his bosses rewarded him and his juniors admired him: but they weren't the reason he spent twelve years in jail – only the excuse. Now I wonder how many members of the *nomenklatura* survived untouched from cradle to grave.

The Eitingons' suffering had many causes, not all of them to do with the Soviet system, though they were all a consequence of Leonid's character, from the grumpiness that must have made him so unrewarding to live with ('We couldn't make merry when he was there,' Zoya once said: 'when we were without him I felt easier') to the womanising that compounded the injury: 'He had no family,' Zoya said at another point: 'he had women who loved him.' Zoya's mother, the unfortunate Olga, lived in a constant state of distress: when Leonid was working abroad she didn't know who he might come back with – Shura, Musa, Caridad – and when he was in prison she didn't know which of them he intended to come back to. As for Zoya, she was in equal measure sorry for her mother in her grief and impatient with the helplessness that came in its wake. I don't think, however, that this was the sort of suffering she had in view when she spoke of 'the tragedy of our family'. In my mind there's a kind of woman who's both sexy and smart and who, because she has no trouble holding several contradictory ideas in her head at one time, finds it easy to get her own way while also accepting that if a man is a proper man his wishes, and his defeats, must always be paramount. My mother was one of those. So is Zoya.

It followed that in Zoya's mind, and in the mind of most of the family, the Eitingons' tragedy was principally Leonid's tragedy, however much the rest of them suffered for it. 'The experience', Zoya writes in her memoir, 'changed my life. I had not realised how privileged my family was. I had the impression that everyone lived the way we did, but now I realised how people could be put down and humiliated every day of their lives.' Used, like her mother or her sister, to being greeted in the street with a sort of bow, she now found there was no greeting at all – only silence. Former friends crossed the road to avoid them or looked down at their feet to avoid catching their eye. As for the few who didn't turn their backs on them there was always, in Zoya's account, a busybody to report them to another, more powerful busybody who'd have little trouble putting an end to the friendship.

And that was the least of it. In 1951, when Leonid was arrested for the first time, his sister Sonia, the doctor, lost her job and a few months later was sent to the Gulag (while her daughters, taunted at school, went off the rails); his brother, Isaak, too, lost his job: once an important engineer, he now couldn't get a menial job in a paint factory. Both Leonid's elder son, Vladimir, and Zoya had been working, like Leonid, in the secret service: they were thrown out immediately. Vladimir made the mistake of returning to his old job when Leonid was reinstated only to be thrown out all over again. 'He had enjoyed only four months of dignity,' Zoya writes, pityingly; she had had the good sense to get out, to find herself a job – at the Institute of Foreign Languages – before she had one foisted on her, and then to stay out. (Whether a woman of her talents ever completely stays out is not something I expect to be told.) As for Vladimir, Zoya writes: 'The district party committee found a job for him as a foreman in a plant where a team of women were manufacturing the wrapping for rice and sugar.' It was a while before he was able to remake himself as an academic.

Olga and her daughters – Leonid's official family – were allowed to write to him once a month and to receive a letter from him every month in return. In Zoya's account his were the 'letters of a staunch Communist who believed in the system'. Presumably a letter written in any other vein would not have got through. Then she adds, enigmatically: 'Leonid had a special feeling for Stalin and how he had made the country strong, but he was an introvert and kept more of his feelings to himself.'

He was released in March 1964, a year ahead of time. Zoya had again waved her wand. A friend of hers, a man with a car, came to pick him up and, as Zoya tells it, with tears in her eyes, the guards all came out to see him off, and as he said goodbye he pointed to each one in turn and told Zoya his name. He had his nicer moments.

CHAPTER 32

Last Wife

Leonid was released from Vladimir in March or November 1964 – accounts once again vary. Had Zoya not persuaded the chairman of the Military Procurator's office to include in Leonid's present term the eighteen months he'd spent in prison before Stalin died he wouldn't have been out until 1966. He was old now and frail, but not that frail: 'The way he fell on his food when he came out of prison', Zoya reported in an unusual moment of candour, 'we could hardly stay in the room with him. And he was an intelligent man, a cultured man, and that made it worse.' In the normal course of things Leonid wasn't a great eater (though he liked sweet things) or a drinker (though he liked brandy). Basically he was a smoker. 'You see,' Zoya said, 'he was a chain-smoker and when he was smoking he was thinking of a lot of things.'

He'd only been back a short while when he nodded to Zoya to come out into the street where they could discuss some of the things he'd been thinking about. 'You know,' he said to her, 'they are valuable, the agents we have out there. We have lost contact with them but they could be helpful to us. The only person they really trust is you because they know you. You tell the comrades that it's important . . .' Zoya was dismayed. 'Of course, of course,' she replied, 'I'll talk to them.' But she knew that the 'comrades' – his former colleagues at the Lubianka – would have nothing to do with Leonid or, *pace* Sudoplatov, with any plan of his devising. 'I didn't have the guts to tell him that nobody was interested in him or in anything he thought of doing,' she said to me on another occasion. His career had come to an end and it was painful for her to have to hide it from him.

I was surprised that she let on that she knew the agents he was alluding to: it's not something she readily acknowledges. She's happy to say, as she did now, that he was 'more outspoken' with her than with anyone else in the family, that he thought she 'was clever and could hold water, so to say it', but the fact that she had worked in the same department under the same boss counted for more and had never been mentioned.

As for where it was safer to talk – inside the flat or out on the street – it was hard to know. Or was it? If none of his former colleagues wanted to hear from Leonid it followed that none of them could imagine that he had anything of interest to say – anything worth their while listening in to. On the other hand, it definitely wasn't safe for him to be seen in the street. He was released early on condition that he stayed in the country somewhere outside Moscow and reported once a week to the local militia. Once a formidable figure in uniform, now a little old man in civvies, he had to spend every night in a different flat and take care not to be spotted on the street by the merest passing policeman.

They had 'a wonderful party' (Zoya's words) when Leonid returned, but Olga, worn down by ill-health, an addiction to painkillers, and the years of not knowing whether Leonid would come back to her or to Musa, was bedridden by that time and died two years later. A much stronger woman than her mother, Zoya had always, by her own account, been impatient with Olga and her gloomy, paralysing sentimentality. And it wasn't only Olga: there was far too much of it, she felt, among the women in her family ('They're all ba ba ba, always seeing things in the negative'). She was different ('I am after my father'), which was why, as she described it, she always had to do everything. It wasn't an entirely happy situation. The rest of the family was both glamorised by her (she taught Leonid's granddaughter how to use lipstick) and resentful, attracted and anxious to escape, while she was exasperated by their incompetence and pleased by the opportunities it gave her to show what she could do.

Her main task now as she saw it was to get Leonid back on his feet. He came out of Vladimir with a soldier's pension of twelve roubles and fifty kopeks a month – just enough, she says in her memoir, to buy ten packets of cigarettes. She had managed to get him released from prison before the official end of his sentence. Now she called on the former head of the KGB Alexander Shelepin, an old schoolfriend, and with his help and a few well-placed bribes got Leonid a job as an editor and translator at Mezhdunarodnaya Kniga, a branch of Soviet publishing that dealt with foreign books, and from there a salary and a pension. He was no longer, as she puts it, an ex-convict.

But Leonid didn't depend wholly on Zoya to get back on his feet. Ten people were living in the flat he came back to: a big flat by Soviet standards, it had three – some say four – rooms. In due course Leonid's daughter Svetlana, her husband, their two children and her husband's sister moved out. Then Olga died and her sister moved out. So that just left Zoya, her American husband – Bernard Cooper, an interpreter (she'd met him at Nuremberg, where she too had been an interpreter) and sports journalist* – and her daughter Tatiana. She didn't expect Leonid to stay with them; even when her mother was still alive he used to disappear for hours at a time: 'I'm going for a long walk,' he said, as so many husbands, or 'husbands', do. She thought he would move in with Musa, but he didn't do that either. He had found a new woman.

Evgenia Puzirova was eighty-six when I met her in 1991. She was still beautiful in the doll-like way old ladies sometimes are, with big blue eyes in a softly wrinkled face; and she was dressed the way dolls used sometimes to be dressed, in a frock with a big lace collar. She'd been married to the manager of the Putilov glassworks in Leningrad, who lost his job and his Party membership in 1948 'for having too many Jews working for him'; and when he got another job and was reinstated in the Party he was criticised at a Party meeting at his new workplace, came home and had a heart attack and died. She'd been an interpreter in Spain during the Civil War, and in Zoya's account – but not in hers – she'd first known Leonid there. Evgenia: 'I knew of him in Spain but we were not acquainted. We met later by chance in Moscow.' Zoya: 'He was not a man who would go out and get acquainted with someone new, so it was easier to re-establish his relationship with Evgenia when he met her again at a reunion of Civil War veterans.'

* Cooper's family, originally part of the Belorussian diaspora, returned to Russia a generation later. Cooper himself studied in Moscow, fought in the Soviet army and, after Nuremberg, worked all his life as a sports reporter for Radio Moscow.

I wondered, but didn't ask, whether Leonid had been as sulky and taciturn with her as he had been with his other 'wives'.

Zoya (crossing herself as she says it) didn't like Evgenia, the only one of Leonid's women she didn't try to get on with. Evgenia was spoiled and asked for too many things: a one-room apartment for her and Leonid, but it had to be a carpeted one-room apartment; then: 'Oh Zoya, could you get me a fridge'; then: 'Oh Zoya, could you get me a phone.' For Leonid's sake Zoya did her best ('I used all my strength and my pull'). But that wasn't all. Evgenia complained too much about the government, calling Brezhnev a fool and a drunk; she was 'enraptured' with her son, an actor and a ne'er-do-well, when it was Leonid who needed her attention; and she was always making 'cookies' – 'all those *pirogi*,' Zoya said with a harrumph.

Worse still, from Zoya's point of view, when Leonid told Evgenia the flat would be hers after his death she got him to marry her just to be sure, yet he'd lived with Olga (on and off) for thirty years without marrying her; then when Leonid died she sold the flat to live with her son and daughter-in-law; and when her son died she had the nerve to ring Zoya and say she wasn't happy living with her daughter-in-law: could Zoya find somewhere else for her? Finally, when Leonid was posthumously rehabilitated (more on that in a minute) she wanted a pension. Zoya told her – probably with some satisfaction – that she wasn't entitled to one given that she wasn't his wife when he was in prison.

Evgenia asked me too if I couldn't get her a pension. During the Second World War she'd worked on the Arctic convoys that brought supplies from British ports to

Murmansk and Archangel – by common consent the cruellest naval campaign of the war. In 1944 she was on a Soviet ship that was torpedoed two days out of Murmansk; she spent some harrowing minutes in the freezing water and was eventually picked up by a British minesweeper. (After several hours in the bowels of the ship drinking whisky and coffee she went up on deck and was looking at her blue face in a mirror when the captain came by and asked if there was anything she needed. 'Only some lipstick,' she replied. It's the sort of remark Barbara Stanwyck might have made in those circumstances.) After the war she was notified that she'd been awarded a medal by the queen. I'm not sure why: in the story as she told it she hadn't saved anyone's life; maybe all the Russians who served on the convoys were later – quite a bit later, it would have to be – given a medal by the queen. Now she wanted to know whether perhaps there was a pension attached to it and could I find out for her.

There were many things to admire about Evgenia. For one thing, she could afford a more disinterested take on the past than Leonid's family. In the 1930s during the Purges, she said, without looking for any kind of excuse, 'We would look in the paper every day and see that individuals we knew of and even rather admired had become enemies of the people and we believed it.' The only thing she didn't believe, she said, was the Doctors' Plot: 'I stopped on the way to work and saw the newspaper on the wall with the list of names and I was ashamed of my country. I walked along with my head down. I couldn't look at my fellow Russians. And when I got to my work, my *sluzhba* – and of course there were many Jews there – I couldn't look them in the eye.'

Whether she said this because it was true or because in her mind it became true after she married Leonid, who can tell. 'Nobody talked to anyone else about these things,' she said. 'Neither friends nor relatives because you never knew who you could trust.'

'Who were you afraid of if you had no bad thoughts about Stalin?' I asked – it was hardly an original question. 'We never thought it through,' she replied. 'We never gave an account of it to ourselves.'

Gorbachev, she thought, was no good: he talked too much. Brezhnev, Chernenko and Khrushchev were stupid. What good leaders had they had? I asked. Evgenia would say Lenin but Leonid's granddaughter said that he never got a university degree. She would rather say Nicholas II (though she was wrong about Lenin). Evgenia dismissed that idea: what did Nicholas know? He wasn't a leader. There were no strong leaders. That's why there was a revolution. Then Stalin wiped out the intelligentsia and they were done for.

Svetlana (Leonid's daughter): 'No foreigners understand us Russians. We have so much patience. We are a nation of martyrs.'

Evgenia: 'It will get better.' (To me) 'Come again in two years' time and if I'm still alive I'll give you a good dinner.'

Svetlana: 'It will never get better. Not in my daughter's lifetime. Not in my grandson's.'

Leonid's name had by now cropped up a couple of times in the West. Testifying before congressional subcommittees, first Khokhlov, then Orlov mentioned him and gave some account of his activities. The article in which Khokhlov mentioned Leonid – surname and all – and the part that he played in Trotsky's assassination appeared in the *Saturday Evening Post* in November 1954.

He is described by Robert Conquest as 'the organiser of Trotsky's assassination' in the first edition of *The Great Terror* in 1968. By the time the revised edition came out in 1990, Conquest knew enough to list him in the index as 'Eitingon, Leonid (N. I.)'. In 1971 his name is cited, though misspelled – 'a mysterious figure named Leonid Etingon' – in the *Chicago Tribune* on the occasion of the funeral in Moscow (which he didn't attend) of his fellow spy 'Rudolf Abel', alias Willie Fisher. There must be other references I don't know of, but they would have been few and far between; there is, for example, no mention of him in the place where one would most expect to find it: in the last volume of Deutscher's biography of Trotsky, published in 1963.

The situation hasn't changed much since then. If you look at any book about the Soviet Union that has come out in the past twenty-five years, pre or post-perestroika, you will find at most two or three references to Leonid in the index, but more often none at all. Ask Zoya why this should be so and she will say, 'He was not like that,' meaning he had no interest in the limelight. Which was just as well given his line of activity. Or she will say, 'It was not necessary' – meaning, again, that however well he did his job it wasn't the sort of job you'd want to make a noise about. More to the point, he was just a functionary; as he told Khrushchev, he carried out the orders other people gave him. He used his own initiative of course, but within the parameters other people had set.

What rankled was the fact that he hadn't been rehabilitated. He'd spent forty years in the service of the Party and the country, on many occasions at some risk to himself; he'd achieved nearly everything that had been asked of him; he'd distinguished himself in the war against the Germans; and he'd disposed of the man whose existence had been seen as posing a greater threat to the Soviet Union than Hitler. In return he'd been judged a traitor, spent twelve years in prison and had his medals, his rank, his Party membership – effectively, his entire past life – confiscated. Friends and former colleagues, for whom he was something of a wounded hero, interceded on his behalf and got nowhere. One of them was Ramón Mercader. Mikhail Suslov, the chief Party ideologue, told him to get lost. 'We determined the fate of those people for ourselves once and for all. Don't stick your nose into other people's business.'

In 1975 Leonid himself, as much a wounded hero in his own eyes as in the eyes of his friends, wrote to Yuri Andropov, then head of the KGB, once more listing the posts he'd held (or some of them), the places he'd worked (or some of them), and many of the things he'd achieved. 'Do whatever is useful to the Revolution,' the great Dzerzhinsky had said to him and that was the precept, he told Andropov, that he'd followed all his life – which made his arrest seem all the more 'difficult to understand, absurd and preposterous'. 'I appeal to you', he said in conclusion, 'as a member of the Politburo of the Central Committee of the Communist Party of the Soviet Union: that is, of the Party to which I have belonged since 1919, and alongside which I fought to shield the October Revolution against its enemies both internal and external. Secondly, I appeal to you as the head of the Chekists with whom I worked my whole life. I beg you to help me secure my rehabilitation

and restore my Party membership as soon as possible.'
Andropov was silent.

He went on working at his publishing job for four years,
until 1968, or for seven years, until 1971, which in either
case was longer than he needed to – Shelepin had said he
could get a pension after two months – and I like to think
that he enjoyed the work, that he found some satisfaction
in the exercise of ingenuity translation requires. It also
gave him a reason to get out of the house, which he always
liked to do. I find it hard to imagine what he did all day
when he stayed at home. Zoya likes to say: 'He would sit
and smoke; that's what he mainly did' – but you can't do
that all day long. He went for long walks 'to clear his
head', while he was still fit enough to do so; he exchanged
hunting anecdotes with his friends from the old days and
played cards with them and complicated games of patience
by himself; and some say he played dominoes and some
say it's out of the question that he played anything as idi-
otic as that. He read the newspaper, but not obsessively.
He read books, but I never got very far when I tried to find
out what books; Alexander Herzen's *Past and Thoughts*,
'the book that was always on his bedside table', is all I
know for sure. A taciturn man, he didn't like a lot of chatter – we know that – and Zoya maintains that Evgenia
'tired him with her talk and her mess', obliging him to go
round to Zoya's house for a bit of peace and quiet. Zoya
quiet? She must have loved him a lot.

He wasn't pleased with the way things were going in
the Soviet Union and perhaps that's why he could tolerate
Evgenia's disparaging chatter better than Zoya imagined.
He may have said in 1957 – in a letter addressed to his

family from Vladimir – that he was 'so happy' that they had all 'lived to see the 40th anniversary of the October Revolution' but by the 1970s he'd lost his illusions. When Sudoplatov wrote that 'in later years Leonid proved to be more cynical than I was', Zoya didn't cross the passage out, as she did many others in my copy of his book. In 1957 he'd called himself Dzerzhinsky's man, knowing it would produce an effect on his audience: in the world over which Brezhnev presided he would have sounded like a sad and sorry old man, a has-been, a dinosaur.

At the end of the 1970s his health began to fail. His ulcer never really got better (all that smoking can't have helped) and his circulation was poor. He could no longer manage the Metro, and his daughter Svetlana, who all her life had been devoted to him like a dog to its master (her words), looked after him as well as she could, visiting him in her lunch hour, going to the chemist for him whatever the time of day or night, reading to him when he was too weak to hold the paper. Ten years later she was still reproaching herself for letting him be taken to hospital to die: but she couldn't help it – at home he would have bled to death. Zoya, as always, had her own, brisker way of looking at these things. Now that he was dying, she told me, 'they' decided it was safe to acknowledge him to the extent of admitting him to the Kremlin hospital. At the time I imagine it made her angry; or was she pleased at heart? Now she seemed amused. Once he was there, she recalled, and this too is very Zoya-like, it was an excess of attention that finished him off. He died – though probably not, as several of his victims had, of the doctors' attentions – on 3 May 1981. 'Go away,' he said, rebarbative to the last, 'I'm an old man.'

Svetlana's flat, May 1994

Svetlana: 'On his last night at home when Evgenia was asleep I sat near him and he told me that people would write about him and that he was recognised as the best intelligence officer there'd been between the First and Second Wars. He knew that I was very attached to him and that it was very painful for me. "With whom will I leave you, little daughter?" he asked. To the others he said: "Cremate me and throw my ashes into the Yauza." I didn't want to hear that.'

Vladimir: 'When I left on the 30th of April he said: "You know I'm sick and tired of life."'

Svetlana: 'To me he said: "Life is no longer interesting."'

Vladimir: 'He wanted to go from the Kremlin hospital to the military hospital, where he felt more at home.'

Svetlana: 'He was a wise man.'

Vladimir: 'He never stopped fighting for the restoration of his title. In the Procuracy where they dealt with his case there is a huge file of his letters and of ours as well. He never stopped fighting for his rehabilitation until his last day.'

Svetlana: 'He was rehabilitated eighteen months ago.'

Vladimir: 'He never thought himself guilty. There are people in that situation who lose their confidence but he believed in himself until the end of his life. He wouldn't allow himself a single thought that diminished his self-confidence. His self-respect was the same whether he was a general or a prisoner or an old-age pensioner. Many people felt that he kept his distance, but that was very important to him. Once we went to a reunion of Omsbon, the wartime commando unit. All the soldiers stood below the leaders on the platform and my father and

Sudoplatov stood to the side. They were asked to come up to the platform and they addressed him as Comrade General though he wasn't a general.'

Svetlana: 'He never lost his head in any situation.'

Vladimir: 'I remember an occasion when he was away on a mission and I came to the Lubianka and the guard said: "Where's your father? It's a long time since we've seen him." And that was just the man who stood guard.'

('That's the sort of story we were told at school about Lenin,' my friend Nadia remarked at this point as she listened to the tape.)

Vladimir: 'That's the way people related to him. He never flattered anyone, never flattered or slithered. He always stuck to the matter in hand and never owed anyone anything.'

Svetlana: 'We weren't afraid of him but what Father said we did.'

Vladimir: 'We didn't even discuss it.'

Svetlana: 'I was already fifty-three when he died and without his advice I'd never undertaken anything. Even now I think: what would Father say? I was very attached to him.'

I asked what he would think of what was happening now.

Vladimir: 'He was always able to foresee political developments, and what's happening now would just have elicited a sarcastic smile.'

What did he think of life abroad?

Svetlana: 'He saw how we live here.'

Vladimir: 'In the first place it was never discussed. If something caught his eye he might make some comment on how things were abroad. We were once in a crowd and he said in France a man might be playing the accordion and you would throw him a franc and he would play for you. And if you don't give him a franc he would still play. A tiny thing like that he might mention but he would never talk in a serious way about how things were here and how they were there. He liked to see new and good things in our life and to show them to us. For example, we were walking with him once in the centre of town – which was something we did very rarely – and a new ice-cream shop had opened on the street. "That's nice," he said. "Let's go and eat ice cream."'

Svetlana: 'He loved ice cream. In hospital he asked me to bring him ice cream – fruit and vanilla. It was the last thing I brought him.'

'When he was in France,' I asked, 'was he there as a Frenchman?'

Vladimir: 'Let's say he was there as a Swede.'

(In other words, as an illegal.)

Svetlana: 'He was exceptionally talented. He knew languages he had never studied.'

Vladimir: 'He liked listening to records and could put the same record on twenty times.'

Svetlana: 'And he had one book that he loved – Herzen's *Past and Thoughts*.'

Vladimir: 'He read constantly and went on reading what he had read in his youth.'

Svetlana: 'On his grave I put lilies of the valley. They were his favourite flower.'

Vladimir: 'He never went to anyone's house without a present. Wherever he went he would buy flowers or sweets or jam. He always brought his mother a present – often jam and sometimes he ate it all himself. I arrived once from school and he was sitting at the table eating herring with cherry jam. I said to him: "Dad, what's wrong with you?" And he said: "Silly, try it yourself. It's delicious."'

Svetlana: 'His favourite jam was blackcurrant. His favourite food: meatballs. That's what he liked best – for breakfast, lunch and supper.'

'It's not that I remember him: it's that I never forget him,' Svetlana had said when I first met her.

There were about a hundred people at Leonid's funeral but only one person apart from Zoya, a former World War Two colleague, felt able to speak. With Leonid's death, he said, 'the chivalric – *rytsarsky* – period in the history of the Cheka had come to an end'. Later several others went up to Zoya and apologised: they'd wanted to speak, they said, but were afraid that there might be repercussions. In other words, they knew he hadn't been rehabilitated.

That final sacrament wasn't administered for a further eleven years, for all the efforts his children made. Svetlana approached the Committee of Party Control a number of times. Officially no one refused and no one helped. Once when she phoned, someone – she didn't remember his name – said that her father was a hero and she should be proud of him. But no one took any steps towards rehabilitating him. Vladimir, who said that as long as he lived (a very Soviet locution) clearing his father's name would be his main goal, joined forces with Anatoli Sudoplatov, the general's son, in pursuit of that goal, while the general, in his own words, 'bombarded the Central Committee with appeals' on his own and Leonid's behalf. Zoya, as always smarter and better connected than the others, concentrated her efforts where they counted: first with the Party Congresses, then with Gorbachev's man, Alexander

Yakovlev, chairman of the Party Rehabilitation Committee. 'I was pushing all the time,' she said. The competition between the three of them as to who was pushing hardest was intense.

I have no idea how much each of them knew about the killings and the poisonings Leonid was involved in. Zoya, I imagine, knows quite a bit, but she also knows what is best blotted out. And in any case what they knew they didn't speak about because 'in our family we didn't talk about these things': it was dangerous then and dangerous now, if only because it might have harmed Leonid's chances of rehabilitation, or so they feared.

Trotsky's death was common knowledge: everything else was passed over in silence.*

Leonid was finally rehabilitated in April 1992, five months after the Soviet Union itself had ceased to exist. I haven't seen his rehabilitation certificate but Sudoplatov's is reproduced in his book. Dated February 1992, the scrap of notepaper on which it's printed comes from the office of the Procurator of the Union of Soviet Socialist Republics, but the typewritten text reveals that he was convicted and then rehabilitated in accordance with the criminal code of the Russian Federation.

The decision to absolve Sudoplatov and Leonid of their crimes was taken at the same time as the murder charge

---

* Remaining unaneled had one advantage: it was much harder for an outsider – a journalist, for example – to gain access to Leonid's files before his rehabilitation. My man Igor had tried to persuade Vladimir and Svetlana to allow him to see documents that were accessible only with the family's authorisation by telling them that he would use his influence in support of Leonid's rehabilitation. I was never sure whether this was just a ruse, but when I said I found it uncomfortable I was told reprovingly that Igor didn't have my 'scruples' where Eitingon was concerned.

against Oleg Kalugin for liquidating Georgi Markov on Waterloo Bridge was dropped – 'since Kalugin was fulfilling his military duty'. 'I was only following orders': is it ever a decent excuse? What if your accuser is the institution that gave you the order in the first place? Can that be an extenuation? As Zoya said, 'My family did some ugly things but I understand why they did them.'

Late one November afternoon Zoya took me to see Leonid's grave in the Donskoy cemetery, next to the Peoples' Friendship University, which was reserved for foreign, mainly African, students and didn't altogether live up to its name. Leonid's grave, which he shares with Zoya's mother (I'm sure Zoya saw to that), is near the perimeter fence and a street light shines over it. The two names are engraved on the tombstone:

OLGA GREGORIEVNA NAUMOVA
1900–1966
NAUM ISAAKOVICH EITINGON
1899–1981

Zoya crossed herself, bent down to remove some yellow flowers that the last visitor had left, took off one glove and swept away the leaves with her bare palm in a ceremonial way. The tombstone is quite modest and it seems that Lonya, Leonid's younger son, wanted to buy something bigger and fancier with an inset portrait of Leonid in the Soviet fashion. Zoya disapproved. Lonya, she said, always wants to show how much money he has to spend. And besides, she added, Leonid made it plain that he didn't want every passing stranger looking at his face.

CHAPTER 33

At the Undertaker's

My mother, inevitably, died in the course of the many years which, on and off, I have spent thinking about and writing this book. My brother and I were at the undertaker's in Geneva, the place where she'd mostly lived for the previous forty years. The undertaker asked us some questions, as well as consulting her passport, in order to fill in the form that had to be sent off to the city authorities so that her death could be registered.

Then he handed my brother the form for him to check that everything was as it should be. My brother read it and passed it to me. Parents' names: Fanya Monosowsky and Boris Eitingon. That was right as far as I knew (I hadn't been sure of the Fanya but 'Fanny' hadn't seemed the thing to say). Date of birth: 30 May 1907. That was accurate, though there had been a time when her passport said '1909' because my father was born in 1909 and she didn't like people to know that she was eighteen months older than him. Nationality: 'Grande Bretagne'. She had taken my father's nationality when the Americans decreed that she'd lived abroad for too long to be allowed to maintain her naturalised American citizenship (a decade or two later they offered it back but by then she said, 'to hell with them' – she often said that sort of thing). Place of birth: 'Lodz (Grande Bretagne)'.

It was a pleasing idea – the city of Lodz (pronounced

'Wudjz'), the centre of the Polish textile industry, transferring its looms to the north-west of England – but I crossed out 'Grande Bretagne' and wrote in 'Pologne' all the same. Then I asked my brother whether, had I not been there, he would have changed it. 'No,' he said. His sense of the ironic stretches further than mine. So much for the historical record, the archives, the documents: they're only there for formality's sake.

A few months later my brother told me that the processing of her will had been held up because the authorities had found two versions of the year of her birth: 1907 (the correct version) and 1909 (the white lie). That she was a year and a half older than my father and that she'd lied about her age in her passport had for many years seemed to be the darkest of dark secrets. Then she decided she didn't care about the age difference or who knew about it – hence the discrepancy between the two sets of documents.

When the civil authorities in Geneva got in touch with the archivists in Lodz, the archivists came up with a date of their own: not 30 May 1907 but 14 October 1907. May 30th had always been an important date to me, bringing to mind my mother in the days when I loved her entirely, as a child does. It seems to me that I would have had a very different sense of her, and of the year and its shape, had I thought (or known?) that her birthday was in October. Be that as it may, the Swiss authorities fretted for a further six months before declaring themselves satisfied that she had indeed been born on 14 October 1907. I shouldn't have been surprised by this new, posthumous arrangement. You're not really an Eitingon without one last trick up your sleeve.

Bibliography

Agabekov, G. S., *ChK za Rabotoi*, Berlin: Izdatelstvo 'Strela', 1931

Agabekov, G. S., *OGPU: The Russian Secret Terror*, trans. Henry Bunn, New York: Brentano's, 1931

Agabekov, G. S., *GPU: Zapiski Chekista*, Berlin: Izdatelstvo 'Strela', 1930

Andrew, Christopher, and Gordievsky, Oleg, *KGB: The Inside Story of Its Foreign Operations from Lenin to Gorbachev*, London: Hodder and Stoughton, 1990

Andrew, Christopher, and Mitrokhin, Vasili, *The Mitrokhin Archive: The KGB in Europe and the West*, London: Allen Lane, 1999

Ascherson, Neal, *The Struggles for Poland*, London: Michael Joseph, 1987

Badziak, Kazimierz, 'Wlokienniczy Koncern Eitingonów wii Rzeczypospolitej', *Rocznik Lodzki*, tom xxxv, Warsaw–Lodz: Panstwowe Wydawnictwo Naukowe, 1986

Bailey, Paul J., *China in the 20th Century*, Oxford: Blackwell, 1988

Baron, Salo W., *The Russian Jew under Tsars and Soviets*, New York: Macmillan, 1976

Beevor, Antony, *The Battle for Spain: The Spanish Civil War 1936–39*, London: Weidenfeld and Nicolson, 2006

Beevor, Antony, *The Mystery of Olga Chekhova*, London: Viking, 2004

Beevor Antony, *The Spanish Civil War*, London: Orbis, 1982

Berberova, Nina, *The Italics Are Mine*, trans. Philippe Radley, London: Chatto and Windus, 1991

Beria, Sergo, *Beria, My Father: Inside Stalin's Kremlin*, trans.

Brian Pearce, London: Duckworth, 2001

Berlin, Isaiah, *Flourishing: Letters 1928–46*, ed. Henry Hardy, London: Chatto and Windus, 2004

Bertin, Celia, *Marie Bonaparte: A Life*, London: Quartet Books, 1982

Bickers, Robert, *Empire Made Me: An Englishman Adrift in Shanghai*, London: Allen Lane, 2003

Borkenau, Franz, *The Spanish Cockpit: An Eyewitness Account of the Political and Social Conflicts of the Spanish Civil War*, London: Faber and Faber, 1937

Brabant, Eva, Falzeder, Ernst, and Giampieri-Deutsch, Patrizia (eds), *The Correspondence of Sigmund Freud and Sándor Ferenczi*, 3 vols, trans. Peter Hoffer, Cambridge, Mass.: Harvard University Press, 1993, 1996, 2000

Braithwaite, Rodric, *Moscow 1941: A City and Its People at War*, London: Profile Books, 2006

Brandenberger, David, *National Bolshevism: Stalinist Mass Culture and the Formation of Modern Russian National Identity, 1931–56*, Cambridge, Mass.: Harvard University Press, 2002

Brenan, Gerald, *The Spanish Labyrinth: An Account of the Social and Political Background of the Spanish Civil War*, Cambridge: Cambridge University Press, 1943

Brent, Jonathan, and Naumov, Vladimir P., *Stalin's Last Crime: The Doctors' Plot*, London: John Murray, 2003

Carter, James H., *Creating a Chinese Harbin: Nationalism in an International City 1916–32*, Ithaca, NY: Cornell University Press, 2002

Castillo-Puche, José Luis, *Hemingway in Spain: A Personal Reminiscence*, trans. Helen Lane, New York: Doubleday, 1974

Churchill, W. S., 'Leon Trotsky, alias Bronstein' and 'Boris Savinkov' in *Great Contemporaries*, London: Thornton Butterworth, 1937

Clausen, Søren, and Thøgersen, Stig, *The Making of a Chinese City: History and Historiography in Harbin*, Armonk, NY: M. E. Sharpe, 1995

Conquest, Robert, *The Great Terror: A Reassessment*, London: Hutchinson, 1990

Costello, John, and Tsarev, Oleg, *Deadly Illusions*, New York: Crown Publishers, 1993

Danto, Elizabeth Ann, *Freud's Free Clinics: Psychoanalysis and Social Justice 1918–38*, New York: Columbia University Press, 2005

De Groot, Gerard, *The Bomb: A Life*, London: Jonathan Cape, 2004

Deutsch, Helene, *Confrontations with Myself: An Epilogue*, New York: W. W. Norton, 1973

Deutscher, Isaac, *The Prophet Armed, Trotsky 1879–1921*, Oxford: Oxford University Press, 1954

Deutscher, Isaac, *The Prophet Outcast, Trotsky 1929–1940*, Oxford: Oxford University Press, 1963

Deutscher, Isaac, *The Prophet Unarmed, Trotsky 1921–1929*, Oxford: Oxford University Press, 1959

Diamant, Adolf, *Chronik der Juden in Leipzig*, Chemnitz–Leipzig: Verlag Heimatland Sachsen, 1993

Dugrand, Alain, *Trotsky in Mexico*, trans. Stephen Romer, Manchester: Carcanet, 1992

Eastman, Max, *Great Companions: Critical Memoirs of Some Famous Friends*, New York: Farrar, Straus and Cudahy, 1959

Ehrenburg, Ilya, *Men, Years – Life*, trans. Anna Bostock, Yvonne Kapp, Tatiana Shebunina, 6 vols, London: Macgibbon and Kee, 1961–6

Etkind, Alexander, *Eros of the Impossible: The History of Psychoanalysis in Russia*, trans. Noah and Maria Rubins, Boulder, Col.: Westview Press, 1997

Feklisov, Alexander, with Kostin, Sergi, *The Man behind the Rosenbergs*, trans. Catherine Dop, New York: Enigma Books, 2001

Fenby, Jonathan, *Generalissimo: Chiang Kai-shek and the China He Lost*, London: Free Press, 2003

Fenby, Jonathan, *The Penguin History of Modern China: The Fall and Rise of a Great Power (1850–2008)*, London: Allen Lane, 2008

Fishman, David E., *Russia's First Modern Jews: The Jews of Shklov*, New York: New York University Press, 1995

Fitzpatrick, Sheila, *Everyday Stalinism*, Oxford: Oxford University Press, 1999

Foner, Philip, *The Fur and Leather Workers Union*, Newark, NJ: Nordau Press, 1950

Fraser, Ronald, *Blood of Spain: The Experience of Civil War (1936–1939)*, London: Allen Lane, 1979

Freud, Ernst L. (ed), *Sigmund Freud–Arnold Zweig: Briefwechsel*, Frankfurt am Main: S. Fischer Verlag, 1968

Frosh, S., 'Psychoanalysis, Nazism and "Jewish Science"', in *International Journal of Psychoanalysis* No. 84, 2003

Gassenschmidt, Christoph, *Jewish Liberal Politics in Tsarist Russia, 1900–14: The Modernisation of Russian Jewry*, Basingstoke: Macmillan, 1995

Gazur, Edward P., *Secret Assignment: The FBI's KGB General*, London: St Ermin's Press, 2001

Gellhorn, Martha, *The Face of War*, London: Hart-Davis, 1959

Gordon, Eric A., *Mark the Music: The Life and Work of Marc Blitzstein*, New York: St Martin's Press, 1989

Gorlizki, Yoram, and Khlevniuk, Oleg, *Cold Peace: Stalin and the Soviet Ruling Circle 1945–53*, Oxford: Oxford University Press, 2004

Harmelin, Wilhelm, 'Jews in the Leipzig Fur Industry', in *Leo Baeck Institute Yearbook* 9, 1964

Haynes, John Earl, and Klehr, Harvey, *Venona: Decoding Soviet Espionage in America*, New Haven, Conn.: Yale University Press, 1999

Hemingway, Ernest, *For Whom the Bell Tolls*, New York: Charles Scribner's, 1940

Herzen, Alexander, *My Past and Thoughts*, abr. Dwight Macdonald, trans. Constance Garnett, rev. Humphrey Higgens, New York: Knopf, 1973

Hobsbawm, Eric, *The Age of Extremes: The Short Twentieth Century, 1914–1991*, London: Michael Joseph, 1994

Holloway, David, *Stalin and the Bomb: The Soviet Union and Atomic Energy 1939–56*, New Haven, Conn.: Yale University Press, 1994

Hosking, Geoffrey, *Russia and the Russians: A History from Rus to the Russian Federation*, London: Allen Lane, 2001

Houseman, John, *Unfinished Business: A Memoir*, London: Chatto and Windus, 1986

Jacobs, Dan N., *Borodin: Stalin's Man in China*, Cambridge, Mass.: Harvard University Press, 1981

Jeffery, Inez Cope, *Inside Russia: The Life and Times of Zoya Zarubina*, Austin, Tex.: Eakin Press, 1999

Jones, Ernest, *Sigmund Freud: Life and Work*, 3 vols, London: Hogarth Press, 1953–7

Karlinsky, Simon, 'Memoirs of Harbin' in *Slavic Review* 48 No. 2, Summer 1989

Kershaw, Ian, *Fateful Choices: Ten Decisions That Changed the World 1940–41*, London: Allen Lane, 2007

Khenkin, Kirill, *L'Espionnage soviétique: Le Cas Rudolf Abel*, trans. Alain Préchac, Paris: Fayard, 1981

Khenkin, Kirill, *Okhotnik vverkh nogami*, Paris: Posev, 1980

Khenkin, Kirill, *Les Russes sont arrivés: L'Infiltration soviétique en Occident*, trans. Louis Lauréat, Paris: Scarabée et cie, 1984

Khokhlov, Nikolai, *In the Name of Conscience: The Testament of a Soviet Secret Agent*, trans. Emily Kingsbery, New York: David McKay, 1959

Knight, Amy, *Beria: Stalin's First Lieutenant*, Princeton, NJ: Princeton University Press, 1993

Kostyrchenko, Gennadi, *Out of the Red Shadows: Anti-Semitism in Stalin's Russia*, Amherst, NY: Prometheus Books, 1995

Krivitsky, W. G., *I Was Stalin's Agent*, London: Hamish Hamilton, 1939, reissued under the title *In Stalin's Secret Service*, Frederick, Md.: University Publications of America, 1985

Kuznetsov, Ilya, 'KGB General Naum Isaakovich Eitingon' in *Journal of Slavic Military Studies*, Vol. 14 No. 1, March 2001

Lattimore, Owen, *Manchuria: Cradle of Conflict*, New York: Macmillan, 1932

Levine, Isaac Don, *The Mind of an Assassin*, New York: Farrar, Straus and Cudahy, 1959

López-Linares, José Luis, and Rioyo Javier (directors), *Asaltar los Cielos*, documentary film, 1996

McCormack, Gavan, *Chang Tso-lin in Northeast China 1911–28*, Stanford, Cal.: Stanford University Press, 1977

McGuire, William (ed.), *The Freud/Jung Letters*, trans. Ralph Manheim and R. F. C. Hull, abr. Alan McGlashan, Princeton, NJ: Princeton University Press, 1994

Maddox, Brenda, *Freud's Wizard: The Enigma of Ernest Jones*, London: John Murray, 2006

Makari, George, *Revolution in Mind: The Creation of Psychoanalysis*, London: Duckworth, 2008

Malcolm, Janet, *In the Freud Archives*, New York: Knopf, 1984

Malcolm, Janet, *Psychoanalysis: The Impossible Profession*, New York: Knopf, 1981

Marcus, Joseph, *Social and Political History of the Jews in Poland 1919–39*, Amsterdam: Mouton Publishers, 1983

Massing, Hede, *This Deception*, New York: Duell, Sloan and Pearce, 1951

Max Eitingon: In Memoriam, Jerusalem: Israel Psychoanalytic Society, 1950

Meier, Andrew, *The Lost Spy: An American in Stalin's Secret Service*, London: Weidenfeld and Nicolson, 2009

Meisel, Perry, and Kendrick, Walter (eds), *Bloomsbury/Freud: The Letters of James and Alix Strachey, 1924–1925*, London: Chatto and Windus, 1986

Mercader Luis, and Sánchez, Germán, *Ramón Mercader Mi Hermano*, Madrid: Espasa Calpa, 1990

Merridale, Catherine, *Ivan's War: The Red Army 1939–45*, London: Faber and Faber, 2005

Meyer-Palmedo, Ingeborg, *Sigmund Freud–Anna Freud Briefwechsel 1904–38*, Frankfurt am Main: S. Fischer Verlag 2006

Michaud, Stéphane, *Lou Andreas-Salomé: L'Alliée de la vie*, Paris: Editions du Seuil, 2000

Miller, Jane, 'How Do You Spell Gujerati, Sir?' in Christopher Ricks and Leonard Michaels (eds), *The State of the Language* Berkeley, Cal.: University of California Press, 1979

Mitter, Rana, *The Manchurian Myth: Nationalism, Resistance and Collaboration in Modern China*, Berkeley, Cal.: University of California Press, 2000

Moreau Ricaud, Michelle, 'Max Eitingon and a Question of Politics', *American Journal of Psychoanalysis*, Vol. 65, No. 4, December 2005, originally published in *Revue internationale d'histoire de la psychanalyse*, No. 5, 1992

Nabokov, Vladimir, *Collected Stories*, London: Weidenfeld and Nicolson, 1996

Neiser, E. M. J., 'Max Eitingon: Leben und Werk', unpublished dissertation University of Mainz, 1978

Orlov, Alexander, *The March of Time: Reminiscences*, London: St Ermin's Press, 2004

Orlov, Alexander, *The Secret History of Stalin's Crimes*, New York: Random House, 1953

Orwell, George, *Homage to Catalonia*, London: Secker and Warburg, 1938

Overy, Richard, *Russia's War*, London: Allen Lane, 1998

Patenaude, Bertrand M., *Stalin's Nemesis: The Exile and Murder of Leon Trotsky*, London: Faber and Faber, 2009

Payne, Stanley G., *The Spanish Civil War, the Soviet Union and Communism*, New Haven, Conn.: Yale University Press, 2004

Polonsky, Antony (ed.), *From Shtetl to Socialism: Studies from 'Polin'*, London: Littman Library of Jewish Civilisation, 1993

Pomer, Sidney, 'Max Eitingon 1881–1943: 'The Organisation of Psychoanalytic Training' in Franz Alexander, Samuel Eisenstein and Martin Grotjahn (eds), *Psychoanalytic Pioneers*, New York: Basic Books, 1966

Poretsky, Elisabeth K., *Our Own People: A Memoir of 'Ignace Reiss' and His Friends*, London: Oxford University Press, 1969

Powers, Thomas, 'Were the Atomic Scientists Spies?' in *New York Review of Books*, 9 June 1994

Quested, R. K. I., *'Matey' Imperialists? The Tsarist Russians in Manchuria 1895–1917*, Hong Kong: University of Hong Kong, 1982

Roazen, Paul, *Meeting Freud's Family*, Amherst, Mass.: University of Massachusetts Press, 1993

Roth, Joseph, *The Wandering Jews*, trans. Michael Hofmann, London: Granta, 2001

Rubenstein, Joshua, and Naumov, Vladimir P. (eds), *Stalin's Secret*

Pogrom: The Postwar Inquisition of the Jewish Anti-Fascist Committee, trans. Laura Esther Wolfson, New Haven, Conn.: Yale University Press, 2001

Schröter, Michael (ed.), *Sigmund Freud–Max Eitingon: Briefwechsel 1906–39*, 2 vols, Tübingen: Edition Diskord, 2004

Sebag Montefiore, Simon, *Stalin: The Court of the Red Tsar*, London: Weidenfeld and Nicolson, 2003

Seidman, Michael, *Republic of Egos: A Social History of the Spanish Civil War*, Madison, Wis.: University of Wisconsin Press, 2002

Serge, Victor, and Trotsky, Natalya Sedova, *The Life and Death of Leon Trotsky*, trans. Arnold J. Pomerans, London: Wildwood House, 1975

Sharapov, E. P., *Naum Eitingon: Karaiushchy Mech Stalina*, St Petersburg: Neva, 2003

Siqueiros, David Alfaro, *Me Llamaban el Coronelazo: Memorias*, Mexico City: Grijalbo, 1977

Slezkine, Yuri, *The Jewish Century*, Princeton, NJ: Princeton University Press, 2004

Smyth, Henry D., *Atomic Energy for Military Purposes: The Official Report on the Development of the Atomic Bomb under the Auspices of the United States Government*, Princeton, NJ: Princeton University Press, 1945

Stephan, John J., *The Russian Fascists: Tragedy and Farce in Exile 1925–45*, New York: Harper and Row, 1978

Sudoplatov, Pavel, and Sudoplatov, Anatoli, with Schecter, Jerrold L., and Schecter, Leona P., *Special Tasks: The Memoirs of an Unwanted Witness – A Soviet Spymaster*, London: Little, Brown, 1994

Thomas, Hugh, *The Spanish Civil War*, London: Eyre and Spottiswoode, 1961

Thubron, Colin, *Among the Russians*, London: Heinemann, 1983

Trotsky, Leon, *My Life*, London: Thornton Butterworth, 1930

van Heijenoort, Jean, *With Trotsky in Exile: From Prinkipo to Coyoacán*, Cambridge, Mass.: Harvard University Press, 1978

Vital, David, *A People Apart: The Jews in Europe 1789–1939*, Oxford: Oxford University Press, 1999

Volkogonov, Dmitri, *Stalin: Triumph and Tragedy*, trans. Harold Shukman, London: Weidenfeld and Nicolson, 1991

Volkogonov, Dmitri, *Trotsky: The Eternal Revolutionary*, trans. Harold Shukman, London: HarperCollins, 1996

White, Stephen, *Britain and the Bolshevik Revolution: A Study in the Politics of Diplomacy 1920–24*, London: Macmillan, 1979

Wilbur, C. Martin, and How, Julie Lien-ying, *Missionaries of Revolution: Soviet Advisers and Nationalist China 1920–27*, Cambridge, Mass.: Harvard University Press, 1989

Wolff, David, *To the Harbin Station: The Liberal Alternative in Russian Manchuria 1898–1914*, Stanford, Cal.: Stanford University Press, 1999

Wynne, Greville, *Wynne and Penkovsky*, London: Corgi Books, 1985

Young-Bruehl, Elisabeth, *Anna Freud: A Biography*, New York: Summit Books, 1988

Index

Abakumov, Viktor, 391–2, 394, 398

Abdurakhman (accomplice of assassin), 337

Abel, Rudolf, *see* Fisher, Willie

Abraham, Karl: death, 189–90; membership of Psychoanalytic Committee, 173; Poliklinik role, 178, 181, 189n, 190, 191; war work, 172; in Zurich, 165

Adler, Alfred, 162n, 185

AFL (American Federation of Labor), 78, 80–4, 87–9, 199, 221

Agabekov, Georgi: on Chinese strategy, 147; in Constantinople, 150–1; death, 151, 286, 345; defection, 151, 152–3, 345; on Leonid, 149; on OGPU, 151, 154–5; on Trotsky surveillance, 158; writings, 151–2

Ageloff, Ruth, 300

Ageloff, Sylvia, 286, 298–301, 307–8

Alexander, Grand Duke, 144–5

Alexander II, Tsar, 43

Alexander III, Tsar, 43

Alliluyeva, Svetlana (daughter of Stalin), 399

Amin, Hafizullah, 419

Amtorg: creation, 66, 84; Eitingon relationship, 315, 327, 365, 373, 376; role, 84–5; US investigations, 198–9, 202; US staff, 326–7;

Andreas-Salomé, Lou, 187

Andrew, Christopher (and Vasily Mitrokhin): account of Soviet espionage, 245n; on Arcos documents, 137n; on Cohens, 358; on Fisher, 357; on Grigulevich, 302; on Hall, 350–1; on Leonid, 336; on NKVD liquidations, 290; on NKVD network in US, 356n; on NKVD role in war, 342; on Orlov, 281, 295; on 'special tasks', 245, 292

Andropov, Yuri, 433–4

Ankara, 335–8

Antonov-Ovseenko, Vladimir, 280

Arcos: British raid, 85–7, 90, 203; creation, 66; Eitingon relationship, 67–71, 73, 90, 203–4; espionage role, 137;

455